Melita Baker was born in Dorset and has spent much of her life travelling and working, as she puts it, at a variety of jobs around the world, while as a very young mother trying to bring up her children and grow up herself. She feels that her favourite counties of Dorset and Devon are combined in the idyllic scenic beauty of the south-west of Ireland, where she has lived for the past six years, and which she describes as the place where her restless Celtic spirit has been able to put down roots, allowing her to devote all her time to writing.

FINAL RECKONING

Melita Baker

POCKET
BOOKS

LONDON · SYDNEY · NEW YORK · TOKYO · SINGAPORE · TORONTO

First published in Great Britain by Pocket Books, 1995
An imprint of Simon & Schuster Ltd
A Paramount Communications Company

Simon & Schuster Ltd
West Garden Place
Kendal Street
London W2 2AQ

Simon & Schuster of Australia Pty Ltd
Sydney

A CIP catalogue record for this book is available from the
British Library

ISBN 0-671-85277-9

Typeset in Palatino 9/12pt by
Hewer Text Composition Services, Edinburgh
Printed and bound in Great Britain by
HarperCollins*Manufacturing*, Glasgow

With all my love to my endlessly tolerant family
And in Loving Memory
of a darling mother. And beloved husband.

ACKNOWLEDGEMENTS

To Raj, Chico, Twitch, King'B, Lynnie, Steve. You all know what for.

To Sara, for the timely kick, et al . . .

Especially to Jani, for sorting out the muddle – and for being there, always, when needed.

To Louise, for shining the light.

To Darley, for those deliciously bubbly pep-talks (and the glass that awaits).

Not least . . . to Jo, for 'daring to rush in . . .'

PROLOGUE

'Gemma, will you please clear off my bed – and go and get ready. There's only an hour before — '

'I can't believe you are still going through with this . . .' Gemma Lloyd's usually vehement voice was muted as she fought to talk past the near-hysteria which threatened at any moment to erupt and blow her mouth apart.

'Oh, Lord . . . please not that again.' Diana Lloyd-Fauvère glanced at her cousin and shook her head, knowing that further attempts at explanation would be pointless. Gemma had formed an opinion, based on God-knew-what, and would not now abandon her gloomy predictions.

'Why won't you at least compromise, you know, timewise?'

'Compromise?'

'Yeah.' Gemma's brown eyes brightened at gaining Diana's full attention. 'Why the damned hurry?'

Diana's eyes had narrowed. 'Gemma, *what* are you talking about?'

'You know *what* – about this damned engagement, about this whole scene, Di. Christ, you've only known these Nazareth men a month — '

'Six weeks,' Diana corrected automatically, knowing she ought not to get involved in this.

'OK, big deal, six whole weeks . . . your life's not a bargain basement sale, Di. How can you make a lifetime decision based on six weeks? All I'm saying is put it off for a while.'

Diana sighed and turned away to her closet. The same argument, over and over. Purposefully she kept her back to her cousin as she selected a shoe-lace strappy dress, and tried not to feel the brown eyes burning holes in her back from across the early-American chic of their hosts' New England guest room.

'Just tell Mat you need more time – give it all more thought— '

'But I don't need more time,' Diana said firmly, turning, dress and underwear in one hand and shoes in the other. 'So there's no compromise called for.'

Gemma gritted her teeth and clenched her fists tighter in the pockets of her cotton jeans. How the hell was she going to make her cousin see sense?

She dared not lose her temper today, not with so much at stake. A shiver of angry helplessness surged through her, but she was not giving in. There had to be a way.

'Well, will you at least put off the wedding date? Get to know Mat better?'

'I've given my decision and the date is set,' Diana said matter-of-factly, heading for the adjoining bathroom. 'Let it go, Gemma.'

The rush of the shower wrecked Gemma's good intentions and rocketed her off the bed and across to the open bathroom door, her pretty features set in anger. 'All right! But tell me something,' she yelled at the glass shower door. 'What's your decision based on? Your loneliness, or theirs?'

Diana pushed open the shower door, her face suddenly bleached of its light tan, her eyes dark with pain. 'That's a very cruel thing to say . . .'

But Gemma was too angry, too afraid, to stop now. 'It's not meant to be, you know me better than that . . . but is it true? Is that what this is all about? Two lonely men rambling about in that mausoleum of a house . . . and you still searching for Uncle Marc. Are you trying to find *him* there?'

'Papa is dead . . .' Diana said tonelessly, her eyes fixed on Gemma's face as if she were suddenly seeing a stranger.

'Goddamnit! Don't you think I know that? Who the hell has been trying to hold you together these past two years since he died?'

Tears sprang to the edge of Diana's eyes, and Gemma, cursing herself and her big mouth, handed over a towel. 'Lord, I'm sorry. Please don't get upset. I'm just so confused . . .' Her face crumpled miserably. 'And you're scaring the shit out of me.'

Diana wrapped the towel around her chilled body. 'There's nothing to be scared about, Gems. It's really a miracle. I've found a kind of peace again. Can't you just be happy for me?'

Gemma bit back her opinion of this particular miracle.

'What about *love*, Di?' She changed her tack rapidly. 'Isn't that supposed to come into the picture somewhere?'

Diana's voice was distant. 'I'm sure it will. I'm going to give it every chance.'

Gemma's mind reeled. Miracles? Peace? Giving love a chance? But with *which* Nazareth, she wondered cynically, Matthew, the smooth, charming son, whose glances at Diana were cold when he thought no one was watching? Or the even smoother, charming father, David, who couldn't keep his eyes, or his hands for that matter, off Diana at *any* time? No. Oh no – no – no – NO! She had to make Diana listen. 'Look, I've never asked anything of you, or questioned anything you do, but as your best friend, I'm asking you to do me one favour. Just *listen* to me; hear me out fully, one last time. I'm begging you, Di . . .'

Diana stepped back and stared at her cousin for a long moment, then she nodded. 'All right, Gemma. I'll hear what you have to say. Now let me get a robe on . . .'

Gemma was, as always, brutally honest. She admitted that she'd damned Diana's mother, Aunt Rachel, for getting them invited to America for the summer. That she'd also damned their hosts, the Goldings, for introducing them to David Nazareth, and specifically she'd damned his son . . . Diana kept her word, as always, and listened. She was curled into a silk-covered armchair at the window, her gaze on the gardens below, and apart from the odd movement of her shoulders, a tensing of her jaw, Gemma had no idea what her reactions were.

'You see, Liz Golding admitted that David quizzed her that night we met him, and she told David you were still grieving for your father. She even told him that her friend Aunt Rachel had asked her to have us for a holiday because you were taking so long to get over Uncle Marc's death. Don't you see? He moved in on you as a substitute. A bloody effective substitute too.

'*Jeezus*, Di, he was good. I couldn't believe how good. He dripped solicitous charm all over you like a flaming wax candle, until he had you eating out of his hand. Then within days he'd fixed up that phoney party, the excuse to get you and his son together. Liz told me it was no secret that Mat wasn't attracting any marriageable women, and it was no secret either that David was worried about that.

'You've got to admit they made quite a duo. Widowed father and bachelor son, both oozing enough charm to sink the British fleet! You didn't stand a chance . . . can't you see that? You were still so vulnerable, Di, and in so much pain . . . I mean, Uncle Marc was your world . . . you hadn't come to terms with his death, and then suddenly you were the centre of all that flattering attention.

'But I don't only blame these Americans, I have to say that I blame Uncle Marc too.' Here Gemma took a careful breath, aware that she was treading on hallowed ground.

'He was so other-worldly, and his refusal to live in the present day . . . well, it kept you isolated, didn't it? I mean, how often did he let you join us at school? For a few short months every second year or so? And that was sheer bloody negligence, everybody said so. You were always top at everything you attempted – but no, Uncle Marc wanted you travelling with him; so what did you get? Foreign tutors with scarcely any English, and all of them as absent-minded as your papa.

'You were never really in this world, Di. God! I loved that man too, but he was out to lunch when it came to life with a capital "L". His life revolved around ancient civilisations and distant lands. OK, I know he was a brilliant archaeologist, but face it, he lived and breathed mythology and legends . . . and that's what you grew up on. A diet of romantic chivalry; honour, codes and mores that were as mythical as dragons and Camelot . . .

'You've never even dated anyone! How can you possibly know that this Matthew Nazareth is the right man for you? Or are you blinded by his handsome father? There's nothing wrong with a mild infatuation with a guy who could fill your father's place . . . so long as you recognise it for what it is, and at least get out in time.

'Di, I've watched David with you, and I'm convinced he's up to no good. It's like some kind of trap. I don't know why I feel that, but I *do*. He's ruthless. I feel it in my bones.

'As for Matthew, he just gives me the creeps. He has shifty eyes, and oh, Jesus, I can't stand the idea of you being here with those two, and me on the other side of the ocean, too far away to be of any help if you need a friend.' Now Gemma paused, exhausted by her effort – and by Diana's total lack of reaction. She hadn't expected co-operation, but some kind of emotion might have at least shown if she was getting through at all.

When Diana did, finally, turn to look at her cousin, the only sign of emotion on her pale, lovely face, was in the luminosity of her eyes.

'Thank you, Gems. You've been very honest – at least about the way you see things. I have to say, though, that I don't agree with you.' Now she smiled, her usual gentle smile. 'But I will promise to think things over very carefully. Does that satisfy you?'

Gemma stared. Had she got anywhere at all?

'You'll put the wedding off, then?'

'I didn't say that,' Diana said, uncurling lithely from the chair. 'I said I'd think everything over carefully. And I will. Now, we're going to be late, so can we both get ready?'

* * *

Gemma tore through her closet, throwing together her hall-mark selection of motley colours and styles, that somehow always blended perfectly on her, and finally crammed her feet into a grotesque, but on her smart, pair of platform shoes and headed despondently downstairs to the waiting limo.

Stubborn, loyal Diana had made it plain. She'd listened to Gemma too late. Her word was already given. To Matthew. And Gemma knew she would go through with the wedding.

All Gemma could do now was pray for her happiness, and give her support.

'This is certainly an auspicious year for romance,' Liz Golding was saying gaily as the limousine David had sent for them turned into the long, beech-lined avenue leading to the Nazareth mansion. 'What with Prince Charles and Lady Diana's wedding next month. Gee, honey, imagine . . . even the same name as yours!'

Diana's smile was tight. It wasn't the first time the name-comparison had been made, but now there was the romantic connection as well. However, her mind was on Gemma's outburst and what, if anything, she should do about it.

'Wouldn't have thought he'd have bin' allowed to marry a commoner,' Sam Golding mused, his keen eyes noting the excellent condition of David's grounds.

'Some commoner!' Gemma retorted, always ready to argue, and particularly today. 'Have you seen her pedigree?'

'Still a commoner,' Sam repeated stubbornly. He had become an expert at winding Gemma up, and relished the sparring matches.

Lady Diana, again providing relief, thought Diana. 'But the daughter of an earl,' she commented diplomatically, hating arguments at any time, and knowing that Gemma and Sam were likely to continue baiting one another at the party – something she definitely did not want today. 'They don't come much closer to royalty than that, Sam.'

'Mebbe so, but — '

'Will you look at those peonies! Aren't they gorgeous, Sam honey . . .?' Liz cleverly distracted her husband. 'Do you think we could get some tips from David's gardener? Ours aren't nearly so good as these.'

Sam begged to differ, preferring to think theirs a different variety, and as Gemma too had taken the hint Diana had a few moments to continue her thoughts.

The references to her father had created a groundswell of unhappiness she was having difficulty weathering. The inference that she was substituting one or both Nazareths for him was a ghastly consideration. She didn't believe it, of course, but she had to examine her conscience and her motives. If Gemma was even remotely correct, she'd have no alternative but to call off the wedding – and live with the shame of that for the rest of her life.

The accusation that her papa had raised her badly had been hurtful, but no one had understood her relationship with her father. The more she saw of the 'real' world, the more grateful she was to her father for sparing her for as long as he had.

Diana's entire musing was on the word *substitute*. That was a nasty word indeed – and if she *were* guilty of employing it, then her own honour was suspect, and for that reason alone she would have to make amends.

As the beautiful Nazareth mansion came into view, Diana saw Matthew and David, both so tall and handsome, waiting at the foot of the wide, marble staircase, and her insides gave a small leap of anticipation. For a moment she closed her eyes and mentally shook the worry from her mind . . .

But later that evening, as the sun was setting on what had been a lovely day, she had further opportunity to consider her 'problem'.

Some of the guests had departed, some had gone into the drawing-room with Mat and some, like Diana and David, lingered talking in small groups on the deep, sheltered terrace that ran along three sides of the house.

For several minutes they had been alone, talking of inconsequential things, comfortable together. Diana knew she should probably follow her new fiancé in to where she could now hear a disco starting up. But for the moment the gardens were mellow with evening shadows and the faintest scent of jasmine and honeysuckle hung enticingly on the air.

Just to sit here with David, even in silence, was enough.

With that thought, Gemma's warnings sounded again, and a cold fear snaked through her body. David was looking away from her, across at the Goldings who, with another banker and his wife, now argued the merits of David's potted palms.

David's face in profile was lit with an indulgent humour, fine laughter lines creased away from his eyes. Was this, she thought, the face that represented a reincarnation of her papa? And suddenly it became vitally important for her to know.

Covertly she studied her father-in-law-to-be. Marc had been tall, but with fine features and a small frame – David was taller, broader-shouldered, muscular. Like her father, David had blue eyes and dark hair, but that was true of many men. No, in looks, at least, they were not remotely alike.

She persisted in her appraisal, but she could find no hint of Marc in the quiet man beside her. Except in her feeling of companionship, of comfort in his presence, the feeling of warmth and safety. Yes, that was it. There *was* a similarity. Now she could laugh at Gemma's fears, her own too. So she felt warm and safe with David – she *enjoyed* his company, *liked* being with him. Good Lord, wasn't she *lucky*, she was actually getting a father-in-law she liked . . .

At that moment David turned back to her, his eyes attentive, his voice caringly concerned.

'Are you getting cold, honey? Ready to go inside' – he grinned – 'and join that godawful noise?'

Diana laughed gaily, glad to have laid her fears and uncertainties to rest. 'Well, I'd happily stay here all night and talk – discos aren't really my scene – but I suspect my fiancé might think it rude of me, so if you'll excuse me . . .?'

'Don't think you're leaving me out here with the "old gardeners".' David gave a mock grimace and jumped up with an exaggerated flourish to offer her his arm. 'I'd rather spin you around to *The Dancing Queen*, or whatever, than pull up an armchair and discuss those darned peonies one more time!'

There it was again, that tug on her heart-strings. But Diana accepted it gratefully. David Nazareth *did* have an attraction, and she was glad of it. It reached that part of her soul that had been frozen since her father's cruelly sudden death, made her feel *alive* again.

Just as Mat's quietness, his old-fashioned reticence, had given her confidence . . .

His proposal *had* been sudden, scarcely a month after they'd met – but somehow it had seemed right, and when he'd found it difficult to ask her, his words stumbling and hesitant, she'd wanted to finish his sentences for him; help him with what he wanted to say. He'd been so shy – more shy even than she. And when he'd explained that he'd never really dated, that his mother's death when he was sixteen had left a still-tender wound, Diana felt she had found a soulmate. It had been easy to respond to his loneliness with all the gentle affection her loving heart held.

She had not minded the chaste inexperience of his kiss, and when he'd quickly drawn back, unable to look into her eyes, and whispered that he'd known from the moment they met that she was the only woman he would ever ask to be his wife, she had accepted him gladly.

Now his mother's ring sparkled on her finger and she knew her heart was beginning to heal. No one could ever replace her papa, but they didn't have to. Matthew and David had suffered a tremendous loss, as she had done . . . but now they would all help one another. Together they would build a strong, new life.

For the first time in her twenty-five years Diana felt that she was needed, rather than needing, and it gave her the warmest feeling she had ever known.

She took David's proffered arm and smiled mischievously up at him. 'Frankly, I'd prefer the peonies . . . but lead on!'

Gemma was wrong. There was no confusion in Diana's mind. Her prospective marriage and future had nothing to do with her father's ghost.

It was something Diana wanted for *herself*.

BOOK ONE

DAVID

CHAPTER ONE

David stared grimly at the celebrations in full swing across his gaily decorated lawns – moodily watching the elite hundred or so guests enjoying the privilege of being invited to his son's wedding.

'Damn you, Matthew!' he swore softly, swirling the dregs of tepid champagne, knowing he cursed not just Mat but all youth on this day.

He had not intended to be alone today, but there was peace, of a kind, in the recesses of the terrace – and so he lingered.

Music, joyful and triumphant, briefly floated across the lawn. Music he had helped to choose, fitting for a wedding day.

A shadow, alien and dark, played over his features, rendering them momentarily ugly. His six-foot-plus frame appeared smaller, hunched as he was as if against an unseen cold. Neither the brilliant warmth of the day nor the joy of his only remaining – correction his only *resident* – son could penetrate the icy chill in his soul.

He had smiled so much today his jaws ached and, he reminded himself grimly, it wasn't over yet.

Sure, he'd go back out and incline his aristocratic head at well-meant congratulations. Yes, he'd accept even more good wishes for the young couple's happiness – and the loneliness which gripped his own heart would be well hidden behind the correct social face.

He grimaced. There was only one person to blame. Himself. So he'd endure, make light of the old clichés about having not lost a son but gained a daughter – and his own crass stupidity would sting him the more.

He glimpsed his daughter-in-law's lithe, provocative form as she moved amongst the guests. Watched as something caused her to laugh and swing back her silver-blonde hair in a gesture he was too familiar with. So often he had wanted to cradle that crown of her femininity in his own hands, but it was not his right. That added to his pain.

Yet he had contrived this match and, with his unmatched flair for scheming and manoeuvring, had brought it off.

'Madness, sheer bloody madness,' he muttered. But had he been mad, or had this whole goddamned nightmare started with his vanity?

Self-consciously he pushed his fingers through his dark mass of hair, whose silver threads were, for once, a source not of modest pride but of bitterness. Damn it to hell, today he felt all of his fifty-seven years.

Once more he wondered if he was deluding himself. Possibly other men went through similar infatuations, urging on to their sons the very women they themselves could no longer have. A tight smile played at the corners of his mouth; why not? There had to be plenty of men who'd enjoy looking at the cake they had no chance of eating.

'Fool, Nazareth,' he cursed himself aloud, unaware of the irony in a third outburst. But yes, he knew himself for a fool. Hadn't his plans for a cosy ménage à trois been a mockery from the start. Just *what* had he thought Mat would offer that he couldn't? Youth? Ah yes, the power of youth . . . firm young bodies, hasty and indulgent passions – and of course heady *promise*; the promise of maturity, usually too early and wrongly spent.

The thought soured him further. Could he have done better at twenty-five, or thirty-five, even at forty-five? Would he have known how to *treasure* a woman then? Someone as precious as he knew Diana to be? No. Not a chance. But by God he knew how now!

He'd never known a woman like her, and yet she'd always been there; somewhere in his dreams.

He'd known it the moment they had met.

*   *   *

The omens hadn't been good for 1981: barely four months in office, Reagan had survived an assassination attempt: Pope John Paul had narrowly escaped death from a gunshot wound in Vatican City; coal miners were still out; and now the major league baseball players' strike threatened the season's games.

He hadn't felt like partying the night he'd met Diana – but an invitation from an old business colleague, a member of the exclusive Locker Room club, founded by David's own grandfather, would have been difficult to refuse.

Boston society knew that D.N. didn't socialise in the normal sense of the word; his status as a wealthy widower made him exactingly cautious and the invitations he had accepted over the years were very few. So he could have refused Sam's invitation without causing offence. For some reason he had chosen to accept.

Sam and Elizabeth Golding were long-standing friends and had no marriageable daughters, no children in fact. So David felt secure enough as he drove into the neat gardens of their colonial country house. It was a while since he'd seen his banking buddy; they could catch up.

Probably Beanie had been invited too. That was the usual form since Ella's death. Boston had been trying to make a match between David and his deceased wife's best friend for the past twenty years or more.

He smiled as he handed his keys to a car boy. They'd never stop trying as long as he remained a widower. He could accept that too. As long as it was *only* Beanie. She had become *his* best buddy years back down the track. There was no threat from Beanie. He was comfortable with her.

The threat, however, existed tonight. Not in the person of Beanie – Beanie hadn't been invited – but in the shape and form of one of the guests, Diana Lloyd-Fauvère.

As Sam led the way from the foyer to the drawing-room, where Liz and their two house guests waited, David had only a few moments in which to realise that his hosts had invited him with ulterior motives.

'She's absolutely go-for-broke luscious, D.N.!' Sam gushed as they walked the long hall towards the sounds of feminine laughter.

'Mat's age, too! Her mother is a famous artist and sculptress. English, lives in Paris. She's an old friend of Liz's. In fact I think the daughter might even be half-French . . .'

David's mouth had already set, even if the woman was a 'match' not for him but for his son. Anger and disgust swept through him, but they were already at the door.

He could hardly back out now.

He drew in a deep breath, controlled himself with long-accustomed discipline, and reminded himself to have words with Sam later.

He'd remember many different things about that night; and he was instantly aware that he would. Though reprimanding Sam would not be among them.

The first impression shocked his senses, all of them, and made him behave even more stiffly than the situation warranted.

His head was instantly full of clichés – the smile across a crowded room being the first. But her smile *did* meet him across the room and before he'd recovered his composure, something in his central being *did* lurch crazily.

David had spent his life undistracted by the many beautiful women of his acquaintance. They were plentiful enough in Boston to be the norm. His long-deceased wife had been a noted beauty and Beanie was a strikingly beautiful woman still. What was it, then, in one gently curving smile, that erased the memory of every woman he had ever seen? In the longest moment of his life, no longer in reality than the sweep of the second hand on his wristwatch, David absorbed and stored every detail of her that his gaze would allow. She was tall, with the legginess of a model, and slender, but still too curvaceous to pass the coat-hanger test.

Her face was a perfect oval of creamy skin, with a small, straight nose, high cheekbones and that smiling mouth. Her eyes, more grey than blue, dark and shining, were huge question marks as she silently returned his stare.

She came across the room to him, graceful and strangely elegant for such a young woman, exuding a maturity beyond her apparent years. Her cream silk dress whispered as she walked, and the gold bangles she wore tinkled and gleamed against her skin.

A Nordic goddess, or a blonde Audrey Hepburn to his Gregory Peck, David thought wryly as she stood before him, tilting her head slightly to look up into his eyes.

He never knew for sure why she captured his heart, but he handed it over on the spot. Unquestioningly, unreservedly, and for all time.

'Hi there,' he'd managed, stupidly. 'David Nazareth, ma'am . . .' He'd wanted to add, 'Your servant.' It was certainly in his mind, but before he could make a complete ass of himself she'd answered.

'Hello, Mr Nazareth. I'm very pleased to meet you.' There was laughter in her voice, excitingly harnessed to the appealing English accent. David's gaze lingered at the upturned corners of her mouth, where impossible dimples appeared. He had to rein in the urge to test their reality against his lips and concentrate on what she was saying. It was irreverently banal. The usual stuff. But he couldn't let the 'Mr' pass.

'David, please . . .'

'David, then,' she replied softly.

Was she mocking him, he wondered. But no, those eyes were as candid as a child's.

This, however, was no child. His next realisation, more of a shock than any other feeling, was that he would trust her with his life.

'My cousin, Gemma Lloyd . . .' she was saying, and although David dimly remembered shaking hands with a

very attractive, dark-haired young thing, he could not later
have recalled anything else about the cousin.

Later, after dinner and a sufficiency of well-chilled Bollinger,
David had cornered Liz for just long enough to find out what
he wanted to know.

'No, not married, D.N.,' Liz had smiled at him, her freckled
face aglow with warmth and genuine friendliness. 'I had a
letter some months ago from her mother, Rachel. She asked
us if we'd have the girls – in fact if we'd invite them. I was only
too happy to agree.' She arranged coffee cups, her face serious
as she added, 'Rachel's been worried about her daughter for
some time. You see, Marc Fauvère, Diana's father, died about
three years ago, on a dig. He was an archaeologist,' she
explained as David began to frown.

'Diana was with him, David. She'd travelled almost everywhere that Marc went since she was a baby.'

'She saw her father die, you mean?'

'Not only that. The real tragedy is that Marc was her world.'
She looked up at David and smiled. 'For God's sake, stop me
if I'm boring you . . .'

'You're not,' he replied honestly. 'I want to know all there
is to know.'

Liz pursed her lips to prevent herself smiling again. What a
scoop, if she could supply David with a real darling for that
brat of a son.

'Rachel is artistic, David. Oh, she loves the girl, but she's
shut off in her own little world, or rather,' she corrected herself
with a grin, 'in her big world. She lives for her work, and Diana
has always come second to that. With Marc it was different.
He loved Diana to distraction and took her everywhere he
could, even arranging tutors when he was travelling in some
outlandish spot.'

'So Diana depended on him for all her needs?' David
guessed, urging Liz on.

'Absolutely,' Liz replied, giving the final touches to an
already perfect tray.

'And . . .?' David persisted gently.

'Rachel's worried that Diana is taking too long to recover,' Liz said simply. 'She won't socialise, except with her two cousins, one of whom you've met tonight and ignored,' she said sweetly.

David by-passed the criticism.

'Three years is a long time,' he said pensively.

'Far too long!' Liz agreed emphatically.

David's thoughts came back reluctantly to the present. Was that what had made Diana so attractive? That she'd loved an older man, albeit her own father, so completely, that the world wasn't bearable without him? But no, he couldn't fool himself on that one. He hadn't known about her father until approximately three hours after he'd already fallen, very deeply, for the unknown girl.

A girl of Mat's age.

He shook his head wearily. Had he been afraid that he'd lose her? So afraid that he'd taken the only logical option, and married her to his son?

He still toyed with his glass, half-closed eyes scrutinising the sunlit wedding scene.

She was so beautiful in her chosen wedding gown. Not white. Not satin and laces. Not even silk, as such. A concoction of her own design, quite the loveliest dress he'd ever seen. The ivory and apricot crêpe de Chine seemed moulded to her slender body, as if created by nature and added to her loveliness.

'Eat your heart out, Pops!' Mat had surprisingly muttered at him this morning. Now he was doing just that.

Somehow the colours and the softness enhanced the luminous pearl-light of the grey-blue eyes, her fairness, and her perfect figure. She looked, he thought wistfully, like a child's picture-book illustration of a fairy queen.

The beauty and the innocence and youth! So carefree, so certain, so blind! As David too had been blind until today.

Today, when Diana had sworn her vows, the church had been hushed in the solemn moment, and his self-imposed blindness had vanished. In the awful agony of silence, he'd known the truth.

Diana belonged to *him*.

And he had married her to his son . . .

Beanie's entrance into the study was so quiet that she had crossed to the french windows and was within touching distance, yet David didn't hear her. Her expression was calm. Outwardly Beanie was always calm. Only the almond eyes under the finely arched brows gave away her feelings. At this moment, knowing she was unwatched, her eyes were sad.

Beanie was petite. Even in her three-inch heels she scarcely made five feet four. But her personality made up for her lack of inches. She was the strongest, most resilient, least emotional woman that David had ever known. She was astute, highly intelligent and as clinically ruthless in business as David had known any man to be.

That she was blessed with a vivacious doll-like beauty had long since been forgiven by Boston's high society ladies. They had learned very quickly that Beanie, despite the provocative bow-shaped mouth, had no interest in their men beyond a platonic courtesy accorded equally to their wives.

Initial fears, occasioned by her startling foreign loveliness, had long, long ago been replaced by respect.

To Boston's certain knowledge Beanie had given her body to no one and her heart to one man. Perhaps the only man in Boston who didn't know she existed as a woman.

Now her stomach knotted with a thousand fears, all of which she instinctively knew were justified.

'Darling?' she called out softly, not wanting to startle him.

He turned at once. 'Damn it, Beanie, you should have warned me. I thought you were some half-pissed guest!'

'Not even slightly pissed, darling. Are you?'

'I wish to God I was,' David said vehemently. Then, aware of Beanie's cool, appraising gaze, he swiftly turned back to the view of the garden.

'I just needed a break,' he muttered apologetically.

'Naturally,' Beanie said dryly, not in the least fooled.

David was annoyed. Beanie saw too damned much.

'Let's get back,' he said curtly.

Beanie moved across the small space and stood beside him. She didn't speak, but silently appraised the scene he had been at pains to view in private.

The bride and groom were together now, not apart as they had been for much of the reception. They formed the centre of a group of young people.

Beanie wondered if the tension she had felt emanating from David in the church had the same source as the one he was radiating now. Her gaze rested on Diana, and she knew that it had.

Her sigh confused David and he half-turned to look at her quizzically.

'I was just wondering about Mat,' she covered swiftly. 'Is it magic we see, darling? Or just that we hope it is?'

David knew what she meant. Hadn't he worried about it himself, over and over?

'This past year, you mean?' He hoped Beanie meant that, and not these past few weeks.

'Mmm . . .' Beanie nodded.

'I sure hope and pray that it's permanent and not magic, my friend,' he replied shortly.

'He's changed, hasn't he?' There was doubt in Beanie's voice, the same doubt that was in David's mind. He turned back to look at the newlyweds.

He frowned. His son lounged in that indolent way he had against a beribboned marquee pole. He seemed nonchalant to the point of indifference. But what did he really feel? Could anyone ever tell with Mat?

Briefly David wondered whose choice his son's cream suit

had been. Not Diana's he was sure. The colour did nothing for Mat, except to make him appear more than usually pallid.

Mat was almost as tall as his father, but with a thinness that David considered unattractive. Admittedly Mat had his mother's fine features, and her corn-coloured hair, worn too long, as David had constantly told him. His eyes were the same pale blue as Ella's had been, and with the same sweep of dark lashes. He also had her pouting bottom lip, but on his thinner mouth it could make him look sullen.

David continued to stare for a few, silent, moments at the hostile stranger who was his son, the heir to the Nazareth empire, who bore no resemblance of any kind to David but every resemblance to the wife David had, years before her death, come to despise.

But, looks apart, had this past year really brought about the 'magical' changes Beanie referred to?

David had to believe that it had.

Nothing else bore contemplating.

'I think he's changed, Beanie,' he said firmly.

'Good. Now, are you composed enough to escort me back into the fray, darling?' Beanie's voice was light.

'Composed, Beanie?' David's voice was suddenly guilty, as he spun round to face her fully.

'That's what I said, and meant,' she said quietly. 'I know that most people are fools, and that fools are blind . . .' Her voice tailed off as she paused to let that sink in. 'But, David, don't think that you can fool everyone. Least of all Diana.'

David's stomach lurched. He couldn't be hearing this right.

'What the hell's that supposed to mean?' His voice dared her to take the subject any further and perhaps, under normal circumstances, she wouldn't have.

'We needn't go into it, darling,' Beanie replied with cool insistence.

'Like hell!' David swore. 'You'd better have damned good reasons for what I think you're suggesting.'

Beanie continued to stare at him, her clear eyes seeing

everything he wanted to conceal. His face was taut with anger and there were dark smudges under his eyes, the kind gained only from many sleepless nights. She shook her head.

'Darling, Diana is not a fool,' she continued carefully.' It might be better if she were, but she is not. She is, however, sensitive. You must be very careful to guard yourself when she is around.'

Beanie heard but chose to ignore the quick intake of his breath. She had to protect David, no matter what it took. He was her greatest friend. That she also loved him was neither here nor there.

She rushed on. 'Diana is gossamer and steel, darling. Fragile, but very strong.'

She brushed at an imaginary fleck on her immaculate grey silk suit, avoiding his eyes. 'You must conceal your feelings better, particularly from her.' Her face grew serious, and the lovely eyes were large in the pale face. 'Diana must never guess what you are feeling, darling, or you will lose her.'

There, it was said.

David stared at his friend. 'You're not joking, are you?'

It was a statement, dulled by the knowledge, slightly sickening to him, that she had guessed his feelings.

'No, I'm not joking.' Beanie moved from the balustrade, and slipped her arm through his. 'If Diana once guesses the truth, you will lose her.' Again the quiet certainty that David found unnerving.

'*I* will lose her?' he tried to play his only card. 'Surely you mean Mat will lose her. He is, after all, her husband . . .'

'Don't play games with me, David!' Beanie was cross now.'I am your best friend, and we have never played games with one another. Let's not start now.'

'You can't lose something you don't have,' David said perversely, still hoping to divert her.

'Nonsense!' Beanie reproved with feeling. '*You* will lose her, not Mat. Matthew has the wife, but he doesn't have the woman.'

'Now who's talking nonsense?' David's face, just a few inches from Beanie's, told her she had hit the target. Bullseye.

'Diana doesn't know her own reasons for marrying Mat – ' Beanie began to urge David towards the door – 'and let's just hope she never finds them out.'

'Whoa!' David pulled up sharply at the door. 'You can't make a comment like that and leave it in mid-air. Damn it, Beanie, what are you playing at?'

Beanie had never been afraid of David and she wasn't about to be bullied by him now. She inched up and pecked him lightly on the cheek.

'Don't be naive, darling.' She gave him her usual sweet smile, and pulled a wry face. 'The newlyweds will be wanting to leave soon, and your presence will be expected, yes?'

'You know it will. But . . .'

'Leave it, darling.' Beanie insisted, her voice cool and measured. 'The future still has much promise.'

Her warm, accented voice took any sting from her words, and David's mask fell briefly away.

'Where will it all end, Beanie?' He spoke tiredly, as if to himself, and he sounded more strained than Beanie could bear.

'With grandchildren, we hope,' she answered briskly, tucking his arm into hers and hugging it gently. 'Lots and lots of little ones, my darling. Many Nazareth heirs, for you to manipulate as you wish. And to keep you, my dear friend, from other mischief!'

David couldn't help but smile. Beanie's light-hearted change of subject had saved him from himself. It had taken the edge off the icy torment within him. And that was sufficient for now.

He smiled down at her and squeezed her arm. She was a damned good friend. The best. Now he could go back to the celebrations with his feelings well disguised beneath the gloss of paternal affection.

In a perverse way he was glad that the marriage had taken place. Glad that the whole thing was almost over and that the knots were securely tied. He could not have borne even one more day without confessing his foolish love.

Soon now the happy couple would leave for Vermont, and during the three weeks they sun-worshipped he would get his emotions back into order. By the time they returned to the wing he had built on to the mansion for them, he would be himself again.

They crossed the marble hallway and rejoined the party as it reached its ebb.

As Beanie had reminded him, perhaps there would soon be grandchildren.

The future need not be bleak.

CHAPTER TWO

Fate was not prepared to be quite as accommodating as David might have hoped. He awoke the morning after the wedding with a heart as heavy as lead. Grandchildren refused to appear in the future he tried to envisage.

He rang his secretary to say he would be at the mansion if needed and absented himself from work for the first time in his life. By the third day he had handed over his pressing work-load to his amazed second-in-command, Jeff Sherman. And remained a truant . . .

Downtown on Slater Street, Nazareth House pulsated strongly as business went on as usual. Nevertheless, the Firm sighed collectively in relief that the wedding had gone off without a hitch.

The flagship of the Nazareth empire was housed in the financial district of the Hub and that was where David's top and longest-serving men held court. Today, in the executive club on the sixth floor, his direct team were taking lunch.

To the rest of the Firm they were known, not unkindly, as the T-EEM, an acronym for The Eyes (Ike Petersen of Press), the Ears (Mark Wheeler of Law) and the Mouth (David's own personal secretary, Jeff Sherman).

No one had dared to let out a breath after news of Mat's engagement. They'd metaphorically held it right up to and including the wedding day itself.

Without exception the staff at Nazareth House were amazed at Mat's good fortune and, for themselves, they had begun to entertain a tiny ray of hope. If there was the remotest chance of Mr Matthew changing for the better, it had to be through his marriage.

The Firm was still celebrating, unofficially, when the T-EEM met at mid-day.

It was definitely still an occasion and the atmosphere had even reached the rarefied sanctum of the club. Jeff Sherman was the first to make a point of noticing, and by so doing tacitly approving, the party spirit pervading the entire building.

He raised his glass of champagne in toast.

'To Matthew and Diana. And to Nazareth House. Long may David prevail.'

'Amen!' his colleagues echoed.

Most of the staff, loathing Matthew and loving David, had been concerned because the boss had seemed a trifle out of sorts just lately. But most of them believed that they could understand his reasons. Winning a prize like Diana, for Mat, must have been quite a feat.

Only the three in the opulent bar-cum-dining-room might have had another opinion as to the boss's behaviour, but if they did they kept it to themselves.

Ike and Mark drank the toast with Jeff and waited for him to begin their lunchtime topic. They had been friends for well over twenty years, but as Jeff was their superior in rank, and closest to David, they waited with easy deference for him to set the subject of the day.

'He's still not in,' Jeff answered their unasked question, his tawny eyes squinting thoughtfully at the pale champagne, which for them was always 'on the house'. 'And no, I haven't been given any reason why.'

'Doesn't need one,' Ike stated matter-of-factly. 'He's obviously exhausted from the relief.' His light blue, Scandinavian eyes, also searched the liquid in his glass.

Mark Wheeler's dark, bespectacled gaze was sombre. 'I sure as hell hope that this marriage will prove some kind of answer.' He shifted his stocky form in the leather club chair. 'But I'm damned if I can see how.'

Jeff gazed from Mark to Ike. 'Petersen?' It was the sign that they could all open up.

'Have to agree with Mark, I'm afraid. It's no secret that Mat's unpopular.' Ike indicated the rest of the building with a nod of his head. 'Getting him married off might well make D.N. feel better, but it sure as holy shit don't lend any brighter light to the future, as I see it.'

'I agree,' Mark stated quietly. 'Married or not, Mat's still moody, weak, selfish, conceited.'

'You've forgotten that he's also paranoid, and a bum. Not to mention incompetent,' Ike added easily.

Jeff Sherman sat back, savouring his champagne and letting the conversation follow its own course. It was better to have the guys air their feelings in here than anywhere else. But loyalty forbade that he himself should openly criticise David or, by the same token, any member of the Nazareth family. However, the T-EEM went way back. There was probably nothing the others could say that he wouldn't agree with. He just had to be more circumspect.

Ike Petersen spoke in a detached voice. 'I don't think there's a single member of staff who sleeps nights when he gets to thinking just how it's gonna be when Mat gets control.'

'David isn't exactly of retirement age, or inclination,' Jeff reminded them.

'Maybe not,' Ike agreed. 'But the day's gotta come, Jeff. And in our time I'd say. Now, if it had been Ben . . .'

There was instant silence, the prickly kind that could make you sweat.

Jeff stiffened, his pleasant face suddenly ashen. 'Damn it, Ike!' He swore quietly and would have left it at that given the choice. Ben was a subject definitely off limits.

The steward poured more champagne, took their lunch orders, and they were again left to themselves.

'Well, it ain't gonna be Ben, so that's that,' Ike said quietly, adding soberly, 'tough though that is for all of us.'

Another silence followed, one in which each of them thought about Ben.

They'd all known Benjamin Nazareth; known and loved

him. Paternal affection was something that he had engendered in the men who worked for his father.

Jeff was hurting the most. He was godfather to both Ben and to Mat, but there was no doubting his preference, even now.

He resigned himself to the fact that an occasion such as this probably made the topic of Ben inevitable. He swallowed a sip of champagne and waited.

'It must be ten years, Jeff?'

'About twelve in fact.'

Ike wasn't looking to upset Jeff, nobody was. Ben's name hadn't passed their lips in years. But in the aftermath of Mat's wedding? Ben was naturally on their minds.

'And there's still been no word from him?'

'Zilch,' Jeff confirmed.

'Not likely to be now, I suppose.' Mark stated, straightfaced.

Ike sighed as he remembered the solemn green-eyed child, who'd grown from a carefree, curious boy into a serious, troubled youth.

Ben had stolen the hearts of the Firm. He had spent every minute he could wandering from department to department, eager to understand the workings of his daddy's business. Ben had been a natural. From a bright toddler he'd become a brighter student, passing all his grades with straight As. And even before his teens he'd uncannily shown the Nazareth bent for law.

It had been uncanny, because Ben had been the son adopted when it was still believed that Ella couldn't have children. He had been the light of David's life and, until his sudden mysterious departure on his eighteenth birthday, Ben's consuming passions had been for his daddy and for Nazareth House.

It was no secret, now, that David had cut him out of his will. There and then. He had erased the boy's name from his vocabulary as totally as if he'd never existed. And from that the Firm had taken its cue.

But it did not stop any of them from wishing things had been different.

The only one who might know the truth was Jeff. But Jeff gave nothing away. Rumour had it that Ella had somehow very badly mistreated the boy – but whatever the truth of that, it was clear only that something had gone badly wrong over at the mansion. No one quite knew what.

'Know where he is?' Ike fished casually.

'He hasn't said.' Jeff's response was instant and sarcastic and he was immediately contrite. 'Sorry, it's the ulcer,' he muttered.

'Biting back, eh? You should get the surgeon to fish it out, Jeff. It's been eating at you for too long.'

Jeff gave Ike a small smile. 'I'll think about it.'

They began their lunch in an unusually strained manner. Mark had lost his appetite and toyed with his swordfish steak. Shit, he thought, the Firm *needs* Ben. He repeated it aloud. 'The Firm needs Ben. Or it will in the not too distant future.' He pushed his hardly touched plate away.

'True,' Ike joined in. 'How long will David give it, Jeff? Can't be more than ten years. Maximum . . .'

'What happens to us then?' Mark was growing nervous now, and it showed. 'After Matthew comes in, I mean . . .'

'What should happen to us?' Jeff answered as casually as he could.

'We're all younger than David, Jeff.' Ike's voice was still cool and detached, reasonable.

'Early retirement!' Mark snapped. It was a thought they'd all lost sleep over. What would happen to them if they couldn't, or wouldn't, work under Mat? If David wasn't around to ensure the safety of their comfortable positions, their pensions, their mortgages?

They weren't self-centred men. Each in his own way had given everything to David and Nazareth House. But at the end of the day they were very well off because of it. So far.

Yet thoughts today kept shifting back to Ben.

'Did Ben ever learn he'd been cut off?' Ike threw the question at Mark, knowing that his own department, Press, had been able to learn nothing second-hand. But that was also good, because if Ike Petersen couldn't learn it, nobody else could. Still, it rankled that he didn't know.

Mark stiffened now. 'My department was never instructed to contact him, so I don't know.' Privately he thought it totally wrong that David had never insisted that Ben be found and told. It was the only matter on which he could fault David in twenty years.

'The lad must know,' Jeff reasoned, aware that here was one area where he didn't know any more than the other two.

'Lad?' Ike had pushed his half-eaten meal away and now his sharp eyes glinted at them over the spiralling blue smoke from his cheroot. 'Hardly that, Jeff. A grown man of thirty!'

'It's a hell of a tragedy,' Mark said dourly.

'And a travesty of natural justice.' Ike gazed levelly at Jeff as he spoke.

'There's no point in raking it over,' Jeff said firmly. 'All it does is stir us up and for nothing.' He rubbed at his diaphragm softly. 'I'm with you guys all the way, but what's done is done. Ben's long gone. Matthew is the sole legal heir – and until his children take over from him he'll remain so.'

He looked at his long-time colleagues. They weren't exactly buddies but they had each earned the others' respect. They didn't socialise together, except for special occasions. But at work they were brothers under the skin.

'Unpalatable as it is, that's the fact we're all stuck with.'

Ike raised his spiky blonde brows. 'Do you think D.N. will be able to haul Mat's ass over here? Get him to pull with the tides?'

Jeff recognised the cynicism but let it pass. They were all staring at the same chasm ahead.

'Not unless someone tells him the score,' Mark interrupted.

'Perhaps we'll manage, between us,' Jeff replied coolly now. David's blindness over Mat's problems wasn't something he wanted to get involved in. But it was becoming a serious matter. How much did David know? No one could even guess. No one dared ask. The subject – like the name of Ben – was never aired.

Jeff had something else to keep him uneasy though, something he couldn't share. The knowledge sat heavily now on his ulcer. As a fairly constant visitor to the mansion he'd gradually become aware, over many years, that David didn't like Matthew. Or vice versa. That in itself had come as a severe shock. But worse was David's blindness to Mat's behaviour, his son's inconsistencies, his lies, his moods and his frequent trips away – to God knew where – at regular intervals.

If David wasn't blind, then he didn't want to know. And that, thought Jeff, is a real problem.

And what in hell could be done about it?

He glanced at his neat gold wristwatch. 'Time I was going. I've a meeting with Sam Golding at three.'

The other two men nodded and he left them, knowing that the subject of Ben would continue more easily with him gone.

Before leaving the building Jeff checked with his secretary, but there hadn't been a call from the boss. He shrugged grimly as he crossed the vast marbled foyer, but managed a smile for the old retainer who held the old-fashioned door for him.

Outside the sun was warm and he entered the air-conditioned Locker Room club with relief. A steward led him through to one of the small cool lounges, and Jeff noted that its only occupant was Sam.

'Ah, Jeff. Right on time! What'll you have?'

'Thanks, Sam. A cold root-beer would be fine.'

'Pull up a pew.' Sam indicated a leather chair and Jeff sat down, amused as always at Sam's use of English phrases. It had something to do with the fact that way back his grandfather had briefly lived in England. That old gentleman had acquired Englishness and passed it onto his grandson rather like a treasured valuable.

Jeff drew some papers from his briefcase and placed them on the table between them. 'I think it's all there, Sam. David had it drawn up before the wedding.'

'Good, good!' Sam beamed. He wasn't, in fact, in any hurry for the transaction, but behind closed doors Boston was talking. Sam was too shrewd to join in, but he wanted to know the truth of it.

'Jeff, I won't beat about the bush, not with you.' Sam paused as the steward brought Jeff's root-beer and waited until he'd left again before continuing. 'You know there's talk about the future of Nazareth House, now that young Mat's likely to be aboard soon.'

'What kind of talk?' Jeff smiled easily.

'Bad, Jeff, bad. They say that in a short while there could be a merger.'

The question was implied in the raised eye-brow. Jeff sipped at his beer. It wasn't a new suggestion – it came up at regular intervals, and it was what commercial Boston would keenly enjoy.

'Rumour, Sam. And, as before, without any foundation.'

Sam watched Jeff thoughtfully. The man was closer than a second skin to Dave, and just as loyal. But Sam's motives were more to warn than to pry. If he just happened to learn something to his advantage . . . well, that would be different.

'Dave's taken a little holiday I hear?'

Jeff could feel his colour fade. Damn it to hell, what *didn't* this club learn? 'Just a break, Sam, a few days.' Jeff's voice was cooler now.

'That's as it may be.' Sam kept his eyes on Jeff's face. 'But folks are wondering, Jeff, Matthew being married now and all. You know how folk talk.'

'No.' Jeff stretched his face into a tight smile. 'How do they talk, Sam?'

'Back off, Jeff. I'm no enemy, and you know it.' Sam's face had reddened slightly.

'OK,' Jeff was placatory. 'What's being said?'

'That Dave will let go the reins – hand over to Mat.' Sam frowned. 'That'd be mighty bad news for Nazareth House, Jeff. Wouldn't you say?'

'Yes,' Jeff agreed. 'If it were true. But it isn't going to happen – not for many years. So there's no problem.'

'It's one of the last family businesses,' Sam mused as if to himself. 'Certainly the largest. Yep, it'd be a tragedy if it were to become a corporation.' He glanced again at Jeff, but saw no reaction. He pulled towards him the papers Jeff had brought and gave them some cursory attention, while he considered the prospects. He personally wouldn't want to see it happen – but as a businessman . . . Nazareth House would be quite a prize.

Jeff cursed David's uncharacteristic behaviour that was fuelling such rumours. No business needed merger rumours: they caused tremors on the market and could easily lead to takeover attempts.

'David's brief absence' – Jeff broke the silence – 'is hardly likely to precipitate a collapse of the Firm. You should know that.'

Sam grunted. 'Oh, I know that, Jeff. The Firm will run as smoothly as an America's Cup yacht – unless the wrong person takes the helm.'

'One of my earliest known ancestors was a good friend of old Josh Nazareth,' Sam said now, 'and talk of the good old days was my grandaddy's favourite topic, learned from *his* daddy, so most of it came down to me. We're a funny lot, we Bostonians.' Sam's smile was whimsical and he nodded his head in approval. 'The past often matters more than the future. Odd that, don't you think?'

Jeff smiled and sat back. He was in for a session so he might as well enjoy it as well as the opulence of the Locker Room which, as a non-member, he didn't sample too often.

'Well, it's no wonder really, is it?' Sam was continuing his theme. 'Our ancestors were incredible men. Fighters one and all. They civilised this place from nothing, turned it into the foundation stone of American democracy.' He paused to take a drink, remembering.

'Old man Nazareth was a *real* legend, my grandaddy used to say. He told me that Nazareth House started out as a wooden hut down on the wharf. Seventeenth century,' he added with a definite pride, a pride he could allow to show when he spoke of David's ancestors, because by implication his own long line was instantly obvious.

'Yep. A wooden hut it was. The original Nazareth came up the river, from Salem, they say. It was called Naumkeg on the old maps. But before that he was from the old country. He was a man of learning, a lawyer like all Nazareths since. But his cleverness lay in spotting an opening for a bright young guy. They say he wasn't thirty-five years old when he was handling disputes among Yankee merchants plying their trade across the seven seas.' Sam shook his head in admiration.

'But he didn't stay in a wooden hut for long?' Jeff encouraged Sam's musings.

'No sir,' Sam agreed. 'He built himself a little brown-stone house on the mudflats.' Now he chuckled aloud. 'Can you imagine Boston as a mudflat, Jeff? Surrounded by an ocean on one side, and inhospitable Indians every other which way?'

'No, and neither can you,' Jeff protested. 'We know enough about our history now to know that the settlers displayed more hostility than was ever shown them.'

'True.' Sam laughed again. 'Still, it must have been something, eh?'

'Very little resemblance to today,' Jeff agreed reasonably.

Sam leant forward. 'It'd be a sad day for Boston if the oldest family business went under.'

'You wouldn't want to see that happen,' prompted Jeff.

'Damn it! Of course I wouldn't. What do you take me for?' Sam looked hurt now.

Jeff smiled easily. 'I just meant, Sam, that if David were

to get into any kind of trouble, he'd be able to count on his friends, wouldn't he? Men like you?'

The meaning wasn't lost on Sam, and his answer was in deadly earnest. 'David himself could count on every man in Boston. But I wouldn't give Matthew the same odds, and that's a fact.' His mouth now set grimly.

'But why?' Jeff played dumb. 'Mat's a Nazareth.'

'Well, he might be,' Sam snorted. 'But not like any Nazareth that's ever been known in Boston. Nope. If David left the helm, it'd only be a matter of time before the foxes would hammer Matthew and wrest the Firm from him.'

His chin wobbled as he nodded vigorously, agreeing with himself.

Jeff saw the glint in the back of Sam's eyes, but he wasn't surprised or too worried by it. Sam Golding was as good a business colleague and friend as any man might have but he was also a natural predator. He would never deliberately try to harm David, Jeff was sure.

But Matthew? Yes, Matthew would be a different story. . .

Nothing was wanted at the Firm and, as Jeff had no other appointments, he left early.

He remained preoccupied as he walked home to his townhouse. Mat's wedding had brought worms out from under the stones, and Jeff had the uneasy feeling that nothing would ever be the same again.

He let himself into his bachelor domain, happy enough with his own company. Jeff wasn't an unsociable animal, but in the main he was a loner and derived his pleasures outside the Firm, from the theatre and an eclectic musical taste. Tonight, though, he had more important things on his mind. Like contacting David.

David was in some kind of trouble and he thought he knew what. No, he was *sure* he knew what. But there was nothing he could do about that.

Was there anything he could do about the rumours? He

doubted it, though Sam's word would pass along the grapevine soon enough.

He recalled David's own words on the subject as clearly as though it were yesterday. Yet it had been over twenty years ago.

'Nazareth House,' David had told him quietly, 'is as old and as revered as the Founding Fathers. As long as there's a Nazareth at the helm, this Firm's future will never be in any doubt.'

To Jeff's certain knowledge it never had been. Until Ben had left. Ben's departure had caused an implosion that had left a gaping crack in the foundations, and now the crack was widening.

He poured himself an iced martini and allowed his thoughts to wander back down the years . . . He seemed to need to reassure himself that Nazareth House was impregnable.

They had been standing looking out of the window, down on to the streets and buildings below. David, handsome and filled with the exuberance of young, strong manhood and the fervour of his ancestors, had been telling Jeff, who'd only been with him a few months, the story of Nazareth House.

'This Firm is as solid as the rock on which the first pilgrims stood,' David had said, his face alight with humour. 'I've never been sure whether my ancestors were Saints, or Strangers, as they were called then, but puritan they were not.' He had smiled to himself, a deep smile which encompassed everything in his sight.

Jeff Sherman had waited politely, but with genuine interest. Already he had an affection for this man, was growing to value everything that David valued.

'True,' David had laughed aloud then, 'religion had a strong hold in my family, at least until I came along. My father wouldn't agree with me, but my opinion is that the Nazareth line was always more merchant than missionary. More the backbone of eventual wealth and culture than soldiers of the Cross.'

He turned and gave Jeff one of the expansive smiles Jeff was to learn were capable of charming total strangers and of winning embittered cases in the court-room and, later, anywhere else.

'Without a strong vein of acquisitiveness, could my ancestors have turned a small brownstone trading post, a one-man law business, into what the Firm is today? No, indeed they could not. But my dear father would like me to believe it all came about through prayer!'

At this his face had hardened and Jeff was later to learn that David's childhood and home life had centred around a strict and zealous bible-worship. Out in the business world, Luke Nazareth was as shrewd a businessman as any Nazareth before him. But at home, apparently, he had assumed a mantle of religious fervour and sombre discipline . . .

The disc came to an end and Jeff stirred to change it. He was unusually melancholy tonight, the conversation at lunch as much to blame as the interlude with Sam.

Jeff had been in his early twenties when he'd joined David, and from that time to this he'd never wanted any other job, or to work for any other man. The business had already begun to show signs of the empire it would become in David's ingenious hands. He had taken an exceedingly wealthy but unwieldly and old-fashioned family business and created a modern empire of both commerce and law.

David firmly resisted any notion of merger or incorporation with any other business house. Yet the offers continued to arrive with monotonous regularity.

'Damn you, Matthew!' Jeff suddenly swore aloud. Because Mat was directly the cause of all the uncertainties flying about the place now.

He glanced up at the clock, wondering if this might be a good time to call.

He knew he was treading uncertain ground even as he keyed David's private number, but his concern was acute enough for him to take the risk.

Sanders took the call on the second ring. He was alert to anything that might disturb his master these days.

'Hi, Sanders. Jeff here. Any chance of a word with David?'

'No, Mr Sherman.' The English houseman spoke quietly. 'Mr Nazareth doesn't wish to take any calls.'

'Oh.' Jeff was thrown. 'I could come over . . .'

Sanders voice was instantly aloof. 'No, sir. You could not,' he warned firmly.

'Hell!' Jeff became annoyed. 'You might at least tell him I'd like to speak to him. On a matter of some urgency.'

'Indeed I will, Mr Sherman. Thank you for calling.'

'Wait a min . . .' Jeff was about to insist that Sanders tell David right now but, to his disbelief, he'd been cut off. Just like that.

He sank back in his chair, puzzled. Since when had David refused calls, or callers?

Jeff nursed his cocktail and brooded. Hell. If only David were more approachable. If he could only talk to him openly. 'Ha!' he muttered aloud. There were more things than the present concern he'd like to be able to discuss with David. Like why in hell he'd ever let Ben leave.

Why hadn't David stopped his beloved son? Or at least brought him back?

And why in hell wasn't it *Ben* who was here, getting married, preparing to inherit one day?

Jeff stared at his empty glass. No, it was no good. If fate hadn't intervened, Ben would still have learned, one day, that all the real power would go to Mat. No matter what David felt, his ancestry had dictated the course he would have taken. There hadn't been a Nazareth yet who'd have tolerated anything other than a blood-child at the helm, and the only honest thing that could be said about that was that it was a damned crime that there *had* been one. Called Matthew.

'God help us all,' he sighed. For Jeff knew that Mat was no more capable of running the Firm than he was of sprouting wings and flying to the moon.

Whatever the situation between David and Diana – and there *was* a situation, however intangible as yet – the future for Nazareth House looked exceedingly grim.

CHAPTER THREE

If David had believed that the marriage would exorcise Diana
from his soul, he was badly mistaken.

He refused all calls and his truancy from the Firm continued.
In fact, after a week he didn't even give it a thought. His
mind was obsessed with thoughts of Diana. Visions of her
and Mat – together – tormented his waking and his sleeping hours.

He brooded in the book-lined elegance of his study, but
read nothing, wrote nothing. The windows overlooked the
gardens and he stood for hours looking into space or across the
lush irrigated lawns, the borders of fine roses and the hedges
intertwined with honeysuckle; down towards the walled garden he stared, through the clumps of lime, elm and pine
trees to the parkland and common land beyond.

His acres, a source of pride all his life, meant nothing to him
at this time.

'*Diana*' was the only word he spoke aloud. And in that one
word was contained his very soul.

Sanders fussed the staff and tended the house without
instructions from his master.

'Shall I light the fire, sir?' he might ask in the cool of the
late evenings. Or, 'Will you have some supper on a tray, Mr
David?'

He barely received a grunt and had to interpret it as he
would.

'You will not disturb Mr Nazareth,' he daily told the household staff. 'No matter what.'

Then, as the days went by, he had to give other instructions
– for instance to Meg, on such occasions as the master's bed
had not been slept in. 'Just tidy up, girl,' he would say quietly.
Or, when the bed looked as if it had accommodated a sleepless

army, he would say calmly, 'The master had a bad night. Strip the bed.'

To the rest of the staff, Mrs Carly the cook-housekeeper and John the gardener, he merely said that he thought the boss had been overworking. They would all, he told them, have to take greater care of him.

Sanders was probably the only member of the small household who guessed at the real problem. He had looked after Mr David for all of David's life and there was little he didn't interpret correctly about his boss's needs.

Unaware of his household's concern, David drove his powerful XJ6 out most evenings, noticing little of the lovely Massachusetts countryside with its hedgerows of glorious colour. Too familiar with fields awash with daisies, buttercups, Queen Anne's lace and lily of the valley, he was indifferent to their splendid displays this year.

He watched the road, just, and drove until he was exhausted, or until he found an out-of-the-way hostelry in which to take a solitary meal. But more often than not to sample a few pain-obliterating short 'n' sharps. He didn't allow himself the luxury of getting drunk, but topped up sufficiently to dull his aching mind.

Mornings found him ashen from nights of haunted, punishing dreams, or slumped in his chair in his study, a half-empty bourbon bottle at his side.

'Mr David, sir?' Sanders called softly to the prone figure one morning. 'Will you take your breakfast now?'

David fought his way up through a dark cloud to find his houseman bending over him, in some apparent concern.

'Breakfast, sir?' The man repeated quietly but with insistence.

'What day is it, Sanders?' David asked drowsily.

'Friday, sir,' Sanders replied. 'Mr Matthew and Miss Diana are due back on Sunday, sir.'

David noted the 'Miss' Diana and didn't correct it to Mrs

Nazareth. He infinitely preferred to hear her addressed as 'Miss'.

'Friday?' He let out a low whistle.

'Indeed, sir.' Sanders smiled. He'd had a feeling that today he would be able to get a response.

'Mmm . . . yes, breakfast would be nice. I'll have it in the dining-room. Oh, and Sanders, make that a full English breakfast. The works!'

Sanders smiled. 'The very best thing, sir. The very best thing . . .'

David stretched his naked body beneath the sheets, and instantly became aware of a new tingle of life, of warmth coursing through his limbs.

Suddenly he laughed, a deep luxurious laugh. 'I'll be damned!' He hadn't felt anything remotely 'male and sexual' in years. The day ahead beckoned pleasantly indeed.

'Friday, huh?' He spoke softly to himself. 'Two more days.'

The houseman smiled across from David's wardrobe. 'Quite so, sir. Now what will you wear this morning?'

David thought for a moment. 'The beige linen . . . oh, and Sanders, I think I'll go into town this morning, to the barber's for a start.' He ran his fingers through his unruly hair. 'I must be quite a sight, eh?'

'The barber would be a good place to start,' Sanders agreed politely and, smiling to himself, he left his master to finish grooming in privacy.

David threw back the covers and strode naked to his bathroom, the past three weeks pushed deliberately from his mind . . . until he caught sight of his reflection in the mirrored walls.

There were lines drawn tautly around his mouth, dark smudges beneath his eyes; and his hair would have done credit to a tramp.

He gave a snort of disbelief. 'Jeez, you look like some kind of alien, pal!'

Sanders, re-entering the room with his master's suit, stopped and would have turned away, but David called to him. 'Sanders, what I need is a kick up the ass. That and a good workout.' He grinned at the surprise on Sanders face. 'Well, it's true, isn't it?'

'Whatever you say, Mr David.' Sanders inclined his head courteously.

David watched his man leave, then turned back to the mirror. It was true. He looked like a love-sick slob of an alien.

The needles of the shower invigorated him. It was as if he'd awoken from a coma. Obstinately he told himself that everything was going to be all right. He'd have Diana in his life and she would fill all the spaces in his emotions. Diana in the house, even married to Mat, was better than no Diana at all.

He stepped from the shower and studied his body dispassionately. Damn it! He was far from over the hill yet. He was in good condition – never better in fact. His powerful frame was still lean and hard; his height well proportioned to his muscular width. As for his stomach, it was as taut as it had ever been.

He glowered at the silver hairs sprinkled generously in his black hair and in the thick expanse of his body hair, but he doubted that they would be a serious turn-off to a loving woman.

The thought startled him. Shit! He was trying to see himself as Diana might. And what the hell chance had he of being naked when she was around?

But his body had responded to the thought and now he gazed down at himself, a rueful twist at the corner of his mouth.

'Buddy . . . you need some action. You live like a bloody monk!' he swore dryly.

The grey feeling disappeared and a twinkle appeared in his eyes.

'Sanders?' He depressed the intercom. 'Get the florist to deliver a couple of dozen white roses to Madame Bérénice, and a message that I'll call her later.'

Had Beanie been worrying? If so the flowers would tell her that all was well. With luck she'd be free for dinner tonight. Who knew, maybe Beanie could point him at some lovely, available lady.

He began to hum as he left his suite. 'Morning, Meg.' He smiled at the maid who was dusting at the top of the wide sweep of stairs.

Sanders appeared, just as David noticed the closed doors at the end of the hall, the doors into the newly built annexe wing.

'Why are those doors shut, Sanders?' David asked, instantly aware of a new knot in his stomach.

'To stop the smell of paint spreading, sir.'

'That paint's been dry two weeks. Get them open,' David snapped.

'Yes, sir.' Sanders did not remind his master that he had demanded they be closed on the night of the wedding.

'And I want them left open. At *all* times,' David ordered tightly.

He hurried down the broad staircase with its twisted, carved banisters and across the marble-tiled hall into the dining-room. The room was high-ceilinged, like all the rooms on the ground floor, and furnished with Chippendale.

The morning sun sparkled on glistening crystal, throwing little kaleidoscopes of rainbow colours on to a snowy white linen table cloth. Highly polished silver reflected the patina of glowing cherrywood-panelled walls.

David had always loved his home, but never more so than today. It had been an empty show-piece for too many years. Soon it would ring with joyful laughter, laughter and the sounds of children. Diana's children. His future heirs.

'This is a lovely room, Sanders.'

Sanders had followed David and now he agreed with him, not remarking that there was anything unusual in his master finding pleasure in a room he had ignored for three decades.

'This table, Sanders . . . it was designed for what . . . twenty people? Yet in my life it has rarely been graced by more than the immediate family.' David glanced down the long table and for a brief moment the joy left him. There had been few memorable moments in his life. Far, far too few.

'We shall change all that . . .' He spoke as if to himself.

Sanders listened.

'Make a note of how I want the arrangements, Sanders. I will, of course, take the head: Miss Diana will be on my right; Mr Matthew on my left. When the children arrive, they will be seated according to age and sex, girls on their mother's right, and boys on their father's left . . .'

Sanders managed not to splutter, and gave a small cough to clear his throat instead. 'I understand, Mr Nazareth.'

David looked up to see who else was about. Sanders only ever called him 'Mr Nazareth' in company. Otherwise he was sir, or Mr David.

Meg had come down and was waiting to ask Sanders a question concerning her chores. Seeing him busy with the boss, she began to turn away.

'Meg, don't go.' David smiled at the young woman. 'I want some advice . . .'

'Before breakfast, sir?' Sanders disapproved mildly.

'Right now,' David replied firmly.

He leaned against a window-sill and addressed them both. 'Now, what would you choose as wedding gifts, if you were young brides? I want to buy something for Miss Diana. She wouldn't accept a wedding present, except a small watch. Now I intend to surprise her,' he laughed softly. 'Yes, so that she'll find it hard to refuse . . .'

Both members of his staff stood, uncertainly, looking at him.

'Meg?'

'I don't know, sir.' The girl shook her head. 'I've never been a bride, sir.'

David grinned. 'Neither have I, Meg. But I just want some suggestions. Anything?'

'Flowers, sir?' Meg coloured warmly under his earnest gaze.

'Not very lasting, Meg.' David chuckled. 'But yes . . . perhaps some flower vases. Sanders, did you notice if Miss Diana has any yet?'

'I think not,' Sanders replied, furrowing his brow. 'And I don't believe there's a clock in the bridal wing, sir.'

'Excellent!' David rubbed his hands with delight. 'That will do for starters. Thank you both.'

'May I serve your breakfast now?' Sanders assumed his normal mantle with relief.

David was whistling softly as he strolled over to Back Bay. His purchases were selective but swift. Neither the very Brahmin store of Shreve, Crump and Lowe, nor the hallowed atmosphere of Firestone and Parsons could tempt him to dally. He ordered an antique carriage clock, circa 1870, a fine set of Steuben wine-glasses; a canteen of silver cutlery, to be engraved with the initial 'N', and left instructions for their delivery on Monday morning to Mrs Diana Nazareth.

Pleased so far, his next stop was at the florist. There he chose a dozen slender brass and copper vases, complete with an armful of apricot and ivory roses to fill them, then made his way more leisurely to Quincey's market. He had to conceal his amusement as several wives of close colleagues gaped. Now, he wondered . . . what would they all make of David Nazareth doing his own grocery shopping?

He was still smiling as he selected a fillet of beef, a kilo of oysters and a strawberry cheesecake large enough to feed a small army. They would go very nicely with a vintage Château-Lafite he had in his cellars.

The morning had passed enjoyably. But now David was ready for something more stimulating. First the barber shop, and then a workout at Zak's.

The gym punished him sufficiently, and the massage followed by a hot shower took care of his aching muscles. Now he needed a drink and some non-taxing company.

Beanie took his call at her home on Mt Vernon. She'd given up trying to reach him and, like Jeff, had resigned herself to the fact that David was out of circulation, no reason given, until he was good and ready to be otherwise.

'Darling!' she exclaimed, delighted to hear at last.

'Beanie.' David smiled and toyed with his bourbon glass, the club's portable phone cradled against his shoulder. 'What are you doing tonight that you couldn't change for an old pal?'

Beanie all but purred with pleasure. It was a long time since David had invited her out. 'I had been going to have supper, all alone and friendless,' she teased.

'Well, honey . . . how about we catch a show at the Wilbur, then some dinner. Fancy Cyrill's?'

It was one of Beanie's favourite restaurants, but she wouldn't have cared if it'd been a hot-dog stand. To cover some of her pleasure she complained lightly. 'But you give a lady no time to prepare, darling! Besides, I have nothing to wear.' Her voice was warm, sexy and mischievous.

David grinned. The lady joked. 'How about you wear something *grey*. Just for me?'

If Beanie noticed the implied sarcasm, she ignored it. 'Oh dear,' she sighed in mock exasperation. 'Very well, if you insist.'

'I insist.' David also mocked lightly. 'I'll call about eight . . .'

He returned the phone to its cradle, leaned back in the club armchair and chuckled at the thought of Beanie, Boston's top designer, with nothing to wear. An MB label was something women would fight for, as essential as their Back Bay townhouses and their country homes, their stretched Cadillacs and their diamonds.

But Beanie would wear grey. Doubtless it would be contrasted with a startling colour – anything from the rainbow – but she never wore any other main colour than grey.

It was part of the enigma that was Beanie.

David had long ago given up trying to discover her background – and to his knowledge no one else had discovered it either. It was a very long time since he'd given it any thought. Yet, for some inexplicable reason, this evening he was consumed with curiosity.

Beanie, as a very young designer, had arrived in Boston from God-only-knew-where just after the war, and had slipped swiftly into its top society. Not an easy thing to do for any outsider, let alone a foreign one. Of course she'd been incredibly young, and very beautiful. David knew of more than one Boston blueblood who'd fallen for the dark-haired, mysteriously exotic beauty. But it had been more than her feminine allure, more even than her air of helpless innocence – and did not concern her undoubted talent. It had been simply 'something else'. Something as tangible then as it was still today.

Whatever the 'something else' had been, she'd opened a tiny shop in one of the poorer parts of town, designing and making exclusive model gowns based on the latest European styles. The fashion-hungry of the city had descended in droves on the little shop, conveying instant status on the then seedy back street. From the start Beanie's patrons had been discriminating and wealthy. Within two years she'd had to move to larger premises in Newbury Street, now the equivalent of Fifth Avenue.

Her business had continued to expand ever since. Yet even though she had more seamstresses than any other designer outside New York, she still did the designing and cutting herself.

CHAPTER FOUR

As David walked over to his garage block, he mused on Beanie's total secrecy about herself and her past. Some – David among them – had in those early days believed her to be essentially 'Parisienne'. She'd certainly seemed as insouciant, volatile and as stylish as Bostonians imagined Parisians to be, but she was neither inconsequential nor intimate, and she lacked the flirtatiousness of a true-born Frenchwoman. The Paris tag had, therefore, never been fully accepted. But it was all they had.

David slipped behind the wheel of his Jaguar, eased the sleek motor into gear and drove out of his long, tree-lined Beacon Street drive, and turned for Mt Vernon, still with Beanie's hidden past on his mind.

Ella had been his new bride, and had quickly claimed Beanie as her best friend. For a long time David had thought it his duty to find out what he could about Mademoiselle B. Suchard. But it hadn't worked, beyond the proof that she had boarded the plane in Paris. It surprised him now to realise that he was still irked and still curious, although why in hell he should care tonight was beyond him. All he'd wanted was a good meal, in pleasant company, nothing that would tax his mind. Yet he'd spent half the day already raking over times long since gone.

Why should he care *now* what Beanie might or might not have been? She'd been his friend for nearly thirty years and had never abused that friendship.

Thinking of friends reminded him that it must be about time for one of Beanie's parties. He navigated the Jaguar into Beanie's private bay in the basement of the plush block of apartments, smiling. Diana would *love* one of Beanie's little dos which were like gold dust, scattered only on the favoured few. They were famous for being as exceptional as snow on the nose of the Sphinx.

David had yet to attend one which did not delight him. The perpetual child in Beanie seemed to emerge through the creative, and unique, themes of her parties.

No one ever knew for sure when the next would be; or who would be there or where it would be held. Only those invited would be told the venue and the date, and they were wise enough to keep it to themselves until after the event. Being among the select few guests was a status jealously sought by many, even though it might be the only time they would ever be invited. Once was enough to make the golden claim. Beanie, with her parties, decided Who was Who.

How she decided her guest list was a secret known only to her. But it was not only the obvious social circles from which she made her choice. Many a young unknown had found success after a mysterious invitation dropped through their door. Yet Beanie chose with uncanny acumen, knowing that she would get immediate loyalty.

Only once had a columnist been invited and that lady could still recall some fifteen years later, with acid clarity, her social gaffe. She had made the mistake of forgetting she was off-duty, and questioned her hostess. The experience, she would still tell one and all, was instant frostbite and a quick cold march out of the door.

This hadn't made Beanie any the less popular, or lesser news. Quite the opposite. Her reclusivity and single-minded avoidance of the media guaranteed that some scribbler was always lurking nearby, obsessed by a vision of scooping a first real interview with the 'French Freezer', as Beanie had long ago been dubbed by the press . . .

They were lucky to be early at Cyrill's. Once the crowd started arriving, they could not have enjoyed the intimacy that was now theirs.

'You look, as usual, very lovely,' David complimented her as they sipped Kir Royales and awaited their meal.

'Despite the grey?' Beanie teased gently.

'Because of the grey!' David replied emphatically, ignoring her light tone. 'You should wear it more often, it could get to be all the rage.'

Beanie smiled with him. There was an inner tension about David tonight which emanated as subtly as the light cologne he wore. If she hadn't known him as well as she did, she might have thought that there was a provocative sexual undercurrent between them. But she knew that to be quite impossible. Years ago she'd learned that David might flirt with her, or she with him, but he never expected it to be taken seriously. On occasions she'd found that unbearably hard, for she'd wanted him for as long as she'd known him.

David appraised Beanie equally thoughtfully. What was different about her tonight? Perhaps a new hairstyle? Another glance at the cap of dark glossy curls, told him it wasn't that. What then? A new perfume possibly?

David didn't know. She was simply stunning. But then, she always was. Was it the outfit perhaps? She wore a silvery-grey chiffon two-piece, with a pencil skirt and a flounced-edged jacket. The vee of the neckline emphasised the small, pert breasts, drawing David's eyes appreciatively. He'd said 'wear sexy' and that's what she'd done. But he'd seen her in sexier clothes, and been less aware of her as a woman than he was tonight.

'Darling, you're staring,' she said softly, almost warningly.

David felt his colour rise, and with it a rush of annoyance. Damn it, they'd been close friends for a bloody long time. Surely long enough for some truths.

'Beanie . . . you irk the hell out of me,' he said suddenly. 'You're sexy enough to bring the animal out in any guy . . . yet here we are, as what, thirty-year friends? You still have the power to attract me but, damn it to hell, you're a closed book! For all I know about you, we could be complete strangers.'

Beanie gazed wide-eyed at the outburst, which was unusual enough. But the burning light in David's eyes warned her to be wary. She'd been right. There was something different about him tonight.

She sipped some more of the Kir Royale, then put her glass carefully on the table, steadying her nerves.

'David, there is nothing more you should know about me than you already do.' She gave him a small smile but her eyes were grave. 'Everything that's happened in my life since I came to Boston, you know about — '

'Honey,' David interrupted sharply, 'I'm talking about where the hell you came from. And why it should still be a bloody secret, at least between us, when — '

He stopped as he saw her beautiful eyes glaze over with tears. Beanie, crying? 'Look, honey,' he said quickly, 'don't get upset. Not with me for Chrissakes. I'm your friend, remember? It's just that, well, hell, I don't know why you still don't trust me after all these years . . .'

Beanie had composed herself swiftly. She'd never let her emotions show to anyone and she wasn't about to start now. But her voice shook slightly as she answered.

'It has nothing to do with trust, darling. I have done nothing in my life to warrant your distrust, I swear.'

'Then what *is* your secret?' David persisted, his voice low with his own feeling of hurt pride, 'And *why* is it still between us?'

'It's not,' Beanie stated quietly. 'The only things I haven't told you are too painful for me to talk about.' Her eyes were solemn again as they met his gaze. 'If I had ever told you . . . even if I told you now, darling, you would feel sorry for me. And the one thing I have never wanted from you is pity.'

She lifted a small hand as he began to protest. 'No, it's all too long ago to remember now. You might say you wouldn't feel differently, but, believe me, you would. I have hidden little from you except a place of birth and a childhood best forgotten. Why won't you just accept that?'

David stared at her, moved by a distress made more obvious by her attempt to conceal it. Pity her? Beanie, his strong friend?

He'd seen her make mincemeat out of competitors, male and female alike, and now he'd just had a shocking insight into her inner vulnerability.

Suddenly, he didn't want to know her secret, not if the thought of it could cause that haunted look. Whatever had created her secret had caused her enough pain. He would not add to it. He reached out and squeezed her hand. 'Forgive me, honey.'

'There's nothing to forgive.'

'I'm an insensitive asshole,' David said wryly.

'No, just a too-curious male.' Her light laugh broke the tension. 'Now, what's this play you're taking me to. I hope that it's a comedy.'

'It is,' David assured her, smiling tenderly. He was relieved that they'd managed to put things back on their old footing. He gave her a brief résumé of the show they were to see and, by the time they'd finished their meal, they were once again flirting lightly, harmlessly, as they'd always done. But they were more than aware of a new tension between them.

As they drove back to Mt Vernon, David had every intention of seeing her to her door, and then getting himself home to bed. And perhaps that's how it would have been, had Beanie not stumbled as he helped her from the car. Her warm body momentarily brushed against his and he held her for just a second or so too long.

Bemused, and still feeling guilty, he could not refuse her invitation to come up to her penthouse for a nightcap.

Beanie was only too aware of the battle going on in David, and her own heartbeat was rapid as they entered her suite. She was more than aware of his frustration, a frustration that had made him act so out of character tonight.

She was also sadly aware that *she* was not responsible for fanning the flame of his sexual needs. Someone else had done that. But she had always dared to hope that *one day* he might turn to her and she was woman enough to recognise her chance when it came. And it had come. Tonight.

Her body trembled with anticipation and anxiety. But she deliberately quashed any guilt over what she was suddenly, feverishly planning. She didn't owe any loyalty to Mat's wife . . .

'You fix the drinks, darling. I'll rekindle the fire.'

David instantly regretted coming up with her. The lights were low; small-hours music played on the stereo. Across the Charles River soft lights glittered, their reflection on the plate-glass windows somehow exotic. The atmosphere was muted, seductive, a perfect setting for lovers.

He busied himself at the bar, determined to have just one sociable drink, then leave.

But he'd underestimated the power of the sexual tension between them. When he brought the drinks from the bar, Beanie was curled like a small dark kitten on the long, mink-coloured suede settee. His body tightened responsively. She'd never looked more appealing than she did tonight.

The almond-shaped eyes with their dark fringes watched him as he approached, and with strangely heightened clarity he was instantly aware that she wanted him. Also that she was scared. That recognition helped him, made him feel stronger, somehow.

'Here you go, honey. Martini. Just how you like it.'

He was careful not to sit too close to her. Christ. This was all his fault. He'd behaved badly and, to make matters worse, he'd openly admitted his attraction. So now it was up to him. He'd have to get them both off the hook. He began to make casual small-talk about business.

Beanie let him. She encouraged him to relax, interjecting small comments from time to time, until gradually he began to unwind.

The warm, sultry atmosphere and the alcohol helped him. He'd needed company, and he had it. He was, anyway, probably imagining anything else. Beanie was his buddy, for Chrissakes. He threw off his jacket, loosening the knot in his tie.

Beanie chatted easily. She had all the time in the world tonight. She'd learned a long time ago how to act, but tonight she was acting for all she was worth. She watched as David grew more relaxed, until she was sure that, for the moment, he'd forgotten his concerns, as well as his desires.

'I have been wanting to talk to you about my next season's Show. Perhaps Diana would like to help me plan the party afterwards, do you think? But wait, I'll just get us another drink.'

David nodded. He was happy to listen to Beanie talk about her business, and proud that she always sought his opinion. He stretched out on the settee, eyes half closed, enjoying the music.

Beanie stood behind him for a while, watching him. It might be a cliché but he did remind her of a large American cougar she had once seen, stretched in that same deceptively unguarded way, relaxed, yet alert. He exuded a feral sexuality, as if it were coiled deep within him, ready to erupt. Tantalised by her imaginings, she shivered.

She brought the drinks over and curled herself on the carpet near him.

'So, what about the Show and the party?' he asked lazily. 'Autumn, I take it?'

'Mmm, but earlier this year. Perhaps just after Labor Day.' She leaned against the settee and looked up at him, searchingly. It might be now or never, she realised. 'There's something I want to ask you, though, nothing to do with business.'

He tipped his head to look at her. Her dark eyes were glowing and he tried to blank out the picture she made – to resist the erotic images of her naked beneath the grey chiffon . . .

'Have you ever wanted to make love to me?' she asked softly.

He forced himself to answer casually. 'Sure.'

'Before tonight, I mean?'

His thoughts raced. Should he lie, or risk the truth being the best safeguard. 'Many times,' he answered lightly.

Her hand gently moved against his thigh. 'Don't lie to me, darling. Not tonight. Please.'

'I'm not,' he said cautiously.

'Then why don't you?'

He pulled himself up and turned round to face her, his expression deliberately amused. But her face was rigid with tension, and again he saw the sheen of tears held back.

A sudden warm compassion flooded through him and he pulled her gently into his arms. 'Honey, I've never tried to make love to you for very good reasons. I've been a bastard this evening, and I'm sorry.'

He spoke the words softly into her hair, soothingly, as if she were a child being denied a special treat. 'I was a selfish sonofabitch earlier. I behaved very badly, and I'm sorry. Can you forgive and forget?'

She buried her head deeper against his chest, and her voice was husky with sadness as she repeated herself. 'Please, darling, make love to me . . .'

He heard the pain and her need and, to his horror, his body responded.

He tried to put her gently from him. 'Beanie, don't do this. Don't make it difficult for us.'

She groaned, and her body shuddered against his. 'Honey!' His voice was more urgent, anxious. 'I'll tell you why I haven't, and why I'm not about to now. It's because I'm too selfish to ruin the friendship we share. I value that just about as much as anything on this earth. I do love you, honey, you know I do, but it's a special kind of love. If we were to become lovers it would . . .'

His sentence remained in mid-air as Beanie suddenly covered his mouth with her own warm soft lips. The shock momentarily stunned him, but it was too much for his long-pent-up needs; hunger exploded within him and suddenly he was in a mindless ecstasy of desire which fired his blood and raged through his body with the power of a high-voltage electricity charge.

He could no longer stop himself.

Her fingers reached inside his shirt, sending arrows of fire from his nipples to his groin. He too groaned hungrily, his need as deep as hers. He *wanted* her.

And somewhere, deep beyond his reach, he hated himself.

His hands moved of their own volition, releasing the belt at her waist, undressing her swiftly, tenderly, exposing her nakedness to his hungry eyes and mouth. His lips sought and found the eagerly swollen buds of her breasts. She began to cry softly with pleasure, and he was deliriously lost.

With infinite skill she was undressing him as he caressed her, then she slid away from his mouth and dropped to bury her head between his thighs.

She heard him moan, almost angrily. But then he was in control of her, his hands in command, exploring. His touch grew more urgent as his fingers and his mouth brought her nearer and nearer the end of her own short fuse. Deliriously she whispered his name, over and over again.

He freed himself of his last clothing, not letting her out his reach . . . and like him she was wild. Her lips and fingertips caressed every inch she could reach, until his body burned like molten steel. Flaming with agonising pleasure. The sweetest pain.

It was like a battle in which neither would release the other. They rolled on the thick carpet, their limbs damp and tangled together. One minute her small breasts were filling his eager mouth, nipples swollen, hot and throbbing. And then she had slipped from him, down, until her tongue was torching his last defences. Her hands gently cradled, fondled, as her mouth held and tormented him.

Suddenly he pulled her easily up to his chest. Then he was towering over her, as her eyes, enormous pools of pain and pleasure, begged for more. He gave it willingly, drunk on her exquisitely sweet body, mercilessly kissing and probing every inch of her loveliness, until she cried out for release.

She lay open beneath him, a precious prize waiting for him to make his final claim. Then, as he started to enter her, his agony rose above his desperate need, and he cried out the name of his one true love . . . and a black despair engulfed him.

When he dared to open his eyes, to beg her forgiveness, the misery in her beautiful brown eyes mirrored his own.

To hide his shame he rolled over and buried his face in his arms.

Beanie lay quite still on the carpet. Only her hands had moved up to her eyes to hide her own despair.

She was still lying like that when David forced himself to move back towards her, his heart aching far more than his body, aching for them both.

Gently he pulled her into his arms. She complied like a small child and he rocked her, holding her against his chest. There was nothing he could say yet, nothing that would help.

After a while she shivered, and David eased himself up. He had never hated himself more than he did at this moment. But somehow, God only knew how, he had to try to prevent the total collapse of the friendship they both valued so much.

He was still shocked and his mind was confused, but he knew that he'd seen love in her eyes. He hadn't known she loved him in *that* way until then. But in the same instant that he'd recognised it, his own love for Diana had burst forth, had acted as a defence; and in that penultimate moment, he'd cried out her name. His brain finally started to function again. Clothes, she needed clothes, as much for warmth as for her self-respect. He struggled silently into his trousers and padded swiftly to her bedroom. In the closet he found a warm robe and brought that to her. 'Here, honey. Put this on before you get chilled.' He marvelled that his voice sounded so even, so entirely normal. 'I'll fix us something to drink before I go.'

He didn't wait for her reaction, guessing that she'd need

a little time to compose herself. So he took longer than was necessary to arrange two cognacs on a tray.

But the tray wasn't needed. He felt her presence at the bar, and turned to press the brandy silently into her cold hand. He could not ignore what had happened. Or what had not.

He came round and eased himself on to a stool next to her small, robed figure. And, taking one of her cold hands in his, he gently pressed it to his lips. His eyes were caring, and genuinely concerned.

'As I was saying, honey,' he said gently, 'before we both got carried away by all that booze and seductive music, I believed, and still believe, that if we were to become lovers everything would change between us. I meant it when I said I'm selfish. I like things the way they are, the way they've always been . . .'

He sensed that she was about to protest but he stopped her by pressing a finger gently against her lips. 'Honey, let me finish. I owe it to you, to us both.'

Her eyes, swollen and red in the white face, focused on him. They held no accusation, only sorrow. She listened intently.

'You might have wanted to say that things couldn't change, that tonight would have made no difference; but, honey, I'm telling you that it *would*. The relationship we have is the best of both worlds. As a man I can fancy you, as a friend I can love you. But the two can't be combined without ruining our friendship. We enjoy one another's company and we each know that the other is there when we're in any kind of need. Substitute a sexual relationship for what we have and you can say goodbye to friendship as we have known it.'

'Why?' Her voice was small, still shaken, immeasurably sad.

David sighed deeply. God, this was hard. But it had to be said, and cleared up forever. 'Because, honey, you do mean too much to me for me to risk losing you over a sexual interlude.' He gazed into her eyes, willing her to see the truth.

'I've always enjoyed your sensuality, the edge your attractiveness gives. I'd guessed you were an exciting woman and tonight has more than proved that. But it has also proved that, much as I might physically want to, I must never again take advantage of your generosity.'

He was careful to edit the word love out of this summary. Tiredness was welling up in him, making him dizzy, but he had to make sure that she understood – and he had to take all the blame himself, before he could leave.

He refilled her brandy glass. 'If you weren't the best friend I've ever had, nothing, and I do mean *nothing*, could have come between us tonight. I'd have fucked you until your mind blew, and' – he gazed at her intently – 'that would have been the end of us as friends.'

Beanie shook her head, unable to believe, refusing to accept what he was saying. 'No. It was Diana. Not me, and not our friendship!'

'You're wrong, Beanie. Very wrong. Diana "happened" tonight, and I'm glad that she did.' He caught both her hands in his and his face was grave. 'Honey, I don't have anything more precious I can offer you than friendship. If we had gone any further, tomorrow I'd have had to wipe you from my mind as a friend.' He saw her about to argue again and stopped her with a warning shake of his head. 'You have to believe I mean that. I couldn't be your lover and your friend without a much greater commitment – it's the way I'm made – and as I *can't* offer you any other commitment than the friendship we already have, that would have been the end of us. Period.'

Despite her desolation Beanie knew he spoke the truth. It was the David she knew, and still loved. To him she couldn't be both lover and friend. Only the woman he loved with his soul could take that place.

She managed a small, shaky smile, and steeled herself to show she understood. Her eyes still betrayed her love, but she raised her glass. 'To friendship, then . . .'

'Until death us do part,' David swore. Truthfully.

Beanie closed the door softly behind him and wandered slowly into her bedroom, acutely aware that she had never felt more alone than she did now. She had at long last enjoyed being in his arms, had known the feel and the smell and the taste of him. In every sense but the ultimate one, they had been lovers.

For the first and last time.

In one way it was cruel, yet in another she now had a special memory to treasure. She knew that the episode would never be referred to again, not by her and certainly not by David.

Although she shivered, her body was still hot, tense with unrequited love and passion. She stepped out on to her balcony, glad of the cool summer night. Below, and far into the distance, the lights of Boston blinked and glittered. She could pick out the lights of vessels anchored in the harbour. It was a familiar scene, comforting in its distant serenity. High above her the sky seemed a reflection of the lights beneath it, ablaze with countless shimmering gems. She drank in the scene, filling her mind with it, willing her emotions back into perspective.

It was, after all, as she'd thought. David was in love with Diana. There was no animosity in her heart towards the young woman. If anything, she too was glad that Diana had come between them in time. Beanie couldn't doubt David's words.

Friendship was all they had, because he had finally given his heart to Diana.

She shivered again, this time with genuine cold, and turned back into her warm suite. How easily she could have lost him, the dearest person in her world, for the price of one night's love. She could bear unrequited love, had done for many years, but the loss of his friendship? No, not that, ever.

Beanie was a practical woman. She would put this memory deep in the background. Nothing that had happened tonight would come between her and David. She wouldn't allow it to.

Poor David. She could pity him more than herself. Life had prepared her for tragedy and disappointment, but David was an innocent. She would bear the hurt and no one would see the scars. But David? She shook her head, filled with new sadness for him. He was a one-love man, and in that they were alike. But she doubted that he would be able to take rejection by Diana. He would suffer terribly.

She remembered his dead wife, Ella, and the secret that she had burdened Beanie with for all these years. It was an irony that Ella's secret had given Beanie a key which could give David happiness. But it was a double-edged key. It could give him Diana. Or it could break his heart.

She sat wearily on the bed. The key could not be used until she was certain of Diana. She would have to wait and watch for the right time. If it came, she would break her vow to Ella – but only if it came.

She would not break her vow lightly. Everything depended upon Diana. If time proved that she cared for David, then Beanie would act. If not, then the secret would go with her to her grave.

She dressed for bed in a dove-grey negligee, her thoughts turning as they did every night, to her own secrets. She lifted the folds of some tissue on her closet shelf, and gazed for the last time on a snowy-white creation that had lain there for many years. Her romantic dream.

It was the only garment she'd ever made for herself that wasn't grey . . . and tonight she had come so near to being able to wear it. It was a chiffon negligee with appliquéd tiger-lilies across its silk bodice. She had made it some months after Ella's death nine years ago, when she had still been innocent enough to dream that David might turn to her. Dry-eyed now, she patted the tissue gently back into place.

Tomorrow she would burn her dream.

She would have liked to pray. Often she wished that she could, and this was one of those times. She had tried in the past, for the sake of the nuns who had saved her and healed

her, and taught her so well. And who had sent her on her way
to the New World, with exhortations to 'remember God, and
be thankful to Him'.

She had never known God, so she could not 'remember
Him'. But she could, and did, nightly bless the nuns. She
had never forgotten them. They were helped to run their
orphanage in France by the cheques she regularly mailed.
With the first one, she had requested that her anonymity be
respected. And with true integrity they had honoured her
wish, graciously accepting their 'God-sent' rewards.

Beanie smoothed her grey silk nightdress over her limbs, and
slid into bed. Her nightly ritual was to run through a list of
facts that she would never allow herself to forget.

She had been ten years old when the soldiers had come to
take them to the camp, twelve when her broken father had
been killed. Thirteen when her mother had died of starvation
and abuse and thirteen, also, when her younger sister had
been torn screaming from her arms. Fourteen when her
own baby had been slaughtered as she watched, the little
girl she hadn't even held. Fourteen and a half when her
reproductive organs had been removed. Fifteen when she
had been mercifully saved and sent on the long journey to
the orphanage in France.

Grey was not an eccentricity. It was the colour of all
those years, the colour of the uniforms. She wore it as a
memorial. Grey, so that she might never, ever, be tempted
to forget.

She turned off the night lamp, and a solitary tear slid down
her cheek. Defiantly she brushed it away.

David was the only man she had ever loved, apart from her
father. Nothing had changed. Tears would help no more than
prayers. She was a practical woman and David might at some
time need her practical help.

Her life would go on. She would will it to. Just as she had
in that grey, but never distant, past . . .

CHAPTER FIVE

The evening had exhausted David beyond thought. He'd just about managed to utter a silent prayer of thanks that he'd managed to save a little face for them both. Tomorrow he'd ring Beanie, have her meet him downtown for lunch. Their friendship would return to normal. He'd see to that.

He threw off his jacket and then fell on to his bed, too tired to remove the rest of his clothes. And as sleep claimed him Diana entered his dreams. He held her tenderly, weeping into her loving arms. She let him cry it all out. Then she made love to him, satisfying him as he slept . . .

Less than half a day's drive away, in Vermont, Diana hadn't even attempted sleeping. Summer in the ski-capital of the east was *hot*.

She had lain for most of the night on the queen-sized bed, still dressed and perspiring in the balmy mountain air. The air-conditioning was full on but her body refused to cool. Every sense was alert for the sound of Mat's return.

At every noise she jumped, her nerves stretched near to breaking point. But as each new sound proved not to be Mat, she felt faint with relief.

Waves of nausea assailed her and she felt more than a little feverish. It could have been the long doses of sun and physical activity, but it wasn't – it was Mat.

She stumbled to the bathroom and retched emptily over the basin. After a few minutes she bathed her face, her hands trembling as she patted herself dry.

She needed food. That would help, and she knew it wouldn't help for Mat to catch her being sick again. It could easily precipitate further ugly scenes. And she could not bear even one more of those.

She brushed her now sun-silvered hair into a ponytail and straightened her cotton dress as best she could. Fortunately the bar and the coffee shop, adjacent to the cabins, stayed open all night. She would slip over, grab some coffee and a bite to eat. She gritted her teeth anxiously as she stepped out of the cabin, but Mat's bright yellow Jaguar was nowhere in sight.

A breeze had sprung up with the dawn, bringing with it the fresh scent of pines. She breathed it deeply into her lungs. Only twenty-four more hours of this hell, and they would be back in Boston. Twenty-four more hours of dodging Mat. If she could . . .

She hurried towards the lights of the complex, glad now that she'd made the effort. Even though she was bone-tired and shaky, she was hungry, and hunger pangs kept one awake. The last thing she needed was to be awake when Mat got back.

Inside the complex she felt safe. Mat and his cronies had been thrown out in the first week, for rowdy behaviour, and they'd steered clear of the place since.

Where they now ate and drank she didn't ask, didn't care, and wasn't told, or invited to go. From the moment they'd arrived, to find Mat's friends already in residence and obviously waiting for him to party with them, the nightmare had begun.

'Yes, ma'am?' A tall young waiter appeared, order book at the ready.

'I'll have the full early breakfast, please,' she said, studying the menu and not looking up.

'Any coffee? Juice? Muffins? Pancakes?'

'Black coffee, and orange juice.' Diana closed the leather cover.

There were few diners, and the place was large enough for her to keep herself apart from the friendly bantering to and fro between distant tables.

What had she done? Or, more accurately, what had been done to her?

Her appetite threatened to vanish again, but her sense of survival was beginning to assert itself. She'd barely eaten for days now, had grown exhausted from trying to keep a distance between Mat and herself. Admittedly she'd won the latest round; or so it seemed, because Mat hadn't been near her for two days. However, in just over twenty-four hours they were due to head back to Boston. He'd have to come back soon.

'Here you go.' The young waiter was already back, putting before her a plate loaded with eggs, ham and skillet potatoes.

Diana fought down the nausea, drank a few sips of the strong, aromatic coffee and then cautiously began to eat. She swallowed a mouthful, not tasting anything, willing her stomach not to let her down. She had to get some strength back, and quickly. She'd climbed and explored and walked for hours in the mountains until her body had rebelled. But anything had been better than staying around Mat.

Fortunately, he wanted little to do with her. But she had become obsessive: it wasn't enough to just keep her distance, she had to get as far away from him as possible, and to come back only when exhaustion had dulled her body and her mind, only when she already ached so much that her bruised body could endure whatever nasty little treats he had in store for her.

She knew she'd reached her own pain-barrier today; it was only the thought of Boston, and David, that was keeping her going.

Why Boston – and David – should represent safety she didn't even question. All she really understood was that Mat *would* behave differently once they were back at the mansion.

Her head ached and her heart was leaden. How could she have been so hoodwinked? And how had Mat managed to disguise what he really was? More to the point, how could she have ever believed herself in love with him?

Gemma had been right all along, at least regarding Mat. She *should* have taken more time to get to know him.

Able to eat no more, she pushed the half-finished breakfast aside, and called the waiter to bring her a large scotch. Tonight, or rather, early this morning, she didn't want to be sober.

The scotch helped. Gradually her tremors eased and her thoughts became more coherent.

She couldn't understand why she had believed in Mat, or why she had behaved so out of character in marrying him in such haste. All she knew was that David was somehow a major factor.

And that was something she wasn't prepared to analyse . . .

She ordered another double scotch. Outside the day had fully broken, and for the first time she was not afraid to face Mat.

He'd had all the fear she was going to allow him: he'd been stronger than she; he'd abused her sexually and physically, and in her shock she'd let him get away with it for almost two nightmarish weeks. But not any more. Today she would warn him that he'd had his last 'good time' at her expense.

If he wanted to keep his activities from being made public, he'd keep his hands off her. Or she'd . . . her thoughts suddenly dried up. She'd what? Tell the police? Tell David?

The thought brought a fresh new twist to her pain. David was everything she admired in a man – everything she had so sorely missed since her father's death; how *could* she tell him? She shuddered as she imagined her own father hearing that his only son was a . . . a . . . she could not bring herself to put a name to what Mat was, but she knew what such a truth might have done to her own father, and in that moment she knew that she could not tell David.

Wearily she swallowed the last of the scotch. David had confessed such pride in having her join his family, a joy almost. No, she would not be the one to destroy his illusions. He might well be immensely wealthy and have few apparent concerns, but she had seen the loneliness, the vulnerability beneath the sophisticated exterior.

Unwillingly she concentrated on Mat. She was quite sure now that no one, apart from his friends, knew the truth about him.

She'd learned the very first night how it really was with him. Shock had kept her from taking the first train or plane out of the place. Then fear. Real, paralysing fear.

She rose, swaying slightly, and headed for the door. There was still one more fear to confront: that through the disgusting, perverted and violent sex, she might possibly be pregnant.

If so, would she endure the pregnancy – for David's sake? To give him the grandchild she knew instinctively he longed for with all his heart?

It wasn't something she could bear to think about just yet.

The cabin was still empty, and she crept inside with relief. If Mat should come back now, she was too exhausted, and too numbed by the alcohol, to be afraid. No matter what he threatened, she would not give in. She would lie about going to the police, to David, whatever it took. But she would not take any more.

And if she was pregnant . . .?

She collapsed on to the bed, her nerves ragged. Her last sleep-laden thoughts were of David. If there was a child of this diabolical union, would she carry it, for him?

Whatever, she knew she had no choice but to face the trauma and the scandal of divorce. Her own considerable sense of honour and, yes, David's too, would have to be sacrificed. *Nothing* would make her stay in this evil marriage.

CHAPTER SIX

David was at the foot of the broad sweep of marble steps to meet them.

Sanders stepped forward to take the luggage; Mrs Carly and Meg hovered nearby.

Diana was out of the car first, lean, tanned, wearing a figure-hugging white linen dungaree outfit.

David swallowed a lump in his throat as stern warnings to himself dissolved at the moment of seeing her. She was lovelier than he remembered, if that was possible. But she was also thinner.

She threw her arms around his neck and hugged him with such youthful exuberance and innocence that for a second he despised himself. But her touch sent shock-waves through his body, and his grip unconsciously tightened.

She made a startled move backwards, her cheeks flushed pink with sudden awareness, but David caught her arm again firmly, and lightly kissed her cheek.

'Welcome home, princess,' he murmured softly, covering her confusion with a gentle squeeze.

She looked up at him, her eyes pools of questioning blue, and at that moment David could have sworn that she had felt the current too.

To cover her discomfort, and his own, he called a forcedly cheerful 'Hi' to Matthew, who fiddled with something in the trunk of the car. His son raised a hand in acknowledgement, and Diana regained her composure sufficiently to speak.

'Have you missed us then?' she teased innocently in a light gay voice.

It was the wrong thing to ask, but David answered without thinking. 'You'd better believe it!' he said emphatically and the look which passed between them was so electric that it silenced them both.

Fortunately Mat chose that moment to join them.

'Hi, pops.' He casually embraced his father. 'How's it bin?'

David winced at the term 'pops'. Today it made him feel old. 'Oh, about as usual, son,' he lied.

Matthew had no tan at all, David noted, and if it were possible his son looked even paler than before he'd gone away, unhealthily pale, in an ashen way.

David shrugged the observation aside. Mat had never been the type to enjoy the outdoors. Nothing had changed in that respect, then. Yet, by comparison, Diana's tan was surprisingly deep, as if they'd holidayed in different parts of the world.

David stole another glance at her as they walked up the staircase. Was he mistaken, or did she look ill under that golden colour? Without knowing why, he felt his stomach muscles knot. Instinct told him that something wasn't right. He couldn't immediately put a finger on what, but the feeling disturbed him.

'Coming through for an aperitif?' He indicated the open french windows on the far side of his study.

'Not for me,' Mat declined. 'I've got some calls I want to make. But I'll catch a cold beer with you later.'

'Don't forget dinner,' David warned firmly. Then he returned his attention to Diana. 'You'll join me, won't you, sweetheart?'

Diana glanced quickly at Mat, but he shrugged his thin shoulders and headed across the wide hall for the stairs.

'Of course. I'd love to,' she responded warmly.

David led the way through to the terrace, where Sanders had arranged a champagne cooler in honour of the newlyweds.

Diana sank gratefully into a plump, brightly cushioned chair. She was so relieved to be home that her sigh was audible on the quiet evening air.

David, at the terrace bar, frowned. He could still feel the

tension coming from her, yet his instinct told him it wasn't from their encounter.

'Here you go, princess.'

Diana smiled, and accepted her glass silently.

'To having you home.' David raised his glass.

'Amen to that,' she said dryly, before sipping at the deliciously cool Bollinger.

David sat opposite her, unwilling to quiz her. Questions could wait – for the moment at least.

Diana felt the coiled spring inside her beginning to unwind. Mat had returned to the cabin only this morning, so she'd had all of yesterday to collect her thoughts and to make decisions. On the drive home she had unemotionally told Matthew that their marriage was over, and was still amazed at how indifferent he had seemed. But the silence on the remainder of the journey had been harrowing.

Now she was home and safe. David was here. She could relax for a little while – until she knew if her period was going to be on time.

David made comforting small talk and she let herself be drawn by his magnetic presence. An hour passed, unnoticed.

The sun had sunk low in the sky, bathing the garden in glowing tints of flame. The fountain made little swishing noises, harmonious and soothing to Diana's stretched nerves. Now the scent of honeysuckle and roses drifted on the evening air, mingled with the heady fragrance of nicotiana.

Again she sighed. It was so lovely here. There was only one other place she could perhaps love as much, and that was Devon, where she'd gone to school with her two cousins on the few occasions when her father hadn't been able to take her on one of his expeditions.

'So many sighs, honey,' David remarked.

'Oh, only of contentment,' she replied quickly. 'This is such a heavenly place to be.'

David nodded, wishing they could be alone like this forever. But a glance at his wristwatch brought him back to reality. 'I think we'd better be getting changed, honey. You know what a stickler Sanders is for punctuality.'

Diana gave a mock groan. 'Shame,' she said lightly. But her heart was far from light. There hadn't been time really to assess Mat's reaction yet, and he was upstairs in the annexe, still to be faced.

For the first time she wished that David hadn't built the separate wing. She'd have felt safer if their rooms were closer together.

'Right,' she said with forced gaiety. 'Let's not keep Sanders waiting.'

David followed her into the house and as far as his own rooms at the top of the stairs. He watched her thoughtfully as she continued down the hall, towards the thick oak doors that Mat had closed behind him; something David would deal with later – he wanted those doors left open.

For now, other things were on his mind. Such as why did Diana look as if she was hiding something, or at least as if something was badly amiss? Not only was she nervy and skittish but her eyes looked strained.

He turned into his suite. Whatever it was, he'd make it his business to find out.

Matthew was sprawled on the bed in their suite waiting for her. As soon as she saw the thin, set lips, she knew there was going to be a scene.

'So, "princess",' he sneered mockingly. 'Finished playing games with the old man?'

Diana drew a deep breath to control her fear and made to pass him for her dressing-room. But he sprang from the bed, caught her arm and spun her round to face him.

'I've thought about your ultimatum today and, like I said, it doesn't bother me any. You might find it hard to accept, but I'm as turned off by you as you are by me.'

His voice was menacing in its tonelessness. 'But I'm going to give you a warning, my little golden girl. Mess up my act with the old man, and your pretty English face will be one great American mess. Is that clear?'

Diana was shocked, but she pulled herself free of his spiteful grip and managed to walk away. She knew that if she argued when his voice was flat like this it would make him worse.

She sat down shakily at the dressing-table and began brushing her hair. She had to act unconcerned, despite the fear enveloping her.

Matthew wheeled after her into the dressing-room, his features colder, uglier, than she had yet seen. He was across the room and had grabbed her from behind before she could find her feet to dash for the bathroom. She forced herself to sit as still as she could, though his nails had raked the skin from her neck and his hold was choking her.

'I'm warning you! Don't think I haven't seen how the old man sucks up to you. The dirty bastard fancies you like crazy. That's the only reason I married you.' He released his hold suddenly, and she had to catch at the dressing-table to stop herself from falling.

'You're talking nonsense,' she spluttered, trying to keep the tears at bay. Her mind was reeling as much from what he was saying as from his assault.

He was instantly behind her again. This time he seized a handful of her hair, and pulled it so hard that she almost screamed. His cold gaze held her eyes in the mirror. 'Don't tell me what I'm talking,' he said through gritted teeth. 'You think the old man didn't set this whole thing up so's he could get you into this mausoleum . . .? He's so damned clever he almost earns my respect!' Now he sneered. 'But I figured his angle right from the start . . . he wants in your pants so bad he'll do just about anything!'

Diana felt the blood drain from her body and waves of revulsion swept through her. Mat had to be insane! How else could he say such dreadful things. Such vile accusations were almost worse than his vicious cruelty.

'Can't take the truth, eh?' Mat's voice was loaded with

contempt. 'Well, "princess", one word from you to my father, and I'll let the whole damned world know what gives between the two of you.' He gave her hair a last yank and let her go.

Diana managed to keep her hands away from her burning scalp, not wanting to show him any more weakness. 'You're mad,' she said as coldly as she could.

'Save your compliments,' Mat jeered. 'Keep em' for when my father makes his move . . . as he will.'

He threw his head back now and laughed dirtily. 'I can't imagine what he thinks you've got between your legs that's worth what it's gonna cost him. But I sure as hell hope he finds it better value than I did.'

Diana's head pounded. She swallowed painfully, tensing as he crossed the room. If he turned back this time, she would make a dash for the bathroom and if necessary she'd scream from the window.

As if he'd read her thoughts, he did turn at the door, but made no move in her direction. 'So, we understand each other, don't we? I'll keep out of your bed. And you will keep out of my life.' He added venomously: 'But you as sure as hell better keep your mouth shut. Or else my father's reputation gets splattered. Get it?'

Diana stared, still unable to believe that the evil person threatening her was the same person as the suave, charming, quiet, gentle man she'd married just over three weeks ago.

'I'll be using the blue guest suite,' Mat continued coldly. 'You'd better find a way to disguise that fact. We wouldn't want anyone asking questions. Now would we?'

Diana found a small voice. 'You wouldn't do anything to harm your father. You're bluffing.'

Matthew leaned against the doorpost, affecting nonchalance. But he left her with no illusions. 'Don't bet on that. It'd do the old man a considerable amount of harm if I were to confess how you'd broken my heart when I found you together, naked . . .on my bed. Boston wouldn't let a thing like that pass, Diana. Take my word for it!'

He stepped into the hall but turned again to add spitefully, 'I'd get that neck covered if I were you. You seem to have caught it on something.'

He pulled the door quietly shut behind him, leaving Diana in a worse predicament than she would ever have believed possible . . .

It was hard for Diana to thank David for the lovely gifts, because Mat watched her constantly. And she found that she couldn't talk to David naturally – not with all the things Mat had threatened racing round in her mind.

'You liked them, then?' David found it hard to believe that she was talking as if his presents had been a bunch of garden flowers.

'Very much. Thank you,' she repeated guardedly.

'Good.' David let it pass. She was definitely out of sorts and he would find out why. When the time was right.

For all his efforts, the meal was wasted. Mat picked at his food restlessly and Diana merely toyed with hers. The vintage wine might as well have been lemonade.

David had great difficulty concealing his annoyance and disappointment, but he made every effort to keep the evening afloat. 'Tell me all about the trip,' he asked, hoping to inject some life into the party. 'I've only been to Vermont in the winter, but I guess it's beautiful even in summer?'

Diana's account told him nothing that he could pin his anxieties on, except that she reeled off the things that Vermont had offered, as expertly as a travel agent.

Matthew added nothing, leaving his wife to answer the few questions David put to them.

David studied them covertly as dessert was served. He could hardly ask what was wrong. But whatever it was was tangible, and unpleasant.

He was relieved when Matthew finally pushed back his coffee cup and declined a cognac. 'I'm beat. See you guys tomorrow.'

Diana didn't look up, but David nodded curtly. One thing was certain. Mat's manners had reverted to bad.

Grateful that Diana hadn't followed Mat's example David suggested brandy in the drawing-room.

Sanders had lit the fire and the logs crackled invitingly. Luke Nazareth had always insisted on fires in the evenings once midsummer had passed, and this evening David was glad that he'd kept up his father's old custom. The room would have been cool by now if he had not, and he was aware of Diana giving an occasional shiver.

He drew her into a chair near the fire and poured her a generous measure of brandy. Perhaps she was coming down with a virus. That could account for the way she looked.

But she seemed to brighten up now that they were alone. She stretched her long legs out before her and put David in mind of a cat lowering its guard. Then she dropped her head tiredly back against the soft cushions, and as she did so the silk scarf fell away from her throat.

David blinked at the ugly red weals.

'Oh, it's so good to be home,' she said with feeling. 'Thank you, David, for the *beautiful* presents; you really shouldn't have done that.' She smiled warmly. 'And what a superb meal! I hope that Mrs Carly won't be put out – we don't seem to have done justice to it . . .'

David thought that was the understatement of the year, but he wasn't about to upset the fine balance of her mood. She seemed almost dangerously edgy. And what about those marks on her neck? He was certain they hadn't been there earlier.

He made a small attempt at humour to hide his growing concern. 'So you're glad to be home. Makes it sound like honeymoons aren't all they're cracked up to be.'

Her face paled and a fleeting expression of panic showed in her eyes. 'Oh, I wasn't going to complain,' she said, almost anxiously. 'But it's always good to come home.'

David bit back the questions that were rushing through his

mind. Like 'What's the problem between you?' . . . 'How did you hurt your neck like that? how come I get the feeling that you're unhappy?' Instead he said gently, 'Well, sweetheart, just so long as you remember that this *is* your home, and –' he paused to gaze into her eyes, willing her to recognise the offer he was making ' – that I'm here to give you support. In any way you might need. In anything that worries you.' He left the sentence with an underlying question mark so that she could share a confidence if she wanted to.

She smiled at him faintly, and unbelievably he thought he saw something like fear in her eyes. 'Thank you,' she murmured. 'But I'm sure that being home is just the thing.'

It was another odd comment, but David let it pass. He wasn't always sure when semantics confused his understanding of her words. Mostly the different ways in which they used their common language were obvious, but this wasn't one of those times.

He changed the subject. 'You're not just staying up for me, are you honey?'

'Of course not.' Diana blushed faintly. 'I always enjoy your company, you know that.'

'Sure,' David retorted lightly. 'But what about the bridegroom. Won't he be missing his bride by now?'

Her laugh was strained. 'Heavens no! Mat needs more sleep than I do. He's usually asleep before his head touches the pillow,' she lied uncomfortably.

David's eyebrows shot up, but again he could hardly comment.

'Let's talk about you,' she said lightly, curling herself into a ball in the chair. 'What have you been up to while we were away?'

'Oh, this and that, you know. Weddings don't halt the wheels of progress entirely.' He grinned at her, then proceeded to concoct a host of activities he'd supposedly undertaken in their absence. He concluded, mistakenly, by mentioning the date he'd had with Beanie.

Her reaction surprised him.

'Have you ever thought of marrying her?' Diana had begun to relax now, pushing thoughts of Matthew to the back of her mind. She would worry about him tomorrow. For now she had the company she had missed so much, and was enjoying it.

'You can't be serious!' David's mouth had tightened.

'Why shouldn't I be? You have many things in common. And Beanie obviously cares a great deal about you.'

He smiled thinly. 'There's such a thing as love, honey. Wouldn't you say?'

'Then you don't love her?' It was perverse, questioning him about love, but it had slipped out.

'Not in the way that you mean, no.'

'Then you must be a hard man to please,' she said guilelessly.

'Far from it,' he said softly. 'I just happen to know what I want.'

'That's present tense.' She grinned.

'So it is.'

'Then there *is* somebody?' She was teasing now, mischievously. But at once she wondered if it was innocently, or if she hoped to learn something that would prove Mat's accusations way off course.

'You could say that.' His voice was harsher than he'd intended, but she seemed not to notice.

She gave a little laugh. 'Anyone I know?'

David drew in his breath, 'Damnit Diana! Have you looked in a mirror lately?'

Diana drew back, stunned. His eyes blazed with raw emotion. No! It couldn't be true. She was misinterpreting his words because of what Mat had said. She paled and shook the thick hair back from her face. 'I'm sorry,' she said. 'I had no business questioning you. Please forgive me.'

She uncurled her legs and would have risen to leave, but David's hand reached out and touched her arm. Her face at once registered confusion and distress.

At that moment he would have given anything to have the right to take her in his arms. To banish that look in the lovely, but strangely haunted, eyes. Instead he gently gripped her arm, and his eyes compelled her to return his gaze.

'Diana, please, don't *ever* tease me. And don't ever play with my feelings, just because you can.' His voice was low and barely controlled. 'Sweetheart, I'll never lie to you about anything that's important to me. *Never*. Do you follow me?'

Her cheeks flamed and her gaze fell away from his. It confirmed to him that she understood.

His voice grew stronger. 'If you can't handle knowing the truth, then don't ever ask me any questions, because you'll get only truth from me, sweetheart. But I'll never knowingly hurt you, or cause you any embarrassment.'

He paused, aware that she was looking at him strangely now. She shook her head slowly. She could not allow herself to believe what she'd heard, could not have Mat's accusations proved. She loved David. He was her father-in-law. He was her friend. She needed him.

He rose, and pulled her gently from her chair. His lips brushed her burning cheek. Then he hugged her very briefly, and put her from him. 'Off you go to bed,' he said, trying to lighten the tension between them.

Diana put her hand to her head. But she couldn't think straight. Everything was so confused.

David sighed to himself. 'Off you go, honey,' he urged again. 'And don't take too much notice of me. I'm just an old fool.'

She reached out and touched his sleeve.

He froze. There were bright, unshed tears in her eyes. It took all his control to keep his arms at his side.

'No,' she said huskily. 'You are not old. And it's me who's the fool.' She dropped her hand again, wearily. 'You'll have to forgive me. I think I'm probably too tired to make much sense of anything tonight.'

David turned away. 'There's nothing to forgive.'

'Then we're still . . . friends?'

David flinched. *That* bloody word again. 'Always,' he swore gruffly.

He heard her light steps hurrying from the room, and as soon as she was out of hearing he slammed his fist against the panelled fireplace. Damn, damn, damn! Why hadn't he let it be?

Long after that interchange he lay awake in his room, staring up at the fine old plastered ceiling. How was he supposed to handle this situation, if every time he got within sight of her he made a fool of himself? How was he going to get through the weeks, months, years ahead? He'd promised himself that he'd stay in control, but the first evening she was home he'd blown it. What the hell did he do now?

He groaned into the silence. David Nazareth, head of a multimillion-dollar business, cool, scrupulous but ruthlessly capable, more than a match for any man in the business world, totally in charge of his emotions for fifty-seven years, was a complete wreck, unable to stand the thoughts that relentlessly reminded him how near she was – and how much nearer to Matthew. The knowledge burned and angered him.

It was no good. He'd have to get away from the mansion for a while, put some time and distance between them – until he could find a way to get on top of his emotions.

He started to plan. He'd have to get himself some fieldwork. Something out in the country.

But it would have to be soon. He just couldn't face the thought of being so near to her. If he stayed, he wouldn't be able to stop himself.

His son would be no match for him; if he ever decided to play a serious hand, Diana would be his. There was strong chemistry between them, and she'd felt it too. It'd been written all over her face, echoed in her body language.

Yes, by God, she'd come to him willingly, given time, if he ever did decide that was the way it was going to be. Oh yes, he could seduce his son's wife all right, break their marriage as easily as if it were a blown egg. And that was why he had to get away before he went past the point of no return. It wouldn't change his feelings, but it might give him chance to control them.

Before they destroyed them all.

CHAPTER SEVEN

Time became a passage of meaningless and monotonous events, as David found himself more and more work to do away from Boston. Days rolled endlessly one into another. Nights blurred into a series of seemingly identical lonely meals and identical lonely hotel rooms.

Diana found that her father-in-law's absence disturbed her more deeply than she cared to analyse. But she was thankful, in a way. Her senses told her that David was a dangerous man to have around, dangerous in ways that Matthew was not. Since their mutual agreement, Mat had kept to his word. Now she hardly saw him.

David was a different matter altogether. When he was home at weekends, she was increasingly aware of him as an attractive man; sufficiently so to be glad he was not around too much.

But it also saddened her. She not only enjoyed his company, but was keenly interested in Nazareth House. She had believed that she would become more involved in that side of David's life, had even nursed a small hope that he might offer her a job of some kind within the Firm.

As the weeks passed her hopes grew fainter. When David was at home, he spent less and less time with her and more time working in his study. They met for meals, but rarely had the conversations she'd so looked forward to.

To add to her loneliness there was also the problem of what she was going to do about her marriage. The pregnancy she'd feared was non-existent, but Mat's threats kept her from doing anything about a divorce.

There had to be a way for her to end this farce of a marriage; but, try as she might, she could find no solution.

Meanwhile, she lived for the small bright spark of David's

weekends at home, those in which he spared any time to spend with her.

For the rest of the time she buried her anguish behind an increasing isolation.

David had been surprised at how easy it had been to distance himself physically. He travelled constantly, rarely spending more than a night in any one place and he threw himself into his work with something like his former zeal.

His contact with Diana at weekends was almost zero. When they did meet he was charming, cool and detached, and Diana was the perfect daughter-in-law. She was friendly and caring, but also quiet and passive. He reasoned that soon it would be safe to return home. But not just yet. Not until he was sure that he could trust himself.

In the four months that followed he made more trips around the States than he had in as many years. He gave himself a gruelling schedule, and wherever he landed his staff found themselves suddenly working heavy, demanding hours.

No one from the Firm commented on his unusual behaviour, at least not to his face. But there was one member of the T-EEM who knew that Mat was less interested in his marriage than David appeared to be. Jeff Sherman had learned some new, disconcerting facts about Mat.

Had David been at home more often he would have known that Matthew was rarely home, that Diana was losing even more weight, that she wasn't eating or sleeping properly.

In short, that she was ill.

As it was, these facts were abruptly brought to his attention early in December.

He'd flown in from Ohio late on a Friday afternoon, and called unexpectedly at the office to collect some papers. Usually he went straight to the mansion on Fridays, and straight to his study. This weekend, though, he had reached a decision. He was tired of all the travelling, tired of being away from home.

The trouble was that he'd created a mountain of work during his travels, and now he needed someone to take it over. Jeff would know if there was anybody ready for a leg-up in the Firm. With this in mind he rode the elevator up to his floor.

He stepped into the deeply carpeted reception area, breathing in the familiar scents and atmosphere of his private domain. His shoulders squared as he crossed the now empty foyer. It was good to be back.

He expected Jeff, perhaps a secretary or two, to be still at work within the inner offices. What he didn't expect, and never would have expected, was the angry voice coming from his suite.

Jeff's voice.

David's lips pursed. There were few rules in the Firm and he expected obedience to those. One was that an outburst from a junior would be tolerated, once. For senior staff it was taboo.

He swept through the door, taking in at a glance the presence of two secretaries and Jeff.

He stared coldly, listening to Jeff berating the younger female secretary for an apparently minor misdemeanour.

'That will do!' His voice cut through the air icily.

Jeff turned swiftly, colour suffusing his drawn features. But he recovered quickly.

'Dave? Boy am I glad you're back!'

'In my office!' David commanded. Then he directed a stern glance at the other staff. 'Leave whatever you're doing. Get on home . . .'

The bustle was instantaneous. Jeff stared, guilty and angry.

'Inside,' David repeated, and walked through to his office.

He slammed his briefcase down on his desk, and stood glaring at his top man. Waiting.

Jeff closed the door behind him.

'What the hell were you doing?' David's voice was that of a stranger.

Jeff swallowed, hard. No one knew better that David Nazareth tolerated no breach of his rules, that even he would not be excused, no matter how good his reasons. Under his breath he swore.

'I'm still waiting,' David said coldly.

Jeff's fuse began to blow.

'Yeah! Well, aren't we all,' he snapped bitterly. 'Look, I'm sorry about blowing my stack, and I'll apologise first thing Monday.' He rubbed nervous fingers at his temple. 'It really had nothing to do with that kid, just a stupid mistake that caught me at a bad time.'

'Go on,' David pressed him.

'Shit, Dave. I blew up because I was in overload. It happens!' His temper was barely held.

'Not on my time,' David replied acidly. 'So you'd better explain, hadn't you?' He removed his overcoat and sat down behind his desk.

Jeff watched the implacable features, his own mouth grim. What did he do now? Colour the truth in pastel shades? Carry the can, and go on keeping quiet? His insides felt raw, his ulcer niggled ceaselessly. But no, he'd done all the covering-up he was going to do. David's face decided him. He'd never been looked at with such contempt, and the injustice of it made his blood boil.

'OK! You asked, so I'm going to deliver it to you straight.' He advanced towards the desk, halting just close enough to grip the chair facing David. 'It's bad news, long overdue, and it concerns Matthew.'

David tensed, but his voice was even. 'Matthew caused that scene out there?'

'No, damnit, Matthew caused my short fuse!' Jeff swore. 'I'm well aware of my actions out there, and that you'll expect me to justify them. But I can't do that without telling you some home truths.'

David leaned back slowly, easing his long legs out before him. 'So tell . . .'

Jeff wasn't dumb enough to believe David had relaxed, but he couldn't go back now.

'I know that Mat's always been my responsibility when you're not around,' he began testily. 'And I've never shirked it. Neither have I come running to you when things were difficult. But lately things have gotten out of control. Mat's always been a pain in the ass, but until recently I could handle most of it. Not any more, Dave!'

He shook his head violently, and tightened his grip on the chair-back.

David's face was deliberately blank.

Jeff's stomach churned. He didn't like any of this, least of all the cold barrier he could feel between them.

'Matthew has been truanting for years, on and off, but things have worsened lately. I've never interfered because he's your son, and he's your problem! Or should be.' He shrugged now, some of his anger seeping away in the sobering revelations of the matter.

'I've been covering up for too long, Dave, and I've grown sick and tired of being his whipping boy, of having to run my butt off on his behalf, chasing all over town straightening out his messes.'

Jeff's eyes never left David's face. 'He's a shit. And I'm through cleaning up after him. You want him to toe the line? Well, *you're* going to have to make him.'

David was rigid with angry shock, but he kept his control. 'Sit down, Jeff,' he commanded tightly. 'And get to whatever point you're trying to make.'

Jeff sat, his eyes and mouth grimmer than before.

'Look, you know that Mat's never liked work, but there was a time I could haul him in here, make him do something useful. Not any more. Not since his marriage.

'Everyone hoped that his marriage would straighten him out, that he'd get it together, come in here more often. Learn the business. Ha! That was joke number one. If it weren't for the cheques, you'd think he didn't exist — '

'What cheques?' David interrupted.

'The rubber cheques I've been covering,' Jeff snapped.

'Until his marriage, whenever he went over his allowance I'd give him time to catch up. But since his marriage it seems he can't spend it fast enough.'

David crossed to his bar and poured two stiff brandies. 'Get outside this.'

He handed Jeff a glass before returning to his seat with his own. 'Now, from the top.'

Jeff swallowed a sip of the liquid. It burned all the way down.

'He's been doing it for years,' he began slowly. 'Taking time out. Overspending. Being a shit. But I never thought he'd go this far. Not as far as bouncing cheques. But he's been doing that for a few weeks now, and when the latest one came in today, I blew.'

David's voice was even, despite being spoken to in a way he'd never heard before. 'What's he spending on?'

'Your guess is as good as mine,' Jeff said frankly. 'But, whatever it is, the cheques are always for cash lately. I had discreet words over at the bank, told Sam Golding that Mat was over the top and that his credit was up. He put the brakes on, I guess. So now Mat's bouncing cheques for cash all over town. They're coming in here like confetti.'

David swallowed the humiliation. He'd deal with the cheques. No Nazareth had ever let creditors down. No Nazareth had ever bounced personal cheques. Matthew had gone too far.

'Okay, I'll deal with that; it's not your problem any more. What about the rest?'

Jeff grunted his relief and shrugged. 'Absences. Period. That might be a bigger fish to hook.'

'The *point*, Jeff!'

Jeff swung out of the chair, his eyes blazing again. 'The point, Dave, is this. If you'd kept a closer eye on Mat, cared what the hell he was doing, none of this need have happened! Are you reading me, Dave? We have a helluva problem, and it needs sorting. Now!'

He raised his hand and began counting Mat's problems off on his fingers, ignoring the warning light in David's eyes.

'One: he's given up any pretence of being interested in the Firm – anyway, he isn't capable of running it. Two: he likes money too damned much, but he ain't gonna work for it. Three: something's wrong in his head – everybody knows it. Four: he ain't even home any more.'

He dropped his hand, and stood, shaking his head. 'I've tried everything I can think of but nothing works any more. Christ, I can't even get him on the phone these days . . .'

David's voice was emotionless as he spoke. 'You could have spoken to me sooner, not waited until things had got so out of hand. I was always available, you know.'

'Not for things like this,' Jeff retorted flatly. 'I'd never abuse my position to tell you how to run your own kid, you should know that.'

'Well, you've done so now,' David stated grimly.

'Only because someone *had* to. I'm sorry it had to be me. I'm even sorrier that it was necessary. But I'm glad that it's out in the open. Now *you* can deal with it, any way you like. I guess I don't need to say that I don't want any part of Mat's affairs from now on. I've had all of Mat I'm going to take.'

He added soberly, 'I guess it goes without saying that I'm damned sorry if I've offended you.'

He moved towards the outer door, stopping with his hand on the tooled-brass handle.

'Matthew *is* a mess, Dave. There was never a time when he wasn't difficult and if Matthew's what Nazareth House has to offer in your wake, God help us all!'

David was anchored to his chair by an anger so solid that he felt drugged by it.

'Oh, and one more thing,' Jeff said bleakly. 'While you're sorting this little lot out . . . take a good look at Diana. Because if I'm any judge that little lady is not only one very unhappy person, she's also ill. Maybe Matthew'll know something about that as well!'

He turned in the doorway, pain and sympathy in the gaze
he levelled at David, and something else, something akin to
anxiety. For himself.

'You're the only one qualified to knock that bum into shape,
but frankly I won't take any bets on you winning. I'll be home
all weekend. If you need me . . .'

The door closed silently on the first confrontation between
them in more than twenty years.

David couldn't have known that the line he'd drawn so
lightly many years before would become, with time, indelible.
He only knew now, as a haze of fury settled around him, that
Jeff had dared to cross it.

He was grim as he entered the mansion, handing his coat
to Sanders without answering his greeting.

'Where's Miss Diana?' he snapped.

'In her suite, sir,' Sanders answered levelly, covering his
surprise.

'And Mr Matthew?'

'I'm sorry, sir, I couldn't say.'

David took the stairs slowly, his humiliation goading him.
Damn Jeff. And damn Matthew. The hell he'd put up with
crap like this. *No one* spoke to him as if he were an imbecile.
No one breached his rules. No one lectured him on his
responsibilities – and no one this side of eternity abused the
name of Nazareth.

As he neared the annexe he forced himself to appear calm.
This had nothing to do with Diana, and he would not let her
be upset by it. Matthew he'd deal with himself. Tonight.

He'd think about Jeff Sherman later.

Entering her sitting-room silently on the sound-muffling
carpet, he was able to observe her writing at her bureau for
several moments before she became aware of his presence. His
anger abated swiftly. God, she was thin!.

He crossed the room swiftly, a small knot of fear in his
throat.

'David!' She started nervously and the eyes that met his were dark with some unfamiliar emotion. She dropped her pen, and a flicker of a smile crossed her gaunt features.

'You made me jump,' she said hollowly.

'Sorry, honey. I should have knocked,' David apologised.

'Nonsense,' she replied. 'I must have forgotten it was Friday, or I'd have been expecting you.' She brushed a strand of hair from her forehead and looked at him blankly. 'It is Friday, isn't it?'

David stared, surprised, but she continued in a rush. 'How stupid of me. Of course it's Friday.' She rubbed her temple distractedly. 'You wouldn't be here if it wasn't . . .'

'Princess, are you feeling OK?'

'Me? Oh, yes. I'm fine.' She turned away from his gaze and tidied up some papers. 'I was writing to Gemma and her sister, Candy . . . I seem to have neglected my cousins lately . . . my mother, too . . .' Her voice tailed off thinly.

David's concern grew. 'Diana, honey, what's the problem?'

'Problem?' She turned to look at him again, her hand moving nervously to her mouth now. 'I'm sorry, I . . . I don't know what you mean.'

'You look ill, sweetheart.' David came closer, touched her shoulder and felt her bones under his hand. 'What's wrong?' he demanded.

She got up quickly, moved away from his touch, and began lighting lamps about the room; avoiding him.

'There's nothing wrong,' she answered tonelessly, busying herself at a distance. 'I'm a bit tired. Silly, I know. I'm not sleeping too well . . .'

She gave a shrug. 'It's my own fault. I don't take enough exercise.'

She crossed to straighten some perfectly orderly cushions. 'I don't know where the time goes. I should get out in the fresh air some more. Yes, that's what I'll do . . .'

David couldn't fathom the way she looked, or her erratic

behaviour. Or the disjointed, staccato sentences. He watched her helplessly.

Finally she perched on the edge of a settee and turned to look at him. He could see how tightly the skin was drawn across her cheekbones. He saw her clasp and unclasp her hands and realised that, whatever was wrong, he was somehow making it worse.

He strode across to sit beside her and took her cold hands in his.

'Honey, what *is* it?' he urged gently.

She looked away. 'I've told you, I'm just a bit tired, or maybe just too lazy . . .'

'Too lazy for what?' David released her hands, and moved to a chair facing her. She was obviously uncomfortable with him so close, and her gaze continually flew to the door.

'For anything,' she said wearily.

He felt even more helpless. What in hell was going on around him? Everything had fallen apart in his absence.

He spoke carefully. 'Well, honey, whatever it is, I'm home now and I'm going to be staying home. Maybe we can take some walks, go over to the health club together . . . get you some of that fresh air.'

She looked up, and now her eyes were alight, as if she was relieved. 'You're going to be staying home?'

'Sure am,' David answered gruffly.

'Oh.' Her voice was warmer. 'That's nice.'

He grew more concerned, but first things first.

'Honey, is Matthew around?' His urgent need to see his son had grown by the minute. Now he was barely able to contain his impatience.

'Matthew?' Diana stared as if confused. 'Er, I'm not sure.'

'Are you expecting him for dinner?'

'Dinner?' Her face grew thoughtful, then brightened as if she'd remembered something important. 'Yes, of course. It's Friday, isn't it? So yes, he'll be here for dinner. He always is, on Fridays.'

David had to let the matter pass, although her manner

and tone shocked him. It was as if she were unable to think rationally.

'Good,' he said quietly. 'I have some business to discuss with him, honey. Will it bother you if I do that this evening? Get it out of the way,' he added with a reassuring smile.

'You did say that you're going to be staying home now?'

David heard the anxiety again, but nodded carefully.

'Then that's fine,' she said with a weak smile. 'I'm sure everything will be fine then.'

David got up slowly. He had to leave her. It was impossible to watch her behaving so disturbingly without wanting to take her in his arms. Another few moments and he would not resist the temptation.

'See you at dinner then.'

She nodded distantly, seemingly wrapped up in her own thoughts again.

David paced about in his study, a three-finger restorative of bourbon in his hand. He hadn't a clue what was going on in his own home. But whatever was making Diana look and behave like that had to be serious.

He toyed with the idea of illness, but deep down he knew that it wasn't a physical ailment that bothered her. Whatever was wrong with her was almost certainly caused by a deep-rooted unhappiness and, as Jeff had said, he didn't think he'd have to look far beyond Matthew to find out what.

His anger returned and grew, and with it a strange relief. He had never enjoyed arguments with Mat, indeed he'd avoided them as much as possible. Not because he was blind but because he had lived on *hope*.

Well that hope had gone. Matthew had had all the rope he was going to get. Now it was time to tighten the noose. Right up to his throat.

There was still a short time until dinner. He cursed the waiting and poured himself another drink, incensed that he was being forced by circumstances to take the steps he should have taken a long time ago, even before Ella had died. Long, also, before Ben had left. Steps which might have altered what was likely to happen now . . .

He was so engrossed in his thoughts that he heard only Sanders after his third apologetic cough.

'Yes, Sanders. What is it?'

'Dinner is served, Mr David.'

The time had come.

'Are Mr Matthew and Miss Diana down?'

'Yes, sir.'

'After dinner, Sanders, see that my son and I aren't disturbed. We'll be in here. And we won't be needing anything for the rest of the evening. Is that clear?'

Sanders inclined his head. 'Very good, sir.'

David walked slowly across the spacious marbled hall, surprised that now the moment had come he was ready to meet it.

He stopped outside the dining-room door, unable to prevent a sudden rush of sadness. The hall was empty but he could still hear the ring of his feet on the marble floor, an echo of the emptiness of his own childhood and those of his sons, Benjamin and Matthew.

He had never known a time when that hall had resounded with children's laughter. And tonight he knew that he never would.

CHAPTER EIGHT

Matthew and Diana both stared as David came into the dining-room and took his place silently.

Matthew's eyes narrowed; he had been jittery since Diana had told him his father wanted to talk business with him. He'd guessed what that might mean and, by the look on his father's face, he was right. The old man's face was grim.

Diana was only slightly disturbed. Obviously David had something on his mind, but her own heart was so relieved by the news that he'd be staying home that she could think of little else.

Dinner was a disjointed affair, and they were all glad when Meg began to serve the dessert.

'Not for me, Meg,' David waved the girl aside. 'Nor for Mr Matthew either.'

There was a small satisfaction in watching Matthew blanch.

'Diana, you go ahead. Mat and I have a lot to talk about, so the sooner we start . . .' he tailed off, suddenly aware of the undercurrent between her and his son. It was as if she couldn't bear to look at her husband. 'It's nothing for you to worry about, princess,' he added gently.

She nodded wanly. 'I don't really want anything else, so if you don't mind I'll go upstairs?'

'Sure, honey. Go ahead. We'll join you for coffee later.'

She slipped from her seat and without another glance at either of them left the room.

David watched her go, furious at her distress and the state she was in. He wheeled round on his son, his icy voice whipping the thin veneer of glossy charm from Mat's face.

'Get your ass into my study!'

Matthew's eyes opened wide with shock. His father had never spoken to him like that before.

'What's up, pop?' He tried to make his voice casual but it came out thin and pitched too high.

'Don't you "pop" me,' David snarled. 'Just move it!'

Matthew affected a look of nonchalance as he sauntered across the hall to his father's study, but beneath the mask he boiled. Whatever the jerk had on his mind, he wasn't about to be treated like a child. He was almost twenty-six, for Chrissakes, not sixteen.

He flopped into a chair near to the door, ready for an early exit.

David closed the door firmly and crossed to the bar. He poured himself a brandy, but did not offer one to Mat.

For several minutes the only sound was of crackling pine-logs, but the atmosphere was heavy with accusation.

David stood before the fireplace and studied his son with a coldly analytical eye.

Matthew lounged, lizard-like. His long legs, clad in black velvet cords, stuck out in front of him like reedy stalks. His shirt was also black and his only gesture towards the 'dressing for dinner' that David insisted upon, consisted of a cravat-style necktie, worn jauntily inside his open shirt-front. On his narrow feet were Gucci loafers, scuffed and tired-looking.

Matthew's eyes met David's, their paleness gleaming with contempt.

David glowered. Insolence was evident in every line of the unkempt figure so carelessly draped in the chair. Mat's straw-coloured hair, worn too long and now only rarely clean, fell lankly over one eye.

'Who in hell *do* you look like?' David queried aloud.

Mat shrugged, not fully understanding. He was used to the old man's negative comments on his appearance. They didn't bother him.

David moved slightly from the fireplace, subjecting his son to another scrutiny. When Mat took the trouble he could be reasonably good-looking; but those days were fewer and fewer. Marriage hadn't changed that.

David swallowed some brandy, fighting the revulsion which his son's person evoked, and which had never been stronger than it was now.

His voice was barely controlled when he spoke again.

'OK, I'm not going to beat about the bush, Matthew. I've pussy-footed around you for all of your life, but that's over. You're in here to account to me, boy. And that's what you're going to do. Without prevarication. Is that clear?'

Matthew's mouth had fallen open, but no sound came from it.

'I want answers to questions that are all over this town and I want them good, understand? I want to know where the hell you spend your time, with whom and why. I also want to know why you're constantly absent from the office. And, not least, I want to know what the hell you're doing cashing bum cheques. Have you got all that? After you've given me those answers, I want to know what's wrong with your wife. Now, start answering!'

Matthew felt the heat scalding his face. Shit, he thought, this was going to be a bigger hassle than he'd expected.

He tried the helpless act – he'd gotten away with it before. 'I don't know what to say, dad.'

David felt his stomach tighten at the wheedling tone. 'Then you'd better start thinking of something, because your ass is on the line. I want answers – and I want them tonight.'

Matthew squirmed in the chair. 'Ah, shit, dad. You know I've got no head for business,' he placated, trying to make it sound light. 'That place bores the pants off me, for Chrissakes!'

David spoke icily. 'What do you think you're going to do with the business, when you inherit – if you're never there to learn anything about it?'

Matthew smiled thinly. This was safer ground. The old man's anger had never lasted out a full row with him; he always wore him down before he could. 'Ah, when I inherit? Well, now that you've asked . . .' His smile grew more cocky, confident that he was on the right track. 'Well, I guess I'll be making a few changes. Yeah. Quite a few changes.' He continued to smile.

'Oh, like what?' David's voice was dangerously calm, encouraging.

Matthew mistook the tone and his confidence swelled. Jeezus, the old man was a walkover, like his mom had always maintained. 'Keep the pressure on your father,' she'd told him repeatedly. 'Never let him think he's got the better of you . . .' Matthew's heart filled with renewed bitterness as the memory of his mother took hold. Why, if it hadn't been for her, that bastard Ben would have stolen his inheritance. But they'd fixed *him* between them, he and his mom. They'd gotten rid of him. He could have laughed aloud as he remembered how they'd done it . . . but that was a different matter, and a different time. His mom wasn't here to do battle for him any more.

But neither was Ben a threat any more. The old man had only one heir now. *Him.* The thought gave him considerable strength.

'Gee, dad, I haven't given it much thought yet. But . . .' he scratched his head thoughtfully. 'I guess for starters there are a couple of smart-asses to get rid of. Then the promotion of a few brighter guys who could run the place without me having to clean their noses for them . . .'

He glanced up at David and, taking his silence for encouragement, warmed to his theme. 'Hell, there's no need for us to work our butts off over there. We pay damned good bucks. Too much if you ask me. Strikes me that some of those jerks should get off their asses and start earning the fat hauls they con us out of!'

He looked across at David and smiled brightly. Perhaps the old man would respect him if he thought he was giving it all such serious attention. And maybe he'd even admit that Mat was right, admit that he could learn a trick or two from his son.

David's face was unreadable. 'Let me see if I've got this right. You'd like to sit back and just spend the money that has taken generations to accumulate? Hand over the reins of our family business to strangers? Pay other people to do your work for you? Does that sum it up?' His voice was toneless, guarded.

Matthew shrugged again, indifferently. If the old man didn't like the idea, that was his tough shit. He wouldn't be around to have any say in the matter.

He shifted restlessly in his chair. 'Oh, I'd go over from time to time. Keep an eye on things. Kick ass once in a while, just to keep them — '

His sentence was knocked unfinished into mid-air as David's hand dealt him a stinging blow which all but took his head off his shoulders.

Stunned, Mat tried to rise from the chair, but David's hands gripped him, pinning him down.

David leaned over his son, his eyes glittering like slivers of cut crystal, his lips curled back in rage.

'You no-good sonofabitch! You arrogant little bastard! Just who in hell do you think you are? What do you think gives you the right to sit on your bony ass while others work to keep you – eh?'

'No one keeps me,' Matthew yelled. 'I've got mom's money to keep me!'

David pulled back from the chair, contempt written all over his face. 'You're pathetic, Matthew, do you know that?' He spat the words out. 'And worst of all, you don't know how damned ignorant you are. Well, sonny, I've got news for you. The money your mother left you wouldn't pay for the gasoline you put in that fancy motor of yours. If you think your allowance comes from the paltry sum your mother left, you're even more stupid than I thought.'

He drew back to a safe distance, controlling his rage, not trusting himself to keep his hands off the stranger he saw before him.

'Let me tell you about your money. I invested it – the few thousand you were left, so's it would give you a half-way decent return. And do you know where I invested it? In

Nazareth House! And I'll tell you something else that you'd know already if you spent any time in the business that keeps you. I make up the difference in your allowance. *Me*, boy. Me, and my business endeavours. *Your* money wouldn't buy peanuts for a miniature monkey!'

Matthew had half risen. A trickle of blood ran from a cut where David's signet ring had caught his lip. He looked ashen, but his eyes blazed. 'You're a shit-assed liar!' he yelled, all pretence gone.

David's heart turned cold, but he stood his ground. If he hit his son now, he'd kill him. 'I think you might have just written your own future,' he said grimly.

'Stuff yourself!' Mat spat contemptuously.

'I'll finish what I started,' David continued coldly, 'and you'll listen, pal. I'm covering your tracks, up to today. Not because I could care a damn if you wound up in jail, but because Nazareth has always been an honourable name and even a shit like you isn't going to be allowed to foul that up. But, as from today, you will live within your allowance. You won't spend one dollar over your limit. Is that clear?'

Mat ignored him, and mopped at his mouth sullenly.

David managed to hold his temper in check. 'You'll have no more cheque-books until *I* think you're fit to control them. And I'll relieve you of your credit cards. You can bring them all to me in the morning. Cheque-books, credit cards. Got that?'

'You can't do that!' Matthew's face blanched. 'You sure as hell can't do that!'

'No? Just don't blink an eye, son. Because you haven't been listening too good. I'll run it by you again, so it's clearer. Your credit just ran out. It's cancelled. As from now your financial status is *zilch*. Now, have you got *that*!' He crossed to pour himself more bourbon to disguise his shaking hands.

Matthew's gaze followed, the flaming mark at the side of his mouth at variance with the cold gleam in his eyes.

David continued, clinically, methodically, 'You've lived here free of charge, without an expense or a responsibility in the world since you were born. Your clothes are provided. Your cars are provided. Your parties and your holidays have always been provided. You've had an extra allowance for your wife, and all her expenses, from the day you proposed . . . Now, if you can't afford your additional toys – whatever they are – on the money you earn, that's going to be your tough luck.

'You'll get paid every month by me, in cash. And to see that you earn it, you'll start Monday morning, with your butt on a chair over at the Firm. On the ground floor, where the humblest beginners start – every weekday, eight-thirty through six, and you'll be clocked in and out.

'You'll learn the hard way. Same as every one of your forebears did. The same as I did. From the ground up. And you won't get promoted until I'm convinced you're good and ready. If you ever are.'

'You're crazy!' Matthew's voice was hollow. 'If you think I'm wasting every day in that hole, you've got another think coming. You might be stupid enough to work yourself to death, but I'm not. And what's more, you can't make me!'

David slammed down his glass and leaned heavily on the mantel. His voice was deadly. 'No? Well, how does this grab you? I'm giving you twelve months to pull your act together. Six of those to get your ass in shape, and a further six to prove you're half-way intelligent enough to learn the business. At the end of that period, I'll review tonight's conversation, to see if you've earned any changes, and — '

'The hell you will! You can't make me go over there unless I feel like it. And you sure as fuck aren't treating me like shit! So what're you going to do about *that*?'

David's anger seared his heart with its ugliness, but he kept his voice even.

'I'll tell you what I'm going to do, and it's something I should have done a long time ago. I'm going to whip your butt into line. You'll be at the Firm every weekday, along with me. You'll come home every night. And weekends you'll spend with your family. Me and your wife. Get it?'

Matthew was growing more reckless by the minute. His mind was whirling with jumbled, spiteful thoughts; thoughts he'd nurtured most of his life, and which were now exploding in his head. His father was gutless. Mat had done what he wanted all his life. He didn't believe for a moment that David would have the nerve to treat his only son like an employee. He was a fanatic where family reputation was concerned.

Although Mat was shaking, he managed to put it down to knowing he was late for a meeting with his pals. The old man was bluffing – hoping to frighten him into submission. Ha, some chance!

'Let's talk about it some other time,' he said in a tone he hoped sounded reasonable. 'When you've calmed down a bit.'

'You've got some nerve! We'll talk again all right. We'll talk tomorrow, and the next day and every day it takes about your duties over at the Firm – and those you'll be taking better care of here.' David willed himself not to lash out. 'Twelve months, Matthew. Take it or leave it.'

'What the shit does that mean?'

'Exactly what it says,' David interrupted evenly. 'Twelve months, Matthew.'

'Or what?' Mat dared to sneer.

David turned away from him, and moved nearer to the fire. 'Or you're *out*,' he stated quietly.

Matthew was stunned. But then his mind began to calculate again. It was an act. He had to remember he was the *only* heir. Mat knew only too well what Nazareth blood meant to his father. He wanted to laugh out loud, but another sudden thought crossed his mind. Why, the cunning old bastard. Of course, Diana! That's what it was all about. The old man was counting on grandchildren.

His hands were trembling now, and he had begun to sweat. He'd have to get out of here soon, or the old man might see him get the shakes good and proper, and that wouldn't do at all. He began to make his way to the door again. If the old bastard thought that he'd get grandchildren and then disinherit him, he was in for a helluva long wait.

Mat's hand reached the handle, but he was shaking too much now to turn it. Somehow he had to get control, get his head clear, or he wouldn't get out of here at all. Pain began to tear at him, but as it did he summoned up all his self-control. He forced himself to think about other things. About that bitch upstairs. And about his more immediate problems.

He needed money, plenty of it. He couldn't manage on the pittance his father allowed him. He needed *big* money. Nazareth money. Not handouts, the real McCoy.

The handle finally turned. Thank God! He couldn't hold out for long now: the pains were increasing. He had to catch Clyde and Fixer on their evening run. He had money for the moment, and the old man hadn't pulled his cheque-book or credit cards in right away. He'd make good use of them over the weekend, while he thought out how he was going to sort the old man out. And he would sort him out, oh yes. David-asshole-Nazareth would regret tonight. Matthew would see to that.

He was half-way through the door when David's voice rang in his ears.

'Where in hell do you think you're going?'

Mat turned. He was too far gone now to be careful: his voice was thin and cracked with loathing. 'None of your fucking business!'

David stared disbelievingly at the clammy, sneering face. What was going on? Was Mat actually walking out? 'Just a damned minute,' he said hotly. 'We're not finished here yet, not by a long shot — '

'Get screwed!' Mat spat, wrenching the door open.

He didn't make the hall. David, realising that his son *was* walking out, was behind Mat in seconds. His grip stunned Mat and to Mat's chagrin he found himself hauled bodily back into the room and thrown into the chair he'd vacated.

David's breath rasped painfully in his chest from his awful anger.

'No one walks out on me. No one, do you hear!'

Mat felt dizzy. The room had begun to tilt and sweat soaked his body. But he had to keep alert, keep his head. If he could.

'What's your game, Matthew?'

'What game?' Mat pleaded innocence once more.

'Did you hear anything I just said. Did you really hear me?' David's voice was a whiplash.

'Yeah, I heard you.'

'You heard me, eh?' Did you hear me tell you that you're on trial?'

'The shit I am!'

David's eyes narrowed, and his fists clenched dangerously. 'You swear at me one more time, boy, and I'll knock your head off your shoulders,' he warned.

Mat heard the threat, but was too far gone to be warned. 'Yeah, I guess that's your style, isn't it?'

David ignored the insult. 'I want to know what you're going to do about the mess you're in?'

Matthew managed to clear his vision, just. He swallowed painfully. He had to get out of here. Nothing else mattered. Not tonight. Tomorrow, when he was feeling better, then he'd be able to handle this crap.

'I want to think about it,' he lied, his voice furred and thick.

'Think about it?' David roared. 'Have you lost your mind?'

'I said I'll think about it!' Mat retorted. 'And I will. When I'm fucking well ready!'

David reacted instinctively. His hands reached out for Mat's lapels and, pulling him to his feet, he knocked him down again.

Mat fell to the floor, the pain in his jaw transcending his other pains for a few moments.

David stood over him, violence surging in his heart, but the sight of his son, bloodied and helpless on the floor, brought him back to his senses.

'God Almighty!' he swore. 'If you don't give a damn for me, or the business, what about your wife?'

Mat levered himself up by the arm of the chair. How he'd love to whip that self-righteous face. But he wasn't strong enough. He was no physical match for David.

But he did have one thing he could use. Diana. He managed to find his feet. 'My wife?' He spat out the words. 'Now that you mention it, why don't you take care of her yourself?' He found the back of the chair and leaned on it for support. His voice trembled, but still it was filled with venom. 'You wanted this marriage so godamned bad, *you* take care of her. Come to think about it, that would probably suit you both, wouldn't it?'

'What in hell's name does that mean?'

'You're so damned smart. You work it out!'

'Matthew, I'm warning you . . .' David's voice had never been so dangerously strained.

'Yeah?' Mat sneered, beginning to feel better. David had played into his hands. 'Lay another finger on me, and we'll see who needs warning — '

'Don't threaten me!' David snapped. He could feel the vindictiveness emanating from Mat now; it was as tangible as the chair between them.

'No threat,' Mat said spitefully. 'Statement. Period. Mess with me one more time and you'll see what I can do to you in court. To the pair of you!'

David froze. What did Mat know? What could he know? There was nothing to know, damn it. But his mind whirled as he finally faced what he'd long suspected and hadn't dared confront. Mat *was* unbalanced – as Ella had been, *had* to have been. The truth he had hidden from, now, in its stark form, staring at him, numbed him.

'I'm going out, and this time don't try to stop me.' Mat had inched away, watching David warily. He knew he'd won. All it had needed was Diana. As he'd thought. It was written all over the old man's face. A small flame of triumph burned in his aching guts.

'Tell my wife she'll see me when she sees me. But it sure as hell won't be tonight!'

David knew that he could stop him, but there was no longer any point.

He turned his back as Matthew eased out of the room, and poured himself another bourbon. He downed the drink in one, the taste bitter in his mouth.

What had he unleashed? Had he really believed a confrontation could undo a lifetime of damage? Well, he had his answer now. It wouldn't. Hadn't. All it had done was tear down the wraps – wraps he supposed he'd used to cover what he couldn't understand.

He sank into his chair and leaned back wearily. And yet it was a relief to know that he need no longer hide what he felt. He'd been forced to face himself and he need never act again.

He lifted his head as a greater truth dawned. From this moment on he need never again hide behind rigidly enforced family rules, codes of behaviour imposed upon him by unknown ancestors. He was *free*. Jeff and, yes, Matthew had freed him – given him a freedom he hadn't dreamed was possible, because until now he hadn't even known that it had been denied him.

He had been kidding himself all these years. Fooling himself into believing that one day he would help Mat to bury the hatred and neuroses bred into him by Ella's sick mind. He had watched from a distance, loth to uncover unpalatable facts about his son; content to fool himself that one day Mat would turn to him for help; convinced that when that day came, he would be able to give him that help.

Well, the day had come, today. Not for Mat to turn to him, but for him to uncover the pit of darkness within himself. The unpalatable fact that he had never liked his son enough to want to help him.

His new freedom gave him the strength to face things as they were. All the battles he'd had with Ella over Ben, and over Mat, made sense to him now. He hadn't fought for equality for both boys as he'd allowed himself to believe.

No, it had been a battle with two clear sides: Ella and Mat, and he and Ben. The last barriers had come down. But it didn't help the rawness he felt.

Even so he knew what he was going to do. And it would be done mercilessly. His new freedom ensured that he wouldn't waste time on a compassion he didn't feel – or on a man he didn't give a damn about.

Exhilarated, he realised he was no longer concerned for the future – that relentless master of his every thought and move until now.

The future, with his very skilful care, would be everything *he* wanted it to be.

Diana was waiting, coffee keeping warm in a small bain-marie at her side. 'Ah, David, I was beginning to wonder where . . .' She glanced past him nervously, brow clearing when Mat didn't appear.

David noted the glance, and knew that everything would be all right. For some reason of her own, Diana was afraid of Matthew. Soon she would have no reason to be. David would make sure of that.

He smiled down at her, before taking a chair where he could watch her, lovingly.

She passed him a coffee, and their fingers accidentally brushed. Diana blushed and looked quickly away.

David smiled gently. His horizons had been irrevocably changed. The future was Diana. It was as simple as that.

'Matthew has gone out.'

Diana's eyes flickered. 'Oh?'

He sipped thoughtfully at the coffee she passed him, before saying carefully, 'I thought you might be able to tell me where he goes.' She shook her head, colouring.

'You don't have any idea?'

'No,' she said in a small voice.

'But you do know that something's wrong with him?' David watched her carefully.

Her colour deepened, but she shook her head again.

No, she didn't know? Or no, she wasn't saying? It didn't matter, he'd find out. 'Honey, I've been very stupid – very blind,' he said carefully, 'but not any more. I know something's badly wrong between you and Mat, and I understand you don't want to talk about it. I shan't probe, but you don't have to go on pretending that all is well. You see, I know that's not the case.'

Diana bit her lip, but didn't respond.

David spoke soothingly, easing the tension between them. 'I don't know for sure what Mat's been up to, but I do know there won't be any more of it.' He watched as her lashes flickered over lowered eyes, guessing from the way her shoulders eased back that she was relieved. 'It's over, Diana.'

Diana looked up at him open-mouthed, her cheeks flaming with embarrassment.

David's heart constricted anew. 'Just reassure me, honey. You aren't sick are you?'

She shook her head.

'Didn't you trust me enough to talk to me?' he urged, still very gently.

'About what?' Her voice was wary.

'About whatever Mat's been doing to make you look so ill.'

Diana stiffened. It was here, the moment she had been waiting for. Yet still she couldn't do it. David was guessing, he couldn't know the truth. Her mouth tightened. He wasn't going to learn it from her. She would not be the one to tell him.

'Why has Matthew gone out?' she managed, changing the subject.

David stared at her, frowning. She wasn't going to open up then. Pity. But it didn't matter. The last thing he wanted now was for her to be distressed any more. 'We had words,' he stated evenly. 'Mat walked out.'

'I'm sorry,' she said woodenly, her heart plummeting at the thought of Mat coming back later, probably in a temper.

'That we had words, or that he walked out?'

'That you had words,' she answered simply.

'They were long overdue.'

'Was it business?'

David didn't miss the covert look; it was one of fear. 'Yes, mainly. Mat hasn't been up to scratch for a long time. We had to straighten a few things out. I'm afraid I was harder on him than I'd intended. So we fell out rather badly.'

'Badly?' Diana eyes were wide.

'I'm afraid so, honey. I'm also not very proud to admit that I, well, I slapped him a little.'

'You struck Mat?' Diana's hand flew to her mouth in dismay.

David interpreted the look correctly, and his hand reached out for hers. 'Honey, stop worrying! Nothing's going to happen to you, I promise. When Mat gets back he and I will finish what we started and that will cure a lot of his problems.'

Diana groaned inwardly. David didn't know what he was talking about. He'd never seen the vicious side of his son.

'Diana, listen to me!' David said urgently. 'Matthew will not treat you badly again. Whatever he's done, it's over. Believe me!'

Diana nodded as if she understood, but her blood had gone cold. If David had abused Mat, she would be in for a rough time. For a fleeting second she debated telling him everything. Then she remembered Mat's threats.

She sat very still, hoping that David would finish his coffee and leave. She would barricade the door to her suite, if she could get to bed before Mat got back. Her thoughts began to whirl feverishly. She would have to get rid of David, then make herself safe. Tomorrow she would decide a final course of action, when she knew how Mat was going to react. She might have to tell David then, and that was soon enough.

As David didn't move, she rose unsteadily. 'Thank you for telling me, but I hope you'll excuse me now. I have a headache . . .'

'Of course, honey. You get some rest,' David said, rising from his chair. 'We'll have breakfast together, say around eight-thirty?'

Diana agreed, and walked with him to the door.

CHAPTER NINE

Later that night Beanie's words at the wedding came back to David; something about Diana not knowing why she'd married Mat. He frowned in the dark, as suddenly his own guilty secret surfaced at the front of his mind. Oh Christ – in all the upheaval of his own emotions he'd forgotten all about it. Mat had *never* wanted to marry Diana. He had been bribed. By David.

Sweating now, he remembered the scene between them. It had been the beginning of the summer, just a few days after David had met Diana himself . . .

'Do I hear an "ideal arrangement" going down here, or are my ears deceiving me?' Matthew was leaning against the banister at the bottom of the stairs, arrested in disbelief.

'Call it what you like,' David replied tartly. 'I'm just asking you to meet a young woman who would clearly be an asset to you, and to this house.'

'You *can't* be serious!' Mat said, stunned, but amazed enough to continue listening.

'You are the right age, so is she,' David continued dispassionately, ignoring his son's sarcasm. 'It's time you settled down, gave your attention to the Firm – and to your future. I happen to think that we have found the right partner for you to do just that.'

'*We*? I haven't even met this person.' Mat said incredulously.

'You will on Saturday. I'm giving a party here, in the garden. Beanie will act as hostess for us. You can invite your friends.'

Matthew couldn't believe this weird conversation, but his father's tone of voice warned him that this was *business* – and, as Mat well knew, in business no one argued with

David Nazareth. In spite of his urge to laugh out loud, he found himself curious, intrigued. 'And then . . .?'

'Then we'll see,' David stated matter-of-factly. 'You are always crying broke, saying you want more privileges – inside and outside the Firm. Here's your chance to get them.'

Mat's hand tightened on the newel post as recognition dawned. The old bastard was going to try to buy him. For a moment his hatred threatened to explode, but the intimated reward urged caution. 'A sort of bargain, you mean?'

His father's eyes narrowed, but he continued as if insulted. 'Damn it, Matthew! She's beautiful, intelligent, classy . . . and I'm busting a goddamned gut for you here!'

Mat made himself frown, as if thinking. 'And the Firm?' he queried. 'What does this, uh, lady, bring to the Firm?'

'You!' David snapped, irritated

Matthew's eyes gleamed. He was on a *roll*. The old man was putting up bait. Filthy, stinking bait – but bait nevertheless. 'And in return,' he said coldly, 'I get what, exactly?'

David's gut tightened, but he would not be goaded. Nothing could be allowed to stop this, it *had* to happen. He couldn't see any other way. 'If you agree, and there's no reason why you shouldn't – she's a very special young lady – then of course you'd have a commensurate increase in your allowance, a raise in your salary, additional expenses – all that sort of thing.'

For a long moment father and son stared at one another in the sun-filled hall, David uncertain of his son, Matthew too certain of his father . . . and of himself. The tension built.

So, Matthew thought, his dad had decided to provide the bride he'd never have brought home himself – and the rewards that went with the deal were the bait. He scrutinised his father through narrowed eyes, and for several seconds he tasted the bitterness of a lifetime. But his quicksilver mind as swiftly erased it, with the thought of what this could bring him. Money. Power. Freedom. But most of all, *money*. 'How, uh, generous, would these extra allowances, expenses, be?'

David met the avaricious question carefully, knowing that

before last summer they could not have had even this, distasteful, discussion. He knew that he had no choice but to haul Mat into line, but until he'd met Diana he hadn't known how.

He coughed behind his hand to cover his disgust – at Mat, and at himself. He didn't like what he was attempting; it went against every grain of integrity in his soul. But fate had provided an unexpected source of hope. Hope for the future; for Mat; for the Firm. He didn't yet add, and for himself.

His throat felt tight, but his answer was unequivocal. 'Just as generous as you are to Diana.'

He was wide awake now, his insides churning at what he had done. Mat had married Diana because he, his father, had paid him to. Jesus Christ, had she found out?

For a moment sweat trickled down his back; the thought was devastating. But no, it couldn't be that. She would have given it away, he was sure of it.

Relieved, he wondered what *could* be making her so nervous, nervous enough to have lost weight, to look so ill. She was hiding something. But what?

The question haunted him, and when morning came he knew he had to have answers: not just where Mat went, but what he did to cause his wife to look the way she did. Suspicions and guesses weren't enough; he needed substance.

Breakfast hardly helped. Diana was tense and as pale as a ghost. All David could get out of her was that Mat hadn't returned.

'Not at all?' he quizzed, disbelievingly.

Diana glanced at him quickly, and shook her head. It was becoming a form of language between them, he mused ruefully. He'd ask a question, she'd shake her head. Well, not for much longer. Today he'd get the truth from Mat.

He excused himself as soon as he decently could.

'Are you going out?' Diana's voice was barely a whisper, tinged with fear.

'Have to, honey,' David reassured her. 'But I'll be back soon. Why don't you stay down here? The house could do with some nice floral arrangements. John will get you whatever you need and perhaps Meg will keep you company.'

Diana grasped at the idea, agreeing swiftly.

'Good!' David rose. He didn't want her alone in the annexe if Mat came back. He turned to Sanders with a meaningful look. 'See that Miss Diana has all that she needs to keep her occupied *downstairs*, would you? And free Meg for the morning so she can help Miss Diana . . .'

All four of the staff had been worried at the amount of time the young mistress spent alone upstairs. Sanders was glad that Mr David had decided to do something about it.

'I'm sure that John would be pleased to show you the choice of blooms, Miss Diana. I understand the peonies have been very fine this year,' Sanders said, taking his cue effortlessly. 'And Mrs Carly is baking, I believe. So elevenses should be most enjoyable, if you would honour us with your company?'

David smiled. Sanders was very quick on the uptake. Diana wouldn't be left alone for a second.

Now he was free from worrying about her and could concentrate his attention on Matthew.

As he drove into the city there was only one thing on his mind. *Matthew*. No matter what it took, he would sort him out today.

In his mind's eye was a stark picture of Diana, robbed of her gentle vitality, gaunt and haunted. It still shook him. He had to know what that bastard had done to her, whether his appalling suspicions were correct. But he didn't dare think what he might do if they were.

His mouth was grim, his intentions pitiless as he toured

the streets of Boston, checking one parking lot after another. Slowly he cruised the streets, every fibre of his being alert for Mat's yellow Jaguar.

No one in the bars where the younger crowd hung out had seen him. Ditto the fast-food places and the coffee shops. There was no point checking the sports complexes, gyms or health clubs, but he did tour the riverside and boating areas, on the off-chance.

On foot he searched the malls and pedestrianised shopping centres, but it was Saturday morning, so he knew his chances of spotting his son in the crowds were slight.

After four hours he'd had enough and drove to Nazareth House, parked in his private lot and let himself into the silent building. A quick call reassured him that Mat hadn't been home, and that Diana would be kept under discreet observation.

He began the time-consuming task of phoning everyone he knew, looking for Matthew. It was difficult enough fending off the effusive greetings and offers of hospitality, but giving nothing away whilst seeking Mat was harder. His suave diplomacy would not prevent the grapevine rustling all over town and country.

Just before five in the afternoon he hung up on his last, futile call.

He sat back to think. Until this moment he'd have sworn that all he wanted was for Mat to do the right thing. Now he wasn't so sure. Until yesterday he'd told himself that so long as Mat sired Diana's children everything would work out just fine. In Diana he had seen the future of Nazareth House, in her character the strength for future generations. She had all the fine characteristics missing in his son and David had believed that she would provide the fertile soil for his son's weak seed. So long as Diana was there to bear the future heirs, David had convinced himself that he could bear his own fate with equanimity.

But that had been before the wraps had come off. Before

he'd recognised Mat's hatred and, yes, his own. Before he'd seen how bitterly unhappy Diana had become.

He drove back home, at a loss to know what to do next. He'd been desperate to kick Mat's butt – but then what? It sank in now that he hadn't planned beyond that moment.

However, he couldn't accept that Mat had walked out on him after all that had been said. It was out of character for Mat to make life difficult for himself. Sure he'd played hookey a lot when he'd been younger, when he hadn't known what was at stake. Now? He sure as hell knew now. That fact bothered David intensely. That Mat had listened, and had still walked out.

He pulled into the garage block at the mansion – still no yellow Jaguar. He frowned in the gloom. It still didn't make sense. Matthew had blown it, *knowingly*.

On Sunday morning David made a personal call to a very trusted friend, Pat O'Rourke, Chief of Police, a man David had known most of his life. Their two fathers had been great buddies and though David and Pat didn't socialise that often their friendship was secure. There was no one he could trust more than Pat.

He caught the chief at home.

'Pat, I need a favour.'

'Sure thing, Dave.'

'Nothing formal, you understand?'

'Wouldn't expect you to call on the Sabbath about nothin' formal,' Pat replied easily.

'It's Matthew. He's missing,' David stated bluntly.

'Missin'? Or gone on the wild side?'

'Yeah, something like that,' David said quietly.

'You want him home? Or just to know where he is?'

'Where he is. Nothing more.' David said firmly.

Pat grunted softly. 'That nice little wife with him?'

'No, she's here.'

'Everything else OK?'

'Fine, Pat. I just need to know where he hangs out. He and

I have a little unfinished business to sort out,' David added grimly.

'Leave it with me, Dave,' Pat replied. 'Now where'd you want to have this information – home, or elsewhere?'

'Over at the office, Pat. And thanks.'

'No sweat, Dave. I'll see what can be done.'

CHAPTER TEN

Knowing that Diana was safely involved with household matters, and that he would be notified when Matthew appeared, David retired to his study.

He worked all afternoon on the draft of a legal document he would give, if necessary, to Mark Wheeler, stopping only when he was satisfied that he'd covered every possible point.

Now his dilemma was what to tell Diana, and when.

How did he break it to her that he'd issued her husband with an ultimatum? And that Mat had called his bluff? He thought it over for a long time before finally deciding to say nothing for the time being. Why aggravate the situation? Diana appeared to be less than bothered by Mat's absence. If anything, she seemed relieved by it.

David was in his office earlier than usual on Monday morning, with instructions to his ground-floor reception staff to buzz him the moment Mat walked through the door. He wanted no scenes when his son did arrive.

There was no doubt in David's mind that Mat would show this morning. He'd given him no choice.

Pat O'Rourke came on the line half-way through the morning. Apologetically he explained that Mat hadn't been seen anywhere in Boston that weekend. He'd had his men quietly check every avenue.

At noon precisely, David picked up his internal phone and called his own legal department.

'Mark? Meet me up in the Green Suite as soon as you can. Use my elevator – oh, and Mark, keep it quiet.'

It was five after noon when Mark Wheeler stepped out of the elevator, bristling with curiosity, and walked the long hallway to the rarely used suite.

Matthew had called David's bluff. Now he didn't get a

second chance. David handed the document he had prepared to Mark.

'Holy shit!' Mark swore when he had read the disinheritance. His face was grave as he looked up at his boss. 'This is it?'

David's face was unreadable. 'That's almost it . . . When he comes here, as he will in due course, he collects $500,000. See that it's kept ready, in cash. He will be escorted to the mansion by yourself and Jeff to pick up his personal clothes, but he is not to be left alone there under *any* circumstances – and wherever I am, I want to be informed that he's there. He can keep his car, but he gets nothing else. *Ever*. Is that all quite clear?'

'This is classified, right?' Mark's expression was of shock and relief, and the combination made his bespectacled eyes huge.

'Wrong. It's not classified. Not after you check out the legalities and ensure that there are no loopholes.'

David was already standing as Mark rose.

Mark knew that any document David had drawn up was watertight. 'I'll make sure there are no loopholes,' he said with quiet fervour.

'Good man,' David said, unsmiling.

As the news was not classified, it spread like a bush fire through the stunned building, just as David had intended it should. By mid-afternoon, no one who was anyone in Boston hadn't heard the staggering news.

Matthew Nazareth had been disinherited and no one in Boston would give him the time of day thereafter. Boston would do what it was supremely good at. It would close ranks.

David refused to see anyone for the rest of the day, including his personal secretary, Jeff Sherman.

There was nothing David wanted to talk to anyone about today. Especially not to Jeff.

He worked on, oblivious of the secondary bush-fire of speculation. Oblivious too of the fact that he had still to tell Diana. He hadn't even thought again about how to tell her what he'd done to Mat.

He had, for the moment, forgotten about heirs.

In his smouldering rage he worked until late, rising from his desk only when all his emotions were spent.

He had not that day given the future a single thought.

But at a deep, subconscious level, a seed had been sown. That seed was not yet in his conscious mind. But it would be. Very soon.

Matthew had vanished.

Pat O'Rourke's reports were few because there was nothing to report. It was as if Mat and his exclusive yellow Jaguar had been swallowed up wholesale.

Life at the mansion went on as normal.

David told Diana that Pat was looking for Mat.

Other than that he told her nothing, and she asked him nothing. If she'd heard about Mat's disinheritance she gave no sign, of interest or otherwise. It was as if she didn't want to know.

David was happy with the status quo; more than happy that she didn't ask any questions; perfectly happy that he had her to himself.

Slowly she returned to health. David was at home every evening, and on some days he cut his diary to be with her.

Christmas approached: the new President of Egypt, Hosni Mubarak settled into his role after his election following the assassination of Anwar Sadat; thousands of people faced arrest under Poland's new martial laws; alarming reports were being collated around the USA concerning a new disease affecting the immune system. But Matthew Nazareth did not return home . . .

Winter passed and the spring weekends were filled with pleasant outings and activities: David and Diana went boating, and Beanie joined them frequently for lunch, or for a trip around the bay; to shop, to go to the theatre or to see a film.

If ignorance was bliss, then those were blissful months for them all. Diana blossomed and became more like her old self. Admittedly there were still occasions when she would suddenly glance around, that stricken look on her face, but those times grew less frequent as the months passed.

It was as if they all held their breaths, unwilling to mention Matthew . . . perhaps pretending he didn't even exist.

David did everything he could to strengthen his relationship with Diana, developing a deep friendship, as warm and caring as they had both hoped for before the marriage had taken place, but with a singular difference; Matthew no longer intruded.

Only Beanie saw through David's fatherly guise, but she wisely refrained from mention of the fact.

Pat O'Rourke kept up a determined search for Mat, regularly checked his sources and just as regularly reported 'nothing' to David.

Diana had regained her lost weight by the time summer reached its end. Her first wedding anniversary came and, although David and Beanie held their breaths, it went without mention.

No one knew that her thoughts occasionally became frantic, or that there were still nights when, hearing a small sound, she would lie awake frozen with fear.

As much as was possible in the circumstances, David was contented. There were still hurdles to overcome, but he was a very patient man.

The halcyon days came abruptly to an end one autumn morning.

David arrived at his office as usual, to find a very subdued Jeff Sherman waiting for him. From the look on his face, David thought Mat had come back. His heart hit his shoes.

But it was a different problem, and one David could handle with his hands tied behind his back, though annoyingly it involved a trip out of the state.

An engineering firm Nazareth House had acquired some years before in a small town outside Philadelphia had recently tendered for, and won, a government contract. It was a small

but extremely prestigious feather in David's, and therefore the
Firm's, cap.

The problem had arisen because of the nature of the contract
which was classified as an official secret and, as proprietor of
the satellite firm, David had to deal with the matter himself.

'Damn!' he swore now. 'I'll have to go down myself.'

"Fraid so,' Jeff concurred.

David's heart sank. The last thing he wanted was for Diana
to have to be alone. He'd done a rough calculation of how long
Mat might last on the money he'd cunningly filtered from his
various accounts on the morning David had expected him to
show up at the office. On David's reckoning, that money had
to be almost gone.

Mat would surface soon. But how? And where?

David studied Jeff dispassionately. It looked as if it was time
to let him back in from the cold.

'Jeff, I need a favour.'

Jeff gazed into the frosty blue eyes, and waited. He'd been
badly wounded by learning of Mat's disinheritance through
rumour. But it had hurt even more that David had never since
discussed the matter with him.

'It concerns Mat,' David said now, his voice emotionless.

Jeff remained silent, but a muscle worked at his jaw.

'When Mat left the house, we'd had an almighty row. I'd
given him an ultimatum the night you and I had that little
talk; the rest you already know. Since that night he's been
missing.'

Jeff knew that, but David himself hadn't confirmed it
until now.

'The thing is, you were right. I think Mat had been abusing
Diana in some way.' David paused to let that sink in, but
there was no gratitude, none of their old friendship in the
formidable gaze.

'He's about due to run out of money, and my guess is he's
going to show up when he needs more. That could be soon.'

'Where do I come in?' Jeff's voice was steady.

David glanced over his steepled fingers, watching Jeff's face intently. 'If it hadn't been for this,' he freed one hand and waved a finger at the papers they'd just gone over, 'you wouldn't come in at all.'

Jeff felt the impact of the words, and a chill ran the length of his spine, but before he had chance to work out exactly what that meant David went on in the same toneless voice.

'My concern is that when Mat does show he might make a nuisance of himself.' He continued to stare at the younger man. 'I'm not asking you to baby-sit him, just to keep a check on the mansion and Diana. To be available. If Mat should come here first, you'll need to know what arrangements I've made concerning him. If he goes to the mansion first, Sanders will have my instructions.'

Jeff was stunned. He'd taken the snub badly at the time, but had worked hard at not letting it show. Now he knew, for sure, that it had been a calculated snub. He'd crossed the line. David had redrawn it, leaving him out in the cold.

'Well?' David asked quietly.

He might just as well have spelled it out, for Jeff knew instantly that David was talking as much about his job as about Mat's reappearance. It was a challenge to Jeff's loyalty, maybe a small bridge back. Very small. But it was on offer. Comply, or goodbye.

'What do I have to do?' Jeff managed in a small voice.

David's look was less chilly now. 'First, you go down to Law. Mark Wheeler will fill you in on Mat's full entitlements. There's not much to know. Second, he's not to get into the mansion alone. If he wants to collect anything, he has to be accompanied by you and Mark. Any trouble and you call Pat O'Rourke!' David paused, aware of Jeff's discomfort, waiting for any comments. But Jeff had none, so he went on, 'I'd like you to check at the house regularly, mainly to see that Diana is OK.'

Jeff nodded.

'Well, that's that. Now, book me a flight down to Philly

tomorrow. And get rooms at a decent hotel. If one of those guys *is* an alcoholic, some ambient R & R should flush him out.'

Jeff pulled himself together and returned to his own office. He hadn't trusted himself to speak.

His wounded pride hurt more than his ulcer. Ever since he'd joined the Firm he'd personally handled all David's private affairs. *Never* had he had to ask any other department for access to private information.

Without a single word being spoken, without a change in his position or his salary, he'd been efficiently, ruthlessly, demoted. And he had only himself to blame.

David and Nazareth House were his life. He knew the rules. He had broken them. David had drawn a line, he had crossed it. Worse, he had been insulting while he did it.

Jeff felt like a child again. And, like a child, he wanted to weep. Instead he crashed his fist against his desk, shattering a crystal paper-clip dish.

Twenty-four years, and his *first* mistake.

There would never be another. There was a lot of lost ground to make up, and the sooner he began the better.

But first there was Mark Wheeler. Better get that over with fast and let the latest rumour get going on its inevitable rounds.

That Jeff Sherman, long-time second-in-command, no longer had the boss's confidence . . .

Diana was apprehensive about David's plan to leave for Philadelphia, all her old fears re-emerging at once.

'Will it be for long?' she asked him at dinner, concealing her dismay.

'Not a moment longer than it has to be, honey,' David said firmly. 'A few days, a week at most.'

'That long,' Diana said bleakly.

'I won't stay away a moment longer than necessary, princess. I promise,' he assured her; but later that night he tossed restlessly, well aware that Diana had become withdrawn almost at once. Once more he damned his son. Why the hell didn't he come back, get the whole business dealt with, and then get out of their lives?

It was what David was waiting for. Praying for.

But it was useless to speculate on when Mat would turn up. It could be next week, or next month. There was nothing David could do about it.

Nevertheless, he was uneasy. Suppose Mat did come back while he was gone? Suppose he demanded that Diana leave the mansion with him? She was still his wife after all. What would she do?

He cursed silently. He couldn't give a damn about Mat, but he did fear his effect on Diana.

Before he finally slept, David reached something of a solution. He'd call Beanie tomorrow, have her come over to the house to stay. At least then he'd know Diana had company, other than just staff.

Later, he would recall his intention. It would come back to haunt him. For the following morning he overslept, and in the rush to catch his plane had to miss breakfast – and therefore didn't see Diana. Temporarily, with the government contract on his mind, he forgot about Mat.

The call to Beanie was never made.

Long after dark the next evening a car pulled into the tree-lined drive. Matthew drove as close to the house as he needed to be, choosing his spot with care.

The first scarlet leaves of autumn scattered into the windy night.

Swiftly he killed the engine and the lights, and waited until his eyes grew accustomed to the dark. The two friends with him knew that it was silence from now on. This was Mat's party, and those were his rules. They sat, tense and sweating in the back of the car, while Mat worked out his moves.

Shielded by trees, Mat knew that he couldn't be seen by anyone glancing from the house. But in the darkness he was clearly able to make out the lighted windows at the front of the mansion.

He waited for fifteen minutes, then slid from the car. His sneakers made no sound amongst the swirling leaves as he moved silently towards the garage. It took only moments to establish that David's car was not there, but that Diana's VW runabout was neatly parked.

Mat grinned in the dark. His information had proved correct. No doubt the old man's car was waiting for him at the airport. Jeez, if his father'd had the sense to use a cab, Mat knew he couldn't have been sure enough to risk this plan. But the knowledge that he could predict his father's likely behaviour in most situations gave him an added satisfaction.

'Friggin' jerk!' he muttered softly to himself, beginning finally to enjoy the sweet taste of revenge. David wouldn't be such a clever ass in future, not after he'd sampled Mat's calling card.

Mat's insides jellied with pleasure as he crept around the building, noting the rooms that were occupied and those that weren't. He was going to be in clover for the rest of his life. Diana would give him everything he wanted, just to keep him away; and the old man would pay willingly for the same privilege . . . he'd make *sure* of that.

Admittedly, he hadn't meant to leave it quite so long before calling and making his intentions clear. But after all that fuss in the papers, he'd decided it was better to lay low for a bit longer. Disinherited! Christ, the irony! As if he gave a shit for Nazareth House . . . he was only too happy to be rid of the burden. There was only one thing he'd ever wanted from his old man – and now he was going to get it. *Money*.

The past year had been the best of Mat's life.

With his pals he'd made an old warehouse habitable and

even comfortable; they'd had everything they needed at a basic level, and all the freedom to do as they pleased. It suited Mat perfectly. And his pals had been good to him – better than any family, certainly any *Nazareth* family. He'd been sick a few times, but they'd taken good care of him, danced attendance on him, fetched whatever he needed when he was too sick to go out.

And why shouldn't they – after all, he was the Big Guy. The *source* of the money. It was a good feeling. Powerful.

But money was short now – his small haul of saleable articles had run out; the last – his gold watch – had bought them a bit more time. He hated the break-ins, the ever more difficult search for new fences – after the last one he'd said, 'Enough.'

This past week had been bad. They'd had to cut back and that had made him mad as hell. Now he sniffed angrily, remembering the cold sweats when he'd thought he'd have to crawl back and beg forgiveness. Screw that! But amazingly his luck had held. He'd gotten into the habit of checking on the old man – calling in different voices. He sneered contemptuously; it was so easy when you knew how. He crept stealthily back to the car, savouring how he'd felt this very morning, when the receptionist at Nazareth House had so politely informed him that 'Mr Nazareth is out of town for a few days.'

One anonymous enquiry and he was able to learn anything he wanted. It was a breeze.

Mat's car had been resprayed black and now, with its third set of salvaged licence plates, was unlikely to attract any attention. Yeah, he felt safe. There'd be cash in the house. Money and jewellery, and other small, saleable items. They would do very nicely for the moment, until he established a set arrangement with his wife. He leaned against the car, glowering as he thought about his wife.

He'd never intended to marry. Only his father's bribe had made him consider it. Christ, he'd been stupid – what had he gained but aggro? What had she brought him but trouble?

He slid back into the car and despite its warmth he shivered. Fucking bitch. It was all her fault. She'd turned the old man against him – just as Ben had. Well, he'd dealt with Ben, now he was going to deal with her.

He watched as the last of the lights were extinguished, knowing that no sound carried from the annexe to the servants' quarters. His face gleamed with perspiration now as he thought of the possibilities in the night ahead. He only wanted money, but he knew his pals would be interested in his beautiful wife as well. He grimaced to himself, sickened.

Mat had never liked women. The only person he'd ever loved had been his mother, and she'd died on him, left him to grieve alone, with a man he feared and hated. He'd never forgiven her for that. Since then, Mat's tolerance of women had been low, lower even than his libido. Mat had no natural sex-drive. He had to be stoned to get it up.

Even for a body like his wife's.

Well, he was nicely stoned tonight. So were his pals and they'd earned their rewards. Maybe it would be fun, a quartet . . .

The house had been in darkness for an hour when Mat turned to his friends.

'OK, you guys. Remember all I've told you? Right? And no one hangs about downstairs, got that?'

He reached in his pocket for a balaclava hood, and his pals took their cue. The three covered their heads.

'Fixer, you watch the time. Sixty minutes, not a second longer.' Mat grinned behind the menacing dark wool. He'd waited most of his life to repay his father for loving Ben more than him. Now his moment had finally come.

'OK,' he whispered, his voice ugly. 'Let's go!'

It was almost dawn when Matthew and his friends fell, panting and swearing, back into the car. Mat stalled the engine several times, his hands shaking and sweat dripping from his face.

'Christ Almighty! What the friggin' hell happened in there?'

His voice was a shriek as he threw the car into gear, and reversed all the way back to the street.

His friends were gasping, still trying to catch their breath. Mat hit the gas. Christ Almighty, it had all gone wrong! He headed for the highway, his brain trying to function rationally.

They had to get far away, and fast. No good going back to the warehouse now. Jeezus! They'd blown it. And all because Fixer had stashed some dope, and insisted they have a little party. He hadn't been able to control them after that. They'd been like rutting animals.

Sure, he'd agreed to party – had intended to. But not like that. He had no stomach for *that*. Now he shivered as he tasted his own vomit again. And Diana's blood – he was sure he could taste her blood.

His self-preservation reasserted itself, made him blot out the scenes of the past few hours. He couldn't think about it. He would *not* think about it. No, he'd think about what the hell they were going to do now. They'd have to get out of the state, head south. Now! Instincts returned, and he drove swiftly, but not erratically, for the state highway. The last thing they needed was to catch the attention of a traffic cop.

As the car sped on into the morning, all three men – now they were far from the crime – were calming down. They accepted Mat's decision to run; there wasn't any choice. Their pockets were bulging with money, jewels and small valuables that would easily sell. But Mat's face was grim. He'd intended setting up an on-going situation, a ready supply of cash. But now?

His anger was all-consuming. He could *never* go back. He shook with impotent rage. That bitch! It was all her fault. She'd caused Fixer and Clyde to flip. If she hadn't kept pleading, they might not have been so rough. If her body, with the nightdress torn off, hadn't been so lovely, so provocative . . . if the slut had given in, taken what she was asking for, instead of fighting like that! It was all *her* fault.

He cursed her over and over again as the powerful motor ate up the miles. Silently, and with tears running down his face, tears of self-pity – and of frustration at having his perfect plans fouled up.

He hadn't an ounce of compassion for the woman they'd left, or a second thought about her condition. Matthew was incapable of thinking of anything other than his ruined plans. And of how the hell they were going to manage when the haul ran out.

He'd intended to frighten her – and the old man. Force them to concede his *rights*; to money whenever he wanted it. And he'd have agreed to stay away, for the right price. Damn, damn, damn! Her fault. *Her* fucking fault. He'd find a way, some day, to settle with her once and for all.

For now he dashed the tears from his eyes and headed towards California.

CHAPTER ELEVEN

It was a typical fall day, cloudless, fine and cold, but with that special hint of wood-smoke in the air, the tangible autumnal scents of apple logs and spruce cones that even city-dwellers, like Beanie, could sniff at and appreciate.

In Beanie's case, more than appreciate. There was no time that Beanie loved as much, for when nature was at its most mellow her mind was most content.

Her heart found its greatest peace when the glorious New England countryside was ablaze with its famous fall colours. Even the tourists, coming in droves to admire the vivid oranges and bright crimsons, against their majestic backdrop of deep velvety green spruce and blue-black pine trees, could not love it more than Beanie did. Somehow, when the leaves turned from gold to russet brown to fiery scarlet, and the sweet chestnuts swelled on the trees, she came alive. Not for her the seduction of spring. Life for Beanie began again, renewed, in the fall.

Autumn heralded beginnings for her, the time of quiet preparation for the hectic winter months to come. Beanie's best parties were those she gave between October and March. She had never enjoyed the boisterous outdoor events so loved by Americans. Summer, to Beanie, was one long air-conditioned pause, lightened only by her Midsummer's Eve party. Perhaps it was something in her ancestry that made her relish the shorter days and seemingly longer nights. Or maybe it was just that her only indulgence, her parties, lent themselves so much more to indoor settings. To the candlelight, and the deep red wines she enjoyed more than the light, summery whites.

Fall and its partner, winter, gave her many excuses for indoor parties. And people were more inclined to dress well when it was cold enough to cover up in an expensive fur. If there was anything that Beanie loathed, it was sloppy dress.

Thinking about dress and furs reminded her that she would have to look in at Kajaz soon, if she wanted to buy Diana a full-length silver fox coat for Christmas. She had given her a silver fox wrap already, but it would be the same fur again. Once Beanie decided which fur suited a woman, her dainty nose turned up if they wore any other kind. Diana was born to wear silver fox, and if Beanie had anything to do with it she would never wear any other.

It had been a most enjoyable morning. Beanie had spent ages in Newbury Street, in Quincey's Market and Boylston Street, shopping for odds and ends for her forthcoming party, and had finally finished up at Eric's, where she'd bought pretty wrappings in delicate pastel shades. Now she almost hummed with contentment as she sniffed the air and made her way, laden with packages, to her car.

Shopping for her parties was always agreeable, but more so when she had the deliciously sensuous prospect of an evening beside a crisply crackling log fire to look forward to as well.

Despite the cold, she was perspiring slightly by the time she had walked to the lot and loaded her car. It would never have occurred to Beanie to question her need to do her own shopping when she was one of Boston's wealthiest women. It was just something she enjoyed. Money was not something Beanie analysed. Neither were the topics of her own position and power ever alluded to. Hard work and an instinctive business sense had earned her enormous wealth and celebrity status. But she was not inclined to pay them more attention than was strictly necessary.

Likewise her car. It was functional. That was all she needed. David was always trying to get her to change it, but she didn't see the point. It was reliable. What more did she need?

Her parties and her daily maid were her only real extravagances. The housekeeper/maid was essential, for Beanie's busy life left little time for domestic duties. The parties were another matter. They were her indulgence and her only vice. Her one excuse to spend . . .

The penthouse was warm and welcoming and, as always, she inhaled its atmosphere as she came in, as if there were perfume in the air. And to her there was. She couldn't have named it, or even recognised it as psychological. To her it was the aroma of security, mingled with the exotic essence of freedom. The most powerful scent in the world.

Spreading her packages on the huge glass-topped table, she hummed softly to herself.

Phyllis, her dour and faithful maid waited for Beanie's coat, tutting at the silky coldness of the fur against her warm arms.

'Coffee's on its way, ma'am,' she said, in mildly reproving tones. 'And a good *hot* luncheon to follow.'

'Thank you.' Beanie smiled, taking no offence. Phyllis had been with her for over ten years and for most of them had tried to mother Beanie. It never worked of course, as they both knew. But tacitly Beanie allowed the woman her small tokens of devotion. Phyllis was a gem, but Beanie permitted none of her staff, at home or at her salons to become close to her. She was as caring and as considerate as an employer could be, but she maintained a rigid personal detachment.

Her only 'family' was David's.

Now her mind was fully occupied as she contemplated her purchases carefully. These were only the finishing touches for a party long ago organised. This party would, as always, have a special theme. Beanie took great pains with her themes, and then with all the minutiae to ensure that they were followed through to the last, tiny, detail.

Every party was an event in Boston's society calendar. And every guest at an exclusive MB party took away memories never to be forgotten, as well as some small, equally exclusive, memento.

For a short time, each guest became like a child to Beanie.

A child, like herself. She created innocence for them and for a while grown men and women would delight in her lavish and indulgent affection.

For a few blissful hours, Beanie escaped the grey prison of her memories, bridged the intervening years and transported herself and her guests back to the fairyland of a childhood she imagined might have been hers.

The telephone began to ring, just as she was admiring the porcelain-on-gold brooches she had received this morning. Her theme for this party was to be a garden, an exotic paradise for butterflies. There would be hot-house bushes and flowers everywhere, and real butterflies, flown in specially, to exclaim over. The culinary delights would be in butterfly shapes and the entire penthouse would be a rainbow of colours.

The gifts were, accordingly, butterflies, in every colour imaginable, delicate and shimmering. They were each individual brooches, one-off designs, handmade at Cartier, to Beanie's innovative and fastidiously expensive taste.

Phyllis answered the phone, whilst Beanie checked that no diamonds or emeralds or rubies had come loose.

Her maid held one hand over the receiver, and called to Beanie.

'Madame? It's Mr Nazareth's houseman. He sounds very concerned.'

A frown creased Beanie's forehead. Sanders? What could he want?

Phyllis shrugged her shoulders in answer to Beanie's raised eyebrows, and handed the instrument over.

'Yes, Sanders?' Beanie enquired courteously.

The voice she knew well was nervous, shaken; her frown deepened.

'I'm sorry to disturb you at home, madame, I've been trying to get you at the salons, I . . . I wonder . . . could you come to the mansion, immediately?'

A cold shiver ran down Beanie's spine. 'What's the problem? Where's Mr Nazareth?'

'Mr Nazareth's out of town, madame,' Sanders said quickly, his voice low and almost unrecognisable. 'It's Miss Diana, she's . . . she's . . . in trouble.'

Beanie forced herself to ask calmly: 'Can you be more specific?'

'Not on the telephone, if you please.' Sanders' normally serene voice began to rise. 'She's very sick. Can you *please* come? It's delicate – and very urgent!'

'Of course,' Beanie replied instantly. 'I'm on my way.'

She put the phone down.

'Phyllis, get my coat again would you. I have to go over to the mansion. And don't wait lunch for me. I've no idea how long I might be.'

She collected her bag, and threw a last instruction over her shoulder at the worried face. It was an instinct, nothing more.

'If anyone wants me, just say I'm not at home. I'll call you from the mansion later.'

Sanders had sounded very alarmed and he was hardly the neurotic type, Beanie reasoned with herself on the short drive from Mt Vernon, but surely it couldn't be something truly serious?

But what could make a man like Sanders frightened?

Beanie pressed her foot urgently on the gas pedal.

Sanders' face should have warned her.

All the shocked faces should have warned her. The other three members of David's small, capable staff stood by Sanders, as if frozen in the hall.

Only Meg, sniffing in her handkerchief, made a sound; little, shuddering sobs.

Beanie's heart began to race, but she kept her voice as even as she could.

'Where is she?'

'Upstairs, madame,' Sanders said, his voice hollow. 'In her suite.'

Beanie's legs were already carrying her swiftly up the stairs and down the long corridor to the annexe.

Nothing had prepared Beanie for what she found. And yet her life had.

She froze for a second, her eyes wide with horror. Then instinctively she closed the door behind her, shutting the stricken faces of the staff firmly out of sight.

Inside the room she leaned briefly against the door, steadying herself, gathering courage and strength. Then, on shaking legs, she crossed to where Diana lay, naked, on the bed.

Beanie wanted to retch but old, savagely won strengths took hold and she became steadier. There was debris everywhere, strewn across the bed and all around the room. And the stench . . . of blood and vomit and urine. Of other nameless, less tangible, ghastly things. She steeled her stomach and very carefully reached for Diana's hand.

It was cold, icily cold, but the pulse was there: shallow and fluttery, but there.

Thank God! Beanie's relief was instant, and with it her mind cleared. Warmth! The girl needed warmth. That was *first*. She turned for the likeliest closet, and again she froze.

'Oh God!' she swore angrily. *Evidence*. She must not disturb evidence. She searched her pockets and found a silk scarf and with that around her hand she made a quick, nauseating, search.

Amongst the sordid mess she found a blanket that wasn't soiled, and crossed swiftly to cover the bruised and blood-ied body.

Her hand trembled badly, but she knew what had to be done. Boston General hospital was nearest and had excellent facilities, but Beanie's instincts rejected it for the discreet Sycamore Clinic. Relieved that the bedside phone was functioning, she keyed in the number.

A cool voice answered. 'Good afternoon, Sycamore Clinic. How may I help you?'

Beanie spoke very clearly in response. 'This is Madame

Bérénice Suchard. I'm calling from the Nazareth mansion, on Beacon Street. I have an emergency. A young woman, badly hurt . . .'

'One moment, madame,' the cool voice replied. 'I'll put you through to the doctor on duty.'

Seconds ticked by. Beanie's gaze remained on Diana's almost unrecognisable face.

'Dr Leyland here. How may I help you?' The voice was deep, with a faint Scottish lilt. Masculine, and thankfully strong.

Beanie described Diana's condition quietly and methodically.

Her mind was now distanced from emotion. Her voice was clear and, despite its accent, clipped and composed.

She ended her brief but thorough analysis, only allowing concern to enter her voice as she added cautiously, 'I hope you will understand, Dr Leyland, that I am a family friend. In the absence of any near relatives I am trying to act with discretion.' She waited a second before continuing briskly, 'The General is nearer than the Sycamore, doctor. I trust that my decision to call you, in preference, was the right one?'

Andrew Leyland was equally brisk, his voice carefully detached.

'I understand, madame. I'll come over with the team myself. We should be with you in less than fifteen minutes.'

There was a fractional pause and then the lilting voice became authoritative. 'It would help if the young woman's blood group could be established. We carry a blood bank on board – if you can turn that information up . . .?' He swiftly gave her his mobile phone number. Just in case.

Beanie gave him directions to the mansion and replaced the receiver.

Diana was becoming clammy as her blood temperature began to rise again. Beanie checked her pulse once more and then gently mopped at the sweat-filmed brow. Anger, white-hot but controlled, coursed through her. Why Diana? In the name of anything good, why *this* gentle girl?

Her heart began to ache. Why *anyone*? Why her mother? Her sister? Herself . . .?

Images of the past rose unbidden and merged with the horror in the room. Hideous images, impossible to connect . . . there was no connection, and yet they came. Distorted, blurred, they broke through her guard and slipped past her into the bright, beautiful room. Barren, broken images of those unholy scenes of so long ago . . . filled with the distance-muted screams of women and girls, some only children, long dead now.

She rose blindly from the bed, tears born of long-ago pain and of remembered terror tearing past her anger, turning it into anguished sorrow.

She stood with her back to Diana, her small figure shaking as she fought to control something she'd never expected to face again. The minutes ticked slowly away, and gradually her strength returned.

She had not expected to see her past again. Not here. Not in America. Not ever, ever again.

It was several minutes more before she returned to David's anxious staff, by which time she was composed again, quietly in control – her own fears and horror carefully erased from her saddened face.

No one would ever tell that she had suddenly aged that day . . .

Sanders, helped by her presence, restored a small sense of normality, rising above the tragedy just sufficiently to take a tiny measure of pride in knowing where the household medical records were kept.

Diana's blood group was telephoned to the ambulance crew, who were well prepared by the time they drove the distinctive, but today silent, blue ambulance up to the marble steps.

Beanie had only one other immediate thing on her mind as the doctor and his two paramedics attended to Diana. To keep the staff busy.

The small group she joined in the kitchen were well aware of the awfulness of the situation. But they were thankful that she was in charge. Not even Sanders could have coped so well.

Beanie summed up the situation in broad terms.

'I will be going to the Sycamore with Miss Diana but I need to know where to reach Mr Nazareth. Sanders, I'll leave you to handle that. Later, when I know for certain how she is, I'll call him from here.'

Her tone and quiet control pulled them together, and they now looked to her to tell them what to do.

'In the meantime, Meg, will you make up a bed for me in the main wing . . . and Mrs Carly, if you could arrange a meal for me, when I get back?'

The cook-housekeeper and the maid nodded silently, glad to have other things to think about.

'Sanders, if you could telephone my maid? Tell her simply that I will be staying overnight here. Nothing more than that.'

Sanders inclined his head. He understood fully. Mr David would expect madame to take charge and his staff to obey her implicitly. Not that that was hard to do, under the circumstances. Sanders thanked heaven Beanie had not been off on one of her fabric-buying trips.

'John, I know you don't live in,' Beanie continued, covering the last member of the staff, 'but I'm sure that Mr Nazareth would appreciate you staying here until he gets back. Can that be arranged?'

The gardener-handyman understood as well. 'Sure thing, ma'am. Only too glad,' he said. 'Besides, that bastard might come back.' He coloured as he spoke aloud the thought on everyone's mind.

Beanie nodded briskly. 'Thank you.'

Sanders glanced at John, and a silent promise passed between them. It was unbelievable that none of them had heard anything. Christ, it was a holy shame! But, if he did come back . . .

John's features were a mask, but beneath the outer calm he

had a prayer in his heart. He prayed that he would come back.
Because if he did, he'd be waiting for him and he and Sanders
would know what to do with that bastard. John hadn't seen the
young mistress, but he'd heard description enough. None of
them had dared mention the name they were certainly thinking
of. But none of them had any doubts.

Now, if only the sonofabitch would come back before the
boss. That would do nicely, thank you, God.

There were sounds of the medical team coming down the
stairs, and Beanie moved towards the hall door to join them.
But before she went she had one last, uncomfortable, point
to make.

'I'm sure you don't need telling this, but I think it better if you do not go back upstairs. And did anyone touch
anything?'

There was a collective shaking of heads.

'Good!' Beanie said, grimly.

Dusk had fallen and still Beanie waited. She had paced the
floor of the visitors' lounge until she was exhausted. Now she
perched on the edge of an upholstered chair, sipping at coffee
brought by a solicitous nurse. Diana had been in surgery for
three hours.

Beanie concentrated her mind on her surroundings in an
effort not to think about what was happening behind the
theatre doors.

The clinic had hardly changed since she was here last. The
cool pink, aqua, green and cream decor had been refurbished
and the furniture updated to the new rage for upholstered,
chunky Portuguese cane. But apart from that Beanie couldn't
detect any real change in the place at all. It was still designer-
chic elegant and, with its exquisite wall-to-wall silk Chinese
carpets, a place where only the extremely well-heeled would
be found waiting.

She stared into her cup, reflecting and remembering. The
last time she had been here was when Matthew had been born.

Although the clinic boasted several similar private reception suites for their distinguished clients, she had waited then in this very one. But then it was for news of her best friend's safe delivery of her longed-for child.

Beanie grimaced with distaste. Thoughts of Ella could still fill her with disgust.

Try as she might, she could not halt rogue memories from over twenty-five years ago filling her mind.

Had she been wrong? Wrong to have kept Ella's guilty secret from David for so long?

It had seemed the kindest thing, at the time, but now . . .what now – what in hell *now*?

Reason again reasserted itself. Nothing was proven about Mat. Nothing at all. She was over-reacting. Wasn't David in for shock enough as it was, without knowing the secret she kept? The thought chilled her.

In her heart she felt the birth of a new hate. For Ella. Ella, pretty, vacuous, neurotic, with her old-Bostonian ways, her so-correct manners. What a hypocrite she had been!

The thought turned inwards. What about herself . . . hadn't she helped perpetrate the evil that Ella had inflicted upon them all – if she had spoken out at the time, might all this have been prevented?

Her misery deepened. Damn Ella, with her monstrous demands. Even from the grave she'd had the power to keep her friend loyal.

Beanie shook her head tiredly. She had given her word and she had kept it. Not for Ella – she hadn't deserved a lifetime's trust. But David had, and for him she had kept quiet. For David she had no choice but to go on keeping the secret.

But right now she couldn't avoid the heart-sinking realisation that she had done him a greater injustice than favour.

She put down the cup shakily. Time would show her what to do . . . if anything *could* be done.

Her features were grave, and her eyes mirrored the ache in her heart.

Andrew Leyland watched her as he momentarily paused at the
door, aware despite his own tiredness that this woman had to
be desperately shocked despite her courageous front earlier.

'Madame Suchard . . .'

The weary, solicitous voice pulled Beanie back to the present. She glanced up and lifted a small hand fearfully to her
mouth.

Andrew Leyland crossed to a nearby chair and dropped into
it. His spirit felt bruised and angry, but to the family of the
victim he could only show professional calm.

Beanie's eyes searched his face, begging for reassurance.

'It isn't good,' the doctor said quietly. 'But it could, I imagine,
have been very much worse.'

Beanie waited, still too afraid to speak.

'Does she have any relatives nearby?'

Beanie shook her head, but found her voice. 'Her mother
lives in Paris.'

'And her husband?' he pursued.

Again Beanie shook her head. 'No. He isn't around.'

Andrew Leyland raised his brows.

Beanie pulled herself together. 'A family upset . . . he hasn't
been at home for several months,' she explained lamely.

There was something 'not said' in her voice, and the
doctor sensed her reluctance, but he moved on. 'So there's
no one?'

'David Nazareth,' Beanie said quietly. 'Her father-in-law.
But he's away on business. In Philadelphia.'

'I see,' he said carefully. 'And when is he expected back?'

Beanie blinked rapidly. 'I should imagine that he'll be here
the moment he can get a flight.'

'Ah, you've been in touch with him?'

Beanie paled still more. 'No, I haven't. I thought it wisest
to wait until you had . . .'

He let that pass. 'You'll give me his contact number? I should
speak to someone fairly soon.'

Beanie's gaze was level. 'I'd like the chance to speak to him myself first.'

Andrew Leyland studied her thoughtfully. She'd come to him – and asked for discretion. He judged he could safely tell her. Some of it.

'It's early days of course, but Mrs Nazareth's a healthy young woman. She should heal . . . in time. At least the superficial wounds will heal. That was some beating she took.'

Beanie kept her expression neutral.

Andrew Leyland went on more briskly. 'The flesh wounds are just that; they always look worse when they're fresh. But at least there shouldn't be any lasting damage to her face. Nothing that time won't erase anyway.

'The fractures will naturally take longer,' he continued. 'She has a broken pelvis, three cracked ribs, two broken fingers and her left wrist is broken . . .' He listed the other injuries, concealing his own anger and disgust. 'There are small fractures in both legs and arms – her jaw is chipped, likewise her cheekbone; thankfully her skull is undamaged, but I suspect some tissue damage beneath the scalp . . .' He paused to rub his temples tiredly. 'However, she won't be walking, I shouldn't think, for some time.'

Beanie's eyes flooded and her head drooped with despair. It was even worse than she'd thought. Poor, poor Diana.

'Quite a catalogue for one night's work!' Andrew Leyland's eyes glowed hotly, but his voice remained cool and professional.

Beanie glanced up, instinct warning her that there was more.

'As for the rest?' Now his gaze bored into her, through her, to somewhere beyond her soul. 'I've had to stitch. She was torn quite badly internally but I hope there won't be any lasting damage.'

His face was grim. This job at any time would have taxed his emotions; coming on top of a twelve-hour stint, it had shattered him.

'The uncertainties . . . the matters beyond my skills are in the greyer areas; her mind, and her emotions. Gang-rape sure as hell won't be the easiest thing to forget.'

Beanie stared at the tired face. Had he said . . .? She felt the shock as if from a long-distance punch. It hit her slowly and with an unreal quality, as if she were dreaming. Or drunk.

'No!' She heard her own protesting voice, small and far away.

'I'm sorry . . .' he rose slowly. 'It's best said now. Confidentially, of course.'

The worst had been said. Now *he* needed some answers; to the questions he hadn't asked.

'I should talk to a relative, but as her mother is so far away, it had better be Mr Nazareth. You say he'll get back straight away?'

Beanie's voice was shaking. 'I'll go home and call him now — '

'I think I'd better talk to him myself . . .the police should be informed pretty quickly — '

'No!' Beanie interrupted sharply, her brain racing into action. 'No, Dr Leyland. This will be a terrible shock for David. He's devoted to Diana. At least let him learn from a friend. Please?'

The doctor pursed his lips, doubt and exhaustion mingling.

Beanie sensed his doubt and hastened to reassure him. 'I will call him now, doctor. I know he'll come back at once.' Her mind was a whirling mess, but some things were instinctive as far as David was concerned. Like publicity. His hatred of it.

She rose unsteadily, but now her voice was purposeful once more. 'I would also appreciate it, Dr Leyland, if you would delay your report to the police. At least until Mr Nazareth has the chance to get back, or to talk to you himself. I know he will be more than grateful. We *all* will.'

Andrew Leyland hesitated. 'I shouldn't have held back this long . . .' He was about to deny the request, but something in Beanie's eyes overruled his reservations. He shook his head gravely. 'Under the circumstances . . . Well, just get Mr Nazareth in touch with me. Before the end of the day.'

He moved to the door ahead of Beanie, opened it and held it for her.

They crossed the plush foyer in silence. At the main doors Andrew Leyland paused to glance at his wristwatch. It was five forty-five.

'I'm going off duty for a few hours now, but I'll be back around ten. My colleague will let me know if Mr Nazareth gets in touch before then.' His hand touched Beanie's arm briefly. 'I'll give him as long as I can . . .' Again he shook his head. 'God knows, I shouldn't wait at all, but midnight. Absolute maximum . . .'

Beanie was grateful. 'Thank you, doctor.' She tried but couldn't quite manage a smile. The pain inside her was too great.

Andrew Leyland nodded unsmilingly.

CHAPTER TWELVE

At the mansion Beanie had to force down the supper made for her, conscious of her responsibility to maintain a show of reassurance, and to tell the household nothing other than that Diana was over the worst, and was in good hands.

Her first call had told her that David was out and not due back until seven-thirty. Her wrist-watch now showed it to be twenty-five minutes past.

Her hands shook as she poured herself a rare drink of spirits. The brandy would help to warm her, but for the moment, as she looked out from David's study, over his gardens, she shook with cold.

She hadn't been able to prevent further memories flooding back. Her carefully built wall had crumbled today, leaving her exposed and raw for the first time in over forty years. The nuns had pleaded with her to repress nothing, to 'Remember, cry, forgive . . . and then let it all go.' And she'd fooled herself that she had. All except for the colour grey, worn in memoriam.

Now it seemed to her that everything in David's garden was grey – as if that colour had taken on life and robbed the autumn of its vibrant golds and scarlets; robbed the earth of its gentle mellow browns. Even the evergreens were ghostly in the floodlights she had insisted on having turned on. The whole scene was grey.

She turned from the window crossed to the telephone, brandy balloon in one hand and a soaking handkerchief in the other. The tears had fallen, but without relief. Tears for her mother who had not wept, even at the end. For her father, who had. For her younger sister, who had died screaming. For her own evilly conceived, but so loved baby, who had not had the chance to cry.

And, not least, she had cried for Diana. Diana, perhaps her

rival. Diana, whom she loved as dearly as she would have loved the little daughter who hadn't been allowed to live. Diana, her friend. And yes, the love of David's life.

Silently, as she punched out the number, she prayed – not to God, but to justice, if indeed that existed anywhere – that Diana would recover fully; in body *and* in mind.

She closed her eyes wearily as the hotel receptionist dialled David's room.

As soon as she heard David's voice her heart was filled with sadness for him.

She'd hoped he would be alone, but the sounds of masculine conversation proved otherwise.

'Beanie? This is a surprise. What is it?'

Beanie took a deep breath. 'Darling, please forgive me, but we must talk. Privately. It concerns Diana. It's serious.'

She heard his intake of breath.

'Hold on, would you . . .'

In the background she heard faint sounds, of doors closing, of a puzzled. 'See you later.'

'Now, what's going on?' David demanded abruptly.

'I can't go into detail on the phone, darling. Diana is very ill. You must get back tonight.'

'Ill, Diana? What's wrong?'

'It's delicate, David. Very, very delicate. Please don't question me. I can't give you details, but it's imperative that you get back to Boston immediately. You're needed, David.'

David digested the fact that Beanie had just used his Christian name twice, something not heard in many, many years.

'Where is she?'

'In the Sycamore Clinic.' Beanie gathered courage. 'She's had surgery and is in intensive care. But there's more, darling. The police are going to be involved. You have to come home. *Now.*'

David felt the knot then, the one which had begun to tie itself around his intestines at the first sound of Beanie's voice. It tightened and jerked.

'You won't tell me anything at all?'

'I *can't*.' Beanie stressed. 'Not until you get here. It's not something I can discuss down a telephone line! This is not something you'd want made public. Now, will you get back here tonight?'

'I'm changing as I talk,' David snapped, and Beanie heard a drawer slam. 'Beanie? You did say she'll be all right. Right?'

'The doctor said so.'

'Where are you now?'

'At the mansion. I'm staying overnight.'

'OK,' he managed. 'I'll get on to the airport here. If I need to, I'll hire a private jet.'

There were no goodbyes, and the line went silent.

There were swirling red mists before David's eyes and a sick feeling in the pit of his stomach. Whatever was wrong was very wrong.

Beanie wouldn't tell him on the phone and that made him very frightened indeed.

Inexplicably, as he packed he thought of Mat. And as fast as the thought entered his mind it took hold. Matthew. It had something to do with Matthew!

The premonition stuck. And, as it did, he remembered. He hadn't called Beanie to ask her to stay with Diana. Cold sweat broke out and ran down his back, soaking his fresh shirt.

He had forgotten.

And whatever had happened to Diana had happened because he'd forgotten.

Although his fear was founded on the little Beanie had said, it was as solid as rock.

Beanie did what David had advised, left her car at the mansion and took a cab across the river to Logan airport. It made sense. David's Jaguar was at Logan and they would drive straight to the clinic.

She waited apprehensively, her eyes scanning the flight board and the incoming passengers. Had he made the flight?

There was little relief at seeing him striding down the arrivals hall towards her. She was too numb. Too afraid for him.

His hug was perfunctory, before he hurried them to the parking bay.

The Jaguar purred softly at his touch and within moments they were nosing out into the steady stream of traffic.

'Right,' he said in a strained voice, 'let's have it.'

There was only one way to tell it and that was the way it had happened. Beanie closed her eyes and began from the time of Sanders' call.

She left out little, and embellished nothing. The deceit, if it could be called that, was that she didn't mention either the gang-rape or the state of the bedroom. Beanie reasoned that David had enough horrors to contend with for the moment and there'd be time enough for facing those additional, loathsome, matters later.

She finished her summary and there was no comfort she could offer him, nothing she could say that would ease his terrible pain.

His knuckles were rigid against the dark leather cover of the steering wheel and his jaws were clamped violently tight. He was beyond speaking, his voice smothered by a rage so great that it consumed him.

He drove automatically and fast, the car slicing through the traffic without him noticing. Soon they would be there where his *life* was lying, broken, in a hospital bed. Diana, unconscious, beaten and abused. Hurting so badly.

And he hadn't been there to protect her.

The car-park at the Sycamore was deserted but David drove up to the main entrance. He would have done so had it been broad daylight and half of Boston there to see him. Gone were the pretences.

He switched off the ignition, and half-turned to Beanie.

'It's my fault,' he said in a voice harrowed with grief. 'My fault, Beanie! I knew that she was scared, and I was damned well scared too. So when I knew I was going to be away I promised myself I'd ask you to stay at the house with her. I knew she shouldn't be alone — '

Beanie began to protest but David silenced her swiftly.

'I forgot, Beanie. For Christ's sake . . . I forgot!'

The tears he now fought against were too much for Beanie. She put her head in her hands and wept softly as he walked away.

Now they were both guilty . . .

Andrew Leyland was in his office working on his reports; waiting for David.

'I'm sorry you've had to come back to such tragic circumstances, Mr Nazareth.' Andrew extended his hand.

David took the proffered hand and nodded stiffly.

'How is she?'

'She's as comfortable as we can make her,' Andrew replied gently. 'Please sit down.'

'Can I see . . .?'

'In a little while,' the doctor assured him calmly. 'She's sedated, Mr Nazareth. She'll be no wiser about your visit tonight – so let's talk first, then I can take you through . . .'

David sat, wary and nervous, while Andrew moved to a nearby cabinet where he foraged about for a moment, coming up with two whisky glasses and a bottle of Famous Grouse.

'Medicinal,' he commented as he poured two measures.

Andrew sat down. How much did Nazareth know? 'You've spoken to your friend, I gather?'

David nodded.

'There is something I didn't feel it politic to tell your friend, Mr Nazareth. Something the police might be tetchy about not having sooner. But I wanted — '

David interrupted coldly. 'I'm not interested in what the police might feel! My daughter-in-law comes first — '

'Quite,' Andrew Leyland interrupted smoothly. 'And so she

does, and she will. But the facts are that she has been very badly beaten and abused. It *is* a police matter, Mr Nazareth, and they *won't* understand why we've left the evidence lying around your home all day.'

David's eyes widened.

Andrew Leyland grunted. 'You haven't been home, then?' The question was rhetorical.

David put his untouched glass down. 'I think you'd better tell me everything.'

Andrew Leyland did just that. His summary was thorough. He listed Diana's injuries with a professional calm that did him credit, particularly as he felt very far from detached. He had given his whole life to healing, but today he'd felt murderous, ashamed of his sex. His normally sensitive nature had been overwhelmed with the harrowing realisation that he could, given the chance, have willingly executed the fullest possible revenge on those responsible for this diabolical outrage who would never suffer anything similar . . .

Punishment would never fit the crime.

David listened with the same intensity as to Beanie's description in the car – but the additional information confused his comprehension.

'You . . . you're sure? About it being a . . . a multiple attack?'

'As certain as I can be.' For a few seconds he studied his glass, giving the other man a chance to recover. 'There's also the matter of narcotics . . .'

'Narcotics?' David sat bolt upright. 'Diana would *never* — '

'Not your daughter-in-law, Mr Nazareth. Her attackers. There were traces of heroin in the, um, the evidence on her body. There's none in her blood, we've checked. Her room will undoubtedly yield further samples.'

'Jeezus H. Christ!' David finally swore.

Andrew Leyland pushed back his chair. 'It's been a long day, Mr Nazareth. Perhaps you'd like to see your daughter-in-law now – then we'd better decide who fronts up to the cops . . .'

*   *   *

Pat O'Rourke took the late call amiably.

'Well now, D.N., and what keeps a solid citizen like yourself from his bed at this hour?'

David wasted few words. 'Pat, I've got an almighty problem on my hands – one that I wouldn't want handled by anyone but you. In the strictest confidence – and in a hurry.'

'Ah!' Pat's voice was gruff. 'You want I should take a night ride over to that nice little pad of yours. Right?'

'I'd be more than grateful, Pat.'

'Nothin' to it, Dave, 'cept the time it takes for an old un' to get his darned boots on,' Pat bantered easily. 'You reckon I should need anythin' other than a steady hand for that real nice Jack Daniels I know you'll press on a tired ol' cop?'

'A notebook and a camera I should think,' David said quietly.

'I'm on my way ol' buddy.'

Thirty minutes later they were together in Diana's bedroom. Pat O'Rourke made a careful appraisal of the scene, while David stared woodenly into space.

He was filled with sickness and rage and a sense of helplessness that rendered him silent. Pat's face was unreadable as he picked his way methodically through the litter and the chaos, all the while making notes on a dog-eared scribble-pad.

Finally Pat was through. He closed his note-book and cleared his throat. Only his eyes burned in the craggy, impassive features. 'Let's just take a little look downstairs, shall we?'

David led the way out in relief.

'I'll lock this door now, Dave, and I'll hang on to this key for you for the moment.'

He pocketed the key in silence, studying the door briefly before following David back down the stairs.

'Why don't you fix those drinks, eh? I'll just have a mosey around outside.' He pulled a battered torch from an oversized pocket and let himself out into the night.

When he returned his eyes lit on the bourbon with a warm gleam. He nursed the generous measure in silence, then swallowed a deep draught of the fine liquor. He sighed. It was at times like these that he wished he'd become an airline pilot.

'Inside job,' he stated finally.

'What!' David exclaimed, stunned.

'No unlawful entrance, Dave. No sign of force anywhere. Had to be someone Diana knew. Often the case . . .'

'You're sure?' David's face was ashen.

'Sure. Either folks she let in . . . or folks who let themselves in. Key job, Dave. Foul night last night, as I recall. High winds, real high – not the sort of night you'd leave your door open . . .'

David was staring at Pat, seeing nothing.

'Guess I need to be lookin' for that young husband again.' Pat's careful gaze was sympathetic. 'Sorry, old friend, have to start with the obvious.'

David shook himself, and poured fresh drinks, not even attempting to control his shaking hands. 'The doctor thinks there was more than one man, Pat.' Despite himself, he couldn't conceal the note of hope.

'Yeah. We'd agree on that all right.'

'He also mentioned that the . . . the attackers were probably on narcotics,' David said quietly.

'Did he now?' The chief said interestedly.

'God Almighty, Pat! What do I do now?' David's big body seemed smaller as he slumped miserably in a chair, looking at that moment like an old man.

Pat gazed at his friend, genuine care and concern on his craggy features.

'You do nothing, Dave. Except what I ask you to do. I'll tread eggs on this one, keep it in my personal pigeonhole until we have something to go on.' He grimaced tiredly. 'I'll have to have some of my boys over here, first thing, but they'll keep it nice and quiet when I tell em' to. No one's going get to hear about any of this until we're good and ready.' He put his glass down a little reluctantly. 'I'll have to put out a pick-up on Mat, but I'll play it nice and cool, don't you worry.'

'I'm more concerned about Diana,' David said harshly.

Pat's eyebrows rose slightly, but he continued in the same toneless voice. 'You might run a check on your household silver and any other items of value, like your daughter-in-law's jewellery and so on. Let me have a list tomorrow. Oh, and check if you're missing any cash.'

David looked at him blankly.

Pat shrugged but his gravelly voice was kind. 'It's on the cards, Dave. Guys on dope need money, plenty of it.'

At the front door, he gave David's shoulder a comforting squeeze. 'I'll go by the Sycamore before I go home, take that doctor's report into safe keeping, eh?'

With practised skill, the police chief conducted an all-states alert without attracting a whisper of publicity, but despite intensive police efforts Mat had again become invisible.

Diana's recovery, though, was remarkable in every way and after six weeks she was allowed to continue her recuperation at home.

She had not been able to help the police in their enquiries, however. She claimed to have no memory of the events of that night.

Andrew Leyland assured the police chief that such traumas could have that effect, and offered the opinion that it was probably the best thing.

Pat O'Rourke definitely agreed. But he knew that in Diana's case, sadly, it was far from the truth. Long years of experience had taught him to recognise a cover-up, and the young Mrs Nazareth, for reasons of her own, was not prepared to remember. And there was nothing he could do about that.

Except wait.

Matthew Nazareth couldn't stay underground forever; he wasn't made of strong enough metal. Pampered wealth and a weak character were never going to cope in adversity. He'd surface soon, Pat reckoned. Had to. Those were expensive habits. And Mat's purse was here in Boston.

Yep. Pat O'Rourke could wait.

Beanie moved temporarily into the mansion to keep Diana company during her convalescence. And while she continued her own routine during the week, Diana was exercised around the clock by a team of therapists – all young, skilled, and dedicated.

It should have been a strained time but, remarkably, it wasn't. Diana refused any discussion of the 'accident', and concentrated on her own recovery. She would accept no pity, and soon that emotion was erased from those around her.

Beanie's love for the girl grew, as did her admiration. What had begun as a pleasant friendship developed into a deep bond. The older woman watched the thin cheeks fill out and saw the brightness slowly return to the luminous grey-blue eyes. Gradually, the occasional taut smile was repeated more frequently until, after four months, Diana could smile without discomfort.

Once that happened, the household returned to something like normality.

David took on two teams of full-time security guards for the mansion. He wasn't taking any further chances.

He dared not think ahead to a time when Mat would come back. When they might have to face up to what Diana had buried.

He lived each day as it came, loving her with everything he had, within the limitations of their relationship. Nothing could reveal the future but in his heart he still held his dream. And patiently he waited.

Diana worked at getting well. She, too, had plans deep in the secret recesses of her mind. Plans which she could not yet confide to the two people she loved so much. Plans for divorce, and plans for returning to England. She was not stupid enough to think that it would be easy. It would be an agonising step when it came. But her whole being warned her of the dangers of remaining at the mansion, near David. As soon as she was totally well again she would have to go. Before it was too late.

But as Christmas ended, there was a more immediate problem to resolve, one which she confided in Beanie one evening, as her friend helped her prepare for bed.

Beanie had become like an older sister to her. And, as she had confided her own awful secrets during Diana's post-operative state, they had become inextricably linked.

Now she had to ask Beanie to keep another confidence. But was it fair to expect Beanie to divide her loyalties, as she would have to if she became Diana's ally? Diana knew now that Beanie loved David with all her generous heart. How would she react to Diana's news?

Beanie lounged on Diana's peach-silk-covered chaise, a petite figure in her grey silk pyjamas. Diana thought her beautiful, vivacious and enviably ageless. And knowing how Beanie had suffered, she could only admire her all the more.

If anyone could understand, it would be Beanie. But, conversely, it could, because of her experiences, alienate her.

'Beanie, I'm pregnant,' she finally said bluntly.

The shock on Beanie's face was instant. Her hands flew in dismay to her mouth. 'No!' she whispered, her eyes wide and shocked.

'I'm afraid so,' Diana assured her quietly.

'What . . . what will you do?'

'Have an abortion.' Diana's voice was quite calm.

'Oh, darling! Is there no — '

Diana interrupted firmly. 'I have no choice, Beanie.'

Beanie crossed to her and stroked her long hair soothingly, her own thoughts agitated. 'But, darling . . . if it is Mat's, then it is also David's grandchild. Have you considered that?'

Diana stiffened. It was the crux of the matter and the thing that had caused her most anguish.

'I've thought about little else,' she said truthfully. 'But it alters nothing.'

'Darling, there are tests that can be done,' Beanie pleaded. 'Won't you at least consider having them done?'

Diana winced at the pleading tone. Somehow she'd known that Beanie might feel this way – after all she'd been raped, repeatedly, but she hadn't wanted to lose her baby. It was the one difference between them.

But Diana would not carry this child for anybody, not even for David.

'No,' she said resolutely.

Beanie stared at Diana's pale face and saw determination in the large eyes, eyes that were grey and cloudy at this moment as if such a terrible purpose had washed the sparkling blue from their depths.

'Diana, darling. You know what this could mean to David,' Beanie persisted gently. 'You must know.'

'Yes.' Diana's voice was cool. 'And that's why he must learn nothing about it. Ever.'

'But Mat's been disinherited. David has nobody, darling!'

'Beanie, I have done all that I can for David. I protected him from learning about Mat's drug addiction. And his violence. I have refused to name his son in my rape. But I cannot give birth to a child from that night, and then leave.'

'Leave . . .' Beanie gasped.

'Yes. I'm sorry.' Diana's tone was grave. 'I intend to divorce Matthew as soon as I feel strong enough to go through with it. So you see, I would have two choices if I had the child. Either to take it with me to England, or to stay here and raise it in Boston. If I took it to England, David would lose it anyway, and . . .' She shook her head. 'It would be impossible for me to stay here.'

'But why?' Beanie probed more carefully now. 'Why would it be so impossible to stay? If you were divorced from Mat — '

Diana shook her head vigorously. 'No! Beanie, it couldn't work. It would be too . . . too difficult.'

'Because of David's feelings, you mean?' Beanie's eyes were clear and guileless.

Now Diana coloured. She nodded.

'Then you couldn't, ever, return his love?' Beanie pursued, carefully, bringing into the open at last the one subject they had never discussed.

Diana choked back a little sound of distress. 'How could I? I know very little about religion, but I wouldn't want to do something that might be offensive to God. Or morally wrong.' Her voice was filled with sadness and pain but there was strength in her words. 'Anyway, I am still David's daughter-in-law. It couldn't be anything but wrong, Beanie. Very, very wrong.'

'Is not taking life also wrong?' Beanie said softly.

'Oh, Beanie, don't! That's too cruel,' Diana whispered, her eyes filling with tears. 'I have no choice, don't you see? One sin would surely lead to another and who would know which was worse? No I can't and I won't live like that!'

Beanie put her arms comfortingly around the trembling girl, hushing her. And her own sadness overflowed into her voice. 'It's all right, darling, I understand. Of course you must follow your own conscience. And you are right. It is all too much to ask of you.' She tilted Diana's troubled face towards her and with enormous effort spoke in her more usual, no-nonsense fashion. 'So, come. Cheer up. We shall settle everything, darling.' She somehow managed a smile.

It was a bitter pill for Beanie, to have to hold two secrets from David, either one of which would have given him a fighting chance with the woman he loved. But Diana had made her decision and there was no doubting her intention to carry it through.

Beanie made arrangements the following morning with Andrew Leyland, who was in immediate favour of the decision. Two days later Diana was readmitted to the Sycamore, ostensibly for an overnight check-up.

Andrew Leyland performed the abortion, removing from

Diana's womb a tiny scrap of dormant male life, resembling nothing.

When Diana returned to the mansion it was as if a terrible burden had been lifted from her shoulders. The last reminder of that awful night was gone and now she could begin to concentrate on the future, on piecing her life back together again. She couldn't think about David. Didn't dare. She had to put him as firmly in the past as Matthew, with as much distance between her and them as only an ocean could provide. But first she had to be physically strong enough.

And that took the best part of another year.

CHAPTER THIRTEEN

In a period in which artificial heart surgery progressed, the United States announced a revolutionary defence system dubbed 'Star Wars', invaded Grenada – and lost the America's Cup, after a hundred and thirty-two years, to Australia . . . Matthew Nazareth managed still to evade the police system.

The second Christmas since the attack came and went in Boston, and heavy snows were on the ground before Diana felt strong enough to face the dreaded task of telling David her intentions.

Her physical recovery was complete. Now it needed only the final step and her mental and emotional healing could properly begin.

It was a bitterly cold February evening. They had taken dinner in companionable comfort and were now settled with cognacs round a cheerful log fire.

Diana had warned Beanie that she intended to tell David this evening and now there was an air of uneasy expectation between them.

They made a charming group. David in a dark suit, his urbane good looks enhanced by his inner contentment, his eyes sweeping over Diana at regular intervals, appraising and admiring.

She looked as well as she had two and a half years before, at her wedding. The terrible attack had robbed her of her youthful innocence, but in its place was, to David, a maturity complemented by a naturally serene nature. She was, in short, more beautiful to him.

David openly admired and not quite so openly desired her. Her full, shapely mouth invited his attention as she spoke softly to Beanie. To David it spoke of promise; rich, abundant promise.

He should have realised that the changes he saw were occasioned by the bitter and violent leap from being a lonely child into an confused, violated woman – the maturity forced, the physical improvement the result of bone-wearying exercise and tireless exorcism of the attack his son had led on her. Had he only stopped to reflect, he would have known that, although physically mended, she was still emotionally and mentally wounded. As it was, he marvelled at her courageous recovery and enjoyed her renewed beauty.

Diana chatted with Beanie, uneasily aware of David's attentiveness. Tonight she would tell him . . .

Beanie was planning to return to her penthouse soon now; she would not continue living at the mansion now that Diana had no real need of her, and Diana had to speak to David while Beanie was still there to give her support. The minutes passed and at last she gave Beanie a purposeful look.

Beanie nodded encouragingly. If it had to be done, better get it over with. Diana straightened on the leather chair and turned her attention fully to her father-in-law.

'David,' she began carefully, 'there's something I've been wanting to discuss with you. Would now be convenient?'

'Sure, honey,' he said warmly, unaware. 'Whatever's on your mind, spill it out.' He smiled encouragingly, then frowned and listened for a moment. 'Let me get that damn phone first, sweetheart. The staff are all at their dinner.'

He was gone only a few minutes. They could hear the rise and fall of his voice from the study across the hall, but they couldn't catch any of the conversation.

When he returned the look on his face was enough to make Diana shiver. Instinctively she reached for Beanie's arm.

David stood as if uncertain, leaning heavily against the door. His eyes mirrored some deep emotion. His skin seemed stretched and grey, and when he spoke his words came in bursts, short and harsh.

'That . . . was Pat O'Rourke . . . there's been news . . . about . . . about Mat.' He swallowed the bile that rose to the back of his throat. 'He's on his way over . . . to tell us about it . . .'

He couldn't bring himself to look Diana in the eye. Instead, he crossed unsteadily to the bar and poured a large measure of bourbon, which he downed in one go.

Diana froze in her seat, her heart pounding, her mouth dry. She lifted questioning eyes, dark with fear, to her friend. Beanie squeezed her hand then went to David.

'What is it, darling? What's happened?' Her light touch and soft words caused David to blink. He was far away, lost in his own turbulent thoughts.

'Better wait for Pat,' he said distantly and gazed at her blankly.

'Darling!' Beanie urged him. 'Is it something which might distress Diana? Shouldn't you prepare her?' She began to be afraid herself.

David shook his head woodenly. 'Pat asked me to wait for him.' His eyes moved finally to Diana's face. She was still and pale. 'Honey . . .' His voice was tight. 'Pat says . . . he . . . has to bring the news himself . . . I guess he has his reasons.'

Diana stared back, speechless with shock. Oh God, yes! She was sure that Mr O'Rourke had his reasons. He knew she was guilty of concealing Mat's part in the attack, she'd sensed it at the time. Probably he'd found Mat and had got the truth out of him. Now he would want to know why she'd lied.

Was the law the same as in England? If so, she couldn't be forced to testify against her husband. At least she might be able to spare David that much. But now David would know everything. A cold shiver ran down her spine. Would he also want to know why she hadn't told him? And would she be able to conceal the truth, yet again?

It was all beginning again, the nightmare she had allowed herself to think was over.

Beanie saw the fine beads of perspiration break out on Diana's forehead and poured her a fresh brandy. This was the last thing Diana needed – it might be all it took to bring about the breakdown which Beanie had thought averted. She forced the glass into Diana's lifeless hand. 'Drink it!' she commanded briskly.

The door chimes startled them all, even though they were expected. Beanie pulled Diana closer to her and gripped her wrist firmly. 'It's all right, darling!' she said, hiding her own anxiety. 'He can't hurt you again. Don't be afraid. We're here with you!'

Pat O'Rourke followed David into the bright room, leaving a wet trail behind him. His great fur coat made him look like a polar bear, laden with snow, thick and fresh from the driving storm outside.

He struggled out of the garment without a word and, finding no hand to take it from him, dropped it into a wet heap by the fire and stood warming himself silently at the blaze, his eyes fixed on his feet.

David poured him a bourbon, which Pat took and downed without his usual banter.

'There's no point making a fancy speech, ladies, Dave. So I guess you'll forgive me if I speak plainly.' Pat reached into his pocket for a notepad and his craggy face was expressionless as he began consulting his notes.

'Last night state police down in Tahoe got a call out from a guy who runs a casino there. Appears he'd been having some trouble with a bunch of youngsters. Well, the officers arrived, and this trio high-tailed it into a beat-up motor.

'The officer in charge told me it wasn't a night to be playing cops and robbers.' He shook his head, remembering. 'No one in their right minds was out on those mountain roads in that weather. But those guys took off like they had the devil up their tail, taking treacherous corners and bends on two wheels. It was snowing, and the fool was pushing that motor over a hundred.

'Pretty risky business, chasin' motor cars on ice.' Pat tutted and shook his head, giving them time to absorb what he was telling them. 'Then they hit a real daddy of a bend way up in the mountains . . . went straight over the edge.'

He looked at them impassively, allowing his detachment to make it impersonal.

'The sheriff told me it took a long time and a lot of machinery to get the bodies out of the wreck . . . It was dark an' the snow kept getting the best of them. Anyway, this morning, come daybreak, they hauled the last one out. All lives lost. As expected.'

He cleared his throat, wishing he'd sipped his drink. Or had another to warm his insides and make this miserable chore easier to handle.

'Forensic reports are still coming in, but those guys weren't just drunk, they were full of heroin.'

He straightened up and replaced the notebook in his pocket.

'Sorry, David, Mrs Nazareth. But I can't alter the facts. One of 'em was Matthew.'

In the silence, Pat O'Rourke walked over to the drinks cabinet and poured himself another bourbon. Then he took the liberty of pouring three more and purposefully passed them around.

To David he said gently, 'It'll help, Dave.'

Beanie sobbed now almost silently, her heart broken for the two people she loved most in the world. But her heartbreak was for what could have been between them and her tears were of relief for them both.

Diana had no tears for Matthew, and across the room David found it impossible even to think.

Pat O'Rourke downed his drink. They'd all feel better when he was out of the way.

'Folks, right now you're probably feeling kinda strange . . . but when some time has passed you just might feel that this accident was for the best. It seems that everybody, including young Mr Mat, has been spared an almighty nasty ordeal!'

Pat looked at Diana and saw the guilt he'd always known about.

'Diana, however you look at it, justice has been done. Don't waste tears on the past . . . that's my motto.'

He turned to David and they walked together to the door. 'There will have to be a formal identification, Dave. The body will be here tomorrow. You'll stop by, sometime in the afternoon?'

David managed a dumb nod and, with an effort, tried to thank Pat.

'No thanks needed, Dave. And just one more thing: the past died last night on those mountains, with Mat. I've shredded everything, whether known or merely suspected. The slate's clean. Accidental death, period. Goodnight, Dave.'

David stared for a long time after the police chief's car had steamed through the snowdrifts in the drive, until the swirling clouds of snow forced him back into the warmth of his house.

He stood with his back against the door, facing the room where his love sat waiting. It had been Mat, Mat and his friends, who'd raped her. And Diana had kept it locked up in her mind so that he wouldn't be hurt. He now knew, with a fierce sense of wonder, that she loved him and the joy transcended any grief he might have felt for his son.

CHAPTER FOURTEEN

The funeral took place as privately as David had requested on a bitterly cold Friday morning a week later.

There were fewer than a dozen invited mourners to witness the hired pallbearers lowering the plain coffin into the snow-laden ground of the family plot beneath the stately cedars as Matthew was laid to rest among his Nazareth ancestors, after the simplest ceremony that David could persuade the minister to accept.

A journalist, huddled well-concealed in abundant wood-land nearby, recorded on video the strangely unemotional moments.

The absence of grief puzzled him. He noted the pale young widow, simply dressed in black, without wreath or prayer book; the father, also in black, hatless and remote.

Top designer, the chic Madame Suchard, and Jeff Sherman, legendary for his long service as David Nazareth's P.A., were sketched summarily into the audio-system. Chief of Police Pat O'Rourke's presence was given more space, but there was little else of the mourners to record.

They came, they buried, they left.

Later the journalist would film the floral tributes and there were surprisingly many, almost all worded in deference to David, rather than in remembrance of Matthew. There was a simple wreath from Nazareth House and one from the staff at the mansion, equally bleak and stark.

David's sheaf of white, waxen lilies, lay on the soil at the foot of a temporary wooden cross. He had agonised over a farewell message, but couldn't bring himself to pen hypocritical endearments; neither could he use a paternal signature with any ease. He had resolved the situation with the terse inscription, 'Reunited with his beloved Mother.'

The journalist had to wait until the mourners left to find the only tribute that lay on top of the coffin. It was a single white rose with a black-bordered card attached. He zoomed in to film the poignant words.

Matthew. Rest in Peace. Diana.

The funeral report the next day, heavily edited to remove speculation, would be as brief and remote as the event itself. It would pass unremarked. And the only person who would wonder why the shocking, accidental death of such a young, rich, only son, and husband, had failed to evoke any emotion or grief would be the journalist himself.

There was no wake after the ceremony. Neither David nor Diana could have borne it. The long black Cadillac carried the two of them, in silence, back to the mansion. David had insisted that no one, not even Beanie, returned to the mansion, reasoning that Diana needed privacy and time to recover from this new ordeal. There had been only essential conversation between them since Matthew's death, but he was sure that, with this day over, they would be able to talk. They needed to discuss the future.

She was pale but composed as they entered the empty house. He had given his staff twenty-four hours' leave, to visit friends or family, instinctively aware that it would be easier all round if no one had to make polite noises.

Diana stood at the foot of the stairs and turned dulled eyes to him. 'I'd like to shower and perhaps rest until lunch-time,' she said flatly.

David nodded understandingly. 'Do that, honey. We can eat when you're ready.'

He went into his study and was drawn to the window to stare out at the ghostly white gardens. Unfamiliar landscapes formed by thick drifts of snow brooded beneath a threatening, swollen sky. All was still. Silence pressed heavily on David where he stood at the french windows overlooking the terrace from where he had such a seemingly short time ago watched the wedding scene. He gazed bleakly, sensing that if he could have wept it might have helped. But he had been denied the normal grief of a father for a beloved child. Instead, he knew only a legacy of guilt.

He could not cry for a man he had never liked, a man who had abused the only woman he had ever loved. He could only hurt for any part he had played in the making of what Mat had become.

He couldn't even cry for the child that Mat had once been . . .

He continued to stare unseeingly, praying for tears. He wanted badly to weep, to cleanse his heart and soul of guilt and bitterness.

But tears for Matthew would not come.

His breath clouded the pane, obscuring further the frost-distorted view, yet for a few fleeting moments he saw the garden as it once had been, on a long-ago summer's day.

There by the fountain, in the cool of its lee, he could see Ella, stiff and proper in her hard garden chair. Two little boys played at her feet: Benjamin, dark and robust, holding out a toy to the frail, fair and truculent Matthew, who smacked it out of his hand and screamed so that Ella delivered a resounding slap on the side of the darker head.

David shook himself, but the years fell away before his gaze and he saw his bride, Ella, on his own wedding day.

He'd married Ella just after his twenty-fifth birthday. It was what his father had wanted for him, to be properly settled and with a family, and Ella had all the right qualities. She was slim, fair, pretty and from an old but impoverished Bostonian family. A proper 'Brahmin' bride.

Socially, the marriage was deemed an excellent match and for the first few years David had been as happy as he knew how to be. It had not been an exciting relationship, but with most of his adult life taken up between Harvard and the Firm, David had no yardstick by which to judge his marriage.

But his wife had. She desperately wanted a baby and after the second year could talk of nothing else.

When David's father died quite suddenly in that year, only six months after his mother, she became frantic, driving David to distraction on the subject of a child.

Finally, exasperated, he'd agreed to go with her for fertility tests and later, when Ella told him that she was probably barren, his wife's very real distress drove him to seek a solution. He found it through Pat O'Rourke, who had a friend in the New York police force who in turn had a friend in a New York agency specialising in providing orphaned children for selected homes.

At first Ella had refused to consider an unknown child, but gradually she relented and then grew excited as they waited for the arrival of their baby.

David was just under thirty when the call came to say that an European boy of eight weeks was theirs and they travelled to New York to collect the baby with total joy in their hearts. He'd already been named Benjamin by his mother before her death, a name David approved, knowing it from the Bible to mean First Born or Favoured One.

Ben was everything David could have wished for in a son. Dark like himself, the baby passed comfortably as his own, and he grew to be a bonny, happy child.

The Nazareths were told little of the child's identity; only the few bare facts that the agency had learned from the convent in Switzerland where he'd been taken by an elderly spinster aunt when his mother had died soon after his birth. The nuns assumed the child to be illegitimate as there had been no mention of his father. The aunt, however, had been an aristocrat, so the baby had good blood.

It had amused David, and sometimes Ella, to speculate on the blue blood that ran in Benjamin's veins. But it was not a speculation that lasted very long. Ben became completely theirs, so much so that by the time he was two years old David, at least, had forgotten that the boy was adopted. To him, Ben *was* his son, his pride and joy. And he had no qualms at all in naming him his heir.

But then Ella started pleading again about having a child and would not be reminded that they had a son, or that she could not conceive. Daily she begged David to make love to her, regardless of how he was feeling. Her aim was pregnancy, nothing else, and she got rid of David as abruptly as she could when he'd done his 'duty'.

However, when she deliriously announced her pregnancy some months later, David had been genuinely delighted. Now his beloved Ben would have a playmate.

Matthew's arrival had changed their lives completely.

Overnight Ella became a doting, possessive mother with eyes only for Matthew. She was not at that stage cruel to Ben, merely indifferent. It was only when Mat began to toddle around that David noticed how reticent Ben had become, and then he'd witnessed Ella slapping the boy that summer's day in the garden.

The truth had dawned: his wife's love could not encompass both boys, and so Ben was pushed further and further out of her neurotic little world. It had been a landslide situation. No sooner had he mentioned his distress over Ben than matters became much worse. Before long he'd had to hire a nanny for the discarded child, someone to be with him whilst he went to the Firm.

After a while it sickened him to know that the only care Ben had, apart from his, came from a hired help. David himself tried to treat both boys equally, but it was impossible. Ella practically lived in the nursery wing with Mat, and Ben was banished to distant rooms with his nanny.

It had torn David apart when, on Ben's fifth birthday, the little boy told him that 'Mommy only loves Matthew.'

David watched grimly now as the scene was re-enacted his mind's eye. He had rushed home early to join the birthday tea, but instead of the boisterous party he'd expected, he had found Ben alone, sitting on the stairs.

'Hi, champ!' he'd greeted the boy, moving to the staircase, his instincts hammering a cold suspicion home to his heart. 'Have I missed the party?'

Ben lifted his gaze from the carpet. Tear stains marked his pale little face and red-rimmed eyes met David's. 'Wasn't any party,' the child had said, his voice hollow.

'No party?' David tousled the boy's curls, but a frown deepened between his brows.

'Nope,' Ben replied, ducking his head away from David's caress.

David stared down at the child, aware of the little boy's manful battle to hold back his tears.

'Where's your momma?' David controlled his anger tightly.

Ben's chin came up and, despite his efforts a tear slid silently down his cheek. 'Mommy doesn't love me,' he said in a whisper, his eyes now fixed on David.

'Nonsense!' David spoke briskly but his heart was in his mouth. 'Where did you get that crazy notion?'

'Mommy said so,' the boy said, and David could hear the dull certainty in the small, trembling voice.

'The hell she did!' David said softly, his anger burning furiously. Controlling himself for Ben's sake, he lifted the now unresisting child into his arms and hugged him reassuringly.

'I'm sure it's a stupid mistake, son,' he said gently. 'Daddy will sort it out, don't you worry.'

'Mommy only loves Matthew. She told me,' Ben repeated stubbornly, his voice muffled against David's chest.

'Did you get your presents?' David changed the subject, carrying the child towards the kitchen where, hopefully, there would be cookies and ice cream to help ease the wounds.

Ben wriggled suddenly, angrily, so that David had to put him down, surprised.

'Didn't want any,' the boy muttered tremulously, and before David could stop him he had turned and was running away to the garden.

It had caused the first blazing row with Ella and given him

his first true insight into her frail state of mind. She'd actually screamed at him that Ben had to go, that no adopted bastard was going to deprive *her* child of his rightful inheritance.

It had been all downhill after that.

Mat had grown more precocious and Ben more withdrawn. Ella excluded Ben from everything she could, and the rows grew more frequent. She demanded better clothes for *her* child, more toys, a better and a 'different' education for *her* son. That had been one of the worst times. She'd been like someone possessed, raving about an 'adopted bastard' going to the same school as *her* son. How she wouldn't 'stand for it'.

David, shaken badly, had stood his ground. But the problem had only just begun.

Mat had always been frail, a petulant child suffering from one childish ailment after another, while Ben had been hardy and strong. But even Ben's solid strength was not enough to cope with Ella's spite and, in time, Matthew's goading.

Soon Ben grew solemn, taking refuge in his room and his books, unless his father was around, and before long that wasn't often. Every time David set foot in the house, the rows started . . . and always on the same subject. Mat had to be the sole heir.

It was more than David could take. He'd been scrupulously fair, altering his will to give both boys an equal share in everything.

He hadn't yet become inflexible.

But, unconsciously, he had started taking the easy way out. To keep the peace he found more and more work to do at his office.

The boys became teenagers, and they couldn't have been more different. Mat grew from a petted, spoilt child into a sullen, moody youth. His work at school was indifferent and he lazed away his leisure hours. Goading his older, studious brother became his greatest pleasure, driving Ben to the limits of his endurance. And Ella picked on the quiet teenager at every chance she got.

Matthew could do no wrong, not even when he took his foul tempers out on her. Her *darling* boy was highly strung, while, to her, the bastard Benjamin was a crafty and alien interloper whose sole intention, Ella swore, was to deprive Matthew of his God-given rights.

The years raced by and only David, more and more rarely at the mansion, was blind and deaf to the increasing fury of the cauldron of emotions bubbling away at the heart of his home.

It boiled over on the day before Ben's eighteenth birthday. In one of her unprovoked rages, Ella attacked him with a new viciousness, demanding to know when he was going to stop scrounging off them and go back to the 'peasant father' who'd obviously sired him. As her taunts grew uglier, Mat joined in, and it took every ounce of Ben's considerable strength to keep his hands off the younger, weaker teenager.

David remembered with cold clarity calling Ben to his study, late in the evening, to present him with his birthday cheque, remembered how proud he'd been of the tall, handsome lad who'd stood before him.

David faced the teenager across his desk and a satisfied smile lit his features.

'It's your best report yet, son. Top of your year.' He glanced down again with pleasure at the latest glowing report of his son's achievements. 'You'll come into the Firm with better qualifications than I had, and mine were damned good!'

Ben's face was unreadable. His eyes, dark as any ocean, watched David intently but gave away nothing of his feelings. He stood even then as tall as David, impassive, remote, almost indifferent.

That was what David sensed as he stared again at his unsmiling son. Ben was always courteous, politeness seemingly inherent in his nature. But today David recognised the strength of that courteous indifference. And with recognition came a sudden fear.

'You'll make a fine lawyer one day,' he added quickly, to

fill the increasingly uneasy silences that followed everything he said. 'Yep. You'll follow me, your grandfather, your great-grandfather, et al, to Harvard. Hasn't been a Nazareth yet that didn't graduate from the home of the Ivy League.'

David's words fell heavily into the polite silence. Flustered and uncomfortable, he flourished his pen over his cheque-book and allowed his voice to become deliberately hearty.

'This cheque is for your birthday, and is also a reward for all your hard work.' He filled in tomorrow's date, and signed it with a degree of relief that the interview was almost over.

'Here, buy yourself a car, son. You've earned it.'

Had he known then what Ben's reaction would be, he would never have allowed the situation to develop. With the hindsight of today – that mountain peak from which all the past is so clearly seen – he was convinced that he could have changed things, could have kept Ben from leaving.

But on that day nothing had forewarned him that Ben was about to shatter his world.

David's outstretched hand held the cheque, waved it slightly as his irritation mounted.

Ben remained motionless, ignoring the hand, not even glancing at the cheque, and, as he finally began to speak, a curious emerald flame burned deep in his eyes.

'No, thank you. I won't be driving until I can buy my own wheels.'

'Don't be an ass!' David chided, failing at first to hear the undercurrent in Ben's softly spoken rejection. 'It'll be years before your allowance will match the price of a car.'

'If by allowance you mean "salary",' Ben said quietly, 'you're probably right.'

'Salary?' David queried, puzzled.

'I'll buy whatever I need with my own money,' Ben said.

'What money? You don't have any money,' he said reasonably, 'except what I give you, your allowance.'

'That's right,' Ben agreed. 'Or was right, until now . . .' His voice tailed off and he hesitated for one last time, outwardly calm, not wanting to betray the terrible ache in his heart.

David, fighting a tremor of anxiety, forced his voice past a sudden lump in his throat. 'OK. You have something on your mind. You'd better tell me about it.'

He dropped the cheque on to his desk and leaned back in the leather chair, trying not to recognise his son's purposeful tone and demeanour as threatening.

Ben's pale-olive skin seemed too tightly stretched over his finely planed bones. There were parallel shadows down his cheeks, creating a gauntness both alien and menacing. With an increasing awareness of Ben as a presence, an almost physical force not encountered before, David made a vain attempt to avert the collision his instinct told him was coming.

'If you're not well, son, sit down.' His voice was guarded now.

'My health is fine,' Ben replied shortly. 'And I won't sit, thanks. Sitting down would be too cosy for what I have to say.'

David's eyebrows shot up. He wasn't used to this attitude from anyone, and he didn't like it one bit. 'So shoot,' he said, calm for the moment, still reining in his emotions.

'I'm leaving,' Ben said.

A snake-like sensation slithered down David's spine. 'Leaving?'

'Yes, sir. Leaving. On my eighteenth birthday. That's tomorrow.'

'I'm damned well aware that it's tomorrow!' David snapped. 'Didn't I just offer you a cheque for tomorrow! An open cheque,' he added meaningfully.

'Ah, that . . .' Ben moved closer to the desk and David, confused as he was, still noted proudly the graceful movements of Ben's long, muscular limbs. Ben had never gone through a gangly or awkward stage. He hadn't ever had a hint of shyness, or that confidence-destroying teenage scourge, pimples. It seemed to David that the bonny child had made all the transitions invisibly, and had arrived at a fine, promising young manhood effortlessly.

Ben made no attempt to touch the cheque, but he looked at it briefly, then raised his eyes to meet David's.

'I have a college friend who's planning a trip to California. I'm going with him. Tomorrow.'

David breathed again. 'Why didn't you say so, son! OK, so we'll get your car when you come back! How long do you plan to be on this trip? You'll need an extra summer allowance. I can —'

'I'm not coming back,' Ben interrupted, his voice even and deep for such a young man. 'I don't want to prolong this, there's no point. So I'll tell you how it is. I'm leaving. Period.'

'Not coming back?' David echoed stupidly, still not really registering the finality in Ben's voice.

'That's right, sir. I'm not coming back. I'm leaving, leaving this house, leaving everything to do with this house . . .' Ben faltered for a second in his flat monotone, emotion close to the surface. But he knew he had to stay cool, cool and totally in command. If he didn't, David would break his determination. If he once showed how much he was hurting, he would be lost.

'I'm leaving Boston. For good.'

There, it was said. At last he had freed himself.

To David it was as though a volcano erupted inside his head and blazing lava flowed through him. A wild screeching voice repeated over and over, Ben . . . Ben . . . *Ben*!

Ben continued, with the utmost courtesy, to destroy him. David listened, appalled, to Ben's litany.

Ben wanted out. Out of the household, out of Nazareth House, out of Boston, out of David's life. *Out.*

Now, with an almost maniacal determination, David reasoned, cajoled, fought with everything he had to keep the only son he loved.

Before he knew what he was admitting he promised to make

a stand against Ella and Mat, begged Ben to forgive him for the lifetime of suffering he'd endured.

Ben stared at him in silence. And frustration caused David to lash out.

'Don't you think you at least owe *me* something? Wasn't I the one who gave you a good home? Haven't I given you the best education? The promise of a rich, successful future? Ben, I *love* you! You are my life! For the love of God, be fair!'

'Fair!' Ben finally snapped, unable to hold back now that the word 'love' had come into it. 'Were you fair to me when I was lonely? When I was hurting? When I *needed* you?' Ben shook his head angrily, not wanting to be goaded into showing how he really felt, deep, deep inside.

'What are you talking about?' David demanded. 'I've tried to be there for you. I've done everything I damned well could for you!' His voice rose in protest.

'Including leaving me in the care of a lunatic!' Ben snapped coldly, leaning suddenly on the desk, his façade of indifference disintegrating rapidly. 'Because you do know that's what she is, don't you?'

David's mouth fell open in shock, but Ben wasn't waiting for a discussion now, his blood was beginning to boil.

'I'm tired to death of being that woman's scapegoat and a whipping boy for her demented son!' Ben's eyes now sparked fire. 'And I'm tired to death of the daily round of viciousness that passes for a so-called home life! *When* have you ever given any time to sorting out the mess your family's in?' Bitterness edged his old-young voice. 'Don't talk to *me* about fair! What's fair about having to call a woman who hates you "mother"? Where's fair in a life ruled by a spoiled, vindictive brat? Because that's the least of what Mat is!'

As suddenly as it had come Ben's anger collapsed, and he drew in a deep breath. 'You just don't know the half of it,' he said tiredly, 'because you don't want to know. You have never been able to face it, have you?'

David's shock was so intense he could only stare, mute and wooden.

Ben pulled himself upright with an effort, and his next words were in a voice hollow with weariness, emotionally exhausted from years of sustained mental and verbal battles.

'When I was small, I thought you were *God*,' he said emptily. 'I worshipped the air you breathed, and loneliness was the price I happily paid to live in your world, to know you loved me as your son. I took all the crap Mother and Mat dished out, I accepted their meannesses and cruelties, because I had *you*, my daddy, at the centre of my world.'

Ben's voice grew colder and more distant. 'Right up until I was fourteen, I tolerated the fact that only the servants cared if I had enough to eat, cared if I lived or died, because I had my daddy's *love*. And until then that kept me company enough. The belief that *you* cared helped me live an entire childhood of rejection.'

David prepared to argue against such a monstrous picture, tried to find words to deny, to placate. But Ben had turned to the door, was at the door.

'Since I was fourteen I've tried damned hard to keep my respect, my love, for *you*. I've battled with everything I had to keep you on your pedestal. But I've run out of excuses for you. I've run out of strength to fight mother and Mat on my own. Even for you.'

He had the door open now, his knuckles white against the polished oak.

David tried to rise but his body was leaden, pinning him helplessly in the chair. 'Ben, don't!' he managed hoarsely.

The face of a stranger stared back at him.

'It's too late now, father. I can no longer live under the same roof as a man who is too weak to control the sick, greedy minds that run the house.

'Mother and Mat have rammed it home for years that I'm in the way, that I have no right to any expectations, that I'm not worth a damn to you. Well, when I finally faced the truth, that you couldn't love anyone except yourself, they won.' Ben's eyes were remote. He was beyond recall. 'The last time I pleaded with you to sort it out was four years ago. I've waited until now, until I'm no longer a minor in your guardianship, to see if you would, could, deal with it.' His voice dropped even further, until it was almost a whisper. 'Perhaps you could have. But you didn't.'

At last David was on his feet, the full horror of Ben's words compelling him to move.

But Ben wasn't quite finished and as David crossed the room, his arms outstretched to embrace the only son he loved and whose heart he'd unwittingly, *unwillingly*, broken, Ben delivered his final blow.

'I hope in time, David Nazareth, that I will forget I ever knew you.'

David had been too hurt and too angry to try to prevent him leaving after that, too hurt to recognise the truth, too proud to go after Ben and bring him back.

Matthew had blossomed in his brother's absence. David, weakened from years of fighting and running, and still in shock from the loss of his beloved Ben, had allowed the manipulative Ella to convince him of what he needed to believe, that Ben had been the cause of all their troubles. Soon she'd returned to David's bed and, after years of frustration, he was allowed the occasional relief that her body offered.

In a new mood of gaiety, Ella had pointed out the difference in Mat. Couldn't David see it? Why, the poor boy had only been held back by that cunning bastard who'd won all David's affection for himself, leaving Matthew bereft of a father's love. She reminded him regularly how they'd all suffered. All because of Ben. And so David had allowed himself to be convinced. He cut Ben out of his will – and a part of his heart died.

The strange new peace lasted for two years, until Ella died of a tumour on the brain. A slow tumour that, the doctor said, could have been growing for many years. David was faced with the unwanted ghost of Ben's claim that Ella had been insane.

With this came the dreadful realisation that he should have seen it, should have got her help. He wrestled with, and finally refused to accept, that he could have done something about it all. It would have put the blame for Ben's rejection of him squarely on his own shoulders and David was not prepared to accept that. He buried the entire matter. Or so he'd thought then.

Matthew had idolised his mother, and his grief was an awful thing. For six months he retreated into a solitary world in the old nursery wing. By the time he emerged from his shell, the pattern was set. Their relationship reverted right back to childhood days. Matthew was barely civil, and he began staying away from the mansion, sometimes for days on end. Before too long, David didn't care.

All he wanted was peace – and peace only came when Mat wasn't around.

That tortuous situation lasted for over a year and then was replaced by what David had grimly called the Jekyll and Hyde period, when Mat would change his mood more frequently than his clothes. One day he would be moody and foul-tempered, the next day apologetic, charming and kind. The see-saw lasted until the summer before Diana had come into their lives.

That last summer had given David the first hope in almost a decade because Mat suddenly seemed to grow up. David had held his breath and waited for the tide to reverse.

But Matthew had played his part brilliantly, and by the time David met Diana and her cousin Gemma, visiting Boston on holiday, David was convinced that Matthew too had buried all the ghosts and finally settled down.

David stirred from his reverie; his hands were numb with cold and he was stiff from standing in one place for over an hour. The fire had died down and the room was chilly. He added fresh logs, bending nearer to catch the little warmth. His heart felt restricted, tight, as if it were banded in iron, heavy and cold.

He trembled, and knew that it was as much from his own painful memories as from the cold. Diana, in her innocence, had stepped unwittingly into an illusory, gilded trap. And *he* had been largely responsible for that.

Wearily he poured himself a straight whisky, and eased his tired frame into a leather chair. There was nothing left inside himself now that he didn't know about.

He'd wanted her from the first moment he'd seen her. Pride and fear of rejection had confused him, so he'd done the next best thing and manoeuvred her into marrying his son. Would he ever be able to forgive himself for that?

The logs caught and the fire began to crackle with life and warmth. He shifted in his chair. Matthew was dead. Ben was gone. Nazareth House, for the first time in its history, had no heir.

But there was still Diana. The thought of her, upstairs in his house, stirred the blood in his veins and lifted the bleak cloud from his mind.

Diana! What could he offer her that she might, just conceivably might, accept?

At last there were no barriers, nothing coming between them. His son was dead. The thought echoed around his mind. Matthew *dead*. Diana *free*. Now, if he played his hand very carefully, she could be his.

He swallowed more of his drink and forced his attention back to the present. It was *now* that mattered. The past was gone. Only the future remained. His future, and Diana's. Damn Ella and Ben and Matthew!

The tightness around his chest eased. What the hell, maybe it was *not* too late for heirs.

Diana joined him soon afterwards for the buffet lunch that had been left for them, and his heart leaped with pleasure at the sight of her.

She had changed into a soft wool dress of a cornflower blue that intensified the deep blue lights in the smoky depths of her eyes, eyes that fascinated David with their changing colour and thick, sensually sweeping dark lashes edged with gold. The mane of platinum hair was tied casually back at her neck with a wisp of ribbon. She wore no make-up and, as always, David marvelled at her beauty.

He scrutinised her covertly as she served them from an array of silver platters. She was far too young to have suffered so much, but he'd make it up to her in every way there was.

Did age really matter that much? She was nearing twenty-eight now. Was the difference such a big deal? There were many young women married to older men these days, and vice versa, he thought wryly. No, age was unimportant.

It was compatibility that counted. Besides, he knew that with Diana he would be ageless.

He felt the stirrings of desire again, and with difficulty accepted the plate she offered.

They picked meagerly at a lunch neither really had any appetite for and then at David's suggestion took their coffee into the now warm study.

They sat either side of the fire in companionable silence for a while and David felt most of his tensions drain away.

Although Diana excited him there were times, like this, when just to be near her was enough, times when her gentle presence afforded him peace. There was time enough for other needs.

The room was becoming warmer, and David's winter suit felt uncomfortable. He loosened his black tie, removed his jacket and undid a few shirt buttons.

Diana was silent, watching him cautiously. Her mouth was dry. She had to tell him. A film of perspiration dampened her hands. He unnerved her so.

His strong, slender fingers as he'd opened his shirt had

invited her attention. Now the dark hair of his chest against the crisp white shirt drew her eyes. She ran her tongue lightly across suddenly dry lips. Their eyes met and she knew at once that he wanted her. Her stomach contracted and she could not prevent the flush of her own desire staining her cheeks.

She had to tell him. Now, before it was too late.

'David, we need to talk.'

'Yes, sweetheart, I know,' he said huskily giving her a smile of encouragement. 'So who begins?'

She swallowed hard. 'I think I should begin. What I have to say might affect whatever you have on your mind.'

She ignored his sudden frown and rushed on swiftly, forcing herself to resist the tingle coursing through her body. 'I think you'd better know right away that I am leaving Boston.'

Her words fell heavily into the suddenly echoing silence.

David's face drained of colour and he stared, shocked, as Ben's face appeared, superimposed on hers. He shook his head and the vision disappeared.

'Leaving, honey? You're not serious?' He kept his voice marvellously even.

'I'm afraid that I am.' Her voice was firmer now that she'd managed the first move.

'Is this some kind of joke?'

'Do you think I would make a joke on a day like this? And at your expense?' she said hollowly.

David ran nervous fingers through his crisp dark hair, then a thought occurred to him and he almost laughed with relief.

'Of course, honey. I get it. I told you I'm an old fool! You need a little break. Right? Away from all this for a spell. Well, that's only natural sweetheart, of —'

'I'm leaving Boston, David,' she interrupted and he couldn't mistake her tone. 'I _have_ to leave. I have to get away from . . . from Boston.'

David groaned beneath his breath. 'Why? You know I'll take good care of you. You'll feel better soon. We'll go away . . . take a good long holiday. A few weeks somewhere in the sun with no problems to worry us. That's what we need . . . that's what *you* need . . .'

'Stop it, David!' she cried. 'That's the last thing I need, you and me alone in some idyllic paradise! How do you think *that* would help!' Her voice had risen and tears loomed near.

'I can think of several ways!'

'That's just the problem!' Now there *were* tears in her eyes.

'What's the problem?' he persisted stubbornly, his heart beating rapidly.

'*Us!*' Diana snapped nervously. 'You know that! That's why I have to leave . . . Please, don't make it harder for me?'

'Harder? For you? Now I know you're joking!' David was suddenly angry, afraid, his breathing ragged. 'What about *me*, Diana? Don't I have any feelings? I've just buried my son, and you tell me you're leaving?'

'It's for the best,' Diana said woodenly.

'Best? For what? For whom? Not for *me* it isn't, Diana, and not for you either. If you think it is, you're fooling yourself!'

Exasperated by his stubbornness, Diana snapped back. 'I have to go, David! Please understand!'.

'Understand? My God, honey! What are you talking about? Are you trying to tell me that you don't feel anything for me?' Suddenly he leapt up and crossed to her chair, dropping to his knees in front of her. 'Because, my love . . . if you are, I'm going to have to show you just how wrong you are.'

'No, don't. David, please, you mustn't!' She shrank into the corner of the chair, and buried her head in her hands.

He stared at her, stunned. Was she *afraid* of him? He was confused, and yet her nearness inflamed him. With a considerable effort he controlled the urge to force her into his arms. It was hard, because he knew that she *would* respond. The chemistry between them couldn't be denied forever.

He stood up unsteadily. She needed time. Pushing her like this, when she was overwrought, wouldn't do either of them any good.

'It's OK, honey,' he said gruffly. 'Don't hide from me like

that. You make me feel like some kind of monster. Look. No hands!' He raised his hands in the air, and made an effort to smile.

She looked up, and he saw the relief in her eyes. Why was he such a fool with her? A damned impatient fool. What was the matter with him, rushing her like that? Christ, they'd only just buried Mat!

'Sorry, sweetheart. I guess we're both overwrought,' he soothed. 'I think a brandy would do us good . . . help us to relax. What do you say?'

Diana nodded. Anything to keep him at a distance. She'd been so wrong to think that it might be easy . . . that he would understand. She should have kept her plans to herself . . . left him a note to find after she'd gone. But she'd wanted to do the decent thing, to tell him herself.

To get his blessing? Well, that would probably have been expecting too much. But she had hoped for understanding.

Now she realised miserably that she would get no help from him. Only hindrance.

'Here you go.' He held out a glass to her and the look on his face suddenly inflamed her. 'You'll feel better for this,' he said smoothly.

'Don't bloody well patronise me!' she swore, lashing out angrily and knocking the glass he held with trembling hands, spilling some of the amber liquid over her dress. 'I'm not a child! And I refuse to be treated like an imbecile. What's more, I don't need alcohol to help me judge right from wrong!'

David blanched and recoiled. Not only had he never heard her swear, mild though it was, he'd never heard her voice raised in anger. His shock was greater for that.

She had risen from the chair and, mopping at her dress, was stumbling across the room.

'Wait, honey! Don't go! Look, come back here by the fire . . . your dress will soon dry. Please! Let's just sit down and talk this thing over rationally. Don't you at least owe me that?' He caught up with her, reached out and held her arm.

Diana paused, trembling. Oh God, poor David! What was she doing? He didn't deserve tantrums, especially today. Guilt crowded into her tired mind.

She let him lead her and didn't protest when he eased her gently on to the soft leather settee facing the fire. And she silently accepted the brandy glass he refilled.

'Now, tell me what this is all about,' he said gently, seating himself beside her. 'Whatever it is, I'm sure we can work it out.'

Diana swallowed some of the brandy, again unnerved by him, his closeness, the sensual male heat of his body so close to hers. She took a deep breath and tried to calm the sudden erratic beat of her heart.

'I don't want to lose your friendship, David . . . I . . . it means too much to me,' she stammered. 'But you have to accept that . . . I . . . am leaving.'

'Have to? Hell, sweetheart, you're not making any sense.' His eyes were narrowed, but Diana saw his pain and flinched from it.

'Honey,' he said quietly. 'You're just confused right now. Don't try to make decisions yet. Wait until you're feeling stronger, until you've had chance to think things out, unemotionally . . .'

'I've had plenty of time to think.' Diana snapped, prepared to explain but not to wait. 'I've had more than a year to think, and there is no other way.'

David reached out and rested his fingers lightly on her arm. 'There *is* another way, Diana. If you'll give it time,' David insisted, his voice low and pleading. 'Don't leave me now, sweetheart.' His hand moved to her chin and he gently turned her face to look at him. 'I don't think I could bear it. What will I have left if you leave me? You're all I've got now.'

'Don't!' she warned quickly. 'Don't blackmail me, David, it's not fair.'

'I'm stating the truth,' he said bleakly.

Diana lowered her eyes, blotting out the desire and pain she

knew were in his. But he moved nearer, his fingers refusing
to release her chin. She felt his warm breath, uneven, on her
cheeks.

She tried to turn but his hands dropped to her shoulders
and held her in a firm, steady grip.

'Oh God, David! Please! Let me go. Don't do this,' she
begged, frozen to the spot.

'Don't what my love? Don't kiss you? Don't touch you?
Diana do you think *I'd* hurt you? I love you for God's sake.
And I am *not* Mat!'

'No!' she cried, pushing at his chest. 'Don't say you love
me. Don't even think it. It's wrong!'

She tried again to twist out of his hold, but it was already too
late. His hands were sending shock-waves through her body,
and she only knew how fragile her guard had been when it
collapsed as his mouth sought hers.

At first she struggled, with him and with herself, but the
power of feelings long repressed was greater than she'd ever
imagined. David was the first man to have awakened desire
in her. Now her body responded hungrily. His mouth was
gentle, searching her lips, her skin, evoking fierce shivers
of erotic pleasure. A soft moan escaped her now as David's
fingers traced a tingling path from her shoulders to the loose,
scooping cowl neckline of her dress. The wool material sprang
aside as if designed for this very purpose and David's fingers
dipped beneath it to the cool satiny skin. His stroke was
light but sure, spiralling maddeningly slowly down to the
lace-covered swell of her breasts.

Diana's pulse raced and her fingers instinctively entwined
in his hair as he grasped the frothy garment and wrested it
smoothly from her body. She gasped as her breasts sprang
free, and gasped again as his fingertips circled her breasts
with the softest of touches that teased and enticed her nipples
to thrust upwards towards the source of pleasure.

Her breath came in quick little gasps, her lips parted invol-
untarily and her teeth grazed against her suddenly sensitive

tongue: she was lost, trembling when his fingers feathered across the aching pink points. She had never been cherished like this, didn't know what to do; but her body did. As David's lips caressed her throat and his fingers tantalised, she strained towards his hands and unconsciously her pelvis arched upward.

David leaned in to her, easing her down beneath him, fully alert to her every move. His hard body felt her next move towards him and he eased his hand behind her to the small of her back and pressed firmly. She responded perfectly. Her hips lifted and he felt her legs part slightly to draw in the shape of him. He nestled very gently into the small valley she had made and as he did the swollen tip of him pressed forward against the soft silk guarding the entrance to her. This time when she gasped, her eyes flew open and he gazed into their passion-filled depths with all the love in his being. She shuddered against him; her eyelids drooped heavily and a great swell of love surged through him. She could be his. If he took the greatest of care.

He knew now that he would be her first real *lover*.

She would be his to pleasure and to protect for the rest of his life. If he could reach past her guard and claim her today, *now*.

He held himself steadily in his present position, not forceful but maintaining the gently dominant thrust against her, waiting for her to proceed further. His left hand remained at her lower back, ready to encourage when she was ready. His right hand continued to feather over her nipples, resisting the urge to tug at the sensitive peaks, to feel the swollen nubs between his thumb and forefinger. A little longer, he reasoned, and he would be able to ease the wonderfully pliant dress off. He wanted nothing between her skin and his when he took her, after he had tasted her, knew every intimate fold and crease, every soft undulating curve of her. His tongue tingled in anticipation and his body tightened.

Diana's hips arched and she moved herself forward, feeling

the bulging weight indenting itself further. She was hot and her breathing had become irregular, short little panting gusts. Her breasts ached with need, and the exquisite sensation of David's fullness, expectant against her, excited her still more. The word 'surrender' hovered deliciously in the tiny part of her mind that still functioned.

David tugged with his mouth and chin at the neck of her dress, pushing the material down until at last he could see his fingers above the creamy skin. One more delicate move and her breast was free to his eager mouth.

Diana's momentary shock as her naked breast was exposed faded as his warm breath fanned her nipple, sending rippling waves of pleasure through her body.

David's lips closed over the tender nipple and she groaned helplessly, unable to stop herself pushing harder into his mouth. His teeth gently gripped the hard little bud and his tongue slid over its surface and lapped at the captive treasure. Diana bit down on her lip to stop herself crying out with pleasure, but the strength of wave after wave of almost unendurable ecstasy forced her mouth open and little mews of joy filled the room.

David's heart and loins leapt. Nearly there. Oh God, nearly there. He groaned longingly and lovingly as he suckled intensely now. Diana's body was moulded, writhing, against his and it was all he could do to keep a check on his own needs. Her fingers entwined in his hair, tugged his head harder to her breast, and then she was pulling at her dress, unable to bear the unequal attention. She wanted his love, his kisses, everywhere.

He could have wept with joy, but it was still too soon to show his own vulnerability. However, it seemed the moment he'd longed for had come. His precious love wanted him. His mouth roamed against her insistently as he waited, as impatient as she for the other, not quite emerged prize. At last it too was free and for a moment he could only stare, marvelling at the perfect, upturned breasts.

Diana threw back her arms, basking in his loving gaze. Her breasts rose proudly high above her ribcage and the dusky pink nipples hardened. David leaned hungrily to the one as yet untasted. As the fresh soft peak tightened in his mouth, Diana moaned urgently.

David's hand moved skilfully to her waist, then over her stomach, his touch still careful but firm. When she didn't resist, his fingers moved more boldly, skimming caressingly down her thigh to her knee, then back up more slowly on the inside of her leg. His touch was sure, stroking her silky skin in long, leisured movements towards his ultimate goal. Her dress rode up easily on the hook of his finger.

Suddenly she shivered from head to foot and all his movements stilled. He held his breath and waited, but she thrust her nipple immediately back against his tongue. More nervous now, fearful that this spell they were weaving might suddenly break, his hand renewed its quest determinedly.

When his sensitive fingers brushed against soft lace he paused, while he increased the pressure of his other hand on her lower back, just sufficiently to move her forward and up slightly so that she was centrally positioned against the broad width of his pelvis.

Diana was feverish, her body out of her control. David was its incredible master. No thoughts could now invade her barricaded mind. She was abandoned, gloriously, to his touch. She felt the weight between her legs shift, astonished at the new sensations – unbelievably, more powerful still – coursing through her veins.

David held her suspended against him, her pleasure arcing into his body. He eased his thumb gently beneath the lace, pulling himself back slightly, in readiness.

Diana was becoming dizzy, faint from the ferocity of her own responses to David's concentrated skill. Her body ached all over and *still* the pleasure surged. She was beginning to feel desperate for release.

When David's thumb suddenly slid into place and his fingers

below gently parted her, her gasp was violent. At that same moment his mouth and tongue worked feverishly and an insanity of ecstasy almost overwhelmed her. His hand on her back urged her still further forward and she opened herself wider, wanting his hand, his fingers, his hardness, all at once; everything; his mouth, his hands; his beautiful, masterful mouth and his hot swollen tongue and his long, strong demanding fingers; all of him.

She began to cry softly. He was everything, and she was everything to him. Her forbidden lover. All that she had feared or dared to dream of – and more. And this was just the beginning. How could she bear knowing all this, and know it could never be hers . . . that he was her *father-in-law*!

David had frozen at the sound – and now, although his breath was ragged and his heart pounded, he knew, crushingly, that he had somehow lost the moment. For a few seconds he couldn't breathe; everything in him stilled. Then he forced himself to raise his eyes. Diana had turned her head into the scatter cushions and was sobbing as if her heart were broken. For a moment he felt his own heart stop, then it thumped back into rhythm with a painful shudder.

What had he done wrong?

He pulled himself upright and gathered her into his arms, holding her head close to his chest, all his pent-up longings diverted to her distress. His own ache was severe, but he could not hurt her. He would die first.

'Sweetheart, don't. It's all right,' he soothed. 'It's OK, honey. Don't cry.'

Diana's sobs wracked her body. For herself. For him. In frustration, but also something else. A hot surge of anger broke through her pain. She hadn't wanted this, had fought against it from the moment they'd met. She'd done everything to prevent it. But today, in the mind-numbing shock of Mat's funeral, her guard had slipped.

And David had moved in for the kill. It was emotional rape. Her hand began to push at his chest, at first weakly, then strongly. She fought her way out of his treacherous embrace and all her crazy, turbulent longings turned to rage.

Finally she was free and gasping for air, her face drained of all colour, shocked; her eyes wide with horror and anger.

David drew back, stunned by the wildness in her eyes. His hands fell helplessly to his side.

Diana scrambled up, frantically smoothing her dress, her hands shaking. She raked her fingers through her tangled hair, backing away from him, breathing heavily with fear and rage.

'No *more*, David. I warn you . . . stay away from me!' She backed to the door, her heart racing, her mouth dry and her whole body aching. 'You bastard!' she spat at him. 'You cunning bastard! You . . .' Her voice tailed off. She couldn't find words to express her disgust at him. Or at herself.

David's eyes were glazed with pain, but he didn't move. 'Diana, honey,' he pleaded heavily. 'I'm sorry. Goddamnit, I'm sorry! I rushed you, sweetheart. Forgive me . . . I know it's too soon, but the business with Mat . . . it must have — '

'Don't say any more!' Diana snapped, her trembling hand reaching for the door handle behind her.

David recognised the fear behind her anger and it shocked him. Did she think he would . . . Jesus! Suddenly he had to reassure her, take that terrible fear and accusation from her eyes.

'Please, don't leave like this,' he begged. 'I swear I won't touch you again. Let's just talk, let's deal with this for God's sake!'

Diana twisted to open the door. She had to get away. She must not let him persuade her back into his arms.

'Talk? Talk, David? Do you think I would trust you now just to talk? I don't think I shall ever trust you again!' Now, with the passage of escape so near, she drew a deep breath, tried to calm her voice. 'This is exactly what I was afraid of. And I was right to be. Now perhaps you'll see why. This is the reason why I have to leave.'

'Oh no, Diana. You can't . . . For Christ's sake, be real! We're adults here. Two normal human beings who love one another. We just need time, that's all.' David rose shakily and moved nearer to the fire, needing warmth, and to give her the clear message that he was no threat. That she was safe. He wouldn't follow.

Diana paused warily. Half of her wanted to deal with it. To resolve the damned problem. To restore their friendship. She didn't want to leave with this awful mess between them, but still she hesitated. She didn't trust him now. In fact, she realised with a dull shock, she could not trust either of them.

'Will you accept that I'm leaving, not try to talk me out of it?' she demanded.

David's eyes flashed. 'Oh no, my love. I'll *never* accept that,' he declared. 'I'm not going to let you do that.'

'I don't think you can stop me,' she retorted coldly. 'Unless, of course you intend to use physical force. As Mat and his friends did.'

David felt the words like a stab in his heart and for a moment he could only stare, winded. 'That was a pretty nasty blow,' he said finally.

Diana knew it was and she instantly wished the words could be recalled. 'I'm sorry,' she admitted. 'I shouldn't have said that.'

'It's OK, honey,' David replied. 'I know you couldn't really mean it. You sure as hell know I could never hurt you. I love you too much to do anything against your will.' He ran his hand tiredly through his hair, searching his mind for the right words to clear this nightmare up, to make her see the truth, and accept it.

'If you hadn't responded the way you did, then I guess I'd be less certain. But now I know without any doubt that you care . . . that you want me as much as — '

'Oh you *are* a bastard!' Diana gasped. 'You aren't going to give an inch, are you!' She held the door, finding courage.

'There's obviously no point in us talking. If I can't trust you to see the facts, as they are, then I've clearly overestimated your intelligence,' she said quietly.

David was on his guard again instantly and he spoke quickly, moving towards her. 'You can trust me with your life, Diana! Damn it you must know that. It's you who won't face facts.' He forced himself to stop as the light of fear came back into her eyes. He leaned heavily against the back of a chair, feet from her.

'I've told you I'm sorry, and I mean that. But I'm only sorry to have rushed you, not for having wanted to make love to you. You can't go on fooling yourself, honey. Not for much longer. You can no more hide your feelings than I can.

'But I won't push you. This is a bad time. You're over-wrought right now. I'll wait, Diana, for you to heal. I know that in time, when all this ugliness over Mat has faded, you'll be ready to begin again. *Time* is all I ask for, my love. Time to prove to you that my love is real and strong. And time for you to accept that our love is the most beautiful, the most important, thing in this whole damned world. Is that so much to ask?'

Diana had been listening with a sinking heart. There would be no reasoning with David today. So now she had somehow to placate him. Just for today. Just for long enough.

She managed a small, hopefully reassuring, smile, and a slight shrug of her shoulders. 'Well, let's leave it for now. I am really very tired and my head does ache. Perhaps you're right. The funeral *was* probably more of a strain than I realised.'

David relaxed and smiled and came across the small distance. His hand touched her arm carefully and he brushed her cheek with a cool, non-threatening kiss.

'Haven't I been saying you're all wound up? Why don't you get some rest? I could bring you something on a tray later — '

'No! Really, I shan't want anything. I think it's best if I crash for today,' Diana said hastily. 'I'm too wound up to do anything but sleep.'

'Fine honey,' David replied with a forced smile, hating this new situation between them, wanting to resolve it for all time. 'We'll talk tomorrow. You get some rest.'

Diana edged through the door, still not trusting him. 'Fine. I'm sorry, David . . . I — '

'Forget it!' he interrupted swiftly. 'Go to bed. Everything will look better tomorrow. Trust me . . .'

CHAPTER FIFTEEN

Alone in her room at last, Diana surveyed the row of packed suitcases and groaned.

There was far more than she could take now.

David's behaviour, and her own reaction to him, had changed everything. There would not be the luxury of farewells.

She rummaged in the top of her closet and found a lightweight overnight bag. It would be about as much as she could manage on her own.

Carefully she began unpacking the cases again, hanging things back in their former places, returning her belongings to their old homes.

The overnight bag took a few toiletries, things she would need immediately; a change of clothes, underwear, pyjamas. She zipped it shut, and the awfulness of her situation whirled in her mind.

She sat heavily on the bed. What had she ever done to deserve such misery as this? But she instantly shook the self-pity away. There was no time for it. The truth was she had stayed on too long. She should have got out while Beanie was still in residence, instead of becoming trapped by Mat's death.

What had she thought she could do for David anyway? Cure his pain with a few smiles? God, it had taken all her time dealing with her own problems. No, she'd left herself wide open for today. It had been on the cards too long for her not to have seen it coming. And God – when it had finally happened she'd wanted it as much as David!

She shivered as she remembered how it had been. Then resolutely she halted the treacherous thoughts. *No more*. She was getting out now. Ending it. As it should have been ended a long time ago.

Darkness fell at last, and she welcomed it.

She felt nothing but contempt for herself as she sat at the desk. The action she was about to take was wrong, pathetic, but David had refused to understand. He would not willingly let her go and if she stayed she would be a prisoner of her own insane, intolerable need for him.

The only certain cure for what was between them was distance. She would put that distance into effect and hope that time would heal them both. But she couldn't prevent the tears that fell as she at last folded the shakily penned note.

Everything was done. She set her alarm clock and lay down on the bed in warm travelling clothes . . .

CHAPTER SIXTEEN

David left the mansion early the next morning with a smile on his face and a whistle on his lips. He'd thought of a perfect answer overnight and was anxious to set the wheels into motion straight away.

It was noon before he got back, carrying with him an armful of Diana's favourite roses and a pile of travel brochures. He was whistling softly again as he ran up the marble steps. He hurried inside, excited by his plans. There would be time to talk to Diana before lunch.

A month's cruise perhaps? He took the staircase two steps at a time. Or a tour of Egypt? He knew she'd like that. She'd loved the place as a little girl, and she'd told him that one day she'd like to go back.

It was just what they *both* needed. A holiday away from Boston. A complete break from everything, away from prying eyes, and away from the need to pretend a mourning that neither of them felt. A month? Better still, two? It was the ideal solution. A holiday, alone together.

His insides felt weak as he momentarily succumbed to the memory of how she'd felt in his arms. His steps quickened. *How* he'd love her, when she would let him. He'd felt the response in her body, tasted the love in her kisses. He wanted her so badly it was almost an embarrassment. Of course he forgave her the curses – she'd been overwrought and fearful that it was too soon. She hadn't meant any of it. He knew that.

He paused outside her sitting-room, willing his heart to steady. He'd have to court her so carefully, but it was only a matter of time . . .

He wandered through the suite, dazed with shock and disbelief . . .

The note told him she had gone, but still he sought her in the empty rooms.

The bed was carefully made, the room neat and orderly as if she'd just stepped out for a while. He opened her closets, transfixed by the rows of clothes hanging neatly inside.

She'd gone. Leaving all her personal belongings.

Her perfumes and some cosmetics adorned the dressing-table in the dressing-room. Her robe hung on the door. Stiffly he turned to her jewel-case and lifted the lid. Matthew had stolen only the modern, easily disposable stuff: he was too clever to have taken distinctive pieces. The cameo brooch that had been his grandmother's was still there; and the ruby and diamond necklace his mother had so loved. Automatically he catalogued the contents; the antique white sapphire engagement ring, also his mother's, was in its box; his grandmother's single strand of pearls glistened like tear drops on its velvet bed. There was more. He looked, but did not touch.

Finally he lifted a tray, knowing that Diana had kept Mat's ring there, out of sight, since it had been brought back from his smashed body. His eyes focused with difficulty. Mat's ring was there all right, and beside it, glinting coldly, was Diana's wedding band. The gold watch that he had given her on her wedding morning gleamed from a side tray.

She had left it all, everything connected with her life as a Nazareth.

He struggled from the room, his legs heavier than iron, closed the door behind him, and leant heavily against its polished wood.

She'd left him. Diana, his only love. She'd gone.

He stumbled blindly to the stairs, unaware that Sanders had frozen at the sight of him. He staggered the length of the hall, holding on to its walls; unaware that he moaned as he lurched down the staircase – crippled by a searing pain that threatened to tear him apart.

He didn't see Meg or hear her gasp as he hurled himself into his study. He was in terrible pain, pain that burned him to his very soul. Night-black, dense terror of the soul pain; leaping, obliterating, hellish-red pain. The pain of all his losses, the hurts of a lifetime, condensed into one ball of agonising fire.

Ignited by Diana.

With the door locked against the concern of his staff, the pain and the rage burst forth. For the first time in his life, David Nazareth wept. Like a demented child he cried and roared, battered by the intensity of his grief. For an hour he keened, and to those outside it was as awesome and fearful as the sounds of torture.

David's tears were for himself. Bitter tears of regret, and of guilt, and of frustration – of loneliness, and of love. Unrequited love.

When the storm passed, he slumped in his chair, exhausted, and closed his eyes.

By the middle of the afternoon he knew what he had to do. He sat down at his desk, a half-empty bourbon bottle and glass within reach. His hands still shook as he held Diana's terse note. He'd read it until he could have quoted it backwards, but still he read it one last time.

> *David,*
>
> *Forgive me for leaving in this way. I so wanted to leave in friendship, but you have made that impossible. Beyond all else, I regret that. It hurts me to do this, but you give me no choice. What we feel is wrong, it can never be.*
>
> *You said that 'Time heals', then let it do so please; for both our sakes.*
>
> *I cannot deny that I will miss you, nor that you will always be very special to me.*
>
> *I have to deny anything else.*
>
> *I will send you an address once I am settled somewhere. And I will write. But only as a friend.*
>
> > *Ever,*
> >
> > *Diana.*

The single page was stilted, the phrasing staccato, and he could see the stain of her tears on the page.

His proud, stubborn Diana, with her wondrously stupid sense of honour. Did she really believe that he would accept her goodbye? She had written him a farewell note, expecting him to behave according to her quaint codes. Well, he had news for her.

He folded the note and stowed it in his desk drawer. Then he pulled his private telephone towards him, and grimly dialled his office.

Jeff Sherman answered.

'Jeff, it's me. Switch to private.' David heard the series of clicks and knew that they could not now be overheard.

'All yours,' Jeff said easily, unaware of events that were about to alter their lives forever.

David's voice was strained but clear, and he came straight to the point.

'Jeff, sometime last night Diana left the house. I want to know where she went. Try the cab companies first because she didn't take her car. Come back to me when you have something . . . and Jeff, keep it real close!'

If Jeff was startled, he didn't let on.

'Okay, Dave, I'm on to it. You're at the house now, I take it?'

David affirmed that he was and rang off.

Within fifteen minutes Jeff called him back.

'She took a city cab to Logan at six this morning. Then she boarded flight BA 313 to Paris at 0700 hrs. Her ETA there is in one hour's time, US. That's around 9 p.m. in Europe,' he added helpfully. 'There's no onward booking, although the flight was a scheduled Boston–Paris–London. Looks like she's planning on staying over in gay Paree?'

He couldn't help the question mark. Every bone in his body was alert, for a reason he couldn't yet determine.

'Good,' David answered thoughtfully, as if satisfied. 'That means she's gone to her mother. She'll be safe enough there.'

His heart was in his mouth, but now he delivered the basic facts unemotionally. Jeff would have to know them if he was to help.

'Diana was very distraught yesterday, you see, and intimated that she might leave. I thought I'd talked her out of it, but it seems she decided to avoid further discussion with me . . .'

Jeff fixed his attention, hearing the quiet distress behind the casual words. 'Strong-minded lady, Dave, you know that. But . . .' he mused aloud, 'perhaps not quite herself – with the funeral and all. She was pretty rigid at the service.'

'That's what's worrying me,' David responded quickly. 'OK, great job, Jeff. I'll want to talk to you later, when I get a few things straight in my mind — ' He was about to hang up, when Jeff interrupted.

'Hey, Dave. I'm just thinking here, what about a press release? Someone might have noticed that she was on that flight?'

David's stomach contracted. 'Good thinking! I'll get on to Ike right away, then he can buzz you with a copy. Thanks, Jeff.'

'No sweat,' Jeff murmured.

Ike Petersen, the Firm's press secretary took David's call. 'Hi there, D.N., how's it going?' Ike would not mention the funeral. Few people would.

'Coming together, Ike, slowly. They keeping you busy over there?' David enquired politely, knowing that Ike would have had numerous calls for information on Mat's death to contend with, and the added problem of insisting the funeral was to be private.

'You'd better believe it,' Ike's deep-timbred voice chuckled richly. 'Just about everyone's up to somethin' in our little empire.'

'Good thing they are. Keeps you in work, old buddy.'

'Too right there. Now, what can I do for you, Dave? Anything in particular you have in mind? That little sort-out you had down in Philly worked out nicely, according to my sources.'

Ike didn't know about the high level of secrecy, but he could second-guess and knew it was a delicate operation.

'Cairo looks set for take-off, with the usual maximum aggro, so I'm told,' he said dryly. 'Oil is bubbling up 'neath the desert sands, waiting for someone to kick ass. I've been thinking of getting a camera crew out there – keeps our guys on their toes if they think that *Time* or *Newsweek* might be interested in their ugly mugs. Or Venezuela's interesting, if you really want some strife.

'Or did you want to know one of the half-million or so things I *don't* have at my workworn finger tips?'

David couldn't help a tight smile. Ike did a difficult job with a great deal of patience, tact and foresight. David had always liked the man, and that helped him now.

'Nothing beyond your geriatric abilities today, Ike,' David quipped. 'Just a little social gossip to add spice to the media's dull rhetoric.'

Ike was instantly alert, his pen poised.

'Right, this is it, I'll leave you to fill in the obvious yourself. Ready? "Mrs Matthew Nazareth, recently widowed, etc, etc, flew to Paris this morning to over-winter with her mother, the well known artist-sculptress, Rachel Lloyd-Fauvère, etc; Nazareth House spokesmen say that the young widow will be much missed at the mansion, etc. Mr David Nazareth will remain in residence, but following the death of his son will not be extending or accepting any social invitations during the coming months . . . etc, etc. Got all that?'

Ike whistled slowly. 'That should frustrate the gay widows and society hostesses no end! Sure you wouldn't like me to add that you've gone fishin', just to play safe?' He didn't add what he was thinking, that D.N. would be even more sought after, now that his heir was dead.

The thought sobered him. Dave was as good a guy as they came. But shit, the guy'd had enough tragedy to last a lifetime. And what did the future hold for him now? Or Nazareth House? He shook his head with unusual gloom.

'How does that read?' David was asking.

'Just fine. You ever need a job, call on me.'

David laughed, genuinely if a little shakily.

'I'll do that. Right, get a copy over to Sherman. Oh, and see that the Firm gets a memo. I don't want my employees reading second-hand gossip in the newspapers. One other thing, Ike, see that a copy of the local papers gets to Paris. We don't want Mrs Nazareth thinking we've forgotten her the moment she takes a little holiday, eh?'

David sipped grimly at his tenth bourbon that day.

He'd covered the social tracks – done the duty bit. Later he'd call Beanie, before the story broke. What next? He still couldn't believe that Diana was in Paris.

Yesterday already seemed a million years ago. What had happened to his plans? Everything had depended on Diana remaining with him, or at the very least in Boston. He sure as hell hadn't a hope of courting her by mail. He debated going over to his Paris office, but dismissed the thought instantly. She wouldn't thank him for following her.

No. The fact was she'd have to *want* to come back.

He groaned aloud. What a mess. Honour, ethics, morals. Screw them all! He wanted Diana: and he knew she wanted him.

His dulled brain began slowly to function again. There had to be a way, somehow.

But how?

He had more wealth than he could ever need, but fat use that was to him in this situation. Diana would not be bought. He'd have to come up with something foolproof, a plan which couldn't fail. He tapped his pen thoughtfully on his blotter.

He mentally listed his assets. He had the money. He had the brains. He had the determination. And, damn it to hell, if necessary he had the time. A way would present itself. It had to. He would never give her up. Not now.

Not ever.

To the relief of his subdued staff, he came out of his study and took a light meal that evening. His own acute sense of survival told him that he must maintain not only appearances but also his own strength.

In the morning he awoke with the beginnings of a plan forming in his mind. Tentatively he explored it as it took on a hazy but identifiable shape. It was a very new seed-form and he'd have to cultivate it with extreme care.

It was a helluva long shot.

It was also monstrous, cunning, even foul. But it just might damned well work.

He was impatient for Jeff to be at his office, and called the moment he knew he'd be there.

He wasted no time on pleasantries, coming straight to the point. 'Jeff? Good! A couple of very private jobs for you. I want them on priority. Shelve everything else.'

Jeff Sherman listened in silence, concern growing by the second.

'Number one, I want you to keep tabs on Diana. I want to know where she is, where she goes, and with whom, from now on. Got that? Right. Number two, get me an update on Ben. Yes, you heard it, on Benjamin! That shouldn't be too difficult.'

His voice hardened at Jeff's small protest. 'He originally went to California. Start there. Nazareth is not a common name . . . go straight to "N".

'OK. When you've got him, I want to know everything there is to know about him. His job. His prospects. His social life. Financial situation. Everything. In fact I want to know if he catches cold. Got the picture?'

'D'you like to run that one by me again?' Jeff enquired in a deceptively calm tone.

'You got it first time, buddy,' David said flatly.'The priority on him is his prospects. What they are, what they're likely to be.'

'He could be out of work,' Jeff mused, beginning to think he was getting a picture of Dave's intention.

'Ben? Ha!' David snorted. 'Not a chance of that. Not with his brains and determination,' he added on an edge of bitterness. 'But, Jeff, you're to work only with the best on this. Get whatever agencies you need, but no cowboys. I want results, Jeff. And I want them yesterday!'

Jeff Sherman whistled under his breath, while his razor-edged mind calculated what this could mean.

'Right, you'll get all that, Dave. Anything else while I'm at it?'

'Yeah,' David spoke thoughtfully. 'That empty office down on sixth. Move whatever you need for this job into there. Have a private line fed into it, so you can take any reports etc there. You and I will have the only keys to that suite. I want no leaks on this one. And Jeff, I want action, not talk . . . and I want it *now*.'

'You've got it, Dave,' Jeff replied as coolly as he could. 'Shall I expect you?' he queried as an afterthought.

'In a few days. I've got things to do myself,' David said dismissively.

He hung up, leaving Jeff to make of it what he would. He didn't at this moment give a damn what the guy thought. He had only one thing on his mind, Diana. He didn't care what it might cost, or what methods he had to use. This was war, and he would stop at nothing. Without Diana there was nothing to live for. Not for him. Not for Nazareth House. They both needed her.

Diana *and* heirs for the Firm.

His obsession was all but complete. He *would* have her children at the head of Nazareth House. However he had to do it, whomever he had to use.

And Benjamin, as a tool, would be expendable.

For the last time he dropped his head in his hands, and wept for what might have been.

When, finally, he was able to control the last of his gut-racking tears, he raised his head and swore out loud with all the agony and force of his tormented soul.

'I *swear* before God Almighty, Diana. I *will* bring you back. You will *not* escape our destiny!'

BOOK TWO

DIANA

CHAPTER SEVENTEEN

'*Marais, s'il vous plait,*' Diana instructed the driver, ignoring his far from amiable shrug. She was glad she was able to speak French as well as she could English – and although she never spoke of France, nor in French, except when she was in Paris, it was reassuring to be able to slip from one language to the other. However, despite being born here, and her father a Frenchman, she had no natural affinity with the country. She didn't dislike France, or Paris, she was just detached from its familiar, overwhelming and seductive capriciousness.

Maybe, she thought, as the taxi screeched to a halt, a hair's breadth from the Citroën in front, in the Place Charles de Gaulle, towered over by the magnificent Arc de Triomphe, she had a built-in resistance to a people who exasperated her.

She gazed up at the illuminated beige stone of the Arc, its coloured spotlights casting giant rays of red and blue into the night sky. Yes, it was lovely, but her admiration was perfunctory, a token homage to a marvellous piece of architecture; she felt no *frisson* of national pride.

The Place de la Concorde was as always thronged with sightseers. Arguably the most beautiful square in Paris, it boasted not only the Obelisk of Luxor, but also several statues representing the major provincial capitals of France – and two huge fountains, with their sprays lit and softened by lamplight from globes on their tall, wrought-iron posts. Despite the amazing views, all the way back to the Arc de Triomphe, she always found it hard not to be reminded of the bloody years of the Revolution, when the guillotine had been the gruesome centrepiece.

But now they turned off to the left and came even more speedily along the Rue de Rivoli, past the Tuileries and the

Louvre, finally turning beside the Hôtel de Ville – the city's council offices – and they were almost there.

Her stomach was in knots as the cab drove into the beautiful square where her mother had her gracious mansion and studio – yards from the Picasso Chez Lui; she had the distinction of having lived there long before Picasso's museum had transformed the neighbouring Hôtel Salé.

Diana placed her bag on the step and stood back for a few moments, looking up at the mellow golden building, with its glossy green double door and its steeply pitched, black-slated roof. She always felt tense before meeting her mother, even though she knew it passed the moment she saw her. She supposed it was because this house, this square, reminded her instantly of her father, of her childhood journeyings away from this place, whether to school in England, or visits to her cousins on Dartmoor; or to some exotic place where her father was working. She couldn't see this house without thinking of him, and feeling the aching loss of his company and his love.

She had wondered in the past how he had coped with Paris: He had been a quiet, philosophical man, who needed peaceful surroundings; yet as a budding archaeologist from the Dordogne, he had been enraptured with her mother, Rachel, an English student of art, and they had settled down here, where she had wanted to be. They had made an odd couple; equally talented, equally in love, but so very different in their natures.

And yet theirs had been a great love – a sustaining love . . . and their differences, their many, long, separations, had not mattered to them.

From very early in her life, Diana had known two quite separate lives, the one with her father, and the one here.

The one with her father, which had formed her character, had shielded her from the frivolity of Paris and any hunger for its bright, brittle lights. With him she had learned to ignore the pressures of Parisian society – a society that demanded one be seen in all the 'right' places, with all the 'right' people.

Her father had protected her by taking her with him on his expeditions around the globe, for as often and as long as he could. And when she was not with her father, she was at boarding school in Devon, with her two English cousins, Gemma and her younger sister, Candy.

At twenty-three, she had still been his constant companion, until the freak accident which had killed him, in Africa, had separated them forever.

She brought herself back to the present – to that other existence, the one with Rachel at its centre. Rachel's house was brightly lit, but that was no indication of her being there, as Diana knew. But tonight she prayed that her mother was at home. She didn't relish the thought of a hotel room, even for the night.

Rachel Lloyd-Fauvère was not a conventional mother – and she was notorious for her exasperating eccentricities. But no one was as detached as she; no one more singularly disinterested in other people's problems, including her daughter's.

She was exactly what Diana needed at the moment.

The front door opened in response to her tug on the bell, and behind the maid, Jacquie, she was relieved to see her mother.

Rachel came forward immediately, noting both Diana and her small bag in a brief glance. Her voice was just as her daughter expected. Light, non-curious, slightly vague.

'Darling, how lovely. Is that all the luggage you've brought? Goodness, you can't be staying long. Do come in, darling, we're warming the streets. I expect you'd like some coffee?'

Diana couldn't help smiling as she followed her mother.

Rachel turned briefly in the marbled foyer. 'Leave that with Jacquie, darling.' She indicated the small bag without interest. 'The green room's made up . . . you know where it is, of course . . . you can settle later. Café crême, yes?'

Her voice floated off as she made her way towards the back of the house.

Diana slipped of her coat and gave it to the maid. Rachel made anyone feel normal, just by comparison.

Ten minutes later she was sipping the scalding chicory-flavoured coffee her mother always favoured, and biting with a suddenly astonishing appetite into a hot buttered croissant.

Rachel perched on the edge of a lime-green silk-covered chaise and gazed speculatively at her only child.

'Well, darling, whatever else has happened since you phoned me, the funeral alone hasn't given you those dark circles.' She glanced over Diana's slight form. 'Nor taken so much flesh from your bones. Not enough time,' she stated matter-of- factly. 'So if and when you want to, you can tell me about it . . .' She glanced away at a clock, and tutted before saying, 'How's David?'

'Fine, considering,' Diana murmured.

'Good.' Rachel dismissed him, duty done. 'I was glad not to be expected to attend the funeral, all that morbidity. More coffee?'

Diana, thinking how little morbidity had been attached to Mat's burial, could only nod. She was already beginning to relax in the peculiar calm of the house.

It was peculiar – because Rachel's life-style was chaotic: the house was regularly filled with people coming and going to Rachel's studio at the back of the house, or attending one of her parties or dinners; noisily debating the latest art fads, or holding forth on this new artist or that new medium.

Rachel had long held court in an elite group of Paris artists. Her life was a continuous round of work, exhibitions, parties and more work; all of which she undertook with a quiet passion that was as truly Parisian as it was possible for a non-native to display.

Her home sometimes resembled a station, alive with the bustle of passing human traffic, yet, contrarily, it reflected a deeper inner quality that was also uniquely Rachel, a peaceful detachment from everything not connected with her own work.

Diana knew that the comment about the funeral was as near to condolences as she was likely to get. Also that, unless she chose otherwise, the subject would not come up again. Her mother would listen, willingly, to anything her daughter might wish or need to say. But she would ask no questions.

Rachel had an amazing ability to let go of anything remotely unpleasant or unalterable. She would not allow or encourage emotion on any subject. She abhorred it; and had no time for conventionalities for the sake of them. If her daughter was grieving, she would respect it and leave her to get over or through it. If she wasn't, then why pretend?

Rachel now rose from the chaise, glancing again at the clock. 'Sorry, darling' – she didn't look the least bit sorry – 'I'm already late. You'll excuse me. I must change.'

Diana smiled. 'Of course. Lunch tomorrow . . . any chance?'

'If I can.'

They brushed cheeks and Rachel flew upstairs, a light, elegant woman, ever in a hurry.

Diana curled up on her velvet chair, finding the last vestiges of her anxiety drifting away.

Her mother would not reorder one second of her life for her, but she had found out long ago that that suited them both. Diana knew she was genuinely welcomed, and that her mother loved her. But Rachel lived by her own rules. The moments they spent together would be the more precious and rewarding for their total independence of one another, for their freedom from suffocating bonds.

Diana loved and respected her mother, but more as a good and wise friend. Her father had been her only real family. He had been the one to nurse her small hurts, to heal her disappointments, to soften the little blows of her life. He had been the one to hold her when she cried, to kiss away the tears.

And he had taught her to love Rachel for what she was: a very talented, single-minded artist, who simply didn't have an ounce of maternal instinct. Home had been wherever her father was. Paris was just a place where her mother lived.

She wondered about her mother's private life. Did she have one? Were there any lovers? Diana gave the thought up. If Rachel did have lovers, she would probably never learn about them, for Rachel would certainly never confide in her daughter.

Thinking about lovers brought David back into her mind. But she was not ready to think about him yet. It was still all too fresh. She needed to be distanced from him, by space and time.

Tired as she was that night, sleep eluded her for a long time. The sounds of Paris by night drifted into her room, their vibrant energies echoing her own restlessness.

She felt cowardly and guilty for leaving David the way she had. But, she reasoned, if she'd stayed she would have given in. There was no question about that. He confused all her emotions.

Why hadn't she recognised that it was the father, not the son, that she had fallen for? If she'd understood that, would she still have gone through with the marriage, to be near to David?

She shook her head. Who could know? As it was, she'd gone through hell trying to protect him, trying to conceal his son's perverted behaviour, and his ugly character.

She'd gone through all that trauma just to stay near to David. Even after the rape, when she should have left, she'd stayed, masochistically enjoying the pain of being near to him, so afraid that David would find out what Matthew was really like; putting him before herself, because of her love for him.

Love. What could come of love between a man and his daughter-in-law? Nothing but trouble, and the heartbreak she already knew.

She turned into her pillow as bitter tears spilled on to the satin pillows. She'd been the biggest fool under the sun, and she'd made David one. Now he would be suffering hurt pride as well as everything else – and she knew enough about David to know that his Nazareth pride would not recover easily from such a blow.

Her tears flowed freely at last; tears for the heartbreak and the physical suffering, she had endured; tears for the new loneliness she could already feel.

The pinkish glow of a brighter Paris morning found her with a colossal headache, and a weariness in her bones that even a long bath did nothing to dispel.

The call she'd intended to make to her cousin Gemma didn't get made that day, or on any of the several that followed. She was numbed in mind and spirit, unable to think straight, and she needed to be very certain of what she intended to do with the future before she saw Gemma.

Meanwhile she went for long walks along the banks of the Seine – or sat, wrapped up against the cold winds in the lovely cobbled square of the Jardin des Tuileries.

She walked in the rain, in the sleet, and, as winter receded, on dry, mild nights.

Often the distinctive rich aroma of roasted coffee drew her from the street into a bustling, warm café, or she might order a bowl of soup, steaming hot and pungent with garlic, in a bar where the haunting saxophone of a jazz group playing the blues had pulled her off the street by her heartstrings.

She would sit well into the small hours, searching in her heart for all the emotions she must weed out if she was to begin her life anew.

She dined twice with Rachel and talked of nothing consequential, but the time came three weeks later when they were together in Rachel's studio.

An easy silence lay between them. Diana's book lay unopened on her lap as she watched her mother deftly mixing oils on her palette. She'd always found her mother's craft fascinating.

She watched as blobs became scenes, dark patches turned

to light and shade. As she had inherited none of her mother's talent, the whole process remained a wonder to her.

Rachel glanced over her shoulder, her artist's eye noting the drawn brows, the luminosity of eyes too large and serious in such a pale face, and she frowned. Wastage of beauty appalled her.

'Darling, are you feeling any better yet?' she mumbled through teeth clenching a brush.

'Much, thank you,' Diana said, but her voice was expressionless.

Rachel ignored the answer, moving her brush to mix more paint. 'Well, it's not Matthew, that's certain. The accident is too recent to have caused shadows that deep. What then . . .? Boston? David?'

Diana paled and stiffened. It was so out of character for Rachel to pry that she was surprised.

'Hum,' Rachel continued. 'Whatever it is, *petite*, it's time you resolved it, or put it behind you. If you can't solve it, darling, let it go.'

Diana shifted uncomfortably in her seat. She was not ready to be drawn into any kind of confession. Not about Mat, and certainly not about David. She changed the subject.

'I'm toying with the idea of changing my surname,' she said evasively but truthfully.

'Good idea,' Rachel responded, unperturbed. 'Do your own thing under your own steam. Nazareth's a famous name, even here, ' she added.

'Lloyd-Fauvère's not exactly unknown, mother,' Diana said drily.

'Not quite the same connotations for you though, darling,' Rachel stated evenly. 'Go back to being a Lloyd-Fauvère for the public, and in private your friends can call you what you like.'

Diana nodded. It was what she'd decided to do anyway.

'Diana?' Rachel only used her daughter's name when she was serious, so Diana looked up at her expectantly. 'Do you intend to stay here much longer? I'm not being rude . . . you know you are welcome for as long as you wish . . . forever if you'd like. But, you have no friends here, and few interests . . .'

She tutted as she ran her expert eye over Diana's blue jeans and jersey. 'And you have so few clothes. Unless you want the whole of Paris to start asking questions, you will *have* to do something about your wardrobe.'

Diana grimaced. 'God, you're right! I'm sorry, it just didn't dawn on me. I've been doing a wash and wear routine.' She gave her mother a small smile of apology. 'But, as for staying here. No, well, not for much longer. But before I finalise my plans, would you mind if I had Gemma over for a few days?'

'Of course Gemma can come. It will be good for you to have some company, and she's certainly lively!'

It was a response of affection. Rachel was fond of both her brother's daughters, in her own way.

Diana thanked her. 'I'll get out shopping, as soon as I've spoken to Gemma.' She gave a wry smile. 'If I don't, she might insist on helping me choose my clothes.'

'Mercy!' Rachel's eyebrows arched upwards. 'That you don't need.'

'Don't remind me.' Diana was grinning now and Rachel smiled for a fleetingly warm second.

'If you're calling, give them my love,' Rachel said and, closing the conversation, went back to her work.

Diana went through to the salon, feeling more relaxed. Thinking of Gemma had cheered her, so obviously she was ready to face her now.

To her delight, her Uncle George answered the telephone. He was delighted to hear from her, but shyly at a loss for words about Matthew. Diana cut into his mumble of condolences gently, and heard the relief in his kind voice. She assured him that she was very well and hoped to see him and her Aunt Charlotte, soon.

'That'll be nice, Diana,' George said warmly. 'You know how welcome you always are here. But I expect you called to speak to Gems?'

Diana confirmed that she had.

'Well, can you give me a minute? She's helping with the milking . . . no, don't worry, it won't take a moment to fetch her.'

Diana smiled as she waited. Chalk and Cheese, that's what Rachel and George were. Uncle George was as retiring and shy as Rachel was gregarious, his great loves being his family, his pub and his small herd of milk cows.

It had often puzzled her that, with his aversion to crowds and his love of privacy, he'd married an outgoing Australian girl, who'd insisted they buy a pub. Now he was a popular 'mine host' in a sprawling eighteenth-century inn, where they'd raised their two, Australian-born, daughters, deep in the Devonshire countryside. The pub's success was no doubt due as much to George's easy-going manner as to his wife's culinary expertise.

All the same, Diana knew that George and Charlie wanted to sell up . . . and Charlie longed to go home to Queensland, which they both loved. But neither of their daughters wanted to leave England. Gemma, at twenty-five, hankered after a career in fashion design, which she swore she wouldn't be able to get 'down under'. Candy, at twenty-three and already established in a career in nursing, lived in the hostel at Plymouth hospital. And despite the fact that both girls were old enough to fend for themselves, Uncle George was a worrier and didn't want to leave them.

Perhaps Diana's half-formed plan would be the answer for them all.

Gemma came breathlessly to the phone and shrieked: 'Di! How fantastic! Where *are* you?'

Diana laughed. 'I'm with Mother.'

Gemma blew a loud raspberry.

'Your manners don't improve with the years,' Diana said

drily, feeling as if she herself was shedding years by the minute.

'Does Aunt Rachel?' Gemma returned smartly.

'Touché! And no, not a chance.'

'Well, why are you in Paris then, and not here? You'd better have a good excuse,' Gemma growled in mock anger.

'No excuses, Gems. But some very good reasons,' Diana said quietly. 'What are you doing with yourself this weekend?'

'Oh, this and that . . . you know. Why? What are you cooking?'

'How about pizza in Paris?'

'Yippee!' Gemma yelled. 'Can't think of anything better.'

'Then could you make tomorrow?' Diana asked.

'Can I last that long?'

'Great! Okay, I'll get on to a travel agent here and come back to you with flight details. You might have to pick your ticket up on departure — '

'Di, look,' Gemma interrupted, suddenly embarrassed. 'I'm pretty boracic at the moment — '

'It's my treat,' Diana insisted swiftly. 'I need to talk to you, Gems. Away from the bosom of your family . . .'

They strolled along beside the Seine on a brisk, cold afternoon, their breath forming little clouds in the air.

They were so different in looks that any resemblance between them should have been slight or non-existent, but for some reason people had always perceived them as being alike, so much so that they had often been presumed to be sisters.

Diana, with her mother's ash-blonde hair and her father's grey-blue eyes, was head and shoulders above Gemma in height and half again as slim. And although there were only two years between them, Diana was the natural elder, appearing more sophisticated, elegant and mature.

Gemma was as dark as Diana was fair, with a shock of unruly chestnut curls and enormous brown eyes. Hers was a vivacious personality, lively, zany and mischievous, exuding an innocence that was highly misleading. She lived life to the full, changing her lovers at least as often as the seasons.

Gemma was as talkative as Diana was reserved and, even though they shared a familial directness, Diana's was tempered with a natural diplomacy, while Gemma's could be dynamite.

Fortunately, Gemma thought the world of her cousin, giving Diana a decided influence over her cousin's impulsive nature and her whiplash tongue. At least, for some of the time, for Gemma could no more control her natural sassiness than she could the Queensland accent she had adopted at her mother's knee.   As they walked, they talked animatedly.

Gemma adored Paris and could never get enough of it. She drank in the dash and daring of its people, the sensuous hedonism, the presumptuous, disdainful style of the city-dwellers. Gemma would fit perfectly into Paris.

Diana had hesitated at first about telling her anything other than the facts of Mat's death but, knowing that Gemma would have a thousand questions anyway, had decided her to unburden her heart.

Now, as she finished the story, Gemma scowled darkly.

'Shit!' The younger girl swore for the dozenth time in the past hour. 'Those bloody Yanks! They really messed up your life.'

'Swearing won't help, Gems,' Diana said easily, knowing that the worst was over. Telling it all had been difficult. But it had been a relief.

'It might not help you, Di, but it makes me feel better,' Gemma said mutinously. 'What the hell was David thinking about? God! He's as old as dad!' Her lovely face was clouded by the knowledge of her cousin's suffering. 'For two pins, I'd go over there and sort that bastard out myself.'

'Attraction's a two-way thing you know, Gemma,' Diana said drily.

'Yeah? So what were *you* attracted to? Not his money. I know you better.'

Diana frowned. 'I don't know, Gems. David's a very attractive and magnetic man.'

'I suppose he's not bad for his age, but he took advantage of the mess you were in. That's sick,' she said in disgust.

'No. He didn't,' Diana corrected her. 'He kept extremely good control if you ask me, considering that it must have been obvious that I felt something for him.' She smiled wanly. 'I've told you that I care deeply about him, too. There were plenty of occasions when we could have, well, got together, if we'd wanted.'

'Why didn't you, then?'

It was typically Gemma, blunt and to the point.

'Because it was *wrong*. That's all there was to it.'

'For you, yes. But not for David it seems, not once he'd got the opportunity.'

'That's unfair,' Diana protested. 'I've told you he had other chances.'

Gemma's face blazed, partly with cold and partly with fury. 'Ha! That clever jerk was waiting for the right moment, Di! You must see that! I'd put money on Davie-baby playing a real low-profile game, waiting until you were too weak to hold him off any longer, marking time until you fell into his lusting arms.'

'No! You make him sound so false and contriving.' Diana's chin went up proudly. 'He's just not like that. And,' she gave Gemma a scathing look, 'I shall wish I hadn't confided in you if you're going to be so condemning.'

'Diana, that man's shrewd. He has to be. Look at what he did with his father's grotty little firm.'

'It was never a grotty little firm, don't exaggerate,' Diana said firmly, striding away, back towards the city and the first lights of dusk.

'Heck, Di. Slow down! Perhaps it wasn't a small business,' Gemma admitted. 'But it was still far from what it is now. And you don't get to play in the international league with a cabbage for a brain.'

Diana slowed, but refused to comment.

'Do you remember when we first met him? Because I do,' Gemma said now without rancour. 'He couldn't take his eyes off you, remember? It's a pity you ever met them. He had you married to that stoned son of his so fast you didn't know what day it was.' Now Gemma was scowling again, her face dark with controlled anger.

Diana halted, and turned to her cousin with a helpless look in her eyes. 'You're wrong, Gems. David didn't know about Mat's problems and I think he has been desperately hurt in all this. And I think you're wrong about his intentions towards me. I'm quite sure that his feelings just crept up on him.' She frowned thoughtfully. 'Anyway, if he really did care for me in the way you suggest, why didn't he just court me himself? Why go through such a charade?'

'You've got to be kidding! He's too damned smart for that.' David was what? Almost sixty! And you were twenty-five. How could he have hoped to pull that off? No, Di, he *used* Mat, there can't be any doubt about it, and nothing you say will change my opinion.'

Diana slipped her arm through Gemma's. 'Gems, it's *over*. It's been a nightmare, but it *is* over. Sniping about what might or might not have been is a waste of time. I've told you everything because we've always shared, and I wanted you to understand how impossible it was to put any of this in a letter, or even in a phone call.' She hugged her cousin's arm. 'I intend to build a new future – and you figure largely in my plans. If there's a hope of it working, there can't be major secrets between us.'

Gemma's whole being burned with indignation. Diana had suffered, was *still* suffering, and yet here she was still defending that asshole, still refusing to face the truth. 'Okay – you say it's finished, that it's all over with the Nazareths, but I have one point to make. You walked out on David, right? After he'd tried to make you stay – and after you were almost lovers. *You* pulled back. *You* walked out. You say it's all over, but what about him? Has David Nazareth finished with you?'

'He doesn't have much choice,' Diana said.

Gemma snorted. 'David Nazareth? Without a choice? *That* I'd like to believe!'

Diana smiled faintly. 'Believe it!' she said. But her heart felt suddenly constricted.

The dusk gathered rapidly around them, lights springing up everywhere, and Diana felt a shiver that was something more than just the cold.

'Come on,' she said, pushing David firmly out of her mind. 'Let's indulge ourselves. How about the George Hotel and a nice hot chocolate?'

Gemma's mind was far from easy, but she capitulated with a grin. 'Luxury and luxury. My two favourite words!'

Diana laughed. 'So we'll wallow. And I'll tell you my plans.'

CHAPTER EIGHTEEN

It was cold in Boston. Colder than in Paris, colder than in London. To David it was colder than the Antarctic wastes.

He'd swivelled in his chair to watch Beanie's face and now, even if he couldn't have overheard part of the clear responses she was getting from the telephone, he'd have known from her face.

The chill ran deeper in his veins, setting his features into a frozen mask.

'You're quite sure, darling?' Beanie kept her eyes lowered as she spoke into the instrument. 'Well, I'm sorry too. But you'll keep in touch?'

David turned stiffly back to some papers on his desk.

'She won't come back,' Beanie stated quietly.

'I gathered.'

'It's early days, darling,' she stressed soothingly.

'Not for me it isn't,' he said grimly.

Beanie gathered her coat and purse. There wasn't any point in lingering. The key she held was of no use to him. Diana was adamant she would not return. Why aid his destruction? He seemed capable of engineering that without her help.

She kissed his ice-cold cheek and left the office in silent despair. David had changed: no longer the man so loved by everyone, more a stranger to be feared. In two short weeks he had developed a dark aura, a brooding inpenetrable cloak.

For the first time in their very long friendship Beanie felt that she didn't know the man he had become. And she was afraid for him.

So was Jeff Sherman.

As Beanie left the suite, David buzzed Jeff to come through.

'Sit down, Jeff,' David said briskly. 'What's the latest report?'

'I've been giving you all that I get, Dave,' Jeff said quietly. 'There's no more today than yesterday.'

'Run it past me again.'

'He's a junior lawyer in an old-established firm,' Jeff repeated carefully. 'Top drawer, but a small firm. Long on reputation, but short on potential. The usual sort of stopgap for a beginner. He's gaining himself a reputation nevertheless.' He watched David's face curiously as he spoke. 'For fairness, and for being on the ball. Nothing you wouldn't have expected as it's Ben.'

David gave him a stony stare, but made no comment.

'He lives alone. Has a nice apartment overlooking the ocean, an occasional female friend, but nothing serious.' Jeff shifted before concluding, 'It seems to be local opinion that he's cut out for better things. There has an offer from L.A. but he turned it down flat. No one knows why.'

David studied Jeff's face. That last didn't ring quite true. 'I'll have that again, Jeff. As you heard it this time.'

Jeff shrugged. He'd tried to ease it. But nothing was that simple any more.

'The story goes that he's bitter, hurting, lonely . . . or all three.' His tawny eyes scanned David's face for a reaction, but there was only the tightening of a jaw muscle. The cold yet strangely electric blue eyes bored through him unnervingly. 'Anyway, whatever, he's a loner. Seems to prefer the life in a small beach town. He's never been known to go into San Diego or up to Los Ángeles. And the rumour is that he's wasted.'

David's face was impassive. 'It's still not enough. It's bare skeleton. I want meat on those bones. Good red meat that I can get at.'

Jeff blanched, but he murmured, 'You'll get it. Just as soon as I have it.'

'Time's at a premium,' David snapped.

'Yeah, but it takes time all the same,' Jeff argued reasonably.

David threw down his pen, his face now creased with anger.

'Time? Damn it to hell! How much time do I have?'

Jeff wondered if this was the moment he'd waited for. But who could tell? However, he saw the opening and decided to seize it regardless. 'Look, Dave, you can shoot me down in flames if I'm out of line, but you know, it just might help if I knew what the hell you were up to. For one thing' – he shifted again uncomfortably – 'it could spread the load. And that might help you get things into perspective.'

David's face had whitened, but Jeff plunged on. 'You're so goddamned uptight no one can speak to you these days, and it's affecting the entire workforce. Your people are too nervous to say "Hi" to you. That's bad news for the Firm, Dave.'

David's face went from white to purple and then back to chalk again. From a bristling lion to a badly winded old man. He slumped down in his chair, and for a long moment there was silence in the room.

Then he began speaking, very quietly at first, as if to himself.

'You're right, Jeff. I owe you an apology. You and everyone else.' He managed a ghost of a smile. 'But the staff aren't going to hear any of this. They'll just have to put it down to a father's grief, won't they?'

He gazed up at the ceiling before continuing. 'I have the worst goddamned problem of my life on my hands, and I'm expected to behave like Mr Nice Guy! Well, that's just tough shit!' He stared at Jeff as if trying to see him clearly.

'That workforce out there.' He nodded his head in the general direction of the rest of the building. 'They could be faced with a whole set of worries in the near future. Like a corporate body for a boss!'

Jeff listened carefully, disguising his tightening nerves beneath a bland exterior as David continued.

'I'm not immortal, Jeff! If I don't come up with an answer to maintain the status quo, Nazareth House, as we know it, is finished.'

David's eyes were cold and cutting as he summed up.

'Without an heir to take over from me you can imagine what would probably happen: in here would sit a load of fat directors, organising everyone else's work and money. Strangers, deciding who would and who wouldn't have a job. And most of those good guys out there would be on the line. Out on the streets, no more mortgage facilities, so no more homes. Guys who don't know any way to work but mine would be expendable. So much garbage to be swept away in the usual post-takeover clean-out.

'Do you get the picture, Jeff?' His voice was raw now with undisguised emotion. '*Everything* my ancestors worked for, everything I've worked for, everything we've all worked for would be just so much crap!'

He rose unsteadily and walked to the window. Across the street were buildings nearly as old as his. But squeezing in amongst the lovely brownstone and warm red-brick buildings were newer, uglier edifices, all glass and no substance. He considered them full of psychedelic promises but he'd still seen too many of his business associates crumble under their monstrous advances.

He turned to gaze at his second-in-command. 'I might be down, Jeff. But I'm not beaten yet! As long as there's breath in my body I'll fight for Nazareth House. Every inch of the stinking way!' His eyes had glazed and his features took on the resolve of a zealot. 'I'm about to go unethical for the first time in my career. But frankly, for the first time I don't give a shit for ethics!'

Jeff continued to stare at his boss, his mind reeling from the undercurrents of power and fierce emotion. There was nothing he could say.

David leant on the vast expanse of oak desk between them. 'I won't let Nazareth House go under the hammer. Not while two other people out there in that wide stinking world carry the name – and the responsibility of the name – Nazareth.' His eyes were gleaming now. 'Two people, Jeff. They're out there, and they *owe* me. Because of me they're both Nazareths. Only

because of *me*. And, by Christ, they'll perpetuate that name,
and this Firm. So help me God!'

Jeff felt his insides turned liquid. Jeezus! Was the man mad?
Or was this a temporary insanity occasioned by fear? He stared
at David and knew the answer.

It was obsession.

'Those kids?' he queried softly. 'Ben and Diana?'

'I sure as hell don't know any other Nazareths!' David
retorted.

'I'm not sure that I follow.' Jeff made his voice casual.

'I've told you,' David said flatly. 'I don't intend to merge
this Firm with any other. Not while I live. Not now. Not at
any time. Is that clear enough for you? Nazareth House will
never go public. And, like I said, out there are two people who
can help pull this shooting match back together again.'

'What if they aren't interested?'

'They aren't going to have any choice,' David said grimly.

'You've got to be kidding!'

'Don't put any money on that!' David's voice was a whiplash
of steely determination.

'Just what *do* you have in mind?' Jeff enquired gravely.

'Are you with me, or against me?'

The question was so direct it momentarily threw Jeff. He
leaned back and tried to read the face he'd known so long.
But it gave nothing away.

He sighed inwardly. Whatever it was, he was in already. Up
to his neck. After the funeral his own true colours had surfaced
and they'd not been a pretty sight.

He remembered it now, his inner elation and power hunger.
Mat's death had brought them out, focused them at the front
of his mind where he could no longer ignore them, or pretend
they didn't exist.

Matthew dead. Diana gone. Nazareth House without heirs.
It had been a heady combination.

He recalled now how he'd felt then. He'd actually been glad,
happy that David would now have to merge, in time. For a few

days he'd lived on a floating cloud of anticipation. He'd been second-in-command for well over twenty years. That had to be worth a seat on the board? A directorship?

Power, at last!

When realisation had dawned, it had sickened him. He had taken a few days off work – unheard of in his entire career, and had got himself methodically drunk. Pissed on his own self-loathing.

David had done everything for him, David and the Firm.

David and Nazareth House had been his life. Yet, for a Judas purse of shares and privileges, he would have sold them out.

He'd felt the worst kind of heel, the biggest sonofabitch in history. But he'd pulled himself together.

The hunger, once faced, had passed.

He lifted glowing amber eyes to his boss. He was with him, whatever it cost, whatever it took. For as long as he was needed.

'I'm with you Dave. All the way . . .'

CHAPTER NINETEEN

Diana, wearied at last from her lone walk and disturbed thoughts, turned from her distracted views of Cox and Staple Tors. Hours on the moors had done little to clear her head or ease the numbness in her mind. The granite Tors, brooding in the distance seemed symbolic of her dilemma.

It was growing dark and a freezing February wind sprang up, bringing with it the thick, eerie grey mist for which Dartmoor was notorious. Fortunately she knew her way well, and she hastened back towards Tavistock.

Life had been so peaceful during the last two years. She, Gemma and Candy had settled into a large rented house in Glanville Road and between them they had made a comfortable nest. Although a pot-pourri of colour schemes and furnishings reflective of their very different tastes, the house was undoubtedly their home. And in it they had become almost idyllically settled.

It had been too good to last.

The rain which had held off for the latter part of the afternoon now began again, causing her to sigh in exasperation.

She hurried off the moor-track, down past the golf-club and on through the busy market town. The rain was coming down in sheet's now, and the wind snatched at her flapping coat. She turned right and covered the last short distance at a sprint, arriving home breathless and soaked to the skin.

Gemma hailed her in the hall, her face pale and anxious. 'Good grief, Diana! Where've you been? I've been going crazy with worry.' She paused, bright eyes noting Diana's distress. 'Okay, bath first, questions afterwards.'

She ran up the stairs ahead of Diana, and while Diana stripped off her wet things Gemma filled the bath.

Diana slipped gratefully into the foaming water. Her head ached, her body ached, even her mind hurt, and none of her thoughts made any sense. She closed her eyes and slid further down into the warm silky depths.

'The walk didn't help, huh?' Gemma said.

'Not a lot.'

'What are you going to do?'

'Apart from getting legal advice? I just don't know, Gems.'

'Jesus wept!' Gemma's eyes glowed with anger and frustration. 'We might have known this would happen.'

'Oh, don't, Gems,' Diana sighed tiredly. 'Push off, and let me think.'

'Right. Tea then. Will you be long?'

'No longer than it takes to get my blood circulating again.'

Twenty minutes later, in pyjamas and dressing-gown, Diana padded barefoot into the sitting-room. With her still damp hair swept up into a ponytail she looked young and vulnerable.

Gemma made her voice light. 'Tea coming up. Don't know what you'd do without me to wait on you hand and foot.' She handed over a fine china cup.

'So enjoy, servant,' Diana retorted lightly. 'You know you love the luxury you live in.' She frowned. 'Talking of which, when's that job of yours going to start to pay you some decent money?'

Gemma pulled a face. 'I agreed to work on commission, you know that. And as long as Tavistock's too mean to recognise a first-class designer dress shop, I'll be earning peanuts.'

'Can Penny hang on?'

'I don't know, Di. I doubt it. She's too talented for this dump; she'd be better off in Plymouth.'

'I have to agree with that,' Diana concurred, sipping her tea. 'Tavistock's a strange place.'

'Amen!' Gemma exclaimed. 'But I told you that when you wanted to settle here. I wanted Plymouth, remember?'

'I know,' Diana agreed without rancour. 'But we had such

good times here in school holidays, and when it's not raining it's a very pretty town.'

'Yeah. So's Princetown!' Gemma retorted drily. 'And I expect Dartmoor prison's quite a fetching place in the sunlight . . .'

Diana gave her a wan smile.

Gemma put down her cup and glanced at her watch. 'Candy's late,' she commented.

'Gosh, is that the time already?' Diana looked at the clock in dismay, then her gaze flew to the pile of documents lying on her desk. 'I shan't call Boston again tonight. Pity,' she said grimly. 'I'd hoped to come back and find those were all a bad dream.'

Gemma looked at the papers with a sense of helplessness. She could almost taste the trouble they contained. 'Fat chance,' she said, her voice dull. 'You should have believed me when I said David hadn't finished with you.'

'I still can't take it in,' Diana murmured.

'Well, if you follow that shit over there, you're going to be taken in good and proper,' Gemma said without humour.

'Then why don't you try to be helpful instead of just sniping?' Diana asked. 'What I need is constructive advice.'

'Take the money and run.' Gemma's tone was deadly serious.

'What do you suppose that would solve?'

'Financial difficulties,' Gemma declared.

'I don't *have* financial difficulties,' Diana said firmly.

'Correction, Di. You didn't have. You do now.'

Diana groaned and sank back in the comfortable print-covered armchair. Gemma was right, she did now have money worries, but not through lack. Quite the opposite.

She closed her eyes in an attempt to ease the pounding in her head. The money was only the tip of the iceberg, though she neither wanted or needed the two million pounds she had just been informed was in her bank account, her part of Mat's estate.

But that was a trifling matter, compared to the other news

she had received; that Tavistock was to get a financial injection, to the tune of ten million pounds – courtesy of David Nazareth.

And an unknown American to oversee its expenditure – on the town's most 'worthy cause'.

It was crass, vulgar and obscene. It was also perhaps typically American. But it was *not* typically David. And that bothered her as much as anything else.

Why her? Why Tavistock? And why the hell couldn't he have tested his resurrected adopted son in some American town? Why did it have to be England?

The questions that had torn at her mind all day haunted her again. What was he trying to prove? Was he, as Gemma had suggested, trying to buy her good opinion of him? She shook her head disbelievingly. There were far easier ways of doing that. Twelve million pounds could have bought a lot of courting time.

No, it wasn't that simple. Yet he couldn't have pulled this thing together overnight. He had to have worked it all out very carefully. And that's what didn't make sense.

She'd had a letter from him not more than six weeks ago. A chatty, informal letter. They'd restored something of their friendship a long time ago. When David had written, asking how she was, Diana had responded warmly, and there had never been a hint that he was planning something like this. He'd never so much as made a reference to Ben. In fact, she couldn't recall him ever talking about Ben. Yet surely he should know how happy she would have been for him? To know that Ben was back in his life, that he had someone again.

Why hadn't he told her about his hopes, his dreams for his adopted son? Why spring it on her in such a mysterious fashion, without warning? And what he'd sprung on her was too unreal for words. Why had he done it?

Questions without answers. Yet. And the whole thing stank.

*　*　*

It was growing late when they heard Candy's key in the door. Moments later she rushed into the sitting-room, dripping water everywhere, her eyes huge with worry.

'Have you heard it yet . . .?' she managed breathlessly.

'Heard what?' The other two spoke at once.

'The news. It was on the radio. Of course old Mrs Wills had to go and wet her bed again and I couldn't get away, but it was on the radio . . .

'I didn't catch everything but oh, they had a lot to say.' She stuck her small chin out fiercely. 'It was awful hearing them talking about your private affairs like that.'

'Like what, Candy?' Gemma urged impatiently.

Candy's eyes rounded solemnly. 'All about your marriage to Matthew, Di . . . and about his death – and you changing your name back, and about David's adopted son coming to Tavistock . . .' She paused for breath and then continued gravely, 'They said he's on his way here, right now.'

Diana frowned, that couldn't be right!

'What else?' Gemma demanded.

'They know where you live, Diana. They gave our address on the radio.'

'You aren't serious?' Diana said faintly, her hands moving nervously to her throat.

'Totally serious,' Candy said unhappily. 'I heard that bit quite clearly. They said they're hoping to interview you soon.'

Diana crumpled in her chair. It had begun.

Gemma's mind was racing along with Diana's, but on quite a different track. That bastard had tricked Diana. Jeff Sherman's letter had warned Diana that the news could break soon – he'd even suggested that she should perhaps get out of town for a while. That slimy jerk Nazareth must have known Jeff's warning would come too late. Damn it, the letter had only arrived this morning.

They gathered silently, holding their collective breath, in front of the television later. If the local radio had the news, then so would Television South West's local coverage. A few minutes of the continuing horror over the tragic deaths of the crew of the American space shuttle, Challenger, was followed by reportage on Mikhail Gorbachov's first party congress since becoming the Soviet leader almost a year ago. Nearer to home, dozens of deaths were reported as freezing blizzards swept western Europe. The Westland affair got its usual mention, and there were fresh troubles brewing over the government's plans to introduce a poll tax in place of rates. And David Nazareth had come back to haunt them.

The local news opened with the name they had all dreaded hearing. Prepared though they were, it still shocked and mesmerised them.

'Mr David Nazareth, one of America's wealthiest men and an eligible widower, is reported to have sent his adopted son, Mr Benjamin Nazareth, to England on a benevolent mission. Reliable sources confirm that Mr Benjamin Nazareth is expected to arrive in the market town of Tavistock very shortly, where we are told his remit is to establish a trust for the town's worthiest cause. It appears the trust will have ten million pounds at its disposal.

'Speculation is growing over why Mr Nazareth has chosen a small town in England for this unusual gesture. It is, however, known that Mrs Matthew Nazareth, the widow of David Nazareth's only blood son, now resides in Tavistock under her maiden name of Lloyd-Fauvère.'

The newscaster glanced briefly at her notes before concluding. 'It does seem that Mr David Nazareth expects his widowed daughter-in-law to assist his adopted son in this unique venture.

'Mr David Nazareth was not available for comment this evening – but we will bring you any further developments in Tavistock's unexpected windfall as they come in.'

To Diana's dismay, it was not left at that. Following the announcement, a whole series of film clips and photographs were shown. Of David, of her and Matthew at parties and at their wedding. Then, sickeningly, the funeral they'd thought so private – close-up film of Diana's rose and terse message on Mat's coffin, concluded the review. The newscaster then began to detail David's business interests around the world . . .

'My God,' Diana groaned. What had he done to her? Candy jumped up and switched the set off, her face pale and worried.

'Bloody hell!' Gemma cursed angrily. 'Hanged, drawn and effing well quartered.'

'Gems . . .' Candy looked at her sister warningly, her eyes solemn with concern.

'It's true.' Diana's voice was edged with bitterness. 'It's been accomplished with a single stroke. He didn't even wait for my reply.'

'You can still tell him to go to hell,' Gemma said more reasonably. 'He can't force you into this charade, Di.'

'That's true Diana,' Candy joined in, her bright young face clouded. 'You aren't obliged. Are you?'

'Of course she's not, don't be stupid.'

'Don't start arguing you two,' Diana warned. 'We've got more important things to spend our energies on.'

'What now?' Candy asked, bemused.

'Not much we can do until tomorrow, Candy. David's away, and Jeff wasn't at Nazareth House when I called. Even Beanie's off buying fabrics somewhere.' She pretended a nonchalant shrug. 'I'll try again tomorrow. When I've had some legal advice.' She gave them a tight smile. 'Let's sleep on it. Who knows, tomorrow things might not look so dramatic.'

She was awake soon after dawn, a sudden premonition causing gooseflesh all over her body. Carefully she peered from the window. They were there, a group of shadows huddled near the sodden, tree-edged border of the lawn.

She let the curtain drop and shivered. The heating hadn't come on yet and the house felt cold. Rapidly she threw on jeans and a roll-necked cashmere sweater and, despite her own trepidation, felt a momentary sympathy for the people outside.

She forced herself to forget the pity. They were paid to get a story – and that's what they would do. Whatever it took.

Diana had no illusions about the media. She'd lived most of her life in the shadow of people who attracted public attention. And if who you were, what you did or how you earned your living was of public interest, the media did a damned good job of letting the public know about it. Now the ruthless camera-eye would focus on her and her cousins.

Over breakfast Diana explained the situation.

'But I have to go to work,' Candy said in dismay. 'I'll get the sack if I don't turn up, we're short-staffed as it is.'

'I'm the only staff there is,' Gemma put in, her dark eyes searching Diana's face.

'I know, and I'm sorry, but we have journalists and goodness knows who else camped outside, and we don't know how long they will stay there. Certainly until they get some kind of story. I shan't be opening my shop today either.' For a moment she thought of the tiny boutique, selling expensive chinaware and crystal, in the lobby of a local hotel. She had needed something to do and had built a nice little business, but it wouldn't do any good to worry about that today.

'Look, for the next few days you'll have to trust me and take my advice. I'm truly sorry, but there's not much choice for the moment.'

'I'm all for not working,' Gemma said cheerfully. 'Doesn't help relationships with my bank manager though.'

'Don't joke, Gems,' Candy said. 'But Diana, it's you they want to interview, not us. Isn't it? Why should they be interested in me?'

'Not just you and Gemma. Your parents, and my mother. If those people can't get a story out of me, they'll start turning over stones. You two will make a pretty pair to be going on with.'

'Maybe you're making more of it than there is,' Gemma said, only half-hopefully.

'Don't hold your breath,' Diana stated. 'By tonight those charmers out there will know what colour your undies are, how often you bath, when you go to sleep and who with.' She glanced meaningfully at the vivacious brunette.

'Oh lord,' Candy sighed glumly.

'Stuff David and his poxy money!' Gemma scowled.

'Amen,' Candy added spiritedly.

They laughed for the first time since the letter had arrived, breaking the tension.

'We'll have to organise ourselves,' Diana said, thinking aloud. 'No opening any of the doors. That's number one. No one comes in or goes out without my agreement. OK?'

They nodded dumbly.

'And the curtains stay closed.' Her voice was so grave that neither of them commented.

'We'll talk to as few people as possible – less chance of them learning anything through others that way; so, apart from ringing in with excuses for our absences, no unnecessary calls.'

Gemma stared at her. 'Is it really going to be that bad?'

'I think so,' Diana replied honestly. 'And if I'm any wiser from past experiences, we still won't beat them.' She shook her head again. 'They'll most likely be crawling up the waste pipes before the day is through!'

'Jesus!' Gemma raised her eyes to heaven.

'We're prisoners,' Candy said in dismay.

'More or less. But hopefully not for too long,' Diana said briskly.

'Aren't you going to talk to them at all?'

'Not until I speak to David, or get legal advice.'

'Get that first,' Gemma retorted. 'David will only box you in tighter.'

'I intend to,' Diana said as she rose from the table. 'In fact, I'll call that latest lover of yours; what's his name again?'

Gemma grinned. 'Alan Brookes-Browne.'

'I hope he's competent,' Diana said drily.

'If he's as good a lawyer as he is a lover, you're home and dry.'

'You should know. I suppose he'll be at home with his live-in wife?'

Gemma avoided the direct gaze and looked at her watch. 'Guess so, it's still only eight. Probably having breakfast.'

'And you hadn't a pre-breakfast appointment anywhere?' Diana couldn't help the dig.

Gemma frowned, but her answer was light. 'What? And miss my beauty sleep.'

'It wouldn't be the first time this week,' Diana said tautly.

'Wow! Are you mad at me?'

'No, just constantly disappointed,' Diana said quietly. 'What's his number?'

Gemma muttered the number, hating to be in Diana's black books.

Candy busied herself tidying up, her cheeks aflame with embarrassment. Gemma's love life was the only real friction between them and, like Diana, she wished that her sister would confine her affairs to single men.

At eight-fifteen Diana dialled the number and, to her chagrin, had to speak to the solicitor's wife. She gave her name and apologised for the intrusion, saying only that it was extremely urgent that she speak to Mr Brookes-Browne on a legal matter.

After a short wait a careful, well-modulated voice came on the line.

'Brookes-Browne here. How may I help you, Miss Lloyd-Fauvère?'

He obviously already knew that she was Gemma's cousin. As clearly as possible she summarised her situation. Brookes-Browne had dined out the previous evening and so had no idea of the colossal weight which had descended on the little market town. When Diana had finished her brief story, he was silent for several moments, thinking.

'You're already under siege you say?' His voice was steady, professional. Diana confirmed that they were. 'Very well. Give me an hour or so to bring myself up to date with what's what, and I'll join you at your house. You obviously don't want me to make any comment on your behalf yet? No, quite so. Let me see what I can learn. I'll be with you as soon as I can.'

Gemma had come into the sitting-room and was again her flippant self.

'Did he send me his love?'

'He was very cautious and thoroughly businesslike,' Diana said coolly. 'Gemma, you really will have to stop playing around with married men.'

Gemma gave a mock groan. 'What other kind are there?'

'Single men!' Diana exclaimed.

'In Tavistock? You've got to be joking, Di. You know as well as I do that this is the town where that famous book originated – *The World Is Full Of Married Men*'.

'Gemma!' Diana sighed with exasperation.

'Come *on*. How many single men have invited *you* out lately?' Gemma persisted.

'Point taken,' Diana admitted drily. 'But you don't have to accept the invitations, you know.'

'What, and lose all that experience? Not everyone wants to live in celibacy like you.'

'And Candy,' Diana corrected absent-mindedly, as she began plumping up cushions.

'Why pick on me today?' Gemma questioned irritably.

'I'm sorry, Gems. I guess this business with David has made me edgy. Still,' she crossed the space and hugged her cousin, 'you do worry me so. It's such a mean thing to do, and you're not a mean person. I guess I just want better things for you.' She gave the girl's shoulders a quick squeeze. 'And now that this thing has come up, I don't want to see your name plastered across some smutty tabloid's pages.'

'Cheers,' Gemma said, chastened by the thought.

'Well, don't let's think about it for now. We have enough to concern us for the time being.' Diana sifted through the documents on the desk, her gaze thoughtful. 'But after this is all sorted out, Gems, do yourself a favour and calm down a bit.'

'Calm down?'

'Yes.' Diana looked up. 'If we're lucky enough to keep your affair with Brookes-Browne secret, it won't mean that we can keep future affairs quiet. Our lives might never be the same again, you know. You and Candy will be in the spotlight – and people will notice you in future, in ways they never have before.'

'Celibacy it is then,' Gemma quipped, a little tremor in her voice.

'Well, just not married men!' Diana smiled.

Diana was relieved that the solicitor was not all good looks and charm, as she had feared might be the case. Gemma seemed not to mind what was under the skin. Looks were her priority. Looks, and a good body.

Alan Brookes-Browne appeared to have both, but he was not flaunting them today. Despite Gemma being in the room, he gave her only the most civil of greetings. His manner was crisp and concise.

'Fortunately one of my junior partners caught the news broadcast last evening, so between yourself and him I have a fairly clear picture.

'I took the liberty of making a call on your behalf, very discreetly. I spoke to a secretary at Nazareth House, who told me that David Nazareth hasn't been into his office all week, and that his personal secretary, a Mr Sherman, wasn't available to talk to me. Is Mr Nazareth in the habit of being absent?'

'Mr Brookes-Browne,' Diana said, ignoring the question, 'in future don't take any liberties on my behalf without checking with me.' Her voice was cool and unequivocal. 'I have already checked with Boston myself today; you could have saved a phone call. But no, Mr Nazareth was never in the habit of being absent.'

Brookes-Browne sat back in his chair, chastened by his client. He'd only seen Gemma's cousin from a distance, in the gift shop she ran in the Russell Hotel; now he gave her more considered attention.

He'd never been a man for blondes himself, in fact he'd always thought their Nordic colouring rather cold and insipid. Now he revised his opinion. This blonde was stunning, and far from any dumb stereotype.

Diana had spoken softly, her voice lightly husky and accentless. She was obviously well-educated, and equally obviously well-heeled financially. But quite apart from immediate appearances there was something more subtle about her attractiveness.

She was totally unflirtatious, yet she exuded sensuality; something in the movement of her hands, the toss of her hair, the depths of her extraordinary grey-blue eyes.

It was also in the way she moved her body.

But there was strength in that gaze and voice. It fascinated him. He was so absorbed in his study that he had mentally to shake himself out of it when she stopped speaking. It was one of the few occasions in his life when he had been overawed by a woman, and it was an interesting experience.

'It's very strange indeed,' Diana repeated, frowning at him.

The solicitor cleared his throat, suddenly conscious that he had been staring and that Gemma was looking daggers at him from behind her cousin's back.

'Yes, quite. Well, you know Mr Nazareth very well, so I'm sure you're right,' he said stiffly.

Diana's gaze was cool, expectant.

'Um . . . yes, well . . . if I could just glance at the documents?'

Diana handed them to him, and he concentrated his mind.

'Extraordinary,' he murmured at last. 'Most unusual.' His professional interest was back to the fore. 'And have you reached any decision?'

'Then she's not obliged to do what that bastard wants?' Gemma couldn't conceal her glee.

'Obliged? No. It's an unusual request, but however couched, it is only a request. The choice is Miss Lloyd-Fauvère's — '

'I'm well aware of that,' Diana interrupted coolly. 'What I want to know is whether we can, in fact, establish a trust of this nature – whether David Nazareth has the power to impose his will on a town in this way.'

The luminous eyes appraised him seriously.

'Anyone can spend their money as they wish, if that's what you mean?'

'I'd just like to be certain,' Diana repeated.

'Of course. I'll do some checking. Meanwhile, is there anything else that I ought to know?'

'Such as?' Diana asked cautiously.

'Well, do you think your ex-father-in-law has any ulterior motive in making Tavistock his beneficiary in this way?'

The solicitor noted the sudden undercurrent of tension in the room.

'Plenty,' Gemma muttered under her breath, as Diana glared at her.

'I'd like to think not, she replied carefully. 'But I can't be one hundred per cent sure.'

'I see,' Alan Brookes-Browne said, aware that he didn't see at all. 'And you've never met this adopted son?'

'No. Never,' Diana said frankly. 'It's one of the things that bother me most. You see, it's out of character for David to behave in such a high-handed manner, and I admit to being angry as well as puzzled.'

'That's hardly surprising,' Brookes-Browne said drily. 'You are expected to take on a venture of this complexity, out of the blue, and with a man you have never met – correct?' His keen eyes studied her openly now.

'It's bloody blackmail,' Gemma blurted out angrily, unable to contain herself any longer. 'And you know it, Diana.'

'Blackmail?' The solicitor's eyebrows rose attentively.

'Not the kind you could take that to mean,' Diana replied swiftly. 'Gemma's just over-protective.'

'Any form of blackmail, Miss Lloyd-Fauvère, is distasteful,' he said carefully. 'And if it might affect the people of this town, then perhaps I should know about it.'

Diana glanced angrily at her cousin. It hadn't been necessary to involve anyone else in such a personal matter. But she would have to reassure him now.

'It is a purely private matter between David and myself,' she said wearily. 'Something that happened a long time ago, and is totally irrelevant.'

'Can I be the judge of that?' the solicitor said smoothly, his curiosity whetted. 'I really can't act properly without all the facts.'

Diana shook her head with annoyance. Was she never to be allowed to forget the past?

She stared into space as she began to summarise the situation as best she could.

'I cannot say that I was immune to him as a man,' she finished. 'And because of that I decided to leave Boston. I came here to build a new life, and have done so successfully. End of story.'

For a few moments the solicitor digested her words.

'And to the best of your knowledge that, um, affection, is historical, rather than current?'

'Certainly.'

'Rubbish!' Gemma said scornfully. 'That's bullshit, Diana, and you know it.' Gemma turned flashing dark eyes on the solicitor. 'It's only true as far as Diana's concerned. David has *never* let her go, and *will* never let her go. This cock-up is the proof.'

'You don't seem to agree on the finer details of these matters,' the solicitor said pleasantly, skilfully drawing the two women out.

'Gemma's talking nonsense,' Diana said lightly, wanting the subject closed once and for all.

'Like hell I am!' Gemma declared angrily. 'If David's not planning to use Benjamin in some way to get you back, then I'm not Gemma Lloyd.'

'Even if that were the case,' Brookes-Browne said carefully, 'there's no law against against it to my knowledge — '

'I just don't want to see her hurt again,' Gemma said mutinously.

'Me neither,' Candy declared, speaking for the first time, and causing them all suddenly to notice her presence, which made her blush furiously.

'Coffee anyone?' she said over-brightly, jumping up nervously.

'I thought you'd never ask,' Brookes-Browne said with a smile, dispersing the tension.

Candy disappeared through to the kitchen and Gemma, feeling suddenly ashamed, followed her.

'They seem very fond of you,' he said kindly.

'It's mutual,' Diana replied. 'I know that they worry about David's intentions, but I wish that they would accept that I'm old enough to manage without wet-nurses.'

'Quite,' the solicitor responded comfortably. 'But that's typical family for you. However, now that we are nurseless, so to speak, do you believe that your father-in-law is making this gesture solely to regain your affections?'

'Hardly,' Diana said. 'There must be plenty of other ways he could have done that.' She lapsed into a thoughtful silence for several moments before continuing as if she were talking to herself. 'But I don't understand it. If David had wanted my help with Ben, why couldn't he have asked for it? Why this intrigue? And why this grotesque business about a trust?'

'Perhaps we both need answers to that,' the solicitor commented gravely.

'I would have understood.' Diana ignored his comment. 'I would have been glad to help.' Suddenly her eyes flashed. 'But I *am* angry at the way this has all happened.' She made a helpless gesture with her hands. 'It could affect Gemma and Candy's lives, and that makes me *very* angry.'

Alan Brookes-Browne closed his briefcase and gazed at the young woman speculatively. He wondered if she realised that most people would give their eye-teeth to be in her position, and that few people would be showing such concern for relatives at such a time.

'This, um, separate inheritance of yours – from your husband's estate, wasn't it? Why do you suppose that it has taken so long to administer? Two years is a long time – particularly for a man with a whole team of lawyers at his disposal.'

Diana felt the cold fingers of the iron hand in the velvet glove. But she knew that encouraging any further speculation would not help establish the right relationship between her and this man.

'David knew that I didn't want anything of Mat's,' she said quietly. 'Why he has chosen to forget that fact, I don't know.'

'You mean you might have refused it, given the choice?'

'No might about it.'

'Two *million* pounds, Miss Lloyd-Fauvère?' The man's voice rose in disbelief.

'Two, or ten,' Diana stated emphatically. 'I have no need of Mat's money, and no desire for it. My father left me very comfortable financially. I work because I wish to, but I don't need to, Mr Brookes-Browne.'

'But it is still quite a coincidence, isn't it – your inheritance arriving at the same time as this other event?'

Diana knew exactly what he meant.

'That's something else to resolve when I speak to David,' she said dismissively. It was, after all, no concern of his.

Alan Brookes-Browne sat back, openly curious. Despite the enormity of these events she seemed almost detached.

Ten million pounds to lavish on some worthy cause, and two millions pounds, plus whatever else she might be worth, in her pocket. He shook his head. It would be an interesting case – and that was the understatement of the year.

Soon after that the solicitor left the house, only stopping to comment to the press that his client was not ready to make any statements yet.

He had with him the documents from Boston, ostensibly to photocopy them for the record. But he was keen to study them more fully in the privacy of his own office. He'd have a colleague run over them, see what he made of them.

He strode cheerily despite the drizzling rain. Mr David Nazareth had certainly injected some excitement into his humdrum daily routine. Pity about the little affair with Gemma. It was over, of course. He couldn't afford to damage his reputation now. And he didn't doubt that the event would boost his career considerably. Now, if he could also win the handling of the trust . . .

He felt extremely optimistic as he made a brief detour to the local vicarage. He had suggested asking the young vicar, Pritchard Gilwin, to call on the household in Glanville Road. There would undoubtedly be errands to run, and the women could be under siege for days.

Later that day, Diana sat broodingly by the phone. It was already after eleven in the morning in Boston and still she hadn't been able to reach David. All she could learn was that he wasn't there, but that Jeff Sherman would be available after lunch. It meant she'd have to ring again in the evening.

On Martha's Vineyard, an island off the coast of Cape Cod, New England, David was taking a call from Jeff Sherman in Boston.

'We're on our way, Dave. All systems go.'

'She's had the letter, and all the documents?'

'Yep. She's called several times already. I'm counting on talking to her myself pretty soon now.'

David's voice was tense. 'You've covered the supposed "leak"?'

'Well, I shall do when I speak to her.'

'And Benjamin?' The strain was more noticeable now. 'He's bought all of it?'

Jeff gave a short laugh. 'You worry too much. Didn't I say every guy has his price? Relax, Dave. I put him on the plane myself, an hour ago. In just about eight hours' time he'll be on his way from London to Devon.'

There was a small silence.

Jeff Sherman broke into it, jokingly. 'He sure doesn't like you too much right now. But he's on his way, OK? He's bought the whole package. Didn't like the wrappings, or the price, but he sure wants what's inside.'

'Damned fool!' David snapped, irrationally.

'Yeah. Well, you'd better be glad he is,' Sherman said easily. 'If he wasn't, this little scheme of yours would still be on the drawing-board.'

'Never would've taken Ben for a fool,' David muttered.

'He's not,' Sherman contradicted himself evenly. 'You're just much smarter than he is, that's all.'

David sighed audibly, then snapped again. 'He's damned lucky to even get this much of a shot at the pot, after what that jerk did to me.'

'Too right,' Sherman agreed amicably. But he felt sickened, with pity for Dave, and for Ben – and with loathing for himself. Ben didn't deserve this crap. Sure, he'd walked out all those years ago, but not without damned good reason. No, it wasn't fair on Ben. He was one very nice guy. And clever. The memory of how he'd had to work on Ben made him sweat.

It had taken every ounce of cunning he could muster. David had allowed only one meeting between his estranged adopted son and himself. The rest had been down to Sherman.

Now Jeff only had one consolation. At least Ben would come out of it a wealthy man.

He pulled himself together to catch what his boss was saying. Either the line was bad or Dave was having a hard time as well.

'No Dave, there's no sweat,' he replied to the faint question.

'No one has any idea where you are. The official line at Nazareth House is that you're on a delicate government job. That'll keep anyone from asking or answering any questions inside the Firm.'

'When do we hear?'

'My guess is soon,' Jeff said placatingly. 'You just enjoy the fishing out there and stop worrying. But stay close to a phone. If all goes to plan you should be talking to Diana yourself later today.'

David replaced the receiver and wandered out on to the terrace of the rented beach home. It was too damned cold to go down on to the beach, never mind go fishing. He stared out across the ocean.

The sea was swollen, dark and angry. Somehow it reassured him. It matched his mood exactly. The ocean met a grey and navy sky, sombre and threatening. David shivered and pulled his collar up closer around his neck. There was still more snow out there, plenty of it.

He turned back into the house, too distracted to enjoy the intricately carved fretwork canopy of the timber cottage, a famous feature of the homes here in the wealthy beach area of Edgartown. Instead, he returned to the warmth of the blazing log fire and settled himself on a sheepskin-covered settee. He'd brought several books for his short exile and one of them lay unopened by his side.

He poured himself a large dose of bourbon, his third that day, from the well-stocked tray by his side and picked up the paperback idly. The glaring title and cover picture blurred and danced before his eyes. He swore quietly and threw it to the far end of the settee.

He rubbed his eyes. Sometime he'd have to get an optical test. He'd had several of these odd visual disturbances lately.

'Tension,' he muttered to himself. 'Nothing that having Diana back wouldn't cure.'

But, even as he spoke the words reassuringly aloud, a hard knot of fear formed inside him. He had never been a man for idle health worries, and surely he'd been under greater stresses, worse pressures, during his business career? What then could account for his sudden concern?

He shook his head, angered with himself. This was no time to start fretting like an old woman over a stress-related symptom. When he got back to the mainland he'd get his eyes checked. He grimaced. He'd probably have to start wearing spectacles. Now that'd be a nice ego blow.

Despite the vanity behind his thoughts, he frowned. Was he worried about his appearance? Did he really consider that wearing glasses even came into the problem he was facing?

No, he wasn't that vain, or that stupid.

It might have been the bourbon, or the warmth of the fire, but a small trickle of sweat ran under his collar. He was conscious of it. Lately he was acutely conscious of everything.

He could even pinpoint the precise moment of his new self-awareness.

It had been when Benjamin had walked into his office.

David had never had reason to feel unequal to any man in his life, had never met a man he envied, never met a man he knew he couldn't handle. But Benjamin at eighteen and Benjamin at thirty-two were two entirely different people. David hadn't expected the lad to have turned into a freak. But neither had he expected what he'd got.

Not at the time. Since then he'd realised his own mistake. But on that day?

On that day David had recognised the first flaw in his plan, the first, and the biggest. But it was only with hindsight that the recognition had registered for what it was. At first he had merely been temporarily stunned. He'd covered his own confusion swiftly but the shock had gone deep.

His fingers clenched around the whisky glass. Ben's face seemed to be etched on to his retinas. He couldn't look anywhere without seeing that face, the face of his once beloved child.

Ben's face. Not merely handsome; something more than handsome. Infinitely more.

His hand shook as he reached distractedly for a refill; then he recalled Ben's eyes, and he pulled back from the bottle as if he'd been stung.

No! He couldn't afford to drink any more today. *Especially* not today. He had to keep his wits absolutely clear now because soon Ben would be arriving in Tavistock.

A low oath erupted from his frustration, the sound strange and hollow in the silent room. Ben in Tavistock, with Diana. And he was entirely responsible, just as he'd been once before, with Mat.

The glass crashed into the stone fireplace, causing the logs to hiss and spit as the remnants of whisky hit the flames.

He rose swiftly, ignoring the swirling mists before his eyes. He couldn't sit any longer. Goddamn it, why the hell didn't the phone ring? He began to pace the long room.

He knew now that he'd been every kind of fool under the sun. Oh sure, his plan was workable. It was, he was sure, just about foolproof. Except for Ben. Ben was the unknown factor, the one thing David could not be sure of. Worse, for the first time, the only time ever, his certainty of Diana had faltered.

Whatever David had expected of Ben, it wasn't what he'd got. What he'd got was The Enemy, a cool, ruthless, brilliant enemy. His own son. The man he'd pulled back out of obscurity for his own ends was the one man in this whole world who should never have been used.

He ceased pacing, pausing before the window to stare out beyond the gardens to the angry, swollen waters. An ocean the colour of Ben's eyes. Dark, passionate, filled with hate, burning with tempest.

If the sun were to slash a brilliant ray down upon that seething mass right now, it would be just exactly the same flash of menacing green brightness that had blinded him so recently in Boston.

He turned away from the view, shaken to his very soul by

the knowledge of what he had brought into being. Ben's hatred had been a bitter enough pill, but he'd expected to have to swallow something similar – so it was not that alone that he feared. It was Ben himself: his beloved Ben, his hated Ben.

If it weren't such a tragic irony it might have given him something of satisfaction. To have raised a foundling to such standing, to such a brilliant future, could, once, have been a reward greater than he could have dreamed of.

But not now. Not any more.

He had provided his own arch-enemy.

Ben was more than capable of destroying the only thing David had left, his increasingly desperate hope of a reunion with Diana. Now he had only one hope left, and that was that Diana would be immune to Ben, as immune as she had been to all other men except himself.

He moved a chair closer to the fire, and pulled the phone on to his lap.

The double agony of his love-hate for Ben and his consuming love for Diana tortured his mind.

Surely Jeff's call would come soon?

CHAPTER TWENTY

Benjamin Nazareth pounded along the sand, the noise of his breathing and erratic pulse drowned by the thunderous waves of the ocean as they broke along the shore. Sweat ran into his eyes, and he dragged a sweatshirt sleeve across them to clear his vision, sufficiently at least to make out his path. He'd been running hard for over half an hour and his lungs were beginning to feel as if they'd soon burst. Sense dragged at his subconscious and he slowed his pace, easing out of the run into a jogging stride.

Although it was winter and the Pacific was today surfed and swollen, it was still clear enough for him to make out the headland of distant San Diego. It was a day to match his mood, grey and unsettled.

He gentled down to a fast walk, and eventually stopped altogether, dropping to the sand in a heaving, sweating heap.

He stretched out, struggling to regain his breath, fighting to overcome the fury still raging in his heart. Gradually his breathing eased and he was able to take air without gulping it in laboured bursts. The hammering in his temples slowed to a dull throb and he lay quite still on his back, letting the distortions of his pulse and heart settle to a more regular rhythm.

Several minutes passed before he felt inclined to sit up, and when he did he was more annoyed than surprised to see how far he was from home. What in hell had made him take those calls from Boston? He shook sweat from his hair as he sought answers within himself. He needn't have done it; no one had forced him.

A large naval vessel appeared on the horizon. He watched its progress absently, his thoughts far away in another world.

Europe . . . He tasted the word and knew that he should feel something. Interest? Speculation? Something. But he couldn't. Not at the moment. Not while he was still reeling from shock.

Europe was a dream he'd had for a long time, so long, in fact, that now, when it was within reach, he couldn't experience anything. All he could think of was how he'd reacted to seeing the old man again, and the promises the meeting had spelled out.

Nazareth House. His one-time life, preserved in a glass jar labelled 'The Past', was now offered to him on a plate.

For a price.

The price was that he'd have to live in England for at least five years, carry out David's orders, put into action David's plans.

He'd have to try to work with a woman he'd never met. Matthew's left-overs.

It stank beyond belief.

What in hell was he doing even considering it?

He began the journey back, jogging gently this time, letting the quiet rhythm build up until he was breathing easily in tune with his body movements. He was a powerful man with a lot of stamina, but he'd pushed himself enough today. Anger had given him impetus. Now the anger had gone, to be replaced with a sense of impotence.

In the apartment he called home his answering machine light glowed. He stared at the machine thoughtfully. It could be Sherman, wanting his answer. Or it could be anyone.

He turned on the shower. He knew it was Sherman, and he'd just have to wait. Right now he was incapable of talking to him.

For the second time in Ben's thirty-two years, David Nazareth had reached out to pluck him out from obscurity, to set him upon a course already planned for him. The only difference this time was that he had a choice.

The shower only served to cleanse his body, it did nothing for his mind. Neither did a cold beer erase the bitter taste in his mouth.

He arranged a stack of light symphonies on his music centre and stretched out on a sofa. Music was soothing, something he sought for pleasure, for company and, as now, for distraction. But memories of the brief meeting with David ran around and around in his head, refusing to be put aside even for a moment.

It had been surreal . . .

Three weeks ago, midway through the evening, he'd been working on some papers when the telephone had rung. He'd been slightly annoyed at the disturbance and resolved to put the caller off briskly. The papers had been needed for the next morning's court session.

'Nazareth,' he'd answered curtly.

'Ben?' A familiar voice, nothing more.

'That's right.'

'Jeff Sherman, Ben. Remember me?' The voice had been easy.

'Sherman . . . of Boston?' He'd felt a sudden pull at his insides. He'd covered a lot of distance and years since he'd last heard that voice. He'd stiffened, his senses suddenly alert.

'None other,' Sherman had said, still in that easy way, as though it had only been yesterday. 'How're you doing Ben?'

'Fine.' What else could he have said?

'That's good. Glad to know that, Ben.'

Ben had shifted uneasily. 'Is there something I can do for you?' he'd asked cautiously.

'I hope so, Ben. I hope so,' the voice had repeated quietly. 'As I hope you will forgive this intrusion. I know it's been a long time . . . and you, uh, haven't been in touch . . .'

'Could you come to the point?' Ben had interrupted. 'I have paperwork to clear for a case tomorrow.' He had not been cold but not warm either. He hadn't even really grown curious yet. It was as if someone outside himself was talking through him, listening through him. He'd felt a slight but detached interest, nothing more.

'Your father would like you to come to Boston, Ben,'

Sherman had said. 'If you can manage it? He has something of importance he'd like to discuss with you.'

Ben had felt the knot then, looping around his gut. 'I don't have a father,' he'd said very quietly.

Jeff Sherman had sighed deeply. 'I know, Ben. That's how you feel. Can't say I blame you.'

'Right,' Ben had replied. 'So you have my answer.'

'You do know that Mat's dead?' Sherman's voice had been almost apologetic.

That had silenced him. He made a point of not reading any of the society papers or Boston-based newspapers. He hadn't wanted to know anything about Nazareth House.

'Two years ago,' Sherman had continued. 'No heirs . . .'

Ben felt the knot again. 'I don't see what that has to do with me.'

'Your father is a sick man.' Sherman had pulled his ace. 'Ben, he needs you. More to the point perhaps, Nazareth House needs you.'

Ben had grown icy cold, but then beads of perspiration had broken out on his forehead. 'Look, I don't know what this is about, Sherman. I left Boston, and everything in Boston, a lifetime ago. Nothing's changed.'

Jeff Sherman's voice had been gentle. 'Yeah, I know, but circumstances can change, Ben. People can change. I know it's asking a lot, but all Dave wants is to talk to you. Don't give me an answer now, sleep on it.'

'There's nothing to sleep on,' Ben had responded stiffly through his constricted throat.

'Just think about it overnight, Ben. David is sick. There are no heirs. Nazareth House is wide open for grabs, unless . . .' He paused. 'But, like I said, all Dave wants is to talk things over with you. Just, please, give it a lot of thought. I'll call you tomorrow.'

He hadn't been able to concentrate on work again that night, but had paced his apartment until very late. He'd never contemplated anything like this. As far as he'd been concerned, Nazareth House was dead and buried, beyond his reach, gone.

He'd thought his old dreams long spent, but that night he relived them: his old longing to be part of that great old Firm; his dream to be everything his father would respect and love, to be a good lawyer, for David; to be the son David would be proud to have at his side. At the helm of Nazareth House.

It had been a night of anguish and pain. Greater than the pain he'd suffered years before, when youth and pride had sustained him through desolation. Now he was a man, a man who'd been raised in success and luxury in Boston, and had given it away for sweat and tears and the toil of many lonely years.

He was a man with a solid career ahead of him, a career he'd carved out for himself. He was a solitary man, but with longings for family and roots. In his heart he belonged nowhere, but belonging was what he wanted more than anything else. His life now was well-planned, executed with studious care. He worked harder than anybody he knew, for the rewards he remembered only too well.

He had built himself a perfect retreat, had the job he wanted for the moment, the apartment he'd slogged to pay for.

He'd chosen the small company he worked for with great care, knowing that he could get all the experience he needed in splendid isolation. His leisure time was clear-cut. Daily, he swam, jogged, worked out. He kept himself in peak condition physically – and mentally. Sexual liaisons were an indulgence he rarely allowed himself.

Love was a luxury he hadn't yet been able to contemplate.

All the defences of his life had crumbled that night. All his far-reaching plans had fallen apart. In the stark light of dawn he'd gazed out across the ocean, towards the East Coast. Towards Boston. And David.

And he was filled with self-loathing, knowing that it had taken only one call to break fourteen years of his proud, miserable exile.

The stack of records came to an end and the sudden silence brought him back abruptly to the present. The light on the answerphone still glowed reprovingly, but his memories rolled on again.

The meeting had been easier than he'd imagined it would be. David had looked all of his sixty-two years, but his illness had not diminished him either in appearance or in presence. He was still the same magnetic man, electric in voice, compelling in charm.

It had been later, after the initial edges had been cautiously skirted, that he'd learned just what it was that David had in mind.

He should have walked out then, but he'd felt pity for the old man, pity enough to hear him out. He still should have left after that. Yet the web had been spun, and he had stayed glued to its surface.

There had been several moments for the truth. He'd let them all pass, and had kept on listening. True, he'd shown his disgust, his distaste – but he hadn't walked out.

Now it was as if his anger burned at a small altar deep within him, the flame controlled before the greater deity of ambition. David Nazareth had outlined his crazy conditions, conditions that no one in their right mind would accept, but he had not refused him.

He could not.

Nazareth House had been dangled as bait and nothing else would have kept him there, listening. Nothing else would have made him promise, coldly, to consider it. But he knew he was going to sell his soul to David in return for Nazareth House. He was only stalling so that the old man would sweat; stalling in order to kid himself that he had to think it over.

But there was nothing to think over. There never had been. David knew it. Sherman knew it. Now Ben himself knew it.

Before he had returned Jeff Sherman's call that night, a new flame joined the first. Together they burned white in Ben's heart.

Anger. And hate.

The first born of injured pride, and years of loneliness.

The second born out of what had long ago been unconditional, devoted love for the father he had adored.

The man he now hated with all his soul . . .

The first-class cabin lights were dimmed and Ben's fellow passengers slept, but the steady humming rhythm of the jet engines kept Ben wakeful – and very aware of the momentous journey he was making.

'Diana Nazareth.' He tasted the sound in his mouth, and found it dry, insubstantial. If, as he suspected, David was in love, or lust, with her, then why the preposterous marriage clause? He'd got no answers in Boston, just a take-it-or-leave-it attitude. He'd taken it. Had to. Or he wouldn't be here now.

But it still didn't make sense to him.

It was one of the first things he intended to get clear in his mind. Very clear.

And if this Diana Nazareth had any designs on the Nazareth empire via him, he'd damned sure put her straight. Ben had no intention of marrying anyone, let alone David's choice.

Consider marrying Mat's widow? *Never.*

He'd stick the five years out, yes. But David could whistle for any other hopes.

Celibacy, if necessary, Ben could handle.

CHAPTER TWENTY-ONE

It was afternoon in Tavistock before Diana reached Jeff, whose immediate friendliness and informality seemed markedly out of tune with the chaos surrounding her. She had to cut through his greetings, the unnecessary enquiries after her health.

'Jeff, I don't have the time to waste on banalities. Just tell me where I can reach David.'

'Ah,' Jeff's voice was like silk. 'You've had our missives, then?'

'I most certainly have,' Diana retorted. 'And I'm far from amused, Jeff. I want to talk to David. Immediately.'

'Not possible, I'm afraid,' Jeff lied easily. 'But I'm sure I can help you; what's the prob — '

'What do you mean, not possible?' Diana interrupted. 'Where *is* David?'

Jeff allowed himself an audible sigh. 'Uh, there are things going on here. Serious things.' He slipped effortlessly into his rehearsed role. 'I'm under a lot of pressure here at the moment. Things are difficult, Diana, with David so — '

Diana stepped neatly into the trap. 'What's happening, Jeff? What's going on? Where the hell is David? Damn it, Jeff, I'm under siege from the press; a virtual prisoner in my own home.'

'Jeezus! How the . . .?' Jeff swung into pretended horror. 'What in hell made you involve the press?'

'*Me*?' Diana's astonishment was total. 'You mean *you* didn't tell them, Nazareth House didn't tell them?'

'Christ, Diana, do you think we're that stupid? God, David will freak. Some bastard has leaked that info. We'd hoped to get your consent back by now, then we'd have gone to press,' he added in pained shock. 'Ben will have to be told – he's on his way right now. He'll walk into it unprepared — '

'On his way . . .?' Diana's voice echoed down the line. 'What are you talking about? Why would Ben be on his way now?'

'I don't understand this,' Jeff stalled. 'You *did* get the note telling you Ben was arriving in London this evening?'

Diana was stunned, her head spinning. 'This *evening*? Jeff, I only got the request to help yesterday morning — '

Jeff groaned loudly. 'Jeezus, what in hell's gone wrong . . .? I'll have someone's guts for this — '

Diana snapped back: 'Whatever has gone wrong, pal, had better be fixed. Pretty damned quick! David has no right to do — '

'Honey,' Jeff soothed. 'David would hit the sky if he knew this cock-up had happened. Christ knows how I'm going to keep it from him.'

'Keep it . . .?' Diana's voice became stony. 'Where the hell is David? I want to talk to him, *now*.'

It was time for Jeff to deal the ace. 'In his condition, honey, that wouldn't be wise.'

Diana froze. 'His condition . . .? Jeff, either you tell me right now or I'll take the next plane and come and find out for myself!'

'David will have my balls!'

'You're running out of time,' Diana warned.

'He's sick, Diana. *Real* sick.'

'Where is he?'

'In a clinic. Not here in Boston. Couldn't let anyone know what had happened. But he's recovering, Diana. That's what counts,' Jeff said swiftly, letting his concern show.

Anger and fear misted her vision. She rubbed her eyes, every kind of emotion flooding her body, but her voice was strangely calm. 'Either I speak to him today, Jeff – or I will be on the first plane I can get. That's a promise.'

'Diana, my damned job's on the line here — '

'Today, Jeff!'

Jeff sighed. 'This has to be confidential, Diana, you understand that?'

'Nothing's confidential,' Diana snapped. 'Not unless I speak
to David today. So get off the line and get David to call me –
or put me in touch with his doctor. Either one, Jeff, and you
haven't much time, so you'd better move.'

Diana hung up, shaken to the core of her being. David ill?
And it had to be kept secret from Boston? She didn't dare to
imagine what it might imply. It was all so crazy: David sick
enough to be in some secret clinic, the press on her doorstep,
Ben on his way here, and this bloody trust.

Why was she letting this happen? She wasn't involved with
the Nazareths any more. God, hadn't she suffered enough
from that family?

But she knew she would go through with it.

She had aborted the one heir David might have had. And
telling herself now that a child born of rape would probably
have been a bad apple didn't help. It *could* have been Mat's
child, in which case it would have had David's blood. But she
had played God; she alone had decided the fate of the unborn
innocent.

And for the rest of her life she would have to bear the
consequences . . .

When she came back into the drawing-room Gemma was
shocked at her pallor.

They were alone, but Gemma wouldn't ask what had happened. When Diana was ready she'd tell what she wanted her
to know.

Diana seemed locked in a world of her own as she began
quietly to pace up and down, hands deep in her pockets, head
bowed in thought.

Gemma watched, fuming, damning David Nazareth to hell.
Diana was falling apart again.

'You'll wear the carpet out,' she finally said.

'Nonsense,' Diana replied absently, continuing to pace.

'Diana, you're driving me crazy!'

Diana stopped pacing and stared at Gemma as if only just

noticing she was there. 'Sorry,' she grimaced. 'I was just mulling things over.'

'Get anywhere?'

'Nowhere sensible,' Diana admitted, but she sat down.

'Want to talk about it?' Gemma asked gently, but at that moment the telephone rang.

Diana was across the room in seconds.

'Diana Nazareth,' she answered automatically, and Gemma groaned in despair. Diana hadn't used that name since Paris.

'Oh, Mr Brookes-Browne . . . I was expecting a call from Boston.'

'Still no news then?'

Diana wasn't supposed to tell anyone, but this was her legal adviser. He should at least know in principle.

'David is apparently quite ill, but I do expect to hear from him tonight.'

'Hum, not the best news. Anything else?

'Only that Nazareth House didn't give that release. I spoke to David's personal secretary and he says it was a leak. The requests are supposed to have reached me well before now – I don't yet know what went wrong. Oh, and Ben is arriving in London tonight. Apparently he doesn't know about the leak — '

'How very unlikely,' the solicitor said drily.

'That was my first thought,' Diana admitted. 'But I think there's more to David's illness than I know yet, and whatever his plans were, they might well have been affected by that. Once I have his call, I'll be in a better position to judge.'

'Fine. What I really called about was to tell you that the Reverend Gilwin is going to call on you. I'll pop round myself about ten-ish. Hopefully you'll have had that call.'

In the background Gemma held her tongue, but her instincts were in overdrive. Whatever the bullshit was about David's health, she knew Diana would hear him out. And Diana was ripe for plucking . . .

* * *

The Reverend Pritchard Gilwin turned out to be a delightful young man, and endeared himself to the three of them.

Kind brown eyes shone out from a chubby face, and he made light of the press's reaction to his visit, saying that he'd voiced his concern for their well-being if they were kept hanging about outside in such inclement weather.

'I told them they were welcome to refreshments at the vicarage, but they seem content to take turns at the pub. It's their loss, though. My wife's cucumber sandwiches are all the rage.'

Gemma burst out laughing, imagining a huddle of sensation-seeking journalists making polite conversation with the vicar. 'They wouldn't get what they want at the vicarage!'

'Well, not the beer or the gossip perhaps.' Pritchard smiled. 'And Eucharist didn't seem quite what they sought either.'

Pritchard was a pet, and he was also to be their staunchest ally in the months to come. But for now he was their contact with the outside world; the fetcher of groceries, newspapers and sundry items; and the bringer of laughter and light.

'You seem to be something of a mixed blessing for our little town, Diana,' he said with amusement later, as they all sat around the fire.

'Not by choice,' Diana assured him.

'Not yours anyway,' he agreed. He had listened carefully to Alan Brookes-Browne's brief summary of the situation that afternoon. He had also watched the news the previous evening and, reading between the lines, had correctly assessed the enormity of the problem.

'You have a difficult task ahead of you, if you agree to take it on,' he said mildly, accepting a third cup of tea. 'If you go ahead you will make friends and enemies. And if you don't go ahead, you will make friends and enemies.'

'What?' Diana queried.

'If you become lady bountiful, you will favour some and not others. If you reject this trust, you will upset some of the people already planning to benefit from its coffers,' he explained brightly. 'Either way, you can't win.'

'Charming thought,' Gemma said.

'It's not Diana's fault,' Candy protested indignantly.

'We all know that,' Pritchard said kindly. 'But the devil has his day, I'm afraid.'

'Devil David, you mean.'

'Gemma!' Diana warned.

'Is that how you see Mr Nazareth? How interesting?' The vicar smiled gently at Gemma. 'But perhaps we shouldn't be too un-Christian about a potential benefactor — '

The telephone interrupted him and Diana was out of her seat at once. 'I'll take that in the study,' she said quickly, and hurried from the room.

'Speak of the devil,' Gemma muttered angrily.

Diana's heart began to race as soon as she heard David's warm Boston accent.

'Diana? It's me, honey.'

'David! Where in God's name are you?'

'Now, honey, you're not to worry your pretty head about me. I'm fine, now . . .' He paused briefly. 'Had some problems getting to a phone, though. You know what these people are like, frightened to let you move in case of lawsuits.'

'David . . . please don't do this to me,' Diana whispered, sinking to a chair, her knees jellied. 'Tell me what's wrong.'

He smiled to himself. It was working. 'Nothing that rest and time won't cure. The big man here is pleased with my progress.'

'What happened?'

'Oh, you know how these things go, princess. One minute fine, the next flat on my back. I just have to take things a bit easier from now on.'

He allowed a silence to follow, not too long, but long enough.

'Are you still there? Look, I'm going to be just great. Just have to be more careful in future. But, as the doc says, I'm lucky. I've had a warning. Gives me chance to set my house in order, as they say.'

Diana was shaken. 'Oh, David . . . can I do anything?'

'Not a thing, honey, except be your sweet, loving self.'

'David, I'm sorry, I wouldn't want to stress you, but when I spoke to Jeff about Ben and this trust thing, he was so vague. I *had* to speak to you.'

'That's OK, honey,' David soothed. 'I just wish to hell it hadn't all happened like this. Jeff's told me about the chaos at your end. But, Diana, I can't do a damned thing from here.

'I had intended to talk to you myself, before this happened. Guess my timing was lousy. Not for the first time, eh?' He let the implications of that sink in. 'But this is no time for recriminations or regrets. No time at all. I don't even know how much time there is but, honey, I really need your help.'

'Of course.' Diana's voice was flat, all the things she had been going to say erased by the helplessness she felt.

'Honey, I know this is a lot to ask, but please, meet with Ben, and think it over. Will you just do that for me, princess? I *have* to test him, and you are the only person I trust unreservedly. You know what Nazareth House means to me and now that you and Mat are both gone' – his voice tailed off momentarily, allowing the silence to emphasise his meaning – 'I have to give Ben a chance. He's all I've got.'

'Of course,' Diana repeated. 'I understand that. But, David, why Tavistock?'

'Because *you* are there,' David said quietly. 'Who else could sort a Nazareth out better than you? If Ben's not the guy to inherit, you're the one person I trust to spot it. But, honey, I hope you won't have to do that. Without an heir, generations of hard work and love will be lost.'

'I understand,' Diana said. And the trouble was that she did.

'I'm begging,' David continued, in the same, almost weary voice. 'I don't know Ben any more. We're strangers to one another. He might not be able to handle it. But I have to try with him. He's my only hope.'

'All right,' Diana reluctantly agreed. 'I'll meet Ben, and we'll take it from there. But I'm not making any promises – that has to be very clear. After I've met him, we'll see.'

'That's all I'm asking,' David lied.

'And I do want to know how you're progressing, and when you get home. You have to promise to keep me informed – no more surprises. Promise?'

'You'll know,' David assured her. 'Just one other point for now, sweetheart. You won't mention my, uh, health problems? You know what the grapevine is like; they'll have me in my coffin in no time. And that wouldn't do the Firm any good at all.'

Diana found she had agreed and David had gone before she'd begun to think straight. She replaced the phone with shaking fingers, and dropped her head into her hands.

Oh God! He was really ill. Ill, and alone. And it was her fault.

If only she'd stayed with him!

She thought of the child she had aborted, and tears sprang to her eyes. She had killed the child who could have been David's grandchild for her own selfish reasons. Why in God's name hadn't she found the courage to tell him about Mat in the first place? Maybe Mat could have been helped, maybe later they could have had children?

She had deprived David of everything, had let him down. And she had loved him, in a way.

And yet, unbelievably, he still loved her. It had been in his voice. What had she done to deserve that love? Or the trust he was putting in her?

So she would help him, no matter what it took. It was too late to undo the harm she had done him, but it was not too late to help him with Ben.

She would find a way to repay him for all that she owed him. Somehow.

But she knew that no one, certainly not Gemma, would ever understand . . .

Alan Brookes-Browne stepped into a full-blown row.

'You have to be bloody mad!' Gemma was shouting.

'No! I'm quite sane, Gemma. I've made my decision and I intend to stand by it.' Diana wasn't shouting but her voice was hardened by anger and her cheeks glowed hotly.

'Just because David's ill in some secret clinic?' Gemma stood, hands on her hips, dark eyes glowing with rage.

'That's not the only reason.'

'No? Diana, that bloody creep's got you just where he wants you. One word, and you're putty in his hands. For God's sake, Diana, don't do it. You'll live to regret it.'

Candy watched silently, bemused.

'Whether I regret it, Gemma, is unimportant. But what is important, to me, is are you going to help or not? If you're not, then I'll find a way to get you two safely out of here until things are — '

'That's nice!' Gemma retorted, not letting Diana finish. 'You think you can be Joan of Arc on your own? Well, you can't. If you're stupid enough to get taken for another ride by David-bloody-Nazareth, that's your problem, but this time I'll be along for the ride. That way he'll have two of us to look out for!'

'Three!' declared Candy staunchly.

'Keep quiet, brat,' Gemma said without malice.

'I will not!' Candy drew herself up to her full five feet two inches and declared, 'We're all in this together. Whatever "this" is.' She glowered at her sister and her cousin. 'And I'm twenty-five, not twelve, so you can stop treating me like a baby!'

'Well said,' Alan Brookes-Browne applauded.

'Who let you in?' Gemma demanded.

'Candy, before she became embroiled in your parlour game,' Alan said easily, looking at Diana. 'Am I to take it that you are now willing to accept your role in this trust?'

'I am,' Diana said firmly.

'Then perhaps we'd better all sit down and discuss a few things.'

A short time later Alan Brookes-Browne had his first taste of his client's stubbornness. He had just suggested that she leave all the correspondences between Jeff Sherman and the trust to him to deal with, when she cut him off.

'Stop right there!'

Her cousins stared at her, startled and amazed, as if she had suddenly sprouted horns.

'When I asked you for advice, Mr Brookes-Browne, I did not appoint you either to the trust or to a position as my guardian. When, and if, such positions become available, I'll let you know.'

'Whoa there,' the solicitor protested. 'Hold your horses. I'm only trying to protect your interests. That's what a solicitor is for.'

'On the contrary, I'm paying you to advise, not to instruct. When I want you to intervene on my behalf, I'll say so. In the meantime, I am capable of making my own decisions and conducting my own correspondence without anyone's assistance. If that changes, I'll let you know.'

The chill in her voice and the incisiveness of her attack made the solicitor reappraise her. She had grown steelier, already distanced from the strained, uncertain woman of yesterday.

It was a heady combination: beauty and a good body; intelligence and grace; wealth and, yes, a new power, or the beginnings of it.

He smiled, respectfully. 'You are quite right, and I apologise. I'll be happy to take whatever instructions you give me.'

Diana nodded courteously.

The two sisters gave each other a bewildered glance.

They had just witnessed the rebirth of Diana. A less vulnerable Diana than the one they'd always known. This was a new Diana Nazareth, who would, in time, take all three of them to positions beyond their wildest dreams . . .

CHAPTER TWENTY-TWO

The next morning Alan Brookes-Browne read out the brief statement Diana had given him. After their long wait it was something of an anticlimax for the reporters. It said only that 'Mrs Diana Nazareth will be receiving Mr Benjamin Nazareth shortly, for discussions on Mr David Nazareth's proposals. When the discussions are concluded a further statement will be issued.'

There were grumbles and curses all round as most of the journalists headed for the town to find phone boxes. A core would have to return to their workplaces, but a few remained, taking turns to watch over the comings and goings at the house.

When the local vicar and another man in a cassock arrived shortly after breakfast, the press gave them only perfunctory glances.

The London employees of Nazareth House had done their bit. Not only had they smuggled Ben out of Heathrow before anyone had known of his arrival, but they had also contacted Diana for further advice.

A swift meeting between the vicar, the solicitor and Diana had provided an answer. Meanwhile, Benjamin spent the night at a hotel near Heathrow and left just before dawn for Tavistock – and the vicarage.

It was only later, when the vicar left the Glanville Road house alone, that the press realised they'd been duped. Two men had gone in to the house; only one had come out.

The press were not amused. Benjamin Nazareth had arrived beneath their noses, and they hadn't managed even a photograph. It hadn't helped that no one had been able to get hold of any pictures of him from Boston . . .

* * *

Diana, Gemma and Candy were all silent as Pritchard introduced the tall priest; Diana because she felt a sudden,
astonishing fear. Candy, because she was struck with her
worst attack of shyness ever; and Gemma because she was
instantly, totally, in lust.

Diana found her voice first, and extended her hand. 'I'm
pleased to meet you, Benjamin.' Her voice was clear, her
handshake firm and cool.

He took her hand, held it while he looked into her eyes, and
completely unnerved her with what was, surely, a glitter of
hostility in his intense green eyes.

'Likewise, but the name's Ben,' he informed her, in a voice
as deep and velvety as moss.

She recovered as Ben turned to shake hands with her
cousins, and from somewhere deep in her unconscious mind
something warned her to take control – at once.

'You'll want to change, I'm sure,' she managed pleasantly.
'Pritchard, would you like to take Ben up? For now, his room
is the second on the left.'

Benjamin Nazareth would probably never make such an
impression again. He was by far the most attractive man
any of them had ever seen. But wearing a priest's cassock,
with its connotations of chastity and inaccessibility, he was
devastating.

Pritchard, returning with Ben, now in the clothes he had
carried in a bag, was consumed with amusement and genuine
curiosity as they came back downstairs. No one could remain
unaware of the man's rugged good looks, but Pritchard had
never had chance to witness the effect of such a man on
the opposite sex. He'd noticed, with interest, the sudden
atmosphere. Now he was mischievously eager to witness
further events.

To that end he ushered Ben into the drawing-room first, so
that he could watch the second instalment. And it proved
worth the effort. All three faces turned to Ben, each guarded,
composed into neutral blankness. It was, to Pritchard, as if they

were attracted and repulsed – as if by a magnetic enemy who might or might not attack.

'Coffee?' Diana was first off the mark again, leaping to her feet and heading for the kitchen.

Ben sat down in the nearest vacant chair to Diana's, and Pritchard pulled a small chair close beside him, settling himself expectantly. In the kitchen Diana leaned against the sink, unreasonably anxious for space to breathe, and to quell a nervousness unfamiliar to her. He had reminded her of David . . . which was impossible, yet she had almost cried out David's name. What on earth was the matter with her?

They were not alike, she reasoned with herself, yet when he'd walked in, it had been like a confrontation with one of the photos of David in his thirties. She'd shaken off the weird feeling of *déjà vu*, instantly. But then he'd looked at her with such intensity that the vision of David had reappeared.

And then she had known a deep sadness – almost a longing – something she couldn't name. And that had shaken her.

But she couldn't hide out in the kitchen, so she finished arranging the tray and took a deep breath before returning to her guests and, cautiously subjecting him to a third appraisal as Gemma, in a sudden display of domesticity, poured the coffee, she was able to reaffirm the dissimilarity with relief.

He bore no resemblance to David: he was taller, wider in the shoulders and across the chest, and, she had to admit, better looking than even David had been. His colouring was different too. The dark hair was not black, it was more a bitter-chocolate brown. And his eyes, incredible eyes, were varying shades of green – enviably fringed with a thick sweep of dark lashes. The broad curve of his brow and the squareness of his jaw, complete with a deep cleft in his chin, finally removed any resemblance to David.

Diana was annoyed with herself for thinking the old cliché about Greek gods, but it was impossible not to.

And, damn it, that was the last thing they needed!

'Coffee, Diana?' Gemma was holding a cup out to her

cousin, with a frown that warned Diana she'd been staring.

'Oh, thanks,' Diana said over-brightly.

'Cream, Ben? Sugar?'

Gemma smoothed the moment over and Pritchard, sensing the need for some initial assistance, turned his attention to Ben.

'Did you manage to see anything of the countryside as you were driven here this morning? Probably quite unlike the scenery in the States?'

'Certainly unlike California,' Ben agreed lightly, glancing at Diana with a look she could have sworn was conspiratorial, but God only knew why. When he followed that with a small smile, seemingly just for her, she felt a jolt somewhere behind her ribs.

Resolutely she returned his smile with a chilly, formal one of her own and, to her surprise, he winked.

Confused by the cryptic messages he was sending her, she lowered her head and concentrated on her coffee, while Pritchard began a summary of the recent unusual weather patterns around the world. You could always trust an Englishman to smooth over a difficult moment with a non-confrontational discussion of the weather, Diana thought thankfully.

It gave Ben a chance to wonder about the shock of chemistry between himself and Diana; and about the warning in that cold smile. He studied her as covertly as she had studied him, behind the facade of small-talk.

He *was* shocked by her, no doubt about it. Whatever he'd expected, he had not expected this.

It was something he had never experienced, something he would never have expected to find here. But what was it that he thought he had found? His eyes narrowed slightly as he watched her. She had turned her gaze on her cousin, but she was well aware of his attention.

They were both aware.

So this was the woman Mat had married. Now how in the hell had he managed that?

Then he remembered that she was also the woman David was besotted with, and a sharp pain hit his gut. Suddenly he knew that he *had* to know how she felt about David.

That would do to begin with. And after that, a thousand other questions needed answers, answers that Ben intended to get.

Meanwhile, he sent a silent message out into the ether. 'David Nazareth, bastard that you are, I think I owe you one!'

For just a fraction of time his hatred lifted and he tasted the brief sweetness of gratitude. Then, as quickly, he remembered, and the mantle of hate settled around his shoulders again . . .

Once they'd played the tea-party ritual, Diana put her cup down and turned finally to look at him openly.

'We have a lot to talk about. Are you tired? Or would you like to talk now?'

'I'm not tired,' Ben said.

'Would you all excuse us? I think we'd be better having this initial meeting between just the two of us.'

Ben rose and followed Diana across the square hall to a study.

Diana crossed to a bureau, took some papers from a drawer, and took a seat behind the narrow expanse of polished wood. Ben pulled a chair up to face her and wondered idly why she had chosen such a formal position.

'You have probably been better briefed than I have, but we should go through these together.'

She was unsmiling, her face unreadable as she pushed copies of the documents towards him.

Ben didn't immediately look down, but across at her. 'I suppose you do know we're both insane?'

Diana's eyebrows rose questioningly.

'Dancing like this,' Ben tapped the papers, 'to David's crazy tune. Or did you choose to be in on all this?'

'I don't think I understand you?' Diana said stiffly, having no intention of discussing either her motives for helping him or her relationship with David.

'Come on, Diana. I am not going to bite.'

His ironic smile did little to help her composure, but she replied gravely enough. 'I should hope not. We're all taught, surely, not to bite the hand that feeds us?'

To her astonishment, instead of being put down, Ben chuckled heartily.

'Please, let's not get off on the wrong foot,' Diana said heatedly, unsettled by his provocation.

'Now that,' Ben said, still amused, 'would be very interesting. Which foot, exactly, would a guy have to use to get off with you?' His eyes gleamed with merriment – but Diana paled and looked troubled.

Ben was immediately contrite. 'Look I'm sorry, Diana. Just my damned Yankee humour. Please accept my apologies.'

Diana shook her head, as if to clear something away, and answered in a softer voice. 'Really, it's all right . . . It's just that this whole business has been so traumatic.' She smiled weakly. 'I think I've forgotten how to take American humour.' She raised her eyebrows. 'But I ought to remember, I lived in Boston long enough.'

'Fair enough,' Ben said agreeably. 'So we'll both try to remember the semantics before we shoot off. Agreed?'

Diana nodded.

Ben took up the sheaf of papers. 'Right, let's get on with the Book of David, shall we? And as we go along you can tell me if I break any rules. However, I plead innocent in advance, not having whatever your advantages are, and not knowing yet how you play the rules.'

Diana recognised the genuine plea, and introduced a note of banter herself. 'All right, you're forgiven in advance, for today. But you're far too bright not to have learned by tomorrow.'

'You're going to be a hard teacher,' Ben said dryly.

Diana shrugged her shoulders. 'It's a hard world, Ben. And

we have a hard job to do in it. Hard and serious. Those are real people you've just had to be smuggled past, and this is a real town, with human beings in it who have to be considered when we are playing God with them, people who are going to be affected by the money we are going to dole out on their behalf — '

'Wait a minute here,' Ben frowned. 'What exactly are you saying? That I don't know all that? Do you take me for a complete fool?'

'I don't know what to take you for, Ben. I don't know you yet,' Diana flashed.

Ben stared at her for a long moment before replying: 'Nor do I know you, or have you forgotten that little fact? I don't know your angle, or even what's in it for you. But I do know about small towns, and what the God Almighties can do to them. I've seen plenty of messes in the States – and cleared up a few in court, too.'

They stared at one another, confused by the clash of under-standings, both again resentful.

Diana calmed down first. 'Why don't we just go through the basic facts today, and resolve to get to know one another as soon as we can?'

'That's a damned good idea!' Ben snapped, angry that he was sparring with her when he really did want to get to know her.

Diana, too, was annoyed at the undercurrents of emotion between them. But she would have to make a greater effort to keep control. It would hardly help David if all she could do was bring out the worst in his heir.

'Ben, it's not like me to be so touchy, but to be honest I'm hugely tired.'

Ben raised his eyebrows.

'I don't know when you learned about all this . . .' She waved her hand over the papers. 'But I only received these forty-eight hours ago, and I've had little sleep since then. It was a bolt out of the blue for me, and not a very welcome one. So, if I'm tetchy, please try to understand. You see, I've had only occasional communication with David since I left Boston. I didn't even know you were back in his life until two days ago.

'I'm still having problems working it all out. To be honest, I didn't want to have anything to do with it.' She gave him a weary smile. 'But I've given my word, and I'll keep it.

'And there's that lot out there.' She indicated the closed curtains at the bay window.' They aren't going to sit in the rain forever, waiting for a statement from us.

'But the main point, of course, is that we two have to decide what we are going to do.'

Ben had watched her carefully as she explained and, with his professional training, knew that she was being honest. Yet it didn't make sense. He'd known for over three weeks. How come she hadn't been told until the last minute?

'Mind if I just have a look at these?'

For several minutes he was engrossed in the papers, reading through once, and then again for clarity. When he looked up, his eyes were narrowed. 'They don't need my signature' – he pushed the sheaf across the desk – 'only yours.'

Diana frowned. 'What's the matter now?'

'You've only had those papers for *two days*?'

'I've already told you that.'

'And you knew nothing about any of this until then?'

'Absolutely nothing. What's wrong?'

'That sonofabitch kept you in the dark until the last possible moment — '

'There were reasons,' Diana interrupted, at once on the defence, and irritated to hear Ben bad-mouthing his father.

'Like what?' Ben's voice was grim.

'I'm sorry, I'm not at liberty to disclose them.'

'As you aren't at "liberty" to agree with my decisions over the trust?'

'I don't see what we should disagree over,' she said carefully, hearing the sarcasm in his voice.

'But, if we do? You get the black ball – the Book of David gives you the final word.'

Diana stared at him. 'You didn't know about that clause?'

'Too damned right I didn't!'

Diana began to see the problem. 'And you wouldn't have accepted if you'd known,' she said quietly.

'I didn't say that,' Ben said swiftly. 'But hell, I had the right to know.'

'Oh God.' Diana sighed and slumped in her chair.

'That might be a second way of putting it, yes.'

Diana searched in her mind for a reason for this latest mystery. Clearly Ben's pride had just taken a blow, and that couldn't have been David's intention – so that left Jeff, and she knew that he'd been under a lot of strain. It was the only explanation she could think of. Even so, it must not be allowed to create problems.

'Well, we'll have to try not to disagree,' she said lightly, and stretched her hand across the desk. 'Partners?'

Ben's pause was fractional, and when he took her hand his true feelings about David's dirty dealing were concealed.

'Partners,' he agreed.

Both felt the instant, tingling shock.

Diana quickly withdrew her hand.

Ben's hand lingered a moment in mid-air, then he too withdrew, and his eyes were unfathomably dark.

So it was done. They had shaken hands on it.

But Ben was already committed – to a different contract, one that Diana clearly knew nothing about, one that was at Nazareth House.

Now Diana would sign this contract, in the presence of her lawyer, and they would both be committed – to each other through the trust, to David through both contracts that he would hold.

Committed, but in different ways.

Ben wondered when he would tell her . . .

CHAPTER TWENTY-THREE

Alan Brookes-Browne read the document once again, assured himself that they both knew what they were committing themselves to, and witnessed Diana's signature.

He stood up. 'Well, that makes it legal. You now have joint control of ten million pounds, to be spent in the worthiest cause of Tavistock. Not forgetting that the onus is on you, Ben, to make a profit from the said cause within five years, and Diana has the power of veto.'

Ben and Diana both nodded.

'I'd like to see a copy of the contract you signed in Boston, Ben. For the record you understand?'

'I don't have it with me, but I'll get Sherman to send a copy over,' Ben stalled.

'Good. Now, do you mind my asking if you have any ideas yet?'

'Absolutely none,' Ben said truthfully.

'Then I wish you the very best of luck.'

'Amen,' Ben declared with a tight smile.

While they wouldn't all have agreed that there was cause for celebration, they nevertheless opened a couple of bottles of decent wine when Pritchard joined them later. The solicitor, now insisting they use his Christian name, suggested an impromptu toast.

'To David and Ben.'

'To Nazareth House,' Ben contradicted.

'Perhaps to Diana, Ben, David *and* Tavistock?' Pritchard offered, diplomatically.

'To Tavistock's worthiest cause.' Ben changed the toast again, and this time they all drank cheerfully enough.

The wine helped relax them all, and soon they had agreed on the basic outline of a press release to be given out in the morning. Alan suggested they should both be present when he read it out, and Diana had reluctantly to agree that it was probably the only way they could bring the siege to an end.

For the moment the tensions eased.

'But won't you miss seeing your family?' Pritchard was asking Ben, and with interest the group turned its attention to them.

'I don't really have any family.' Ben's face swiftly shuttered as the spotlight fell on him.

'What about Mr Nazareth senior?' the vicar enquired, bemused.

'No, I shan't miss him,' Ben said flatly.

'Oh, I'm sorry. How rude of me to be so personal.' Pritchard was clearly embarrassed.

'Please, feel free to ask anything,' Ben reassured him. 'But you'll have to get used to the fact that we Yanks aren't renowned for diplomacy. We tend to speak our minds.' He turned to Diana. 'Isn't that right, partner?'

Diana answered carefully. 'Mmm, on occasion.'

'There you have the diplomat in this duo,' Ben remarked lightly.

'But five *years* away from your home country?' Alan observed thoughtfully. 'That's quite a sentence, Ben.'

'It is a very long time.' Pritchard nodded.

'The rewards are worth it,' Ben said drily.

'Quite so,' Alan agreed, losing interest when it was clear the man wasn't about to be drawn. He turned instead to Diana. 'Do you have any plans beyond tomorrow's press release?'

'Not yet,' she admitted.

'We just want to get through the first ordeal, then we'll set our minds to the job in hand.' Ben closed the subject firmly.

There was little else that could be added, and so the group turned to small-talk before breaking up.

Once Diana and her cousins were alone with Ben for the first time, it was apparent that tension still lingered between them all.

Ben, acutely aware of the atmosphere, made the first move

to break the ice. 'I know we have to work together, Diana, but would you prefer me to find somewhere else to live? Or go to a hotel tonight?'

'Of course not.' Diana was genuinely surprised by the suggestion. 'I hadn't thought of you being anywhere but here. Gemma, Candy?'

'Of course you must stay here,' Candy answered at once.

Gemma, swiftly imagining all sorts of delicious possibilities becoming impossibilities if he stayed here, carefully confused the issue. 'Perhaps Ben would be happier with his own space? Naturally he's welcome here, but I thought he might be too polite to say no.' She fixed Diana with her most innocent smile.

'He'd say no,' Diana said drily, not in the least fooled by Gemma's act, but made aware by it that there might be other problems looming on the horizon.

'Just a thought,' Gemma shrugged her shoulders.

'Well, then, the choice is yours, Ben.'

'I'd like to stay,' he said evenly.

'Right, now how about supper?'

'Could I perhaps, first, put you in the picture regarding my relationship with David,' Ben said lightly. 'It might affect your decision to have me as your house guest?'

They were all silenced.

'I don't plan any speeches,' he continued. 'But if we are going to live and work together, then you should know my feelings.'

Diana felt chilled.

Ben noted Diana's cold look and the proud tilt to her chin. Without saying a word she was defending David. His spine prickled.

'I'm an honest kind of person myself, that's why I want the record straight. Fewer problems that way.'

He seemed to be waiting for a response, so Diana said, as casually as she could, 'The floor's yours.'

'It might be expected, as I'm supposedly the heir to the Nazareth empire, that I would worship the man who intends so to endow me. But, so that the issue isn't confused between us, I'll tell you now that nothing could be further from the truth. I stopped caring about my "father" many years ago . . . but before you misconstrue that, you should know that it was long after he had ceased to know that I even existed.'

Ben gradually unfolded his story, unemotionally, with an intense concentration that held them all in its grip. He omitted nothing, yet doled out the facts sparingly.

'I adored David with every breath in my body,' he told them. 'Yet for years I lived virtually alone in one wing of the house. Ella lived for Mat, and he for her. I realised later that they were both disturbed – but when I was growing up I couldn't have known how to handle something like that by myself.' At this point he looked at Diana with something of an apology in his eyes.

'Mat was cruel, quite viciously so; he was always inflicting some kind of pain on Ella, and on me. I couldn't retaliate because I was so much stronger and much bigger . . . however, Ella encouraged Mat to be the way he was. He'd kick, scream and bite, even his mother, until he drew blood. No one could handle that child and, apart from Ella, nobody could stand him.

'David made efforts in the early years, sure. But from around my tenth birthday, he just wasn't around any more. He couldn't handle it, so he avoided it. The best action was no action. He knew how I was treated – plenty of hired helps told him in no uncertain terms – but . . .' He shrugged, leaving the rest of that unsaid.

'That alone didn't change my feelings for him – it was the bus that did that. It became the final straw.'

Now his face was grim, his voice shocking in its bleakness.

'Every single schoolday of my life in Boston, from first grade until the day before my eighteenth birthday, I took the bus to and from school. And every day that Mat attended he was driven to and from school by Ella, my so-called mother. I could have even stood that, if I hadn't had to watch the exercise day in and day out, winter and summer, rain, snow or heat-wave. If I hadn't had to stand at the bus stop, and watch Mat wave as they passed . . .'

Diana closed her eyes, unable to watch the agony that was there for them all to see; the broad, strong shoulders, hunched in remembrance. She knew that if he looked up they would see the haunted look in his eyes.

Her heart went out to him, and at the same time she wrestled with the impossibility of it being the same man they were talking about. How could a man such as David Nazareth have tolerated such barbaric cruelty – and it *was* cruelty – to his son?

Ben had described, by omission, a man who had been at best an indifferent, weak father, and at worst a monster. Yet Ben's tale rang true and she was forced to remember that David hadn't seemed to know Mat at all, while Ben's descriptions of his brother were vividly accurate.

Her thoughts were interrupted as Ben moved from the position he had stood in all this time, and her eyes flew open in dread.

Gemma and Candy were as tense as Diana, and almost as shaken.

But Ben's mask was back in place. He looked cool and quite collected now as he sat down. It seemed he had no more to say about his childhood.

'I don't mind admitting that Nazareth House was always my dream,' he said quietly. 'A dream I freely gave up all rights to, and worked damned hard to forget. Or at least I fooled myself I'd forgotten.

'When Jeff Sherman approached me with this little bombshell, I told him I wasn't interested. But I guess I must have wanted to be persuaded otherwise.' He managed a tight smile. 'I knew I'd been cut out of David's will . . . maybe my pride forced me to see if I could make him capitulate.' He shrugged. 'Anyway, you've heard how it was . . . and I have to add that there isn't a hope in hell of things changing between me and David.'

'You'll still go through with it anyway?' Gemma asked. 'After what he did to you?'

'For Nazareth House,' Ben gazed intently at her, 'I'll do whatever it takes.'

'It really means that much to you?' Diana couldn't help asking.

'Next to David, it was my life,' he said simply.

And in that moment they all knew just how much Ben had suffered. And for how long.

Candy, unable to cope with thoughts of the lonely little boy without bursting into tears, excused herself and fled from the room.

Gemma, too, rose, and her voice was unsteady. 'Don't mind us,' she said, feigning mockery. 'We're an emotional family. Candy's not rude, she's just out of her depth here.' She crossed and bent to kiss him on the cheek. 'We're glad to have you with us, but I'm for my bed as well. See you in the morning.' Then she too fled.

'And then there was one,' Ben murmured. 'Or will she too flee, run away and leave me alone with my memories? Or is she, like me, made of stronger stuff?'

His look filled Diana with a disquiet she had thought long behind her, left in Boston two years previously.

She stood up, unwilling to be alone with him while her own emotions raged; but she didn't want him to feel rejected. 'I think your story has disturbed us all, but it makes no difference to our agreement. You are very welcome to stay here. But, Ben, after the past forty-eight hours, we are exhausted. So for that reason, and no other, I'm afraid that I too will have to say goodnight.'

Ben caught her hand as she passed his chair, and lifted her fingers to his lips. Their gaze locked for just a moment, but it was enough for Diana to know beyond any doubt. Ben was dangerous, just as David had been. They were in some strange way intermingled in her mind – almost as if they were one and the same person.

She drew her hand gently back from his fiery touch. She had been burned before. It would not happen again.

Not with a third Nazareth.

She turned at the door, and had to steel herself against the lonely picture he presented.

Willing her voice to a lightness she didn't feel, she said, 'Family. Friends. And partners.' Then she added very softly, 'But nothing more. Sleep well. Goodnight, Ben.'

The morning dawned bright, cold and dry. It was reason enough to feel positive about the day ahead.

They had it all worked out. Alan, Diana and Ben would meet the press outside, and Alan would read the release. Alan would allow a few photographs. He would also parry any questions Diana or Ben might not wish to answer, or which he deemed an infringement of their legal or personal rights.

Diana dressed carefully, with Gemma hindering more than she helped.

Gemma sat Buddha-like on the bed, scrutinising and commenting on every step of Diana's cosmetic routine, while carefully sounding her cousin out.

'Wear the poppy lipstick I loaned you. It goes marvellously with your ivory skin, and it will bring out the yellow in that cream dress. God, he's just a dream isn't he . . .?'

'The coral suits me better, and my skin isn't ivory, it's just pale. Who's a dream?'

'Don't wear the pearls, Di. They're so *boring*. Wear the jet beads. Ben, of course, who else?'

Diana ignored her and hunted through her jewellery case. She selected a long single strand of creamy pearls. 'Depends what your dreams are made of.' She slipped on the pearls, knotted them just below the cowl neck of her black jersey dress, and stood back to judge the effect.

'The gold chains would be better. My dreams are made of that . . .' Gemma sighed theatrically.

'Good luck then.' Diana tried an earring of twisted gold and pearls, wishing Gemma would shut up.

'Oh, Lucifer! Not those, Diana. Wear your diamonds, give 'em all a flash. You mean you're not interested?' Her tone was disbelieving, hopeful.

'Right first time. He's all yours.'

'Carte blanche you mean?' Gemma was grinning.

'Would you accept him any other way?' Diana deliberated between pearl clusters and the twisted earrings; the last thing she wanted was to look like a dumb blonde on Ben's arm.

'What about the silver fox?' Gemma watched, surprised, as Diana pulled a cream wool coat from her wardrobe.

'Not appropriate.'

'For a millionairess? You have to be kidding!'

'Nope,' Diana pushed the fur to the back of the rail. 'Time for it to go to charity – preferably somewhere in sub-zero temperatures.'

'You've gone mad,' Gemma declared. 'Charity begins at home — '

'Not this time,' Diana said firmly. 'The animal rights activists have a very good point.' She twirled round in her wool coat, ready at last. 'Animals needn't be killed to give us coats.'

'Bloody hell. The soya brigade strikes again,' Gemma laughed. 'But, Di, did you mean it about Ben?'

'Whatever I said, I meant.'

'Blimey, you're serious today. That worried, eh?'

'About this press meeting? Or about your prospects with Ben?'

'Diana, come on! Look, I won't chase if you're interested . . .'

'You're too gracious, love. But I'd be careful if I were you. Ben doesn't strike me as the type who'd be flattered at being in a lottery.'

She moved towards the door. 'Now can we please go

downstairs? And do stop chattering about Ben. His room's only across the hall, you know.'

'Don't I know it.' Gemma sighed deeply enough to make Diana hesitate at the door.

'What's the problem now?'

'You are for a start,' Gemma said hopelessly. 'I mean, just look at you. All legs and beauty, plus riches and brains, and where do I stand?'

'For goodness' sake, Gems, will you stop that? You are *very* attractive and getting men has hardly been a problem for you.'

'I know,' Gemma admitted. 'But, Di, I think Ben might well be my match. And seeing as I'm the smitten one, at last, I have this awful feeling that he'll be the one that gets away . . .'

She looked so crestfallen that Diana tousled the dark curls.

'What man has resisted those toffee-brown eyes, and that glossy head of curls?' she teased. 'Brighten up, sweetie. And try playing it cool. I have the feeling he likes his women that way.'

'That's me out then.' Gemma linked her arm despondently through Diana's. 'I can't be cool for two minutes.'

Diana closed the door behind them, aware that something in her mind was muttering clichés about 'protesting too much'. But she *was* sure she didn't want anything to do with Ben romantically. Wasn't she? Forcing a smile, she pushed the dangerous thought aside.

'If you are smitten enough, Gemma, you'll learn.'

But, despite her reassurances to Gemma, Diana could hardly fail to notice that Ben looked frequently at her. Neither could she miss the fact that Gemma saw it too . . .

As soon as she, Ben and Alan emerged into the sharp, frosty air, her spirits quailed. It seemed to her that half the town had turned up in the street, and, despite being shielded on each side by Ben and Alan, she felt naked, exposed.

The flash of cameras from every direction made her put her

hand protectively to her eyes, trying to block out the blinding glare. It was only seconds before Alan stepped directly in front of her and raised his arm as a signal that the photographs must stop, but it felt much longer.

Then, as the questions were hurled at them from every direction, Alan took up his earlier position, but with his head bowed. Pencils poised over notepads, rustling and pushing ceased. Silence was restored.

Alan began to read from their carefully prepared statement and, as he did, those who knew that a copy would be handed out afterwards ignored him to concentrate on the young couple themselves.

They were to be news as much as the money and the trust. Within hours they would decorate newspapers under such awful banners as 'Beautiful Benefactress and her Debonair Consort'. And, worse, 'Prince Charming and the Fairy Godmother take Tavistock to the Ball'.

Regardless of the preposterous headlines, they were definitely 'an item'.

Even with Ben and Alan in tight control, it took every ounce of their considerable skills to keep the press within the bounds of the subject matter proper. Personal questions flew from every direction, until Diana began to wonder whether anyone was interested in the trust at all.

Journalistic interest in the trust itself was confined to the local media. But a small contingent of national journalists, looking for a sensational story, found this one handed to them on a plate.

They were outside for less than ten minutes before Alan, realising that interest was becoming a shade too provocative, ushered Diana and Ben back into the safety of the house.

But he remained in the garden for a while longer, concealing his delight beneath a calm composure. As the trust's solicitor he was home and dry. His business, already brisk, would now gallop. Behind his bland smile he day-dreamed of larger premises. A new car? A yacht?

Diana changed her clothes and wished she could sleep forever. She felt utterly wrung out. The thought that she had, for a time anyway, given away her rights to privacy, lodged a dark shadow in her heart.

Ben, in his room, seethed. Not for himself – he could take as much as was given out – but for Diana. In the few hours he'd known her, he'd recognised her honesty and integrity. He'd say she was the last person to deserve public annihilation such as this morning's fiasco could bring.

Once more the flames were fanned in his heart. David Nazareth had engineered Diana into a situation as loathesome as it was insane. But, Ben thought, David had underestimated his adopted son by a million miles. As Ben had underestimated himself. Without knowing why, he was already prepared to champion the woman he had expected to detest.

Now why the hell was that?

They were gathered again in the drawing-room as Alan came striding cheerfully back into the room.

'Well now, that wasn't too bad really. Nasty lot, but I think by and large we came out fairly well.'

'Do you now?' Ben stared, a muscle working vigorously in his jaw, a steely light in his eyes. 'Well I'd say that we were neatly herded, hog-tied and damned well branded.'

Alan could only stare back, speechless.

'Was it awful?' Gemma demanded, bristling.

Diana nodded but said nothing.

Ben had to warn himself against reacting in an overtly anti-David manner. He couldn't yet be sure how that might go down with Diana. She was protective, yes, but he still had to learn why.

He forced himself to relax.

'Well, it's over now. The deed's done and we're committed to making the very best of it. Isn't that right, partner?'

Diana smiled stiffly. 'Of course.'

Ben's brain swung back to the task in hand. First, he

thought, they should learn as much about the town and
its environs as possible. He gave Alan a list of items
he thought they might need to be going on with, maps, a list
of local charities, names of local dignitaries, and as soon as
Alan had left, Ben brought up a related matter.

'I don't know how much lawyers charge in England, but if
Alan's going to work for the trust, as opposed to either or
both of us personally, don't you think we should employ him
only in that capacity?'

'I don't quite follow,' Diana said.

'The trust can pay his fees for any employment connected
with that, but he's likely to be a very expensive errand boy.'

'True,' Diana said, thinking rapidly. 'But who else can do it?
None of us should go out just yet.'

'Why not ask Pritchard if he knows anyone?' Gemma had
come back into the room carrying a bundle of mail, and had
caught the tail end of the conversation.

'Good thinking, buddy,' Ben smiled.

'Shall I telephone him?' she asked.

'Yes, do.' Diana eyed the bundle in Gemma's hands. 'What
on earth is that?'

'Fan mail,' Gemma said cheerfully, setting the pile beside
Diana. 'I'll go and call Pritchard. Have fun . . .'

Diana picked up the first letter gingerly. 'I can't believe this,'
she said faintly.

Ben strode across to glance at the pile, and his grimace said more than his words. 'Not slow around here,
are they?'

Diana opened the first letter, read it and passed it to Ben.
Her astonishment grew with each new letter she read.

'Begging letters. My God!'

And they were. Some amateur, many very professional, but
each with a case to present as worthy of their attention.

'Can you believe this?'

'I should think it's just the beginning,' Ben replied.

'But what do we do with them?'

'Answer them all, vaguely,' Ben suggested. 'And keep a list of everybody who writes.'

'What's vaguely?'

'You know, "Thanks for the letter, etc; but we aren't making any decisions yet." In other words, stall.'

'Lord. And you think we might get more?'

'Guaranteed,' Ben stated. 'So we might as well work out a standard reply for them all.'

'Good thinking,' Gemma said, returning from the telephone. 'And Pritchard says he thinks he can find someone. Can I read any?'

'Help yourself.' Diana handed over a pile. 'I think they're rather sad, really.'

'Don't,' Ben said matter-of-factly. 'The moment you feel sorry for individual cases, your business judgement goes out of the window.'

Diana was prevented from answering by Candy coming to the door. 'Diana, telephone for you. It's David.'

Ben's stomach instantly churned.

'I'll take it in the study,' Diana said quickly, aware of Ben's sudden scrutiny.

She was gone only minutes, but to Ben it seemed far longer. His face was set, his eyes dark, as Diana returned and announced over-brightly, 'That's it, then. David knows that I've accepted, and that we've given out our first press release.'

'Damn him to blazes. Is he going to keep daily tabs on us?' Ben's face had set mutinously.

'That's hardly fair, Ben,' Diana chided him carefully. 'He had the right to know what decision we'd made. I suppose I should have called him, or at least Jeff.'

'Like hell you should! He set this damned business up, let him do the running.'

Diana felt a cold shiver run down her spine. If Ben was going to be so prickly over David, how on earth were they going to live and work without problems? David was bound to be a central figure in whatever they did. It was his money, his baby. But then, come to that, so was Ben, in a manner of speaking.

She decided against mentioning that David had just asked her to write him weekly reports on their progress, and on Ben's progress. Neither was it the time to mention that she'd just promised to visit Boston on a regular basis. It was part of the unwritten promise she had made. To do everything David asked, if it would help him with Ben.

She withdrew silently to the study, ostensibly to type up a standard letter, but also to get away from the anger Ben could not conceal. He would just have to learn, and quickly, that she would not allow him to involve her in the tragic, but private, matter of his past.

Ben remained edgy for the rest of the morning, his mood only lifting with the arrival of Pritchard.

The vicar knew just the lad to help them out, a boy who'd passed all his exams with excellent grades and who was still unemployed.

Chris Parkes called on them the next day, and at once they knew they'd found a treasure. He threw himself into the job with intelligence and enthusiasm, bringing information by the armful and helping sift through it with a quick and lively mind. Day after day they pored over facts and figures, while the list of potential causes grew longer as more and more appeals flooded in.

Hospitals, doctors, churches, institutes; numerous local appeal groups; two orphanages, playgroups; ecological societies; families with sick children, or elderly relatives; private businesses sent their accounts and plans for expansions. The chamber of commerce sent reams of advice, and offers to help run the trust, as did the borough council and the local council; and everybody who had anything to do with anything wanting money wrote in.

The list was enormous. And for every local appeal there were at least two from other parts of Devon and a few from further afield.

Ben left all the mail-sorting to Diana and her cousins, while he spent the greater part of each day learning everything he possibly could about Tavistock. By the end of three weeks he knew it as well as he had known the beach town where he'd lived for years.

They were all growing weary. Every letter had to be answered, and that was taking up the better part of most days. Worse was the fact that no issue they debated, however keenly, really answered the description they needed. While many were worthy, none seemed to merit an investment of ten million pounds and none seemed remotely likely to return the kind of profit they sought.

It began to look impossible.

The press had grown tired of the lack of events, and now the family were only bothered by the odd telephone call, or the occasional reporter at the door, asking was there any news yet? Life got back to as normal as it could be under the circumstances.

Ben began to wander the town, always questioning, always searching. Social invitations, at first a deluge, slowed to a trickle, as did the mail. Gradually it had sunk in that the group were not going to swayed by pity or bought by flattery.

A month passed, then another; and spring arrived, decking the town's gardens with golden daffodils and the moorland with budding heather and gorse.

They seemed to have reached the end of the road.

One evening, as they were finishing the latest batch of letters, Candy looked up at Diana and quietly said, 'I think I've just about had it.'

It was so unusual for her to be negative that Diana was at once contrite. 'I know, love. But something has to turn up soon. What about the maternity hospital,' she said brightly. 'Didn't you feel that might have some merit?'

''Fraid not!'

'Couldn't you just give them all something?' Gemma chipped in, bored to death by the relentless regime – and the forced celibacy.

'That's not what we've been asked to do,' Diana reminded her.

'No, and I can't see you succeeding. My bet is that David's given his heir apparent a red herring to chase,' Gemma said. 'Has it occurred to you that David might not want Ben to inherit?'

'What a crazy thing to suggest,' Diana protested. 'David couldn't have the first idea that it would be this difficult. Wouldn't it seem fairly reasonable to suppose you could dispose of ten million pounds quite easily? And why send Ben if he didn't want him to prove himself worthy?'

'Oh God, not that word worthy again. I swear I never want to hear it again after this bloody farce.'

'Me neither,' Candy added fervently.

'I reckon it's time you threw the whole thing back at David,' Gemma said. 'He's had quite a slice out of our lives now, and I'd willingly tell him where to shove it.'

'I'm sure you would, Gems. But that wouldn't change the reason for your boredom,' Diana said directly. 'And you'd still be of some interest to the media, so your love life would remain curtailed.'

Gemma grunted and would probably have taken the issue further, but just then Ben burst into the room, his excitement palpable.

'Get your coats on. I think I've found it!'

They were dressed and out of the house in minutes, all asking questions at once. But Ben would only shake his head and say, 'Follow me.'

He hurried them down into the town, stopping only when they got to Bank Square.

'All I want you to do is to observe what I point out, OK? And save all the questions until later. I want to know if you see what I'm seeing.'

The shops were closed, the town deserted except for a few youths hanging around aimlessly in the growing dusk. The air was still and silent. Bemused, they followed Ben up Duke Street and its continuation, Brook Street. There he stopped and nodded towards the only sign of life: two take-away shops, one on either side of the road, each filled with youngsters playing listlessly on ball-game machines or drinking Coca-Cola. On the street were a few bicycles and motor-bikes.

'Just take note of that,' Ben said enigmatically, striding out now for Vigo Bridge.

They turned along by the riverside and on into the pannier market, where Ben nodded his head again at a group of young people standing around talking. On he took them, into Bedford Square, where more youths lounged along the church walls.

He shepherded them up West Street, and down into Russell Street, across the main Plymouth Road and finally into the Meadows. Scattered around in the pale light of evening were yet more young people, huddled in the shadows. They wore uniform blue-jeans and parkas; a few held cans of beer, a few smoked. Some skimmed pebbles over the river. They looked up at the group, and then away again, uninterested.

Diana began to sense what Ben was considering. She studied the youngsters more carefully. There was little to get excited about. Ordinary bored kids, fairly typical of the generation.

Once back at the house, they all wanted to talk at once.

'You can't mean those idlers?' Gemma dropped, bored, into a chair.

'I know,' Candy declared. 'You're going to build an amusement hall!'

'I sincerely hope not!' Diana exclaimed.

'Yes, those youngsters. Not entertainment though. A future. A great big Future, with a capital F.'

They stared at him.

He strode to the table and stood gazing at the pile of maps and reams of notes, but he was miles away. Eventually he spoke. 'I've been studying those kids for weeks now. *They* are the answer. I've talked to dozens of them: I've talked to the local schools, the education authorities, the adult education department, the employment office, the Department of Social Security.

'I've also talked to shopkeepers, some of the parents, a lot of the townspeople, the police, the probation officers. Everyone who could give me any answers in fact.' He paused, and looked directly at Diana. 'I didn't want to raise any hopes until I was sure.'

'And are you?'

'Absolutely. All it needs is your agreement.'

'To *what*?'

'I can't say at what point I became aware of them, or of their needs,' he began quietly. 'I only know that sometime between the time when Tavistock was a thriving Stannary town and today the young people began to be overlooked. I've searched back in the archives even as far as Cromwell and the Abbey, and nowhere can I find any provision for the next generation.

'However, coming back to those idlers as you call them, Gemma. They are no more idle than you or me, they're just beaten by the system. I'm talking about kids who don't quite make A-level material, kids who come out of school at sixteen knowing that they don't have any place to go. Do you suppose that they enjoy being regarded as trash? Or, worse, being ignored in the hope that they'll go away? That's where *I'd* like to spend the money. It's the most worthy cause this town has got.'

Now he waited for their reactions.

'I think it's a lovely, generous idea, Ben. But how do you propose that we invest ten million pounds in those kids, and make a profit?' Diana was guarded, willing to be persuaded but afraid of a wild-goose chase.

'I haven't worked it out in fine detail yet, but I do have the skeleton of a plan.'

'Well, let's hear it?' Gemma said impatiently.

'Not so fast. I said it's only a skeleton,' Ben protested. 'I need to do more homework, but my basic idea is some kind of centre that will provide jobs. But it has to provide for all the kids, including the handicapped.'

'That's a tall order,' Diana said, thinking carefully. 'But it has possibilities. Let's work on it.'

'Good.' Ben relaxed.

'Great,' Candy enthused, liking the idea.

'Lunacy,' Gemma retorted, unsmiling. She didn't even like children.

Ben's plans took off from that moment. They spent the next few days talking it over, and the seed grew. By the end of that week they had a basis, in many ways still undefined, but sufficiently encouraging for Ben to want to make a real start.

They were outside having tea on the lawn, enjoying the luxury of a fine warm day.

Ben was lazing on his back on the grass. 'Our first target should be a house. A very big house. And a lot of land.'

'What's wrong with this house?' asked Gemma, sandwich half-way to her mouth.

'It's rented,' Ben replied patiently.

'So what? Are we planning something illegal?'

'Ah, Gemma,' Ben teased, 'always suspicious.'

Gemma was stung into silence. Ben smiled at her, hoping to take the edge off his remark. He would have to be more careful with her, although she frequently riled him, because he still wasn't sure how much influence she had over Diana.

Come to that, he wasn't any closer to knowing any of the cousins beyond a superficial level. He'd been too involved to discover the personal depths in the three women. And he'd spent minimal time alone with Diana, though that, he assured himself, would change.

But bantering with Gemma had already become a habit. Something about her watchfulness made him flippant.

'You don't trust a soul, do you, sexpot?' he half-joked. 'At least, you don't trust me.'

'That's not true,' she protested, blushing at the back-handed compliment. 'I trust a helluva lot of people. But I don't trust any Nazareth, that's for damned certain!'

'You know, you're not so wrong, young Gemma.' Ben let his eyes rove over her lazily, and was rewarded with yet another self-explanatory blush. Inwardly he groaned. He didn't want the wrong cousin getting ideas. He ignored the dig about his name. 'We need a very large property to come up with the miracle I'm intent on – that's all I was saying — '

'Ben!' Diana interrupted sharply. 'Are you out of your mind? We're talking of helping a few youngsters, and you're talking of miracles?'

'No, Diana. We're not talking about a few youngsters. We're talking about all the kids in this town,' Ben corrected her firmly. 'And we *are* talking miracles, by any other name. I want us to give these kids a future which their children will inherit. I'm not talking about a short-term carrot or a once-off handout. I'm talking about total commitment. That's why we have to get it right. Because if we don't, someone, somewhere, will screw it up.'

Diana could see tiny beads of sweat on his brow. Just the heat of the day, or the sweat of a visionary? For a moment she was afraid. Yet she was becoming convinced of his purpose and of his ability; she was being drawn in to his wild, ambitious, wonderful plan.

'Tell me how you see this miracle working. And, equally to the point, making a profit.'

'Just by making David's money do something really useful,' Ben said fervently. 'I'm an old-fashioned capitalist, and a pretty conservative one, but I feel in my guts that the trust can make money. And more than that, the rewards for those youngsters will be a real achievement for us.

'I want to take those kids and stretch their imaginations as far as they will go – but more importantly I want to give them an active part in a very realisable future.' He paused to look directly into her eyes. 'That's why *we* have to work hand-in-glove, as a dedicated team.

'We might have to fight the town itself to give its kids this chance. We might have to fight jealousy and prejudice, greed and envy even, the kind that can get nasty.

'That's why it is vital that we all pull together, that we agree, and that when we don't we discuss it rationally without going off at emotional tangents. I say we need property and land, but if anyone wants to argue that point, then let's do it openly and without sniping.'

Diana saw at last that Ben was an idealist, but, paradoxically, also a realist. He was no more radical than she was. He just had a radical plan to alter the destinies of a town's young people.

He was shrewd, with an innate understanding of his fellow men and their failings. And he had been given an opportunity to leave his mark, albeit a small one, on the world.

As she met his intense gaze, she had an extraordinary thought. Would Ben actually accept his inheritance from David? She was beginning to believe that Ben had a burning desire to do some good with his life. It was strange feeling – but she couldn't help doubting that anything less would satisfy him.

She gave him one of her rare warm smiles, a smile that forgave him everything and asked forgiveness for herself.

'So what do you want us to do? I'm with you all the way, no matter the trials ahead. What do you say Gems? Candy?'

Her cousins both nodded.

'For starters we could give it a name. How does "The Youth Trust" sound? And if that's agreed, as we have a quorum we could vote on giving Gemma and Candy official jobs in the trust?'

Diana nodded her agreement to both suggestions. The girls just stared, delighted and nervous.

'Then I'd like to announce our decision as soon as possible. That will take care of all that mail we're getting. Agreed?'

'Agreed. Anything else?'

'Yes. Let's begin house-hunting in earnest.'

'I take it that the trust headquarters will have other purposes besides housing us?'

'Of course.' Ben smiled again.

'OK, let's vote the girls in.' Diana stretched, glad to have finally got somewhere, if only to the starting post. 'Now can we *please* take a break from this, at least for the weekend?' She stood up. 'I'll just rough out a letter for our admirers, then I'm for a rest. My brain needs to recover.'

The three cousins went into the house together, all of them suddenly drained.

Ben stretched out in the late sunshine. He believed in the plan with his soul, but didn't believe that it would be any easier than he had outlined. It could be much harder. All at once he uttered a silent prayer, to a God he was uncertain existed, that the plan might work despite the colossal odds against it.

The letter done, Gemma followed Diana upstairs, out of Candy's hearing.

'Do you really believe this is all possible?'

Diana stopped at her bedroom door. 'I believe in Ben's belief in himself.' Her glance at Gemma was curious. 'Don't you?'

'I suppose it has a certain appeal,' Gemma murmured non-committally, and moved off down the hall.

Diana stretched out on her bed, her mind raking over Ben's idea. She liked it very much. What she didn't like was the lack of substance, the absence of a really concrete plan. How on earth was the idea going to become a sound investment? Ten million pounds wasn't exactly peanuts and how did a large house and a townful of youths fit together?

Resolutely, she closed her eyes. Ben was the one who had to prove himself. He was also the ideas man. Let *him* work it out.

CHAPTER TWENTY-FOUR

Ben and Diana let it be known around the town that they were searching for suitable premises for the trust. Other than stressing the need for large premises and land, they gave no hint about their plans.

Soon they were viewing houses, farms, converted barns, just about anything which looked even remotely interesting.

The press, tipped off, waited.

The town's interest also picked up, and people cautiously began to speculate on the nature of the trust. Behind closed doors less civilised debates raged, as hopeful beneficiaries planned battle strategies against rivals.

While Ben and Diana tramped from one property to another, the town divided itself into distinct camps. Personality and business interests clashed all over town, and long-term friendships came to bitter ends. Only a smattering of people, without any cause to promote, watched the proceedings with indifferent curiosity.

The hunt continued through the summer, but nothing was what Ben wanted; even though he couldn't say exactly what he did want, it was never what they saw. But, as they wearily turned away from one place after another, his plans were growing.

One plan in particular he kept to himself. Once they'd found the right place, he knew it would all fall into place . . .

Time passed, and as the lists from the estate agents grew fewer and smaller, they began touring in Ben's new Jaguar, through the countryside and villages, in the hope that they might spot something the agents had missed.

The last day of August shimmered with heat as they all sat around, listlessly riffling through brochures they had studied endlessly already. None of them dared voice their growing sense of failure, or say that their faith in Ben's dream was ebbing.

The telephone interrupted their lethargy. Diana took the call from Pritchard and the others listened.

'I don't know if that's a good idea, Pritchard,' Diana said, frowning. 'I'm not sure Ben would be interested in a lease. What was the man's name again?' As she wrote it down something jogged her memory. 'You did say Adrian Lawrence, the solicitor? Heavens, he must be in his eighties by now. He was elderly when he was one of the governors at Larchwood . . . Yes, that's right, my cousins and I all went to school there.'

She listened again carefully, then shrugged her shoulders. 'Well, I suppose anything's worth a try, What can we lose at this stage?'

She came back to the table, the frown still evident as she studied the note in her hand.

'Interesting?' Ben asked.

'Mmm, intriguing,' she replied, sitting down at the table, her thoughts for a moment far away.

'Well?' Gemma prompted.

'I'm not sure it's of interest to us,' Diana said thoughtfully. 'It's only a lease, on part of an old estate. There are barns and cottages, but apparently all in need of "sensitive" restoration.'

'Sensitive?' Ben queried, 'As in period, or just in style?'

'I should think period. Pritchard said it's the oldest manor in the county, but not a stately home as such. More feudal country seat, whatever that means. And if it's "feudal", that reads "needs a fortune" to me.'

'We've *got* a fortune,' Ben said drily. 'And so far nothing to spend it on. Let's go see.'

Adrian Lawrence was delighted to hear from them, and happy to see them at four o'clock that afternoon.

The sisters agreed to go for a walk once they were at

Yelverton, even Gemma admitting that four eager house-hunters might be a bit overwhelming for an elderly man.

Diana and Ben rang the doorbell of 'Hawthorne' with two minutes to spare, and were met by Adrian Lawrence, looking no older than when Diana had seen him last. Only his clothes, hanging loosely on his tall, thin frame, conceded his eighty-plus years.

He led them through a series of tastefully furnished, if old-fashioned, rooms, to a sitting-room with open french windows and a wonderful fragrance of lilac and late-blooming damask roses drifting on the air. Only the lazy drone of bees disturbed the still, mellow peace.

Adrian Lawrence ushered them into chintz-covered chairs grouped around a low table which was covered with a lacy cloth and tea things: golden scones; a bowl of deep yellow clotted cream; rich, darkly red strawberry jam; crustless triangular sandwiches and Victoria sponge cake.

'This is kind, Mr Lawrence,' Diana said warmly. 'But I hope you didn't go to all this trouble just for us?'

'Not at all, m'dear,' he reassured her. 'I always take my tea at this time. Years of habit, you know. But your appointment coincided nicely.' He smiled benevolently at them both, an innocent twinkle in his hazy blue eyes. 'Can't manage dinner so easily these days,' he continued, putting them at their ease, Diana realised, as he poured the tea. ''Fraid I tend to nod off by about nine, but that's no reason why I can't still enjoy good food and good company.' He passed small bone china cups to them both, the Lapsang Souchong's delicate fragrance blending with the summer perfumes in the room.

'I play "mother" quite a bit these days, though not with the frequency my dear wife did, bless her. She's been gone ten years now,' he said quietly, pausing for a moment, a lost look on his thin, patrician face.

'You have a very good cook,' Diana said, gently changing the subject.

'Thank you, m'dear,' he said softly, then brightened up

again. 'Yes, she's a wizard in the kitchen, comes in every morning during the week, does her baking, prepares me a fine luncheon. Couldn't manage without her.'

But he obviously had to in the evenings and at weekends, Diana thought sadly.

'Perhaps you could tell us some more about this lease, sir?' Ben's voice was also gentle.

'Ah, yes, the lease.' Adrian Lawrence was at once professional, setting his cup down with care, and straightening his shoulders with obvious relish.

'I suppose I really must begin with a note of caution, in as much as I don't have an actual lease to offer, just a willingness on the part of my young friend Simon Tamerford to open, shall we say, discussions.'

Ben's brows met in a frown. 'If you'd clarify the precise situation?' he said, slipping comfortably into a familiar role.

'Of course, of course,' the old man nodded. 'There *is* the possibility of a lease – I am merely stressing, for all parties concerned, that this is a tentative approach; that no lease has existed before; that we are not discussing a tenancy, only the consideration of such a possibility.'

'I don't understand,' Diana admitted. 'Reverend Gilwin said you had a lease for us to consider!'

'More a meeting to discuss a lease,' Adrian Lawrence said kindly. 'If you are willing to consider a limited lease, on a limited area of a large estate, then I can arrange for you to meet the owner.'

'We'd need to know a good deal more than that before agreeing to anything,' Ben said firmly.

The old man turned fully to face Ben, his gaze now thoughtful. 'Ah, yes, Mr *Nazareth*.' Ben was surprised by the emphasis, and by the gaze levelled so intently at him.

'Does my name bother you, sir?'

'Yes,' the old man replied succinctly. 'It most certainly does. But bear with me, young man, and I'll tell you why.'

*　　*　　*

'It was the painting, you see,' Adrian Lawrence beamed, as if delighted with himself. 'I learned of your trust and I thought I might be able to help you out, while helping my young friends. It was while I was with Simon Tamerford that I suddenly remembered the painting . . .' He paused for a moment, distracted by his thoughts. Diana and Ben exchanged discreet puzzled glances.

'I haven't seen it in many, many years, but all of a sudden I remembered it. I'd been racking my brain over where I'd heard the name Nazareth, and there it was. Just like that!' He smiled at them both, sure that they understood something that was perfectly clear to him.

'A painting reminded you of a name?' Ben queried encouragingly.

'Yes, dear boy, exactly that,' Adrian said with satisfaction. 'It was after the annual spring-cleaning at Tamerford, oh, a very long time ago . . . They don't do that any more, haven't the money these days, but they did do it then, and that's what I remembered.' Adrian Lawrence caught Ben's glance at Diana. 'Ah, you think I'm rambling, but I'm not. It was then, you see?'

'Not really,' Diana said apologetically.

'Well bear with me, my dear, it is all relevant. Now, where was I? Oh, yes – the spring clean. It was before the younger Tamerfords' time, but the aunt would remember, I should imagine. The spring-cleaning had all been done when there was a devil of a row. One of the old family portraits had disappeared and it was Simon's uncle who discovered it. Oh, sorry,' Adrian said, noticing their blank faces. 'Simon's the master now, but he wasn't born then.

'Well, there was such a to-do about it, but it never turned up. Anyway, I happened to ask Simon about it, and that's when I remembered . . .'

'Yes?' Ben encouraged as Adrian Lawrence tailed off, obviously to follow his thoughts.

'Yes, it was the name Nazareth. That's what reminded me.

The lost portrait was of one of the very early ancestors, way, way back. And I recalled that his middle name had been Nazareth.' He beamed again, pleased with himself.

Ben didn't know what he'd expected, but somehow he was disappointed.

'Why was that so important?' he asked, curious in spite of himself.

Adrian smiled widely. 'Because the young man emigrated to America.'

Ben thought for a moment. 'Do you know when?'

Adrian Lawrence frowned. 'I can't recall exactly, but certainly after the Pilgrim fathers. Late seventeen hundreds, I think. Yes. Definitely.'

Ben shook his head. 'Well, even if there is a coincidence of name, that's all it is. David Nazareth's family were in Boston at least a hundred years before that, and there's no Tamerford in their background. I used to be fascinated by their history – I'd remember a distinctive name like that.'

'But Nazareth's an unusual name too,' Adrian Lawrence pointed out. 'And that young man went off to America. Broke his mother's heart . . .'

'An interesting coincidence,' Ben said lightly, not wanting to spoil the old man's hopes.

'Pity,' Adrian Lawrence said, sadness in his voice. 'I was rather hoping you were related.'

Ben smiled pleasantly. 'I couldn't be anyway, sir. I'm adopted.'

'Oh, I'm sorry,' Adrian Lawrence apologised at once. 'I was told that and I must have forgotten. How stupid of me . . . so thoughtless.'

'It's not a problem, sir,' Ben reassured him.

Diana said nothing. For the moment there was nothing to say. But something wasn't right, an elusive something that she couldn't pin down.

'So, what about this lease?' Ben enquired.

*   *   *

Outside, later, a light breeze had cooled the car's interior enough for them to sit inside comfortably. Diana put a hand on Ben's arm before he could start the motor.

'Do you suppose there could be some connection between David and these people?'

'Not a chance, I should think.'

'Well, you must admit it's odd. An emigrant from here with the same name? I mean, it's not a common name is it? Are you quite certain that there were no Tamerfords in the Nazareths' background?'

'Positive,' Ben stated firmly.

'It is fascinating though.'

'The only thing fascinating me,' Ben said matter-of-factly, 'is this lease. As it stands it doesn't look possible. But I am curious to meet this Simon Tamerford and see what he's offering with my own eyes.'

'We'll know tomorrow,' Diana said. 'But right now we'd better find the girls.'

The directions they had seemed less than accurate when it came to finding Tamerford the next afternoon. They had taken the turn where instructed but after ten minutes they were manoeuvring through pot-holed lanes, too narrow for two cars to pass, completely mystified. Ben drove slowly, in fervent prayer that they wouldn't encounter anything coming in the opposite direction. Devon lanes were a whole new world to him – and this particular lane didn't seem to be leading anywhere at all.

As it was, they must have driven another mile without passing a single habitation before they came to a left-hand fork in the road. They looked at one another, shrugged and took it. It led them on a mile-long scenic tour to river boundaries and a disused quay.

Ben stopped the car and they both got out. They'd given themselves time so, as it was a fine afternoon, they enjoyed a few moments of exploration.

The countryside here was lovely, dense with trees and lush vegetation; the river wide, its clear waters moving swiftly;

and across its silky green expanse they could see Cornwall. At any other time they might have enjoyed exploring the deserted buildings dotted about the quayside, but there were so many; even a scattering of cottages, now derelict, which had obviously housed workers in some long-ago time. The scene was picturesque and peaceful, but with regret they knew they had to move on.

'Which way did we come?' Ben asked, momentarily disorientated.

Diana pointed, uncertainly. 'That way, I think. These lanes all look the same.'

Ben chanced a right-hand fork.

But it was a mistake the road led them only to a T-junction. Ben swore. 'What now, left or right?' Again his sense of direction had deserted him, and Diana admitted she didn't know.

They drove on again, cautiously, for a further couple of miles, on a twisting single-lane road not much better than a cart-track, banked thickly with sycamore and beech on either side, when suddenly it came to a dead end. At least, the road didn't go any further. Instead, in front of them rose enormous wrought-iron gates set into massive granite pillars, which in turn supported high stone walls that stretched as far as the eye could see in both directions.

'This can't be it.' Ben stared at the forbidding gates.

'Shouldn't think so – there would be a nameplate, or something, I'd imagine,' Diana said.

Ben was bemused. What did he do now? There wasn't room to turn, and he didn't fancy reversing all the way back down that narrow road.

He switched off the ignition.

'Perhaps there's someone about. Maybe they'll let us turn in their drive,' he said.

Diana followed him to the gates. They were fastened shut by a padlock on a rusty chain, but instinct drew her closer.

Ben drew in his breath: beyond the gates a long sweep of turfy, pitted drive wound beneath majestic horse-chestnut trees. To their left, rolling fields of velvety green stretched to the horizon. Dotted about were ancient oaks, massive maples and copper beech trees. Hedges, thickly leafed, divided open pasture lands where cattle grazed in the afternoon sun.

But it was the house sprawling in the distance that drew their attention. Ben remembered the binoculars in the car and was back with them in seconds.

'God, that's magnificent!' he exclaimed from behind the glasses. 'Diana, take a look at that beauty.'

She focused on the house, or rather the mansion. This surely had to be Tamerford? The house itself resembled a small castle, a splendid, almost medieval building of slate and granite.

Sunlight caught the muted colours of the buildings and cast back a soft hint of purple and grey, and here and there a sparkle from pink and silvery-grey felspar crystals in the aged stone. Diana could make out many windows that were mullioned and lead-paned. There were turrets at each wing of the main building, and a large courtyard of grey cobbled stone. The outbuildings were too numerous to count. At last she gave in to Ben's insistent tug at her sleeve, and handed the binoculars back to him.

Ben's gaze travelled carefully over the house again, over the turrets and towers, the lead-paned windows, moulded granite arches and huge, Gothic-style studded doors. He was enchanted. He'd seen pictures and film-sets of English stately homes, but this was different. It looked as if it belonged to another time, a romantic era only read about in history books.

The walls of a stable block were still covered with summer colour. Ivy scrambled with late magnolia and twisted, gnarled wisteria up the old walls. The cobbled courtyard was decked about with moss. He was mesmerised.

'There's clearly no one expected here,' Diana said, and shivered as a sudden cold breeze sprang from nowhere. The sky overhead had become dark and threatening.

Ben glanced up at the looming clouds.

'OK, better go then,' he said, and turned away from the gates reluctantly.

They had barely reached the car when they heard the sound of an engine nearby – and seconds later a loud crack of thunder, followed by a flash of lightening. Rain would not be far behind.

As they stood, not certain what to do next, an old Land-Rover pulled up behind them, with a small, nondescript car in its wake.

In dismay, Diana realised that the youngish, fair-haired man climbing out of the Land-Rover, with a stern set to his jaw, was probably the owner of the land on which they were parked.

Seemingly unperturbed, Ben crossed to the newcomer, and smilingly held out his hand.

'Hi, are we in your way? We seem to have met a dead end here. I'm afraid we're lost.'

The man ignored the hand and his answer was brusque.

'If you are Mr and Mrs Nazareth, you're late. Otherwise you are on private property, signposted as such.' Despite the clipped, well-modulated voice, the man was clearly angry.

Ben shrugged expressively. 'I am Ben Nazareth, yes. And this is Diana Nazareth, but she's my sister-in-law, not my wife.' Ben's tone was light, but Diana knew his exaggerated courtesy covered his own temper.

'If you are Simon Tamerford, then our apologies. We have been on an enchanting trip to an old jetty – unintentional, I can assure you. But I found no signposts of any kind.'

'No. You wouldn't from there,' the man granted in a tight voice. 'The quay is private property too. I suppose you didn't see those signs either?'

Diana was annoyed by his high-handedness. 'No, we did not. We came across it by accident, looking for your house, and have been lost ever since.' Her voice matched his own for coldness.

The man gazed levelly at her. 'I've been out looking for you.

Our appointment was for thirty minutes ago,' he informed her stiffly. 'But you're blocking my drive, and as I don't intend that either my sister or I will reverse for three miles to let you out, it seems I shall still have to see you.'

He ignored the astounded looks on their faces and pulled a large bunch of keys from his pocket.

Diana bit back a sharp reply as he turned away and unlocked the gates.

'Lead the way,' he said curtly to Ben. With that he jumped into his battered old vehicle, and revved the engine impatiently.

'Charming man,' Ben said in a strained voice.

'Arrogant sod,' Diana retorted stiffly.

Ben eased the car forward. 'Breeding has that effect on some folk,' he said enigmatically. 'Anyway, don't let it rile you. We'll get to see that house from closer quarters.'

Diana couldn't have cared less. The unnecessary rudeness had spoiled any interest in the lease.

'We are *not* staying,' she declared heatedly. 'I wouldn't have anything to do with that man if you paid me!'

Thunder continued to crackle noisily overhead as Ben followed the long drive curving around and down towards the buildings they had seen from a distance.

As they approached the house, Ben was so busy trying to see everything that he failed to notice the obstacle in his path until it was too late. Only the sound of his tyre blowing and the sudden slew of the car told him what had happened.

'Oh Christ,' he swore, pulling the vehicle over as quickly as he could. 'That's all we needed.'

'Get the spare on and let's get out of here,' Diana muttered angrily.

'No can do.' Ben was grinning. 'I forgot to put it in. Now I shall have to ask our genial host to let me use his phone. Don't think he'll like that, do you?'

'Ben!' Diana exclaimed warningly. But Ben was already at the Land-Rover door.

Diana sat woodenly in the car, with absolutely no intention of speaking to Mr Simon Tamerford – even if they bumped into one another head-on – ever again. She fumed as she recalled his rudeness. If it took two hours for a garage to send someone out, she would not budge from the car. The rain began to fall, small drops at first, which, in true Devon fashion, suddenly turned into dollops and then a mini-monsoon. In moments she could only just make out the other cars, and a shape she assumed was Ben's. It was just their luck to be caught here with a storm gathering momentum by the second!

The door opened and Ben was suddenly yelling at her above the noise.

'Diana, just *trust* me, please? We've been invited to take tea . . . now don't argue, there's a good girl.'

Ben was soaked to the skin, the rain running in rivers down his face. But she couldn't mistake the twinkle in his eyes. She would have refused, but Ben practically lifted her bodily from the car.

'Oh!' she gasped, as the rain hit her square in the face, blinding her momentarily.

Ben pulled her through the pouring rain towards the house.

Diana's next view was after a towel had been passed to her, and she'd mopped the water from her eyes.

A young woman with a lovely face smiled warmly at her. 'You poor thing. First getting lost on that awful road, and now this puncture. Please, come in out of this dreadful weather. It will be warm in the kitchen.'

Despite her earlier anger, Diana was charmed by the woman's genuine sympathy and good manners. The sister, at least, was worth knowing.

Their host stood inside an arched interior doorway gazing darkly at them. He turned and they automatically followed. At least, they followed at half his pace. He was leading them through the most enormous hall, or was it a room? Diana followed Ben's incredulous stare. The house was a mixture of grandeur and decay.

It was as if they had stepped back hundreds of years: Flagged-stone floors rang with their tread, and everywhere they looked were antiques, most badly in need of repair. There were suits of armour ranged along the walls; paintings in frames as large as doors, their gilded edges peeling, watched over them. Tapestries, once rich and fine, hung limply, their beauty faded. A fireplace as big as the drawing-room at Glanville Road yawned at the end of the hall, its cavernous mouth filled with cast-iron pots. Fire-irons, as big as any man, stood against a blackened granite hearth.

They were ushered without ceremony through a small oak door at one side of the fireplace, and on through a series of dim rooms unlit by any source, so it was all they could do not to stumble, and their concentration rapidly centred on keeping up.

Finally they were led into a huge kitchen-living-room, whose warmth, light and heavenly aroma of stew assailed them all at the same time. They both blinked, accustoming themselves to the light and to their strange surroundings.

Their host crossed to speak with a tall, very elderly lady, dressed from head to toe in black. She turned briefly from an ancient cooking range to gaze at them, then abruptly turned her back to busy herself over the range.

Diana interpreted Ben's raised brows, and agreed to herself that this must be where the man had learned his manners.

However, the sister made the introductions.

'I'm Gabrielle Tamerford, but please call me Gabbie. You've met my brother, Simon – and this is our Great-Aunt Ruth.

'Please sit down, if you can find anywhere.' She grimaced apologetically, moving clutter from the few chairs; some small tapestries, a sewing box and a skein of coloured silks. 'We rarely have visitors,' she confided, 'so we tend to be very untidy in here, much to Great-Aunt Ruth's eternal dismay. There, now please do sit down. Tea won't be a moment.'

'Thank you, Gabbie. We didn't mean to intrude,' Diana said, wondering where the meeting have been held had they arrived at the appointed time. But she dismissed the thought as they all shook hands.

Simon Tamerford reluctantly took Ben's proffered hand, eyeing the difference in their heights – Ben stood a head and shoulders above him – and, looking even more uncomfortable, Simon, too, sat down.

The great-aunt brought a pot of tea to the table, set it carefully down, and then gazed at them both again before turning without a word and walking silently from the room.

'Please excuse Great-Aunt Ruth,' Gabbie said swiftly. 'She really lives in a world of her own most of the time. We're lucky still to have her, and with most of her faculties intact.' She smiled and poured the tea.

'Is your aunt very elderly then?' Ben asked conversationally.

'Yes, almost ninety.'

'Good heavens.' Diana felt ashamed of the comparisons she'd been making between Simon and his aunt. 'She doesn't look anywhere near that age.'

'No, she doesn't,' Gabbie agreed proudly and with obvious love.

Ben finished his tea and turned to Simon. 'I realise we can't expect our meeting to go ahead, but I'm embarrassed here . . . Obviously we're holding up your meal. If I could just use your telephone, then we can wait in the car.'

Simon coloured. ''Fraid that won't be possible, old chap.' His voice was edgy. 'We don't have a telephone.'

'No phone?' Ben repeated.

'I'm afraid not,' Simon said tersely. 'And it's too dark to go ahead with our meeting.' He made an vague gesture with his hands, which could have meant he was sorry – but which Diana interpreted as meaning he was only too glad to get rid of them. 'Perhaps some other time,' he added, without interest.

'Fine,' Ben said, concealing his disappointment.

'How do we get home?' Diana asked pointedly.

Gabbie didn't hesitate, 'I'll drive you – and you could

perhaps get someone out to look at the car tomorrow.' She gave them another apologetic smile. 'I don't think you'll find a mechanic willing to come to these wilds on an evening like this.'

Diana smiled her relief.

'You'll do nothing of the kind.' Simon stood up purposefully. 'I will not have you out after dark in that death-trap of a car.' He turned to Ben. 'If you are ready?'

Ben tried to converse with the man on the journey, but all he got was monosyllabic answers. Diana's first impression was reinforced. Gabbie was a delightful person – her brother was not. At Glanville Road he refused Ben's invitation to come in, clearly impatient to be gone.

'Well, thank you again. We'll see you tomorrow,' Ben said courteously.

'I'm only in for tea for half an hour, at four, but no doubt my sister will be about somewhere,' Simon replied dismissively.

They stood in the rain, watching his tail lights disappear.

'Well, I'll be damned.' Ben chuckled. 'Did you ever meet the likes of that . . .?'

'Not before. And, I hope, never again,' Diana said feelingly, amazed that Ben was so amused by it all.

CHAPTER TWENTY-FIVE

Later, after a welcome meal, they recounted their experiences to Gemma and Candy.

'I wish I'd been there,' Gemma moaned. 'It sounds like something out of a horror story. Just my luck to miss it.'

'I'd have liked to meet Gabrielle. She sounds nice,' Candy commented. 'And their house must have been fascinating.'

'Fascinating owner,' Diana said with a shudder.

'Yes, very,' Ben agreed, that odd smile still on his face. 'In fact, I shall enjoy getting to know Mr Simon Tamerford.'

'You must be joking!'

'Not at all,' Ben replied with surprising conviction. 'I think that guy might need a friend.'

Diana couldn't believe her ears. Simon Tamerford had made it perfectly clear that he was not interested in entertaining them again. Whatever the lease might have offered, it had clearly been written off now.

'Ben, you are being stupid — '

'I'm not, Diana. That man has a lot of problems. We might just be able to solve some of them for him.'

She could only stare at him incredulously.

'Here!' Candy exclaimed excitedly, pausing in her search through a pile of ordinance survey maps. 'I've found it, look . . .' They all gathered around her, even Diana, in spite of her declared lack of interest.

'Here. It's called Tamerford Manor.' Candy spread the map on the table. 'Golly, it has hundreds of acres of land, some of it forested . . . and look here, there's a river, quite a big one. It must be quite a place.' Her finger pointed again. 'And look at this, even the village is named after the manor. It's called Tamerford.'

'Exactly,' Ben beamed. 'The perfect place.'

'Ben, *no* — '

'Oh *yes*, Diana,' he said seriously. 'It's perfect. All we have to do now is persuade the Tamerfords to sell.'

'You're crazy. Why would they?'

'Money, Diana. A simple financial equation. Did you get a good look at that place?'

'Of course not, and neither did you.'

'I did see how badly they need money,' he said quietly.

'With all those antiques? That land?' Now Diana's disbelief was total.

The girls watched the argument with interest.

Ben's gaze was steady. 'Simon's clothes were all but threadbare,' he persisted. 'The place is falling down around them and they can't even afford to install a telephone.'

'Maybe they just don't want one,' Diana said stubbornly.

'As much as they don't want electricity?' Ben asked softly.

'They have electricity,' Diana said shortly.

'Nope. They have a *generator*,' Ben corrected. 'And the only room in that whole place that appears to be wired is that ancient kitchen. And not for appliances, only for light. I checked,' he added soberly. 'And I listened. There's only a small generator, and I think I know why. Generators are very fuel-hungry — '

'Lots of country folk still don't want power,' Gemma interrupted, becoming bored.

Ben stretched his long legs out under the table and watched their faces. Diana's showed disbelief, Candy's excitement, Gemma's poorly disguised interest. He was inwardly trembling with excitement and wanted to shout at them that he was right. But he knew enough about them now to know that they would not be won by pressure, particularly Diana. Persuasion was the key to her – and without her agreement he couldn't do a thing. He still needed to convince her, and he was shrewd enough to realise that gaining her cousins' sympathy would be a step in the right direction.

'I believe Mr Simon Tamerford wants electricity,' Ben smiled warmly at Gemma. 'You see, I studied our arrogant host, and I'd lay any odds that his anger at the world is caused by frustration. I admit to knowing very little about the man's actual situation, but I wasn't trained as a lawyer for nothing. Observation of human behaviour is one of the first things you learn – and there's no better training ground for studying stress in all its forms, than the courtoom.' He had their complete attention now, as he had intended. 'And I might add that I had eighteen years' tutelage under the best psychologist there is: David Nazareth. I started my training by watching him from the time I could see his face, and while I'm not finished learning by a long shot, I'd say I was pretty qualified to judge the behaviour of an irrational man.

'And Simon Tamerford is an irrational man. His behaviour today was appalling, and unnecessary. He displayed classic signs of chronic shyness, or insecurity on a grand scale, or both. Now, when you think about it, as the owner of an estate the size of Tamerford he should exude confidence; and courtesy would have been bred into him.

'As he wasn't able to manage anything other than rudeness and anger, I'd say he's a man with more problems than he can handle; problems that he sees no way of overcoming; almighty money problems. He's haunted, harrassed beyond his ability to cope.'

'That's awful,' Candy said in real distress.

Ben didn't hear her: he was engrossed in the map and in his thoughts. He'd even forgotten his ploy to involve them.

'I'd say he's probably also younger than he looks, but that years of hard work and worry have aged him.' He gazed thoughtfully at the map. 'It must have been a sharp kick in the ribs when he found us at his rotting gates in a new and very expensive car.' Now he did look up, at Diana. 'His reaction was one of pure humiliation.'

Diana's hand covered her mouth. She felt dreadful for the things she had thought.

'It wasn't personal – he was choking. Then, when he was

forced by circumstances to show us how he lives in that outwardly grand place, it was more than he could take. That man was dying slowly. Of embarrassment.'

'Oh, I was so rude to him — '

'That's natural,' Ben said. 'He asked for it, so don't feel bad. You couldn't know what his situation was.' He grimaced. 'I didn't feel too good myself, sitting there in an expensive suit when he can't afford a decent jacket. He'd taken off his topcoat by the time we got inside and, as he had been expecting us, the jacket he was wearing had to have been his best.'

'I don't follow,' Diana frowned.

'It was patched, Diana. Very cleverly, yes, but everywhere. And his cord trousers were too far gone to be patched any more. They were threadbare. And when he thought I wasn't aware, he was staring at my clothes.'

The silence in the room was heavy with emotion.

Ben rubbed his eyes tiredly. 'Believe it or not, I liked the man. He's proud, but that's not unnatural with his birthright. I'd also say that under that arrogance he's a decent, honourable type. Look at the way he wouldn't let his sister come back out in that old car. No, I'd say he's just over his head in worries.'

'And you're going to try to take his home away from him?' Candy's voice was pain-filled.

Ben swiftly remembered what this was all about and silently blessed the girl's caring nature.

'On the contrary, how I see it is that if we, the Youth Trust, were to offer him a chance to keep his home and improve his own circumstances, while aiding a very worthwhile cause, he might be more than willing to listen.'

'I don't see how — '

'Diana . . .' Ben stopped her. 'Think about it. There's just no way that family can restore the ancestral home to its former glory – and I'd guess that would be their prime concern. Supposing we could show them that it *could* be done, even on a 'you scratch my back and I'll scratch yours' basis, don't you think they'd be at least interested?'

All three gazes were fixed on his, Gemma's with doubt, but definite interest, Candy's with open excitement, Diana's, through narrowed eyes, showing a glint of understanding.

'I do believe, Benjamin Nazareth, that you might not be totally mad after all,' she said.

'Thank you, ma'am.' Ben made a mock bow. 'I think you might be totally right.'

They sat up late into the night as Ben explained his ideas. They were daring, possibly frightening, but the more they were thrashed out the more it began to look as if they could work.

An hour before dawn they agreed on their immediate plan of action and it was a tired but determined quartet that arrived later that day at Tamerford Manor.

Diana's two-door BMW was hardly ideal for four people, and they piled out in some relief. Candy fell in love with the house instantly, while Gemma revelled in the tapestry of colours and textures of the setting.

Their first ploy had been to arrange for a mechanic to arrive at least an hour after them, and at least one hour before Simon was due at the house for his tea. This was to be not only a recce but also the start of their plan.

No one came immediately to greet them, so they had a few minutes in which to gaze around, minutes in which Ben's initial perceptions proved sound. As he had been sure, the house and outbuildings ranged over a very large area, and in the distance even more buildings confirmed his hopes.

Now he hammered again on the massive door, praying that it wasn't all going to go wrong. Suppose Gabbie wasn't, after all, at home? A bead of perspiration glistened on his forehead; the girls began to look worried.

But then a brightly dressed figure appeared at a distant wing of the house, waving at them to come that way.

Gabbie greeted them cheerily. 'I hope you haven't been there too long? We don't often use that entrance,' she explained. 'It was just the nearest yesterday in that sudden storm.'

Diana made the introductions, and they were all welcomed warmly.

Gabbie seemed unfazed by the extra company. 'How nice! We rarely have company and it's lovely to meet you.'

'We don't seem to have got our timing right,' Ben lied with an apologetic smile. 'The mechanic doesn't appear to be here yet.'

'Good!' Gabbie wrinkled her nose as if mischievously. 'Then you can take tea with me. We'll hear him arrive if we sit in the old dining-room. Please come in.'

Ben winked at the girls and fell in beside Gabbie, enthusing about the house and its grounds. She was totally unlike her brother, her own enthusiasm evident in her happy chattering as she led them through a bewildering maze of cobbled yards and small, shaded quadrangles, finally leading to a walled herb garden, through which they entered the kitchen, now empty, where they had been made to feel so uncomfortable yesterday.

But Gabbie didn't pause in the kitchen, merely led the way through a series of halls, some square, some narrow, into a part of the building beyond the great hall. The door they took was tucked away behind the massive fireplace, and led them beneath a Gothic granite arch into a beautiful wood-floored hall.

'It's far too big for us,' she said with a laugh, 'and not easy to run. I imagine it was a nightmare for the servants in the old days . . . but I doubt that the family were greatly inconvenienced. Not that I'd have a clue how to manage servants, even if we could afford them!' She pulled a wry face. 'And of course one wouldn't call them servants now, probably staff. Quite right too,' she added gaily.

Yet another hall, but this one made them all stop, just to stare at the old stone-flagged floors, a sweeping staircase, wide enough to take a coach and four, rising to a galleried hall above

– far too wide for them even to glimpse the doors that must lie
beyond.

On every available foot of wall hung enormous paintings –
very definitely not of any recent time.

Diana began to feel uneasy. Perhaps they'd been too quick to
judge. There was no shortage of wealth here. On the contrary,
the furniture and furnishings they had glimpsed, never mind
the paintings here, had to be worth more than they could begin
to imagine.

Gabbie led them finally into a room dominated by a central
refectory table and massive oak carver chairs; the walls
were entirely hidden by ancient Flemish tapestries.

'Do sit wherever you like. I'll fetch some tea,' Gabbie said.

'Good lord. All that way again?' Diana couldn't help a look
of dismay.

Gabbie laughed widely, showing perfect white teeth. 'Ah,
but across from here, I can reach the kitchen easily. From
where we came in, that's a different story. Look . . .'

She pulled open a wide door to reveal another courtyard,
this one bright with flowering shrubs. 'That's the outer pantry,'
she pointed to a whitewashed door in a far wall. 'Through
there, and I'm next to the kettle in no time.' Now she gave them
that mischievous grin again. 'It's one of the lesser walks . . .'

While they waited, their curiosity taking in all the details
of the room, they each mused about Gabrielle. Diana thought
her one of the nicest young women she'd ever met, quite
unaffected and natural. She knew that she could like the girl
very much, given the chance.

Ben had similar thoughts, but tinged with business interest.
The sister would be a good ally to have on their side, and
already he was sure that Diana would establish a friendship
quickly.

Possibly she'd have to. He, too, had noted the antiques and
the paintings, and he had to admit they worried him.

Candy was too overwhelmed to do anything more than stare
around her.

Gemma was intrigued, but not by the house, which to her was creepy, over-large and hideously old-fashioned. Her interest was in Gabbie herself. Not only was she charming, tall and as slim as any fashion model, but she wore her clothes as if they were designer garments instead of the home-made outfits Gemma knew them to be.

Gemma thought she recognised a soulmate, someone with a similar passion and flair for clothes. Her own ambition, to design and market her own designs, was something she instinctively felt that Gabbie would understand.

Gabbie was true to her word and soon they were drinking tea, with Ben's ears fine-tuned for the arrival of the mechanic. Once the man arrived, what possible excuse could they have for staying longer?

Gabbie was saying matter-of-factly, 'It's not the most comfortable room, but it has the advantage of facing south, so as well as being warmer than most, one has the light for longer.'

'You don't have electricity then?' Ben asked, his voice innocent.

'Lord, no, far too expensive, I'm afraid. And there are far greater priorities for Simon.'

'Such as what?' Ben enquired, with a smile.

'Well, the repairs, the running expenses, the farms. A hundred things that you would find boring,' she said simply. 'I honestly don't know how he keeps up, poor thing.' For a moment her face was shadowed with sadness, but she swiftly recovered. 'I help as much as I can, but there's the house to run, furnishings to repair – not that I ever seem to get anywhere with those – and, of course, great-aunt to care for. I'm not as great a help to him as I'd like to be.'

'No doubt things will improve, in the future.' Ben tested carefully.

She shook her long dark hair, and her green eyes were clouded. 'Not in our lifetimes, I'm afraid.'

Diana was uncomfortable. It no longer felt ethical to discuss the future of Tamerford in this way.

'We were hoping that you and your brother would have dinner with us,' she began. 'Nothing formal, just the six of us, and of course your great-aunt, if you think she would enjoy it?'

'Oh, how lovely,' Gabbie was instantly cheered, her face softening with pleasure. 'When?'

'Whenever it suits you,' Gemma responded swiftly.

'I would have to check with Simon first,' Gabbie pulled a face. 'He's not a great socialiser, as you noticed yesterday, but I'm sure I can persuade him. He's always saying that I should get out more.' Now her smile was conspiratorial. 'So he's not likely to object, is he?'

Diana had her doubts, but could hardly say so.

'But great-aunt never leaves the house now. I'm sure you understand . . .'

At that moment they heard a car outside, so Ben had to excuse them.

'I'll be sure to have a spare tyre in future,' he promised Gabbie.

'I'm glad you hadn't this time,' she grinned.

'You will call?' Diana handed Gabbie their phone number, having been assured that there was a phone box in the village.

'I promise,' Gabbie said firmly.

There was nothing they could do but wait, knowing that if Gabbie couldn't talk Simon into meeting them again they were in trouble.

Even Ben quailed at the prospect of having to make a further, direct approach so when Gabbie called the very next day, there was a collective sigh of relief and Saturday evening was agreed.

'Let's down-play the visit,' Ben warned. 'No fancy dressing, and keep the meal simple. We don't want Simon bolting before the race . . .'

No one could have said who was most nervous as the six of them sat down to a soup starter – although admittedly Simon was courteous from the moment of his arrival. He couldn't have been described as talkative, but his behaviour was less arrogant. He listened to the small-talk, gave the occasional half-smile or nod.

At least he wasn't scowling, Diana thought as she cleared the dishes for the roast to follow, though whether he would join in the conversation remained to be seen.

Simon wore the tweed jacket again, with much-pressed grey flannel trousers, and an old school tie. Gabbie delighted Gemma in an ankle-length jade green chiffon dress that was beautifully copied from the current handkerchief-hem styles.

Ben was at his most charming and the girls chattered unself-consciously.

Only Candy seemed as tongue-tied as Simon, her cheeks remaining red for far longer, Diana mused, than their stint in the kitchen warranted. In fact Diana began to wonder . . .

As dinner neared its end, Ben went to get more wine, leaving Simon free at last to talk to Candy. Diana deliberately joined the conversation with Gemma and Gabbie, now advanced to the latest fabrics – but couldn't help but be aware of the current passing between her youngest cousin and their guest.

When Ben returned Diana gave him a quick, meaningful look, indicating the pair with a slight nod. Ben's eyebrows rose, but he got the message quickly enough.

It was as if Simon had undergone some sudden character change. They spoke in soft tones, but his eyes were alive, and, at something Candy blushingly said, he laughed.

But pudding was Candy's pièce-de-resistance, and so in time she had to excuse herself.

Simon turned back to Ben and Diana, but now his face was less strained.

'I'm afraid I owe you both an apology,' he said ruefully, colouring slightly. 'I can't really excuse my bad behaviour, except to say that it had been a trying day, one way and another.'

'No problem,' Ben said easily. 'We were late, we were at the wrong entrance . . .'

'No,' Simon's hands moved expressively, 'I was very rude. Unforgivable of me . . .' He reddened still more. 'But I ask your forgiveness nevertheless.'

It was so simply put, so without guile, that they both smiled.

'And I was concerned,' Simon continued, his voice still taut, but determined to explain. 'Adrian Lawrence is an old family friend, but I admit to having resented his interference. Although, God knows, we could use the money — '

'There's nothing wrong with that,' Gemma put in, having tuned back into the conversation.

'Do you have much livestock?' Ben steered the subject back on to safer ground.

'Too much, and yet not enough,' Simon grimaced.

'How's that?' They were on a roll and Ben didn't want to let the moment escape.

Again Simon coloured. 'I have the land for a great number of animals, but not the funds to hire the labour and expand. In truth, it takes me all my time managing what I have now . . . and the rewards are non-existent.'

'That's a shame,' Ben commiserated. 'Farming is always a risky business – even if you have the capital.'

Simon gazed at him, his look clearly asking what Ben thought he knew about it.

'I worked my last years through college, and later worked summers to pay for law school.' Ben settled easily into a subject he was comfortable with. 'Only as a hired hand,' he added hastily, 'but even so you get to learn a lot.'

Simon's attention was caught. 'What kind of hired hand?'

'First on a pine farm – the guy grew Christmas trees. Not much variety in that . . . but later on an arable and livestock farm. Part prize beef cattle – Charolais and Limousins imported from France – and the rest was corn and beet, feedstuff basically.'

Simon and Gabbie were both listening intently, and it was obvious that the two men had found unexpected common ground. Soon the talk was all of farming.

Diana, as surprised as anyone, wondered why Ben had never mentioned his knowledge; but at the same time she realised that Ben was still very much an unknown quantity. How had they all lived together for seven months, and learned so little about one another?

But the answer was obvious. The trust had excluded everything.

As well as watching Simon and Ben, now conversing in great depth, she covertly watched Candy. The girl hung on Simon's every word. Had Gemma noticed? Diana doubted it; she had returned to monopolising Gabbie, as if the others didn't exist.

Altogether the evening was turning out well.

But as midnight approached, Simon reluctantly said they would have to go. 'I have a six o'clock start,' he apologised.

'Oh Lord!' Gabbie exclaimed. 'Great-aunt! I hope she hasn't needed anything . . . I've never left her before,' she added in dismay.

'She'll be sound asleep,' Simon reassured her, then, just as Ben was about to make his play, Simon turned suddenly to Candy. 'My most valuable heifer is due to calve soon. Would you be interested in seeing her? I rather think it could be tomorrow or the next day.'

Candy nodded, tongue-tied, her cheeks twin spots of flame.

'Might I collect you around lunch-time?'

Candy nodded again, strained at being the sudden centre of attention.

Thank you for a lovely evening, and a super dinner.' Gabbie filled the silence gaily. 'We'll return the compliment very soon.'

The Tamerfords moved towards the door.

'Oh,' Ben said, as if he'd just thought of it, 'would it be any trouble if I were to come over sometime, Simon?' He managed a mocking smile. 'I'm fresh out of decent exercise, and as you can see, it's fairly over-womanised around here. I'd enjoy the chance to help out,' he added hastily.

Simon looked surprised. 'Are you here permanently?'

'For several years. I'm involved in running a trust with my, uh, sister-in-law here . . . but as we don't have that up and running yet, I have time on my hands. Perhaps,' he added carefully, 'we could even talk around the idea of that lease?'

'Fine,' Simon said non-committally. 'Why don't you pop over the day after tomorrow? I'll be glad to show you around.'

Ben smiled his thanks.

As he got into his Land-Rover, Simon turned one last time to Ben. 'But if you expect me to take you seriously . . .' he looked at Diana and gave her a wink . . . 'I suggest you find something suitable to wear.'

'Still waters run deep,' Gemma quipped as they returned to the house.

'They certainly do,' Diana agreed cheerfully. 'He's not such an ogre after all.'

'Quite a dry humour,' Ben mused. 'And I don't think our Mr Simon Tamerford is anybody's fool.'

'You mean he's sussed us?' Gemma asked, wide-eyed.

'No, not yet. But he knows we're up to something.'

'He's up to something himself,' Diana said meaningfully.

Ben frowned and looked at the closed kitchen door, where Candy had closeted herself with the dishes. 'Mmm, interesting.'

'Absolutely,' Diana replied. Then, with a warning frown at Gemma, she added, 'Don't make any wisecracks to her, Gems. Let it take its course. Whatever that might be.'

Gemma stared at her as it all began to truly sink in. 'Of course. That's why he didn't want you over there tomorrow, Ben.'

'You know, Gemma, I think you've got a brain after all,' Ben grinned.

Candy returned the next evening glowing from her day in the fresh air; she could barely conceal her excitement over the successful delivery of the heifer calf Simon had hoped for.

With difficulty they refrained from questioning her about the personal side of the day but, knowing their joint mission, she volunteered her impressions of the antiquated farm.

Ben was at Tamerford with minutes to spare the next morning, suitably attired in traditional country clothing.

Simon, coolly appraising him, could have said that a new Barbour, olive wellingtons and a smartly checked cloth cap might have been more appropriate for a weekend country gathering than for farm work; but he refrained and Ben strode with ease beside his host, genuinely interested in the land and the work and appalled by the worn, outmoded tools with which Simon had to work.

They worked steadily until noon, when Gabbie brought them a thermos of hot soup and bread still warm from the oven. It was only as they sat to eat on a hay bale, that Ben winced as a stab of pain hit his lower back.

'Out of practice, eh?' Simon's smile was still a little reserved.

'Looks like it,' Ben admitted.

'Well, don't overdo it today,' Simon warned. 'You won't be much help flat on your back. Call it a day and come by another time.'

'Not on your life,' Ben grimaced. 'How'd that look to the girls?'

'On your own head, then . . .'

By four in the afternoon, though, Ben had almost had it. He was very fit, but he wasn't used to all the bending yet. As they reached the last post on a stock-fence they were repairing, he eased himself straight gingerly. 'Perhaps I should take your advice now. But before I go, could we talk?'

'I wondered if we might, eventually,' Simon said drily.

'I hadn't imagined you wanted to do this for the love of it.'

'I *am* enjoying it,' Ben contradicted wryly. 'But enough is enough for one day. And yes, I'd hoped for the opportunity to talk.'

'Fair enough.' Simon returned to the job in hand. 'But I've told you how I feel. I can't see how Adrian's suggestion would work – and,' he added cautiously, 'I don't know what you have in mind.'

'You have a lot of outbuildings,' Ben began, 'and, from what you say, a lot of land you can't afford to work. For starters, would you tell me which buildings Adrian was talking about?'

'There's the quay – there's a mill building there, and some cottages you must have seen; a number of barns, various stone outhouses, all dilapidated. And there's the lodge at the western gate.'

Simon squinted at the last stretch of fence, checking the line-up. 'On another approach to the quay there is an old coach-house, some very tumble-down servants' cottages; near the area we call Cherry Walk there is a large sorting house, where the fruit was once sorted for the markets and then there is the gardener's cottage, above the walled gardens that once produced vegetables.'

He put his tools into a bag, and watched Ben's face. 'Old glasshouses, storage rooms. There's even an old ice-house, which you can still get into although it's very grown over – and it's still damned cold down there.'

'I see. And how much of the land itself is still productive?' Ben asked, his brain racing.

'About twenty acres,' Simon said angrily, the humiliation again showing.

'How come?' Ben said gently.

'I don't know . . . bad management.' Simon managed a shrug, but Ben was not fooled.

'A careless ancestor or two, a couple of gamblers, death

duties . . .' His face was grim now. 'Advances in technology we couldn't keep up with. Ours is not the first estate to fall victim to trends.'

'Have you ever thought of selling?'

Simon stared, and Ben thought he'd gone too far, too quickly.

'No. My father talked about it, but I believe Ruth talked him out of it. I think she was right,' he added. 'It's one of the few medieval homes left in the country. If anything, it should be a national treasure' – he leaned against a fence post – 'but it happens to be our home.'

Ben could feel the man's pride and frustration seething, but he knew he had to go on while he had the chance.

'And you couldn't sell any of the furniture, or the paintings, or the tapestries?'

'No, I damned well couldn't!' Simon snapped. 'It's probably hard for you to understand, but this land, the house and everything in it have belonged to my family, by direct descent, for more generations than I can keep track of. I could no more sell a chair than sell my soul.'

Ben felt a strange compassion, strange because he knew he was getting involved, compassion because he was feeling more for Simon than for the trust.

'But how long can you go on?' he asked gently.

Simon's burst of anger had burned out. 'I don't know,' he said wearily. 'I honestly don't know.'

'What do you reckon it would cost, to put it all right?' Ben's gaze was intense.

Simon straightened up, and sighed. 'Millions,' he said emptily. 'At a guess.'

Ben stared across the patchwork of ancient land, deep in thought. If he'd understood everything correctly, it could be that more than the trust could benefit. And, unexpectedly, that mattered to him. It mattered that Simon should keep his home.

Suddenly he wanted to tell him the truth, to confess his

plans. He wanted Simon to agree to be helped. Perhaps it even mattered more than the trust?

He had to shake himself. He was getting sentimental. Maybe it was the atmosphere around the old place? There was a magnetism here, and he was falling under its influence. But he didn't mind.

'Supposing I were to tell you that I think we could help,' he began cautiously. 'Help to save Tamerford, and at the same time help give employment to all the young people of the area. Would you be willing to listen?'

Simon turned back to him. 'I'd be a fool not to.'

Ben told him everything as they walked slowly back towards the house. He left out nothing, including his own feelings about David Nazareth. He told him what he knew of Diana's marriage to Mat, and his conviction that David was more than besotted with her.

Simon listened intently until Ben came to the final part: their search for premises, his vague ideas, and their meeting with Adrian Lawrence. If he objected when Ben described his feelings on discovering Tamerford, he kept it to himself.

Now they stood beside Ben's car, Simon's face a mixture of fascination and uncertainty.

'I don't think I'd care to upset your Boston benefactor,' he said finally. 'He sounds a thoroughly nasty piece of work. Hmm, I'm not certain I'd care to put my future in those hands.'

'Ah, but you wouldn't. The trust is ours legally, and we spend the money as we see fit,' Ben reassured him.

Simon's blue-green eyes were perplexed. 'It's a massive undertaking, Ben. And although it's a very attractive idea, I'm not convinced it could work.'

'But if Diana and I came over, brought my plans, we could have a proper look around the estate – and then discuss it fully. Would you at least agree to that?'

Simon scuffed at the ground, thinking. Then eventually he looked up, and his face was grave.

'Bring Diana over for the weekend. There's no harm in talking.' He waved his arm in the general direction of the farm, and smiled tightly. 'I don't remember a weekend off . . . I'll get a local chap in for a couple of days. Probably do me good to take a break.'

Ben went to shake his hand, but Simon stopped him with a step backwards and a shake of his head.

'No promises, Ben. We'll talk, but I'm making no promises.'

'Agreed,' Ben smiled. 'And tomorrow I'll be here to help out as agreed.'

'See how your back is,' Simon commented drily.

CHAPTER TWENTY-SIX

Candy and Gemma were disappointed not to have been included in the invitation, but they were excited and optimistic over the news. Candy had told them nothing about her second date with Simon. All they knew was that she was seeing him again soon and if it was unlike her to be so close about her feelings, none of the others commented.

Diana thought about David as she packed a few essentials in an overnight bag. She hoped they would have news for him soon now. She'd spoken to him a couple of times and written her reports as promised, but she was finding it harder to be comfortable with him since Ben's revelations about his childhood. As far as she was concerned, the sooner the entire situation with him and Ben was resolved the better. Perhaps then she would finally be free of the Nazareths. The power of veto she held over the trust also distressed her. It made her feel like Ben's minder and, conversely, David's spy. Neither position was tenable for very long.

Gemma watched her cousin preparing for her brief weekend, and was ashamed of the jealousy that gnawed at her.

They might indeed have been engrossed in the trust, but not so exclusively that Ben's increasing attraction to Diana wasn't obvious, at least to Gemma, and Diana was not as immune to Ben as when he had first arrived – although it was not discussed between them any more. Gemma had seen Diana laugh with Ben; watched her eyes light up sometimes when he was particularly attentive. Now they were going to be together all weekend in that great rambling house . . .

Diana looked up at that moment and caught her frown.

'Something wrong, Gems?'

'Uh uh,' Gemma denied, wishing she could dare to say 'please leave something for me'. But it was out of her hands

and she knew it. No, Diana hadn't encouraged any flirtation
. . . but Gemma shivered.

'Cold?' Diana asked, mildly surprised.

'Goose-bumps,' Gemma stated, and shot out to her own
room before she could say anything more.

Diana frowned after her. Gemma was behaving a bit oddly
this week. Perhaps she was coming down with a chill?

They had walked their feet off around the estate for most of
the afternoon, until the setting September sun chilled the air
and chased them in to the comparative warmth of the house.

They ate a simple supper in the kitchen – no sign of the
great-aunt anywhere which, to Diana's surprise, pleased her.
But she couldn't help feeling uneasy in the room. It was a
relief to find the library fire glowing and dozens of candles
illuminating the floor-to-ceiling bookshelves – a chance for
Diana to shut off the trust for just a few minutes, to explore
the literary treasures.

But she was soon recalled to the duty before them. The two
men had spread the table with maps and notes, and Gabbie
poured cognacs as their after-supper treat.

Diana watched Ben with great interest. He'd had a good
idea of what he wanted, but it was as if Tamerford had been
the catalyst, bringing substance and form to the skeleton of
his dream. Now he had seen what was possibly available, he
was on cloud nine, one idea after another tumbling into the
melting pot of the grander scheme.

As she witnessed both Simon and Gabbie become cautiously but ever-increasingly involved, Diana had to admire
Ben. Not only was he in sight of a solution for the trust, but
he had extended their interest to include the preservation of
Tamerford. Listening to him now, it was already difficult to
see where the demarcation lines, if any, would lie.

The brandy flowed as freely as their discussions; candles
guttered and were replaced. Still the momentum gathered. In
the soft pools of light, Ben's features were becoming blurred.

Diana rubbed at her eyes, unwilling to admit her tiredness, or the effects of the drink. Or, more especially, the effect Ben was having on her.

He constantly drew her into the conversation, wanted her comments – and from time to time it seemed as if he smiled a secret smile, just for her. At first she had thought it merely a sign of his delight with their progress, but now, after another intense and surely intimate gaze, the smile was there again. This time her stomach flipped and her toes curled.

She tried to warn herself that it could only be the enforced intimacy of candlelight, her pleasure in the progress they seemed to be making, and the combined haze of warmth and brandy. But her reasoning powers were blunted; her body responded to the sexual chemistry – and the next time he glanced over Simon's head at her she couldn't look away.

Ben's eyes had grown dark, but a flame flickered in their depths. She should have had the sense to scowl – or to shrug coldly. But she could do neither. His lips parted slightly in an undoubted invitation. Her own lips trembled and Ben's eyes softened beneath a raised eyebrow.

Diana was barely aware of Ben bringing the late night to a close – unaware that they were mere technicalities away from concluding a mutual arrangement with Simon; or that the trust and Tamerford had somehow become synonymous.

She was just grateful that neither Gabbie nor Simon appeared to have noticed how silent she had become.

Diana was light-headed as she and Ben made their way to the wing shown them earlier. The oil lamps placed for them cast long shadows in the dark halls, causing her to stumble and lean more into Ben's guiding arm.

An arm that caressed as it steadied.

'You're drunk,' he whispered in her ear.

'Am not,' she slurred.

'Remember you said that, tomorrow,' he said, his voice husky with promise.

At last they found the rooms they'd been given, and Ben led her carefully to her four-poster bed.

'I thought these rooms were nearer,' he laughed softly. 'Next time we should bring the car.' He fell on the bed, still laughing.

She couldn't help an attack of mild hysterics, and soon they were entwined in a ball, laughing for so long that her sides began to ache.

'Don't,' she managed between fits of laughter. 'I'm not shure that shleeping here is shomething to be repeated . . .'

'Those long dark halls,' Ben groaned in mock fear. 'I'll bet they're haunted.'

'Ohhh,' Diana squealed, curling closer to him.

Ben's body relaxed against hers. It was nice, Diana thought vaguely. Hard and soft, and he smelt good.

'I should go,' Ben whispered, holding her that little bit tighter.

'Uh, uh.' She shook her head against his chest. 'Ghoshtsh'll get me.'

'Then let's go to bed,' he said softly, his lips against her hair. 'It's getting cold.'

For answer Diana shivered. Ben's mouth found her lips and, although something was trying to make itself heard in her mind, it was lost in the tenderness of his kiss. Desire won over everything else. Even though Diana wanted to protest when Ben undressed her, his mouth on her body drew hot little shivers instead: the combination of alcohol and Ben's skills were too much; her mind and body fused into an aching need.

Her faculties began to fade; Ben's whispers, her own molten limbs, the slip-sliding room, became one dizzying plateau – then a precipice of pleasure and confusion. Everything was falling, and she was going with it.

She passed out quietly.

Diana woke, startled. Something was different. Her eyes hurt, but there was more . . .

She stretched tentatively, memories filtering into her muggy brain. Instinctively she sat bolt upright, her eyes flying open wide. Lifting the covers, she stared at her naked body, and groaned.

My God, she and Ben . . . they'd . . . Now her head pounded. She lay back on the pillow, her hand over her mouth, trying to untangle her thoughts from the thump of the hangover. Had they gone all the way? They'd been naked, she recalled that. Ben's touch and his mouth . . . She gulped, there was no chance of forgetting those. But, had she – had they . . .? Her mind seemed to stop short of total recall, and although she tried desperately, she couldn't fill in any more details. Again she groaned. Facts were facts. She did remember their nakedness, the feel of Ben's body, and yes, her own responses. God, *how* she'd responded.

She closed her eyes, trying to think. *How* had he got past her guard? *When* had that happened? *Had* she encouraged him? Slowly the earlier part of the evening came back to mind. The euphoria of their success, so far, with Simon. The wine and the brandy; the warm fire; the candlelight – and the intense, sensual interchanges between them.

Oh yes, her guard had been down. She had let Ben see how attractive she found him. Damn it, she'd made it bloody obvious. Eight months in the same house and she hadn't made one slip-up – but one evening at Tamerford had destroyed the wall she'd so determinedly built against him.

She had recognised the dangerous chemistry between them on the very first day they'd met. Now it seemed she had thrown everything away and given in to her feelings; knowing how she felt about Nazareths, knowing how Gemma felt about Ben.

In disgust she rolled to the edge of the bed and gingerly put her feet to the ground. The room remained steady; only her head and her heart were disorientated.

As she dressed she thought soberly. Whatever the final outcome had been, she needed to make sure that it wasn't misconstrued. She could not afford for Ben to take the episode seriously, or to think it could happen again. The ache in her head matched the pain in her heart, but she was adamant. Ben must never know how easily she could love him. One, because it would break Gemma's heart, and, two, because it would be too cruel to David.

She silently prayed that Ben, too, had been intoxicated; that he would prefer not to remember. She slipped into his room, and her heart almost stopped at the sight of him. He was sleeping soundly on his back, his chest and arms bathed in the early rays of the sun.

Looking down at him, Diana knew the dawning of a new pain. Every part of her yearned to express the tenderness of the love she felt. But it couldn't be. It was another of life's heartbreaks to be endured.

She bent to shake him.

'Uhhh,' he moaned softly.

'Ben, wake up.' She shook him more firmly.

His eyes opened, and for a moment she could have drowned in the warm green depths.

'Hi,' he said softly.

'Ben, we have to talk,' she whispered urgently.

'Uh huh,' he smiled sleepily. 'Sure. Come on in.' He rolled back the bedclothes invitingly.

Diana covered him again, her heart thumping in her mouth. 'Wake up,' she urged.

'Not till you tell me again you love me . . .' Ben's voice was husky with memory.

Diana went rigid with fear. Had she said . . .? Now anxiety took over, forcing her to be sharp. 'Wake up, damn it. I want to talk to you. Now.'

Ben reached for her hand. 'Name the day, honey. I wouldn't compromise you, you know that . . .'

Diana had to sit on the bed to stop her knees buckling. Perspiration broke out on her forehead. 'This is no time for joking!'

'Who's joking?' Ben tried to reach for her, but she ducked in time. 'Marry me? I asked you over and over last night, but you were too involved with other things,' he teased.

'Now I know you have to be joking,' Diana said as lightly as she could.

'Sweetheart, I don't *have* to be anything,' Ben said quietly, propping himself up on one elbow and staring at her. 'Do you think I would take such an advantage of the woman I love?'

'Stop it!' Diana exclaimed, jumping from the bed, her heart and head pounding.

But Ben had neatly caught her hand, and now he drew it to his lips, kissing her fingertips lingeringly.

She shivered in the cool of the room. This was dreadful. Madness. It had to be stopped.

'The old man will think I'm a rapid operator,' Ben murmured against her hand, his eyes on her face, sparkling.

Diana's blood ran cold. She stared at him, every fibre of her body alert. In the same instant Ben let out a long groan. 'Oh Jesus . . .' He had forgotten the clause in his contract, the one she didn't know about, the one he had been meaning to tell her about, to laugh over with her.

'Diana . . . honey, I should have told you. I meant to tell you . . . Christ, it slipped my mind — '

'Tell me what, Ben?' Diana had drawn back from him, her face closed.

'Jesus,' Ben swore again. 'This is going to sound awful now . . .'

'Tell me,' Diana demanded.

Ben's face had clouded with anger, and now he pushed back the covers and strode in his shorts to the window. The muscles of his back were tense and he locked one taut fist against the window.

'I had to agree that *if* I should marry during my five-year contract, it would only be to a Nazareth,' he said, his breath harsh and ragged. 'But — '

'A Nazareth?' Diana interrupted, her face pale and her eyes

enormous with the implication of his words. 'What Nazareth would you be expected to meet, apart from me?'

Ben's voice was bitter with memory. 'You were the Nazareth the old man meant,' he said, turning to face her. 'But, as I was about to say, the damned clause meant nothing to me . . . I had no intention of marrying anyone, and,' now his eyes darkened, 'you'll understand that, in particular, I wasn't about to marry Mat's widow.'

He came back across the room, chilled to his soul by the look in Diana's eyes, but desperate that she should understand.

'I don't know exactly when I guessed what it was all about, but I did. The old man only ever intended for there to be one mother of his future heirs. You.'

Diana's indrawn breath halted him briefly, but he was afraid she'd misunderstand, so he went on. 'If he couldn't have you himself, honey, he was at least hedging his bets about his grandchildren.'

She stared at him woodenly; confused, angry, hurt. But still silent.

'Damn it, Diana, you know how I feel about him! When I signed that crap my only intention was to make him suffer. No way in this world was I going to help him in his cosy plans. You see, he banked on my believing that I had a better chance if I married you. But I could see how it really was . . . I was his last resort. The estranged son. Until he *met* me again,' Ben grimaced. 'Then I got the impression he wasn't quite so keen.'

Diana found a chair and sank down on to it. Nothing Ben was saying made sense.

Ben saw her confusion and tried to explain. 'I did mean to tell you, but the time never seemed right. Then I started to fall for you myself, but you made a good job of keeping me at bay — '

'Just a minute,' Diana broke in. 'Why would David use you? You've just said he intended to get me for himself.'

'I think he wanted a way to get you back to Boston, so that he could try again.' Ben shrugged. 'The trust ensures that, presumably. Then, if that didn't work, as a last resort he'd accept your children. But only *Nazareth* children. Nazareths at the helm . . . you must have heard that expression?'

'But how would marrying me be an advantage to you?' Diana managed evenly, trying to understand the bizarre picture Ben painted.

Ben's gaze was solemn. 'Because I don't think he intends me to inherit. And he knows that at some time I'd work that out – so if need be, you were the bait to keep me on the hook.'

Diana shook her head, the alleged marriage clause on 'hold' for the moment in a bigger scenario.

'How?'

'I was also given a disclaimer to sign.' Ben's voice dropped, almost wearily. 'It means I don't automatically inherit, even if the trust is a success. The ball is still in David's court.'

Diana frowned, not understanding.

'He figured I'd accept second best, rather than zilch. Second best being, in this case, marriage to you and, I presume, some control through our children.'

'But the contract — '

'Ha! Your contract and the one I signed in Boston are not identical. That's why I stalled Alan on seeing a copy. I intended to tell you about it first.'

Diana's mind was reeling. Could all this be true? This monstrous twisting and manipulating of people's lives? Something niggled at her mind – a small but important factor.

'Why would you agree, if you saw these clauses, and understood them? You are a lawyer, Ben.' Now her voice sharpened. 'How *could* you agree?'

Ben's brows rose and beneath them the green eyes had hardened. 'For Nazareth House? I'd have walked on fire if I'd had to.'

Diana stumbled from the chair, horror blinding her. She had

almost been fooled by his soft words. This man, who by his own admission would do whatever it took to get Nazareth House.

'Diana.' Ben rushed to cut off her exit. 'Honey, it doesn't matter any more. Don't you see? We don't need David Nazareth. We don't ever have to go back to Boston. At the end of the five years, I get a three million pay-out, regardless of anything else. And I'm a good lawyer, I can work. We don't *need* him.'

Diana tried to twist out of his grasp, her thoughts incoherent.

But Ben held her tighter. 'Honey, I can live without Nazareth House if I have to,' he said urgently. 'But I *love* you. I don't want to live without *you*. For God's sake, you must feel that?'

She heard the words, but they made no sense to her. Nothing did.

'Dreams can change, Diana. People can change,' Ben said urgently.

'Can they, Ben?' Diana choked. 'Can such *big* dreams, over a lifetime, be unimportant after less than a year?'

Ben stared at her blankly. 'You don't believe me,' he said flatly.

Diana felt for the door handle; she couldn't think straight yet.

'I don't know what to believe.'

Ben turned and walked away, towards the window. Without looking back he spoke very proudly.

'Well when you do, let me know. Until then you can be assured that I won't bother you.'

Diana's thoughts were so agitated that she didn't notice where she was going, and then she realised she'd taken a wrong turn somewhere. She stood still, trying to get her bearings, determined not to think about Ben or anything he'd said until she was safely back at Glanville Road.

Had they come through that large door last night? It was
impossible to tell. But she wasn't going back, so . . .

The door was heavy and it creaked. She had to push it with
all her weight, and ended up almost falling down a short flight
of stairs.

It was another of those halls. Square, with brightly coloured stained-glass windows and, at the far end, another
stout door.

It all had to lead somewhere, she thought grimly, and as
long as it was out of Tamerford she'd be happy.

Not half a dozen steps into the room, a strange sensation
arrested her. She stood still nervously, the hairs on the back
of her neck prickling. It was as if somebody, or something,
were in the room with her. She glanced cautiously around,
but there was nothing to see.

She felt a compulsion to move away from the windows,
nearer to the inner walls. Her body felt ice-cold. She drew
closer to the wall. When she backed into a solid object, it
was all she could do not to scream. Turning, she saw to her
immense relief that it was only the edge of a large painting.

Imagine being frightened by a load of old paintings!

But suddenly her spine tingled. Portraits? Of Tamerford
ancestors? Instantly she was interested.

There had been something in the story of the missing
portrait that Adrian Lawrence had told. What exactly was
it? Something that hadn't gelled with her.

Allowing her curiosity to overcome apprehension, she
moved closer to get a better look.

The portraits were very stylised. Old men, young men,
dressed in various costumes of their times. She bent forward
to look at the inscription beneath the painting of a particularly
handsome, fair-haired man in a tight blue satin breech-suit
adorned with lace ruffles.

Startled she read. 'Thomas (The Willow), VIII Earl of
Tamerford', and a date. She continued down the row in
amazement, gazing at stern, noble faces and titles. 'Matthew,

XI Earl.' 'Zacharias, XII Earl.' 'Simon, Viscount II. 'Joseph, X Earl.'

Ancient men, ancient titles . . .

Forgetting her own concerns, she followed the inscriptions. Then she was facing the earliest painting. Her heart did a somersault. There, but for the fair hair, the greenish-blue eyes and the seventeenth-century costume, was *David*.

Her shocked gaze flew to the legend beneath the painting, on a worn brass plaque. 'Jeremiah, III Earl of Tamerford.'

She stared again, perplexed by the strange likeness. Why should a portrait of a Tamerford remind her of David? Or did she have David on the brain?

At the end of the row, next to the portrait of Jeremiah, was a dark, empty shape. Beneath it a simple wooden block proclaimed the missing painting to be of 'Joshua, 1690. Beloved second son of Samuel, II Earl of Tamerford'.

The space intrigued her. Was this where the missing Tamerford should be? The one with the middle name of Nazareth?

She turned again to the portrait of Jeremiah – presumably the elder brother – still fascinated that the painting should remind her of David. But, on her third viewing, she was disappointed. The likeness was not great. Possibly the light had played tricks with her imagination, which was certainly aroused in this huge old place. She turned away, occupied with another interesting facet of this discovery. Had the family lost its title? She was pondering this when a voice made her jump violently.

'You have no business in my part of this house, Mrs Nazareth.'

The great-aunt stood at the far end of the gallery, formidable in her long black dress, snowy hair severely dressed into a coil at the nape of her long neck. She looked, Diana thought irrationally, like the housekeeper in a Daphne du Maurier mystery.

Diana found her voice. 'I'm sorry, I'm afraid I lost my way, and found myself here by accident. I didn't mean to intrude.'

Strangely hawk-like eyes swept over her, and Diana recoiled from their animosity.

'This gallery leads only to my private quarters. Kindly leave the way you came.'

'Could you direct me?' Diana asked, trying to sound pleasant through faintly chattering teeth.

'Go back the way you came. Turn left, follow the hall to the end and turn right. There you will find a staircase which leads to the ground floor.'

The old lady had not moved from the far doorway.

'Thank you,' Diana said nervously, anxious to be gone. But again the imperious voice halted her at the door.

'Don't *ever* come this way again.'

Diana's hand froze on the door latch, shocked. The woman's voice dripped venom.

'If you have any influence with that American, get him away from Tamerford and keep him away. There is nothing here for him. Nothing!' she hissed.

Diana backed up the last stair and all but ran from the gallery, the instructions as to the way she should take forgotten. Her heart pounded as she fled along the dark, narrow corridors. The sooner they got out of this place the better. What had they become involved with? Her problems with Ben faded from her mind.

When she at last found the staircase, she hurried down it. Coming into a small lobby she found an open door, and with a gasp of relief glimpsed Gabbie preparing breakfast in the kitchen.

No one else was about yet. She crossed the hall and dropped stiffly into a kitchen chair, her pulse still racing. Gabbie turned from the range and, seeing Diana's face, was instantly alarmed.

'Goodness, Diana. Whatever is wrong? Are you ill?'

Diana shook her head, but found that she was still trembling. Gabbie poured hot black coffee and urged her to sip it. When she was calmer, Diana described her encounter with the old lady.

Gabbie was clearly puzzled, but keen to put Diana at ease.

'I can't think that she actually meant any harm by it, Diana,' she said thoughtfully. 'She *is* a great age. Please don't let it upset you any further. Perhaps Simon will speak to her – he's the favourite. The men always are in our family,' she added with a pleasant smile.

Diana wanted to protest, feeling foolish now, but it was too late. Ben and Simon had come into the room and caught the tail end of the conversation. Gabbie told Simon while Diana kept her eyes averted from Ben's face.

Simon listened, and he too frowned.

'Gabbie is probably right,' he agreed. 'Nevertheless, our dear aunt will have to be gently reminded that it is not she who gives or rescinds invitations here. I do apologise, however, and hope that you will put it down to the vagaries of extreme age.'

Diana nodded uncomfortably. That lady might well be old, but she seemed far from senile . . .

'Tell you what,' Simon added cheerfully. 'Ben and I are going to do some more walking, so why don't you show Diana around properly, Gabbie? That way she'll know the lay of the house, and,' he grinned boyishly, 'can avoid Ruth's quarters in future. Now do start breakfast . . . I'll just take a tray up to her and have a quick word now.'

Diana felt more than a little depressed. She'd made an ass of herself with Ben, and now she felt foolish in front of their hosts. Also, she'd omitted to mention Ruth's weird command about Ben, and it was too late to tell them now. They'd think she was trying to make trouble for the old woman. But maybe Simon would learn about her nasty swipe at Ben, and explain it away.

No such luck. He was smiling cheerfully on his return. 'As I suspected, Diana, she doesn't even recall seeing you this morning. We'll have to take greater care of her.'

Diana remained convinced that Ruth was well in command

of her faculties, but she was in no position to argue the matter.

Gabbie's tour concluded in a study adjacent to the old dining-room.

'Meet some of the modern paintings,' she said brightly.

Diana's depression had lifted a little in Gabbie's cheerful company, and now she walked over to the small group of paintings with interest.

These were from Victorian times to the last generation, Simon and Gabbie's own father.

It was hard not to sympathise when Gabbie told how their parents had drowned on a rare sailing holiday, when much of south Devon's coastline had been battered by a devastating storm.

The two children had been very small, Gabbie explained, and were then raised by Ruth. They were singularly unfortunate in having no other relatives. Diana thought of her own father, and how lucky she had been to have him for so long. But sadness misted her eyes, and she squeezed Gabbie's hand.

'It's all right, really. It's all such a long time ago now. And to be honest,' Gabbie added with disarming honesty, 'I don't remember much about them. This portrait of daddy was painted just after his elder brother died. Don't you think he looks a little sad? I've always thought so, although Simon very naughtily insists it is because he was obliged to inherit this old place.'

Diana gazed at the tall young man, standing beside a fine bay mare; he had Simon's features and colouring, almost nothing of similarity to Gabbie. But no, Diana didn't think he looked sad. She'd have said he looked angry.

'What happened to his brother?' she asked, to avoid giving her opinion that Simon was probably right.

'Killed too. Crashed his friend's plane. He shouldn't have been flying at all – he'd lost all sensation in his right hand after being wounded in France . . . but he thought he could manage a tiny twin-engined job. We don't really know what happened, but he lost control . . .'

'How awful,' Diana murmured. 'So then your father had to inherit, without choice?' She was reading the gilded card – no expensive plaques for these ancestors, she noted.

''Fraid so,' Gabbie replied.

'It says 'Bartholomew, XV Earl of Tamerford,' Diana commented. 'Is there something you haven't told us, Gabbie?'

Gabbie smiled innocently. 'Nothing of the slightest importance.'

'But shouldn't we address Simon – and you of course – with a little more courtesy?' Diana pressed.

'Oh goodness, no. Simon would hate it, and so should I. Si's always said that titles are a bloody nuisance.' She grinned mischievously. 'And they would be in our case. We have neither the money nor the inclination to live up to them.' Now she laughed. 'It doesn't stop the village folk, though. Old habits die hard. Apparently daddy hated the title; it drove him mad.' She shrugged good-naturedly. 'People do tend to assume that money goes hand in hand with titles. It makes one rather a target and when one can't help at all, well, that does make one sad.'

It was all said matter-of factly, but Diana hadn't missed the note of wistfulness that had crept into Gabbie's voice.

Gabbie dismissed the subject, saying, 'Let's go and find the men. Aren't you just longing to know if Simon is going to become a partner in your wonderful venture? My curiosity is killing me.'

'Did you realise that Simon's an earl?' Diana asked thoughtfully, as they drove home to Tavistock.

'What?' Ben's face registered total surprise.

'Yes. That makes both Gabbie and that awful aunt ladies.'

Ben whistled softly. 'No kidding. Are you sure?'

'Positive.'

'Well . . . I'll be damned. Simon hasn't said a word to me.

Now why do you suppose that is?'

Diana explained Gabrielle's reasoning.

Ben gazed thoughtfully at the road ahead. 'Hmm. I wonder. Maybe I'd better have a little talk with the lord of the manor. A title could be very useful to the trust.'

'Is it going to work?'

'Very well, hopefully. Simon's going over all my notes again; but I'd say he's sold on the basic idea. My guess is that we'll be getting this show on the road.'

Diana couldn't have cared less at this minute. She was achingly aware of the emotional chasm between them. They'd hardly exchanged two words since Friday night.

But she couldn't bring the subject up.

And she knew that Ben wouldn't.

CHAPTER TWENTY-SEVEN

Simon surprised them all by giving them his decision three days later. It was positive.

At the same time, Diana told them she had booked a flight to Boston for that weekend.

Gemma wanted to go with her, but was firmly refused. Candy, delighted by Simon's news, made no such demands. Ben was icily cold.

'It might as well be now,' he said curtly. 'Get it over with.' His gaze rested on her for several moments. She had withdrawn from him totally and they hadn't exchanged more than half a dozen words since Tamerford.

'Do us both a favour while you're there — '

Diana looked at him cautiously.

'Take a look at my contract. Check it out for yourself.' His jaw was set, but there was a glint of hope behind the clouded eyes. He got up from the table. He was due to meet Simon shortly.

'Remember my offer last weekend?' He shrugged into his jacket, then gave her a long, intense look. 'It still stands.'

The door closed quietly behind him.

'What was *that* about?'

'Nothing, Gems,' Diana said uncomfortably.

But she thought about his words later, as her Pan Am flight approached Boston. Why did he think she had made such a sudden decision to see David, if not to check out what he'd said?

Yet he'd made her feel guilty, as if she shouldn't need to question his word, as if there could be no question in her mind that his word was more honourable than David's, that she should automatically believe her own contract to be different from Ben's.

But how could she unless she saw the proof? Ben, by his own admission, had wanted to punish David, while all the evidence she had was that David wanted to welcome back his son.

She closed her eyes as the aircraft began to descend, mentally preparing herself to meet David again. It was nearly three years since she had run away from him in the night and she hoped fervently that there would be no awkwardness between them. Her stomach knotted as the plane touched down at Logan; and, to her annoyance, her hands trembled slightly.

'Hi there, sweetheart.' The velvety voice had not lost its power to make her feel special.

'David. How nice of you to meet me.' Her own voice was surprisingly cool; distant.

The charade had begun again.

His lips brushed her mouth, bringing infuriating blushes to her cheeks. She recovered quickly. 'And Beanie. What a lovely surprise.'

'Welcome back, darling,' Beanie hugged her warmly.

'Welcome *home*,' David proclaimed firmly.

Diana refused to look into his eyes, and only studied him covertly when they were safely in his car. He had lost weight and, probably due to his illness, there were strain lines around his mouth. Apart from that, David Nazareth looked remarkably good for his sixty-three–plus years.

Beanie chatted away to her in the back seat, keen to make this reunion as easy as possible.

'You'll be able to attend my next party, darling. It's in four weeks' time, and now that you are here I shall make it very special indeed.'

'Oh, but I shall only be here for a few days,' Diana said quickly, adding, 'Perhaps another time.'

'A few days? Nonsense!' David declared. 'We shan't let you leave so soon, shall we, Beanie.'

'Certainly not.' Beanie smiled affectionately.

'I'm afraid my reservations are made,' Diana told them in her firmest voice. 'I have left Devon at a crucial time for the trust.' She smiled sweetly for David's benefit, knowing he was watching her in the mirror. 'I can't be away for a minute longer than I've allowed – you know how it is, business has to come first.'

'Touché,' David said lightly. 'And spoken like a true Nazareth.'

'Actually, like a Lloyd-Fauvère,' Diana parried, her eyes wide with innocence.

She saw David wince.

Beanie took over the conversation then, skilfully ensuring that a confrontation was avoided – exactly as David had asked her to. He had brought her along because this meeting was crucial. Three years of hell had been long enough, he'd told her – and he'd added that he intended to make Diana change her mind on this trip. Or bust.

Beanie kept them entertained for the of the drive.

The staff were at the bottom of the steps, unable to conceal their pleasure at seeing Diana again.

'Miss Diana, welcome home.' Sanders shook her hand vigorously.

'Only a brief visit, I'm afraid,' Diana said apologetically. 'Mrs Carly, how are you? I've missed your cooking. Meg, you are looking well. And John, how lovely. Are these from the garden?' She buried her face in the crysanthemums, to cover the pang of guilt she felt. These were people who had cared about her; had cared for her. People she had discarded without a word.

She had been wrong to come to the house; she should have booked into a hotel. Wisdom with hindsight, she thought, was becoming a particular forte of hers . . .

Beanie and Jeff were to join them for dinner that evening, but now Diana was alone at the house with David.

For a moment she was nervous, but she swiftly reminded herself that Ben's contract was her main reason for being here.

'Tell me about Ben's contract.'

David put his teacup down carefully and looked at her in mild surprise.

'Ben's contract?'

'The marriage and disclaimer clauses,' Diana said coolly. 'I don't like their implications.'

David stared at her. 'I'm sorry, you've lost me . . .'

Diana gazed back, determined to be strong. 'No crap, David.'

His eyes darkened, forbiddingly.

'I want the truth – and I want to look at Ben's contract.'

'Certainly you can see the contract – but I'm not sure I know what's bothering you — '

'You're not?' Diana's voice was incredulous. 'Come off it, David. You can't have thought I'd be flattered that Ben was expected to marry me!'

'Expected . . .? What in hell are you talking about?'

Diana kept her gaze level. 'It was very clever, but it's not going to work. I will not marry *any* man on your whim.' Her temper rose suddenly. 'Just who do you think you are – God?'

David's face paled, and he put his hand to his chest.

Diana froze in fear. Was he going to have an attack? But slowly the colour returned to his face.

'That contract was private,' he said stiffly. 'Ben promised never to tell you about it.'

Diana's heart plummeted.

'I think you owe me an explanation,' she said more calmly.

David stared down at the floor for several moments. When he looked up again, his eyes were empty, his voice drained. 'Isn't the explanation obvious? You left me, Diana – threw my love in my face and walked out.' Now his face was grim. 'But I wanted your children to inherit the Firm. I've always made that clear.'

Diana wanted to run; to get far away from this can of worms she had reopened. But she couldn't: it had to be dealt with.

'You were going to use me? Use both of us?'

Now David stood up, and Diana could see the tension in his body. He moved stiffly to the window and stood with his back to her.

'Perhaps it was wrong. Maybe it was unethical, but nothing could have happened unless you were willing.' His voice was distant, and when he turned his face was unreadable. 'Is that what all this is about? Has Ben asked you to marry him?'

Diana shook her head to try to clear it, but David obviously mistook the gesture.

'Then what's all this about?'

'I can't believe you have made that clause part of Ben's contract. It's monstrous, David. It must be removed.'

'Oh no.' David's reply was strong and firm. 'I'm not having some gold-digger get her hands on Ben and end up as mistress of this house. Ben marries you or nobody. Leastwise, while I have any say in the matter.'

Diana listened, shock silencing her.

'Don't you realise?' David continued, his voice husky now. 'I love you so damned much, I couldn't *live* with the thought of any other woman here. For Christ's sake, Diana, when you turned your back on me, Ben was the only hope I had.' Now there was fire in his eyes. 'And Ben knew it. He knew my reason when he agreed — '

'You told him?'

'Too damned right I did. I told him straight, "If Diana won't marry me, then you marry her if you want to inherit".'

'You told Ben *that*?' Diana repeated stupidly.

David came across the room and dropped into a chair beside her. He took her hand between both of his, and held it carefully.

'Sweetheart, Ben knows the deal. He's a pretty smart lawyer, you know? What do you think he did, sign that contract blindfolded?'

Diana was stunned. Ben had said 'during the five years'. He hadn't told her that it was a permanent condition of his inheritance. He had lied to her!

She felt betrayed, abused. She had come here to plead for a release from the five-year clause. But now? What could she ask now that she knew Ben had agreed to everything David had demanded?

'Jeff was with us the whole time, honey. You can talk to him tomorrow. He'll show you the contract, and he'll confirm everything I've told you.' He was again concerned as he spoke. 'Has Ben been making a nuisance of himself?'

'I want that clause removed. If it is not, I shall instruct my solicitor to extricate me.' Diana had never been more determined about anything.

David was silent. For a while their gazes locked like horns.

'Very well,' he replied at last. 'I'll deal with it. And I'll give you a letter to take back with you, notifying Ben.'

Diana hadn't finished yet. 'And the disclaimer?'

'What disclaimer?'

'The one you had him sign – that he wouldn't make any legal claims on Nazareth House.'

David laughed softly. 'You are kidding me! Ben told you something like that, and you believed him? Jeez, honey, what's happened to your brain?'

Diana pulled her hands back, stung by his insult. He sighed and shook his head.

'I've just admitted that I told Ben he would only inherit if he married you. What would a disclaimer do, for Christ's sake? It doesn't make any sense.' He rubbed his forehead as if puzzled. 'I just can't think what Ben hoped to gain by a yarn like that.'

'Neither can I,' Diana said grimly.

David stood up. 'Enough of this crap, honey. You can see Ben's contract tomorrow. Meanwhile, let's forget all about it until then. We have dinner guests soon – don't you want to change?'

*			*			*

Dinner was a strained affair. Both Beanie and Jeff were as charming as always and they treated her as if she had never walked out on them all but Diana was unable to relax. The brief conversation with Ben ran around and around in her mind. She passed a restless night and awoke with an unusual feeling of irritability; but also of resolve.

She should never have come back. But she was here now, and there was still one other matter on her mind. Ben was a problem she'd have to confront later. Meanwhile, there was the *other* mystery to consider.

She mentioned it at breakfast.

'Tamerford?' David thought for a moment. 'The folk in Devon? No, honey, the name doesn't mean anything to me. Should it?'

'I didn't think so. But I was fascinated by their ancestors. I felt I'd seen some of the names before . . .'

David watched her carefully.

Diana hesitated – for some reason she wasn't willing to tell him of her strange experience, but she wanted a look at his ancestry.

'It's become something of a hobby – family trees are interesting, aren't they? Would you mind if I looked at yours?'

'The only family tree around here is in the old Bible. You're welcome to look at that.' David's eyes appraised her speculatively. 'It's locked in the glass bookcase in the library.'

'Thanks,' she murmured, adding, 'I'm also interested in old portraiture. If I could see the paintings at Nazareth House, I could compare the early American and English styles.'

'I'll be going over to the office in about an hour,' David said evenly. 'You can come along.'

Diana thanked him and took the key to the glass bookcase in the library, aware that her explanation had sounded weak. But David hadn't seemed very interested. When he excused himself to make some calls, she went in search of the Bible.

It was extraordinary. There were so many similar names that

she felt goose-bumps on her arms and neck. But common sense soon took over. The similarities were all way back, and, as she'd learned from her father, ancient names were commonly taken from legends and mythical gods – or, in more modern times, from the Bible. She closed the book, deep in thought. It had to be coincidence. But still something gnawed at her, something indefinable.

'Find it all right?' David met her in the hall as she was coming out.

She smiled. 'They were such lovely names in the old days . . .'

He shrugged. 'I've never noticed. Are you ready?'

As they drove the short distance to State Street, she wondered why she had lied. Strange things were happening to her lately, things that defied her logic and denied her her natural integrity. In short, she was becoming an accomplished liar.

But for what? Or for whom?

They were greeted with broad smiles. Everyone remembered Diana and no one knew why she had left. But her return had caused speculation. It was no longer any secret that the boss was in love with her. But was she with him? She was half his age, but that was no criterion these days.

David left Diana in the Green Suite, in the boardroom.

She had never had occasion to be here before, and curiously she looked around. The heavy maple furniture matched the quarter-panelling on the walls of the masculine, functional room. The only relief was the grape-green walls, adorned with ornately gilded paintings.

She moved closer cautiously.

It was there again. That same sense of *déjà vu*, a snaking chill up her spine. And the equally sudden admission to herself that this time there *was* a likeness. She was not imagining it, the light was not playing tricks with her. It was there.

Admittedly not in recent portraits. But the old Nazareth ancestors bore an uncanny likeness to the early Tamerfords. And for the first time she was able to acknowledge what she had hoped to find. That the missing Tamerford had unmistakeably founded the Nazareth line.

She stared for a long time at the first portrait, of Joshua Nazareth. The family resemblance was absolute. If she could only find the missing painting at Tamerford, she knew it would be of the same man. She sat down at the table, not taking her gaze from Joshua's face for a moment. She wanted to imprint it on her brain. It was overwhelming. And it was something else, something more elusive. It was as if Joshua's eyes were trying to convey some private message to her.

She shivered. *What?*

At first she had wanted to rush out and get David, bring him in here and spill the story out. But now, as she stared into Joshua's compelling eyes, she felt that he was urging caution. But why? Her brain raced. The Tamerford painting had mysteriously vanished, according to Adrian Lawrence. And there was a space, with Joshua's name beneath it, in the gallery where she had met with such animosity from the great-aunt.

What did it add up to?

Something more than just a long-ago relationship, she was sure. She tingled with premonition, just as she had used to when her daddy had gathered all the known facts of an important 'find', only to declare them incomplete. He used to say that he could always feel it when he had the final key.

Now Diana felt that she had the key, but didn't have the door, or parts of the door, that it would fit – despite the evidence to the contrary. And instinct warned her to keep quiet about her 'find' until she had all the facts. Instinct that Joshua was encouraging? Now she really shook her head. Here she was, staring at an oil painting of a man who'd been dead for almost three hundred years – and believing that he was placing some secret trust in her hands.

'Interesting?' David had come silently into the room, his eyes glancing from the portraits to Diana.

'Oh . . . very,' Diana said brightly, jumping up at once. 'But the styles are quite different.'

'Really,' David said drily. 'So have you finished sleuthing?'

'Yes, thanks,' Diana said, forcing herself to act normally. David was right, she was acting like a sleuth. Now she would think like one and keep her mouth shut. For the moment the amazing discovery would be her secret. And meanwhile, she had other problems.

Men. Of the living variety.

'I'm sorry I can't stay,' David apologised, showing Diana into Jeff's office, where Jeff smilingly awaited her. 'Something that won't be put off. I'll be in my office when you're through. Don't leave anything out, Jeff. Diana knows the whole story.'

Jeff coloured, but his eyes were clear. 'Sit down, Diana. I've got the contract here.'

David closed the door behind him.

Diana read the papers carefully. Twice. Then she read them again. It was all as David had said. Ben's signature was on the document David had described.

And there was no disclaimer.

Sickeningly, she was reminded again of Ben's initial venom towards David – his desire to hurt the man he felt had neglected him.

'Dave told me you were a bit worried about these.' Jeff waved his hand over the papers. 'Anything I can help with?'

'Not unless you can tell me why Ben lied about a disclaimer,' she said quietly. 'I've a pretty good idea why he misrepresented the rest.'

Jeff grimaced. 'Ben's a good guy, Diana. But . . .' he steepled his fingers against his chin, as if thinking '. . . I'd say a man with a mighty chip on his shoulder.'

'Like what?' Diana tested the waters. What did Jeff know?

'He could never handle the fact that Mat was the natural heir,' Jeff answered blandly. 'Ben was in love with the Firm all his life. That's why it was fairly easy for me to get him involved in all this.'

'You?' Diana asked, surprised.

'Well, it was my idea in the first place,' Jeff said. 'Things were bad here, honey. You have to know that.'

Diana waited, watching him.

'Dave's feelings for you aren't a secret any more. And I have to tell you that I hope never again to see a man suffer the way Dave has over you.'

Jeff's voice was unemotional, a catalogue of facts as he saw them, Diana thought. She braced herself for more of the same.

'He was pole-axed, plain and simple. So I eventually came up with the idea that if he and Ben could be got back together, maybe they could forgive one another. Maybe Dave could get reinvolved with the Firm. Through Ben, you know?

'I traced Ben, then I approached David. From then on you know the rest — '

'Whose idea was the trust?'

'Dave's.'

'It's monstrous,' Diana said simply.

'Well, different,' Jeff agreed. 'But a good way to prove Ben, in the melting pot of a charitable cause. Quite original in fact. And it gave Dave the chance to stay in touch with you.'

There were no denials, Diana noted.

She watched him intently. 'Did Ben agree happily to this incredible marriage clause?'

'Sure did,' Jeff replied easily. 'Had to, I guess.'

Diana ignored that. 'Was he aware of how David felt about me?'

'Dave couldn't have been straighter.'

'And there's no disclaimer – of any kind?'

'None whatsoever.'

Diana thought for several moments. 'And when Ben signed this – was he expected to make a play for me?'

'Not at all,' Jeff said firmly. 'He was made very aware that

Dave had not given up on you. No, Ben was told he was to wait until you had given Dave a final refusal.

'As I've said, Dave wasn't about to give up easy. Ben was a fall-back, a last resort. You *know* how the Nazareths are over heirs. And you also know that Dave doesn't have a lot of options. But he sure intended to make his own attempt first.'

Diana studied Jeff's grave face. 'What is it that I feel is missing here? Something that sticks in my throat,' she said softly.

'Mutual hatred, I expect,' Jeff answered levelly.

'Maybe — '

'Anyway, that's all past history,' Jeff said quickly. 'What concerns me now, Diana, is Dave's health.'

She at once felt guilty for not enquiring sooner. 'I'm sorry, how is he?'

'When he took that tumble last year, it wasn't the first,' Jeff said carefully. 'He'd had two other attacks, which we managed to keep quiet. But what we, Beanie and I, are really worried about is what this visit could do — '

'In what way?' Diana was cautious again.

'When he knew you were coming over, he was like a kid in a candy store,' Jeff said gravely. 'And yesterday he was a different man from the one we've watched this past three years.' Now he looked at her with an intense light in his amber eyes. 'What will it do to him when you leave again?'

'That's not fair,' Diana said coldly.

'Life's not fair,' Jeff said quietly. 'But there is chemistry between you, it's obvious a mile off.' He raised his hand slightly as she started to object. 'No, honey. Let me just say what I feel. I believe you do care in some way for Dave. All I'm saying is, can't you work the problems out? If you care at all, then surely there has to be a way? Dave's a sick man, Diana. Do I have to spell that out for you?'

* * *

Diana was very subdued as she changed for the dinner-dance David insisted on taking her to, although how a sick man intended to dance, she hadn't liked to ask.

But she was also distracted by Ben's lies.

The marriage clause, far from being the threat she had assumed from his description, had read as a straightforward, non-negotiable deal. Wicked and barbaric most certainly, but the terms were clear.

And to her it was an agreement that should never have been signed. Not by anybody in their right mind. So Ben obviously wanted Nazareth House on *any* terms. And just as obviously he had come to realise that she would never have had any part of it. No wonder he'd been so distressed when he'd slipped up and mentioned it!

As for the alleged disclaimer, it did not exist. The only reason she could find for Ben's invention of that was that he wanted her sympathy, wanted to alienate her from David. She could come to no other conclusion than that Ben's motive was revenge.

The scalding pain of humiliation burned in her heart – a pain she had thought never to know again after Mat.

For a raging moment she cursed David. Everything rotten that had happened to her had come through meeting him. But her anger with him was short-lived. It was against her nature to be unkind. It seemed to her that David's only crime, foolish and far-reaching though it was, had been falling in love with the wrong woman. Her.

Now he was gravely ill. She still had her life and hopes ahead of her, but she had destroyed any hopes David might have had of seeing the future of his beloved Nazareth House reflected in the face of his grandchild.

She would never forgive herself for that.

Guilt and pity swirled alongside her confusion. And beside them, a renewed tenderness. She would not help Ben destroy his father. David had suffered enough. As she finished dressing, she hardened her heart and mind against Ben. Whatever the truth of his history with his father, it was something that only they could work out. Ben would not use her again.

David was as charming as he had ever been, and while avoiding the more rigorous dances nevertheless danced as sensual a waltz as he always had.

Diana had firmly put all her concerns aside for this one evening, determined that this, possibly last, evening together, would be as pleasant as she could make it.

He was still the most charismatic man she'd known. He was intense and then light-hearted; serious and then filled with fun. He held her as a lover would, but voiced concerns over the trust as a father might. And never once did he mention Ben as they swirled through champagne and waltzes, laughing and flirting as the evening wore on.

It was as if, like Diana, he was determined to make the most of every second.

By the time he helped her, laughing and stumbling, into the car, Diana couldn't remember when she'd enjoyed his company more.

'Nightcap,' David proclaimed, as they fumbled along the darkened halls to his study.

Diana's body-clock protested that it was five in the morning, and she hadn't yet caught up with the jet-lag. But she was past exhaustion, caught somewhere in a haze of tender sympathy and warmth for this caring, troubled man. She took the brandy and sank on to a chair, feeling its cushioned depths envelop her.

'God, my feet . . .'

David sank on to the carpet beside her and pulled off her shoes. She laughed, but didn't pull away from the caress of his hands.

'How are you feeling?'

'I guess heaven will have to wait,' David quipped.

'Don't joke about things like that,' she said quickly.

'Why not, my love? Matter to you?' David's voice was deceptively lazy.

'You know it does,' she tried to say it lightly, but her voice was husky with tiredness and genuine concern.

'Yes,' David gazed at her. 'I know it does, but I wondered if you would remember that.'

'I have forgotten nothing,' Diana said, thinking of other, unpleasant things.

'Good. Saves us having to start over again.'

Diana was at once alert, and looked down into eyes that were shockingly edged with tears.

'No . . .' she whispered. 'David, don't do this to yourself again.'

'I can't hide my love, Diana. Not any more. It's too late for me to play games.' He brushed the moisture from eyes that pleaded for understanding.

'I shouldn't have come,' Diana murmured sadly, unable to bear his pain again.

David took her unresisting fingers and pressed them to his lips for a long moment.

'There is nothing left for me to live for,' he murmured despairingly against her hands. 'All I have hoped for is your love . . .'

'Don't!' Diana pulled back her hands as if she'd been burnt.

'Don't what? Don't admit what I feel? It's too late for that, my love. I told you plainly enough when Mat died . . .' His voice was low as he gazed intently into her eyes. 'Am I to die without ever having made love to you?'

'Oh no, David — '

'Am I so repulsive, sweetheart? Were all those emotions you felt in my arms three years ago some kind of pity?'

'No.' Of course they weren't. But — '

David's eyes were dark with emotion now. 'Everything I'm doing, Diana, is for you. Nothing has any meaning without you. It's like living on the edge of hell.'

'Please,' she begged. 'I can't bear to see you like this, David.'

She did nothing to stop him taking her in his arms. It was as if her own pain and sadness had joined with his. As if they were both grieving for something precious they had lost. He held her tenderly, his arms strong and comforting, his chest a strong boulder against which she could lean. He stroked her hair gently, murmuring endearments she couldn't quite hear. And when he tilted her chin and sought her mouth, she did not resist.

His tears had achieved more than words could ever have done . . .

When he carried her to his bedroom, her senses were as intact as an evening full of champagne and brandy would allow. They were both lonely and unhappy. They had both drawn the short straws of love in this life, but David's loneliness was the greater. If she could give him one night of love and happiness, where was the harm in that?

And no one need ever know . . .

But whatever altruism drove Diana was not what David intended to take. He laid her on his bed with tenderness and a firmness that surprised her, and when she tried to sit up to undress he just as firmly took control.

'No, sweetheart. I have waited a lifetime for you and I won't be denied a moment of this night.'

She gave in without a murmur, even though the colour rose in her cheeks as he removed the last flimsy garments and sat back on his heels to gaze at her.

Would she disappoint him? She knew so little of love. She began to tremble, unaware that her creamy skin shimmered in the soft glow of the bedside lamp, and that her shivers entranced him. Gently he laid her back against the pillows and then with just his fingertips began to trace the outline of her body as if he had all the time in the world. His fingers stroked her throat, paused at the hollow, then moved slowly downwards to the swell of her breasts. She caught her breath as he stroked their contours, then took their weight in his hands, every movement languid and gentle.

His fingertips traced her nipples and the span of his hand spread over them, testing the feel of their erectness against the soft skin of his palm.

She pushed gently, wanting more. But his hands moved down, held her waist, feathered across the slight swell of her stomach, reached the blonde triangle – and stroked through it, down to the insides of her thighs.

She wanted to touch him, to begin to share in this sensual game – but his insistence was total. For some unfathomable reason, David wanted this for himself.

She tried to watch him, the wonder in his eyes, and the almost worshipful way he touched her. But his fingers, and now his mouth, were experts. Her small shivers gave way to deep, shuddering waves, as his lips and tongue explored every surface, and now sought every crevice.

Her body began to writhe as the pleasure intensified. His head moved down to her thighs and his hands reached up for her breasts. In a rhythm she had never known, exquisite sensations flooded through her; alien, wonderful. In feelings she had never known, she started to drown.

And, just as she thought she might scream, he would pause, begin again, slightly differently. Slower rhythms, variations of touch; he played her as if she were a violin, and he its master.

And she wanted him never to stop.

Her body writhed wantonly, craving the pleasure this man gave. It was as if she had never known her own body until she had offered it to David. But she wanted something else. Something his resistance was refusing. She wanted *him*.

On and on went the pleasure until she could bear it no more. She was aching for him to enter her. At last she broke the silence, to beg.

'Tell me, my love,' he demanded. 'First tell me what I want to hear.'

She tried to move away from him, some small voice clamouring to be heard in the back of her mind. But he held her firmly, and began the torture again.

At last she cried out, 'David! Please . . . for God's sake . . .'

He moved his body against hers at once, and she arched her back against the hard swell of him.

But he held her there, imprisoned against him, taut, but not entering her.

'*Tell* me, Diana!' His hands held her shoulders, his hips relaxed against her pelvis. Only his eyes bored into hers. 'I have to hear you say it,' he whispered urgently.

She felt suddenly afraid. He wanted the ultimate avowal. If she made it, he'd expect it to be unreserved. Desperate, she tried to move again but only succeeded in pushing herself harder against him.

And her body screamed out, louder than her conscience.

'I can't!'

David smothered her with kisses, gently swivelling his hips against hers, teasing her with his hardness until she felt faint.

'You can, princess,' he said against her mouth. 'Try.'

She wound her arms tightly around his neck, for this moment wanting only him, only this.

'I do love you,' she compromised, closing her eyes tightly against his searching gaze.

'That's all I ever wanted to hear,' he said exultantly, and thrust into her.

She gasped at his size and strength, and then the pleasure began again and she gave herself to it . . .

David held her tenderly against his chest, gently stroking her hair.

They were both exhausted. Diana tried to speak. She wanted to explain that there could never be anything more than the beautiful experience they'd just shared.

But he put his finger firmly against her lips, and she was too spent to fight him.

Finally, she fell asleep in his arms.

When she awoke, she was in her own bed, naked but covered warmly.

As memories came flooding back, she blushed deeply. Then she groaned and turned on her stomach. History had repeated itself with remarkable speed. For the second time in just over a week, she had drunk too much and given in to a sexual interlude. She'd have to get on the wagon pretty damned quickly. Clearly she wasn't to be trusted near anything more alcoholic than perfume.

She'd broken her own private rule about never having sex with a man she wasn't serious about. And worse, she didn't know about the episode with Ben, but David had definitely worn no protection.

She rolled over on to her back and stared at the ceiling. Possibly there was a partial excuse for her behaviour with Ben. After all, they were both young and free – if she didn't count Gemma, and she didn't dare, at this moment, think of Gemma – they had been high on their hopes for the trust, and simply she'd drunk too much.

She also knew that, had this situation been different, she might now have been thinking of marrying Ben. But Ben was turning out to be someone she didn't know.

None of which excused last night with David.

If Ben was complex and troubled, how was she to describe David? Given the way he felt about her, he was the last man on earth that she should have gone to bed with. And the only excuse she could offer, even to herself, was that she had been genuinely moved by his tears. At the beginning. Because, in the final analysis, she had fully responded to his expert love-making. There had been no pity in those reactions; they were plainly and simply driven by sexual needs she hadn't previously known she had.

Angry with herself, she got up and showered. As she dried off, she stared at her face in the mirror. She didn't see her own beauty, only the outward signs of distress. The grey of her eyes had darkened until it almost obliterated the blue. There were shadowed hollows in her cheeks. Her skin was too pale, the natural colour drained.

She looked as Gemma had claimed she looked when they'd first heard from David. Haunted.

She closed her eyes. It served her right.

CHAPTER TWENTY-EIGHT

'I promise it will be worth the trip.' Beanie hugged Diana.

The boarding call was relayed again; around them the last groups of people were bustling towards the departure gate.

'You have promised to be here, so don't forget.' David's hug was tighter.

'I shan't.'

Already Diana was regretting her rash agreement, but it had seemed easier to agree than to argue the point, during the last turbulent day.

'Six weeks, darling!' Beanie blew her a kiss as Diana handed over her boarding card and ticket.

Her face ached from smiling, but she dutifully smiled at them both; then escaped with relief on to the tarmac.

During the onward leg of her journey from London to Plymouth the next morning, Diana's concern grew.

Had David been extraordinarily gallant after their night of love – or was he simply giving her time to assimilate their new situation? Whatever, he had been solicitous, but not overly so.

She looked out at the grey-green waters of the Sound as the Dash-7 made its approach to Roborough airport. She had been surprised at how easy he had made it for her. Or had he? Her frown deepened. She had expected some kind of morning-after reaction, something that would give her a natural opportunity to apologise and explain her behaviour. But David had filled their day with activities. Beanie had joined them as soon as David was free for lunch. And they had not been alone after that.

They had still been chatting away when Diana could no longer keep her eyes open.

And she had been at the house when Diana came down for breakfast, packed and ready to leave.

There hadn't been a chance to talk to David alone.

And now she had to deal with Ben.

But fate had been kind. Only Gemma and Candy were waiting in the arrivals hall, obviously with something on their minds. The two of them were mysteriously giggly as they packed Diana's suitcase into the boot of Gemma's car.

'Are you going to share the joke?'

'No joke, Di. Deadly serious,' Gemma grinned.

'How was Boston?' Candy asked, her face scarlet with merriment.

'Boston was fine. I'm fine. You both look fine,' Diana replied. 'So what's deadly serious?'

'Candy's being committed to an institution.'

'What?'

'Marriage.' Gemma pulled a face. 'Holy sanctity and all that.'

Diana caught on. 'Goodness. Anybody I know, Candy?'

'Local rabble aren't good enough for her any more,' Gemma laughed. 'Only the lord of the manor for our Candy.'

'Gemma! Give her a chance to speak for herself.'

Candy could only nod happily.

'That's wonderful news!' Diana leant over to kiss her cousin's flushed cheek. 'When did all this happen?'

'Soon as you took your beady eye off her.'

'Do shut up, Gems,' Candy said mildly. 'Only on Friday, Di. But we had sort of talked about it.'

'I'm thrilled for you both, Candy. You seemed suited from the moment you met. Is it too soon to know when the wedding will be?'

'Next month,' Candy beamed delightedly.

'Next — '

'It's Simon's birthday then, and he thought it would be a nice time.'

'He's also going to be thirty. I told Candy she shouldn't wait till he's past it!'

'Gemma!'

'It's all right, Diana. She's been like this ever since we told her.' Candy beamed.

'Well, it's the loveliest homecoming,' Diana said happily. 'But I hope you aren't planning anything elaborate, if there's only a month to prepare.'

'Oh but she is – you know, specially made dress, cathedral-length, hand-crafted lace veil . . .'

Diana grinned as Gemma gunned the engine of her ancient car and headed at a giddy speed towards the moors.

It was good to be home.

'You're being left on the shelf, Gems.'

'Me? No, I'm putting my career first.'

'Oh, which career is this?'

'Catching Ben,' Candy half-joked.

Diana joined in the laughter; but she was reminded with a jolt that her cousin was becoming seriously interested in Ben. As much to catch her breath as anything else, she suddenly declared, 'Lunch? My treat. Let's stop at the Moorland Links.'

In the lovely bright dining-room overlooking the hotel's gardens, she listened to Candy's wedding plans. The marriage would take place in the tiny chapel adjoining Tamerford Manor; and as neither the manor nor the village had its own incumbent vicar, Pritchard would do the honours.

Candy had wasted no time. Already she had cabled George and Charlie in Australia, and a phone call had assured their youngest daughter that they would be present. Diana's mother had been sent a similar cable, but had yet to reply.

Diana assured Candy that she would use whatever influence she might have to ensure Rachel's attendance. But the greatest excitement was over the bridal gown, which Gemma and Gabbie were to make.

'Are you sure you trust those two?' Diana had to smile. 'I mean, has either of them made a wedding gown before?'

'We're quite capable,' Gemma frowned.

'I won't let them choose the material, don't worry,' Candy assured her. 'I don't want to end up dressed in green – or in patchwork!'

'Gabbie has done some beautiful needlework, Di. You should see some of her clothes.'

'They are making it as their joint wedding present to me,' Candy added proudly.

'And nobody gets to see it beforehand. Not even you,' Gemma warned.

'Just keep both eyes on them,' Diana laughed.

As the sisters chatted merrily about fabrics and styles, Diana's thoughts were on the interesting news about a chapel at Tamerford. But it was not weddings she was thinking of. Of course it was logical that an old place like Tamerford would have a chapel, even though she hadn't been shown one. But if there was a chapel, then wouldn't there also be a graveyard? Or a family vault? Or something, anyway?

Somewhere that would record the lives, and deaths, of the Tamerford ancestors. She made a mental note to follow it up, then she rejoined the lively conversation.

Ben had sent a message that he was staying at Tamerford, but hoped to see her later if she came over.

Gemma helped Diana put away her things, clearly with the intention of quizzing Diana about her stay.

'Did you succumb to his charms then?'

Diana held her breath for a moment. 'We talked business. And Beanie's winter party. I've promised her I'll go over for it.'

'When?'

'In six weeks.'

'That's a bit soon, isn't it?'

'Yes. But I've promised her for so long. And you know, she cancelled all her parties when I was so – well, after the trouble with Mat.'

Gemma eyed her thoughtfully. 'Why can't you say gang-raped? That *is* what happened.'

'I don't even think about it, let alone give it a name,' Diana said briskly.

'Perhaps you should.' Gemma handed Diana the last item, and closed the suitcase. 'It might help.'

'No, Gems. It wouldn't.'

'I disagree. But you know me, call a spade a spade, in direct Australian fashion.' She moved to the door. 'So David behaved himself?'

'As always,' Diana said, straight-faced.

'Good. Now, are you going over to Tamerford with Candy this evening?'

'Should I?' Diana followed her downstairs.

'Ben's waiting.' Gemma's voice was small.

Diana saw her chance. 'Ben can wait until I'm ready,' she said easily. 'There are only minor matters to discuss with him. Nothing important. Now you can tell me what's been happening with the trust since I left.'

To her relief, Gemma's face cleared. In that respect Diana was glad it was over with Ben. How would she have felt if she'd ever had to tell Gemma that she and Ben were an item? She gave a small shudder. It would have been one of the worst moments of her life.

She linked her arm through Gemma's affectionately. 'I'm for a quiet evening and then bed. Jet-lag will soon be catching up with me.'

Fortunately, Gemma knew nothing about Diana's reasons for visiting Boston so suddenly. Now there was no need for her ever to know. Later, after they'd both gone to bed, Diana heard Candy come in. After a few minutes there was a light tap on her door.

'It's open.'

Candy came in quietly and closed the door behind her. Diana switched on her lamp, surprised.

'Everything all right?'

'Ben gave me this note for you.'

Diana took the note and thanked her.

'I wasn't prying – but he gave it to me unfolded. I couldn't help seeing what he'd written.' Candy's face was serious. 'It's not my business, but I know Gemma has fallen for him,' she said softly. 'I didn't want her to see this.'

'Wait . . .' Diana skimmed the brief lines quickly.

> *Diana,*
> *Maybe now we can talk rationally?*
> *I can't wait!*
> *All my love,*
>
> > *Ben.*

Diana looked up at Candy's troubled face, and did some quick thinking.

'We argued over some of his ideas. This is nothing for you to worry about, Candy. It's a bit over the top, that's all.'

'Then you aren't involved with him?'

'Most definitely not.'

Candy smiled broadly. 'Sorry, I guess I misread it.'

'Easily done,' Diana said lightly.

'Stupid of me. Well, goodnight then.'

Diana switched off the lamp. She'd be talking to Ben 'rationally' all right. And the sooner the better.

When Gabbie phoned just after nine the next morning, no one was further from Diana's thoughts than Ruth Tamerford.

'Diana? Glad to hear you are back with us. All well in Boston?'

'He hasn't withdrawn the trust money,' Diana laughed, aware that so much at Tamerford depended on the trust now. 'How are things, Gabbie?'

'All's well. But, surprise surprise, great-aunt would like to see you.'

'Whatever for?'

'I haven't a clue. Maybe she wants to apologise,' Gabbie said mischievously.

Diana doubted that. 'When?'

'Would today suit you?

What could she say? That she hadn't the slightest interest, on any day?

'Fine.'

'Lovely. Would tea suit you – say around three?'

'Three it is,' Diana agreed, wishing she'd had the courage to say a simple no.

That desire was reinforced when she drove up the deserted drive that afternoon. Where was everybody?

She gritted her teeth, and climbed out of the car.

'Hi.' Gabbie appeared at the door, smiling gaily. 'Perfect timing.'

Diana smiled stiffly.

'Was Boston beautiful? Of course you weren't there for long. I've always wanted to visit America,' Gabbie chattered, as they entered the house.

'Have you? Well perhaps we can go together sometime,' Diana said, half seriously.

'Some hope.' Gabbie pulled a face.

They crossed the kitchen to a far door, and Gabbie whispered, 'This is great-aunt's wing.' She winked. 'Her private territory.'

The stairs that rose from a tiny hall were covered in thick carpet and brightly lit by lamps in sconces on the walls.

Diana's surprise must have shown.

'We have a small generator at the back of this wing. We try to keep it warm and light here, for safety and comfort,' she explained. 'Great-aunt is quite cosy, really.'

Cosy was not the word Diana would have used to describe the opulent, ornate Victorian apartment she was shown into.

Apart from a four-poster bed and huge carved wardrobes, there was a sitting area larger than any of the rooms in Glanville Road.

Ruth Tamerford rose from an old-fashioned bureau and came across the room to greet them.

She was really rather splendid, viewed amidst the elaborately rich furnishings. Her frock was of black shot-silk, with immaculate ruffles of ivory lace at the throat. Beneath the hem of the long gown, Diana could see ancient, but highly polished, black buttoned boots. The only adornment to the severely elegant outfit was a heavy gold locket on a brooch pin attached to her dress.

Diana was still wary, despite the haughty smile and the extended hand. Close up, Ruth's carved features implied great beauty in some earlier time, but now her unblemished skin was yellowed. The eyes that stared back at Diana were bright, but of indeterminate colour.

Diana drew her hand back cautiously.

'Tea's all ready.' Gabbie covered the silence. 'And great-aunt has her own store of stronger medicine. Now here's the bell, Diana.' She pointed to a faded velvet rope hanging by the door, and another by the bed. 'If you need anything at all, give it a tug and I'll be up in a jiffy.'

Some of Diana's apprehension vanished.

'Thank you for coming, Mrs Nazareth. We'll be fine now, Gabrielle.'

Diana glanced around as Gabbie left. A tea-tray lay on a table between two sofas, in front of a cheerfully blazing fire.

'Please sit down.'

Diana sat. Waiting.

Ruth moved to the sofa opposite and began pouring tea from a silver pot.

'Milk first, or last? Or do you prefer lemon?'

'Milk last, thank you.'

'Was your trip profitable?' Ruth asked, without looking up.

The question was so strange that Diana could only stare.

'To America,' Ruth added. 'To David Nazareth.'

'What do you want?' Diana asked directly, not willing to discuss her affairs.

Ruth passed the tea, unperturbed. 'Did you find him in good health?'

Diana took the fragrant tea, and placed the cup on the table. For someone of such an age, Ruth had a remarkable memory.

'There has, of course, been no further issue – since the death of your late husband, Mr Matthew Nazareth?'

Diana couldn't hide her annoyance. 'I think we'd better get to the point of this meeting.'

'You think it none of my affair?' Ruth sat back and sipped at her tea. 'Perhaps I shall prove you wrong.'

'It is *not* your affair,' Diana said with as much courtesy as she could muster.

'We'll see,' Ruth replied levelly. 'Would you bring me the package in the top drawer in my bureau?'

Diana brought the package, something bundled in very old cloth.

'Thank you.' Ruth's long, fragile finger tapped the bundle as she gazed, seemingly lost in thought, at Diana.

'I am tired, Mrs Nazareth,' the old lady said at last. 'My physician tells me it is time to lay all this down.' Her gaze went fleetingly to the bundle in her lap. 'I have no one else, you see . . .'

The change in her voice was disturbing; she suddenly sounded very, very old. Diana listened warily.

'I can't leave Simon unprotected,' she said as if to herself. 'Not with David Nazareth's interests so close at hand. I have to trust someone.'

Diana felt suddenly chilled.

'Benjamin Nazareth was the last straw.' Ruth looked evenly at her, strength returning to her voice.

'I'm sorry, I don't know what you are talking about.'

'You will. Please bear with me.' Ruth tapped the bundle again. 'In here lies the future of Simon and Tamerford Manor – or of David Nazareth.'

Diana wished she hadn't come.

Ruth's voice changed to a lower register. 'I have asked you here to seek your help, but first I must reassure you that I am not senile, mustn't I? Very well. My behaviour when we met on the gallery was caused by shock. I apologise for my rudeness, and my denial of it to Simon. Now you shall learn the reason. But I need your word that you will not disclose what I am going to tell you.'

'That's not possible until I know what you are talking about.'

'Mrs Nazareth – Diana. May I call you Diana?'

'If you wish.'

'I have taken the time to learn a great deal about you, Diana. And I have concluded that you are the one person who can be trusted with this.'

Diana stared at the bundle again. What on earth was in it? Maps? Documents? Or was it a parcel of dreams – the fantasies of an old woman?

Ruth interpreted the look, and unwrapped the bundle.

Now Diana could see that there were papers and small, leather-covered books, all of a great age, on first appearance. Ruth riffled through the pile and, finding what she wanted, passed it wordlessly to Diana.

It was an old letter, so badly faded in places that only small sections could still be read. The handwriting and style had been distinctive and artistic, clearly the work of an intelligent mind. Attached to the original was a more recent but still very old copy. And this was legible. There was no address, but the date read 1631.

Diana skimmed the page, then read it again more slowly. Finally she looked up, questions tumbling over themselves in her mind.

'That was written by Joshua Nazareth Tamerford to his mother, Rebecca Tamerford,' Ruth said quietly. 'As you have read, it is the lament of a younger twin who believes his older brother is destined to diminish the family fortunes. Jeremiah was, by all accounts, an inveterate gambler. Joshua was the one with the greater love for his home and lands and, rather than stay and witness the downfall he was quite certain his brother would bring to Tamerford, he left for the New World and became David Nazareth's ancestor.'

Diana's animosity had vanished. She hadn't been wrong! Here was the proof.

'But – I don't understand,' she admitted. 'Why is this such a problem? If the Tamerfords and Nazareths are related, however distantly now – surely that could be beneficial to Tamerford?'

'Ah. That's where you are wrong.' Ruth took the letter back and placed it carefully on the sofa beside her. 'These are Rebecca's diaries – ' she handed the pile of leather books to Diana. 'You can look at them later. They will tell you better than I can the reason for later events.

'I want you to look at this next.' She handed over a page from a yellowed sheaf of papers. 'This is the last page of Joshua's father's will. Unintentionally, we are quite certain, this small codicil has been the downfall of Tamerford.'

Again Diana read, this time the wishes of Samuel Tamerford for his beloved lost son, Joshua.

Now she looked up, totally bewildered.

'It is a very old story, you see. One handed down from generation to generation, to the eldest child. I learned of it from my brother by accident. Both his sons were dead, and Simon was just a child – so my brother was obliged to tell it to me.

'You see, this is not just a tale of separation and grief, although it is also that. It is the record of Samuel's unwitting folly. Samuel grieved as deeply for his youngest son as his wife, Rebecca, did. But it was Samuel who caused that same lost son still to haunt this house today.

'Jeremiah *did* gamble heavily, but it was Samuel who tied his hands in the end. He left half of his estate to his missing son. Or to *his* heir. Samuel seems to have believed, even at the end, that Joshua would return, with a strong son, and strengthen his weaker brother's character.

'Of course Joshua didn't return. Neither did any son. Joshua never wrote to his parents again after that first letter. They died still grieving for him.'

There was a lump in Diana's throat, which grew as Ruth told the tragic tale.

'Tamerford grew poorer, and the account set up for Joshua grew fatter. The family kept strict records of Joshua's bank balance.' Ruth's eyes were glazed as she said, 'Can you imagine what it must have been like, to watch that account growing obscenely rich, while Tamerford deteriorated, generation by generation?'

Diana rubbed at her forehead, the beginnings of an ache forming.

'Why didn't they just use the money?'

'Samuel's Will expressly left that money to Joshua and his heirs,' Ruth said patiently.

'But — '

'The key words are "and his heirs".' Ruth's voice was hushed. 'Think about it. "His heirs". There has been no end to "his heirs". Until *now*.'

'You mean — '

'That's right. David Nazareth is Joshua's *last* heir.'

'Might I have something stronger than tea?' Diana asked faintly.

Ruth poured a large brandy for Diana and a tiny measure for herself.

'So David, and then Matthew, would have been entitled to claim that money . . .' Diana was trying to think with a brain hazed by possibilities.

'That's right.'

'Then why haven't they? Or David anyway?'

'Because he doesn't know about it.' Ruth rose stiffly and began to walk about the room. 'Excuse me, I can't sit for long periods – another trial of old age . . .'

Diana nodded, miles away. If David was the heir, but didn't know he was, then he couldn't claim the money anyway.

But what did that matter? He had such enormous wealth already.

But was that the point?

'The Nazareths have never known about any of this?'

'*Never.*'

'But, how could — '

'The family have never informed them.' Ruth ceased walking to lean on the back of the sofa, watching Diana carefully.

'The family? You mean this has never been in a solicitor's hands?'

'No. The will was entrusted to the family. I don't know if that was common practice in those times, but it was in this household.'

'Well, surely the family could have taken that money at any time?'

'Maybe so,' Ruth agreed. 'But they wouldn't do that. It was Samuel's will, after all. Not something to tamper with lightly.'

'But it *has* been tampered with,' Diana protested. 'No one has followed Samuel's will.'

'There was no clause of duty upon any of them to seek out the heir,' Ruth said shortly. 'Only the awful knowledge that while a Nazareth heir remained alive they were honour bound to leave that account alone.'

Diana closed her eyes. Honour? Yes, and no. The most archaic honour to leave the money while the house fell down around their ears – but not the honour to tell the rightful heir. What a bloody insane, dishonourable mess.

'Simon knows nothing of this.' Ruth had returned to her seat. 'And neither does Gabrielle. I don't intend them to know while David Nazareth is alive. That's why I asked for your help.'

'I couldn't! Whatever it is you want me to do — '

'Listen to me, Diana. I ask only that you do nothing at this moment; nothing more than take away Rebecca's diaries and these letters, and that you read them in private. After that, you can give me your answer.

'But I'd also like you to consider this – think of how Simon and Gabrielle are forced to live. Consider David Nazareth's fortune, and the fact that he is a sick man who might not have much longer to live. Even if he does make his adopted son his heir, do you not think that the Nazareth fortune is miracle enough for a man who does not even carry Nazareth blood?'

Diana ignored that. 'Why can't you tell Simon?'

'Because my great-nephew is an honourable man, as his father was before him.' Now Ruth's face was strained and tired. 'He would unquestionably hand the lot over. He must not know until David Nazareth is dead.

'Please, take these items away. Read them. Think about everything I have said. I am dying, Diana. There is no one else I can trust to safeguard Simon's future . . .'

Diana slumped back against the cushions. It was preposterous. And yet . . . 'Simon would probably find my action unforgivable,' she stalled, wanting more time to think.

'You are only helping me. You need not mention knowing what any of this package contains. I beg you, Diana, Please help Simon and Gabrielle . . .'

Ruth stood up again, and pulled the velvet cord.

'Forgive me, my dear. I am very weary. Do let Gabrielle know when you will come again —

'Ah, Gabrielle, I have kept Diana far too long. She has been charming company, though I fear I have bored her with my nostalgia. She is even good enough to show an interest in my collection of old magazines.'

Gabbie was delighted, hardly noticing the bundle Diana had tucked furtively under her arm.

'Come again soon, won't you?' Ruth said ingenuously, as if it were an invitation for further gossip.

By the time she reached Tavistock, Diana's head was aching miserably. Glad that the girls were still at the manor, she took herself off to bed with aspirins and a warm drink. She could not have borne any chatter about Tamerford this evening; and could not have guaranteed she would not burst out with the whole insane business. The weight of this new knowledge seemed an unbearable extra burden.

She sought a cool spot on her pillow and buried her aching head in it. David-bloody-Nazareth. Why was it that all of the worries of her life led back to him?

She sighed aloud. What wouldn't she give to be able to turn back the clock of her life. By five years and four months . . .

In the morning she awoke after Gemma and Candy had left. Gingerly she sat up, but was relieved to find that her head no longer ached at all. In fact, she felt exceptionally well. Somehow the worry and conflict had resolved themselves while she slept.

She would read the old papers, keep an emotional distance from them. Then she would give them back, and say, 'Sorry – but no, thanks.'

Of course the incredible story of the Tamerfords and the Nazareths had touched her deeply. But how could she possibly be involved in such a deception? Not only would she be denying David young relatives, she would be an accomplice in something more sinister than she cared to think about. Ruth could not live much longer. Then the truth would have to come out anyway.

David would learn of his thoroughly aristocratic English roots – and of his somewhat corrupt ancestors; but he would forgive all that once he understood it. And he would have the delight of knowing the young Tamerfords.

She smiled to herself as she pictured his reaction. He'd always had an admiration for things English. No wonder. And he had no need of that secret bank account. No doubt, when he learned how things had been at Tamerford because of it, he'd immediately release it to Simon and Gabbie.

Diana hummed, despite the grey, late October day, her thoughts in a dozen pleasant places at once. But suddenly a shadow dulled her thoughts. There was still the situation with Ben to resolve. And the Youth Trust. It had taken the trip to Boston for her to realise she could not work hand in glove with Ben. She would do whatever needed doing to finalise the setting up, which was now imminent, and then she would ask David to release her.

Simple. Clean. Honest.

Candy looked settled; Gemma would have full-time work with the trust – and the fates would decide what, if anything, would happen to Gemma's dreams of Ben.

And she would have the luxury of her own life back again. She would reopen her boutique, perhaps somewhere else; and could keep a friendly interest in the trust. From a distance.

It was perfect.

She was clearing up after the girls when the door opened and Ben walked in.

He stood inside the kitchen door, speculation in the deep, dark eyes.

'Mountain to Mohammed?' he said softly. 'Now I wonder why that has to be.'

Diana moved to the far end of the table, her heart suddenly pounding; this was the part that would not be easy.

He watched, frowning. 'Not expecting me?' His voice was guarded. 'Or not wanting to see me?'

Diana had stupidly frozen. Ben was one thing at a distance, but something totally different close at hand. She clutched at the tea-towel, all her plans to greet him coolly, in a businesslike manner, vanishing into thin air.

He stared for a moment longer, then pulled out a chair and dropped into it, folding his long legs beneath the table. 'Any coffee?' he said evenly.

Diana managed to nod, and turned to the percolator. Something was tugging at her heart.

'The wedding news is wonderful.' She finally managed to free her tongue. 'Sudden, but perhaps not unexpected.'

'Yes, to both observations.'

Diana poured coffee and set a mug in front of Ben. He had the most extraordinary effect on her; as if she felt her knees were beginning to buckle.

She sat down quickly. The scent of his after-shave lingered in her nostrils, bringing back unsought memories of his body close to hers.

'All going well with the trust?'

'Fine. We should be able to make a public announcement in a couple of weeks.'

'That's great,' she said, meaning it. The sooner the better. 'All the plans ironed out?' Diana knew she must sound as uncomfortable as she felt; and as foolish.

'Better than that.' Ben's face was impassive, the green eyes hard to read. 'Simon's introduced several ideas of his own. He's a diamond.'

'But it will still all take a while to sign and seal,' Diana said, thinking of her own plans.

'Sure. But the kids will be working from day one, that's the main thing.'

Diana looked down at her coffee, away from those penetrating eyes. How could he sound so honest, and so noble, when he was neither? But then again, perhaps he was – in all matters not directly concerning David.

Suddenly she wondered what would happen to all the bright plans and all those jobs, if David pulled the rug out from under them? Or if Simon did, for that matter? She stared into her cup. If the hatred was mutual, as Jeff had suggested, then was it possible that David might find, in his new relatives, an opportunity to ease Ben out?

And what about Simon? If he were to suddenly come under David's protection – or alternatively find himself in possession of a great deal of money – would he be quite so keen to have strangers directing his affairs? Youngsters crawling all over his property? Inwardly she groaned. There were things she had not yet considered fully.

'A lot could go wrong,' she said aloud.

'Nothing's going to go wrong, honey. Is that what you are worrying about? Simon is a man of his word. And so am I. We'll see it through, whatever obstacles are put in our way.'

Diana glanced up, her eyes clouded with worry. Two weeks ago she would have trusted Ben with all her heart. Now? Now she wasn't certain about anything. Or anyone.

'We'll see Alan next week, tie up all the loose ends. That's one of the reasons I'm here. As you are avoiding me, I thought I'd better check that nothing's changed'

Diana heard the underlying emphasis on the 'one', and her stomach lurched. Any minute now things would get personal. It was all getting muddled again.

'I'm sorry. No, nothing has changed. The Trust goes ahead.'

'I wouldn't want to go into a public meeting with my back uncovered,' Ben said grimly.

'I know that,' she said defensively.

'And you are sure nothing's changed?' The question hung in the air between them.

'Nothing to do with the trust – but David sent a letter with me.'

Ben's mouth instantly compressed. 'For me?'

'I'll get it.'

Diana hurried from the room. She had forgotten the letter in all her other concerns. How crazy. She should have sent it with the girls. Now she had to face him with it. She found it in her bag, and held it for a moment, a silent prayer in her mind. If he took this well . . .

Ben paced the kitchen and Diana could feel the white-hot rage pouring from him. It was like being trapped too close to a volcano.

Finally he spoke. 'I didn't ask you to wet-nurse me. It wasn't bothering me any. Why did you get him to change that clause?'

She shrank at the change in his voice. It was ugly. And something else. Dangerous?

'No? Well it was bothering *me*,' she said frankly.

He stared at her, fury rigidly controlled. 'So you *did* think I was trying to use you!'

'No. I wanted it off our backs,' she said, hating this, not wanting to say the hurtful things that must follow, but knowing she had no choice.

'You don't trust me.'

'What do you expect?' she said quietly. 'I've seen the documents you signed.'

'Hold on a minute – what is this?' He stood in front of her, eyes hard and questioning.

Diana couldn't believe the pain in her heart. It was so sudden and so unexpected that for a moment she was stunned. When she could speak, her voice was filled with sadness. 'You lied to me.'

Ben's face registered instant shock, and he drew in a deep breath. 'I don't know what you think you mean by that, but I sure as hell hope you have some kind of explanation.'

'Me? Don't you have that the wrong way round? I *saw* your contract, Ben. I saw everything, and I was told everything that was explained to you. You twisted it for you own purposes – I won't even give a name to what those appear to be. And there was *no* disclaimer, Ben. Nothing. *Why* did you lie?'

Ben closed his eyes briefly. 'Diana – honey, I don't know what you were shown, but I have never lied to you. *Never*. So I don't know what you have seen, but it sounds to me like you've been given a pile of heavy bullshit by my father.'

'Ben, don't! I saw the papers you signed. And David didn't show them to me, Jeff did. He cares about you — '

'The hell he does! Sherman might have shown you some papers, but they sure as hell don't sound like the ones I signed. Don't you know anything about David Nazareth? Sherman wouldn't sneeze without the old man's approval. No, Diana, if you weren't shown the papers I described, then you've been taken for an almighty ride. You've been suckered.'

'Don't do this,' Diana said, her convictions weakening by

the second. What was it with these two men? They were both
equally believable. Suddenly she knew that she wouldn't have
a moment's peace until they were *both* out of her life.

'You saw a document, Diana. How did you authenticate it?
How well do you know my signature?'

She stared at him, astonished. Would he go so far as to
suggest that someone would deliberately forge supposed legal
documents, for her benefit? When she'd barely given notice of
her arrival?

'For God's sake, Ben!'

His shoulders slumped and he moved to the door. 'If you
didn't see the disclaimer, then you didn't see the other pretty
rider. The condition that I would not return to Boston during
the terms of the contract — '

'Not return? Oh no, not more lies.'

'I didn't tell you that one – it didn't seem to matter,' he said,
his voice strained.

Anger crackled in the air between them.

'So I'm neatly hog-tied, aren't I? I can't go to Boston to get
those documents and prove to you that I'm right. If I do, I
forfeit everything I'm doing for those kids.' His face had paled
to a deathly white. 'But I will prove to you – however long it
takes – that there is only one Nazareth who's a liar. And it
sure as hell isn't me!'

The door slammed behind him.

Shaken, Diana sat down. He sounded so sincere. Did he
believe what he was saying? Could he have talked himself
into such conviction of his fantasy? She shook her head. It
was all becoming too much for her.

And yet she trusted him entirely where the Youth Trust was
concerned. Was that perverse of her? No. He had a lot to lose.
Only the trust stood between him and Nazareth House now.
Nothing else.

She should have been relieved that it was over. Instead, a
deep sadness settled over her heart.

It was mid-afternoon before she was controlled enough to

ring Alan. Perhaps not surprisingly, it was the thought of those kids, and Tamerford, that gave her courage.

'Alan? I need to see you privately, before we go public with the Youth Trust.'

A week later Diana had concluded her instructions and signed an interim agreement. All that remained was for her to tell David. She reached him in his office.

If he was surprised by her decision, he covered it well. But his delight was obvious.

'It's your choice, sweetheart. And that's fine with me. You know I'll go along with whatever you feel is right. I'll have the legal department here notified. Now tell me, when can we expect you? Beanie hopes you'll get here at least a week before the party. She's cooking up something really big, sweetheart, and she says she needs you here to make your costume.'

'I'll come immediately after the wedding,' Diana promised, glad that she would have something to fill the weeks ahead.

At last it was all arranged as she had wanted.

Why was it then that she felt she had betrayed someone?

CHAPTER TWENTY-NINE

As they gathered that crisp November evening, they were all glad that the weather was fine. Already the hall's seats had been filled and the comprehensive school's headmaster was assuring people that they would hear everything over the PA system, even in the grounds.

The trustees were satisfied. The whole town was there, s were the media. And not more than a handful of people knew what the trust was going to do. They still had the delightful element of surprise.

Pritchard and Chris had gathered most of the town's young people; no mean feat, considering their apathy. Ten trustees sat on the stage at the front of the hall: Diana and her cousins; Ben and the Tamerfords; Pritchard and Chris; Alan and Adrian Lawrence.

On the stroke of eight, Ben rose, walked to the lectern and began . . .

In Boston, David and Jeff were back in their offices after lunch.

David glanced at his watch. 'Well, he's beginning about now.' He beamed at Jeff. 'It's all going to be easier than I'd thought.'

Jeff raised his eyebrows. 'There's no telling, Dave. Not with Ben.'

'Ha! Giving him ten million was like dropping a boulder in the bottom of a rusty pail. It'll go straight through and leave him with nothing.'

'The rust is a great idea,' Jeff argued.

'Sure. If you have endless capital. But a derelict manor and a townful of outta work kids?' David leaned back in his chair, satisfaction written all over him. 'Nope. Ben's well tied up for the next five years, and no way will he make a profit from that mess. Christ, he's talking about running it like some national heritage – but without the kind of money those people need.' David's laugh was hard.

'I liked the idea of restoring all those old trades though,' Jeff persisted. 'And building the hotel, and holiday cottages, not to mention the marina down at that old quay.'

'So the idea's good – but, Jeff, he's talking major renovations, major building programmes.' David began to list them on his fingers. 'First, that manor will absorb a fortune, as it has to if it's to attract tourists as a prime feature of his plan. Then he has to house the family in that lodge that has no water, no power, no sewage. He has to get all those same utilities down to the hotel, the cottages, the quay.' He shook his head. 'He's talking of a luxurious marina and clubhouse, restoring a chandlery on the spot, setting up permanent workshops for the boatyard – *and* building that hotel and those cottages at the quayside.'

'Well, he's got the labour on the spot,' Jeff pointed out.

'Yeah. But, Jeff, all that labour has first to be trained. Workshops have to be set up, tradesmen employed to train those kids.'

'In a country with high unemployment, that needn't be a problem.'

'Admittedly, but you're forgetting that old manor. That's a medieval house, Jeff, with medieval furnishings. For that read experts, and for those read damned costly. You're talking art experts and restorers; specialists in those old, fragile tapestries; and don't forget the furniture Diana described – it sounds as if it came out of the ark, so again read very specialised work.'

Jeff shifted uncomfortably. 'Well, he could make a start on one of those projects, bring in some capital.'

'You are not hearing me,' David said patiently. 'Diana says his first project is going to be the farm. Christ aAmighty, there are hundreds of acres there, all in need of fencing; the guy doesn't have a shed that isn't patched; he hasn't got stock for that much land; he hasn't even got a tractor. What do you think Ben is going to have to provide for all that?'

Jeff was frowning. He'd thought the whole idea sounded wonderful. Now, he wasn't so sure.

'Then there's "youth accommodation", Jeff. Flats for those kids, and a communal kitchen – *and* a youth club as well.' David stared, wide-eyed out of his window. 'It's dead before it even begins.'

'It might work. Stranger things have happened.'

'Yeah? Well not that strange when it comes to money,' David said drily. 'Nope. Ben's not gonna win this one. And already Diana's out of it.'

Jeff watched David, saddened. Dave was practically rubbing his hands with glee. 'That doesn't mean she'll come back here,' he said carefully.

'I agree. But she *is* coming for Beanie's party. That'll give me the time I need. Ben's made his own bed – now he'll have to stew in it for five years.'

Jeff waited, but there was no more. Dave seemed lost in his own thoughts.

Perversely, he hoped Ben would prove him wrong.

Ben was winding up his speech. He'd held his audience in thrall for an hour. It was enough.

'Here in Tavistock we are going to wage our own war against youth unemployment. There can be little doubt in any intelligent mind that violence, hooliganism, vandalism, are the products of hopelessness. If a man has no job, no hope of a job, he sees no future; if he sees no future, he is desolate; and desolation is perhaps the worst form of distress there is.

'So those, ladies and gentlemen, are our reasons for making the young people of the area our cause. We are not holding out temporary carrots, but a trust that will be run in part by the young people themselves, and which will have, as its longer-term aim, the goal of becoming a private company, a company which all these youngsters will help to build, and in which they will have a financial stake, eventually, as shareholders.

'Of course this can't all be achieved overnight. We're talking a very long-term commitment: ten, maybe twenty, years before we get to that stage.'

He moved to the front of the stage.

'But we are going to begin building that dream on Monday morning. Buses will leave the town at eight, sharp. Those who want a share in this, will be on them.'

Outside, a swell of applause began; then it merged with a standing ovation inside the hall. Photographers moved to the stage; flashguns exploded. Half a dozen microphones were pushed into Ben's face.

He turned to his companions. 'Well, we've done it. Now let's go home!'

Candy's wedding was only days away when the news of Diana's decision broke.

There had been no occasion for them all to meet together since Diana had given her instructions to Alan. Those instructions had since gone to the Nazareth House lawyers for final checking and it had taken time.

Tonight the Lloyds were arriving from Australia, and tomorrow Diana would be picking Rachel up from the airport. Amidst all the chaos, the final papers still had to be signed and, as these concerned only the immediate quorum, the four of them met Alan in the library.

Diana shook her head when Ben offered her the papers to sign first. His mouth tightened, but he said nothing. Simon and Gabbie signed after him, then he passed them back to Diana. She pushed them across the table to Alan, who signed with a flourish, in her place.

In the tense moment that followed, only Ben's eyes betrayed his feelings. They ranged from initial surprise to the darkness of bitter understanding.

'Diana has withdrawn from an active role in the trust,' Alan said smoothly. 'I have her signatory rights, when the three of you reach agreement over anything.' He lowered his voice slightly. 'Mr David Nazareth would not agree to anyone else having her power of veto, therefore she maintains that.'

Simon looked faintly puzzled but not unduly concerned. Gabbie's eyebrows rose slightly.

'Why?' Ben's single word rang in the silent room.

'There is no need for me to be directly involved,' Diana said quietly. 'But I have not lost interest and I will follow the trust's work with great interest.' She stood up and gathered her things. 'I'll see you at the wedding.' Diana nodded to Simon and Gabbie, and escaped from the room.

It was done. She felt an emptiness instead of the relief she had expected. But her day-to-day contact with Ben was severed. That was the main thing.

He caught up with her at her car.

'Wait just a minute!' he thundered, catching hold of her arm and spinning her round. 'What the hell do you think you're doing?'

'You've seen what I've *done*. Please let go of my arm!'

'Not until you explain.' Ben's fury was palpable in the air between them.

'My reasons aren't your concern,' Diana said with more courage than she felt. 'But I've done as I was asked – which was to help you to find a cause and set up a trust.' Her eyes met his steadily. 'I did that for David.'

Ben dropped her arm as if he'd been stung.

'You've betrayed me, Diana.'

'Betrayed you? Nonsense,' Diana said briskly. 'You have an unhealthy fixation, Ben. I'm not reneging on anything; I've kept my word.'

'Not to me,' Ben said very softly.

Diana stepped back and stared at him, her mind weary with helplessness. 'There is nothing more to say.'

'Oh? Maybe not for you, Diana. But I have plenty to say. Like what *did* the old man say to you, or show you, in Boston?

Whatever it was, it was lies. Damned lies! I told you the truth, but you have chosen to believe him. That tells me plenty about *you*, doesn't it?'

'Be careful,' Diana warned.

'Just tell me one thing,' Ben continued in the same, cold voice. 'Do you sleep with every man who wants you?'

Diana slapped him hard across the face.

'How dare you! You don't *begin* to know me, Benjamin Nazareth. But if the day ever comes when you *do*, you can apologise.' She jumped into her car and revved the engine furiously.

Ben stared down at her, an ugly red weal across his cheek. 'I could say the same to you. Word for word . . .' He stood back, his head held high. 'But we'll see, won't we? In time, Diana, we'll see which one of us owes the other an apology . . .'

With Diana staring after him, he turned away and strode across the cobbled yard.

Diana felt her anger drop away, to be replaced by a feeling of utter misery. It seemed that she and Benjamin Nazareth were destined only to fight with one another and, as she drove away from the manor, she wondered on which of them it would take the greater toll.

On the last Saturday in November, Candy Lloyd married Simon, Earl of Tamerford.

After a beautiful but simple ceremony amidst a small, hushed congregation, the party gathered for the wedding breakfast in the old dining-room.

The room had been immaculately cleaned, decked with flowers, it was alight with hundreds of candles. Candy shone beside her handsome groom, he in a rare new suit, and she in her lovely gown. The dress was a dream and Diana and Rachel stood together, discussing the remarkable talent of the two amateur dressmakers.

Purest white lace and satin, combined with a panel of snowy

velvet, floated out into an integral train. On her head, Candy wore an exquisite coronet of stiffened lace, covered with seed-pearls. The same pearls glistened abundantly in the long, scalloped veil. A simple velvet muff had kept her hands warm during the ceremony.

'Talented young pair,' Rachel agreed. 'Pity they are wasted in this backwoods,' she added, reaching for her ever-present camera.

'Hmm,' Diana observed thoughtfully. 'Maybe not for much longer, mother.'

Rachel shrugged slim shoulders, already interested only in catching a good enough shot of the bridal pair to reproduce in oils. She'd already told them that a painting would be her, belated, gift.

Now she decided to make an extra copy, but in water-colours. The young designers might enjoy a painting of their first joint venture.

'Take some photographs to Beanie when you go over next,' she said to Diana as she snapped away. 'It will be interesting to hear what she thinks.'

Pictures taken to her satisfaction, she was attracted to the unusual light and colours on the buildings outside.

'May I photograph, do you suppose?'

Diana looked at the bare buildings. 'I don't see why not.'

It was typical of Rachel to be less interested in seeing her brother and his wife again than she was in the scenery around her. Though, of the few people gathered, she had taken special note of the great-aunt. 'Ideal sketch for a Victorian composition,' she whispered to Diana. 'Perhaps even superimposed a modern office block . . .'

Diana offered no comment. Her mother was off in her own world; she wouldn't even hear a reply.

'And that dashing American,' Rachel said. 'Now he's something. Couldn't you fall for that? Strange, though, for an adopted son he bears a remarkable likeness to David . . .'

Diana hoped no one noticed her cheeks flame.

'Younger, of course. But a much nicer face. I'd trust that face. Can't say the same of David, for all his charm.'

Diana's blood alternately boiled and chilled. Thank goodness no one was near enough to hear.

'Look at those chiselled features, that square jaw and those expressive eyes. Mmm, I like the openness and honesty about him, never mind those looks. Now that would be a good match for you, darling. Pity there seems to be enmity between you.' Rachel shook her head. 'Still, young Gemma's champing at that bit. Shame.'

To Diana's utter relief Rachel turned away, her eye caught by the champagne light on a nearby turret.

'I must get that, darling. See you later.'

Diana had time to conceal her own confusion. It was not easy being around Rachel at the best of times. She saw too damned much.

The newlyweds relished being surrounded by their family and friends, and the promise of a weekend free from chores. They positively shone all day.

Gabrielle gave the wedding guests a tour of the house and, later in the afternoon, Ben explained their plans for the trust. He studiously avoided Diana, and she pretended not to notice him, but Gemma hung on his every word.

Candy and Simon took George and Charlotte off, to somewhere they could catch up on news and gossip. But Diana eventually had to hunt for her house-party, to take them all back to Tavistock. She had looked in several rooms, when she stepped into the library.

Ruth was standing alone before the modern ancestors, with a look of such sadness on her face that Diana pulled the door closed behind her and came to stand beside the old lady.

'Why so sad?' Diana asked lightly. 'Hasn't it been a lovely day? And aren't you delighted for Simon and Candy?'

'Yes indeed. Candy will make a perfect wife for him,' Ruth said. 'But my thoughts are often in the past, my dear. A hazard of one's winter years.' Her gaze returned to the painting of the stern young man with the bay horse.

'I was just thinking that it is a great shame we don't have a better likeness of Bart. He was my favourite nephew, you know. This is not a good likeness at all.'

'Is it because his brother died so young that there's no painting of him? Nathan, you said?'

'Oh, there is. Somewhere. I had it taken down,' Ruth said dismissively. 'He was not popular.'

Diana was surprised. With whom, she wondered. Ruth?

'Simon is very like his father,' Ruth continued. 'Taller, as is often the case, but they came from the same mould.' She sighed deeply. 'Nat intended to seek David Nazareth out, to ask for his help, but his death prevented that. And Bart simply refused. We were terribly poor – and no doubt there were many things Joshua's fund could have done for the children.' She smiled secretively. 'But Bart would not beg a penny. He was a Tamerford through and through. Honour before all else, thank God.' Ruth pulled her shawl closer about her thin shoulders. 'His brother, Nat, would have given the lot away. Imagine . . .' Now she shivered.

Diana was all but open-mouthed.

So there had been *one* Tamerford who would have followed Samuel's will. She would most definitely have liked to see a portrait of him. Strange, Joshua and Nat, both portraits spirited away . . . Pity she would no longer have the opportunity to look around. But perhaps one day – when Ruth died.

'I was looking in the little cemetery,' she said hesitantly, her mind on another track. 'There doesn't seem to be a grave for Nat.'

'No,' Ruth replied shortly. 'His body was never found.'

She started to leave, but Diana had one more question to ask. 'Tell me, is there any reason why there are no portraits of your female ancestors?'

Ruth's laugh was dry. 'An idiosyncracy, my dear. Peculiarly Tamerford. There are probably small portraits – the lofts are full of old stuff. But no, only the heirs were ever hung, so to speak.'

'How chauvinistic,' Diana retorted.

'It's growing dark, my dear.' Ruth changed the subject. 'You have your guests to get home, and I can't be standing around in idle chatter.' She put one long hand on Diana's arm. 'But I am still waiting for you to call on me again, Diana. Please do not leave it too late.'

Long after her mother, aunt and uncle and Gemma had retired, Diana paced her room. Simon was so like his father. The thought ran repeatedly through her mind. So like the father who had refused to claim any help from his only relative. Yet Simon had been denied that same right, or at least the knowledge of it. Was she right not to intervene?

She sat on her bed, deep in thought. What if David should die before Ruth? The implications were obvious. If she told him of Joshua's fund, and he claimed it, then after his death Ben would inherit that as part of David's estate.

That didn't seem quite fair somehow. Ben with all the money, Simon with none. And Ben with no Nazareth blood.

Her sense of fair play was roused. Under those circumstances, it would be kinder to let the money revert to Simon . . .

Gabbie left Diana with Ruth as before, but this time Diana politely declined refreshments.

'I have come to tell you that I will keep your secret. But only because Joshua's money is likely to go to Ben.'

She explained her reasons briefly.

Ruth listened intently.

'Good. And thank you, my dear.'

Diana drove back to Tavistock wishing she had not become involved in such deceptions. But it was too late for regrets now. She had other things on her mind as well. Like her pending return to Boston – and how she would keep David at arm's length during her stay. Never mind. She would manage somehow. And she would be safely back in Tavistock for Christmas.

Her mind wandered to her boutique and whether she would reopen it in the New Year. She couldn't get up any enthusiasm for the idea. Perhaps she needed a change of direction. Possibly some other kind of business. She still hadn't touched Matthew's money. Maybe she would use some of that to encourage Gemma's talents . . .

CHAPTER THIRTY

Diana accompanied her mother to Paris, stayed overnight with her, and then journeyed on to Boston. She had never felt so low-spirited. The past weeks with their tensions and traumas had left her drained.

She gave the head steward instructions not to wake her and pulled her complimentary eyeshades down. The gentle hum of the aircraft lulled her, but not to sleep. Her thoughts were back at Tamerford, with all its problems. Gemma, nothing short of furious at Diana's imminent return to Boston, had called her a bloody fool. A few short and hot words had flown between them after that, ending with Gemma storming out in temper. It was their first real quarrel.

She pulled the eyeshades off and sat up. It was impossible to sleep with a headache and a sick stomach. She asked for champagne. That was known to help unsettled stomachs.

The champagne eventually helped. Diana arrived paler than usual, but without the queasy tummy and headache of earlier in the day.

She needed a holiday, a complete break from Tavistock with all its difficulties. But would she find peace here? Wasn't she just exchanging one set of problems for another? She would go back to Paris after Beanie's party, she decided. The calm of her mother's house would do her good.

She accepted David's kiss of welcome and on the way to the mansion gave him all the news about the trust, unaware that a note of pride had crept into her description of Ben's triumphant public meeting and the subsequent good coverage he had received in the media.

David changed the subject to Beanie's party and her claims that it would be her best do *ever*.

'You are very pale, darling,' Beanie said quietly.

'Mmmm, I must have some kind of bug.' Diana explained her symptoms, but didn't notice Beanie's look of alarm. Later that evening, after Beanie had gone home and Diana had gone unusually early to bed, David called Beanie, as she had requested.

'I want to make some small changes to my party theme, darling. I think you will have to be in on them.'

David listened first with surprise, then very carefully. Beanie's suggestion was insane. Mad. Maybe mad enough to work?

'I don't know what I'd do without you, old friend,' David concluded gratefully.

'Neither do I,' she said flatly. 'But I believe there is more than one reason why this could be truly your last chance. I will do everything I can, darling. But you have to work with me. Every step of the way, from bottom to top step,' she said, knowing a misuse of the English language would amuse David. And knowing he needed humour, as much as anything else.

He chuckled deeply. 'You know I will. Thanks, honey.'

He replaced the receiver, his face strained. So Beanie, too, had noticed that pride in Diana's voice. Pride in Ben's achievements. Well, to hell with that. They'd soon show that bastard where he stood!

Beanie poured herself a martini and took it out on to the balcony. It was a clear, cold December night and the sky was a sparkling backdrop to the glittering stage of Boston by night.

She shivered in her velvet dressing-gown. It seemed the time had come to tell David Ella's secret. It wasn't the perfect moment to use the key she held, but fate was moving against him. If she didn't tell him now, it would very soon be too late.

'David, my love,' she spoke softly into the star-filled night. 'This is all I can give.' Then, suddenly and starkly, her accent was all-American. 'For Christ's sake, don't screw it up!'

* * *

Diana was intrigued by the theme of Beanie's party. A medieval banquet with all the guests in suitable costume. She was also thrilled to know that she would wear a frock Beanie was making for her. She knew that Beanie had done the cutting and that a team of seamstresses would finish the garment to a perfect fit. She began to catch the infectious party mood. Beanie had measured her again this morning, but she was not to see her dress until the day.

'You are my guest of honour, darling. It would never do for you to appear in less than the prettiest gown there. But it's also my surprise,' she declared gaily, refusing Diana's pleas for just a hint of the style.

Diana tried to pump her for more details of the theme or of the guest list. But she was firmly told to 'wait and see'. All she did know was that the venue was the opulent and swish Plaza Hotel.

David was extraordinarily busy over the next few days so there was little time to spend together. Diana enjoyed her time walking, reading and chatting to the household staff. They loved having her back with them and were just as curious as she was about the mystery party. David made no intimate moves towards her, although he was as affectionate as ever. But as he seemed to be preoccupied with work most evenings, Diana was able to get several early nights which helped her regain her good spirits. She still had odd spasms of nausea and the occasional headache, but was certain that the rest would eventually settle her overwrought system.

She did have a moment's real anxiety, though, when on the eve of the party David came home looking as if he'd seen a ghost. He was so pale and shaken that Diana wanted to call a doctor at once. He would not agree.

'It's all right, sweetheart. Nothing to get wound up about. I guess I've caught one of your headaches, that's all.' His smile was strained. 'Nothing that an early night won't cure.'

* * *

The morning dawned bright, clear and cold.

David not only looked better, but was inwardly exuberant. At first he'd been shocked to his soul to learn of Ella's treachery, but as the night wore on his humiliation turned to jubilation.

In the end, through her boastful vindictiveness, Ella had given him the chance of true happiness. Admittedly it hurt to know that Beanie had kept the secret all these years, but he understood that she'd done it to protect his pride. And wasn't she doing everything in her power to make it up to him?

Not that he minded what he'd learned. Far from it. It was the most wonderful relief of his life. Only the deception itself still rankled, and he could live with that.

He had been given the chance to remove Diana's objections. Finally.

Now he laughed gaily as he swung her around the marbled hall in an impromptu waltz.

'Tonight, is going to be the best night of our lives!' he claimed extravagantly.

Diana had to beg him to stop whirling her as it was beginning to make her feel sick.

'And you'd better save some of this energy for tonight,' she reminded him.

He ground to a halt and before she could protest he embraced her tightly, just for a moment, then held her away from him and looked deeply into her eyes. 'Honey, I have never loved you more than I do right at this moment,' he said passionately. 'Remember that!'

Then he was gone.

She spent a leisurely day and, late in the afternoon, showered and washed her hair. Beanie was due to arrive at five. Diana could hardly wait to see her dress.

Punctual as always, Beanie was followed into Diana's bedroom by one of her senior seamstresses, who carried an enormous white box.

Diana gasped with delight when the gown was revealed.

It was palest peach chiffon over snow-white silk, flowing to the ground. The neckline was almost off the shoulders; the bodice fitted tightly into the waist, with a point where it met the fullness of the skirt. Down the front of the bodice were a row of tiny pearl buttons, from neck to just below the waist.

The sleeves were a work of art. The undersleeves fitted closely, ending in points like that at the waist, but this time the point reached the centre of the back of Diana's hand. The oversleeves were draped so that they fell from the wrists, wide open almost to the floor, and they too ended in points.

The dress was completed with a darker, richly-embroidered sash belt, that sat just above Diana's hips. It was exquisite, and Diana enthused excitedly over it. But the final touch, and the one which afforded them all the most pleasure, was the crown. It was a tall filigree work of gilded metals, diamanté and pearls, and flowing from its base was a long filmy veil of shimmering white and peach chiffon.

'Oh,' Diana breathed. 'I shall really look the part of a princess. Thank you, Beanie.'

Beanie waved the thanks aside.

'Now, don't forget that this party is my little dream. We need dreams in our sad world, yes? You are my special guest, so I might ask you to perform one or two little honours with me, darling.' She smiled affectionately. 'You look every inch a princess, so please try to help my fantasy-party be a success. *Be* a princess for tonight, for me. If I ask anything of you, please humour me.'

Diana returned the hug. It would be hard not to playact in such a costume. She kissed Beanie's cheek fondly then hung the costume carefully and began to try out the hairstyle Beanie had suggested, not even noticing that her dream outfit was almost identical to her wedding-day choice of colours. She had just about got her hair right when David put his head round the door. Diana thought that a little of the previous evening's pallor had returned to his face, but he denied that he was feeling unwell.

'It's just this,' he said, his face a picture of embarrassment as he held his costume out for her to see. 'I'll look like a bloody fairy in this!' he said mutinously.

Diana laughed aloud. His outfit was of a dark, burnt orange colour, obviously made by Beanie to match Diana's costume, but there the similarity ended. David's costume was a long, pleated tunic, with elaborate sleeves puffed out at the top and narrowing at the wrist. The material of the sleeves was cut away in diamond shapes to show snowy-white silk beneath. The belt was wide and made of gilded medallions strung together; and a similar chain of medallions was to hang around his neck. But, it was not the tunic, or the jewellery, which bothered David so much, It was the tight cream leggings, the soft brown velvet boots and the hat, a strange round affair, with a mass of snow-white plumes which all but obscured his vision on one side.

'I'll never live this down. Look at it!' he exclaimed, dismally.

'You *and* all the other male guests,' Diana grinned. 'Don't forget that they all have to wear medieval costume as well.'

'What's the betting half of them don't show?' David growled.

'Oh pooh!' Diana mocked. 'You'll probably feel better when you've seen it on.'

He still looked mutinous, so she said, 'Well, we can always not show up. If you are game to risk Beanie's wrath?'

David's face cleared at once. 'Not on your life! Miss out on tonight? Not a chance. I guess I'll just have to grin and wear it,' he punned.

In fact David had the height and build to carry the costume magnificently. He jokingly agreed with Diana's delighted opinion that he would be the most dashing man there and, even though he felt self-conscious in his peculiar outfit, he knew that Diana looked enchanting as he proudly escorted her into the Plaza.

They were greeted by doormen, all dressed by Beanie in

brown satin tunics and brown leggings. David winked down at Diana.

'Not much competition there,' he grinned.

A man in a grey silk outfit took over at the door of the ballroom.

'Your name, sir?' he enquired politely.

'Nazareth,' David replied.

The man stepped into the ballroom.

'Mr David Nazareth and Mrs Diana Nazareth,' he bellowed. 'Guests of honour,' he added, reading from the card in his hand.

Voices quietened as hundreds of faces turned to see the only guests of honour.

'Damn!' David muttered quietly to Diana. 'She gave us a late timing. Obviously we are expected to make an entrance.' He smiled down at her nervous face. 'Ready, my love? Let's give 'em an eyeball at this!'

He stepped into the room and made a sweepingly extravagant bow. Diana went along instantly by dropping into a deep curtsy, hiding her blushing face. Everyone laughed and cheered at once, then Beanie was coming to meet them, clapping and smiling. She wore a long silver dress, with a high hat of lace trailing a grey cloud of veil.

'Bravo! Magnificent!' she cried. 'That was clever of you, darlings. And very courtly. Now come and see what you think of my little theme. Then I'll introduce you to any guests you don't know.'

There was little to do but marvel at the scene before them. The ballroom had been transformed into the interior of a medieval castle. They were standing in a very lifelike banqueting hall, complete with long tables and heavily carved chairs. Even the walls had been covered with stage backdrops so that they took on the appearance of mellow stone. There were artificial tall narrow mullioned windows high up in the walls. Huge mock-iron chandeliers hung from central points, ablaze with golden candles. And at intervals around the walls were massive glass torches, cunningly contrived to look as if they were lit by flames. At the far end of the hall, in front of a huge tapestry curtain, a group of minstrels played galliards on authentic-looking instruments.

'It's beautiful!' Diana proclaimed. 'And just look at the costumes!' Her gaze travelled the room, delighting in one gorgeous ensemble after another. David followed her gaze, relieved to find that he was far from being the only male in fancy underpants.

A young man dressed as a page passed them goblets of wine and, drinks in hand, they were introduced to a great number of people, people who smiled and whose eyes reflected curiosity. Then Beanie led them to their places beside her at the top table. A trumpeter sounded a brief fanfare that would have woken an army, and maids in heavy dresses of black satin, with daringly low cleavages, entered. They carried jugs of wine and champagne, and were followed by portly costumed chefs, bearing enormous platters of whole pig and lamb to carve at the tables.

The spectacle was greeted by cheers and soon the party were enjoying a truly medieval feast. The centre of the room had been left clear and, while the partygoers waded through ten small main courses before the desserts, jesters clowned and dancers danced, as act after act came on to entertain the diners.

There was much laughter at the tables because true to style Beanie had provided only carving knives, so that everyone had to cut and eat with a knife, or use their fingers. Fortunately, there were plentiful finger-bowls of water scattered with rose petals, and enormous square linen napkins.

Diana speared a tender piece of lamb fragrantly tossed in rosemary, wondering as she ate where on earth Beanie had found the gold-coloured plates and all the gold-plated goblets and jugs?

Nothing had been omitted. There wasn't a hint that they were not actually in another time. Beanie's invitations had been very precise. 'No watches, jewellery or other modern items to be worn.' And, to the letter, her guests had obeyed.

Beanie kept one careful eye on proceedings, and one on the six-foot-high sand-timer she'd had placed at the end of the hall.

Finally, it was time.

Beanie gave a nod to the man in the grey silk, and within seconds the maids reappeared to swiftly clear the tables of all but handmade sweetmeats and jugs of wine. Then a hunting horn sounded and slowly the tapestry curtains were parted. The lights around the hall were carefully dimmed and, to the delight of the guests, a stage was revealed. The setting was a lake in the supposed castle grounds.

Beanie eased out of her seat and tiptoed on to the stage to take the microphone. 'Ladies and gentlemen, to add to my fantasy this evening, and I hope to yours, I would like to present for your entertainment the fairytale of The Sleeping Beauty.'

Her guests applauded, hugely enjoying the novelty of being transported back, not only in time, but also to childhood.

Anticipation settled over the hall as Beanie slipped back into her seat.

Diana squeezed Beanie's hand in delight.

The play commenced. A beautiful young queen wept at the side of the lake, and handmaidens could not console her. Suddenly a child-sized frog, dressed all in gold, appeared to glide across the lake sitting on a lily leaf. He asked the queen why she was so unhappy and she replied that it was because she and her husband had no children. The frog made her a promise that she would bear a beautiful baby girl.

The play moved on in time, into the interior of the castle where the queen had just been delivered of a lovely daughter. The handsome king announced that they would hold a party for their beloved child's christening, and invite all the fairy queens in the kingdom.

Once more the talented set-designers changed the scene,

dropping yet another backcloth, which showed a throne room; a small child in a crib was surrounded by ethereal fairies. Each in turn granted the child a blessing and a gift.

It had just come to the twelfth fairy's turn when suddenly on to the scene burst a black-gowned old crone, bewailing the fact that she was the oldest fairy in the land and she'd received no invitation to the christening. She ranted and raved and would not be placated and finally, amidst stage moans of horror from the audience, cast a curse upon the child, that she would prick her finger on a spindle and would die.

The acting held Beanie's guests enthralled. Grown men and women enthusiastically booed the old witch as she left the stage. Then the twelfth fairy, who had been pushed aside by the crone, gave her blessing and gift. She wept because she could not undo the wicked spell, but she could cause it to be altered. She kissed the child and proclaimed that, as her gift, the princess would not die, but would fall asleep for a hundred years, and then be awoken with a kiss.

The audience cheered the young fairy and Beanie smiled at Diana. 'We are all children at heart,' she whispered, as the scene changed to a garden, where a pretty young child danced and sang and played. In the background, palace courtiers ran around destroying every spindle in the land, while the king and queen watched carefully over their special child.

The scene changed again. A teenage princess alone, exploring an old deserted tower in some far reaches of the castle. An old woman welcomed her into a tower room. When the girl asked what the old woman was doing, she offered to show her how to use a spindle. The princess was curious; she'd never seen anything like it. And so, as predicted, the young princess pricked her finger and, stumbling to a nearby sofa, fell into a deep, enchanted sleep.

All around the castle people fell instantly asleep, and the curtains closed on the sleeping cast.

Everyone began to whistle and call for the next act. Beanie took Diana's hand and whispered urgently to her. Diana

blushed furiously in the dark but, remembering her promise
to act her part, she followed Beanie backstage.

David remained where he was, for now.

The curtains slid open again to show an inpenetrable hedge
of thorny bushes surrounding the castle.

A young man stood at the front of the stage, trying to hack
a path through the dense hedge, but all he got for his efforts
were cuts and bruises, and much audience heckling.

Various other young knights came on to the scene, swords
flashing, but to no avail. The hedge held back all the princes
in the land.

The scene changed, and an old man sat beside the hedge,
announcing the arrival of another prince.

The audience gasped, and then cheered loudly as David
dashed across the hall and climbed on to the stage.

The old man told this new prince the story of the famous
Sleeping Beauty, and of all the efforts to free her from her
prison of sleep.

David grinned with hammed-up enthusiasm, whilst the
guests whistled and stomped, greatly amused by his good-
natured willingness to go up on the stage. He began to
hack at the hedge and, as he did so, a narrator told that
a hundred years had passed, to the very day. Suddenly the
hedge parted, the thorns turned magically into roses and the
prince was through into the castle itself.

The scene returned to the tower room, but now instead of
the young girl, it was Diana who lay on the couch. More
whistles and roars went up around the room, and very modern
cat-calls of 'Go for it!'

David crossed to the sofa and dropped a quick kiss on the
princess's mouth.

Now the noise was tremendous.

Diana sat up blushing and yawned and stretched nervously
just as Beanie had instructed and, when David went down
on one knee and asked the princess to marry him, the party
went wild. 'Say yes!' guests yelled to Diana. 'Go on, put him

out of his misery!' cried one knowledgeable wit. And so the Sleeping Beauty accepted the prince's ring and the audience clapped and yelled and banged on the tables. Then Diana and David bowed and all the cast came forward to tremendous applause.

Flashbulbs popped all around the room, and the guests gaily joined in the merriment and the supposed engagement of the prince and princess.

Diana had never been so nervous in her life, but the cheering crowd were so charming, so completely supportive, that, carried away, she linked arms with David.

He smiled down at her. 'I love you, princess.'

She grinned. It was *only* a party.

Flashbulbs popped, and they laughingly rejoined the audience to applaud the cast of the play.

The curtain closed at last and Beanie stood at the front of the stage. Diana watched her, delighted at her creativity and the pleasure she had given so many people. Beanie waited until the hall had quietened down.

'Ladies and gentlemen, I'd like to thank you for your appreciation. I'm sure you'll agree that my guests of honour made a romantic prince and princess and did justice to the play.' She smiled mischievously as the cheers died down. 'Let us hope that they will live happily ever after.' Another cheer greeted her inference.

'But now, before we turn the time back to the present day, I have a small memento of this evening for our lady guests, something which I hope will help them to hold this evening amongst their fonder memories.' She took a large plate from a palace courtier and called to Diana to assist her.

Together they went around the room, laughingly pinning brooches to the costume bodices of the lady guests. A gasp of delight went through the room as the little gifts were examined. They were twenty-two-carat gold frogs, encrusted with diamonds and emeralds, handmade at Cartier, and very expensive.

A roar of approval greeted Beanie's final gift, a frog for the Sleeping Beauty, which Beanie pinned on Diana's bodice herself.

'A token of good luck,' Beanie grinned.

Then she signalled to someone, and the curtains rolled back again, to reveal a modern dance band.

'Would our guests of honour like to lead the dancing?' Beanie cried above the cheers.

David led Diana on to the floor to great noise and merry-making. Cameras clicked away as the laughing couple swirled around the empty floor. Gradually other couples joined them, and soon the dancing was in full swing.

Beanie gave a discreet signal to the man in silver, and he quietly gathered the newsmen and ushered them out of the party.

Diana was exhausted and elated. The strange tiredness had crept up on her again in the past hour; but now she forced herself not to think of it. It had been a lovely party. Certainly, she had never known one like it. And her temporary star status was a heady experience. Admittedly, it was all a little over the top, but everyone was having fun, and as that was Beanie's intention her hard work had paid off.

She blushed against David's shirt when she remembered his kiss and proposal in front of all these people. And her acceptance. But it was all innocent fun, and this laughing, teasing crowd were David and Beanie's friends.

He squeezed her gently and she smiled up at him. 'Enjoying yourself, sweetheart?'

'Hugely,' she said gaily.

Diana awoke from a dream of the fairy-tale party. What an amazing event it had been. She grimaced, unable not to be glad it was over. She had done all that was asked of her. Now she would be able to make her excuses and leave for Paris.

She stretched tiredly. It had been after three when they'd finally got away. It had been fun, but she could not have danced another step or drunk another goblet of champagne. Neither could she have taken any more of the congratulations.

Dear Beanie. So much work, just to give an evening's pleasure. She stretched out lazily, and wondered about Beanie's other dos. They surely couldn't all be so extravagant? So costly? She made a mental note to ask David about past parties.

She was debating making the effort to get up when there was a tap at her door, and David, fully dressed and looking as fresh as if he'd slept a full night instead of just a few hours, was grinning down at her. He dropped a bundle of newspapers on to her bed.

'Well, princess. We made the headlines!' He grinned from ear to ear, as Diana sat up and pulled a paper towards her. 'These are just the early editions. Can you imagine what the later ones will have to say?'

Diana was too stunned to answer. There were photographs of her and David right across the front page of the 'early' she was holding. She was laughing up into his face as he was placing the ring on her finger. The caption blazed. 'Nazareth pulls off Proposal at Fancy-dress Gala!' The next paper showed them dancing cheek to cheek, the ring on Diana's finger flashing in the light. That headline ran, 'Will the lovely Princess wed her Prince?'

Diana read a few paragraphs, a sick feeling growing in her stomach.

'Last night at a spectacular party arranged by their closest friend, fashion maestro Madame Bérénice, David Nazareth and his deceased son's widow, Diana, dramatically announced their engagement in front of over three hundred specially invited guests.

'In an authentic medieval castle setting, the Nazareths, dressed in period costume, joined the actors on stage in the last scene of the ever-popular fairytale of Sleeping Beauty, and themselves performed the closing act. As David Nazareth, dressed as the story's prince, proposed to the Sleeping Beauty, their friends cheered and congratulated the engaged couple. Later gifts were distributed to all the ladies present, to mark the special occasion.'

Diana read on in utter disbelief.

'To honour her friends, Madame Bérénice created a precedent unheard of in her many years as Boston's top society hostess. This reclusive lady personally invited members of the press to record the engagement of her two closest friends.'

Yet another paper demanded, in capitals blazing across its front page, 'Is it Fact or Fantasy? Can David Nazareth Marry his Son's Widow?' It went on to describe the party in detail.

Diana thrust the papers aside. Her face was shocked, her eyes as grey as pewter.

'This is nonsense! David, these lies must be stopped!'

'Do you want it to be nonsense, honey?' David asked very softly.

'Of course it's nonsense, you know that,' she declared emphatically.

'You don't really mean that, sweetheart. You've got my ring on your finger. Shit, honey, we're in love! So, now the world knows. So what?'

Diana stared disbelievingly at him and then down at the ring, still where he'd placed it. Now in the daylight she could see that it was not the paste article she'd thought, but a very real and very large square emerald. She shook her rapidly thumping head. This wasn't happening to her. It was still part of the dream. It had to be.

But David's hand on hers was very real.

'Darling, listen to me. You told Beanie that the only thing that prevented you marrying me was Mat. Right?'

Diana stared blankly at him.

'Matthew was not my son.'

'What?'

'It's OK, honey. I've had two days and nights to absorb it,' David soothed.

'Mat *not* — '

'I know, it takes some getting used to. Ironic, huh? Something that would have crucified me if I'd known years ago is now only a relief. It couldn't be anything else, after what Mat did — '

'I never — ' Diana began.

'You would never have admitted it was him? Yes, I know that too. And it makes me feel very humble, to have such love and protection as you and Beanie have given me.'

David stared into space for a moment, while Diana fought futilely for something to say. But what? Commiserations? Congratulations?

'My pride's hurt,' he admitted quietly. 'But that's nothing I can't live with. Particularly now.' His eyes were grave and tender in turns. 'Not if it gives me the moral right to marry you.'

Diana had not moved. She could not, because the nausea caught her in waves. She closed her eyes, and her mind screamed a silent *no*! But she couldn't speak.

David's voice faded in and out of her mind. 'I've always regretted contriving to marry you and Mat, you must know that. But hell, what would you have wanted with an old man?' His face fell and he stared down at the bed. 'I loved you from the moment, the instant, that we met – but I never intended telling you, believe me. It was fate that moved, in some strange way, and showed me you could care for me too. That's when I started to fight for you.'

She wanted to tell him that she had been confused, that she had mixed him up with her father, that somehow he had brought her papa back; but the memory of the night she had gone to bed with him, out of pity, silenced her.

'Knowing you *could* care for me has kept me going these last years, I can tell you. But when you left, I started to die. It was then that Ben came into the picture. I don't mind admitting that it was my intention to get you back through that trust – and for a while I even kidded myself that, if you two got together, I'd be happy with your children. That damned fool notion was short-lived, I can tell you. It didn't take me long to wake up to the fact that I'd go to the chair for killing Ben, if he laid a finger on you. And that still goes.'

He moved closer and she held her breath, afraid to hear any more. The sickness was becoming insistent.

'It was Beanie's brainwave to use her party to give you the opportunity to see that you would be accepted, that our marriage would be acceptable. I know it was underhand, but it was a last-ditch effort, honey.' He took a deep breath, 'I don't know how much longer I have . . .' He ran his fingers absent-mindedly through his hair, his eyes appealing. 'I don't know what I'll do if you turn me down now — '

'That's — ' she was going to scream 'Blackmail', but her stomach muscles had done all the holding back they were going to – she could no longer fight against nature. She pushed back the covers and ran for the bathroom, only just making it in time.

When her stomach was empty, she sat down on the toilet seat, shaking and feeling utterly wretched. After a while she needed her bed. The sickness had not, as had been the case until now, made her feel better. If anything she felt worse.

David helped her solicitously into bed. 'Honey, why didn't you tell me you had a hangover? This little talk could have waited . . . Still, it's all said now.' He covered her carefully. 'I'll go fix you an iced tonic water – you'll feel better in no time.'

But Diana was not better in no time. She was not better that evening or the next morning.

David called Beanie from Diana's room.

'Beanie, honey, I have to go into the office, but Diana's suffering some almighty hangover. I've rung the clinic – you couldn't come over?'

He came back to Diana's side. 'Don't worry, princess. Andrew Leyland's coming by, and Beanie's on her way now.'

Diana's symptoms of dizziness, headaches and vomiting alerted Andrew.

He took her blood pressure and frowned. 'I think a couple of days in the clinic are what you need.'

His examination at the Sycamore was more thorough and finally he straightened up. 'Well, young woman, we've weathered worse than this before. Much worse. Nothing this time that bed rest and care won't put right.'

Diana started to protest, but Andrew brushed her words aside.

'You have some hypertension. Nothing we can mess with. Not with the baby to think of as well.'

Diana's eyes were enormous in her pale face.

'Just routine. Better safe than — ' he broke off, registering her look of absolute astonishment.

'You didn't realise you were pregnant?'

Diana felt numb. How bloody stupid! Of *course* she should have known. But she hadn't been ill like this before – it had thrown all her perceptions.

She shook her head. Pregnant . . . The word ran woodenly through her mind. Pregnant . . . As in having a baby.

Andrew nodded. 'It happens. Don't feel bad. Every baby introduces itself in a different way.' He stretched out his hand. 'But my congratulations. It will be an added bonus for you and David.'

He called his nurse. 'I'm admitting Mrs Nazareth – if you'd take her to her room . . .'

He watched them leave, a furrow between his brows. He'd have thought this particular young woman would have had enough of the Nazareths in the past. Still, that was not his concern. The coming child was.

He chewed thoughtfully on his pen. Now where had he seen something about David Nazareth? Something which tugged at the back of his mind? He continued to stare into space.

Then he remembered. Clearly. He pressed the intercom on

his desk. 'Sister, can you get down to Records for me, right away? Yes, there's a file I'd like to look at, two, in fact.' He gave her the details and settled back to wait.

Beanie sat in the chair beside Diana's bed and listened carefully. It was as she'd thought. Diana had slept with both men within a short time. There was no way of knowing which of them was the father.

Beanie's thoughts raced. David could be here at any minute. If he was given the news, he'd immediately start celebrating.

'Don't tell David yet — '

'I don't intend to,' Diana interrupted. 'Don't you think I know what he'd be like?'

'I mean, don't tell him about Ben. It would put his shot at Nazareth House at zero.'

Diana sank back on the pillows. It was exactly what she had been thinking. She picked up her bedside phone. 'I'd like to speak to Dr Leyland, please. Yes, it is urgent.'

She listened to the voice, and replaced the phone.

'It's too late,' she said to Beanie. 'David is with Andrew now.' They stared at one another. Helpless.

But David, far from helpless, had rushed from the clinic after Andrew Leyland's news. He had business with Ike; to prepare a press statement that would give Boston a second sensation – the revelation that Mat had not been his son. That he, David, was not only free to but *would* marry Diana.

Andrew Leyland made his way to see his patient.

'You wanted to see me, Diana?'

Beanie had left, as Diana had asked; now she faced the doctor alone. 'I was going to ask you not to tell David. But I presume it's too late?'

Andrew coloured. 'I'm sorry, he came straight to me to know how you were.' He looked uncomfortable. 'You should have told me . . .'

'I didn't really have time to think,' Diana replied quietly.

'He would have learned, Diana. You can't keep something like a baby quiet. And you're already three months gone; by the time you leave us, I doubt that someone who knows you well wouldn't realise.'

'Of course,' Diana said automatically.

'You must try not to worry.' Andrew's face had resumed it's professional mask. 'It's not good for your blood pressure.' He patted her arm sympathetically. 'I can assure you that David was over the moon, if that's what's bothering you?'

Diana thanked him. What else could she do? It wasn't his fault that he'd assumed what everybody else would assume: that her pregnancy had precipitated their sudden engagement.

David was ecstatic, his joy complete. He hovered lovingly over Diana's bed, tucking her in and fussing her until she could hardly breathe.

'Whoa!' She pushed him gently away. 'Let me grab my breath.'

'I'm sorry, honey. Trust me, huh? Andrew tells me you need rest, and I barge in here and chat your head off.' He kissed her pale cheek. 'Don't you worry about a thing. I've told Andrew you are to have the best care . . . so all you have to do is rest up and get strong. OK? We'll make all the arrangements as soon as the doc gives the word about your health. Meanwhile, you and my baby get well.' He beamed at her and stood up. 'You couldn't have made me prouder, princess. Or happier. How am I ever going to thank you?'

Diana slid down beneath the sheets.

'Look, you're tired – I'm out of here. But I'll come by this evening, just to see if you need anything.' He blew her another kiss and started to leave. 'Oh, honey, anyone I can call for you in England? Your mother in Paris?'

Diana started up, anxiety flooding through her. 'No! Not yet, thank you. I'd, uh, like to tell them myself. Later, when I feel a bit better.'

'Of course, sweetheart.' He beamed again, and left.

Diana rolled on to her stomach, too dizzy for the moment to make any plans. In a day or two she'd be feeling more like her old self. Then she'd work out what she was going to do. Meanwhile she would have to stall.

Andrew had known there was something, but he hadn't been able to pin it down. Now he knew what the something had been.

She obviously didn't know. But she would have to. No doubt about that. As for David? Well, that was another matter altogether, and not one for him to decide, thank God. But he didn't think this was the right time to talk to Diana. He'd meant it about her blood pressure. Stress was the last thing she needed; but it looked as if she already had plenty of that. He hurried to take a call, already behind schedule. He wouldn't give her any sedation, too dangerous. But he could restrict outside stimulus. And that included visitors. As he walked, he made a note to his secretary. It would be acted upon within the hour. He'd leave his own talk with her for a few days, or until he judged she was well enough.

David was talking to Ike Petersen again, this time on the phone, his smile still huge.

'You got those copies off to England? Good man. Now, Ike, I want you to leak out the news of the baby, strictly unofficial, understand?'

He replaced the phone and grinned at a stupefied Jeff.

'We've done it, Jeff! By God, we've done it! Come on, old pal. Time out. We have some celebrating to do.' As they passed through the outer offices, David's staff gazed open-mouthed at the boss with his arm around Jeff's shoulders.

David paused at the receptionist's desk. 'Honey, send over to De Luca's, order enough champagne for the entire building – oh, and cigars for the guys that smoke 'em. My personal compliments.' David smiled at Jeff as they entered the elevator.

That's how it worked – and without really saying anything.
Long before the 'leak' appeared in the press, Nazareth House
staff would put two and two together.

They'd be more than able to confirm how things stood.

Diana floated through the next week in a haze of dizziness
and sickness. Her blood pressure soared up, and then slowly
began to settle down again. She was too ill to worry about
David, or anyone else and the staff ensured that newspapers
were kept away from her room. Andrew allowed only brief
visits by David and Beanie, no one else. And they were more
than happy to comply with his rule about newspapers.

When Diana had stabilised, she would have to know everything. But while Andrew could protect her, he would.

CHAPTER THIRTY-ONE

Benjamin Nazareth curtly refused a last drink. They would soon begin their descent and he needed his wits about him.

He stared at the paper in his hands, only one of many he'd read, disbelievingly, since they'd arrived, addressed to him, three days ago. The words jarred on him, yet he read them again and again.

No one at Tamerford believed them. None of them could accept that Diana had gone so calculatingly to Boston; that she would deliberately have kept something like this from them. Gemma swore Diana could not do it; Candy agreed. But even without their consensus, which Ben accepted, he would still have come.

Something was badly wrong. Why had Diana not refuted the articles? Why would she not take his calls? His eyes hardened. He thought he knew those answers. Somehow she'd been taken in by the old man. But it was the last time, Ben would make damned sure of that. He shut his eyes, trying to close out the image of the face he'd grown to hate. How had David done it? He didn't ask why, that was too obvious. But he shuddered. David was old enough to be her father – older. The thought made him feel sick.

It was unreal. An unholy nightmare.

His hands trembled violently as he shoved the newspapers into his case and snapped shut the lid. He knew what this trip would mean. Diana had been fooled by those phoney documents, but he knew what he'd signed. This would mean the end of any slender hopes he might have had.

He sat up straighter as the aircraft dipped. What the hell. He was still a good lawyer. He could provide more than amply for them. What was Nazareth House anyway? Just another business when you boiled it all down. He swallowed a bitter lump. So, a dream had ended. So what? He'd ended it himself more than eighteen years ago, hadn't he? It was nothing new, nothing he couldn't handle.

The bitter taste remained in the back of his throat as he alighted from the cab on Beacon Street.

He wanted to walk up the drive for the last time.

The trees were naked overhead, stark and unmoving against the still, December sky. Under his feet an early ground frost crunched.

The mansion came into view, long and sprawling, its marble-chip walls sparkling against the backdrop of ancient trees. In childhood it had reminded him of a sugar cake: it still did.

His steps were firm. Memories came flooding back, but they did not halt him. He surveyed the scene as he walked. There were few houses left like this one, and none so large or so grand. Not in Boston City anyway. He glanced towards the old stable block where only a few cars were kept in all that space. Just like the house, it was half-dead.

When had this place ever rung with happy sounds? Not in his time, that was for sure. Yet he had loved this house and given it his heart. As he'd given David Nazareth his soul. The old mansion could not be blamed for the workings of man, but his heart felt heavy as he approached the white marble columns, the sweeping staircase up to the solid double doors.

He had longed, once, to have friends to this house, to have a party. His jaw tightened. It had all been a long time ago. There was nothing here for him any more.

Except the woman he loved . . .

Sanders answered his ring. Now he stood, thin and hawk-like, his hands firmly on the door.

'Mrs Nazareth is not at home,' he answered the query firmly.

Ben suppressed a smile. Good old Sanders, still the same. But it didn't really amuse him that he was not recognised.

'Where might I find her?' he asked pleasantly.

'You'd have to ask Mr Nazareth that, sir.'

Ben put down his case. 'Well, Sanders, I've had a long flight. So how about letting me in to call a cab?'

'It isn't! You can't be . . .? Mr Benjamin, sir! Come in, come in!' The elderly man held the door wide open, his face suddenly alight.

Ben stepped into his old home, his steps ringing on the marble floor. The house had the sound and the feel of emptiness, but although the small staff greeted him with enthusiasm and pleasure, they were still David's people. Loyalty was as much their byword as anyone's at Nazareth House.

'Where is Mrs Nazareth?' Ben asked again.

Sanders looked uncomfortable.

'I can't tell you, Mr Ben. It would be more than my job was worth.'

Mrs Carly busied herself, her round cheeks red. Meg disappeared, ostensibly to ask John for vegetables. It was like meeting a blank wall, friendly to look at, impossible to penetrate.

'But she was here, Sanders? At least you can tell me that?'

'Yes, sir. The young mistress was here. And she'll be back,' he said.

Ben stared at the man. Would she now? He'd see about that. He put down his cup. No point wasting time here. The cab should be due any minute.

'Will we be seeing you again, Mr Ben?' Sanders asked hopefully at the door.

'I don't know, Sanders. I hope so.' Ben bent the truth a little, and gave the man his hand.

Of course he knew that Sanders would immediately phone Nazareth House, but he sat back easily in the cab. The old man would hardly run away from him. No, he'd think he was getting what he wanted. All along the line.

Ben walked through the lofty foyer of Nazareth House and passed the reception area, anonymous in the early morning bustle. He entered the private elevator and pressed the express button for David Nazareth's suite of offices.

The familiar aroma assailed his nostrils as he stepped out into the richly carpeted waiting-room. It was a mixture of cigars, old leather, expensive cologne, perfume and power. The unmistakable smell of great wealth; one he'd grown up with, and which he could pick up even from a passing stranger on the street. It was not a fragrance that could be copied. And it came only with *old* money.

He couldn't help himself. Despite the gravity of his situation, he inhaled deeply. It was a scent he undeniably loved.

An attractive receptionist watched him with raised eyebrows. He appraised her speculatively. She rose from her domain, at once on guard.

'Can I help you, sir? she enquired politely, poised and ready to press the alarm.

Ben noted the scarlet fingertips, resting on the discreet buzzer. She must be a promotion; she definitely hadn't been here when he'd seen David last year.

'I should think so,' he smiled. 'I'd like to see David Nazareth.'

The receptionist frowned and looked down at her appointments diary. 'I don't see any appointment for this hour. Might I know the nature of your business, sir?'

'No, honey, you might not.' Ben advanced towards her desk and saw the fingers move slightly.

'No need for alarms, just buzz the boss and tell him he's got company. I think you'll find he's expecting me.'

'I'm sorry, but you'll have to give me a name?' The woman was flustered.

'Certainly. Benjamin Nazareth.'

The receptionist blinked. The legendary Benjamin? It couldn't be. He was in the UK for the next few years. Wow! Would *she* have some news for the girls at lunch. She buzzed through to Jeff Sherman's office, confused and not a little unnerved by the magnetic man.

'I have someone here to see Mr Nazareth. He says he's Benjamin Nazareth.'

A door on the far side of the room opened immediately and Jeff emerged.

'Ben! Nice to see you. Come on in.'

Ben stepped into the inner sanctum of his enemy. More faces were raised, curious. They walked the short corridor, past Jeff's office, and came to the double oak doors.

Jeff tapped lightly.

David swung round from the window, his features a mask. 'Come in.'

Ben took the proffered seat, but refused the offer of a drink. Jeff took a chair discreetly behind him.

Without looking at Jeff, Ben spoke quietly. 'What you and I have to discuss might be better done in private.'

'There is nothing we have to say to one another that Jeff can't know.'

Ben studied the man across the desk from him. No, you bastard, he thought, I don't suppose there is. OK, so squirm in company.

'I'm looking for Diana.'

'Are you now. And why's that?'

'That's my affair.'

'Not necessarily.'

'I happen to think it is.'

Each man gazed at the other. Both wore impassive masks, but the tension was a live current between them.

David looked away first, down at the papers on his desk. They were the papers Ben had signed; the others, with an exact replica of Ben's signature, were in his safe at the mansion.

So he hadn't been mistaken. Ben was in love with Diana. And apparently she meant more to him than Nazareth House. He looked up again and, for a brief moment, an old feeling tugged his heart. Once upon a time he had loved this man with all his heart, had even felt badly about Mat's birth, because it would mean Ben wouldn't inherit the Firm. But he'd been going to make sure he was all right, and name him as second in command. If Ben hadn't left, he'd now *be* the heir.

But Ben had walked out on him, told him what to do with his love. He could still taste the hurt at the back of his mouth. Now Ben was a stranger, also a rival.

His eyes glinted. 'I take it that you realise what you've done by coming here?'

'I'm well aware of the facts.'

'Well, perhaps I'd better remind you just to be sure — '

'Save your breath,' Ben interrupted easily. 'Don't bother reading me either of the documents you have. I'm not interested. The only part of your game I'm interested in is the current act. And I'd prefer to discuss that with Diana.'

'Diana doesn't want to talk to you,' David said evenly.

'I'll believe that when she tells me herself.'

'Then you might have a long wait. I hope that your trust can manage without you, for a month or so?' David smiled coldly.

'What's that supposed to mean?'

'That's how long Diana will be away. At least.'

'Cut the crap.' Ben's voice was dangerously calm. 'I'm here to see Diana. Now where is she?'

'I've told you, she's away. Now, if she wanted you to know where she was, she'd have contacted you, wouldn't she?'

'Not if you've got her hidden somewhere,' Ben snapped.

'Don't be a fool. Why would I hide Diana? You have been reading too many romances, Ben. Grow up.'

The sarcastic words rang in Ben's ears but for the moment he chose to ignore them. The last thing he was going to do was let the old man goad him. 'All right, if she isn't hidden, you have no reason for not telling me where she is.'

'No, none at all. But, as she has a telephone and a postal service, I have to assume that her choice is for you not to know.'

Ben grew weary of the game. 'How do I know that she has a telephone? Or any other way of reaching me? I'm sure as hell not taking your word for it.'

'You don't have to. Her whereabouts are known all over Boston,' David said equably. 'You can leave this office now, ask any member of my staff – they all know where she is. But I suggest that you think about what I've said. If Diana wanted you to know, she'd have told you. You might find it an embarrassment to pester a lady who wants to be left alone.'

'Just what are you talking about?' Ben felt his gut knot.

'My fiancée does not wish to see you. It's as simple as that. So I don't know what you think you're playing at, but you'd better think again.'

'Your fiancée!' Ben exclaimed, fury erupting at last. 'Who are you kidding? Look, I don't know how you got Diana to play along with this sick game, but don't you think it's you who should grow up? Do you know something? You make me want to puke! Diana would no more have anything to do with your perverted crap than fly. She'd never let an old man like you near her. Perhaps it's you who should wake up. Before you make a bigger fool of yourself than you've already done.'

David controlled his rage. He would not be ensnared into a dirty word fight. He had all the aces now. He could afford to be magnanimous.

'Benjamin . . .' His voice was steadier than he felt. 'Get a hold on yourself. I may be older than Diana, but I can assure you that many women marry older men. Diana was happy to accept my proposal. I'm sorry that this distresses you so much, but obviously you aren't in possession of the facts.'

Rage burned in Ben. 'What facts?'

'That Diana and I have been lovers for years. But she is a woman of moral integrity – she would not agree to marry me until the facts about Matthew became known. Now that her conscience is clear – '

'What the hell are you talking about?'

A smile played about David's lips. 'I'd known for a long time that Matthew was not my son,' he lied easily, 'but it took time for the proof to become available. Now that it is,

Diana and I will be married. Very soon in fact. Well before our child is born.'

A fuse blew in Ben's mind. Diana, in love with the old man for years? Having an affair? Expecting a child? No, it couldn't be true! He had felt the love growing between them – or he would never have made love to her.

His dreams died.

He had been taken for a ride by *both* of them.

'You don't have to take my word for anything, Benjamin,' David went on in a silky voice. 'It's common knowledge. Ask anyone you like. Diana is in the Sycamore Clinic – you know where that is? Jeff can take you. But you'd better know that her doctor is not allowing any visitors.

'It's nothing serious,' he added almost conversationally, 'just that after those terrible experiences with Matthew – well, the doctor wants to keep an eye on her for a while. And she gets these terrible headaches, you see. A bit of blood pressure . . .'

Memory flooded Ben's consciousness. She had been having headaches; he recalled them clearly. Christ, because she was pregnant!

And he had thought she loved *him*.

But then again, she'd never said so, had she? He raked his memory and found nothing. He'd allowed himself to believe that she cared because it was what he'd wanted. Suddenly his thoughts turned bitter. She'd had to be drunk before she'd let him make love to her. It was he who was the fool. She and the old man, lovers . . .

He felt his hot anger turn to ice-cold humiliation. Slowly he raised his eyes to the impassive, hated face. God! What had he done? He fought for words, and his voice came out flat.

'Everything she did for the trust, for me, it really was for you.'

'Who else should she do it for?' David said.

'But my inheritance. She seemed so concerned about that.'

'No doubt. Diana is a compassionate woman. She gets

involved in other people's problems. She wanted to help, even though I tried to warn her that it would be unthinkable for her to stay over there for much longer.'

He gazed at the tormented face without pity now. 'She wanted very much for me to have an heir, and she agreed to help you establish yourself.'

'Then why the whole business with the marriage clause? It doesn't make sense!'

David shrugged. 'You should know enough about the Nazareths to know that we always hedge our bets. No Nazareth worth his salt ever put all his eggs in one basket. If they had, we wouldn't be in business today. Forgive the clichés, but I'm sure you see what I mean.'

David nodded discreetly to Jeff Sherman and a moment later Ben had a large brandy placed in his hand. He drank it straight down, hoping that it might clear his muzzy thoughts. Something wasn't right, but he couldn't place what it was. The only stark clarity was Diana and his father.

David's voice penetrated the dulled surface of his mind. 'I know you will be very disappointed about the inheritance, but as a lawyer you knew the penalty for coming here today. You knew that the five-year stay-away clause was legal and binding. As a Nazareth, I'd have been bound by honour to leave the Firm to you if you'd kept your legal bargain. It would have left me in a difficult position regarding my own child – but I have enough money to retire, to build the child another business, somewhere.

'But, you have saved me all those difficulties by coming here. However, I am still keen for you to do good things with that trust – and if it proceeds according to our original hopes, you can be certain of the financial rewards that were promised.

'I might even be able to find you a place here in the Firm, but that could be diff — '

'The hell you will!' Ben furiously pushed his chair aside. 'I don't want your damned charity. You know where you can shove it!' He leaned heavily against the desk. 'And don't bother giving my regards to your future wife. You can both go to hell as far as I'm concerned. And knowing you, David Nazareth, that's certainly where you will go!'

He strode to the door, his head high, but he turned and his eyes betrayed the searing pain of his soul. 'I never want to lay eyes on you again as long as you live. So don't bother ever coming over to England, because that's where I shall be making my home.' His chest heaved with rage now. 'I won't lay a finger on you here – I wouldn't give you the satisfaction of having me thrown out. But I swear, before God, that if we should ever meet on mutual ground I'll thrash your damned miserable hide!'

The door crashed shut behind him.

Jeff stared at the floor, unable to believe what he was a party to.

David leaned back in his plush leather chair, pale but unmoved, and unashamed of the deliberate lies he'd told.

All was fair in love.

Ben was mortified. He had made a complete fool of himself and Diana had made a fool of them all in Devon. Exhaustedly, he made his way back to Logan. Nothing could have induced him to stay in Boston for a single night.

He bought a newspaper, more for appearances than anything else, and sat with a cup of coffee in the bar. He had been lucky, if such a word could ever again apply to him: there was a flight leaving for London in a couple of hours. He just had to sit out the wait.

A bargirl approached him and flirtatiously asked if he'd like something a little stronger. Ben brushed her aside, curtly. Then, to guard against further intrusion, he opened the paper. His eyes skimmed the news unseeingly.

The pain inside him threatened to burst out into rage. It took him all his time controlling his emotions and his shaking hands. It was a harrowing experience. Thirty-three years old, and he felt he could weep for a lifetime. His jaw worked as he turned another unread page. His glance fell by accident on the social column. Her name leaped out at him. Unable to stop himself he read the item. It confirmed everything the old man had said.

Growing colder by the moment, he read, 'How thrilled Boston was to hear of the Expected Event in the Nazareth household.' The columnist went on gushingly to say that, 'after the awful news the Nazareths had to bear about Matthew, their marriage and expected child will help to heal the popular couple's wounds.' Ben's face was grim as he read that Mrs Nazareth was expected to announce wedding plans just as soon as she was discharged from the clinic. Silkily the columnist added that, 'no one would expect a big wedding, under the circumstances'.

Ben threw the paper down in disgust. It was still unreal. How could she have done something like this? And with David Nazareth?

He felt as if he had been betrayed.

For the first time in his life he had given a woman his heart. And she had broken it, with the one man in the world he could never forgive.

For the next hour, passengers awaiting flights curiously observed the tall figure, as Ben stalked up and down the departure hall, his expression almost violent.

Ben grieved in despair for most of the journey, but by the time the plane touched down at Heathrow he had hardened his heart. There was nothing he could do about it so he had to switch it off. From now on neither Diana nor David Nazareth would exist.

He had a job to do in Tavistock, and he intended to do it well. Alan Brookes-Browne could handle any future communication with Boston.

For Diana he had swallowed his pride.

And for Diana he had lost Nazareth House.

David whistled cheerfully as he drove over to the clinic that evening. He had good reason to feel in the best of moods. Jeff had reported that Ben had been on the afternoon flight to London. The evening press had announced the news of the baby, but thankfully had relegated it to the social columns.

Life in Boston was returning to normal.

By the time Diana was well enough to start fighting back he'd have it all sewn up. He drove into the clinic grounds and parked the car. Sure she'd be mad as hell for a while, but he hadn't a doubt that he'd soon get her over that. He grinned as he thought about the future. He'd waited a helluva long time to know happiness like this. Nothing and no one was going to take it away from him again.

Soon, Diana would agree to a wedding date. She'd have to, he reasoned. A nice girl like her wasn't going to want to walk up the aisle with a noticeable stomach. He took the steps two at a time.

God, he felt good. It was as if he'd shed thirty years.

Another week passed before Andrew Leyland decided that his patient was stable enough to handle her own affairs again. He glanced over her notes. Her blood pressure had been normal for a week; the giddiness and sickness had stopped. She was currently a healthy expectant mother. With proper care and sensible advice, they could hope for a normal pregnancy from now on.

He found her sitting out of bed by the window. They'd allowed her up yesterday and there had been no adverse effect on her blood pressure. Still, he didn't want her doing too much too soon. He'd keep her in for another week, just to be on the safe side.

Diana greeted the doctor cheerfully enough. She was glad of any company which took her mind off her worries. But it seemed that the doctor had slightly unprofessional matters on his mind this morning. He perched on the edge of her bed, facing her at the window.

'Do you have something on your mind, Andrew?'

'Yes, I do. But it might be embarrassing, so I hope you will understand my reasons for bringing the subject up.'

Diana continued to smile, but more guardedly now.

Andrew Leyland frowned. 'Diana, forgive me, but I have been wondering whether you know who the father of your baby is.'

Diana's heart did a somersault.

Leyland shifted to a different position. 'I doubt that I'd have troubled you about such a personal matter, Diana, if it were not for the fact that there is something you should know.'

'What?'

'As I've said, I'm sorry to bring it up and I don't wish to cause you any discomfort, believe me. But David can't be the father.'

'What makes you say that?' Diana asked faintly.

Andrew sighed. She didn't know then. That made his position all the more difficult. But he'd said it now, so he'd have to see it through.

'Diana, what I am telling you is in strictest confidence, do you understand me?' She nodded.

'Ethically I shouldn't tell you any of this, but very occasionally there are circumstances when a relative has the right to certain facts. As you and David are to marry, I believe this is one of those times. I did wonder if perhaps David had found out in later years, but if he truly thinks that this child is his he hasn't and you must understand that this confidence will have to remain absolute.'

'You have my word.'

'Many years ago, before my time, the Nazareths came here for fertility tests,' Andrew said. 'And when you came in with this pregnancy, and it was obvious that David thought he was the father, it triggered a memory somewhere. Something I had once read, long ago. So I looked up those files.'

'And?'

'I found that Ella Nazareth had asked that her husband not be told of his infertility. There's a note on the files that she expressly wished for David not to be told, unless he asked himself.

'David apparently didn't want to be told, because the files note that he never returned.' He smiled drily. 'Often the case when the man thinks his virility is somehow in question. But the results were conclusive. David is sterile.'

'So if he didn't know, why adopt Ben?'

'Possibly he chose to believe his wife was barren,' Andrew said. 'Of course, if you were to tell him this baby is not his, there is still every chance he won't now find out about his sterility, if you follow me?'

'Don't worry,' Diana said tonelessly. 'He won't find out from me. That would be terribly cruel.'

'And you do know who the father is? That he's healthy, and so on?'

'I certainly do,' Diana said emptily. 'And he's a very healthy man.'

'Thank you,' Andrew crossed to her side and took her pulse. It was racing. 'No doubt you are upset, but you are a sensible young woman. You'll do what's best. For you, and the baby,' he added. 'Now, back into bed.'

Diana curled up when he'd gone. She knew what he meant, but she was far from sensible. She was a complete imbecile. She had spent several years now bouncing from one mess to another, as if she'd never had any intelligence to begin with. It was ludicrous.

She had to pull herself together. For the last five years she had vacillated and procrastinated; let the emotions and needs of others lull her brain into a virtual coma. Whatever the power was that David had over her, it was confused with feelings for her father. And that situation had to be resolved.

David was an intelligent adult who was more than capable of standing on his own feet. Admittedly she cared for him, and she had responded to him sexually, but caring for him and being in love with him were two different things. Responding to a sexually expert lover was also not abnormal.

She had to stop feeling so damned *guilty* all the time.

Since her father's death, she had forgotten how to be her own person. Or perhaps she had never learned how. If not, then it was time she learned. She had needs of her own, needs for her baby – and those needs included Ben.

She fell at last into an exhausted, dream-filled sleep, in which Ben and David were both trying to pull her free from some murky underground cave. She struggled in her sleep. She could not cope with both of them. They were drowning her with their stupid arguments about who should pull her out. She felt herself slipping away from them – down into a dark, deep pool.

The telephone jarred her back to wakefulness and she fought up from the depths of the watery cave. She was trembling and soaked with sweat. The room was darkened and she almost knocked the phone off her bedstand. She swore softly as she found the light.

'Diana Nazareth,' she managed at last.

'Di? It's me!' squealed a voice from a great distance.

'Gemma? Oh God, how marvellous! I've been meaning to call you,' she lied swiftly, gathering her senses.

'Yeah? That's not what we gathered,' Gemma said drily.

'I'm sorry, Gems. Truly I am. I did mean to call, once I'd got myself sorted out. Things have rather fallen on top of me here.'

'It's okay, Di. Ben told us all about it when he got back. I just wish you'd told me, that's all.' Gemma sounded genuinely hurt.

But Diana's mind was racing.

'When Ben got back? Back from where? What did he tell you?' Alarm bells, not unfamiliar, jangled in the back of her mind.

'Oh, everything! He rowed with David,' Gemma said meaningfully.

'What?' Diana cried. 'When?'

'Last week. Di, are you sure you are all right?'

'What were you told?' Diana managed, a choking sensation in her lungs.

'About you and David. You know, being lovers, and about the baby – and you two getting married. Everything, Di. Like I said, I wish you could have trusted me enough to tell me how it really was between you two. I guess I've been making an idiot of myself for years. Warning you off the man you love. I'd say I'm sorry, but damn it, you should have told me!'

Diana heard her own voice making small, apologetic noises. Angry tears were spilling on to her sheet, and she missed some of the next sentence.

But one word filtered through. *Married.*

Her hand went to her throat. 'Could you repeat that Gemma, this is a bad line.'

'I said, it was an ill wind, because Ben proposed to me after he got back.'

Diana forced herself to speak. 'What did you say after that, Gems?'

'Jeez, Di, what's the matter with you? I can hear *you* clearly enough. I said we were married yesterday. Did you hear me that time?'

'I heard you,' Diana replied, switching her mind into automatic, editing data out of the emotion rising from the very depths of her soul. Her voice, clear again now, sounded as if it belonged to a stranger.

'That's wonderful news, Gemma. I hope you will be very happy.'

'Thanks, Di. I'm sure we will be. Look, I was told not talk to you for long, some nurse playing sergeant-major. Are you really all right?'

'Of course,' Diana mumbled. 'Fine, Gems. Just fine.'

'That's OK then. I wish you were here, you know. I miss you. We all miss you.'

'I miss you too,' Diana said bleakly.

'I'll call you again in a few days. Get well soon – then we can have a normal conversation!'

Diana replaced the phone very carefully. She rose unsteadily from the bed and with deliberate care walked into her bathroom and ran a bath.

An hour later she was sitting up in bed, her make-up perfect, hair brushed until it gleamed. She concentrated on the magazine in her hands, willing herself to think about absolutely nothing.

David had his first surprise for quite some time when he visited her a little while later. As he bent to kiss her forehead she lifted her mouth to his. And buried all her plans in his kiss.

Dazed with pleasure, David broke off the embrace to ask, 'Did something good happen that I know nothing about?'

By way of answer Diana responded, 'What date are you free to get married?'

CHAPTER THIRTY-TWO

Diana had more surprises in store. Far from wanting the quiet wedding David had accepted would be his lot, she gave him free rein to plan the wedding exactly as he wanted it. And, to his joy, she took the greatest interest in everything he planned.

On one of the coldest January mornings in recent Boston history, David Nazareth and his four-months-pregnant bride were married in a private ceremony at the mansion. Fifty people gathered to witness the momentous occasion and to share the wedding breakfast at the house. Another three hundred were invited to the wedding supper that evening, at the Plaza Hotel, chosen, David said, because of its lucky vibrations.

Not only did Diana not object to press photographers, she positively blossomed for their cameras. No one present could remember a happier couple.

It was dawn before David made love to his bride, and she responded with greater abandon and passion than he could ever have hoped for. At last their damp, tangled bodies were still and David could no longer fight the weight of sleep. His hand grew leaden on Diana's breast. Carefully she slid from his embrace and, turning into her own pillow, silently wept . . .

Two events combined to prevent Diana from remembering her intention to return the old papers, unread, to Ruth. The first might well, on its own, have jolted her into action, had the second not happened with a seemingly brutal and shocking haste.

Diana kept her monthly ante-natal appointment at the Sycamore with some trepidation. Andrew Leyland wanted to run a scan on the rapidly increasing child. The mystery of a sudden extra weight gain was revealed as they both stared incredulously at the screen. It was hard for Diana to make out the shape, but by following the doctor's carefully pointed finger she did.

Not one set of miniscule hands, but two. Diana's baby was a pair. Twins.

Elated, she dressed and hurried to the phone booth. There would be double celebrations tonight. David couldn't believe it at first. Then he recalled some talk of twins, long, long ago. Diana was exceptionally thankful. There was no history of twins in her family. Hardly able to contain himself, David told Diana to go straight over to the Locker Room club, where he would join her for lunch. He suggested she invite Beanie, and he'd bring Jeff along.

Beanie joined Diana in the cocktail bar, and they laughed excitedly together over the concept of double heirs. Diana was glad that she'd buried everything that night in the clinic. She could not have borne to lose Gemma's friendship; and neither would she have wanted to lose the close relationship she enjoyed with Beanie. This way, she kept them both.

They chatted animatedly over their aperitifs, both aware as time passed that the men were late.

Diana grew restless and after half an hour, gathered her purse.

'I'm going to phone – see what's keeping them.'

Turning, she saw Jeff just inside the door, leaning for support against the frame. His waxen face told them both that something was terribly wrong. They rushed over.

'Jeff! What is it? Where's David? What's happened?'

'He's – in the hospital. No time to get him to the clinic – sorry – too sudden,' he mumbled hoarsely. 'Couldn't make it, Diana – nothing anyone could do – a stroke . . .'

Beanie took charge. 'Steward? A cab, urgently! Diana, go in the cab. I'll see to Jeff and join you there. Go. *Now.*'

The following hours were a nightmare. The stark grimness of total helplessness, of endless waiting, seeing nothing, seeing everything; the real wide-awake nightmare of sudden tragedy.

They were not allowed into the intensive care ward, but sat huddled together in the small, antiseptic waiting area. They spoke only occasionally – in whispers.

Jeff Sherman, David's oldest and staunchest friend, had collapsed, and was at home in the care of a nurse.

It seemed hours before a doctor came to them, his voice distant. 'Mrs Nazareth? Your husband has had a fairly serious stroke. I'm afraid we shan't know the full extent of the damage immediately, but we are doing tests. You can see him now, but only for a minute, you understand?'

Diana nodded.

'The first twenty-four hours are the most critical — '

'And then?' Beanie interrupted, her voice harsh.

'Too soon to tell,' he said shortly. 'Mrs Nazareth, you can come with me.' He looked at Beanie, but shook his head. 'Only his wife.'

'Will he die?' Diana asked starkly.

'It's a possibility you should prepare for – but it's too early to say. Come this way, please.'

David did not die. But after her initial relief, Diana wondered if it might have been kinder if he had. The medical team worked round the clock, and it was as much due to their efforts as to anything that David survived at all; but the prognosis after five days was cruel. He might live for quite some time, or he might not last another week. Nothing was certain.

Except for the facts: he was paralysed; he was unable to speak; he was blind.

Living death.

David was released from the hospital after two weeks, at Diana's insistence. There had been a little progress – movement in one arm.

Diana paid for the finest nursing care that money could buy and, twenty-four hours a day, someone sat with him while he slept, or worked his paralysed muscles when he was awake.

After another month, they were rewarded by a movement in his face – a definite attempt at speech.

Diana pushed his wheelchair herself until her pregnancy was too advanced. He was not ill as such, and appeared to be in no pain. His blind eyes seemed to follow Diana about the place, as if appealing for her help.

Before too long she began to read to him and, on the fine days of spring, she had him wheeled out into the garden, where they spent long hours working the weakened muscles in his arms. Twice a day a physiotherapist worked on his legs, but they refused to respond. A speech therapist worked on his voice, with rewarding results.

His speech, slurred and often unintelligible, was the first part of him to recover. And his arms grew more mobile, the right more than the left. They were the only parts of him that had any life at all.

Early in May, Diana's eighth month, he spoke his first full sentence. Drunkenly, and in an unfamiliar voice; but his meaning was heart-breakingly clear.

It was, 'Thank you for my babies.'

Diana gathered him in her arms, tears streaming down her face. 'The babies need you, darling. Get well for us. *Please!*'

Tears spilled on to David's gaunt cheeks.

It was the beginning of a brief time of respite. Daily he grew stronger. More words came together. At night Diana went briefly into his bed, to hold and soothe him, to ease some of the fear that was often in his unseeing eyes. She banished all her anger and bitterness at his lies and manipulations. He was like a child, lost in the dark; and very afraid.

He became her entire world. Every waking moment was given to him, to his recovery; she bullied and cajoled him to greater effort; and little by little he did improve.

His intelligence was unimpaired, but his frustration with the rest of his body became a zealous determination to overcome his disabilities. His speech remained slurred and at times difficult to follow; but his efforts were always doubled until his listener understood.

By the beginning of June, he could hold short but lucid conversations. He had mastered writing by the sheer power of his will – and spent hours every day communicating with his immediate staff at the Firm, in a childishly inept but perfectly understandable hand – across special paper with raised lines to guide him.

No one doubted the clarity of his mind.

His final triumph was mastering the small electric switch on his wheelchair; enough to propel himself where he wanted to go, in areas he knew by heart.

He had learned to depend on his senses – touch, feel, smell – and as long as nothing was moved, could propel himself around.

Amazingly his sense of humour returned, and he was making small jokes. Jeff had moved into the mansion when he recovered, as had Beanie. Together they backed up the nursing team and, with the household staff, filled his days and nights with loving care and attention.

The only thing he would not discuss was his sight. Mention of his blindness was forbidden.

Because of David's condition, Andrew Leyland found himself setting up facilities for the birth at the mansion. Diana refused to leave David even for a night and Andrew's specialist team were on stand-by as the time approached.

It began at lunch-time on the twenty-ninth of June.

David, with his heightened senses, heard the small groan first. He gave a lopsided grin. 'The new Nazareths are arriving,' he enunciated slowly. Diana kissed him and he managed to squeeze her hand.

By early evening the second stage of labour was under way. Andrew helped Diana into the delivery room, and the midwife arrived soon after.

Diana's labour was hard, but mercifully short. No aids were required to bring Rebecca into the world at three minutes before midnight, nor to assist Samuel's noisy arrival at six minutes past. 'Happy birthday, twins.' Diana smiled tiredly.

No one in the mansion had gone to bed. They all waited anxiously for the news. David heard the cries first and was at the door waiting when Andrew came out to look for him.

'Mr Nazareth, your daughter and son, in that order, have arrived safe and well.' He grinned and let David past into the room, while he went down to arrange for tea to be sent up.

Applause greeted his arrival downstairs, followed by the eager and happy sound of champagne corks popping. Beanie embraced Jeff and set off a chain reaction throughout the house.

Andrew Leyland accepted a small glass of bubbly. His conscience was untroubled. Diana had chosen to keep the secret. So be it.

David wheeled himself as near to the bed as he could get. The nurse held the first bundle against his chest and he felt the baby's head, stroked the silky cheeks, and asked for the baby to be held up to be kissed.

'This has to be Rebecca,' he guessed. 'She smells as lovely as you, darling.'

Diana touched his hand lovingly.

David chuckled softly. 'So. It's to be a woman at the helm. After all this time.'

'Not before time,' Diana teased, well aware that David had sworn to name Ben as his heir. It was the only condition she had stipulated before their marriage, and he had agreed to it. She supposed that with his stroke and the impairment of his memory, he had forgotten. But it was not important. She had seen the will. Ben was quite safe.

She went along with the game. 'You also have a son, you know. What will happen to him?'

The nurse changed the babies over, and David caressed Samuel with equal love.

'Still crazy about these old-fashioned names?' he teased happily. 'But I like them. They'll sound great with Nazareth.'

'You didn't answer me about Samuel.' Diana changed the subject, not at all sure of her own reasons for naming the twins after Joshua's parents.

'Sam? No problems. His mother and his sister will see that he's well provided for.'

Diana laughed. 'What nonsense! Since when did female rule over male in the Nazareth empire?'

David's unseeing eyes gazed at her, and to her dismay she saw they they were misted and pained.

'Since you came into my life, honey,' he said slowly. 'And this wonderful event tonight proves that the wind of change has decided the future.' He took a deep breath, struggling with his words, each one a painstaking effort.

'*You* have restored life to Nazareth House, my love. And as Rebecca left the comfort of the womb first, she has proved herself the natural heir. Only the strong can rule Nazareth House. You just remember that when the time comes.'

The nurse took the baby away. David was growing tired.

'Whatever you say, darling,' Diana soothed.

He rested his head on her breast, drawing comfort from the warm, full roundness.

She stroked the thin, lined face, her heart full.

Sometime soon, she must read those papers Ruth had given her. When she had a moment to herself.

The following day, while Diana and the household rested, David closeted himself with Jeff and Mark Wheeler in his study.

On the other side of the Atlantic, at Tamerford, Gabbie read Beanie's telegram aloud to Ruth. Now unable to leave her bed, the old lady had demanded to be told the moment news came.

'Read it to me again, child,' she said, her voice stronger than it had been for weeks.

'It says, "Twins arrived safely 29/30th June. Rebecca, Samuel, and Diana all well."'

The old eyes held a small fire. It was as she'd thought. The news gave her strength to command her great-niece.

'Gabrielle, I want to see Bob Parsons as soon as he can get here.'

Gabbie went downstairs to the newly installed telephone to call the family solicitor.

Her heart was heavy. Ruth would not live much longer, and she would miss her badly. For, despite the activity and bustle now a part of their daily lives, Gabbie was lonely.

Gemma stayed with the old lady, who seemed to be retreating more and more into a distant world. Half-heartedly Gemma tried to catch the odd word muttered beneath the laboured breath. 'She will see it through,' the old woman mumbled. 'Tamerford is safe.'

Gemma paid little attention to these ramblings; she was locked in her own unhappy thoughts.

'Ben's,' the old lady muttered, and Gemma regarded her curiously. Lady Ruth was not even aware of the woman beside her. 'She'll keep them away. He'll never get it . . .'

Gemma wondered what she was rambling about. But the old woman was almost senile now; she rarely made any sense these days. She was startled when Ruth turned to her, with startlingly clear eyes.

'Gemma, you are a dear girl, but misguided,' Ruth said strongly, and Gemma found herself suddenly chilled by the penetrating, lucid gaze. 'He is not for you. Send him back where he belongs. Follow your own star, child. Or do you always want to trail in her wake?'

Gemma would have asked the old lady to explain, but Gabbie came back and the moment had passed.

Ruth was childlike again.

'Mr Parsons will come out this evening, dear,' Gabbie said gently, and took the frail old hands in hers.

Gemma left the sad little scene and wandered out into the

grounds. There were few places left to find any peace. Builders were everywhere. Youngsters, clean and keen, hurried to and fro, fetching, carrying, learning. Tamerford estate was blossoming.

She carried on, over to one of the old barns. It was wonderful what they had accomplished in such a short time. The barn, newly thatched, rendered and whitewashed, was the special domain of the youngsters. It was to be their own club-house and already they were putting the finishing touches to its interior.

Gemma waved at the group of cheerful teenagers, but the person she sought was not there. He could be anywhere, and at this time of day would not welcome her interruptions, wherever he was. She set off down the lane to their house, not in the mood to enjoy the walk under arches of beech and spruce, oblivious of the profusion of multi-coloured rhododendrons edging the way. All she wished was that she were with Diana and the twins.

She and Ben were temporarily housed in the old miller's cottage, but that couldn't last for long. Already the builders had moved into the derelict mill and the cider-press next door. The days were filled with noise, and there was no escape from the constant dust, the trucks trundling passing her windows.

She entered the house and grimaced. To some it would have been idyllic, even in its pre-restoration state, but to Gemma, a child of the modern age, it was ugly. It was also cold, damp and far from the manor and Gabbie; and from the lodge which Candy and Simon were restoring for themselves.

She sighed as she began to clear yet another ton of dust from the heavy old furniture. In a way she wished that she'd kept the house in Glanville Road. She knew this home was only temporary, that soon they would be moved into one of the finely and handsomely modernised cottages. But it would still be at Tamerford. And that seemed to be where most of her battle lay. It was as if Ben was *married* to the bloody place.

Perhaps if they could have lived elsewhere it would have made all the difference.

She slumped into a chair, depression overwhelming her. Diana had her twins. Candy was expecting her baby in three months' time. But Gemma was nowhere near being pregnant. She sighed deeply. She didn't even have a real marriage. How could you have babies if your husband was too tired, too occupied, or too disinterested to make love?

Not that it was the 'baby' bit that she wanted.

She got up and went to the sideboard, where she poured herself a double measure of gin. She swallowed a large gulp. It wasn't a good thing, drinking alone during the day, but it helped to dull the pain of knowing that Ben had married her in a moment of weakness brought about by his trip to Boston. She finished the gin and poured another.

It was her own fault. She'd known what she was doing, known that he was in agony over Diana and David. She'd fooled herself that she could make him forget but the opposite had happened. The strange likeness she had to Diana, at first her keenest weapon, had been turned against her almost from the start. She had learnt that her marriage was doomed two nights after their wedding.

Trying to make love to her, Ben had suddenly pulled away. 'I can't, Gemma.' His voice was bitter. 'I keep imagining her, with *him*.'

He'd apologised profusely, but from that time on he'd withdrawn into himself. She tried to brave it out, but Ben became a stone wall. Her many efforts to please him seemed only to make him more angry with himself – and to drive the wedge deeper between them.

Last month, after spurning her attempts to get him into her bed, he'd tiredly offered her a divorce. But she hadn't been ready to give up the fight. Now Gemma's thoughts drifted to Ruth, and her ramblings when she'd heard about the twins. Her strange comment to Gemma had sown a seed of suspicion and now, fertilised by the gin, it began to grow.

Gemma couldn't take very much alcohol, but as drinking maddened Ben, and it was the only emotion he showed, she'd begun to drink more heavily. Today she drank even more than usual, tears rolling down her cheeks. Why had she been so dumb? It wasn't as if she hadn't guessed how he felt? But Diana had been so positive that she didn't care for him. Why?

She drank a third tumbler, neat, and curled up on the bed as waves of alcohol pulled her down into sleep . . .

One afternoon, while David and the twins slept and the mansion was for once peaceful, Diana found herself alone for the first time in months.

Dutifully she took the bundle of Ruth's papers from the back of a drawer, and sat down on the nursery sofa to glance through them.

The sun lit the small room and played on the yellowed papers she held. She took up the old letter again first. The one dated 1631.

It was, as Ruth had summarised, the lament of the younger twin. His anger and bitterness spilled into his words – words full of fears that his brother would bring their parents to ruin – words of despair, that he could not stay and, powerless, witness his brother's excesses.

He told of meeting good fortune amongst Christian and worthy people, but there was no mention of the place he was living, or when he would write again.

It was signed with the initials J.N.T.

Diana put it down and took up the second letter. It was an explanation. The letter was on headed notepaper, bearing the name of a London firm of solicitors, and dated November, 1632.

She skimmed the profuse and flowery greeting, stopping to read the factual report.

It read:

> Your esteemed servantes are happye
> to reporte that youre son did sail from
> this Citie on the goodlie ship named
> 'Talbot', in the yeare of Our Lord,
> 1629, to a place in The New World bye
> name of Naumkeag, otherwise knowne as
> Salem. He did keep companie with
> servantes, disguised amonge them. Youre
> son did prevaile upon the goodlie
> souls of the companie, to knowe him
> henceforthe to be one 'Joshua Nazareth',
> and droppinge the esteemed name of youre
> familie, is thus still knowne . . .

Diana read the last parts quickly. They confirmed only what she now knew. But even so she imagined how Samuel and Rebecca must have felt, waiting three years to learn this much about their son's whereabouts.

She finally turned to the little, soft-covered books, much better preserved within their leather binders.

Rebecca's diaries were pitiful and sparse, five of them in all. The pages were few in each, the feminine script jagged in places, as if written under great stress. The words were mere grief-stricken comments; the whole painting a tragic picture of a bereft mother's loss.

She read . . . 'Joshua's birthday. Maye God keepe him safe.' Then further on . . . 'Stille not one word morre of him. Yet my beloved son lives . . .'

There were other, similarly stark passages. Always brief. Always poignant in their conveyance of loss.

She came to the last entry. It was dated December 31, 1649 . . . its message bleaker than any before: 'Twenty years . . . no morre word. May God grante him a safe return to me soone . . .'

Diana's eyes were misted with tears as she closed the book and held it briefly to her breast. She could feel Rebecca's pain reaching out to her. Had she died after that last entry? Her sons would have been forty, which made her a good age in those times.

Diana closed her eyes. How awful to spend your whole life waiting for a beloved child to come home, and to die without seeing him again.

But a quiet anger also burned in her breast. What kind of man had he been, to let his parents suffer so? Or had there been such scenes over his leaving that he had been unable to overcome them to write again? Pride. The Nazareth pride. The stubbornness and, yes, perhaps the coldness that had run through Joshua's line, even to David's father.

Even to David, when Ben had left him.

Carefully she returned the books and letters to the waxed cloth and wrapped them up again. There was nothing she could do now. But in her heart she was glad she hadn't told David. In time Simon would inherit the fund that old Samuel had left Joshua; the Tamerford money would go back where it belonged, without any help from her.

But would that appease the spirit of Rebecca, or of Samuel?

She couldn't know; but she hoped so. And she was glad that she had named her children after the old couple, even if they were no relation to either the Nazareths or the Tamerfords. It had just felt right to do it.

And now the new Rebecca and Samuel were stirring in their cribs. Diana put all thoughts of the sad past out of her mind, and went to her children.

On a scorchingly hot day at the end of September, David suffered a second stroke.

He was rushed with sirens wailing to the hospital, and back into intensive care. Again Diana, Beanie and Jeff took up a vigil at his bedside. They divided the day into three equal parts, and each took an eight-hour shift, with the twins in the care of their nanny on Diana's shift, so that David was not alone at any time.

After the first few hours, they knew he would not survive. The medical team fought all through that first night, but thereafter it was only a matter of time. He died, without fully regaining consciousness, on the fourth day.

Numbed with grief and exhaustion, Diana was taken home to the mansion and Andrew Leyland came by and sedated her. She was incapable of handling anything.

The new English nanny cared for the twins while Jeff Sherman, gaunt and grieving, made the funeral arrangements. Beanie retired to her penthouse and wept alone.

With the United States Navy patrolling the Gulf, in an atmosphere described as 'very tense', amidst the minesweeping operation and continued aggression from Iran, the film industry at home put off its mourning garb for two of its giants, director John Huston and actor Lee Marvin, as the business world prepared to put theirs on for the loss of one of their central players, David Nazareth.

The gathering for his burial was solemn, and the scene was played, as David would have expected, to a packed house.

Hundreds of mourners packed the lawns around the Nazareth family graves. Civic and government representatives stood shoulder to shoulder with David's friends, and men and women from every profession and business, from every old family, and from among his business rivals, joined with a vast army of his employees, to pay their last respects.

The family stood beside the grave, Diana holding Rebecca, Gemma holding Samuel. Gabbie, representing the Youth Trust, stood between Beanie and Jeff.

Behind them the household staff wept.

The last words had been spoken, a long and fitting tribute to an extraordinary man. Diana threw a single apricot rose into the grave, and wished him God speed.

They moved away silently along the path made for them

by the crowds. Not one word was spoken to them as they made their way to the waiting cars. That would come later, at the farewell supper Diana had asked be arranged at the Plaza Hotel.

Meanwhile, there had to be the reading of David's will.

Gemma and Gabbie stayed with the twins while Diana joined Beanie, Jeff and the household staff in the dining-room, where Mark Wheeler sat stiffly with David's instructions.

Diana squeezed his shoulder, and took her seat.

It was a brief affair. David had not wasted many words.

Mark read the Last Will and Testament solemnly.

'To my beloved wife, Diana, I leave Nazareth House and my entire estates; and in her I invest the future of our children, knowing that she will decide their best interests in the future.'

There were a few small, personal bequests.

To Beanie, David left his brand-new Jaguar, 'in the hope that she will learn to enjoy driving a decent car' – and on a more serious note . . . 'knowing she has no need of additional finances, for all the years of love and friendship, I leave her the Abden painting of Boston she has always admired'.

To Jeff he had left . . . 'in recognition of his loyalty during many difficult times, the sum of five million dollars, and charge him to remain as adviser to the new mistress of Nazareth House, so long as that may be her wish.'

Sanders received a large sum of money and a pension for life when he was ready to retire. The other members of the household staff were bequeathed smaller sums of money and the same pension rights.

That was it. All that remained were personal letters for Diana, Beanie and Jeff, which the lawyer handed to them.

Diana took hers without a word, and put it in her purse. She was silent with shock and guilt.

David had broken his word.

He had left *nothing* to Ben.

She had, naturally, hoped for the house, but had not expected it if Ben was to inherit the Firm; it had after all been his home. But she had expected a sum of money, enough to buy a house and raise the twins; perhaps even a trust for their future.

She had not expected that she and Ben's children would inherit everything, including Ben's home and Ben's dreams.

Mark closed his briefcase. It had been a simple will, even if there had been some devious engineering to get it that way.

Now he held out his hand, noting the disbelief, the shock on her face.

Diana forced herself to accept his handshake.

'May I be the first to say that, if Dave had believed that there was anyone better for the job, you would not now be my employer. May I offer you my condolences in your very sad loss; but also my congratulations? I will do my best to help you in any way that I can . . .' He tailed off, uncertain if he was saying too much or too little.

Diana knew what he was trying to convey. She nodded wordlessly.

She faced the two old friends after Mark had left.

'He swore to me that Ben would inherit,' she said coldly. 'He knew that I wanted Nazareth House not for myself but for Ben.' She stared past them into the distance. 'He carried his lies and his manipulations right to his grave . . .'

Jeff and Beanie exchanged glances.

'Diana,' Jeff said quietly, his own face strained with grief, 'Dave was a complicated man; try to understand that, after Ben rejected him, spurned his love, Dave would never have left him Nazareth House. No matter what he agreed with you.'

Diana stared at him, her gaze icy. 'What if I hadn't married him? What if I had rejected him? What would the clever David Nazareth have done with his precious Firm then?' She knew she sounded spiteful, but she felt spiteful. David had tricked her into becoming part of his betrayal.

Jeff squirmed uncomfortably, but he caught Beanie's look and interpreted it correctly.

'It would have been left jointly to Beanie and myself,' he said, very quietly.

Diana was floored. Her eyes flew from one to the other, seeking confirmation.

'To you two? Not ever to Ben?'

'Not ever,' Beanie assured her gently.

It was almost a bigger shock than the one she'd just had, and infinitely more confusing.

She gazed at them both, bewildered.

'But, if you knew that *you* would inherit – why did you help him in his plans to marry *me*?'

'It was what he wanted,' Jeff said simply. 'I guess, for both of us, that's what counted. Anyway, what could we have brought to the Firm? Certainly not fresh, young blood for its future. That's what you and the children have brought.

'Sure, we could have enjoyed the power and the wealth for a few years, but in the end, what?

'With us the Firm would have had a limited future and a certain end. Now it will continue, just as Dave wanted. He could not let his ancestors down. In you, Dave secured the only thing that mattered to him beyond all else: a Nazareth at the helm. Now, and in the future.'

CHAPTER THIRTY-THREE

Somehow Diana got through the days that followed.

Jeff and Beanie were unstinting in their support, although perhaps they, more than Diana, had reason to grieve.

Meetings with heads of departments had to take place; and executives who came from all points of the globe, wherever David's interests reached, had to be seen or spoken to.

Diana played only a nominal role as head of Nazareth House. Guilt racked her and drove her. For the moment she had to be seen as the figurehead; she could not leave a space for speculators to fill with damaging gossip. It had, of course, begun instantly, and she was forced to deal with it quickly; to kill any idea of Nazareth House being 'up for grabs'.

She gave her first instructions to Ike Petersen, and the following day a press release concerning her inheritance and succession to the head of the Firm was published in the national and international news.

Overnight she became one of the world's wealthiest and most desirable women.

And Ben read all about it at Tamerford.

Two weeks to the day after David's funeral, a cable arrived telling Diana of Ruth Tamerford's death. It jolted her memory about the secret.

There was no longer any reason to put it off. She would go to Tamerford and tell Simon herself.

Then she would see Ben.

Jeff assured her that he would keep her informed of all business matters by telephone.

It was Beanie who suggested that, after all the months of trauma, it would do Diana good to take a break. Rachel had not yet seen her grandchildren, Beanie reminded Diana. It would be sensible to stop in Paris, she suggested, and go on three days later for the funeral, when she was rested.

Diana, frantically trying to pack and arrange things for herself and the twins, sent cables to Simon and to her mother. The British Embassy sympathetically issued emergency visas for the two nannies Diana now had to employ full-time – and for the twins, who had yet to be put on their mother's passport.

Rachel accepted the entourage with equanimity. She had installed the twins and their nannies at the farthest end of the house, so the disturbance to her would be minimal.

While Rachel worked on sketches of the twins, Diana rushed around the shops, choosing presents for Beanie and Jeff and the household staff; and for Candy's son, Timothy, now just over a month old.

On the penultimate day of her visit, Rachel surprised her daughter by asking if they might have the morning to themselves. Diana despatched the nannies with some extra spending money to a morning's delight of shopping, and settled down with the twins in her mother's studio.

Rachel did not immediately come to the point of her request, but after sketching for a while she looked thoughtfully at Diana.

'They make such good models at this age. None of the fidgeting that comes as they grow older.'

Diana gave her a small, tight smile. Indeed they were quiet and still, head-to-toe in their portable crib, fast asleep in the morning light.

'It's quite extraordinary how like her father Rebecca is. His features, his colouring, his eyes.' Rachel glanced at Diana's suddenly flushed cheeks. 'While Samuel is the image of you, so fair and such grey-blue eyes. How do you expect to get away with it, darling?'

Diana melted under her mother's knowing gaze, and was silent.

Rachel went on in the same light vein. 'If Ben doesn't know those children are his yet, he will once you arrive at Tamerford.' She continued drawing as she spoke, deftly sketching in Rebecca's dark curls, allowing no licence in these portraits. 'Even if she weren't his double, two blue-eyed parents would find it hard to make an emerald-green-eyed child.'

She sketched for a moment longer in the silence and then turned the block for Diana's inspection. 'These sketches are only for my guidance, as you'll realise. I shall do them properly later – in oils if you'd like?'

When her daughter still didn't speak, she continued, not in the least perturbed. She'd give Diana all the room in the world to tell her about it, and if she didn't want to, that would be that.

'It's just as well David never actually saw his little heirs. It would have finished him sooner, I should think.

'Now what about young Gemma? She was at the funeral; undoubtedly she saw the twins? Did she comment on Rebecca's likeness to her husband? Ah, but then she's young, and possibly didn't think about it. Or the twins were too young then for it to be so noticeable. Babies' eyes are deceptive at such an age, aren't they? I remember waiting for your eyes to establish their true colour, to see if they were the grey-blue of your father's or the violet-blue of mine. Such things are always of interest to an artist.

'Strange though, young Gemma is very artistic. I would have expected her to notice.' She gave a little sigh and went on with her work.

'Oh Mother!' Diana exclaimed at last. 'You always were too wise. How could one hope to deceive you in anything?' Rachel ignored the outburst and turned her attention to the sketch of Samuel.

'I have so many guilty secrets,' Diana went on. 'So many confusions in my life. I hardly know what is best any more,' she sighed deeply. 'And here I am, half-way to Tamerford, intent on undoing at least one bit of damage, and you present me with a further problem, one I hadn't even thought about. God, I've become so stupid it's untrue!'

She went over to look at the sketch of Rebecca. 'It is obvious, isn't it? You have caught the look so precisely. So yes, they are Ben's as you know – and no, Gemma doesn't know. How can I take them there now? I wouldn't hurt Gemma for the world.'

Rachel carried on with her sketch of Samuel as she answered. 'Darling, you can leave the twins here if it will help. But let's go into the salon and have our coffee, shall we? If you need a shoulder, you can borrow mine. People often do you know.' Rachel smiled ruefully. 'It's one disadvantage of being known for one's ability to keep a confidence.'

Soon Diana was unburdening herself, grateful for her mother's detachment. And it was easier than she might have thought to tell her mother everything.

'Do you have those papers with you?' Rachel asked when Diana had finished.

'Yes, of course. I'm going to give them to Simon.'

'Would you show them to me, darling? I think that there might just be something that you have overlooked.'

Diana hurried to collect the papers from her room and, after a while, Rachel looked up from her study of them.

'Just as I thought,' she said quietly. Then gazed levelly at her daughter. 'It's distasteful from beginning to end – but David's part in it all is monstrous. You know, I find it sad that you were so taken in by him.'

'Not at the end,' Diana said grimly. 'But yes for a long time, I was. What's the matter with me, mother?'

'Your dear papa's genes,' Rachel said easily. 'Marc was always a soft touch for a hard-luck story, and he suffered enormous guilt over things that were not even his affair. Pity you inherited that. Still, maybe this will be all the lesson you'll need.'

She sipped at her chicory coffee and studied her daughter. 'But David is dead. He can do no more harm, thank goodness.

But tell me, *who* do you hope to help with all this?' she pointed at the waxed cloth bundle distastefully.

Diana put down her coffee in surprise. 'Why, Simon of course.'

'How?'

'Mother!' Diana exclaimed in exasperation. 'I've told you everything, and you've read the documents, it's obvious how.'

'No, darling,' Rachel said firmly. 'It is far from obvious how it will help Simon.'

Diana gazed, wide-eyed. 'I'm not sure what you mean.'

Rachel leaned forward on the satin-covered sofa, and took a long, very thin cigar, from a monogrammed silver box.

'Who else has a copy of these?' Rachel tapped the bundle of papers.

'No one,' Diana replied. 'Ruth was insistent that these were the only existing documents. That's another reason why I'll be glad to hand them over.'

'So,' Rachel continued, stopping briefly to inhale the aromatic smoke, 'David's dead. Ruth is dead. No one need know.'

'What on earth do you mean?'

'Simply this, darling. If you take these over to Tamerford, Simon will almost certainly want to do the honourable thing. Had you really overlooked the fact that your children now appear to be the current generation of Nazareths?'

'God!' Diana's hand flew to her mouth.

'How fair would it be, Diana, for Ben's children to inherit Joshua's money? And what if your legal advisers decide there is a greater claim against the entire estate, after all these years of deception? Then even the Youth Trust would have to be put on hold while it was all sorted out. It could take years. And short of you admitting in court that the children are Ben's, not David's, it seems to me that lawyers could have a field day with this.'

'Oh my God!' Diana pressed her hands to her face, dazed by the implications.

'I see no hand of God in this,' Rachel said drily. 'It's very much the work of man. And a thoroughly nasty piece of work at that. In fact, it's a good job Ruth is dead, or she and I would have had words.'

Diana turned a stricken face to her mother. 'What do I do?' she asked helplessly.

Rachel ground out the half-smoked cigar, and took her daughter's hand in her own. 'Darling, I have never advised you in your life, I've only ever been a sounding-board. But I want to give you some serious advice now.

'Until such time as you can admit the twins are Ben's, bury this lot. If, as you say, Ruth swore there was no other documentary evidence, she won't have left any hint of *her* part in this wicked deception. So Simon need not know about the Nazareths' rights. Need he?'

'But — ' Diana tried to interrupt.

'No, darling. Leave it all alone until you have made your own decisions concerning the twins.'

'Mother!' Diana said insistently. 'Simon *needs* that money. It could free him and Tamerford, don't you see?'

'Free him from his commitment to Ben, you mean?' Ruth regarded her daughter curiously.

Diana's heart gave a protesting extra beat.

'No. Yes. Oh, I don't know! It just isn't fair that he shouldn't get this money, however much it turns out to be, and I'm sure he wouldn't renege on his deal with Ben.'

'Are you now? Diana, have you ever seen someone who's stony broke come into money?'

No, Diana hadn't. But she'd read stories about such things. Her heart fell like an express lift. But the misery hadn't quite ended.

'As for Gemma and Ben,' Rachel shrugged, 'it's an unequal match, and time will show that. Gemma's is calf love, and Ben's . . . well, let's just say his is probably rebound. Anyway, it can't last,' she said firmly. 'Think of it this way, darling. None of this would ever have happened if David hadn't become so obsessed with you. You wouldn't know any of this existed. My advice is forget it – until the day comes when you can deal with it openly.'

'And if it doesn't?' Diana said dispiritedly.

'Then bury the lot.'

Rachel stood up, her smile more cheerful. 'Now, what are you going to do about Ruth's funeral?'

In the end Diana didn't go. She couldn't, as she said later to Rachel, go that far and not see Candy and the baby, or show her the twins, without a jolly good reason.

Rachel provided it by telephoning Tamerford to say that Diana and the twins had caught a bad chill. Diana posted her gift to Candy en route to the airport later that week. There was no reason why Candy should be neglected, just because she had made such a mess of everything.

The journalist who spotted the group arriving at Logan airport, noted that the young millionairess, so fair and fragile in her black silk frock and black cashmere coat, was still showing her grief at the loss of her beloved husband.

The picture of Diana, grave and unsmiling with her twins and their nannies, appeared beside the article that Ben read in Devon two days later.

Ben slung the newspaper across the table. When would he be able to open a paper without *her* name or face leaping from the print? He was sick of reading whatever she was doing. Yet still he scanned the international press regularly.

His features were set as he left the cottage. He was becoming a masochist. Why did he take the Boston and Paris papers every day if it weren't because he wanted to know what she was doing and with whom? He pushed the thought aside, unwilling to look at it more closely. And besides, he had plenty of other things to think about. Ruth had been buried in the family vault in the chapel yesterday and Simon and Gabbie were both still upset.

They had accepted Rachel's excuses, even though they were disappointed. But it was obvious to Ben why she hadn't come. She'd made it to Paris, but then couldn't face him, knowing that she'd betrayed him with David and destroyed his fragile dream of owning Nazareth House. Instead she'd sent a wreath and condolences to Simon and Gabbie.

The reading of Ruth's will was to be this morning, and he'd offered to keep all the workers and the noise at bay. He had other matters on his mind as well. His marriage, and Gemma's drinking. And the unpalatable fact that the two were synonomous.

Gemma's drinking had become a real problem. She was hardly sober these days.

And that too was his fault. *He* was her problem, and it didn't sit lightly on his conscience. She needed help – and freedom from him, he thought grimly. He had brought her nothing but heartbreak.

Old Bob Parsons read the will in his clipped toneless voice. It was not a long or complicated affair, despite its author's complex character in life. Ruth Tamerford, spinster, had wisely invested the little money she'd had from her father's estate, and now on her death it was to be paid out.

To Simon and to Gabrielle she had left a third each. Her personal furnishings and most of her private paintings, all very valuable, she left to Simon and the Tamerford estate.

Her jewellery, mostly antique and also valuable, she had divided between Gabrielle and Candy; Diana was left a large gold locket and chain on a brooch pin; and a crated painting, stored in the attic above Ruth's rooms, which she was to be given only by Simon in person. As if that weren't enough surprise, Diana had been left the final third of Ruth's small legacy.

The whole sad little sum gave them fifteen thousand pounds each.

Simon and Gabrielle stared at the solicitor and then at each other.

Simon recovered first.

'Thank you, Bob. It's all very straightforward,' he said kindly, sensing the man's discomfort.

'Indeed, my lord. Shall I attend to the other matters concerning Mrs Nazareth?' He cleared his throat. 'Perhaps if I could have the item of jewellery? There was also a letter, which is in my keeping. I can forward them both together.'

When he had left, Simon and Gabbie remained in the library, both deep in thought. Gabbie tossed back her dark curls at last, in a gesture of nonchalance.

'You shall have my share, Si. What on earth do I want with fifteen thousand pounds?' She managed a light laugh, her eyes filled with affection for her brother. 'It will be of much more value to you.'

Simon's blue eyes lit up with warmth. How generous his sister was. All her life she'd given unstintingly of whatever she had, which had never been much. Yet now, when she could make some small independent future for herself, she would make the final sacrifice.

'Dearest girl, I would no more accept that magnificent offer than fly. Don't be such a goose, Gabbie! Fifteen thousand pounds won't make much of a difference to this old place, I can assure you.'

Gabbie knew that when Simon made a decision, nothing would budge him. It would be fruitless to argue and would only anger him. She tried a different tack instead. 'If my fifteen thou' won't help, what good is yours going to do?'

'I'll invest it in the Youth Trust, of course,' he stated matter-of-factly. 'The trust is as much my baby as Ben's now. And our entire future is invested in it anyway. A further fifteen thousand will help things along a little.'

That was all the answer she would get, she knew.

'What painting do you suppose is in that crate?' she wondered at last.

'Haven't a clue,' Simon replied, not really interested.

'Will you take it to Boston, or should I?'

'Great-aunt wanted me to do it, so I shall,' Simon replied. 'Lord knows when, though. Still, maybe she'll manage another visit before too long.'

'And we're not even to mention it beforehand? Odd, don't you think?' Gabbie said, mildly curious.

'Old people have their little whims, Gabbie. Great-aunt probably just wanted to surprise her.'

'It is strange though,' Gabbie reflected.

'Well, frankly, yes. But great-aunt did seem to grow very fond of her.'

'Yes, that's true. You don't mind then?'

'Good Lord, no! Why should I?' Simon's face softened. 'Despite everything, I'm still fond of Diana. And as we both know, sister dear, if it hadn't been for her, David Nazareth would never have set up the trust.' His fine features grew serious. 'No, Gabbie, Diana's personal life is her own affair. I bear her no ill will whatsoever, and I hope you don't either?'

Gabbie shook her head. 'Far from it. I feel she was badly used by David Nazareth. I'm inclined to accept Gemma's view of things, and I find her a delightful person.'

'Good,' Simon said evenly. 'That makes two of us. And, as for great-aunt's legacy, it was hers to leave as she wished. It seems small recompense for what Diana has done for us.'

'Of course I don't hold any grudges, Si,' Gabbie stressed at once. 'But I do find it odd about the portraits in that locket.'

Simon got up and stretched his long legs. There was work waiting and he'd already had half a morning off.

'Portraits?' he enquired, only mildly interested.

'Yes. In the locket. You probably didn't take as much notice of those things as I did. But in that locket were two tiny portraits. Strangely, I'm not sure that I ever knew exactly who they were, but I do remember that they were Tamerford ancestors. Don't you think it eccentric that great-aunt gave those to Diana?'

Simon frowned. 'Hmm. Yes I suppose it is, but great-aunt also realised Diana's part in all that we are now achieving. The old marbles only slipped at the end.' He shrugged into his coat. 'Forget it now, dear girl. Life must go on.'

'Simon, before you vanish into the thick of restorations again, can I ask you something?'

Simon halted, already mentally elsewhere.

'It might seem a bit frivolous to you, but I would like to visit Diana and to see the babies again. And it would give me the chance of my first real holiday.'

Simon grinned. Gabrielle's face was a picture, hopeful, nervous, stoic, already expecting to be told that she was too needed to be allowed to gallivant off around the world.

'Dear girl, that's a marvellous idea. Of course you shall go.' He hesitated, frowning. 'There's just one thing, though. If you could help Candy find a reliable nanny – for company as much as anything else? Gemma's not much use to her in that way at the moment . . .'

Diana stared at her hair in the mirror. Antonio had cut it beautifully. She would miss her long hair, but this style was more practical for her new business life. She completed her make-up. The new style made her look twenty-five again, a disconcerting factor when she was dealing with older, distinguished clients, but a definite advantage when it came to making business deals or handling ruthless competitors. No one expected the chic young blonde to have a clue about business. But in that they were badly mistaken.

She was, admittedly, still learning the ropes, but what she lacked in detailed understanding she was already making up for in intuition and a gut instinct for getting to the kernel of a problem. It was early days, but already rumour had it that David Nazareth had chosen more wisely than people had been led to believe. Business competitors decided that Nazareth had schooled her for years.

After a few minutes in the nursery, where the twins gurgled

contentedly in the care of their nannies, Diana went down to breakfast. Meg, promoted to Diana's personal maid and replaced in the house by two others, had put Diana's mail beside her place. Diana scanned the pile as she drank her black coffee. She recognised Candy's hand, and also Gabbie's.

The square package postmarked Plymouth, Devon, she did not recognise.

Curious, she opened this first. It contained two sealed letters and a flat velvet box. She was reluctant to open the envelope with the spidery handwriting, so put it to one side with the box and opened the manila envelope.

It was from Ruth's solicitor, enclosing the items 'Lady Ruth Tamerford bequeathed to you in her Will. These include the enclosed sum of money, and an item of jewellery she wished you to have . . .'

The cheque disturbed her considerably. Why had Ruth left *her* this money? Or was it some kind of conscience payment? Diana shuddered and put it to one side. She would, of course, return it to Tamerford. Tentatively she picked up the faded velvet box. A tiny card covered with the same spidery writing as on the envelope fell out. It read, 'I hope you will hand this down to Rebecca, with my love, when the appropriate time comes.'

It was signed simply 'Ruth Tamerford'.

Diana held the oval locket for some time. It was unique and of exquisite piece of workmanship; delicate traces of the original floral engravings could still be seen. It was very worn, but with care Diana could make out the initials 'R.T.'. But why would Ruth send her own locket for Rebecca?

In spite of everything, Diana smiled. It was a generous gift and she would treasure it until Rebecca came of age. It would take some explaining, but then that was a long way into the future.

She pressed the tiny catch at the side, worn to all but nothing, and the locket creaked open. Diana gasped, her hand flying in its customary nervous habit to her throat.

Inside the locket were two miniature portraits, and she knew at once who they were. The pale, oval face framed with dark curls was Rebecca Tamerford. She knew it without question.

The dark, solemn eyes stared up at her and Diana saw again the tragic little diaries with their stark, haunting words. She had to force herself from the compelling face, to the portrait opposite. It was of an older man, fair-haired and pale-eyed. His face, too, conveyed an inner sadness.

Samuel Tamerford and his young wife, Rebecca? It had to be. The unknown Tamerford ancestors she had named her children for.

She snapped the locket shut, her hands trembling violently.

This was no ordinary gift. Lady Ruth was reaching out to her from her grave, reminding her of her promise. She thrust the locket back into its box and, gathering up the unopened letter and the cheque, she hurried into her study. Her hands felt as if they were on fire as she unlocked a drawer in the desk and pushed the lot inside.

She looked down in dismay. The waxed cloth bundle mocked her. She pushed it further to the back, revealing a file marked confidential – and the unopened letter from David. She slammed the drawer shut and turned the key, her heart racing crazily. The drawer felt like a secret sin; a private enemy – in it so many of her guilts. She turned and leaned against the desk to catch her breath. It was irrational to feel and behave this way, but that didn't stop her moving quickly away, as if she feared that at any moment it would leap up, roar with fury and reach out for her.

She reached the dining-room and leant against the door, her heart still thudding against her ribs.

Meg was putting a fresh pot of coffee on the table when she looked up.

'Ma'am, are you all right?'

Diana smoothed her skirt, her palms damp, and nodded. 'Fine, thank you. I must have stood up too quickly.'

'Your blood sugar dropped, I dare say,' Meg said easily. 'Come and drink this.' She spooned sugar into Diana's coffee. 'Aunt of mine used to get that. She swore a sugar cube'd cure it. Carried 'em everywhere.'

Diana dropped into her chair and drank the coffee gratefully. By the time she opened Candy's letter she was again composed.

Diana read . . .

We so missed not seeing you at Ruth's funeral, not that you missed much there. Sad affair, really. Pritchard did the honours, bless him.Some of the older villagers came, and of course the family solicitor – you should have met him! He was so thin he rattled, and in his black clothes he looked like a ancient bat.

Simon and Gabbie were both sad – Ruth had been their mother really; but I was the emotional one, you know me! They're really very practical and much more down-to-earth than I am.

Anyway, Timothy is becoming a thumping weight to carry around; how do you manage the twins? But he's a good baby and is very robust. Hopefully you'll see him soon.

We are quite excited about moving into the lodge fully now that it's finished. You should see it . . . it really is lovely, and, with the extensions giving us five bedrooms and four reception rooms, we shall be very grand! It has all been kept in character so it's quite something. I'll send you pictures soon . . .

Which brings me to the heavy bit of this letter. It's about Gemma. Poor Gems, Di. She is in such a sorry state. I do wish you could talk to her like in the old days . . . she always listened to you.

She's drinking, Di. I mean *heavily*. I am beginning to fear for her health. Can you suggest anything that might help?

Last but not least . . . thank you for the beautiful romper

suit and the lovely cot blankets. I've never seen anything so *fine*. They will be super in the summer – if I'm not too afraid that I might spill something on them to use them!

Okay, better go and do some work. Please think about Gems. I'll try anything . . .

Diana was disturbed by the reference to Gemma and drinking. What could that be about? She shook her head and opened Gabbie's letter. She'd phone Gemma later . . .

Gabbie's letter was bright and gay and quite cheered Diana up.

She wrote . . .

and so Simon has agreed that I can take some time off from the old place, and I wonder if you might consider having me for a little while? I wouldn't get under your feet, and would so *love* the opportunity to get to know the charming Madame Beanie (is that right?) and perhaps see her workrooms, if she'd let me! So perhaps after Christmas, if that would suit you?

Diana grinned. It would be good to have young company, and Gabbie was as dear to her now as Gemma and Candy.

She pressed the bell for her maid.

'Meg, get me the telephone would you? Oh, and as I'm not going into the office until later, I wouldn't mind some fresh coffee.'

She dialled the Tamerford number and waited, fingers crossed that Ben would not answer.

Simon answered sleepily, and Diana cursed herself. For the first time ever she had forgotten the time difference.

'Simon? It's me, Diana. Look, I'm so sorry, I forgot the time!' she groaned. 'Do please go back to bed, I'll call again later.'

'No, it's all right Diana, really. I'd have to be up in an hour anyway. It's good to hear from you. Anyone special you want me to wake up? I can now put you through to Gemma's cottage, or to Gabbie's room – that's an improvement on the old days, isn't it!'

Diana laughingly agreed.

'Well, if you're sure Gabbie won't mind being woken, I was ringing to speak to her . . .'

'Not at all. You do realise, I suppose, how much these girls miss you?'

'As much as I miss them,' Diana said warmly.

And it was true. Hearing that Gemma was in trouble, that Candy was lonely, that Gabbie, bless her, wanted to come over for a holiday, had all made her very homesick.

Diana prepared for the office, her thoughts already flying to Gabbie's visit. She could wait until then to learn what had gone wrong for Gemma. Early morning on the telephone was hardly an ideal time to discuss a drinking problem.

The anticipated visit did not happen for two more months. Gabbie had found Candy a nanny she was happy with, but didn't want to leave until the girl was settled in. She cabled that she would arrive on the twenty-fifth of February.

Diana took a much-needed break to show Gabbie the sights of historic Boston.

Gabbie and Gemma had only flown in for three days for David's funeral, so Gabbie felt this was her first *real* trip abroad.

Their feet hardly touched the ground as Diana enthusiastically escorted Gabbie from one historic spot to another. She began with the Freedom Trail, to get them in the mood, including a stop at the Bunker Hill monument, and continued through some of the great buildings, the Customs House, the old State House, St Paul's Cathedral . . .

They tramped the lovely public parks, the beautiful gardens, and even took a very choppy trip around the bay.

Gabrielle was mesmerised, enchanted, and inside a week

had done what many Britons before her had done, fallen in love with Boston.

'I love it! All of it!' Gabbie enthused, as they lunched on fresh seafood at Nino's Place at Maitre Jacques, enjoying even the rain-obscured views across the Charles River. 'I wish I could stay here forever.'

Diana laughed. 'Not at this pace, sweetie. My feet have just about had it!'

'Ah yes, but if one lived here one could take all the time in the world to see the many places you've mentioned that we haven't managed to get to,' Gabbie said wistfully.

'This is true,' Diana agreed, enjoying the beginnings of an idea.

'Oh, Diana. Do you suppose I could ever live here? Even for six months?'

Diana smiled thoughtfully, 'I don't see why not.'

That evening Diana left Gabbie with the twins and went over to Mt Vernon. Not only was Beanie delighted with Diana's idea, she promised to help as much as she could.

'She'll need to come over to my workshop every day for a few months so that I can assess her abilities. When I think she's ready, I'll tell you. That is my condition,' Beanie warned.

'You are a fantastic lady,' Diana grinned.

'So I've been told,' Beanie said dryly.

Gabbie could hardly contain her excitement.

'You'll really help me to start a boutique of my own? Here in Boston?'

'Yes, Gabbie. If and when Beanie says you are capable. You've had no training, remember, but if you are as talented as I think, Beanie will soon iron out the creases. Meanwhile I might look around for a suitable shop for you.'

'I've got fifteen thousand pounds,' Gabbie said excitedly, then her face fell. 'Oh, less my fare and a few expenses.'

Diana's smile was gentle. 'I don't think that fifteen thousand pounds would even get you a lease on a shop, let alone purchase all your materials, shop fittings, et cetera. And you would need enough working capital to carry you over the first three or four years.'

Gabbie looked crestfallen.

Diana soothed her. 'Now don't start worrying. I'm sure you are going to be a great designer, so I will put up the capital, and work out a repayment scheme that won't cripple you. And Gabbie, perhaps you'll let me advise you where to invest the remainder of your money, so that it brings the highest returns?'

'Gosh, can you do all that?'

'Well, Nazareth House can,' Diana replied. 'It was one of the first rules I learned. "Diversify as much as possible". The old, don't-put-all-your-eggs-in-one-basket rule.' She poured them both a glass of wine. 'Now, can we forget you and boutiques for the moment? I'd really like to know what's happening at Tamerford, and in particular what the problem is with Gemma?'

Gabbie curled up by the fire, her pretty face serious.

'Gemma first, then. I'm not really sure when she started drinking, but it can't have been very long after they were married.' She went on to give Diana her account of the situation, ending her summary with surprising information for Diana.

'I know great-aunt didn't appear lucid a lot of the time, but I believe that she was very bright right up to her death. It was her belief that Gemma's drinking was due to Ben's rejection of her. She told me that Gemma had come to her one day and cried on her shoulder. Apparently it was because Ben had told her he wanted a divorce.'

'A divorce!' Diana exclaimed, shocked. 'For heaven's sake, why?'

Gabbie coloured. 'Well, we have our theories. It's a bit embarrassing, Diana. But we thought – well no, we all *knew* – that Ben was in love with you. It was quite a shock when you got engaged to David, and Ben married Gemma.'

'Ben married Gemma first,' Diana said stiffly.

'Yes, I know. But great-aunt said it was a rebound and that it wouldn't last.' She looked at Diana, her lovely green eyes clouded. 'I know she was a very old woman, but she had such an uncanny insight into things, and I found that she was often right. She was in this case too, it seems.

'Gemma never actually confided in me, which was strange really, because we'd grown so close, but I was so busy with all the sewing and repairs for the manor, I just fell into bed each night exhausted. I might have been able to help – if I'd only had more time . . .'

She shrugged her slender shoulders sadly. 'None of us had much time for Gemma, really. Oh, I don't mean that as callously as it sounds! What I mean is that we were all so busy we didn't even take a Sunday off. The Youth Trust and Tamerford are hard taskmasters, they don't let up on us for a minute. It would take a very strong marriage to survive the chaos and total involvement they demand.'

'Simon and Candy's marriage seems to be doing all right,' Diana said carefully.

'Yes, but they're different. I mean – Candy was always involved. She worked out on the farm, about the house, just about anywhere. And of course, now that the youngsters are there every day, she's involved with supervising their meals, and generally being mother to everyone . . . and thank God she is. She's an absolute brick.

'But Gemma never really fitted in, Diana. It wasn't that she didn't try, well, not in the early days anyway, but she couldn't find a niche of her own. I tried to involve her with the work I was doing, but Gemma was afraid of such very old materials. She had a horror that she would ruin some antique Flemish tapestry, and so she wouldn't even try.

'Then of course the youngsters came into the picture, followed hotly by all the experts: the builders, the carpenters, the roofers, the masons, the plumbers, electricians, interior decorators, and all the dozens of others. She was left out in the cold. She just couldn't handle it. I don't mean to be unkind, but Gemma never really belonged at Tamerford – she had no feel for old things, no interest in the past.'

Gabbie sighed. 'She was sort of stranded, if you can understand what I mean?'

'Yes, I can, but surely that didn't break their marriage? Or cause her to drink? Gemma's made of much stronger stuff than that,' Diana said firmly.

'I'm sure you're right,' Gabbie said quickly. 'No, I can't say what caused the initial problems between her and Ben, but it's almost certain that they started her drinking. Being at Tamerford was probably an aggravating factor. And, of course, if there were difficulties right from the beginning, Ben's driving love for the trust and the old place can hardly have helped. He certainly didn't have much time or energy left over for Gemma.'

Diana gazed into the glowing fire. Poor Gemma. What on earth could she do to help?

'If I give you a letter to take back, could you see that she reads it – when she's sober? I'll invite her over here for a break. Maybe she will open up to me.'

Gabrielle shook her head doubtfully.

'Of course I'll try, but finding her sober these days is going to be the thing. And I perhaps shouldn't say this, but do you think she will let you help her, under the circumstances?'

'What do you mean?' Diana frowned. 'Gemma and I have been like sisters, and the best of friends all our lives.'

Gabrielle gave her an old-fashioned look. 'Isn't it said that nothing can come between best friends better than a man?'

'That's nonsense!' Diana exclaimed, with more conviction than she felt. 'Whatever their personal problems are, they have nothing to do with me. And if I can help Gemma, I will. That's all there is to it. Now what about Ruth's money? Was Simon able to do much with it?' Diana changed the subject.

'He's going to invest it in the Youth Trust,' Gabbie said cheerfully.

Diana frowned. She didn't want to be the one to burst that little bubble, but she was sure she'd seen a proviso that no additional money could be added to the initial capital. She made a mental note to talk to Mark Wheeler in the morning.

'How does Ben fit in to the long-term plans you've told me about – if I recall, his obligation is for five years, and two have passed already?'

Gabrielle smiled brightly. 'Oh, there's no problem there. You know they intend turning the Trust into a company at the end of the five years? And not only giving the youngsters places on the board – and shareholder rights – but employing them in the company in the same way as the Trust?

'They've even decided to name it "The Tamerford Youth Company". If all goes according to plan, those youngsters will be running a commercial business in five years or less, and their futures will be secured for generations to come. Ben has said he will stay on and head the company with Simon.'

'Has he now,' Diana said quietly, her face unreadable.

They spent another half-hour chatting about Tamerford and its bright future, before Diana brought the evening to a close.

'I'm going to look in on the twins before I go to bed, Gabbie. And tomorrow we must discuss how we are going to move you out here to live. First there is the work permit . . .'

CHAPTER THIRTY-FOUR

The next day Diana made her call to Mark and, after a brief conversation, re-established in her mind the salient facts. Whatever else Simon might want, he could not put money into the Trust. It was still Ben's baby, and the only money that could be used for the five years was the sum established by David, plus any earned profits.

Diana instructed Mark to call Alan in Tavistock and bring the subject to the attention of both Simon and Ben immediately. She stood by the telephone, thinking. It would be a blow for someone as proud as Simon not to be able to use his little windfall. But there was nothing she could do, not at this moment anyway, unless she could find a loophole.

She arranged to meet Mark later in the day.

What she didn't dare think about was her own treachery. If it were not for the twins being Ben's, she would be able to tell Simon about Joshua's money – and that the twins were not possible Nazareth claimants.

It was too unjust for words. And Simon was the unwitting victim.

Mark Wheeler was apologetic.

'I'm not sure that it would be a good thing to try to alter the situation now,' he mused. 'Even if Ben swallowed his pride and accepted a share in Nazareth House, he's still tied to the trust for the full five years.' He took off his glasses, rubbed his eyes as if to see the situation more clearly, and replaced his glasses. 'Can't see how it would help. Sorry.'

'You mean there is nothing I can do? Nothing at all?'

'Not for the trust anyway. You could lend them personal money but, as they can't put it in the trust, what's the point?'

'Couldn't we somehow undo that bloody trust – that whole

crazy scheme of David's?' Diana persisted, determined to try to find a way to give Simon money.

'I don't think so,' Mark said candidly. 'Dave set that up himself, I doubt there'd be loopholes.'

'You don't sound one hundred per cent sure?'

'I'll look into it and get back to you,' he said, chastened.

Simon and Ben faced each other in the lodge at Tamerford after Alan had left.

'What do you want to do now?' Ben asked kindly.

Simon grimaced thoughtfully. It was difficult any way you looked at it.

'Well, it was only fifteen thousand pounds.' Simon played it down. 'I'll invest the money and we'll use it in three years' time to help start up the company. But it's a damned nuisance. I'd have liked to put it into the trust now.'

He got up from his chair and crossed to the window where Ben stood, his back to the activities outside. He placed his hand on Ben's shoulder and gave it a small squeeze. 'Don't worry, old buddy. We'll see it through. Now how about we get back to the job in hand?'

Ben smiled despite his nagging anxiety. The money was burning up faster than he'd have ever believed possible. 'D'you know, Simon, you're beginning to sound like an American?' he said lightly.

'And you, my friend, are beginning lately to swear in English . . .'

Grinning, they went out to the grounds, to the young workers, and to the many problems of turning a decaying estate into a full working concern.

Ben hadn't yet confided the full truth. He had only just finished working through the receipts of architects and builders, not to mention the restorers' and renovators' estimates for ongoing, never mind future, works. He was already beginning to feel like a fool for thinking that such an enormous sum of money would complete their plans. But not being an expert in any of the fields he was now working in, he'd taken original estimates at face value.

If it hadn't been such an ancient house, such a badly run-down estate . . . If, if, if . . .

The manor itself was the closest to completion, but apparently more time and money were still needed.

More experts and specialists were restoring the mills, boat-house, cider-press, small foundry: a new marina was still in skeleton form and the inn wasn't even beyond the foundations. The hotel, holiday flats, restaurant, and staff quarters were only at planning stage.

They had completed approximately one-third of their plan, and had already said farewell to two-thirds of their money. Soon he was going to have to warn Simon that they were losing ground. And how long it would be before he had to admit defeat, he didn't dare to think about.

Seeing Gabbie, soon to be leaving them permanently for Boston, coming across the lawn towards them he managed to force a welcoming smile.

Gabbie approached slowly, her heart in her mouth. She held a note, and this she now gave sadly to Ben. Ben stared at her, uncomprehendingly. Then he took the sheet of paper she held and read the few words.

'Don't look for me. I'm not coming back. Gemma.'

His eyes were questioning when he looked up.

'I'd gone down to the cottage to see if she'd like to come shopping with me. I need a few things for my departure on Thursday,' Gabbie said quietly. 'I found the note on the table. It wasn't folded or anything. I'm sorry, I couldn't help seeing what it said.'

'Where in heaven's name can she go?' Ben said at last, concern in his voice. 'She has no money, or at least not much. She has no friends that I know of.'

'She took her car,' Gabbie offered.

'Great! Where will that get her? No money, no friends, no home, no job. Shit! Why didn't she talk to me about it? I would have helped her if she wanted to leave. I don't understand; she refused even to talk about a divorce. Now she's done a damned fool thing like this.'

'Perhaps Gabrielle should ring Diana?' Simon suggested. 'It's possible that she has paid her fare to Boston.'

Ben frowned. He doubted that Gemma would go to Diana, but he didn't want to get into that.

'Let's just leave it until this evening, or better still tomorrow morning. She might be back by then,' he said, but without conviction.

But they all began to panic when she did not come back that day, or the next.

Diana answered the phone in her study.

'What do you mean, missing?' She listened carefully to Gabbie's worried voice. 'No,' she replied, 'she's not with me, and I haven't heard from her. But look, leave it with me for a couple of hours. I might be able to think where she would go.'

She pushed aside the work she'd brought home, and concentrated on Gemma, looking for a clue. Where *would* Gemma go, if she was feeling trapped?

What would be in her mind – that contradictory mind, complicated and yet direct?

And possibly drunk. Diana shut that thought out of her mind.

Gemma, alone and unhappy. What would she be seeking? Escape, obviously. But what else? Not oblivion; Diana could not imagine Gemma being suicidal. She was strong, strong and a survivor.

Diana suddenly smiled. Of course. Where else?

Rachel answered her phone.

'Yes, darling. She's here with me. All cried out, and hopefully drying out. No, she's not in a fit state to talk to anyone. I've just put her to bed, or at least Jacquie did.

'But listen, darling, I don't think Gemma should go back

to Devon, and certainly not to Tamerford. I think she should come to you. She's rather badly in need of a friend.'

Rachel rushed coolly on as if she'd forgotten the subject they'd discussed not so long ago.

'There is no hope for the marriage, so there's no point in her going back to more pain. She needs to be occupied, doing something to heal her wounds. And really, darling, she needs total *divertissement*, yes?'

'What about the twins? How will that affect her, mother? Or have you now forgotten your claim that Rebecca is the image of Ben?' Diana's voice was edged with her own pain.

'Darling, I never forget important things. No, regardless, I think you are the very person she needs. Everything else will sort itself out as it should.'

She gave a little light laugh by way of apology. 'Darling, I am in a hurry. I was due out five minutes ago. Now, I shall keep Gemma with me until she's completely over this drinking nonsense – and regains her self-esteem. Would you ring the folks at Tamerford, darling? I so hate these long-distance calls. Tell them all she's safe, and not to bother phoning or coming over. She doesn't want to see anybody and doesn't need the hassle. All right? 'Bye, darling . . .'

Diana hung up on the already dead line. Really, her mother was sometimes too much. But Gemma was safe so what did it matter if Rachel was already organising their lives?

Bracing herself, she put her call through to Devon. She could not be certain how the news would be received, or who would answer the phone. But it seemed that there was only genuine relief, that Gemma had been found and was well.

Gabbie took Diana's call, and assured Diana that she'd give the message to Ben – and she would herself be in Boston a few days later than planned.

Gabbie was already well established at Beanie's workshop when Gemma's arrival was announced, ten days before Christmas. As Diana drove to the airport she enjoyed the bright displays of fairy lights on Christmas trees in many of the homes she passed, trying not to hum the words to a song that ran around in her head, 'There may be troubles ahead'.

Indeed there might, she thought, hearing the tune over and over. So? They'd 'Face the music and dance'.

Rachel had more than kept her promise to dry Gemma out. She'd kept her in Paris for nine months, and during that time she had sent Gemma to a small school for seamstresses – to give her the basic grounding in dress design. She'd been marvellous, Diana reflected, not only keeping Gems occupied and dry, but providing the exact diversion needed.

Gemma had written sporadically at first, in a stiffly formal way. But gradually her letters had livened and lightened up, yet there had been no mention of Ben.

Diana negotiated the heavy traffic, reminded briefly of Mark's eventual reply to her queries. He had found David's contracts watertight, as expected. But there had been one surprise; the five-year clause began not from the time Ben arrived in Tavistock, but from the actual start of the trust. That meant his contract would end in October 1991 – and not February as Diana had assumed. Cunning David had gained an extra eight months of Ben's life.

Diana parked at Logan, locking David back out of her thoughts. She would *not* start thinking about him now. Some day she would have to confront her feelings about the many dreadful things he'd done in the name of love, but she wasn't ready yet.

Gemma was pale and thinner, and so conventionally dressed that at first Diana almost missed her.

'Here, Gems!' Diana called, pleasure in her voice.

The next minute Gemma was in her arms, crying as if her heart would break. 'I've been such an ass, Di, and I've made an almighty mess of everybody's life,' she sobbed.

Diana held her at arm's length, and gazed into the large brown eyes.

'Sweetie, we've all made messes, and I think mine could probably outstrip yours.' She gave her another quick hug. 'So don't get any ideas about having the monopoly on foul-ups.' Seeing tears spring to Gemma's eyes again, she added quickly, 'Let's get you home and get some food into you. You look as if you've starved on mother's nouvelle cuisine.'

Gemma threw herself into her cousin's arms, and hugged her tightly.

'Di, you have no idea how badly I've missed you!'

Diana returned the hug warmly. 'That goes both ways, Gems. Now, do let's get out of here or the *Boston Globe* will be flooded with your tears in the morning!'

When Gabbie got back that evening there were more tears of reunion and happiness. For tonight, though, the only emotion was joy. Gemma was tired from the long flight and Diana shooed her off to bed early.

Next morning Diana was in the nursery playing with the twins when Gemma found her.

'That's better,' Diana said cheerfully. 'You look more like your old self!'

Gemma grinned sheepishly. The fuschia jersey and sun-flower-yellow leggings had been confined to the back of her wardrobe at Aunt Rachel's, along with most of her other 'happy' outfits.

Gemma picked Samuel from his crib. He was a perpetually smiling child, eighteen months old and deliciously chubby.

She took him on her lap opposite Diana, who held the more solemn Rebecca. Gemma gazed across at her exquisite little niece, with her tumbling curls and wide green eyes, and when Gemma spoke Diana almost dropped the child in shock.

'She is so beautiful, Di. So like Ben, too. You know you ought to tell him. He has the right to know.'

Diana held her breath, but Gemma went back to crooning to Samuel, who was engagingly absorbed in his efforts to get her fingers into his mouth.

'How long have you known?' she asked at last, her voice choked with embarrassment.

'For certain? Since I saw the paintings Aunt Rachel has done. But I think I had an idea the first time I saw them. Then Ruth strongly hinted that they were Ben's. Actually seeing Rebecca now, though, confirms it.'

Diana's voice was a whisper.

'Oh, Gems, my dearest friend. What can I possibly say? I had hoped you might never notice.'

Gemma smiled across at her, and there was no animosity in her face. 'What were you going to do, hide them each time I visited?'

'I don't know,' Diana said honestly.

Gemma put Samuel back in his crib. 'Can I hold her?' she asked.

Diana handed Rebecca over, her heart in her mouth.

'Umm. She smells good. Just like you,' Gemma said delightedly and kissed the soft little cheeks.

'That was one of the last things that David said about her,' Diana said, surprised.

'Well, maybe he wasn't all bad then.'

'Gems? Shall we go downstairs and talk this all over?'

'Yes, let's. I shall feel better when I know that you know that I hold nothing against you. Far from it. I love you just as much as I ever did, maybe even a little more now that you have these treasures for me to play with.'

Diana took Gemma's thin arm and together they went down to breakfast.

Gemma really did mean it. She talked for a long time about her foolishness in marrying Ben when she'd known all along that he was in love with Diana.

'I was mad, Di. It was only an infatuation really. I mean, he's so darned good-looking and you know what I'm like. . . Well, I've learned from that mistake. A handsome face is nice to look at, but not when the eyes are cold, and always seeing beyond you to someone else.' She screwed up her face but Diana didn't comment. 'He only made love to me, after a fashion, once.' Now she was matter-of-fact. 'The second time, two days after our wedding, he just couldn't do it. And he told me it was because he couldn't get you and David out of his mind.'

Diana felt her cheeks flame.

'Please don't be upset, Di. I only want you to know the truth, and I won't burden you with intimate details. Suffice to say it was me who was stubborn. I just hoped things might change.

'Anyway, I started drinking. More to blot out my feelings of inadequacy than for any other reason. That was at first. Then I'd drink deliberately to get drunk, to get any kind of reaction from Ben. Aunt Rachel gave me a couple of drinks, I think to test me or something. But I didn't need to bury myself any more and there was no craving for it. I've only ever really enjoyed it socially, and then in small doses.'

She passed her cup over for more coffee, relaxed in the serenity that Diana, like Rachel, created around her.

'Aunt Rachel's been damned good to me, but oh, Di, it's so *good* to be myself again.'

Diana smiled. 'And what will you do now?'

'Let him divorce me for desertion. We've talked on the phone. It's what I want,' she added, seeing a protest begin on Diana's lips. 'No really, it will be quicker and less messy than dragging him through the courts because he denied me my conjugal rights. And he did offer me a divorce right at the beginning, so it's as much my fault that it dragged on. Then . . . well, before then, I have to start a new life. If I can find one to start!'

'That's no problem, Gems. Your life is here with us, for as long as you want it to be. But can I ask you one thing? Do you still love him?

'No. I still think very highly of him, and always shall. But, I don't think it ever was really love. As I've said, more of an infatuation. When it came down to it we didn't have a thing in common – except our love for you.'

Diana stiffened. This was something they'd really have to clear up. It could not be allowed to become a regular topic of conversation between them.

'Gemma, I know this sounds crazy, but I'm certain Ben does not love me. There might have been a time briefly, yes. But it was a long time ago, and only one drunken night together at Tamerford. A lot of bad feeling has been caused since then. So can we please stop any further references to Ben's supposed love for me? They can't lead anywhere.'

'But surely they could now? I mean, those are his kids, Di! You can't mean never to tell him? He'd want to marry you if he knew.'

'Precisely! Do you think I'm interested in marriage for convention's sake? I've had my fair share of problems too, you know. I was tricked into that engagement fiasco.'

She told Gemma all about Beanie's party and the farcical engagement.

'So he *was* a bastard all along,' Gemma said acidly.

'My own reasons for going ahead with the marriage were far from noble,' Diana said evenly. 'I was drugged up in the clinic when your call came telling me you and Ben had married.' She shrugged her shoulders as if it wasn't important now. 'So I married David to cover up the fact that I was pregnant.' Now she stood up and grabbed Gemma's hands. 'OK, subject discussed and closed. Now let's get moving. You and I are buying all new trimmings for the Christmas tree. We will make a fresh start together. And I haven't done any shopping yet! We have lots of gifts to buy.' She shook her head merrily. 'We'll have Beanie and Jeff over, and there's Gabbie, too. A real family Christmas. How does that sound?'

There were tears in Gemma's eyes as she came and gave Diana a hug.

'Like the most wonderful idea you've had for years. But you've side-stepped my question and I want an answer.'

Diana stared directly into Gemma's eyes.

'No, Gemma. I don't intend to tell Ben, not for the moment. Maybe, if the time is ever right . . . but that will be my decision, nobody else's. Is that clear?'

Gemma nodded, sadly.

Christmas at the mansion was the gayest it had been in anyone's memory, and it was hard for them all to settle back into routine after New Year had passed.

Harder, too, for Diana on her first afternoon at home in February, when snow clouds gathered ominously and she had finally to face the task she had put off for so long.

Reading David's and Ruth's letters.

It was pathetic not wanting to face letters from two people who had died. What was the matter with her? They could do her no more harm.

In a way she could explain away her reluctance to read whatever David had said: after all, he'd lied to her, and, in doing so, had denied her the expression of grief she might have found helpful in the loss of his friendship and company. He was locked up inside her, feeding on her anger and all the other emotions she could not unleash on anybody else. But she had waited until she felt her immunity to him was total. For she hadn't wanted to read any more declarations of love. Pity she hadn't known President Reagan's now famous Russian phrase, 'Doverai no Proverai'- repeated again at the historic treaty with President Gorbachov in Washington last December, when the two superpowers had agreed to cut their nuclear arsenals – when David had been alive.

'Trust but verify' would have been an apt maxim to measure her own life by.

The study was dark and still. She switched on the lights, glancing out of the window as she did. She studied the sky for a few moments, trying to judge how soon the snow would fall. It was still enough, and the temperature had risen slightly.

There was such an oppressive feel about the place that she

rang Beanie and asked her to keep an her eye on the weather and get the girls away early if it started – and not at their usual time lately of after nine'o'clock. Then she added a fresh log to the fire and turned to the drawer.

It was just as well that she did not expect the girls early, because after reading the letters she was in no fit state to see anyone.

David's letter was loving – but also, worse, a record of his guilt.

Ruth Tamerford's letter was a confession of a very different kind.

And both concerned Ben.

Two people, one on each side of the Atlantic, with such determined but diverse reasons for wanting one man destroyed – and neither of them had been able to take their secret to the grave. They had, instead, piled them on to Diana's bowed shoulders and the past was not, could not be, buried. It was horribly, cruelly alive.

Ben, betrayed by them both, but in the end more devastatingly by *Ruth*.

And Diana was the only person living who knew.

Diana sank into the armchair, put her head down on its wide arm, hid her face and wept.

Snow began to fall heavily and quickly turned to swirling clouds as the wind got up and turned the snowfall into a blizzard. Diana didn't notice. She was trapped in a dark world of her own, so deep in the misery of her new, unwanted knowledge that she did not even hear the buzz of the telephone.

Meg brought her a tray at tea-time and relayed Beanie's message that she would keep the girls at Mt Vernon until the storm had passed. Diana did not even look up.

Sanders removed the untouched tea and set down a supper tray, concern creasing his elderly features. Diana was huddled back in the chair, her eyes closed as if she were sleeping. He put more logs on the fire and left quietly, to tell the household to stay away from the study that evening. It was a scene he was familiar with from Mr David in days long past.

Boston was at a virtual standstill. Nothing except snow-ploughs moved on the city streets. By nightfall the ploughs had been withdrawn. Continuous snowfall and a keening, icy wind made the work hazardous and pointless. The city resigned itself to the powerful hand of nature and retired behind drawn curtains.

Beanie and the girls were worried. They had managed to get to the penthouse in time, but despite the relatively short distance to the mansion the weather was too bad to attempt the journey. The darkness and fiercely swirling snow brought visibility down to nil and they couldn't have found their way to Beacon Street if they had tried.

Whatever was upsetting Diana and, according to Meg, keeping her shut in her study would have to wait until tomorrow. If she wouldn't answer her phone, there was nothing they could do about it.

They were a desolate little group that evening. None of them liked to think of Diana in some kind of trouble. But, as Beanie warned both Gemma and Gabbie, they might not get to know what the problem was anyway. Diana had a way of shutting down on personal problems that excluded outside attempts to probe. If it was something she wanted them to know about, she'd tell them.

If not? Well they only had to think of Mat and the horrendous assault to recall that Diana would not confide lightly. Sanders had assured them that she was well and it would have to do.

The storm lasted for two days, during which time Diana grappled, and came to some kind of terms, with her latest monstrous burden so that when the concerned trio finally got to the mansion it was a subdued and distant Diana who met them. When questioned about not answering their calls, she made light, evasive comments about having got over-involved with her plans to add a swimming pool extension to the back of the house. She'd drawn a line and no one would be allowed to cross it.

They all noticed the change in her. As the weeks passed she spent more and more time at the office and, when at home, in her study. She was, as always, polite and attentive, but her manner was distracted.

Gradually, almost imperceptibly, the changes became more marked. She left earlier for the office than was necessary, came home later than usual, and often with a short fuse. No one could understand her sudden flare-ups. She lost her temper with the builders, who had finally come to execute plans Diana had long worked on to make alterations to the mansion, and now found her about-turns and sudden unexpected demands very wearing. One day all was well, the next she wanted them to redo some time-consuming job. She changed the colour scheme in what was to be the new family room three times, each time after the decorators had finished the job.

The swimming pool that she'd designed in an annexe to the house was stripped back to its bare concrete after the mosaic tiles she'd chosen were hung but failed to please her. It was a time of chaos and none of them dared question her. If they did she was at once resentful and hypersensitive.

She spent little time with the twins, and even less with Gemma and Gabbie. Beanie watched her, and bided her time. She knew that Diana could not stand up to the increasing mental pressure for much longer. Something would happen to blow it all wide open.

And the day came as the twins approached their second birthday.

What started out as a discussion of when to hold their party soon developed into an argument.

Diana wanted the party on the twenty-ninth of June; the others protested that that wasn't fair to Samuel who was born six minutes into the thirtieth.

Beanie suggested a compromise. Two parties, one on each day.

Gemma and Gabbie thought that was silly and expensive. They proposed the first of July for the party, and each child given special attention on their actual birthday.

Diana listened impassively for a while, then rose from her seat. With a stony face she remarked coldly: 'I'll decide what is best for my children, thank you. I'm sick to death of being told how to run my life, and my children's, by people who can't mind their own business!'

It was not the first time that she had snapped at one or other of them, but it was the first occasion when she had lashed out collectively and hurt them all.

Gabbie quietly left the room.

Gemma gazed woodenly, hurt and angry by the outburst. 'I think that was bloody well uncalled for, Diana. We love you, and those kids. But, if that's the way you feel about it, send me an invitation when you've decided. If you want me there, of course!' Then she slammed out of the room.

Beanie remained sitting on the sofa, checking her nail polish attentively.

Diana drooped her head, suddenly ashamed of her outburst.

'What is eating so badly at you, darling, that you must hurt your family so?'

'I don't know what got into me, Beanie,' Diana said tiredly. 'I can hardly control my temper these days.'

'Won't it help to talk it over with your old friend?' Beanie offered.

Diana looked up, her eyes unutterably weary. 'Beanie, I don't know who is my friend any more,' she said flatly.

'Well, that's the worst thing and the stupidest that I've ever heard,' Beanie said crossly. 'Some terrible catastrophe must have happened to make you talk such rubbish.'

'Make that several catastrophes,' Diana said dispiritedly.

'Start at the beginning,' Beanie said.

'Well, we could start with Matthew, go on to David, then to Ben, add the Tamerfords, particularly Ruth, mix the whole lot together, and come up with a delicious cocktail of self-perpetuating disaster,' Diana said vehemently.

'Darling,' Beanie countered quietly, 'Mat, David and Ruth are dead – so if this is grief, I can't believe it is for them. You are furious with your friends, temperamental with employees, are avoiding your own children, and destroying your own plans for the mansion.

'And you are making yourself exhausted working so many hours at the office. It isn't necessary. You are the mother of young children: no one expects you to leave them for all hours of every day. That's what you pay Jeff and other key members of staff for. Darling, you are burning out on some anger, and it's affecting you in the worst possible way. Do you know you are becoming a tyrant? And for all that you might think David was, he was never cruel to people who cared for him.'

'Ha!' Diana exclaimed, seething now. 'That's what you think!'

'No, Diana. I do not think. I know.'

The two women faced each other across the room. It was the nearest they'd ever come to crossing swords.

'You don't know the terrible things that David did!' Diana declared hotly.

'I think that I do,' Beanie said very quietly.

'Oh, no! Your so-fine friend, Beanie, was not content with tricking me into marrying him and cutting Ben out of his share of Nazareth House, he also aided in some other deceptions; to deprive Ben of even his roots! Did you know that David had a good idea about Ben's background?'

'Yes. At the end he had an inkling, but that was all,' Beanie said unexpectedly.

Diana hadn't expected Beanie to know what she was talking about and this new surprise made her feel even more bitter.

'So! He even told you about *that* did he? What *didn't* David

Nazareth tell you, I wonder? He certainly seems to have always told you things he couldn't tell his wife!'

'He told me what he believed in the letter Mark gave me after his death.'

Diana gazed in surprise, seeing for the first time how tired – tired and sad – Beanie looked.

'In *that* letter? But that's how he told me! How come you've never mentioned it before now?'

'Probably for the same reason that you haven't, darling. What could one hope to do about it?'

'Something has *got* to be done!' Diana cried hotly. 'I didn't read David's letter until that bloody snow-blizzard and it's been eating at me ever since. But it wasn't just David's guesses that really overturned me. It was Ruth's letter.'

'I don't know anything about your letters,' Beanie said quietly.

'No? Well, that's bloody amazing!'

Beanie rose slowly from the chair. 'Diana, don't do this,' she warned. 'Get it off your chest. You can't go on hurting and being bitter like this – you'll burn yourself out. Explain it to me.'

Diana's anger subsided.

Beanie was right and perhaps together they could find a way. Probably David had only been guessing. He surely couldn't have dreamt the actual truth about Ben . . .

'I'm sorry, Beanie. Please forgive me? I am overtired. And I feel so damned helpless! Come into the study with me, and I'll tell you the whole sorry story. You might be able to see some daylight in it, because I can't. And I have churned it over for months.'

Over an hour later Beanie sat back in the deep leather chair that David had favoured, and shook her head. Diana was not wrong. It was the most awful mess.

'That was a cruel and unforgivable act,' she finally said. 'Ruth had no right burdening you in this way. It's as if she unloaded the guilt of centuries on to you. And I agree,

David's manipulations were unforgivable; they both behaved abominably.' She sipped at her martini, thinking. 'It's extra-ordinary, though, that neither could die without confessing their crimes.' She shook her head. 'It's the most wicked abuse of your good nature.'

'I agree,' Diana said wearily. 'So did my mother, and she didn't know half of it then. But it's all there, Beanie, and I can't be an impartial bystander. That's asking too much.'

'How are you supposed to bring justice to that situation, darling? You can't.'

'That's what my mother also said and I agreed, at first. But this new knowledge has tormented me night and day, until I know that I have to do something. My God, Beanie, I *have* to find a way. For all their sakes.'

'Then at least let me help you,' Beanie offered. 'If you do get involved in this, you must have support. It's as lethal as dynamite and it could blow up in your face . . .'

They finally agreed that neither Gabbie nor Gemma should know anything about it all yet. It could take time to find a solution – and meanwhile the fewer people who knew the better.

It was, in fact, several weeks before Diana suddenly conceived a possible solution, and days after that before she could get Beanie alone to tell her about it. She felt a growing excitement, and was hard put to disguise it from the rest of her household. The brief discord when Diana had been so bad-tempered and worried had been resolved; but now their lives were extremely hectic, so she was able to conceal her inner elation for the moment, behind a show of enthusiasm about the girls' new shop.

But getting Beanie alone was no mean feat.

If she wasn't in the new boutique directing the builders and shopfitters, she had either or both of the girls in tow.

Diana had found the ideal premises for the boutique, an old hardware store near to fashionable Newbury Street. It was a lovely old building of mellow stone. They'd had to open up several poky, dark rooms on the first floor to make one large showroom with changing rooms nearby, and this entire floor was now carpeted and fitted with wall-to-wall mirrors. On the second floor they would keep their stock, while the third housed the design and cutting rooms, and the fourth their fabrics and haberdashery.

The ground floor had burgundy-tiled floors with the initial 'E' for Elan, the name they had chosen, worked in gold into the centre.

Here they would show only a few select garments. The rest of the street level was designed as an elegant coffee lounge, with a catwalk weaving through its centre. This was where intending buyers could browse through the in-house catalogue, or watch the garments modelled; or park bored husbands, with daily newspapers.

They were all thrilled with their new baby and none more so than Diana.

But at this moment her mind was far away at Tamerford.

At last Beanie was able to get away to meet her for a quiet lunch at Zak's and Diana carefully outlined her plan.

Beanie listened without commenting until Diana had finished. 'It's extremely risky, darling,' she finally said, adding thoughtfully, 'Simon seems a very upright and honourable young man. Do you know what his response is likely to be?'

'Yes, I can guess. But Beanie, don't forget Ben, too, is honourable. And that's what I'm counting on.'

'What if it goes wrong?'

'Not a pleasant prospect.' Diana grimaced. 'But a chance I have to take – or I'll have this on my conscience for the rest of my life. My biggest concern at the moment is that Ben is still cutting me dead,' she said tersely. 'I have written several times, notes about the Youth Trust, nothing more, hoping to build on that really. But the last one came back with a very curt note. He said: "We have nothing to say to one another. Talk through Alan in the future." That really hurt!'

'Not like Ben,' Beanie commented. 'And it does make this, um, mission, more difficult.'

'Damned near impossible you mean! But I won't be beaten by his pride.'

She fished in her purse and brought out a letter. 'This came today. It's from Alan. He says that Ben isn't going to make it – that the trust is almost out of money, but the plan is far from complete. It was almost the last straw. He *has* to hang on there, Beanie, until next autumn, until the end of that bloody contract, or — '

'Or you would have to make your move earlier,' Beanie said firmly.

'I couldn't. Don't you see that then Ben would think my part was charity?'

'How will you feel, darling, if he, or they, should turn your plan down?' Beanie said, scrutinising Diana shrewdly.

'Truthfully? I dare not think! But at least I shall have resolved my own conscience and laid those ghosts to rest. You know, I'm quite haunted by the original Rebecca. It's as if she's reaching out to me, pleading with me to give her soul the peace it has never known.' She shrugged her slender shoulders, her eyes clouded. 'If all else fails, I shall have answered those pleas.'

'Well, I have to hand it to her – that cunning Ruth Tamerford chose you well.'

Diana frowned questioningly.

'If it had been left in my hands,' Beanie explained. 'I should have burned the lot and let them get on with it.'

Diana smiled at last. 'You are an old phoney, my friend. I don't believe you for one moment.' She squeezed Beanie's hand, her eyes warm with affection. 'There have been injustices in both our lives, things we could do nothing about. You have suffered more than your fair share of those and don't think I don't remember that. But with this plan, Beanie, we can put *two* injustices right, David's and the Tamerfords'. That has to be worth something!'

Beanie smilingly shook her head.

'I only hope that everybody else feels the same way as you do, darling, when this amazing event comes to pass. Now, as I no longer feel like discussing plastering and woodwork, why don't we go back to the mansion and you can give me the rest of those diaries to read? If I'm up to my neck in this, I might as well be as steeped in it as you are. But I warn you, if *I* start seeing ghosts of ancient, grieving mothers, you will have full responsibility for those protégées of mine. And that, darling, requires dedication that would stretch even yours!'

CHAPTER THIRTY-FIVE

The twins' fourth birthday arrived. And it was time to bring
Gabbie and Gemma in on Diana's plans for Simon and Ben.
The alfresco birthday party was well under way before they
could all gather beneath a sunshade on the terrace.

Gemma, in a scarlet silk jumpsuit, watched the twins. 'Becky
and Sam are loving those clowns.'

'Yes, aren't they? But you two shouldn't have spoilt them
with those lovely outfits, you know. You'll have all the
Boston mothers demanding Elan designs for *their* children
next.'

Gabbie's eyes twinkled. 'Well, we've been thinking that it
might be fun to have a range of tots' outfits; we both so love
designing for the twins.'

'Not in the same boutique?' Beanie looked up, horrified.

'Marketing is Gemma's baby,' Gabbie said. 'But there does
seem to be a trend we could usefully exploit . . .'

'Can we can discuss it later?' Diana said amicably, passing
them both iced fruit cups. 'I'm counting on you two being home
for dinner tonight, anyway. There's something important I want
to talk to you about.'

'We'll be in,' Gemma said. 'It's such a luxury to get a whole
day away from the drawing-board.'

The designers eventually wandered off to enjoy the children
and the party and Diana watched them, her delight in them
tinged with just a little concern. They were so young to be
married to their work. She hoped they would soon make time
to play.

Diana shook her head. It wasn't her business. But even
so she would at least like to see them both with caring
partners.

'You've set your date then?'

Beanie's quiet voice brought her back to the present.

'Mmm . . . I think Christmas would be appropriate. What do you think?'

'It's a family time, so it's certainly apt,' Beanie said. 'I just hope, darling, that they will feel like giving you thanks for all your trouble.'

Diana gazed across the garden before answering gravely. 'Thanks are not what I have in mind.'

Beanie raised a delicately arched eyebrow, but was diplomatic enough to keep her thoughts to herself. She knew Diana almost as well as she knew herself; knew that she had contained her pain, and her need, for a very long time. Her only hope was that Diana was not destined for a life of unrequited love. As she had been . . .

Gemma and Gabbie were by turns amazed, outraged and angered by Diana's story. They questioned her avidly, long after Beanie had gone home and the staff had gone to bed. In the end, though, they were excited. And both committed themselves to helping in any way they could.

Gabbie, knowing that her dear brother had the most to lose, had to confess her hope that he would not suffer *too* much. But she was a Tamerford to her soul, and did not hesitate to agree that something must be done.

Honour demanded it.

'It will be very hard if they don't see sense,' she said later. 'But of course you must do it. Whatever I can do, you know I will.' For a moment her eyes failed to meet Diana's. Then, as if gathering courage, she blurted out . . . 'And I thought Rebecca looked like *me*!'

'*You*?'

Diana and Gemma both stared at her.

'I know, crazy isn't it? But I thought, well, um, with the, um, family likeness . . .' She broke off miserably.

'Gabbie! How *could* you!' Gemma exploded.

Diana was mystified.

'She thought you and Simon . . . well, you know!' Gemma said, anger changing to laughter by the second.

'Oh mercy! I'm so sorry, Gabbie. Why didn't you say something?'

'I couldn't really, could I?' Gabbie said, controlling her own laughter now. 'But it was just like looking in a mirror, so who else was there to blame?'

She and Gemma collapsed in a giggling heap, and at last Diana, seeing the funny side of that, joined in.

When Gabbie had finally excused herself, yawning her head off, Gemma and Diana curled up by the remains of the fire.

'Dearest, Di, you are simply amazing,' Gemma said softly. 'But I could kill you for not sharing this awful worry for all this time. OK, I know you've had your reasons, and I have to accept them. But you are a little crazy, you know. We'd all have helped before now.'

Diana smiled warmly up at the pert face, thinking how tragic it had all been. Neither had known happiness with the Nazareth men. Gemma was almost divorced and she was a widow. Twice over.

'Thanks, Gems. The thought means more than anything. But I still need your blessing, as much as Gabbie's.'

'You know you don't even have to ask. But as you have, the answer is I wish you all the blessings in the world. And all the luck!' Gemma grimaced. 'You're taking a helluva gamble with those two, and I don't envy you one bit. But I'm with you all the way. It's time to bury the dead.' She gave her cousin a quick hug. 'If the living will let you!'

In the end, Diana's letter to Ben was sent via Mark to Alan. It was the only way she could be sure he'd read, or be told, the contents. It asked him to join the family for Christmas in Boston, when Diana wished to discuss the winding up of the trust.

She was equally careful in the note she sent Alan Brookes-Browne, but to him she added that she wanted to see the full accounts, as soon as possible. She knew that information would be also be given to Ben. It concealed her real intentions nicely.

Next she sent a letter to Candy, urging her to persuade Simon *and* Ben to come over for Christmas, with her and Timothy. In this letter she hinted at some deep secret that was of concern to them all, which she could only tell them in person.

Gabbie had also written to her brother, and Gemma had written to Candy.

They'd fired all the ammunition they had; now they could only wait.

Mark was preparing the papers to dissolve the current Youth Trust and Ben's contract. Ben had no pay-out to collect because the trust hadn't made the necessary profit. Even one cent would have done.

Meanwhile, Thanksgiving was only two weeks away and if they noticed that Gabbie was subdued, they didn't relate it to Diana's plan . . .

In Devon a few days later, an extraordinary meeting took place in the lodge at Tamerford.

Simon had asked Ben to join them for dinner, which was not unusual, but with features so grave that it became unusual. Ben hadn't pressed him and now sat on one of the sofas that stood on either side of the huge granite fireplace, a glass of fine old port, salvaged from the cellars at the manor, in his hand.

He watched Simon leaning against the oak lintel, and noted a questioning look pass between him and Candy.

She quietly knitted a jersey, the garment resting against her stomach. For seven and a half months, she hardly looked pregnant at all. But she was pale, as pale as Simon.

At last Simon spoke.

'I'm not quite sure how best to put this, Ben, but something rather important has come up. It concerns both us – you and me – and Tamerford.'

'So shoot from the hip,' Ben said easily, although he was wary. He'd never seen Simon look so haggard, or was it haunted? As if he'd had a bad shock. Had something happened to Gabbie?

'I had a phone call from Gabbie yesterday,' Simon said carefully.

Ben thought . . . not Gabbie then. And his stomach contracted. Who else? He forced himself to think of nothing; to blank out his emotions; to let nothing show, not even to Simon, his best friend.

'Go on,' he managed stiffly.

'It's not easy,' Simon replied, his own voice guarded. 'Gabbie was distressed – and the damned pips kept interrupting — '

'The pips — '

'She was calling from a public telephone – didn't want anyone to know she was ringing.' He paused as if seeking words. 'She says Diana has some information – God knows where from – that we . . . you and I . . . that we're somehow related. She didn't say how . . .'

Ben stared, speechless.

'I'm supposed not to tell anyone, especially you,' Simon said quietly. 'She's apparently given her word to Diana, you see — '

'See what?' Ben found his voice. 'What on earth are you talking about?'

'Tamerford,' Simon said softly. 'The estate – and the title.'

Again Ben stared, as if Simon had sprouted antlers. But Simon's face was not the face of someone playing games. He looked ashen.

Ben shook his head. 'I don't follow — '

'I'm not sure that I do either,' Simon admitted. 'The thing that makes it something other than just a bad dream is the fact that my sister was so worried about breaking her word. That, coming from Gabrielle, takes away any possibility of there being a mistake.'

'Tell me everything,' Ben said grimly.

'I didn't know that Candy had a letter from Diana yesterday. We were too busy during the day, and Candy forgot until this morning. You can see the letter, but it doesn't say a great deal. Just hints, really.' He paused briefly. 'I know I should have checked with you first, but it felt imperative to call Alan — '

'So?' Ben interrupted.

'I knew we wouldn't get chance to talk until this evening,' Simon continued as if Ben had not spoken. 'And he'd heard from Diana as well. We all have an invitation to go over for Christmas, apparently. But Diana has asked for the accounts to wind up the trust.'

'She can't do that!' Ben stopped, not certain. The contract was due to expire soon.

'Alan says she can, and seems to be — '

'Well, we damned well need to know,' Ben snapped. 'She can't just drop everything and leave us in mid-air. What's supposed to happen to all the workers? The kids? And you?'

He scraped angry fingers through his hair. He hadn't wanted to face this possibility.

'Christ! I promised this wouldn't be a here-today, gone-tomorrow venture. What am I supposed to do now? What are *we* supposed to do?'

'I don't know,' Simon admitted.

Candy passed the letter to Ben, her face white and drawn. 'There has to be some very good reason for it all, Ben. I know my cousin very well; she's not capable of hurting people.'

'Ha!' Ben exclaimed. 'That doesn't sound like the Diana I know.' He skimmed through the letter. As Candy said, it contained only a hint. Something 'important' that concerned them all.

'I'm sorry,' Candy replied firmly. 'I know that things went wrong between you, and I've always wondered about Diana's side of that story. But I can't accept that she did, or intends to do, harm to anyone. It's just not Diana.'

Ben glanced at Simon, who shrugged his shoulders and grimaced. Clearly he'd been listening to this line of thought for some time. 'Well, regardless of that, are we going to sit here until Christmas to find out our fate?'

Now it was Simon's turn to look puzzled. 'What else can we do?'

'Confront her.' Ben's voice was hard.

'We can't do that,' Simon said, aghast. 'Gabbie confided in me! If we do anything, Diana will know that Gabbie broke her word.' He looked appalled at the thought.

'Diana says she has information that proves us related *and* threatens your home and title, and you're worried about Gabbie's word being broken?'

'I don't see what I can do,' Simon said flatly.

'Simon! Our entire future is on the line here. For God's sake, man!'

'I do agree with Ben,' Candy said. 'It's too big a worry to have it hanging over our heads. We should find out what it's all about, then we'll know what we have to deal with.'

'What about Gabbie?' Simon said stubbornly.

'I'm sorry, Si. Gabbie will understand, I'm sure she will. But whatever it is that's happening over there, it's not expected to involve us until Christmas, right? So maybe there's time to see Diana – forestall it, or something.'

'That's how I'd want to play it,' Ben agreed. 'Catch the baby in the bath, before it's thrown out with the water. We could be over there and back in a couple of days.'

Si was such a straight guy; it was typical of him to be more worried about his sister's word of honour than his own neck. And Ben was quite certain that the 'relationship' bit was someone's fantasy.

'Have you come up with any ideas for a cash input?' Simon finally asked.

'When the contract runs out? Apart from selling my apartment and car, and bringing my savings over, not really,' Ben admitted. 'But I had intended checking out the banks for a loan.'

'With what collateral?' Simon's face was gloomier.'A half-finished project here isn't much in the way of security!'

'Go and see Diana.' Candy faced them both. 'And if you, Ben, will swallow some of that pride of yours, you never know, Diana might surprise you yet.'

Ben bristled. 'I doubt that. But I'm game if you are, Simon.'

'Well, if we really must — '

'I think we most definitely should,' Ben replied emphatically. 'Not just for the sake of the Youth Trust either. It seems we have a little matter concerning you, me and Tamerford to sort out.'

'I hadn't forgotten,' Simon assured him.

Four days before Thanksgiving, Diana was taking the two designers to the theatre and was dressing in her room when Gemma came in. She immediately crossed to fasten the tiny buttons at the back of Diana's black crêpe cocktail dress.

'Good timing, ' Diana said. 'I never can get those things to fasten.' She held an earring against her ear. 'Mmm, these or the fakes?'

'Whichever,' Gemma replied magnanimously.

'Are you all right?' Diana pretended absolute bewilderment. 'You normally have a very decided opinion.'

'Sorry . . . What did you say?'

Diana repeated herself, at the same time realising that Gemma's eyes sparkled and there was a hint of merriment about her mouth.

'What are you up to, Gemma?'

'Just judging whether this might be a good time to tell you my news,' Gemma tried to sound nonchalant and failed.

'News?'

Gemma took a deep breath. 'Jeff has asked me to marry him.'

'Jeff *Sherman*?' Diana's eyes were wide with astonishment.

'How many Jeffs do we know?' Gemma retorted mildly.

'But you don't like old – sorry I mean older – men.' Diana swivelled round, earrings forgotten.

'Oh, is he old? I hadn't noticed.' Gemma coloured.

'Gems! Are you serious?'

'Deadly serious. He asked, I said yes.'

'This isn't some impulse, Gems?'

Gemma grinned. 'Yep. The impulse to marry him! It's not some passing passion, Di. It's warm and very meaningful. He's a great guy and I enjoy his company. He's the first man I've ever known I can be myself with. You know what I mean . . .'

'No. Tell me.' Diana was still anxious.

'Well, it's not like with some younger men. I mean, he's not all hot and grabby — '

Diana laughed. 'I thought that's how you liked them?'

Gemma's face at once became serious. 'We seem to hit it off on all levels, and I can't think of any other man I've known that I'd rather be around. He's even sworn he doesn't want to change me!'

Diana could see it was serious.

'When did all this happen?'

'Not suddenly, if that's what you mean. I've been seeing him two or three times a week for over six months. I didn't want to say anything before I was sure.'

'And you are sure?'

'Very,' Gemma said confidently.

Diana had to think for all of ten seconds.

'Then I am thrilled for you both. Jeff's a lovely man and he'll be very good for you. And you, of course, will be a perfect wife!'

They grinned at one another. 'Who'd have thought it! My little cousin with her aversion to anything over toy-boy age, and my confirmed bachelor personal assistant. Darling girl, it's quite marvellous!'

'Thanks,' Gemma said almost shyly.

'So when's the announcement?'

'I don't want to say anything until after this business with Tamerford and the trust is settled,' Gemma said, 'so we'll wait till after Christmas. Then, I'll tell anyone who'll listen!'

Diana smiled, then a rogue thought crossed her mind. 'How lovely, Gems. The twins might have cousins nearby.'

Gemma shook her head and said very firmly, 'Not from me, I'm afraid. I don't want children, Di. And I know Jeff isn't particularly bothered. We've agreed we're both too selfish to want to share one another.'

She saw Diana's crestfallen face and swiftly added. 'We're both too career-minded, Di. I shan't give up the boutique now, and Jeff's life is Nazareth House. Children would be a very poor second to our real interests. End of story.'

Diana felt momentarily sad.

'Has your divorce come through?'

'It came through in the middle of all that chaos last year,'Gemma said, checking her own appearance in Diana's mirror. 'Which reminds me – I suppose you and Ben will marry at some point?'

Diana returned the look and the frankness. 'I doubt that he'd have me. But would it matter to you?'

'Nope,' Gemma said. 'I'm a realist. You two should have married in the first place.'

'Maybe,' Diana replied. 'But after Christmas I shouldn't think he'll want to renew our acquaintance.'

'I should hope he'll be damned grateful.' Gemma turned and picked up her wrap. 'And you know something? I think when he knows what you've gone through, he will be. He is an honourable man, Di.'

Diana collected her purse and they headed for the door to look for Gabbie.

'Gemma,' Diana said warningly. 'no interference! He has to work it out for himself.'

Gemma grimaced. 'That's asking a lot from someone who thinks you betrayed him, and also believes that you loved

David Nazareth so much you married him and had his children.'

Diana sighed. 'I know. But he *will* know the truth. After that he has to make his own decisions, without any help from anyone.'

'And if he has problems understanding?'

'Then he's not the man I hope he is. In which case, I shall be well rid of him.'

Diana wrapped up the last of the morning's business and was free to go home for the holidays.

It was Thanksgiving tomorrow, Thursday, and she had made it a four-day holiday so that her staff could make any necessary trips to see their families. She was idly flicking through the papers after lunch, luxuriating in doing nothing in particular, when Sanders came into the room.

He crossed to the sofa, looking flustered.

'What is it, Sanders?'

'There has been a call from security at Nazareth House, Miss Diana. It seems you have company, madam.'

'Well? Who is it?'

'Mr Sherman had already left, so — '

'Sanders! Do we have burglars, or what?'

'No, Miss Diana. It is Mr Benjamin, and with him the young English earl. They are at Nazareth House.'

'Holy shit!' Diana jumped up, tea things flying in all directions.

'Quite,' said Sanders. 'Shall I tell the staff to prepare rooms?'

'No! Yes! I don't know, Sanders. Let me *think*. Fetch me the phone. No, I'll *go*, it's quicker.'

She ran from the room, her thoughts in a dozen places at once.

Where would Beanie be? Where were the girls? Where was *anybody*? She wasn't prepared.

Gemma answered at Elan. They weren't closing until six.

'Gemma? Thank God! You have to come home. No – get Gabbie – I mean, you must both come. Hurry, Gemma. They're *here*. Ben and Simon!'

'What? No, of course I don't know why they've come early. They're at Nazareth House. Just get here fast!'

She clattered the phone down, taking deep breaths to restore her jangled equilibrium.

Sanders came in. 'Madame is on the other line.'

Diana exhaled. 'Thank God!' She snatched up the phone. 'Beanie? Ben and Simon are at Nazareth House. What shall I do?

'Darling?' Beanie's brain was ticking rapidly. 'Get Sanders.'

'Sanders, wait right there,' Diana commanded.

Sanders waited.

'Now,' Beanie said. 'Stop panicking. Get Sanders to phone back and tell them to delay them at Nazareth House — '

'Sanders, get on the other line — ' Diana shook the second phone at the poor man. 'Call the office back. Delay them —

'How, Beanie?' she interrupted herself.

'Tell them you are on your way over there from town. You'll meet them there, in your office — '

'It's closed!'

'Unclose it. Get them in there to wait!' Beanie snapped.

'Sanders, tell security to open my office, put them in there – tell them I'm coming from town, and I'll meet them there – what else, Beanie?'

Sanders was already speaking calmly into the other phone.

'Get hold of Jeff. He can stall them for a while. No, *I'll* get Jeff – you calm down – take an aspirin or something. I'll be right over.'

'What if you can't find Jeff? What then?'

'I'll find one of your other secretaries, never fear. You just put your feet up until I get there – or you'll be in no fit state to carry this all through. Do you understand me, Diana?'

Diana started thanking her, but Beanie had already hung up.

Diana dropped the phone on its hook.

She was suddenly very, very afraid.

Diana paced the drawing room, her insides churning. She wasn't ready for this showdown. She wasn't organised, wasn't prepared. Had Mark gone away? What if he'd left town?

That thought made her rush for the phone again.

Mark's voice came on the line.

'Mark – thank God! Are you at home for the holiday? Yes? Brilliant! Listen, Mark, no time for explanations: those papers concerning the Youth Trust? I need them here – yesterday. No, don't come yourself, call a courier – but look, could you be available if I need you? Yes, either this evening or tomorrow. I'm sorry to do this, but you'll see why — '

She heard a car on the drive. 'Mark, have to go. Thanks a trillion — '

Not waiting for Sanders she rushed to meet Beanie, and wished she hadn't.

Alighting from a cab were all her fears.

Clearly, expecting Ben to wait had been wishful thinking.

There was nowhere to run. Simon had seen her and Ben looked up from paying the driver. As their eyes met, even at that distance, a current charged the air between them.

She could only watch as they took overnight bags from the trunk, and a large, square parcel that they had to manhandle between them; it was obviously a painting.

Before they reached the second step, a Citroën pulled up, Gemma blasting away and Gabbie waving madly.

Diana could have kissed them both.

And, with superb timing, Beanie's Jaguar swept round the curve and, skidding slightly, careered to a juddering halt, miraculously, just short of the Citroën.

Ben immediately dropped his bag and strode over to open Beanie's door.

'You still drive like a maniac then – despite the improved weaponry?'

Beanie jumped from the car and, to Diana's amazement, threw her arms around Ben's neck and hugged him tightly. Ben wasn't exactly holding back either, she noticed. He hugged her fiercely, then stood her at arm's length.

'Let me look at you. Oh, yes! Ravishing as always!'

Beanie did a little pirouette, laughing. 'Be careful, darling. I might take you seriously!'

Diana was momentarily stunned. This was the Beanie they had all known when David was alive. And in that same moment she realised how much Beanie had lost when David died. How much of *her* had died with him – and how much she had aged since his death. Diana fought back tears. How easy it had been to forget everything but her own troubles . . .

Then Simon and Ben were hauling the package up the steps, the three women hanging on their coat-tails – Ben and Gemma even laughing together.

Diana could feel the loneliness settle around her shoulders. 'Diana . . .' Ben's hand enveloped hers, but there was no light-hearted smile for her. Nothing but the sensation of staring into the sea on a particularly glacial day.

She withdrew her hand swiftly and turned to Simon. He, too, shook her hand formally; although not as hostile as Ben, he was nonetheless reserved and cool.

So it wasn't a social visit. What had she expected? Well, not this exactly. Reservation, yes. Curiosity, certainly. But animosity? Why?

Her letter via Alan had only hinted at some matter of importance. She had given nothing away about the Youth Trust, she was sure. And the invitation had been for Christmas.

Why were they here now – and clearly ready for a fight?

She held the door to let her uninvited guests struggle through, and at the same moment caught Gabbie's guilty start.

So that was the way it was! Diana sighed inwardly, but she could understand and forgive. She should have realised

Gabbie would try to protect her brother's interests. But how much had she told them?

Panic welled up in her as she faced the two men in the spacious hall. So much was riding on this meeting – pre-emptive though it was. What if she had over – or under-estimated them? Either of them? Or both of them? What if . . .?

Beanie crossed to her side and tucked her arm through hers, giving her a discreet squeeze.

Gemma and Gabbie, too, came to stand beside her, a mite belatedly, but it helped.

Diana had not managed a word.

'Coffee anyone?' Beanie said brightly. 'Or something a bit stronger?'

Diana shook herself out of her trance.

'Good idea! Gems, why don't you take the men through to the drawing-room, I'll get Sanders to bring refreshments through. I have one or two matters to attend to, and then I'll come through myself.'

With Beanie hot on her heels, she escaped to the kitchen, where, to the amazement of the staff, the two women proceeded to talk as if no one else was there.

'What am I going to do?' Diana's voice was ragged with fear. 'I can't face them, Beanie. I can't!'

'Yes, darling, you can and you will! Now will you stop worrying? Just remember what you are going to do for them.'

'You saw their faces, Beanie! They already hate me!'

'Darling, they are worried stupid. Use your head! What do you think has brought them here? I'll tell you – sheer panic. *You* hold all the aces, and they know it.'

'Gabbie did it,' Diana groaned. 'She's told Simon something . . . that's why they're here.'

'Well, if I know Gabbie, and I believe I do, she hasn't said very much,' Beanie countered. 'She's far too sensible, and far too grateful to you. So forget about that.'

'Seeing them – seeing Ben again – in the flesh, it didn't seem easy any more . . .'

'It was never going to be easy,' Beanie said dryly. 'And you know that, darling. Just remember what you are going to offer them.'

'It makes me feel as if I'm playing God! It's awful. Like David did with me — '

'Stop it this minute!' Beanie snapped. 'Pull yourself together, Diana. You are going to tell them the *truth*, and offer them a future, for God's sake! Tell them it how it is – that's my advice. Go straight to the heart of it. No more velvet gloves, darling.'

'I can't – I'll get Mark over. He can tell them.'

'No, Diana!' Beanie's voice was husky with passion. 'There's been too much deception, too much treachery, remember? Those were your words. You decided to end all that. Now you will do it.'

Diana heard the words and gradually they began to make sense. Beanie was right. It had all gone on for too long.

'It's so different, planning it, from confronting the reality . . .'

'I know,' Beanie soothed. 'But you have only to think of one thing, darling. None of this is *your* fault. You are simply the messenger – the medium used by David and by Ruth to conceal the truth. You must try to stand back from that part of it. You must not carry the responsibility for David and Ruth's manipulations any longer. Once you have told them the truth, then you can tell them the wonderful plans you have for the future. Then let *them* decide where their future is to be. You can do no more than that – so do it.'

'Just like that? No warm-up? Launch into it cold?'

'That's your choice, darling.'

Diana considered. It was true, she was only the messenger. As to her own part, her plans, as Beanie said – they were an offer. It would be up to them whether they accepted that offer.

She nodded, calmer.

'If today is to see the end to all those secrets and worries you have been forced to carry,' Beanie said lightly now, 'it should be a day for gladness, not sorrow, darling. And definitely not for fears. Keep that thought in mind.'

Diana hugged her. 'Thanks, Beanie. I needed reminding of that.'

Beanie smiled. 'Now, shall we join our guests?'

Diana decided to act as if all was well between them and, to convey that impression, she laughed as she entered the room.

'What on earth is that great package in the hall?' she asked cheerfully.

Simon's smile was nervous, but it was there.

'A gift from great-aunt. Sorry it's very late, but her instructions were for me to give it to you in person.' Now his smile was sheepish, the old Simon that Diana remembered. 'There hasn't been a chance really – oh and this . . .' He put his hand in his inside pocket to pull out a long envelope. 'Sorry, Gabrielle – great-aunt swore me to secrecy over this.'

He handed Diana the envelope, which she took with a small shudder, and put to one side. She'd face it today, whatever it was. There would be no more secrets. But she would still read it first in private. Just in case.

'Will you open the package?' Simon asked. 'We have all been rather interested to know what is in it.' He blushed at the admission.

The ice was broken, at least with him. Ben just sipped his coffee and watched.

'Of course,' Diana said at once. 'But I give you fair warning: if it is another of your family heirlooms, you'll be carting it back across the ocean.'

They all followed to the hall, even Ben.

'Do the honours,' Diana said to Simon, including Ben in her invitation, suspecting this package might hold more interest for him than he could guess.

Simon stripped the outer wrappings while Ben held the thing steady. Beneath the paper was a stout wooden crate.

'Needs a claw hammer or a fine chisel or something to lever the nails up . . .' Ben looked up at Diana and again their gazes locked.

Her heart lurched wildly.

Ben looked away first. But Diana knew he had felt it too. It had been in his look of surprise, as if he hadn't considered that they might still be attracted to one another.

'I'll get the hammer and stuff.' Gemma broke the tangible silence and was gone only a couple of minutes.

Now Ben held the crate and Simon took the securing pins out. The last one came away and he lifted the top.

'Good grief! This must be the lost twin! Gabrielle, what do you think?'

Gabbie moved closer and peered at the portrait. 'Yes, it is,' she said, colouring brightly. 'So great-aunt had it all the time. I wonder why?' She smiled at Diana, a silent message passing between them.

Diana, too, stared at the painting, her heart beginning to race. All of a sudden her last concerns dropped away. This was taking it all back to the very beginning, to Samuel and Rebecca and Joshua. Ruth Tamerford had finally done the decent thing.

'Well, Joshua,' she murmured, gazing in wonder at the handsome young man. 'You've finally come home.'

Simon and Ben exchanged blank looks.

Simon's face had reddened again. 'What's going on? If that's the lost twin, it should really be at Tamerford. Shouldn't it, Gabrielle?'

Gabbie smiled but shook her head. 'No, Si. Not really. He has more reason to be here.'

Diana willed her pulse to slow down. Ruth's persistent meddling had given her a posthumous hand, whether she'd intended it to or not. She'd been imagining all kinds of nightmare scenarios, in which the family would gather and she would play Inspector Poirot; they would ask the relevant questions and she would explain the long, complicated saga of their family intrigues.

Ruth had finally done something useful.

If Diana could only find the right words.

But what came out was . . . 'Simon, Gabbie of course, and yes, Ben – meet your troublesome ancestor . . . Joshua *Nazareth* Tamerford.'

Simon stared at her as if she'd gone potty.

Ben just gazed blankly.

'Wonderful!' Beanie laughed, and Gabbie and Gemma joined in.

Diana grinned, almost overwhelmed by the exultant feeling of triumph sweeping through her veins. She'd carried all this too long not to enjoy the taste of freedom that she'd just been handed, on a painting, as it were.

Ben's narrowed eyes and Simon's mystified stare no longer worried her.

She laughed lightly. 'This handsome young buck ran away from home in 1629 – you can read the whole story yourselves later – but for now it's sufficient to say that Joshua here founded the Nazareth line.'

Simon was speechless.

'I fail to see where I come in,' Ben said quietly.

Diana crossed her fingers, because she rather hoped that her instincts were right, and that Ruth had done them a double favour today.

'Would you say that crate looks a bit big for *one* painting?' she said, ignoring Ben for the moment.

They all looked at the crate.

'It does,' Gabbie agreed excitedly.

'Would you take Joshua out, Simon?' Diana asked, still crossing her fingers.

He did, and underneath in thick corrugated paper was a second, smaller painting.

'Megabrilliant!' Gemma was almost dancing on the spot. Beanie moved closer to Diana and gave her arm a quick, hopeful hug.

'Let's see who we have here,' Diana said.

She held her breath as the second portrait was revealed. She exhaled sharply when she saw she had been right. It *was* him.

'I don't understand,' Simon said, shaking his head. 'I've never seen this painting. Have you, Gabrielle?

Gabbie shrugged a 'no'.

Diana stared at the portrait. 'I'm afraid Ruth's propensity for mischief, for want of a more accurate description of her unsavoury behaviour, seems to have known no bounds.'

She continued staring at the big man on an Arab steed for a moment. 'You wouldn't have seen this one. Your great-aunt hid it before you were born. It saved having to answer awkward questions, you see — '

'I jolly well don't see,' Simon said tetchily.

'This is Nathan, elder brother of your father, Bart,' Diana said gently, aware that she was about to tread on even more dangerous ground.

'You haven't answered *my* question.' Ben was watching her, observing her as if across a courtroom; his face tight and closed.

'I have, in a roundabout way,' Diana met his gaze levelly. 'It's here, in front of you.'

Ben's facial muscles twitched, as if he'd had a sudden rush of adrenalin.

His voice wasn't quite steady. 'This portrait?'

'He's your father,' Diana said simply.

There was instant, shocked silence. Ben leaned against the banister for support.

'In mitigation, if there can be mitigation, this was not all Ruth's doing,' Diana said swiftly, giving Ben time to recover, to catch his breath. 'Hiding Joshua's portrait was her brother's idea and Ruth simply did as she was told – there was certainly more than one Tamerford ancestor with reason not to want to be reminded of Joshua, as you will learn. But Nat was all Ruth's own work. Ruth's personal wickedness was giving you up for adoption, Ben, after your mother died in Switzerland. It made it simpler, you see, for her favourite nephew's son to inherit Tamerford.'

Ben's eyes glazed, and Diana longed to go to him, to hold him – as Gabbie was holding Simon.

For long, anguished minutes the two men stared at each other, both deeply shocked, both inexorably drawn to the same moment of recognition. Metaphoric swords were half-drawn.

'This means we are cousins.' There was a new note in Ben's voice, hope and disbelief intermingled.

Simon's voice was marvellously even. 'I rather think it means that you are the rightful Earl of Tamerford, cousin.'

There was an instant drop of temperature in the hall, an icing-up of emotions. Swords remained half-drawn as Ben and Simon faced one another. On guard, and overwhelmed.

'Can't be that, old chap,' Ben managed levelly. 'Tamerford already has an earl. A damned fine earl,' he added firmly.

'An impostor it would seem.' Simon let his guard down slowly.

'Not as far as I'm concerned,' Ben stated, his voice clearer. 'Not *ever* as far as I'm concerned.'

Diana felt she heard the clang of steel as the swords were sheathed.

They were spellbound witnesses to the awesome arc of emotion between the two men, as it discharged itself between the two conductors.

The moment they had feared had happened in a flash; a lightening bolt that had found no target.

'We have a lot to discuss, Ben.'

'That we do, cousin.'

Simon's gaze was remarkably impassive. 'I'm sure Diana has a great deal to tell us. Shall we hear that first?'

'Absolutely,' Ben said easily.

'I'm afraid you'll have to wait, Diana said apologetically. 'Before I can give you my undivided attention, I do have some urgent business matters to tie up. Shall we all meet for dinner, at say, eight? Perhaps you could rest up after your long journey meanwhile — '

'We're rested,' Ben said smoothly. 'We got in late last night and caught up this morning, to be on the safe side . . .' His look was full of meaning, but Diana couldn't interpret it.

'We're flying back tomorrow,' Simon added. 'It's not just the trust. I don't like to leave Candy, with the baby due next month. If she's not watched, she works too hard.'

'Well, fine.' Diana was momentarily thrown, but recovered speedily. 'I'll see you at dinner and we can talk all you like then.' She turned to Beanie. 'You'll be here won't you?'

'I wouldn't miss it for the world,' Beanie said dryly, her gaze speculative.

'And you'll bring Jeff, Gemma?' Diana didn't wait for a reply. If it was going to be all over by tomorrow, they didn't have time for niceties. 'And Mark will be here, so I'll tell Sanders to expect eight for dinner.'

She fled from the hall, leaving them all staring after her.

CHAPTER THIRTY-SIX

Diana had needed to get away. She did have other matters to see to, urgent matters. She didn't want the twins wandering about and bumping into Ben by accident – she wanted that meeting strictly under her control.

And she wanted to speak to Candy.

Beanie left at once and the girls took their cue with excuses about dressing and such. If Diana wanted the two men left alone together, she had her reasons.

Upstairs on the wide landing, Gemma gasped a lungful of air and clutched her chest theatrically.

'What's wrong?' Gabbie cried.

'Joseph's beard! That was tough!'

'Yes, wasn't it.' Gabbie's cheeks were pink.

'What made you do it?'

Gabbie stared at her friend, about to deny it, but knew that Gemma would see through it.

'Do you think Diana knows it was me?'

'Of course,' Gemma said matter-of-factly. 'If I guessed, you can be certain Diana did too.'

Gabbie pulled a face. 'I didn't think they'd drop everything and fly straight over. I just thought it would give Simon time to prepare himself if he knew there was a relationship involved.'

'Cor blimey!' Gemma exclaimed. 'What in Fred's name were you thinking of?'

'Who's Fred?'

'What? Oh, Fred. How should I know? Fred Flintstone maybe – or Freddo Frog . . .' Gemma grinned at Gabbie's serious face. 'He can be any Fred you like!'

Gabbie burst out laughing and Diana came out from the nursery, her fingers to her lips.

'Sssh, you two. You'll bring everybody upstairs!'

'Christ, my heart!' Gemma said dramatically. 'It was all that tension, Di. Bloody hell, I thought they might kill each other.'

'Or me,' Diana said ruefully. 'Come in here. I'm about to call Candy to see if she can talk them into staying longer.'

She called the lodge but was put through to a woman with a broad Devonshire accent.

'May I speak to Lady Tamerford?'

'Who's callin'?'

'Her cousin, Diana Nazareth.'

'Ah, Mrs Nazareth, I weren't to tell nobody but you, mum. But I'm surprised 'er Ladyship 'in't wi' you already.'

'What?'

'We told 'er not to go flyin' off about the place in 'er condition. 'Er says next month, but I reckons that baby be ready to drop.'

'She's coming here? When? Do you have any details?'

'I wrote'n all down, mum, if ee'd gi' me a minute . . .'

Diana held her hand over the mouthpiece. 'She's on her way already!'

'Good old Candy,' her sister said. 'I couldn't understand her letting Simon come without her.'

'Yes?' Diana wrote down what the woman told her, thanked her and hung up.

She looked at her wristwatch. 'Crumbs, she must have only just let them get out of sight. Her plane is due in in an hour! Gemma, you get hold of Mark – his home number's in my book – tell him to make it dinner tonight. And he'll be sending some papers over – put them in my room, will you?' She hurried to her room for a coat. 'And not a word about Candy. Let's not spoil her surprise!'

Diana found a dollar coin, yanked a trolley from its tangle and headed for Arrivals.

Candy was looking around, her bright eyes worried. The gleam of her golden curls would have marked her out, even if she hadn't been marooned by an armful of toddler and two huge bags, in the midst of a hall full of festive travellers.

Diana grinned and waved. 'Stay there, I'm on my way!'

'Di! How did you know?'

'Yer loverly secretary,' Diana laughed. 'Was my call fortuitous, or what?'

'She's the housekeeper and she's a poppet – but what made you call?'

'Hoping you'd talk these crazy guys into staying a day or two. But are you insane? Travelling with the baby so near! How did you get away with it?'

'A small misdemeanour,' Candy laughed. 'I told them I was just six months. They weren't really interested after that – and I couldn't stand not being here.'

'No, well, just as well,' Diana laughed. 'But who have we here?' She knelt down to the shy little boy hiding in the folds of his mother's coat.'

'Tim, this is your Auntie Diana. Say hello.'

Tim smiled a Simon smile, peeping up from Candy's huge blue eyes.

'He's the image of you both!' Diana exclaimed delightedly. 'Far better looking than his photos. Gosh, the twins will be thrilled to meet him at last!'

'Does everyone know I'm coming?' Candy gasped in dismay.

'Only the girls,' Diana promised, standing up and giving Candy another hug. 'But thank God you did come, Candy – there's too much at stake here for it to be rushed into an overnight visit.'

On the way home she brought Candy up to date, and got her promise that she would, somehow, help keep the men here for as long as the delicate negotiations might take.

They made it to Simon's room without being spotted by Ben.

'Will you have some tea?' Diana whispered at the door.

'No, thanks. I really need a nap, Di, and Tim should be in bed – he had his tea on the plane.'

'Will you make dinner at eight?'

Candy grinned mischievously. 'You bet!'

As Diana tiptoed past Ben's room, she heard Simon saying, 'Darling! How lovely – but what . . .?'

Smiling, she returned to her own room.

She still needed to recover from the shock of it all, to get her thoughts in some kind of order.

The nannies were now primed to have the twins ready to be brought down for dinner – when she came to get them. Now she had a little while to herself. Time to think what to do next.

In his room, Ben stared over the darkened shapes of the garden to the almost leafless trees and the smudge of the common beyond. All his impressions were shadowy and shapeless he reflected, everything slightly obscured. 'Through a glass darkly,' he quoted whimsically to himself.

That's what it felt like.

He had gone through a range of feelings: from hope to wonder, from awe to fear; and desire. Yes, he admitted, desire.

It wasn't enough that he'd been given the right to break the heart of the only man he'd loved as a brother; or that he'd been handed the key to his heritage on a platinum platter; or that he'd learnt that he was related to David Nazareth, albeit with a few centuries of watering down. No, none of it was enough to keep him from wondering about the powerhouse of feelings that Diana had aroused.

He'd only had to see her for his pulses to race and his brain to scramble.

Yet he'd convinced himself he was well over her; that he'd try to strike a deal for the trust, and then get the hell out of her life.

Now his careful plans were in tatters. His heart felt as if it were in pieces; his future was wrecked. He glowered at his shadowy reflection in the window. He'd just learned that his blood was British blue, had gained a family – a real family – yet in spite of all that, Diana was uppermost in his mind.

Mat's widow. The woman he had intended five, no, almost six, years ago to spurn at all costs. The woman who had taken his heart, and his hopes, and tossed them like confetti into her obscene marriage to David.

Yet today, after all the pain of rejection, he had looked at her and wondered if it really was too late.

Now, when he should be thinking about the shattering revelations that had followed the opening of those crates, he was standing here in a dark room, feeling utterly desolate. He shook his head wearily and at last turned away from his gloomy meditations to the only immediate consolation of a shower.

He stood beneath ice-cold jets until he couldn't think any more then, shivering, wrapped a towel around his waist and lay face down on the bed.

Shock and fatigue took over and he became drowsier. Welcome oblivion pulled him deeper and deeper down into a warm, soft place, where the only sound was of gentle tapping . . .

It was a while before his consciousness registered that the tapping was external – and a few more moments before he recognised that the sound was at his own door.

For a few confused seconds he debated ignoring it, but he was half awake now, so he padded reluctantly to the door, a discouraging frown forming between his brows.

Diana gazed at him uncertainly.

He held the door wide and she slipped into the room.

He closed it and turned the key, afraid she'd hear the pounding of his heart. But she was sitting on the edge of his bed, trembling so violently he could hear her teeth chattering.

Against all the logic of a mind overflowing with questions, he took her silently in his arms and held her, rocking her as gently as a baby.

For several minutes it was all he could do, all he wanted to do. Hold her. Hold his breath. Not think of a single, damned thing. Gradually she responded to the warmth in his embrace and the trembling eased and stopped. Still he held her, stroking her hair. His physical responses were in neutral, suspended somewhere in a timeless space where doubts dissolved, worries ceased, and only this perfect, beautiful moment existed. Here, where their souls met and entwined in an infinity of love so perfect it needed no earthly, no physical expression. There was no sound in the room but the steady rhythm of their breathing.

It was a jolt when she stirred, tilted her head and reached up to cover his mouth with cool, satiny lips. The kiss was chaste, innocent – and in it he felt her promise, implicit and binding, of a lifetime of other pleasures – none on offer now.

But now, right now, they only needed this, the unspoken affirmation of mutual trust and tacit pledge. To have made any other physical advance would have damaged the integrity they both needed desperately to confirm.

Ben's pain lifted. Diana was here, and she had shown him she wanted his love. It was enough.

'Ben?' she whispered a long while later.

'Sssh . . .' he murmured softly, tilting her chin and looking deeply into her eyes. 'Not now, my love. Later . . .'

'But you might not . . .' Her voice was heavy with doubt.

'There's nothing I can't handle now,' he promised. 'Nothing in this world.'

Diana smiled dreamily and snuggled back against his chest for a long, precious moment. Then, with a deep sigh, she eased herself from his arms.

'I have to dress for dinner,' she said, reluctant to leave him at all.

Ben clutched her urgently, his hand too tight, suddenly afraid again. 'Will you find your way back here?'

She stood up and her eyes caressed him lovingly.

'How could I not?' she said simply. 'My life is in here.'

When Ben walked into the drawing-room an hour later, Beanie was watching him. She saw him greet Jeff and Mark with cautious assurance. But he wasn't ready for small-talk with them.

He took a glass of champagne and moved to stand alone in front of the fireplace.

Beanie had tucked herself away at the far end of the room, resplendent in a long silver gown. She didn't want company, so she was glad when Ben tilted his glass to her but made no attempt to join her on the long sofa.

Beanie knew Jeff and Mark couldn't expect warm greetings, not after the hand they'd been forced to deal Ben. She studied them compassionately. They were nervous. They must be wondering if Ben would be magnanimous. If he wasn't, they might both be looking for new jobs very shortly.

And Jeff had another reason to be uncomfortable. Beanie was well aware that he was courting Gemma, and she could tell from Jeff's face that he was wondering about Ben's reaction to that. Silly man! It wasn't any of Ben's business any more. Anyway, it had been Ben's choice to end the marriage.

She returned Ben's reserved greeting, wondering about his sudden restraint.

Beanie had chosen her position in the room well, not far enough away to seem rude, but distant enough to have an advantageous view of the proceedings. She had learned a good deal about people over the years, just by observing. But her particular interest this evening was in what she would see in Ben's face when the twins were brought in. Was he astute enough to be able to recognise himself in those two little faces?

At the moment, though, she was content to sip her champagne and ponder on what thoughts lay behind the chiselled, slightly arrogant face. If anything, she thought he seemed less intense than earlier. Nervous, yes, but not afraid. No, he was remarkably confident, she assessed shrewdly. So either something had happened that she didn't know about, or he'd made his decisions already and, regardless of the outcome, was determined on the course of action he would take.

She shivered slightly and momentarily crossed her fingers.

Gabbie and Gemma arrived together, chattering away in their usual manner, but thankfully breaking the ice that had settled in the room.

Beanie smiled delightedly at Gabbie. Diana had said, 'Dress up' for dinner, and Gabbie had excelled. Dramatically chic in ebony satin, with strands of palest pearls, she was a picture against the men's dark dinner suits.

Gemma, of course, had her own idea of 'formal'. She was in baggy blue harem pants and a flowing silk shirt. Her one concession to co-ordination was that her Arabian-styled shoes matched her shirt. Beanie had to admit that she looked sensational.

And Diana arrived on the stroke of eight, the twins on either side of her, the two nannies hovering behind. Diana was lovely in an ivory silk strapless gown, its ballerina-length skirt billowing around her knees. With only a few diamonds at her throat and wrist, it was elegantly understated and Beanie smiled her approval. Sam wore a wine-coloured velvet jacket and cream knee-breeches, his unruly blond hair setting off his cherubic smile.

Becky wore a velvet frock the exact shade of her mummy's, her dark curls swept up and secured with a bunch of ivory ribbons. Her heart-shaped face was solemn and those give-away dark green eyes swept the room and settled on the one face unknown to her . . .

Ben immediately crossed to greet them, his feelings again in neutral.

'What have we here?' he said gallantly. 'Why, I do believe we have fairies at the party!'

Rebecca peeped up at the smily man with the sparkly green eyes, and at once detached herself from Diana to place tiny fingers in Ben's hand.

Knowing something was expected of him, he kissed Rebecca demurely on her upturned cheek, and gravely shook Samuel's small, proffered hand. At once some unrecognisable emotion stirred within him and he stood up quickly, confused.

He gazed quizzically into Diana's luminous eyes, searching for answers there. But a tiny tug on his fingers demanded his attention. And, as he looked down into Rebecca's solemn green eyes – mirroring the colour and the curiosity of his own – some deep, unfathomable part of his being lurched crazily with joy.

Simon and Candy, whom everybody had met before dinner, and who had in turns been ticked off, congratulated, welcomed – came into the strangely silent room carrying Tim and immediately felt the wild charge of electricity that bounced from Diana and the twins to Ben, and back again.

They hovered silently in the doorway.

Ben's eyes were moist and his voice almost non-existent as he held Diana's gaze, oblivious now of the other people in the room. 'Mine . . .?' was all he could manage. But his soul was revealed in that single, anguished word.

'Yours,' Diana answered shakily, her own eyes filling with tears of happiness.

Ben's world tipped, rebalanced, and then steadied, strongly.

Sanders, transfixed by what he'd just witnessed, managed to croak huskily from beyond the doorway, 'Dinner is served.'

Beanie smiled triumphantly at everyone, and allowed both Mark *and* Jeff to escort her in to dinner.

CHAPTER THIRTY-SEVEN

Tim was asleep in Simon's arms, so he was no trouble to get back to the nursery, and Diana kissed the twins and they went obediently with their nannies. Ben watched them go, his heart full, his mind reeling.

Later, while they were skimming through the copies Diana had had made of all the documents, Simon was as flushed as Ben was pale.

Neither did more than toy with the lobster bisque, the tender medallions of beef, the airy lemon mousse or the light claret served to wash it all down with.

Both men were impatient to talk, but neither did so while dinner was in progress.

At last the table was cleared, coffee was brought and Sanders placed brandy and port decanters on the table, swept his staff out of the room and withdrew.

Then they both looked questioningly at Diana.

'Questions or answers?' she said gravely.

'I've got the general gist, have you, Simon?' Ben's voice was now impassive. Only his hand, drawing circles on the white damask table-cloth with a coffee spoon, revealed his distraction.

Simon was supremely in control.

'Hard not to have,' he agreed. 'But it leaves a million questions.'

Diana admired them both. Simon for his stoicism and Ben for his restraint.

'Are we going to discuss these private matters with non-family members present?' Ben questioned, before Diana could continue, his soft tone carrying a warning.

Diana's eyes were candid as she replied. 'Yes, I think so, Ben. Everyone here is, in one way or another, involved, not only in what has already happened, but in what could happen in the future.'

Ben shrugged his shoulders. 'As you wish,' he said.

'This business of Ben's birth. Dreadful, despicable affair,' Simon said vehemently. 'I think that has overwhelming priority, despite the very interesting tale of the old ancestors. But how did great-aunt involve *you*, Diana?'

Diana looked at Ben and again he shrugged silently.

'It began with that meeting in the gallery, when Ruth was so hostile,' Diana recalled, 'and progressed very quickly from there. When she first asked for my help, I was very much against it because it meant keeping secrets from you, Simon. But Ruth was very persuasive and when she told me that David was the sole remaining claimant against Joshua's inheritance, I'm afraid I fell for it completely.'

'You deliberately kept David from learning he had an interest in Tamerford?' Ben asked cautiously. 'Why?'

'It seemed at the time the lesser of two evils,' Diana said simply. 'He had all the money he could ever need. Simon had none.'

'I wonder that Ruth considered I might have more honour than my predecessors,' Simon said dryly. 'It isn't much of a record of honour!'

'It is a good record of survival, though,' Ben said shrewdly. 'And we wouldn't be discussing this today if honour had won the day.'

'I'm all for survival, stuff the honour!' Gemma butted in cheerfully. 'I mean, the original twin buggered off; why should his descendants get anything?'

'Because Samuel wanted it that way,' Candy said innocently.

'Then why not make both his sons heirs in the first place?' Beanie wondered.

'Don't think it works quite like that,' Simon said uncomfortably.

'The title, house and land always go to the eldest male child,'

Gabbie agreed.

'Monstrous injustice!' Beanie declared. 'Imagine that happening with Rebecca and Samuel. It's barbaric.'

'Peerage rules *are* a bit archaic,' Simon agreed. 'But it's all about protecting the estate really.'

'And you were only interested in protecting Simon?'

'At first, Ben, yes. I had no idea you were involved,' Diana admitted, her voice clear. 'But if I had known about you then — '

'When did you guess about Ben?'

'I didn't, Candy,' Diana explained. 'Not until I got a letter from Ruth, via her solicitor, after her death. She told me all that she had done then.'

'But that was almost three years ago,' Simon said, puzzled.

'Yes, but I didn't read the letter for over a year. I locked it away with some stuff David had left.' Diana blushed. 'Stuff I didn't want to handle because I was too angry over his treatment of Ben.'

'So why have you waited two years since then?'

Diana faced Ben's penetrating gaze, unafraid now. 'Because of your contract with David. I had to know you were free of him, free to make a choice.'

'What choice?' Simon stared from one to the other, aware of the renewed tension but not the reason for it.

'And if I'd stayed married to Gemma?' Ben asked into the sudden, electrified silence.

'The same choice, different circumstances,' Diana replied tautly.

'I see.' Ben's gaze was remote, his emotions concealed.

'Ben, listen.' Beanie charged in defensively. 'Diana has done nothing for herself. *Everything* has been for you and Simon. She made David sign a prenuptial agreement that he would leave Nazareth House to you. But he didn't: he broke his contract and her heart. She has been coerced, emotionally blackmailed and manipulated by both Ruth and David. Don't think she has enjoyed one moment of this hideous fiasco, she hasn't. It put her through hell!'

'It's all right, Beanie,' Diana said gently. 'It must all come out now. Everything.'

'But it sounds as if you weren't concerned for Ben,' Beanie insisted indignantly. 'He has to know that isn't true!'

'I think I begin to see that, old friend,' Ben said quietly.

'Ruth and David were a perfect pair. They were both fiends,' Gemma said helpfully. 'Only now I know that Ruth was the worst.'

'She was confused,' Gabbie couldn't help saying, embarrassed by all these revelations.

'Great-aunt was never confused in her life,' Simon said shortly. 'But she was obviously deeply disturbed. What she did to Ben, to her own nephew, is beneath contempt. It makes her little short of a criminal.'

'Steady on, Simon. I was a baby, old pal. What did I know about it? Anyway, if she hadn't written that letter to Diana we would never have known. So in a way Ruth made atonement,' Ben said softly.

Diana grimaced. 'And I probably did everything wrong. But I believed it was for the best.'

'So what happened to the prenuptial agreement?' Ben had swung his attention to Mark, his gaze hard.

'After the twins were born, David called me in to draw up another will — '

'And that one ousted me,' Ben guessed. 'But where did the prenuptial agreement go?'

Now Mark was conscious of beads of sweat under his collar. Maybe this was when he'd get fired. 'He made me destroy it,' he said as calmly as he could.

'And of course you didn't think to tell Mrs Nazareth about it?'

'No, I didn't. I'd just witnessed her and the twins being made the heirs. David had made his mind up. Nothing would have made him change back, or alter, this new succession,' Mark said as honestly as he could.

'That sounds about right,' Ben said drily. 'So OK, you were doing your job.'

Mark's face cleared.

'Jeff? You were in all this from the start?'

'I'm afraid I have to say yes,' Jeff answered, his tawny eyes clear of guile. 'I did whatever Dave asked of me.'

'But you did it *for* David,' Beanie said sharply. 'As we all did. Come on, Ben! We all loved David, but he was just a man, with a man's human frailties; not so different from the frailties in the other branch of his family, it seems. But, Ben, we'd all do the same for you, you know that!'

'Thanks, Beanie. I think I get the message.' Ben turned back to face Diana and his eyes were dark with the pain of so much betrayal. 'Would you like to tell me why you married David, if you knew the twins were mine, or is that too personal for right now?'

Diana stared at him, wondering why he'd chosen to bring this up here, why he couldn't have waited until later when they were alone. And then a flash of understanding came to her. Ben felt cuckolded. Now, in front of his friends and the two top men at Nazareth House, his male pride sought vindication.

But what about *her* pride?

'It *is* too personal, Ben,' she said evenly. 'I owe you an explanation, as you owe me one. But, as Gemma is here, I won't ask you why you married her as soon as my back was turned.'

Her head was high now, and a note of angry pride tinged her words with irony. 'I didn't know you'd been to Boston; that you'd believed David's lies; that you didn't even come to the clinic to ask *me*. I intended coming home to Devon as soon as I was well enough. But Gemma's phone call, to say you two had married, certainly put paid to that! And I could not have made my cousin unhappy by turning up pregnant by her husband!'

'But you were engaged to David!' Ben's eyes flashed fire now as he remembered the agony of that day. 'It was front-page news, damn it!'

'I was not engaged to David, as Beanie will tell you, from *choice*. To me, that party was just that, a party. Nothing more. I couldn't know that I was being set up, manipulated again.

'As you, too, were manipulated to believe David. If you cared enough to come all the way to Boston, breaking your contract into the bargain, why didn't you at least check with *me*? Did we *all* believe David Nazareth? Why didn't any *one* of us query what he was doing?'

She looked round at them all, and her glance fell on Gemma.

'It seems that Gemma, of all the people who knew him, was the only one able to see through him. However, if I'd taken her advice there would have been no Youth Trust, no meeting with the Tamerfords; I'd have sent the whole nasty package back to Boston and we wouldn't now be sitting around this table as a family.

'So, as there was an element of collusion with most of us here, I'm inclined to the preferable belief that fate, not David Nazareth, brought us all together – and let's leave it at that.'

Beanie, Jeff and Mark were shamefaced. Ben, too, looked decidedly uncomfortable.

Candy, who hadn't been there at the opening of the crate, but had since been told what was in it by Simon, suddenly remembered something that had been on her mind. To do with ancestors.

'Did you get the money, Si?'

'What money?'

'The money Ruth talked about,' Candy said innocently. 'The money you were to have when David died. Samuel's money?'

All eyes were on Candy now, and she blushed furiously.

'David left no money for Simon,' Diana said.

'I know *that*,' Candy said indignantly. 'It was from Ruth to Simon. She told me he would get it when David died.'

'The fifteen thousand, you mean?'

'No! No. From Ruth. Not her own money. Tamerford money, she called it. She wrote it down in that letter.'

'What letter?' Simon was still frowning.

'The letter you were to bring with the portraits,' Candy said, exasperated.

'You knew about the money and didn't say anything?' Simon was surprised.

'Well, she asked me not to tell you. It was to be a surprise.' Candy coloured brightly at the inference in her words. 'Lord, she hooked me too!'

'All this time — '

'Tamerfords are not the only ones who don't break their word,' Candy reminded her husband.

'Good lord, an honourable Tamerford!' Simon was smiling wryly.

Candy blushed happily.

'Simon, that letter you brought me – what did we do with it?' Diana pushed her chair back and hurried from the dining-room, followed by Simon at her heels and the rest in conga fashion behind him.

The letter lay on the top of a walnut bureau. Diana took it down and tore it open.

Her immediate reaction was pleasure, followed by disbelief. She sat down.

Everyone else sat too. Except Ben. He stood by the fire, his face betraying a feeling of uncertainty, of doubt in his ability to take more revelations.

Diana finished the letter and turned to two documents. One a bank statement, the other a birth certificate.

'Lord,' she said at last. 'No wonder she didn't want Simon or David getting hold of this.'

'There's more?' Simon said blankly.

'You could say,' Diana nodded.

'What is it? I can't stand not knowing,' Gemma said, voicing everyone's thought.

Diana looked up at Ben and then at Simon. Again she shook her head. 'No matter what else she was, she was certainly playing God. Ben, this I think is yours.'

Ben frowned but came and took the paper, then, a smile starting, he read aloud.

'Benjamin Tamerford . . . Mother: Blanche. Father: Nathan Tamerford. Informant: Ruth Tamerford, relationship, aunt. Birth registered in L'Oriel, Geneva, Switzerland. It's nice to know I exist as a real person,' he added, humorously. 'There were times when I felt as if I were a creation of David's imagination.'

Simon's smile was genuine. 'I'm so glad for you, Ben.'

Diana stepped gently into the eerie silence between the two men.

'This is addressed to me. Shall I read it aloud? Does anyone object?'

No one did, and so she began. 'The letter is headed Tamerford, and dated three years ago.'

My dear Diana,

When you read this I shall no longer exist in the flesh. Simon will deliver this in person, and who knows, perhaps Ben will be present. In which case, 'two birds', etc.

You already know about Ben's birth from my first letter; that I took away his rights – now you may choose to restore them. The choice, my dear, is yours. Somehow I believe you will be fairer that I have been able to be.

Blanche was very ill with T.B. and I was with her in Switzerland, when the news of Nat's death came. She lost her will to live after that. But she did not die until she had delivered her child – and named him Benjamin.

You will see the situation I was in. I was asked if I wanted her body taken to England or buried in Switzerland. Everything was suddenly, and overwhelmingly, in my hands. (It was easy later, to tell Bart that she and the baby had died; they had no money to make trips to graveyards in Geneva.)

The nuns at the convent were most obliging. They could see that a spinster lady could not care for a tiny baby, and I certainly did not inform them of another nephew and his wife, who could have.

They had an adoption agency in New York, one in England and one in Geneva. Naturally I asked for the one at the furthest distance . . .

The rest of my sordid secret you now know.

As to Joshua's fund – I kept my word to my brother and did not disclose it during my lifetime.

But I have no qualms about handing it on to you.

You are not a Tamerford, but you are a lady of honour. I know you will do what you believe to be the best thing.

For my part, since the arrival of Benjamin Nazareth at Tamerford, I have been made aware of the price I shall pay. Most certainly the 'Gentleman Above' directed Benjamin's feet here, and indirectly warned me of *his* displeasure.

The price *was* too high in the end . . .

I can only apologise to you all,

And leave you with my deepest affection.

                              Ruth Tamerford.

'Evil old bitch,' Gemma said hotly.

Simon was too shocked to comment and Candy sat at his side, hugging his arm to comfort him; while Gabbie sat on the other side of her brother in case she was needed.

Jeff perched on the arm of Gemma's chair.

Beanie sat on the *chaise longue*, Mark by her side.

Only Ben stood.

They all waited. It wasn't over yet.

Diana still had the other document in her hand.

'Anyone else want to reveal David or Ruth's secrets?' Ben said drily. 'They seem to have spread them around generously enough.'

Diana looked at Beanie, her eyebrows raised questioningly.

Beanie shrugged. She didn't mind if Diana didn't, so it might as well all come out into the open.

'I can share Ella's secret,' she said now. 'She burdened me with it for long enough.'

'Ella?' Ben frowned.

'Yes, Ella,' Beanie said firmly. 'It might explain why David suddenly became so certain that Diana would marry him. Or perhaps could marry him would be a better way of putting it. After all, he'd been in love with her for almost five years.'

Ben's eyes narrowed. 'Go on.'

'Matthew wasn't David's son – he was the child of Ella's lover, if that word applies; she only used him to get pregnant.' Now Beanie's face was grim. 'He was a maintenance man at the house at the time. Ella was particularly pleased about that. It was as if she enjoyed him more knowing how scandalised David would have been.'

'Why didn't she have any children by David?' Gemma asked.

'David couldn't have children,' Beanie replied quietly. 'But Ella never told him that. After the clinic confirmed that he was sterile, Ella enjoyed keeping that knowledge to herself and letting David assume that *she* was barren.

'It rather spoiled her fun when David insisted on adopting a child, and she was determined to have her own child after that. Ella loathed Ben before he even came to the house.'

'What an awful woman!' Candy said with a shiver, remembering Ben's own story of his childhood.

'More sad than awful, I think,' Diana put in. 'She had a brain tumour that no one knew about until her death. I remember David telling me that the doctor said that could have caused her manic moods and long depressions; she was a tragic figure really.'

'But to lie like that,' Gabbie whistled softly. 'That's just about as evil and rotten as anything Ruth or David did.'

'I don't know,' Ben said, his brows drawn close. 'I did try to tell David, once, that she was mentally ill. But I was just a kid

. . . still, I think I would have forgiven her if I'd known how ill she really was.'

Diana smiled softly at him. 'That's a lovely thing to say, Ben, after she hurt you so much.'

'So when did David find all this out?' Gemma couldn't conceal her disgust.

'He knew about the tumour after she died,' Beanie said, thinking back. 'But he didn't know about Matthew until just before my Sleeping Beauty party. I hadn't wanted to hurt him with that knowledge if there was no cause to do so.

'I'm sorry, Ben,' she said, not wanting Ben to be upset again. 'But I *did* help David. I set that party up.' Her voice dropped to a low key and her discomfort was evident to everyone. 'And I involved Jeff and Mark a great deal more than David knew. It seemed the right thing to do at the time. David had known so little happiness in his life.' She paused to collect her emotions. 'You see, I knew David was dying. And I told Jeff and Mark. I'd seen all the signs before – the strange visual disturbances and loss of balance on occasions. I wanted him to see a consultant, but he wouldn't agree. He was quite convinced it was an optical problem, nothing more. You can't take the mountain to Mohammed, can you . . .?' Her voice tailed off as memories came flooding through her mind.

'He knew complete happiness for a short while. So it was worth it,' she murmured defiantly.

No one spoke for several minutes, each remembering.

Ben spoke again. 'Beanie, you were the best friend that any man could wish for. David was a very lucky man.'

Tears glistened in Beanie's eyes, and her voice was husky as she answered. 'Thank you, Ben. That's the nicest thing that anyone could say to me. He was my life, you know.'

'Yes, I did know,' Ben said and crossed to pull her gently from the *chaise*, into his arms.

He held her for several minutes, until she herself stepped back, to press a lacy handkerchief to her eyes.

Ben turned back to the room, his own eyes dark and moist.

'Now,' he said abruptly. 'Where were we?'

Diana looked up, saw them waiting. 'I think you'd better take a deep breath for this one,' she said warningly. 'I have here a bank statement from a Swiss bank, in the name of Joshua Tamerford.

'It's a very old statement, but there's a note pinned to it, do you see?' She showed it around the room. 'The note says that the account is only of the balance at the last request for it, which was in 1953 . . . and that there has been no statement requested since then. Up to and including Ruth's death, and until today.

'The statement is dated 1953.' Now she swallowed nervously. 'And the credit balance stood then at £1,500.000. And this is a deposit account,' she added helpfully. 'Accruing interest — '

'Jee-zus!' Mark muttered, astonished.

'Nice one, Ruth,' Ben said drily.

'She was something else, all right,' Jeff spoke for the first time.

'That's about how I'd see it,' Ben agreed.

'One and a half million pounds,' Simon echoed, stunned.

'The Nazareths grew richer, the Tamerfords poorer – and the fund in Switzerland kept on growing,' Ben said wryly. 'And no one any the wiser about any of it. That's quite some secret.'

'This is 1991. That balance is thirty-eight years old!' Mark was still doing sums.

'That's what I was thinking,' Diana agreed. 'So there's thirty-eight years of interest to add to that. What should we do? Give Sam Golding a ring at home tomorrow, ask him what it might be worth?'

'We could make a fair guess at it ourselves,' Ben said cautiously. 'If nobody minds? The suspense could kill us by tomorrow . . .'

Diana glanced around. No one minded. All else was, for the moment, put on hold. There had been a release of tension – a bonhomie engendered by the treasure chest.

Diana found pens, papers and a calculator. Mark gathered them up and trooped off to the dining-room table, with Ben, Simon and Jeff in tow. Diana smiled and indicated the drawing-room. 'Shall we retire, ladies? We seem redundant for the moment.' Then she smiled with relief. 'Thank God!'

Diana added fresh logs to the fire before flopping down on a sofa, emotionally wrung out.

'Phew!' Candy breathed a sigh of relief. 'I don't know about fortunes, but I've gained a ton tonight. And my shoes are so tight . . .'

'Can I get you anything?' Diana asked sympathetically. 'Brandy? Tea? Water?'

'A painkiller, and a glass of water would be great,' Candy winced.

'Are you in pain?' Beanie asked, alarmed.

'No, just aching a bit. Probably the journey, and it has been a very long day.'

'Living in Devon doesn't help,' Diana said drily, returning with the glass and an analgesic. 'It takes half a day just to get anywhere from there. And that's before you begin your journey proper.'

'Too true.' Candy accepted the water and tablet gratefully.

'Shall I massage your shoulders?' Gemma jumped up from the chair, not waiting for a reply.

Diana sat down again, next to Beanie, and closed her eyes momentarily. 'God, what a day!'

'It's going well though, isn't it?' Gabbie queried. 'They're both taking it all marvellously, I think.'

'Bloody marvellously,' Diana agreed. 'Let's hope it lasts!'

'Amen,' Beanie chimed in.

'Will they work it out, d'you suppose?' Candy's tired face was still concerned.

'They'll have to, love,' Gemma said firmly. 'No other choice.'

Diana couldn't rest. She went to the dining-room door. 'Finished yet?'

Ben shook his head without looking up. For a few moments Diana watched him, savouring the knowledge that the muscles she could see through his shirt – he'd abandoned his jacket – would soon be under her fingertips and her lips. It was delicious, watching him. Tiny quivers of pleasure darted through her body just thinking about touching his back. Lord knows how she'd feel if he exposed anything else to her longing gaze.

He glanced up just then and she smiled, a soft secret smile. He interpreted the smile correctly and his eyes threw out a sparkling challenge that caught her neatly in her stomach. She took a deep breath, as a sudden heat soared through her limbs, and had to lean against the door.

Ben raised his eyebrows wickedly.

Diana forced herself to return to the drawing-room, a warm glow in her heart and body. Whatever else might happen, Ben had forgiven her – and had accepted the twins. There was all the time in the world for talking.

'I don't know if I shall be able to stay up much longer,' Candy said, covering a yawn, and then rubbing her back ruefully. 'It must be jet-lag, my back is killing me.'

Diana and Beanie were both alert at the same moment. 'You still have that ache?' Diana queried, her thoughts racing.

'In the same place, low down?' Beanie wanted to know.

Candy's hand flew to her mouth, and her eyes widened, shocked. Then she shook her head. 'No, don't worry. I'm not due for at least another month —'

'I'd say, darling, that you are due now.' Beanie said wryly.

'Oh Lord,' Candy said lightly. 'That's the absolute end, isn't it?'

Simon had heard and came to the door looking worried. 'It's too soon, darling,' he said hopefully. 'Maybe you are just overtired, why don't you go to bed?'

'And miss all this excitement?' Candy retorted, wide awake now. 'Not on your life!'

'At least put your feet up,' Gemma declared, swinging

Candy's legs up on to the sofa for her. 'There you go. Now, what happens next?'

They all burst out laughing, including Candy.

Gemma pouted crossly. 'What's so funny?'

'Oh, Gems! You are,' Diana laughed warmly. 'You are so clueless sometimes. Haven't you ever seen or read anything about giving birth?'

'I don't read horror stories.' Gemma retorted, but she couldn't help a small smile. 'Okay, I'm a dummy. So you experts tell me, what *does* happen next?'

'Nothing much for a long time,' Candy assured her gently. 'Don't take any notice of them, Gems. You can stay with me and watch the birth, then you'll know all about it.'

'Oh no!' Gemma leapt up from the end of the sofa. 'I'll boil the water!'

The men came back into the drawing-room and Ben shook his head. 'We're all guessing different sums. It's probably best left to Sam Golding tomorrow.'

'Far better,' Simon agreed, his face pale.

Beanie watched them all carefully, wondering if this mightn't be just the moment for Diana to put her plan before them. In fact, wasn't it possibly the only moment? Or had Diana forgotten? Changed her mind even? But no, she couldn't imagine her doing that. Beanie had watched Ben and Simon the whole time and had assessed the very strong relationship between them, even though they'd only discovered their blood ties today. Now she had to agree that Diana's plan was workable. A little tingle of excitement spread down her spine. It would be the most marvellous thing if Diana could pull if off. She began to feel very much better.

She caught Diana's eye, and tried to convey what she was thinking with a series of little frowns and eyebrow movements. It would be too obvious if she took her aside to whisper in her ear. But Diana didn't seem to be getting her message.

So Beanie decided that she'd better help things along, prod Diana as it were. 'Isn't there just one small problem.

A point under consideration. About who this fund truly belongs to?'

Diana half-frowned. She had thought about it, but it was so late. Was it a sensible time to bring it up now? But Beanie had done so, no doubt with good reason. A knot of tension formed in her stomach.

Ben answered for a silenced Simon. 'There's no question at all, Beanie. The money belongs to Simon.'

'I disagree, darling,' she said sweetly. 'No offence to you or Simon, but really this is a difficult situation. You, it seems, are the heir to Tamerford and Diana and the twins appear to be the heirs to the Nazareth line.' She smiled innocently. 'You see, there is a slight problem.'

Ben stared at her, a muscle twitching in his cheek. 'I thought you heard me clearly, Beanie? I don't see any changes at Tamerford, now, or in the future. Does that need some other verification?'

Beanie continued smiling, encouragingly.

'Ah,' he said amiably. 'You'd like that in legal prose? Well, the best I can do for you at the moment, for the record, is to state again, I'm not running for election at Tamerford. I don't need time to think about it, you can take that as final. The twins are my children, I'm sure everybody witnessed that revelation – so what is your problem?'

'Are you prepared to sign over any rights to Tamerford?' Beanie asked carefully. 'Legally, I mean?'

'If necessary,' Ben replied, shortly. 'If my word's not good enough — '

'Ben, you can't do that!' Simon broke in, indignantly. 'You and I should talk some more before you make a decision like that. And the money, I mean, gosh, that's yours too.'

'The money,' Mark interrupted, 'belongs to the Tamerfords only if there's no proven Nazareth line. I think Diana ought to be in on this conversation, because she does legally represent the Nazareth heirs.'

Ben and Simon both turned to Diana.

Simon looked as if his heart and his head were in his shoes. Diana felt very sorry for him.

'Diana?' Ben's features were again a mask.

'I *do* have a solution,' she said carefully. 'Something you and Simon *have* to talk about.' She looked pleadingly into his eyes, begging him to understand. 'But I must be absolutely sure you are *both* agreed, about Tamerford, the title, all that it entails.'

'I've said all I'm going to say about that,' Ben said firmly. 'The question's not open to debate.'

'But, Ben, I'm not sure that I can continue,' Simon said uncertainly. 'I think it might even be against the law. Or against peerage laws, anyway.'

'No one's going to know,' Ben argued reasonably. 'You're the Earl of Tamerford, and if I don't declare myself, who's to know any different?'

Simon pondered that, troubled. 'But it isn't right, Ben . . .'

'Si, we can talk it all out at some other time. I know what it is to lose everything you have grown up with, come to believe you will always be part of . . .' He paused, the pain naked in his face. 'No way would I put someone I love through that.'

Beanie smiled at Diana. It would work.

Diana took a deep breath, and plunged into uncharted waters. 'Would you both, then, consider an amalgamation with Nazareth House?'

After what seemed like an eternity, Ben spoke first. 'Perhaps you'd explain what you have in mind?'

'We can discuss details tomorrow,' Diana began. 'But a brief summary is this: as we are really talking about only one family, admittedly with two branches, I have been hoping that we might incorporate the two branches under one umbrella.' She began to get into her stride, and enthusiasm shone from her eyes.

'If we were to become one corporation, say headed by the Tamerford-Nazareth Group in Devon, and the Nazareth-Tamerford Group here in Boston, we could really unite the two families, and each could help out the other in different ways.

'I have a long list of items for discussion, but for the moment the main concern is, are you interested?'

Candy, Gemma and Gabbie were grinning hopefully. Simon was wide-eyed, and Ben was shrewd enough to recognise what Diana was trying to do.

'Lay the ghosts, eh?' he quizzed her.

'Something like that,' she admitted. 'But even more than that, we would have chance to build something worthwhile and lasting, for our children, all of them, on both sides of the Atlantic. They'd grow up as part of an integrated transatlantic family business. What do you say?'

'What about the Youth Trust?' Ben said cautiously. 'We're almost broke.'

'You planned to make it a commercial company eventually, didn't you? Well, with my help it could still go ahead. The company could be a subsidiary of Tamerford-Nazareth, and with a strong parent company behind it it would have considerable advantages in the marketplace. It could go public early, and be looking at profits earlier.'

'What about Ben's contract?' Simon asked, his pleasure shining in his eyes.

'Null and void,' Diana said quickly. 'But the trust could still be worked in tandem with the idea that it become a full company, under the main umbrella.'

'How would you propose to run this amalgamation?' Ben's fears were dispelled, any momentary doubt about Diana's integrity dissolved.

'With the family as head, each of its own branch. You and I here, Simon and Candy there.'

'Complex,' said Mark 'but by no means impossible.'

'And how do you propose to make up the board of directors?' Ben asked keenly.

'I would want Beanie, Jeff and Mark on the board here,' Diana said cautiously, aware that he had yet to agree. 'With the children, Gemma, Gabbie and the others having shares. The children will gain voting rights when they come of age.

But,' she said in a businesslike manner, 'that's an agenda item for discussion, not a *fait accompli*.'

Ben continued to stare at her, his eyes filled with respect. 'And the Tamerford-Nazareth group?'

'Simon and Gabbie at its head,' Diana said, hearing her plan at last taking form in reality, 'with perhaps you and Simon as floating votes between the two . . . but I think the majority of the boards would always have to be family.'

'And the central satellite, the controlling company in the early days?'

'You and myself, Simon and Candy,' Diana replied as coolly as she could, 'at least as a point from which to start discussions.'

'What about start-up funds for Tamerford-Nazareth?' Ben was still testing her. 'Were you thinking of Joshua's fund as sole investor?'

'No, I didn't know about it then. That's private money, and not mine to decide what to do with.' Diana felt hurt. Did he think she was that mean?

'No offence, just curious,' Ben said swiftly.

'Tamerford-Nazareth would get all the help it needs in the early days from Nazareth-Tamerford in Boston. Don't forget that the smaller parent group, that's the four of us, would in practice own the three groups anyway, on an equal-share basis.'

'That's amazing,' Simon said happily. 'In fact, as you say, one group owned by its family and directed by them and their trusted family and friends. What a fantastic idea!'

'It does have appeal,' Ben admitted. 'But it sounds complicated.'

'Nothing we can't jointly work out,' Diana said firmly.

'It'll be a big business.' Ben's eyes were lit now with amusement. 'We'd need several more children in a hurry!'

'Talking of which,' Candy moaned apologetically, 'I have the feeling that if I don't get some sleep soon, I shan't be getting any at all.'

'Darling!' Simon was immediately at her side. 'How thought-less of me. Of course you must get some rest.'

'Then decisions tomorrow?' Diana looked from one to the other.

'Of course. We'll talk after breakfast, Ben, OK?'

'Look forward to it,' Ben agreed. 'Now, get your poor wife to bed.'

With tired but elated hugs all round, Diana bade everybody a very late goodnight.

Only Mark had to turn out into the wet night, but as Diana saw him out she could tell, by his beaming fare-well, that he was a happier man than he had been for a long time.

Diana locked the papers in her safe, and turned the lights out. She was tired but elated.

As she crossed the hall, Ben came from the drawing-room and took her in his arms.

'Why didn't you tell me?' he whispered into her hair.

'About what?' Diana teased. 'The Youth Trust?'

'Everything,' Ben sighed. 'Everything you've had to bear, my love: all the worries – the Youth Trust seems least; David, and all those nightmares; the twins; me and my birth; Ruth and Tamerford; and Simon . . . you were so afraid he'd lose everything, weren't you?'

Diana snuggled against his chest, the warm masculine scent of him delighting her senses. 'Mmm, maybe,' she half-admitted.

'And the relationship between David and all of us . . . I'm amazed how you carried so much weight for so long. And Ruth's awful secrets. How did you cope, my love?'

'I just juggled it between Beanie's and Ella's and David's secrets over here,' she said lightly, nuzzling under his chin. 'It was easy really. Once you have one ball in the air, it's simple to add another couple of dozen.'

'You should have come to me, Diana. It would have been

so easy to have just told me what was going on, or what you thought was going on — '

'Ha! You were like the proverbial bear. No one could mention David's name, let alone confront you with all this! Anyway, how was I supposed to know what you'd do if you found out David was related to the Tamerfords? You could have stormed off into the night and left us all holding the trust, or its remnants!'

'I realise you hadn't learnt who I really was at that stage,' Ben admitted. 'But, darling, you should have known me a little. Or do you always sleep with strangers?'

Diana pushed him away, stung, despite the soft tones. 'You accused me once before of that . . . and you seem to have forgotten how drunk I was that night. So you see, Ben Nazareth, you are still a stranger. I don't remember a damned thing about it.'

Ben swept her up into his arms and, holding her cradled against him, gazed down into her upturned face. 'Well, there's something we can do about that right now . . .'

CHAPTER THIRTY-EIGHT

Ben's room was warm, his bed soft, bathed in a golden-rose glow of dimmed lamplight. On the radio an all-night music station focused on a saxophone's low haunting strains, the music lingering, bitter-sweet and sensual, on the air.

Their first crazy, desperate, urgent needs had been wantonly assuaged. They had been equally abandoned, enthusiastic and fervent; feral couplings that had everything to do with the here and now, the single purpose to blot out the past empty, hungry years.

Now they curled together on the bed, content at last to touch, to caress, to learn each other's body with sensitivity; to store for the future the special places, special responses.

Ben couldn't get enough of Diana's lustrous skin, its sheen and satiny feel. He traced his finger along the outside of her jaw, down the slender neck to the hollow of her throat, loving the way she shivered beneath his touch.

'Do you remember we vowed to apologise when one of us was proved wrong?' she murmured, trying to catch one of his fingers with her mouth.

'Mmm.'

'So I apologise.'

'Uh, uh. You weren't wrong, just taken in, lied to. I should have known that you were being fed disinformation, that David would have covered his back. You must have been totally confused.'

'More so when Jeff and Beanie backed David's story,' she said ruefully, twisting his hair around her fingers, studying the depth of colour. 'Do you know your hair reminds me of mocha coffee?'

'Does it? But they're good people; that kind of loyalty can't be bought.' His hand travelled down to her waist, moving

slowly over the sensuous shape of her hip, the curve of
her thigh.

'No. They are very special. Did you know David was going
to leave the Firm jointly to them if you and I didn't come up
to scratch?'

'That would have been an interesting scenario.' His fingers
continued stroking the outer line of her thigh, almost lazily.
'Perhaps I hurt David more than I ever realised,' he said.

'Mmm. It makes it all the more amazing that they tried so
hard to help him succeed. They could have sat back and
waited to inherit.' She rolled over on to her back, wanting to
be caressed all over, knowing where Ben's touch was leading
and welcoming it.

'Talking of inheritance,' Ben said, 'do you suppose Ruth
took my mother to Switzerland with the intention of getting
rid of me?'

'No, darling, I don't. I believe Ruth's letter. It was just an
opportunity too good to miss: to put her favourite nephew on
the throne, as it were.'

'But what did my father, Nat, ever do to her?' Ben asked,
softly.

Diana looked into his eyes, wondering if this was a good
thing to be discussing here and now. But his eyes were warm
and filled with love. Still she wondered. 'Serious talk, darling,
for the small hours.'

Ben smiled wickedly and bent to each of her breasts in turn,
his tongue flicking over the dusky peaks tormentingly. 'Yep,'
he managed, surfacing for a moment. 'I'm beginning a lifetime
habit,' he continued. 'We'll make a pact, to keep all the serious
discussions for the bedroom, for in the bed to be exact, and we
have to be as naked as we are now.'

Despite her arousal, Diana had to laugh. 'You're crazy, do
you know that?'

'But serious, you'll note,' Ben responded with a smile. 'If
we do that, we'll always be in a position to build bridges if
we need them. Do you agree?'

'How can I not, when you are doing *that*,' she murmured, as he ran his tongue over her stomach, sending shock-waves all the way up to her breasts and back again.

'You didn't answer my first question,' he said, his breath fanning the shivery heat of her thighs, his hands gently parting her legs.

'Ben stop . . . I can't think,' she moaned. 'And you're planning this for a lifetime? I shall go potty.' She trembled as he stopped, his face hovering, waiting only for her answer.

'I don't know – people just have favourites, don't they? Why should it be anything more than that?'

Ben listened, and heard and buried his pain in her throbbing body. No more talk now: there was a lifetime for questions, for understanding and forgiving. For healing.

His hands slid under Diana's buttocks and he lifted her towards him while his tongue probed deeper, seeking the core of her pleasure.

Diana arched her back and thrust her pelvis upwards, straining towards that ultimate moment. She grasped his hair, moaning frantically, and then, as she began to shudder, he pulled up and entered her swiftly.

He took her swollen breasts, mastering her with his touch, keeping her on the edge of the tidal wave that threatened to engulf them both. At last he gripped her slender waist and lifted her up, their kisses containing all that there was of their love, while their bodies rose together, until they both surrendered to the anguish of the sweetest pain of all.

They fell back at last, quiescent, bonded in their old-new love.

Ben held her tenderly. 'You will marry me now?' he asked, for a moment sounding uncertain again.

Diana pulled down his head and kissed his lips very softly. 'I have to, don't I?' she smiled. 'We need an honest father at the head of Nazareth House.'

Ben held her tightly, overflowing with love. Slowly their

breathing became even and, entwined in each other's arms, all the trauma of years past melted away, and they slept.

Thanksgiving dawn on the last Thursday in November broke with an early frost-rime dusting the lawns as if with glittering icing.

While Britain rejoiced in the return of Terry Waite, the last of the British hostages held in Beirut, the USA waited for the expected release of its own hostages, stunned to learn that basketball star 'Magic' Johnson had AIDS.

Further afield, Mikhail Gorbachov continued to fight a losing battle against an already crumbling Soviet Union, and the Croatian city of Vukovar fell to Serbian troops after a three–month siege.

But these were not matters on Simon's mind as he sought Diana urgently.

'Candy's in labour, Diana,' he said in quiet concern.

'How far apart are the pains?'

'Still not close enough, but I think we need a doctor, or a hospital.'

'Don't worry,' she soothed. 'She can have the baby here – I'll get Andrew Leyland.'

She managed a quick shower and a change of clothes before the doctor's car pulled up outside.

Andrew Leyland spoke briefly to Candy, did a quick check of the room that was to become a labour ward once again, put his nurse to work, and then firmly shooed Diana, with Simon and Tim, out of the room.

'I'll call you when you can come in,' he said gently to the anxious Simon. 'Nothing for you to worry about right now. Your wife is doing fine.'

They took the little boy up to his cousins, and then Diana linked her arm through Simon's as they went down to breakfast.

'I don't suppose you've had much chance to think about my proposals – or indeed about anything that happened yesterday?'

'Actually, I had most of the night to think,' Simon said ruefully. 'Between Candy's pains and my swimming head, I don't think I had more than two hours' sleep.'

'Poor old Si,' she grinned. 'Who'd be a prospective father, and a newly rich man all in the same twenty-four hours? It's disgusting!'

Simon grinned back at her, and made a playful attack on her ribs. 'You should be punished, young Diana,' he said, diving past her guard and tickling her until she squealed helplessly. 'It will teach you not to keep so much to yourself in future — '

'What's this?' a stern voice said from the bottom of the stairs. 'Manhandling my future wife, Simon?'

'Whoops!' Simon pulled a face at Diana. 'Caught red-handed.'

'Hi there!' Diana said playfully. 'Couldn't you choose a better moment to creep up on us?'

Ben leaned on the banister, dashing in his cream jersey and black cords, his voice full of love and laughter. 'If you'll warn me when you intend to have your better moments, I'll try to oblige.'

'Ben, Candy is in advanced labour,' Diana said happily. 'The doctor and nurse are here, so it looks as if we'll have more reason than ever to be celebrating today.'

'Oh that's great! Is she all right, Simon?'

'I think so, at least as much as a woman can be at such a time,' Simon said happily.

'Right, breakfast first and then let's talk afterwards,' Ben said, putting his arm around Diana's waist and hugging her hungrily. 'So that's where you went - I've missed you like crazy.'

She reached up and kissed his cheek. 'Me too, but babies won't wait for uncles.' She hesitated, a bit confused. 'No, you can't be their uncle, can you – not if they are your cousins.'

Ben gave her a warning squeeze. 'Uncle Ben suits me just fine,' he said easily. 'And it stops any awkward questions.'

'No,' Simon declared. 'We are not going to deny you any

further, Ben. There's been enough of that already – and I shan't countenance any more of it.'

'Fine, Cousin Ben it shall be,' Ben smiled. 'But if someone asks which branch of the family I'm from, we might have difficulties.'

'Nonsense.' Simon's tone was brisk. 'You are a Tamerford. David adopted you when your parents died. Time we paid some of his mischief back . . .' He grinned wickedly. 'David's dead. Who can question him?'

Diana felt the stirrings of victory. Simon was committed. All it needed was their joint agreement and everything could truly begin.

Beanie came down the wide staircase, immaculate as always, and as always in grey. 'Morning, darlings,' she said gaily. 'How's Candy?'

They told her as they went into the dining-room, where Gabbie and Gemma were already waiting, and as Jeff came in then they were able to tell them all together.

'Candy's in the best hands. Andrew is a very competent young man,' Beanie declared. 'Now, how are the summit talks going? Pass the toast, darling.'

Ben smiled to himself. She didn't change. Beanie was Beanie; no side, no artifice. He was beginning to see why David had kept her close to him. You'd always know where you were with a woman like her.

His glance softened as he watched her covertly while she poured coffee for everyone.

'We're starting the summit after breakfast,' he said. 'You should know that we mere males can't handle new babies *and* business on an empty stomach.'

Beanie gave him one of her knowing smiles. 'There's nothing mere about you, Ben darling. You are, what is it they say? A chip off the old tree?'

'Oh,' Ben looked amused. 'Which tree would that be?'

'Both, darling,' Beanie said enigmatically, and passed him his coffee.

Diana smiled to herself. It was lovely the way they got on; rather like Beanie and David in fact.

The thought suddenly tugged at her heart and an unexpected sting of pain winded her for a moment. It was crazy; why should thoughts of David have this effect on her? But she knew the answer. He had become her surrogate father – despite his own determined efforts to be anything else, despite his desperate obsession that had almost destroyed her. Despite everything, she forgave him everything. He had brought her back to life when she thought she could never laugh or love again. Now she could bury all the dishonourable things he had done. And now she could grieve for him, for the loss of a sad and tragically lonely friend . . .

'All right, darling?' Ben's hand touched her wrist, concerned.

She gazed at him, at this gift David had sent her. Now she, too, knew what it was to love with all her heart and soul; and the love in her heart was big enough to leave room to grieve for David.

'Just a shadow. You know, passing over one's grave. Silly old cliché.' She smiled reassuringly.

Ben turned back to his conversation with Jeff, and when Diana could see clearly again it was to see Beanie and Gemma both staring at her.

'Something in my eye,' she said quietly so that Ben wouldn't hear, and frowned at them to make her point.

'Well, darling,' Beanie said, clearly understanding, 'eat some of this delicious fruit. We girls have to look after our skins. You too, Gemma. It's better for your complexion than staring.'

Gemma took a piece of fruit. It was silly, she knew, but just now she'd have sworn she felt David's presence in the room . . .

Andrew Leyland and his nurse managed to join them for a quick breakfast, while Meg sat with their patient. Candy was doing well and Andrew predicted the new arrival in two to three hours. He assured Simon that he would call him in plenty of time to be with his wife for the birth, so the two men were able to wander off for their summit meeting.

Once the doctor and nurse had departed, the four women were alone together for the first time that morning.

Diana exhaled loudly. 'So far, so good, yes?'

'Sewn up and in the bag,' Gemma stated unhesitatingly.

'So long as Ben can keep his foot firmly on Simon's pride,' Gabbie agreed.

'Beanie?' Diana wanted her opinion more than anyone's.

'I agree with both girls,' she said simply. 'Simon and Ben both suffer from a surfeit of pride, it's a family trait presumably. But, yes, I think the price is right. You have offered them exactly what they both want, to head their own house, businesswise, with no loss of face. Also, you've given Ben the out he had to have if he was going to leave the trust. By giving Simon the chance to head his own company and also incorporate the Youth Trust, you've allowed Ben to walk away with his integrity intact. That was essential.'

She paused, thinking. 'He's very much a mixture of both sides of the family, you know. I can see both Simon *and* David in him, and I think he's inherited the favourable aspects of both.'

The younger women all began talking at once, leaving Beanie to sit back and think her thoughts. She had meant what she'd said, about the mixture of characteristics; she'd watched him very carefully, and all the signs she knew so well were there. They'd always been there, in Ben just as in David. At first she'd feared the same fanatical dedication to the Firm; but as the day had worn on, she'd seen other sides of his nature, the Tamerford side; the fierce pride in refusing point-blank, without knowing anything else was on offer, even to consider taking what was truly his own title; refusing to hurt or to compromise a man he loved.

Ben would love Diana and the Firm with as much devotion as David had. But he would not destroy them.

The future looked very good indeed . . .

* * *

Diana was crossing to her study to call Mark and see if he had contacted Sam Golding when Ben and Simon reappeared from their walk.

'Captain,' Ben beamed at her. 'Just the guy. Where do we landlubbers sign on?'

Diana could have turned cartwheels across the hall.

'This way, gentlemen.' She held open the door to her study.

Seated behind her desk, she scrutinised them both for a few minutes, before relaxing.

'I've had preliminary papers drawn up, but before there's any talk of signing those, we'll meet Mark and Jeff at the office, iron out any wrinkles . . . but you know my outlines. Do you have any problem with those?'

Ben leaned forward. 'We've covered most of the ground rules you laid out and we don't see any difficulty.'

'Simon?'

'It's all more than agreeable. I'm very honoured,' he said, a trace of his former shyness evident in his voice. 'But, just for the record, it must be shown that if at any time Ben changes his mind – you know, about Tamerford, he has only — '

'Simon!' Ben said sharply. 'I'm only going to say this one final time. Whatever tenuous legal claim I could have on Tamerford, I don't want it. You have to accept that now as my last word on the subject – in fact I might get that made legal, then it won't give us further trouble.'

Diana watched lovingly as Ben firmly buried his own past, the past he'd learned of so recently.

'It's not gallantry or even pride, Simon. It's just the way it is. I was raised a Yankee, and I'll die a Yankee.' He smiled to take any sting from his words. 'But a happier Yankee: with my English roots, my Swiss birth, my mad ancestors – on both sides of the Atlantic, I hasten to add – and my lovely, half-English children, my utterly insane but beautiful half-English wife.'

Diana threw a desk blotter at him, but he ducked.

'See what I have to put up with? And you think I'd give up all this to be a mere earl?'

Diana depressed the intercom. 'Sanders, champagne, please. In the study. Mr *Ben's* study.'

As soon as Simon left to go to Candy, Ben, still grinning hugely, pulled Diana from her chair and hugged her hungrily. He had everything he could possibly want: the woman he loved, two beautiful children, and at last a chance to earn his place at Nazareth House. His arms tightened round her waist, and his mouth found hers.

'Later, will you tell me everything about your life until we met? Including what happened with Mat? And all the silly details about the twins? Will you tell me everything – so that I can begin to make up for all the sadnesses, and enjoy the successes with you? We have so much to catch up on, my love.'

'As you wish, my lord,' she teased, loving his nearness.

'Don't,' he cautioned quietly. 'Not even in fun, darling. Not ever. It could stick, and you could slip up and hurt Simon . . .' He gazed down at her and she saw, briefly, a glimmer of pain in the depths of his eyes. She swallowed a lump in her throat; so the bravado didn't go all the way to his soul?

She clung to him fiercely. She'd make it up if it took a lifetime.

'I'm sorry, darling. You are right. I shan't slip up again . . .'

Ben shook off his momentary sadness, laughed and swung her up into his arms. 'Now let's go find those gorgeous children of ours and have a romp with them, before lunch and all other hells are let loose down here!'

The turkey was browning gently under its buttered muslin cloth, and the pecan pie was ready to pop into the oven for pudding, its accompanying walnut cream chilling temptingly in the fridge.

'Is there any news yet, Miss Diana?' Sanders asked. 'Of the baby?'

Much as Sanders enjoyed the thought of another blessing on the mansion in the form of a new baby, his priority was correctly with Mrs Carly's concern about a spoiled lunch. The doctor had said another half an hour, one and half hours ago.

'Judging by the awful noises in that department, I should think it's any time now,' Diana assured him with a grimace. 'But we're all gathered in the drawing-room, so would you serve the champagne now?'

'Immediately,' Sanders replied in relief.

Sanders poured the champagne while Meg passed tiny pastry parcels of crab-meat around, before they withdrew to wait anxiously in the kitchen.

Diana tucked her arm through Ben's, and beamed delightedly at her extended family.

'Toasts?' she queried, holding her glass aloft.

No one seemed prepared to take the leading toast from her, so she made the toast that was dearest to her heart. 'Without Samuel and Rebecca Tamerford – and, with no excuse offered, David and Ruth – we would not now be celebrating this wonderfully exciting day together, all of us under one roof. So my toast is, "Old Samuel and Rebecca, Ruth, and David . . . May they all rest in peace".'

The toast was accepted noisily and drunk with relish.

Ben's eyes glittered briefly, his chiselled features more handsome for the proud set to his jaw.

'To my father, David Nazareth,' he said with a sober dignity. 'May he be remembered with love.'

The toast was again called, this time with a quiver of emotion, and drunk long and silently.

Ben topped up glasses in the sombre moment of remember-ance, and returned to Diana's side. She hugged his arm tightly, her eyes filled with tears.

Beanie, her own eyes awash with memories, raised her glass

unsteadily and spoke her toast in a voice jagged with emotion she no longer had to hide. 'To the family, from those of us who have the privilege to count ourselves amongst your friends. Long may you all live and love and work – together.'

'The family!' resounded around the room, followed by a burst of released energies and happy rejoicing.

The champagne glasses were again refilled and the party swung into festive mood. Excited voices clamoured in questions and theories about the pending merger of the two old families after three hundred and sixty-two years of separation.

Simon's head appeared round the door but he wasn't heard above the noise, until he hammered on the old oak doors. 'Can a new father get a word in edgeways?' he yelled, and a great cheer went up, echoed in the kitchen.

'Come and meet the new addition,' he beamed proudly. 'And bring some extra glasses for us.'

Ben grabbed the champagne, Jeff the glasses, and they all trooped, laughing, into Candy's room.

Candy sat up in bed, her halo of blonde curls framing a pretty face made beautiful by her pride and happiness. In her arms a swaddled infant sucked contentedly on a tiny pink thumb, enormous blue eyes gazing as if they saw everything in this bright new world.

Champagne was poured and passed around in a rapt silence as the family and their friends were hushed by the ever-fresh miracle of birth.

Simon carefully lifted the bundle from Candy's arms, love and enormous pride in his eyes. She nodded shyly, and took the glass Gemma handed her.

Ben held Diana's hand; Rebecca and Samuel held their mother's dress. Jeff linked his arm round Gemma's waist possessively. Gabbie held Tim's little hand, and Beanie's shoulder touched hers as they stood together, friends for life.

At last Simon managed to extricate the child from its

wrappings and a soft murmur greeted a tiny dimpled face, and a shock of golden curls.

As he held the precious child up for them all to see, Simon's voice was laced with loving humility, and the tiniest hint of mischief.

'Candy and I would like to introduce you to our new son. Would you like to raise your glasses, and join us in wishing a Happy Thanksgiving Birthday . . . to David Nazareth Tamerford.'